PROMISES

OF THE

EMPIRE

VINCENT E. M. THORN

Paperback ISBN-13: 979-8-9858185-1-2

EBook ISBN: 979-8-9858185-0-5

Cover art and design by Fabrice Bertolotto.

This book is dedicated to all the friends we lost along the way

May we meet again if it's not too late, and remember the good times if it is

CONTENTS

PROMISES

OF THE

EMPIRE

Vincent E. M. Thorn

PROLOGUE

Smoke formed great pillars over what had been a barren desert just yesterday. Captain Corin Lancen was still having trouble reconciling with what he was seeing. He blinked again. Sure enough, it was still there. It was a tree in the middle of the Great Desert, having burst through the volcanic plateau in a tangle of root and body. A single, white tree, taller than a mountain, leaves spanning the spectrum of all conceivable reds and purples that shimmered like stars.

A chill ran down his spine and he turned his attention to the burning ships that had crashed below. It had been a gruesome sight. When he closed his eyes, he still saw the terrified sailors throwing themselves off the decks of their ships to avoid burning to death, others who had caught fire just before they could make the attempt. He still saw the dragons escaping as their Nest turned into a feeding ground for an even greater creature. And of course, he remembered *that* creature, the single most massive thing he had ever laid eyes on, like a giant snake made of stone that appeared as if from nowhere.

His ship, the *Second Chance,* had been lucky enough to escape destruction. He paced along her deck, grateful to feel something familiar beneath his feet amid all the chaos and confusion. Of course, the comfort would end soon enough. He had to meet Dardan, his employer and the mad woman who had orchestrated the slaughter the day before. "Maybe Balthine was right to get himself killed before things got out of hand."

Ander — Corin's younger brother who was a giant by the standards of most people and doubly so for Corin himself who was short next to many older *children* — stomped his massive foot on the deck. "Belay that," he said. "Dying's no good for anyone."

"Quite right, Ander," Corin agreed quickly. "I wasn't ready for yesterday, that's all."

Ander hoisted a jug of rice wine and shrugged before taking a swig from it. "Dragons kill people all the time."

1

"Aye, but how often is something *bigger* than a dragon? I don't know if you were too drunk to notice, but that... that thing *ate* two dragons in one bite!"

Ander belched before answering. "You worry too much."

"I have to! You never worry at all." He sighed. "Let's find Dardan and get our business done."

Ander nodded and made his way to the helm. Corin sat on a step leading to the aftcastle and took several deep breaths. The ship's engines roared to life and the propellers began their rapid *thwacking* as the *Second Chance* began to move. Dardan's ship, the *Martyr's Demise*, was not hard to find, and not just because it wasn't on fire. The ship was painted black as a moonless sky, but for a painting of the Goddess of the Desert and Strife, Daen — which the *Second Chance* and every other ship flown by one of the Daughters of Daen also sported — but what made it particularly obvious was the corpse of a dragon pinned to its bow in lieu of a standard figurehead — the *Second Chance* had a manticore's head mounted to the front, instead.

Despite having been on the scene when the chaos began, Lancen's ship was not the first to meet the *Martyr's Demise*. The *Forgotten Promise* was present, which didn't surprise Corin, but so was the *Knight In Mourning*, which did. The *Second Chance* rose to meet Dardan's ship. Normally for these meetings, Corin was alone, but today he felt unsafe. "Ander," he said, "I would appreciate it if you joined me."

"Fine," his brother replied.

Fala, one of the deckhands, brought down the gangplank for Corin and Ander to walk across. As he passed, Corin patted her gently on the arm. Her brother had been shot dead during their abduction of the princess. For her part, Fala nodded graciously and moved on quietly to resume her other duties.

Stepping onto the deck of the *Martyr's Demise* felt like he had climbed out of a warm bed on a cold morning and, instead of finding the floor, he had stepped into a pile of eels. As ever, Dardan was sitting on a chair that was probably bolted to the deck, wearing a black veil that covered all but her left hand. To her left was Captain Nyrien, a woman with a face so scarred it had become a perpetual sneer — or maybe that was just her way, and the scars were a coincidence — and to her right was San Mina, or "Lucky San" as she was often called, a woman who had lost her nose to a backfiring pistol. San wore a corset over a shirt with no sleeves to showcase the elaborate tattoos depicting Daen and a dragon on the left and right, respectively.

"Captain Dardan," Corin greeted cordially, "Captain San. Nyrien."

Nyrien's perpetual sneer deepened, and San merely gave him a brisk nod before turning back to Dardan, who answered, "Captain Lancen, welcome." Less than a week ago, Corin had had a sword drawn on him. He had felt more comfortable than he did now.

"There have always been five great captains under the *Martyr*," San said, clearly continuing a conversation that had started before Lancen had arrived. "With the *Scorpion* sunk and all her crew with it, let me take Balthine's place."

Lancen couldn't help but smirk. Of course, she would want to be one of the great captains — anyone who didn't know Dardan well enough would want to; they paid a considerably smaller cut of their earnings and got the more extravagant and lucrative jobs. The trouble was, it was a position that made you aware of just how insane Dardan was, and how the Daughters were less a mercenary band and more a personal army she used to meet her political — and occult — agendas.

"Something funny, Lancen?" San demanded of him.

"No, nothing," he said calmly, forcing himself to smile. "Just thinking. Dardan, if I may ask a question?"

The cowled figure waved a hand. "Go on."

"Well, after yesterday, we summoned the — whatever that thing was called."

"The leviathan," Dardan said.

Corin nodded. "Yes, the leviathan. A magnificent beast, truly… big. My only question is, what do you intend to *do* with it?"

Dardan's slender fingers flexed into claws, just for a moment before she relaxed. "My initial plans were thwarted when the princess escaped. Because *you* allowed her captain to follow you."

Corin took a step back, bumping into his brother's leg. "I still don't know how they managed to follow us, but there's no way the merchant captain could have survived long enough to inform her crew."

"She did more than inform them. She *personally* took the girl."

Corin's eyes widened. "You must be mistaken."

"Lancen," Darden said, "never question me again."

He lowered his eyes. "Of course."

"The ritual was incomplete," Dardan continued, "and with the Dragon's Nest gone, it can never be complete. But the leviathan can be brought into line, have no doubts about that."

"This is all very well," said San, "but you never answered my question; why won't you grant me Balthine's position?"

"The *Scorpion* has always been Daen's left hand," Dardan said cryptically.

"But that's just it," San replied, "The *Scorpion* is sunk! Balthine is dead! The crew is dead! If it's so damned important that the last ship be called the *Scorpion*, I'll rename the *Knight* and —" she stopped and tilted her head as if to listen for something.

Lancen heard it, too. It was the sound of a ship approaching, and fast. Lancen peered off to port and saw a black ship approaching, bearing the same depiction of Daen as all other present ships, and the corpse of a rivermaid nailed to the bow. *It can't be,* he thought as he stared.

Thick plumes of acrid smoke and fog rolled off the *Scorpion's* hull as it picked up speed. Scars and pockmarks covered the ship, giving the vessel a haunted visage. Dardan tapped her foot, and a dozen women in black, armored coats emerged two by two from below deck, each with a sword, spear, or pistol at the ready.

"I'm sorry, Captain San," Dardan said, her tone thick with patronizing smugness, "were you saying something about the *Scorpion*?"

The *Scorpion* rammed into the small space between the *Knight in Mourning* and the *Martyr's Demise*, knocking the latter into the *Forgotten Promise* and creating an irritating screeching all at the same time. Lancen lost his balance and would have fallen had his brother not been there to support him. The smokescreen rolled across the deck like fog, choking Lancen with its acrid stench.

He doubled over and began hacking, and around him the sound of the others coughing filled the darkened gloom. The rattle of gunfire rang out, accompanied by the heavy thuds of bodies hitting the deck. The smoke screen dissipated to reveal three of Dardan's crew lying dead and *Scorpion's* captain striding across the deck with his first mate and a trio of strangers in tow.

Captain Zayne Balthine wore a dark half-mask and a scarf, leaving only a quarter of his face exposed, but he was recognizable

4

by his impractically long, raven hair which billowed freely behind him. His black long coat, by contrast, scarcely swayed, weighed down by the small arsenal the man was known to carry. It seemed being dead had done little to change him.

Following Balthine was Nanette Adarin. The *Scorpion*'s first mate was a lithe woman with a hooked nose like a falcon's beak. A grim expression sat heavily on her face. In contrast to her captain, her long hair was bound in a tight tail, and the body of her black coat was shorter than the sleeves. She held a pistol in each hand as they made a line for Dardan.

Lancen didn't recognize the rest of the *Scorpion*'s crew — a noble blooded woman with short hair wearing a knuckle-buster that was also a knife; a Rivien man wielding a crescent shaped blade; a heavily tattooed man carrying a sword and pistol — and he wondered if that was because the old crew were dead, like Balthine and Adarin were rumored to be.

Four of Dardan's people ran at the attackers. Adarin darted forward and raised both of her pistols and fired. Blood exploded from the shoulder and the kneecap of the fastest soldier, forcing her to drop her spear as she collapsed. The avian woman tossed her spent weapons behind her and reached into her coat as she leaped atop the falling soldier's shoulders. She jumped off, forcing the injured woman down as she lashed out with both hands. Her quartet of black knives found themselves lodged in the forehead, throat, chest, and stomach of a man whose sword fell from numb fingers and clattered onto the deck. The next two both turned their spears on Adarin only for the noble blooded woman to cut in. Her knuckle-buster crushed the side of one spearman's face with a disgusting *crunch-squelch* before she dragged the knife across his head and splashed his blood and brains into the second man's eye. He stumbled, and Adarin moved around his weapon and finished him with a knife to the heart.

The Rivien man and the tattooed one broke forward together and pressed the remaining line of Dardan's crew. The former moved with sweeping grace, flowing around counter attacks like a leaf in the breeze and carving through his opponent with an almost casual air. The other assailant used his sword more like a cudgel, throwing his full weight upon his enemies until they gave way under his savage assault. When only one of the *Martyr's* defenders remained, the brute lofted his pistol almost dismissively and shot her in the throat.

The *Scorpion*'s captain had maintained a steady pace despite the carnage around him, stepping over bodies and wading through blood. He drew an ostentatious sword with a broken falcon on its pommel. When the last of Dardan's crew fell to the deck, Balthine broke into a run, shooting at Dardan like a bullet.

Ander — always the one to put an end to violence with violence of his own — stepped in Balthine's path like an insurmountable wall of flesh. Corin had seen bigger men than Balthine pale beneath that shadow. Instead, blood spurted abruptly from Ander's side and the giant fell to one knee. He swiped at Balthine who skittered out of his reach like his namesake arachnid before resuming his assault on the mercenary leader.

Nyrien intersected his path next with a truncheon in one hand and a sword in the other. Balthine didn't slow as he whipped his arm straight at her. Something flashed in the air between them. Nyrien flinched. A stiletto punched into her baton, quivering much as Nyrien was. Balthine slipped past her without resistance. She turned to follow, only for Adarin to tackle her to the deck.

Balthine's sword was leveled at Dardan's face. When he was in range, he thrust the weapon forward, all but leaping to make the kill.

The cowled woman didn't flinch, didn't try to get out of the way. She said one word that sent a shiver down Lancen's spine.

"Stop."

It wasn't uttered in panic or fear. It was a command.

And Balthine stopped.

The masked mercenary stood poised on one foot, leaning into his lunge, the tip of his blade hovering mere inches from where Dardan's nose must have been hidden under that cowl. The blade stopped as if stuck in an invisible plank. The tip of the sword didn't so much as quiver in any direction, though Lancen could see the strain in Balthine's arm as he tried to push past it.

What is going on? Lancen wondered.

"Why have you returned, Balthine?" Dardan asked. Her tone was exasperated, as if she dealt with an unruly child rather than a man holding a sword to her.

The voice that answered was not Zayne Balthine's. "To kill you." *No,* Lancen corrected himself. Balthine's voice *was* there, it just wasn't Balthine's *alone*. There was a second, unfamiliar voice speaking the words at the same time. It made him shiver.

"Of course you did," Dardan replied dryly. "Drop that sword."

Corin didn't expect him to comply, and for a long moment it seemed he wasn't going to, but then he watched as Balthine slowly released his grip on his weapon. The blade stuck into the deck, the broken falcon on the pommel perched, staring at Lancen, as if to demand to know why its master had faltered.

Or maybe Corin was projecting.

A series of heavy thuds and the clattering of iron on wood sounded behind Corin. He looked and found Lucky San standing atop the Rivien man and holding the tattooed one with his burly arm twisted around his back. She pushed hard, audibly dislocating his shoulder before turning on the woman with the knuckle-buster.

The two circled one another for a tense moment before San whipped her leg out in a kick. The strange woman's knife snapped beneath the force of San's boot, and — like a manticore switches attacks between paw and tail — she spun, delivering a backhand that laid the stranger out cold. The nose-less woman cracked her neck dramatically and looked between Adarin — who still held Nyrien by the throat with her own truncheon — and Balthine, who stood defenseless and unarmed before Dardan.

Lucky San drew her own dueling blade and came at Balthine from behind, going for a beheading slash.

"Zayne!" Adarin choked, unable to intervene while wrestling with Nyrien. Balthine ducked beneath San's blade and turned on his heel.

Blinding gold and red light flashed like a glimpse of dawn.

There was a sword in Balthine's hand — not the one he had drawn on Dardan, which still lay stuck in the deck — but one that was slightly longer, slim with two sharp edges. It was a rich looking, elegant weapon, with a filigree cross-guard and a brilliant, red gemstone on the pommel. The blade of the sword was a strange gold that reflected sunlight as a red gleam. The fine tip sat against San's neck and blood trickled down in rivulets with the lightest touch.

Lancen didn't understand how Balthine had concealed so large a weapon, nor how he brought it to his hand so quickly. San seemed just as surprised as Lancen. She gaped belatedly and dropped her sword.

"I yield," she breathed.

Dardan laughed. "Are you going to kill her?" She sounded intrigued. "I would." San's eyes widened and she cast a betrayed look at her boss.

Balthine shifted the grip on his sword and Lancen winced, unsure whether to look away. The masked man stepped away from San, who took a wobbly step back and put her hand protectively at her throat, stanching the wound with her fingers. He flourished the golden blade, and a small trail of San's blood stained the deck.

Lancen blinked. It was only a blink, but when he opened his eyes, the sword was gone. He looked from San, who had just faced death, to Nyrien, who seemed to have forgotten to fight against Adarin in her shock.

"I wasn't expecting you to spare her," Dardan said. Lancen couldn't be sure, but she sounded disappointed.

"I'm not here to entertain you," Balthine said, pacing around the cowled woman like a predator looking for an opening to kill his prey. His voices were so surreal Lancen questioned for a moment if he was dreaming. He decided he had never had such vivid or strange dreams, however, so it had to be real.

"Of course you aren't," Dardan said in a voice thick with condescension, "you've never been that kind. The sword was a nice touch. I see you have traveled far, Balthine. Or should I call you 'Lucandri'?"

"I don't much care what you call me," Balthine answered, "because the first chance I get, I'm going to kill you."

Dardan scoffed. "Then it's a good thing I have no intention of giving you that chance. It's good you are here; I was just about to give the others new orders."

"I don't follow your orders anymore," Balthine protested.

"Oh?" Dardan asked, her voice full of sickly-sweet derision. "Then what do you call *that*?" She gestured to Balthine's discarded sword. "What about the fact that you don't seem to be standing fewer than four feet from me? You may feel a newfound strength, Balthine the lesser, but it was I who gave it to you, and I hold your leash, as ever."

Balthine lowered his scarf to spit on the deck. "How are you even ready to give orders?" he asked caustically. "If your plan had succeeded, your games would be over. I don't suppose the others know why you really wanted the princess, do they?"

8

Corin perked up at that. *What is she hiding?*

"Hold your tongue," Dardan demanded, and he complied. That was even more startling than seeing him drop his weapon. "I always have a contingency plan. Now, the Daughters are called to start a war, and each of you has a role to play. Lancen, you will continue the work you were doing before the business with the princess."

Lancen nodded uncomfortably. "Sedition, riots, high treason," he acknowledged absently, keeping his eyes on Balthine. *What happened to you?* He thought, only to realize that was the wrong question. The question he really wanted to ask was, *What are you?*

CHAPTER ONE

Raw pain threatened to split Cassidy's skull in two. Harsh morning light somehow reflected off every surface of the room and straight into her eyes, despite the curtains. Perhaps it was *because* of them, because the bloom was intense on the side facing the window. She closed her eyes again, but it wasn't enough to block the pain. What had she been thinking, last night?

A finger made its way lazily along her lower ribs. "What about this one?" asked a too-loud voice in her ear. She knew what's-his-name wasn't yelling — in fact, she could tell by the way his breath felt against her neck he was whispering — but in the wake of a night of drinking, it sounded like a thousand cannons firing in concert.

"A duel," she answered through the pain. "A woman challenged me to impress her husband."

The man whose name she couldn't remember giggled effeminately, and Cassidy wanted to hit him for making so much noise. "Did it work?"

She yawned, trying to remember the details. "Maybe if he liked women with missing teeth," she answered. She pried one eye open. The man she laid in bed with had long hair the color of coal and skin the color of milk. Not a sort for the outdoors, it seemed.

He traced a long, slender finger along her upper thigh. "And this?"

Gods take me now, she thought bitterly. He'd been asking about her scars since the moment she woke up — though, on reflection, she realized she wasn't sure how long ago that was. *And this hangover,* she added. *In fact, take this hangover first.* "A pistol shot," she answered after a moment. "Just a graze, but it hurt."

"I'm sure it did," the man replied, shifting around so Cassidy was suddenly underneath him.

He's so skinny, she thought, *what was I thinking last night?* She remembered only that she had been drinking to avoid thinking. She gave another look to the skinny man on top of her. *What was I drinking last night?* He wasn't unattractive, she supposed, though she generally preferred men who had at least seen the sun once in their lives, or men who could carry her to bed or pin her to the wall when they — *Why am I with this man?* She wondered.

Distantly, a door slammed, and Cassidy felt the pain in her head spike. "Damn!" the man hissed in Cassidy's ear. "My wife's home early! You need to get out of here!"

Cassidy forced her eyes open. "You have a *wife?*" she demanded.

"Yes," her strange paramour said in a matter-of-fact tone. "I told you last night. You insisted we do this anyway."

"That doesn't sound like me," she replied. She forced herself out of bed and stumbled for her clothes.

"I think you were very drunk."

"Okay," Cassidy conceded, "*that* definitely sounds like me." She found her trousers and pulled them on with wobbly steps. She heard boots hitting stairs. *Shit.* She was only just getting her shirt on when she heard the doorknob. Her eyes darted from the rest of her clothes to the door, to the window. *Only one way to deal with this,* she thought apprehensively. She took a deep breath and closed her eyes, feeling for a strange part of her senses that didn't belong. It was the power given to her by the Fae. A cold wave ran through her body, chilling her heart and blood. The pain, weariness, and haziness she felt were washed away and replaced with a sense of intense focus. She broke into a run, scooping up her boots and corset in one hand and the belt that held her pistols and sword in the other as she passed by them. Her hat seemed to leap off the floor of its own accord and landed properly on her head just before she jumped, pushing the window open and falling from the second story of a rather fancy house overlooking Clock Street.

Behind her, she heard a woman yell something and a gunshot rang out above her, but it was soon lost to the rush of wind as she fell. She did a flip to arrange herself feet down and braced for impact. She landed in a passing rickshaw carrying large bags of something soft, and she tucked into a roll that brought her to the front of the wagon. The two men that had been pulling the load along seemed to panic at her sudden arrival and one let go and ran away, leaving his partner to be overtaken and run over by the suddenly escaping barrow.

"Shit!" Cassidy yelled as the rickshaw careened downhill along the cobbled street. People scrambled to get out of the way. A vendor's stall selling expensive-looking knickknacks was sent flying.

Cassidy yanked her boots onto her feet as quickly as she could, hoping she'd have time to jump.

She awkwardly rose to her feet, keeping her stance wide to balance on the runaway cart and tried to don her corset. She made it as far as the first hook when the rickshaw dipped forward and the handles struck the cobblestones, sending her careening forward into a crowded plaza. Unsuspecting pedestrians scrambled out of her way, leaving Cassidy on a collision course with a large fountain.

A voice called out from beneath her hat, "Arms up." It was the voice of Hymn; the Fae Cassidy had befriended almost two years ago. Cassidy obeyed the command and felt the wind around her shift. She was upside down when she reached the fountain and her palms landed on wet stone. She pushed off against it. With her muscles made stronger by her elevated state and her body guided by the Fae's manipulation of the wind, she was able to leap with her arms and land on her feet. Her weapon belt skidded along the cobblestones, stopping just beneath her.

Cassidy could feel the eyes on her even before she saw them. Dozens of people stood, many open mouthed, staring at her as if unsure they had really seen what she had done. A boy that couldn't have been more than ten was applauding her. Back the way she had come, merchants were trying to reclaim their wares. Two members of the City Watch — notable for their dark blue uniforms — were talking with a distraught man in expensive-looking silks. The man was pointing at her, shouting something unintelligible to her at that distance.

"I think it is time for you to start running," Hymn advised from the safety of Cassidy's hat.

"Aye," Cassidy agreed. She had no intention of paying for any damages. Further, if she were caught with a Fae in her company, her execution would be within the week. She dropped down from the fountain to pick up her belt and broke into a run. The watchmen had started after her before she even turned around, but she was halfway across the plaza, and she was soon able to make her way into a crowd working their way up a narrow street. Several people snapped and shouted as she forced her way through, and many more came to a complete stop to see what the excitement was about.

By the time she could see the watchmen forcing their way to her, she had already made her way to a shoddily made wooden fence between two tenement buildings. They were almost on her when she reached the top. The fastest of the watchmen began to follow, only to tear a plank completely off the fence with their combined weight. Cassidy nearly pitched over and swayed violently, holding on to the remaining posts for dear life. Beneath her wasn't an alleyway like she had expected, but a stairwell that led down to a lower street.

"Jump," Hymn commanded. Cassidy swallowed a lump in her throat and obeyed just as she felt a flailing hand knock her boot aside. The stone steps below her approached with a terrifying velocity and she braced herself. She felt a warmth envelope her even as a chill suffused her insides, and she felt certain Hymn was protecting her. The landing was not painless — pain ran up from her feet to her hips from the initial impact, and she banged her shins on a stone step — but thanks to the Fae's intervention it was neither fatal nor crippling. She breathed a sigh of relief only to curse in frustration when she noticed blood dripping onto the steps beneath her. She wiped her nose, blood covering her sleeve.

"Are they still after us?" she asked, pushing herself up. She looked up to see the guards breaking the fence open, presumably so they could follow without breaking their necks.

"I assume so," Hymn said dryly.

"Well, we can lose them easily enough," Cassidy said. She pushed herself to her feet and fled down the steps. Below her was Song Street, a busy marketplace just off from the east docks. She made her way into the crowd with greater ease than before.

"You should consider coloring your hair," Hymn suggested. "The red betrays you."

"I'll think about it," said Cassidy. "No." She crossed the street and stood in the shadow of a tea house that overlooked the city docks. "I can get back to the ship easily enough. Tell Kek to start the engines and ready me an alibi."

The Fae chimed like a bell, which somehow sounded like a sigh. "Very well, but I shall return for you as soon as I do." The Fae emerged from Cassidy's hat, a bloom of blue light, and zipped skyward, lost against the light of the blazing sun.

Cassidy looked back for signs of her pursuers. Three watchmen were only just reaching the bottom of the steps. She stepped into the teahouse, instantly awash in the smell of incense and tea. She walked briskly past the low tables occupied by drinkers and gamblers and found the stairs that led to the second floor. She spotted a window and made her way towards it.

Firm, slender hands grabbed her by the shoulders. Before she could shrug off her assailant, she was pulled off her course and shoved down onto a sitting mat. She grunted in surprise as a menu was shoved in her face.

"It's customary to wait to be seated, you know," said a warm, familiar voice. Cassidy's eyes widened at the thick, Rivien accent. "It's also considered rude to walk by old friends without so much as a hello."

Cassidy peered over the menu, seeing a middle-aged woman with dusky skin smiling at her through a transparent, green veil. "Madame — er, Sister Venitha?" she asked. "What are you doing here? Last I saw you —"

"You ruined my vegetable business," the older woman chided, though her smile never faltered. Cassidy grimaced at the memory. She had been staggering through the streets of Andaerhal with broken ribs. Venitha had carted Cassidy back to her ship in a wheelbarrow. She *had* said something about Cassidy ruining her stall, but she didn't remember what. "I took what money I had and came here to take over my friend's tea shop."

"Well, it's very lovely," Cassidy said, "but I really have to —"

"Be quiet," Venitha said, shoving the menu back in Cassidy's face. "And trust me." She plucked the hat off Cassidy's head and placed a silk scarf in its place. A moment later, heavy footfalls sounded from the stairs. "How can I help today, officers?" she asked.

"A woman came in just a few moments ago. She has red hair about to here, dark skin, and was wearing a black hat with a red feather. She caused quite a disturbance on the plaza."

"Hmm," Venitha said, casually positioning herself between Cassidy and the watchman. "Your fugitive might have slipped out through the veranda downstairs. No one's come up for at least a half hour."

"Thank you, ma'am," the watchmen said through a weary sigh. "Come on, maybe Jion caught her."

As they departed, Cassidy set the menu down and traded Venitha's scarf for her hat. "Thanks for that," she said.

"Don't thank me just yet," Venitha said. "You are going to have to jump out the window."

Cassidy laughed, but Venitha merely gestured her towards the window Cassidy had been about to leap from mere moments before.

"They could still be downstairs," the older woman explained, "and I really don't want you to cause a scuffle."

Cassidy sighed and approached the window.

"I'll see you again, Miss Durant," said Venitha, "assuming you don't get yourself in too much trouble."

Cassidy wondered how the woman was always so certain about that. It was uncomfortable, to say the least. As she settled herself in the open window, she glanced back at Venitha. They both ignored the strange stares from the tea house's patrons. The Rivien woman waved politely and returned to work. Below was another street, even further down than Song street.

Cassidy jumped.

The fall was steeper than it looked, and the rush of air was more than a little terrifying. She was barely clear of the window when she saw Hymn zip towards her with urgent speed.

"Bend your knees," the Fae ordered. Cassidy obeyed in the instant just before her feet collided with the drawn, leather cover of a passing rickshaw, which she bounced off. She fell ass first onto the street with a grunt. Soreness broke through the fog of Fae power, and she knew she would regret this morning when she stopped drawing on it.

She wiped more blood from her face and kept going. She wasn't far from the docks now, and she was confident she could make it to her ship and set off before her pursuers could reach her, assuming they were even looking in the right direction.

The docks stank of human sweat, spoiled foods, sex, blood, and a myriad of oddities collected from around the world all gathered in one place. It was a smell that made Cassidy feel at home. Less comforting, however, was the way people in the crowds went about their business. There was a nervousness in the air. Sailors who should be eager to set sail hesitated before stepping aboard their vessels, workers worried about what the next shipment would bring, and families watching the horizon from their perches looked more worried than excited. Cassidy was willing to bet none of them knew why. She wished she didn't.

15

She tried to push those thoughts aside when she reached the berth where her ship, the *Dreamscape Voyager*, was docked. It was a small ship of Imperial design, with a single balloon of dragon-hide keeping it afloat. She climbed the gangplank to find her First Mate, Kek, was listening to the ship's engineer, Lierre.

"… to compensate for the extra weight," Lierre was saying, her Castilyn accent giving her words a lyrical lilt. "Oh, captain," she added upon seeing Cassidy. "Your nose is bleeding again."

"Aye," Cassidy acknowledged, wiping her face again.

"You've been doing that Fae thing, again," Lierre said, "haven't you?"

"Aye. I had a hangover like you wouldn't believe."

"That's no surprise," Kek said bitterly. "You barely said a word last night, just drank and drank, and then ran off with some fop."

Cassidy hung her head. "Sorry, Kek."

"I thought it was supposed to be a night for the crew."

"It was," she said sadly. The night before had marked a year since the death of their former captain, Elyia Asier. "It was just harder than I thought it would be."

Kek's face softened. "Cass… I'm sorry."

"No, you're right. I should have been there."

"I get it," said Kek.

If only you did, Cassidy thought sourly. It had been difficult listening to them praise Elyia Asier as a hero, knowing what she now knew.

Lierre seemed to sense the tension, and she quickly said, "Hymn told us you might need an alibi if the city watch came running?"

"I thought I might," said Cassidy. "I think I lost them, though. Just to be safe I'm going to keep out of sight until we set sail. Anything I need to know before I start hiding out?"

Lierre nodded. "Those new guns were installed this morning. I was just telling Kek that if we don't make some changes to the engines, we'll be a lot slower than we were."

Cassidy nodded. "Figure out what we need and get back to me." To Kek she added, "Let's go see these damn monstrosities." She climbed the quarterdeck with her First Mate two steps behind her. Sitting on the aft was a massive, four-barrel cannon that dwarfed

16

the one on the port side, while on the starboard side was a brand-new flame-tongue. The new cannon bore decorative tigers.

Due to the rise in draconic activity, any vessels with less than five integrated weapons — including a cannon that could probably punch a hole in any of the moons — were not permitted to leave the harbor. In addition to the increased dragon sightings, rumors abounded about large numbers of ships going missing in the past several months. Most people blamed pirates, but Cassidy knew better because she had been at the Dragon's Nest when it was destroyed. The massive monster Hymn had called the 'Leviathan' was one of the nightmarish sights that plagued Cassidy's dreams when she could sleep.

"Pissing waste of money," Cassidy said, giving a kick to the new cannon. It didn't budge. She stared at it and thought about the monster she had seen pull itself out of that brilliant light. Against that creature, with its scales like mountains, this new weapon would probably be as useful as warm bile.

"We'll make up for it, Captain," Kek said. "We'll get what we need."

Cassidy wished she could feel as confident as Kek sounded. After Asier's death, Cassidy had inherited the ship. Unfortunately, the Asarian Empire placed a tax on inheritance based on value. She had only just begun to feel comfortable with the prospect of paying that fee when the Empire also issued the edict about armaments.

"Cass," Kek added, "you need to stop depending on that Fae shit."

"I'm fine, Kek," she replied.

"Well, you've got a trail of blood down to your chin."

Cassidy wiped her face again. She had been lost in thought and hadn't noticed. "Thanks. Are Miria and Nieves aboard?"

"Aye, Captain."

"Make sure everything is ready and set course for Revehaven," she ordered. "I'm going to turn in. We'll go over the numbers after supper."

"Aye, Captain."

Cassidy descended from the aftcastle and entered the door to her cabin and closed it behind her. She wiped her nose on her sleeve again before undressing. Then, she took a deep breath, bracing herself. She sat on her bed and released the Fae power. For an agonizing, eternal moment all her senses were replaced by

17

blinding agony as every exertion and pain she had been holding at bay since she had first leaped from the window this morning came rushing into its proper place. She fell back on her bed and forced her eyes shut. She buried her face in her pillow to hide her whimpering until the pain subsided from unbearable to simply miserable. Her head felt like it was about to split open. The only comfort she could find was the warmth provided by Hymn, who floated overhead.

When she finally found sleep, she dreamed. She dreamed first of the leviathan, and later, Zayne Balthine.

CHAPTER TWO

I am Zayne Balthine, wrought of the First Light, keeper of the — No, that wasn't right. That wasn't right at all. *I am the* Scorpion, *constructed by Jainin and Malinda Caraden —* No, no, no, *I am Lucandri, and I was born the son of the Imperial —* No, no, *no, no, NO! What is wrong with me?*

He put his face in his hands. Human hands. Mortal, flesh and blood. He tried to focus on that. He tried to remember what those hands had done. Acts of violence, or acts of good, or simple work that were neither evil nor benign — the acts of these hands were mortal, human acts. The acts of... Zayne Balthine.

He pulled his hands from his face and stared at the leather, half-faced mask sitting on his desk. Everything had become so confused when he had killed Elyia Asier and... what? He remembered so vividly the strange shock when he had looked down and seen a sword sticking out of his neck. Or were those someone else's memories? He had trouble sorting those out when they came. No, he decided. That was *definitely* his own memory.

Cassidy Durant.

The name fluttered across his mind, leaving rage and discontent in his mind. *She's the one who did this to me,* he remembered. But how? What had he become, and how had she done it? He thought back to the death of Elyia Asier — he had fallen ill, and when he came to, she attacked. He tried to fight back, wanting nothing more than to survive, but a strange woman had intervened. He could see her so clearly even now, and he knew her — or perhaps the *other* him knew her — but her name escaped him, like a whisper on the edge of hearing, tantalizing and irritating. A thousand different titles he had no words for, strange terms in different languages, sprung to mind when he recalled her alabaster face and inverted blue-then-red eyes, but the name was just beyond the edge of his consciousness. The only title he associated with her that meant something to him was 'Fae'.

Cassidy Durant had conspired with a Fae to kill him.

Dardan's weapon had been an imprisoned Fae as well.

Zayne clenched his fist, watching as wisps of iridescent light surrounded it. *What have I become?* He wondered again. He opened his fist only slightly, and the wisps filled the space. He watched them encircle his hand and imagined them flowing in the opposite direction, and they did. He directed them with his mind into the shape of the sword he had used against Lucky San, and in a flash of golden light the weapon appeared in his hand. He looked at his reflection in the impossible blade. It wasn't the reflection he remembered. Scars marred the left side of his face where he'd been burned, first by Cassidy Durant, and again when the *Scorpion* had come crashing down on top of him.

Where had this sword come from?

He remembered drowning, his lungs burning, begging for release. He remembered that deep, impenetrable darkness. He remembered the terrible heat and the oppressive cold. The weight of the *Scorpion* crushing him, forcing him deeper into the black.

He had dreamed of washing ashore in the middle of a city on the ground, in a strange oasis surrounded by ruins of grand stone, staring up at unfamiliar stars in a moonless sky, while waves lapped gently around his body. He had no way of knowing how long he stared at that strange sky before he felt the pull. The water had risen in a wave and pulled him back into the darkness, to drown again.

Then there had been light. That terrible, wonderful golden light that cut through the darkness so completely it left him blind. The pull was strong, a current that brought him back from the depths. He knew not how, but the *Scorpion* itself dragged from the murky depths of Justiciar Lake, and when he tasted the air — the *summer* air — he carried the strange sword in hand.

He sighed and let his hand drop to his side. The tip of the blade touched the floor, and a shiver went up Zayne's spine.

I can feel that, he realized. He could *feel* the floor through the tip of his sword. He could feel the *sword* through the floorboard. The realization made him itch. No, it wasn't the realization. He could feel the crew of the Scorpion below him.

He wondered if the crew had been a mistake. After resurfacing, he had decided to do what he should have done instead of killing Elyia Asier — killing Dardan, the leader of the mercenary group the Daughters of Daen. However, when he got to her...

"Why did I stop?" he asked aloud. He felt the rasp as his voice crossed the scarring inside his throat.

20

His strange sword became warm. A thought echoed across his mind. *Because she demanded it.* The thought came to him in a voice that was familiar, but he could not place it.

Zayne let go of the sword in his hand and it dissolved in a flash of light.

I was there to kill her, Zayne argued. *She had no say.*

Oaths are binding.

"I swore to obey," he said aloud. He remembered standing atop a decrepit tower in the darkest reaches of the Dreamscape, where red clouds swirled against an endless black, where chains made of stars encircled what seemed to be all of existence. He had knelt — *No.* That wasn't right, either. He hadn't climbed any towers; he had *descended* by airship. He had been branded down on the surface, in a wood obscured by gray fog. Yes, that was what happened.

He pulled one sleeve up to see, as if doubting his memory. He thought for a brief instant his arm would be bare, invalidating the memory. But sure enough, emblazoned on his forearm was the Crook and the three crescents that signified his allegiance. He traced the scar with his fingertips to assure himself it was real.

He had been struggling with what was real for a long time now, when he was alone.

The sounds of arguing broke his reverie.

It was strange that he could hear them in the galley below. He shouldn't have been able to. Yet, he could make out every word, and stranger still, he knew where they were. Nanette was standing in front of the door. Before her, shouting over her, was Shen, a noble-blooded pirate Zayne had picked up before going to Dardan. The other three were sitting at the table, occasionally offering a murmurer of agreement when Shen made a point.

"— promised to kill that witch!" Shen was shouting. "I signed on to bring her down!"

"Back off, Shen," Nanette warned. Zayne knew — he could *feel* — her stance. She was standing with her legs braced, a subtle lean. If it came to blows, she would be ready.

The pirate ignored her. "But our 'captain' just bent right over, didn't he? Like a trained kestrel, ready to serve!"

"You're out of line!" Nanette snapped. "You did no better; you were laid out on the deck like yesterday's catch."

"Fuck you! I ain't killing no empress, and I won't serve the Scourge or her little 'Scorpion'."

Zayne wasn't sure how, but suddenly he was standing between Nanette and Shen. The pirate was a head shorter than Zayne and scrawny, wearing a sleeveless shirt that showcased the myriad of black tattoos depicting chains and binds. His eyes widened in fear and his breath hitched as Zayne stared him down.

"No," he whispered to the pirate, the words scraping across his throat. "You won't be killing any empresses. That is my job. But if you are not willing to play along, you are more than welcome to walk overboard. If you're lucky, you'll strike the water and die *before* something emerges to eat you."

Shen took a nervous step back, his eyes fixed on Zayne, shaking with fear, but also something Zayne wasn't familiar with.

Zayne turned to the others. "I assure you, before all this is over, Dardan *will* be made to answer for her various crimes, and she *will* die. But we must first take the course we are presented with. Will there be any other questions?"

Aresh was a Rivien man with a prematurely graying beard. He shook his head emphatically. Xun, a lanky noble-blooded woman with her short hair styled decidedly *upward*, and Tagren, a mute and burly man with mutton chops, both stared at him with their mouths agape, shaking their heads slowly.

Nanette stepped around Zayne uncertainly. She was staring as well. She blinked several times before looking away. "Do you have a plan?" she said, refusing to meet his eye. "I don't think you can expect to break in the same way you did the first time."

"No," Zayne agreed. He flexed his hand and closed it in a fist, feeling the tension of his muscles stretching over the brand on his arm. "We'll have to be more direct."

"What?" Nanette exclaimed.

"We'll discuss the specifics in private," Zayne promised. He turned to his newest crew. "You had best not disappoint me." He wasn't sure why he said it, but he felt a smug satisfaction rise in his chest when he saw them grow tense in unison.

He beckoned Nanette along and they ascended from the galley. At the very moment he stepped out into the open air, there was a break in the clouds overhead and a beam of sunlight landed upon them. The deck — no, the whole ship — still smelled of the odd mix of charcoal and brine. He wondered if that would ever go away.

"What do you mean 'more direct'?" Nanette demanded. Zayne glanced at her, and her breath hitched.

"There are wards on the Imperial Palace," he said. "Old powers. The kind ostensibly forbidden in Asaria, Rivien, and Castilyn by the Iron Veil Order. I won't be able to sneak in."

"You managed fine before," Nanette answered.

Zayne led her to his cabin. He opened the door, letting her in first. She held her breath as she passed him. When he followed, he went straight for his mask, placing it over his face. Nanette seemed to breathe easier after that.

"Are the scars really that bad?" he asked as he sat down. He hadn't looked at them, but he could feel them. She took a seat on a chair across from him.

"Scars?" Nanette asked. "I can handle scars. That's not —" Her brows furrowed as she stared at him with her dark eyes. Zayne felt like she was trying to figure something out.

"No matter," he said with a sigh, though he wondered what was more significant than the scars. "You're right about one thing. The wards didn't stop me before. But we both know I'm not the same."

There was a silence between them.

"What happened?"

Zayne leaned forward, uncertain as to how to answer that. "I killed Elyia Asier," he began.

"That I know," Nanette replied. "Word spread pretty fast. Everyone said you'd died, too. Before the week was out, every tavern in the city was telling the story. I guess the *Dreamscape Voyager*'s crew wanted the world to know they sank the *Scorpion*. But what *happened*?"

"I don't know," he admitted. "I fought and killed Asier, and then her First Mate attacked. She called a Fae spirit against me, and —" He stopped and placed a hand over the scar left when Durant had stabbed him in the gut as he recalled that moment. "Dardan's secret weapon," he whispered.

"What?"

"Dardan said even Asier wouldn't be able to kill me. That's how I survived — Dardan's weapon was... *Lucandri*. I remember now. I was... broken, drifting. Sleeping. And then..." He shook his head, letting out an involuntary growl. "No, *he* was sleeping."

23

A horrified expression crept onto Nanette's face. "Zayne, what are you talking about?"

He sat there, the words on the edge of his tongue. Then he recited the fight as he remembered it, blow by blow, the confusing aftermath. At first, he stopped several times to recollect, but before long the memory became so clear he could remember each breath and injury, and his fingers twitched when he recalled pulling the trigger that ended Elyia Asier's life. It was so surreal, telling Nanette about the battle, because he shouldn't be alive to tell of it. He remembered *feeling* as well as seeing Cassidy Durant's blade lodged in his throat. It had *caught fire*. But he had survived, because before his throat, her sword had pierced his body and broken the concealed weapon Dardan had given him, which he now knew to be a living Fae trapped in some sort of jar.

"And this Lucandri... resurrected you?" Nanette asked uncertainly.

"Death is irreversible," Zayne said by rote, "once a life is snuffed out, it can never reignite. But so long as there is breath, a memory, a single heartbeat, death can be forestalled." He frowned. Where had he heard that before? "I am still here because I never quite died. By rights, I should have," he added, feeling at the wound at his throat, "but..." He hesitated. His next words were an admission of guilt to the most capital crime in every nation. He needed to say it, however. He had been struggling with it since he had washed on that strange shore, and he needed to share the truth. If not with Nanette, then who? "Lucandri is within me."

Neither one of them spoke for a time. Nanette rose from her seat and found a pitcher of water — Zayne never stored alcohol in his cabin — and poured herself a glass. She stared at the water for several seconds before drinking. Then she poured another and drank. She then made her way to his wash basin and hurled. Zayne felt a mixture of sympathy and pity as he watched.

After she emptied her stomach, she wiped her mouth and shuddered. She whispered something he couldn't hear.

"What was that?"

"I said..." she paused. For a while she stood there, her arms quivering as she held herself over the basin, like she was going to be sick again. "I asked 'how do we get rid of him'? How do we get this thing out of you?" Zayne knew from her tone and composure that was not what she'd said, but whatever it was, he wouldn't press her.

24

"Maybe it will resolve itself in time," Zayne suggested, though he knew it wouldn't. He had seen this before, though he didn't know when.

"And if it doesn't? I can't lose you again!"

Zayne was prepared to say, 'you won't', but his lips refused to form the words. Instead, he rose to his feet and walked up to her. He hadn't noticed before, but she had lost weight since being left behind. She had never been large, but now she was gaunt. "I'll need you for what's to come," he said. "Be strong."

Nanette stared him in the eye, an angry retort forming on her lips. But she swallowed it and said, "Always."

CHAPTER THREE

Cassidy awoke to the sound of wood cracking beneath frost. That alone shouldn't have woken her, but the sounds she *wasn't* hearing set her off. The engines weren't roaring. She flung herself out of bed, discarding the warmth of her blankets for cold, frigid air. She dressed quickly, shoving her legs into a pair of trousers and throwing a jacket around herself, forgoing a shirt and corset. She put her boots on and grabbed her gun belt and sword. She looked to Hymn only to find the Fae missing. Her heart stopped for a beat, and she wondered if she should hide. She shook her head. She drew a pistol and flung the door open.

For the duration of a heartbeat, Cassidy hoped that when the door opened, she would find Kek at the helm, having stopped because something was wrong with the engines, while Miria swabbed, and Nieves patrolled. She would see the balloon overhead, and the sun would be shining in the sky. She hoped, but only for a heartbeat.

When the door was open, the balloon was replaced by a standing mast with vast, white sails that stood out against a sky of black and golden clouds that stretched out endlessly into the horizon. Instead of her crew, the only person standing outside was a woman in a purple-black winter dress with golden hair that reached down to her ankles. When Cassidy looked at that dress, it was like looking into a window into a field of strange and beautiful stars. She stared out into the horizon.

"Djian," Cassidy sneered as she drew nearer, keeping her pistol level, ignoring the desire to huddle for warmth. Her hand shook a little, but not enough she would miss if she had reason to fire.

The woman turned to face Cassidy. She was exactly as Cassidy remembered, with her bronze-colored skin, and her distinctive eyes that marked her as a Fae — irises of pure white surrounded by the same shifting, star-filled purple as her dress. She didn't seem concerned by the weapon Cassidy had trained on her.

"We meet again," the Fae said.

"Obviously," Cassidy replied, cocking the hammer on her pistol. "Why?"

"There is no need for hostilities."

"I think there's very much need for 'hostilities'," said Cassidy. "What have you done to my crew?"

Djian sighed theatrically. "Typical human bravado. I am not here to play games, worry not. Your friends are safe — at least, as safe as anyone can be under the circumstances."

"And just what circumstances would those be?"

"The unleashed Leviathan."

Cassidy narrowed her eyes. "What do you know about it?"

"More than I could describe in the short time I have with you," the Fae answered. "However, you know enough already; it is a massive creature capable of untold destruction."

That's an understatement, Cassidy thought. When she closed her eyes, she could still see that *thing*, large as a mountain, pulling itself out of that pillar of light — from the Dreamscape — consuming anything unfortunate enough to get in front of its massive maw, and destroying anything it came in contact with.

"I have come to you now," said Djian, "to warn you. You prevented a terrible evil that was intended to coincide with its summoning, and for that you have my thanks. However, the one responsible has other goals, and because of the one you call Elyia Asier, one of the enemy's greatest weapons has returned to her side."

The three questions that sprung to Cassidy's mind in that moment were '*what does she have to do with this?*', '*what enemy?*' and '*what weapon?*', but all she could bring herself to ask was, "What?"

"Years ago, Elyia Asier broke open a prison meant to lock away a dangerous individual."

Cassidy remembered her former captain telling her the story. She had been a young girl, enticed with the promise of a wonderful gift. The Fae had given her a glimpse of the future which led her to her death. "Len," she said contemptuously.

"So, you know the tale," said Djian. "Yes. Len. She was imprisoned amidst the stars long ago, and it was our hope that she would remain there forever. However, it seems she had enough influence to reach out, enough to enlist an unwitting mortal. Since attaining her freedom, I suspect Len has been gathering power and intends to return to the side of her master."

"Who might that be?"

27

"Though she has carried many titles, you may be familiar with the Desert Goddess."

Daen, Cassidy thought. She lowered her pistol but kept it ready in case she needed it. She didn't speak the name. Hymn had warned her about the dangers of invoking the names of gods in the Dreamscape. "There's a mercenary group," she said. "The Daughters of… her. They were the ones who kidnapped Miria and… what happened at the Dragon's Nest."

"Yes. If I am correct, it seems Len has been busy garnering support for some time."

"So why are you telling me all this?"

"You risked your life, and the lives of your friends, stopping the last calamity. I thought perhaps you would like to know what you involved yourself in."

"Appreciated," Cassidy said sardonically.

"Remember my warning, Dreamscape Voyager," Djian said as she walked to the edge of the bow. "You have dangerous enemies lurking on the horizon. In the days to come, prepare as you would for a war."

There was a crack of thunder and Cassidy found herself facing a brilliant, blue sky. The sun was high and bright. The engines sounded like they had always been running. The frost-covered floorboards beneath her feet groaned as she took a step back. She let her arm drop to her side and put her weapon away. The Fae was gone, and Cassidy had returned to the waking world. It was strange; all her previous excursions into the Dreamscape had been like a dream. She had never woken up in the same place she dreamed before.

"Hey, Cassy."

Cassidy whirled around and punched Kek in the face. "Shit! Don't sneak up on me like that!" she exclaimed at the same time he yelled, "Ow! What the fuck was that for?" while clutching his face.

"Sorry Kek," she said. "You alright?"

"Aye, I'll manage," he said bitterly, rubbing his cheek. "Shit hurt, though. So, what's got you up so early? And armed to the teeth, to boot."

"Sleepwalking," Cassidy lied.

Kek gave her a flat look. "I've lived on the same boat as you for over ten years. You've never walked in your sleep."

"Well, it's been a weird morning."

"Afternoon," he corrected.

"Aye, that, too."

"So, really, what is it? Hymn got you doing spooky rituals?"

Cassidy shook her head. "No, just... I don't know, Kek."

Her First Mate gave her an uncomfortable look. "Alright. Well, when you're ready to talk, I'll be around."

"Aye," Cassidy agreed. "Anything to report this morning?"

"Afternoon."

"Fuck you."

Kek snickered, and Cassidy scowled until she couldn't hold back a snort of laughter. When they got their laughter out, Kek said, "I like the new look, by the way," with an unsubtle look at her chest, which was covered only by her night shirt. She drew her coat around herself and made a face at him.

"Don't get your hopes up," she said. "Anyway," she added, "your report."

"Nothing yet — flare," he said suddenly, and Cassidy turned around to see a plume of sulfurous yellow smoke shooting into the air from behind a cloud. After a few seconds, a second yellow trail was fired downward, spiraling towards the sea below. "Ship on fire," he noted.

A second later, Lierre's voice sounded over the pipeline. "Flares sighted. Yellow flares off to starboard."

Cassidy turned to Kek. "Looks like we're about to pull off a rescue," she said. "Get us in quick," she added before returning to her cabin, though Kek had already taken the helm and was in the midst of turning the ship.

"Where are you going?" he asked.

She acted affronted, "I am a lady. You can't expect me to be seen half dressed. There might be men."

"I see you fine."

"I said 'men', not boys."

"That's hurtful, Cass. I'm two years older —"

Before he could finish, she shut the door and went to retrieve her clothes. Hymn appeared as a small, glowing rose light above her bed, instead of her normal blue. "Where were you?" the Fae demanded as Cassidy shrugged out of her coat. Over the pipeline, Cassidy heard Kek informing the crew of the approach to the distressed ship.

"I could ask you the same thing," she replied. "Djian pulled me into the Dreamscape."

"Djian?" the Fae exclaimed, and her light went from almost pink to crimson. "What did she want?"

"To warn me, apparently. About Len."

Hymn's light grew suddenly pale. "What did she say?"

Cassidy told her what the other Fae had said as she finished dressing. She grabbed the hat that completed her ensemble. She adjusted the red feather in the band before placing it on her head. Hymn was slowly returning to her usual shade of blue. "She believes Len is the one leading the mercenaries?"

"Aye, that's what she said."

Hymn floated slowly over to her. "I cannot imagine Len being bold enough to take such action," she said after a long pause. "She was always a coward."

"Maybe time's changed her," said Cassidy. "Anyway, no time to worry about it, now. Come on, we have work to do."

"Do you really mean to risk your life for strangers?"

"Wasn't how I planned to start my day. But I can't rightly turn my back on a call for help."

"It might be a trap."

"It might," Cassidy conceded. "We'll find out soon. Unless you want to let me charge headlong into danger unprotected." Hymn's light shifted once more from blue to red and back as she floated towards Cassidy, and they left the cabin together.

Miria and Nieves greeted her with sharp salutes. Each was holding a pair of ice canisters — long, tin tubes containing a pressurized alchemical mixture capable of dousing large amounts of flame. Cassidy took the pair Nieves was carrying and tucked them under her arms.

Soon, the *Dreamscape Voyager* was plunged deep into the thick, low clouds and the air became thick with the smell of wood smoke. Over the roar of the engines and winds, Cassidy could hear panicked screams. They were close. Amid the gray and black plumes, Cassidy saw a flicker of what lay beyond.

"Kek! Hard rise!" she ordered. Her first mate pulled the rope that fueled the flames of the balloon, and the ship began to rapidly ascend. When the *Dreamscape* cleared the cloud and the cold rush of air washed upon them, she grabbed hold of the gunwale and watched with bated breath as her ship only narrowly cleared the burning ship beneath her. It was perhaps twice the size of Cassidy's ship, accounting for the fact that the entire port side hull had been cleaved away, leaving charred, splintered, and burning tinder in its place. The ship was of Castilyn design, with the balloon mounted directly atop of the pilot station, so they had to descend to survey the deck. When they could see, they found a screaming woman crawling through the rubble towards a wall of fire that separated her from a man and child. "Nieves, get ready for triage. Miria, get ready to board."

"Aye, Captain," they said in unison.

The moments stretched out for an eternity as they circled the sinking wreckage. Whatever had torn the ship asunder had been thorough — the ship had been four decks deep, and all were exposed and burning. She could see movement through the smoke. Discordant screams and hollers filled the space. They descended carefully until the Dreamscape's main deck was only a short distance above the distressed ships. The two vessels collided with a gentle, yet jarring *thud*, and Cassidy donned her goggles, put a kerchief over her face, and took a deep breath before leaping.

When her feet struck the unfamiliar deck, the wood beneath her boots cracked threateningly. She hoisted the ice canister and squeezed the lever. A jet of white, mint-scented mist spewed out of a narrow opening, quickly smothering the flames in front of her. When she released the switch a large patch of ice cracked on the floorboards before her. She charged ahead and knelt beside the woman who had been crawling. Cassidy's stomach lurched when she saw her left leg had been severed at the knee. There was a trail of blood behind her that extended to the edge, and her body was covered in soot.

The woman grasped desperately at her when she knelt to check on her. She was gasping and crying horrendously, and dread filled Cassidy as she wondered at the state of the rest of the crew and passengers.

"It's going to be okay," Cassidy assured her. "I need to take your belt off." In her shock and confusion, the woman weakly resisted her efforts for a moment before exhaustion took over. Her breathing began to slow when Cassidy removed the belt. "Hey, hey, no! Stay awake, stay with me!" She wrapped the belt around her stump of a leg and drew it tight as she could, the blood on her hands making them slick. The belt slipped off the stump the first time,

31

forcing Cassidy to try again. The woman squirmed, but she wasn't strong enough to hinder her.

The man and child Cassidy had seen were suddenly crowding around her.

"Mommy!" the child — a young boy — screeched. The injured woman reached out and grabbed her son's hand.

Cassidy turned to the man. "How many people are on this ship?"

He looked blankly, his eyes drifting between her and the ravaged deck. Cassidy snapped her fingers in his face and repeated the question. He shook his head as if to clear his thoughts. "We left port with thirty. I don't know how many are still… I don't know."

Cassidy bit her cheek. She wanted to ask what happened, but there wasn't time for it. "Can you climb a ladder?"

"Aye."

"Would you be able to carry your wife and kid to my ship?"

"They're not my —"

Cassidy slapped him hard in the face. Now was not the time to be shock-dumb. "Can you carry them to safety?"

The man looked at the two of them, crying in one another's arms while Miria tried to get the woman on her foot. "I think so," he said.

"My crew will help," Cassidy promised. "Miria, come on."

The younger woman nodded, and they found an open hatch leading below deck. Once more acrid smoke blended with sweet mint as she suppressed the flames that had risen to the stairwell. The wood cracked and groaned threateningly beneath Cassidy's feet with each step. Through the smoke, Cassidy could see daylight from the massive hole in the deck. She tripped over something hidden by shadow. She caught herself on the wall, which crumbled under her, causing her to slip. A splinter cut her arm. As she returned to her feet, she looked down at what had tripped her. Her eyes widened and her breath caught when she realized it was a pair of charred legs. Her stomach churned. She felt bile rise in her throat. She tried to take a deep breath to suppress the urge, but the smoke was too thick, and she was too aware of the smell of blood on her person. Still, she shook herself and carried on.

Together, they sprayed out the fires, eyes open for more survivors. What they found were corpses. Most were burned beyond recognition, leaving only human-shaped lumps of blackened ash.

Some had escaped immolation only to die from shrapnel when the deck had been torn asunder. Cassidy counted eight dead. They could still hear panicked screams, but they were further below.

"What could have done this?" Miria asked.

Hymn flew out from Cassidy's hat and hovered a foot in front of her, her blue light reflecting off the smoke and debris. "This is the work of the leviathan."

The thought of that monster causing havoc made Cassidy shiver despite the heat. She shook herself and said, "There are still survivors. Stow the *whats* and *whys* until we're done."

"Aye, Captain," Miria replied.

There were two doors on the second level, one of which had only a foot and a half of floor separating it from the massive gap in the side of the ship. The other door was on the starboard side, blackened by flames. As Cassidy approached it, a floorboard cracked beneath her weight, and her right leg plunged through it. She yelped. She tried to pull herself out, but she couldn't get purchase with her free leg and when she tried to push against the floor, it threatened to break further.

"Fuck," she muttered. "Miria, find a safe place to stand, and try to help me up."

The princess nodded and began testing the floor with tentative steps. As she did so, Cassidy thought she heard some of the screams dying down. She hoped she was imagining it, or at least the screamers had decided to save their breath. Miria found a pair of solid planks just in front of Cassidy. She stood with her feet further that shoulder width apart and reached for Cassidy's arms. She reached back and slowly she was pulled up. The sounds of tearing trousers accompanied a sharp, scratching sensation along her thigh, but she did her best to ignore it. Once she was able to get her free leg beneath herself, she stood, extracting the other leg with ease.

"We should be more cautious going forward, captain," said Miria.

Cassidy nodded reluctantly. She didn't like the idea of taking her time when lives were on the line, but it wouldn't do the survivors any good if they died too. With careful, measured strides, gently applying their weight to each floorboard, they made to cross the room. There was a loud crack. Miria gasped. Cassidy's heart sank. The captain looked to the princess and found her own tension and terror reflected in the younger woman's blue eyes.

They were still safe, for the moment.

Cassidy let out a breath she didn't even realize she was holding and continued her painfully slow advance to the door. When she reached it, she kicked it open, and flames lapped up to greet her. She reopened the valve on her first ice canister, blasting it into the smokey darkness until all that remained was a sputtering of mint-scented frost that evaporated immediately. She threw the spent canister aside and readied the fresh one.

She took a tentative step into the blackness beyond. She found wall straight ahead and felt her heart sinking when her foot did not immediately touch floor. It was a stairwell. She heard whimpering below. She dropped to a crouch as she descended. She wiped the smoke and ash from her goggles and saw a huddled figure half-way down the steps.

"Are you okay?" she called. The figure shifted, revealing it was two people. She couldn't make out their faces behind the smoke and grime, but they were both women, one of whom was enveloped in the arms of the one on top of her. She reached out to them, and for an agonizing minute, no one moved, the ship groaning around them, screams still ringing distantly. Then they shifted, the woman underneath rising to her feet, the other falling to the floor, limp. *Dead*, Cassidy guessed. The woman who stood stopped to look at her partner, only to turn and run towards Cassidy. She was crying. "Are you okay?" Cassidy repeated. "Are you hurt?"

"Is it over?" the woman asked. Her voice was shaking almost as much as she was.

"I'm going to bring you to safety," Cassidy promised.

The woman met Cassidy's eye. She was a noble-blooded Imperial, Cassidy noticed. "Nowhere is safe," she said. "The gods want to finish what they started. That thing… it drove her mad! The gods are going to kill us all!"

"That won't happen," said Cassidy, though her thoughts went quickly towards the leviathan. Was it a weapon of the gods? When Cassidy turned, Miria was only two steps above her. "Another one. Make sure she gets to the ship. I'm going on ahead."

"We shouldn't split up," Miria said. "This ship is falling apart!"

"All the more reason you should get back to the *Dreamscape*. Hymn is with me, I'll be okay."

Miria looked like she was ready to argue, but instead gave a reluctant nod and led the woman by the hand up the stairs. Cassidy knelt beside the woman on the floor. She was wearing a uniform of some description.

Hymn hovered over the body, illuminating it for Cassidy to see. "Her spine was crushed," she said.

"Aye," Cassidy acknowledged. She looked back to where the women had been lying. "This doesn't seem like an accident."

"No," said Hymn, "it does not. You heard what the survivor said."

"'It drove her mad'," Cassidy repeated grimly. "Someone did this."

"We had best turn back, before it's too late."

"There are still people in danger!"

"And you are one of them."

"I can't leave them, Hymn. Come on!"

The next deck was even more overstated than the ones above, with a gap several feet wide in the floor that spanned its entire length, separating Cassidy from the prow. On the other side of the gap was a woman wearing the same uniform as the dead woman on the stairs, standing with her back to Cassidy right on the edge of the chasm. Beyond her, Cassidy saw a uniformed man slumped on the floor nursing his side, a woman standing between him and the uniformed woman, and a man and woman curled together in the corner.

Both the woman in the uniform and the one facing her down were trembling. Then, the one with her back to Cassidy swung wildly. The other blocked with her hands and began to scream. She had been stabbed in the arms. The uniformed woman took her by the throat and spun, throwing her into the sea below as Cassidy watched helplessly.

Then she noticed Cassidy, who had crept closer to the edge.

"You there! Have you come to revel in my glory?"

Cassidy sneered. "What have you done?"

The woman blinked.

"It wasn't supposed to be like this," the woman said. "They found my altar. So, I gave my blood to be rid of them, but this..." she shook her head. "I called for aid, and it was a *god* that answered! And its word is final — they must all die!"

35

Cassidy drew her pistol and aimed, but the mad woman lunged at her, crossing the space between them as though it were a step. Cassidy was knocked off her feet, her back slamming the deck hard. Her pistol skidded across the floor. The woman was poised over her, knife in both hands ready to plunge it into her. As the woman's knife came down, Hymn was a blur of light that struck the woman's side, and instead of her chest, the knife cut alongside Cassidy's shoulder.

She spat a curse and kicked the woman off. Pain flared in her arm, and she drew on the Fae power to shut herself off from it. *She cut me with iron,* Cassidy thought wearily. She rose to her feet. Hymn had taught her how to use her bond with the Fae for more than hide away her pain; she could also cause any iron she had touched within the past few seconds to ignite. The connection between her mind and her enemy's knife was so potent it almost seemed physical. She tugged at that connection and the knife burst into flames.

The mad woman screamed, staring at the fire in her hand, too shocked to let go even as it burned her, the flames spreading along her clothes. Cassidy ran at the woman and kicked her, sending her flying into the sea. She watched as the woman fell, flames engulfing her. As she watched, she was reminded of how she had killed Zayne Balthine. A sense of unease sent a shiver down her spine. She turned away before she could watch her body strike the water.

She looked to the survivors. "I'm coming over," she called. "No one else attack me." She returned to the stairwell to give herself room for a running jump and landed on the very edge of the precipice. The wood cracked under the strain, and she fell. Her ribs smacked into the jagged wood. A flash of pain flared through the numbness of the Fae trance. She caught herself but was unable to pull herself up. As she struggled, the man and woman who had been huddled in the corner took her arms. They pulled, and Cassidy floundered for purchase, the wood scraping along her stomach. She hissed and groaned, but soon she was fully aboard.

Her breath was labored for several seconds that felt like minutes. Her head was spinning. Removing her goggles, she looked to her rescuers. Both were covered in ash and dust and grime, but she could make out their faces. He was a pan faced man with a nose too short from his face, and she had a broken nose and a long jaw. She could have kissed them. "Thank you," she breathed.

The woman shook her head. "For all the good it'll do us. We're still trapped here. This ship is falling apart fast."

Cassidy pushed herself to her feet. "If you thought it was hopeless, you'd have let me drop. We'll get out of here. My crew will be here. Hymn!" The Fae presented herself, accompanied by gasps from the survivors. "Tell Kek to bring the ship around. Quickly."

The Fae nodded and flew out into the open sky. When Cassidy turned to the others, they had backed away. "You consort with the Fae!" the man proclaimed, poking her in the chest with a thick finger. "You've saved us from one death only to shove us into another!"

Cassidy poked him back. "Listen here, you ungrateful lout! Before me and my crew came along, you stood no chance! Don't you dare accuse me of —"

"The Captain consorted with the Fae, too," the woman interjected. "It drove her mad, and then this happened! We won't let you —"

A new voice broke through the argument. "Leave it." A man nursing a gut wound on the floor spoke with a deep, resonating voice that reminded Cassidy of her father. "You're stressed, panicked." He coughed harshly for a few moments. "You imagined a wisp. Nothing more. Leave it alone. We owe this woman."

The woman blinked and nodded. "You're right, Jean."

The other man, however, sneered. "Are you mad? She's the same as Dahlia, she'll get us all killed — or worse. I'm not going to stick around and watch this happen again."

Cassidy thought he was going to attack her, but he walked right on past and was heading towards the precipice. She caught him by the arm and pulled him back. He was heavier than her, but he was also tired and couldn't fight back. *"Don't you fucking dare!"* she snapped. "I went through a lot of shit to get here, putting not only my life in danger, but my crew's lives, as well. A lot of people died, because we couldn't help them, but if you add your name to the list, I swear I will sing your praises where all the gods can hear them, do you fucking understand me?"

He didn't reply. Cassidy was ready to punch him, only to see tears cutting through the muck on his face. He stepped away from the edge, sat down, and buried his face in his knees. Cassidy ignored him and went over to the man with the gut wound.

"You've got a fire in you," he whispered to her. He chuckled, then winced in pain. Cassidy felt at his wound. Something metal — probably a knife — had been broken off inside him. "What's your name?"

"Captain Cassidy Durant, of the *Dreamscape Voyager*," she answered.

"Were there any other survivors?"

Cassidy bit her lip, remembering the count she had been given when she came aboard. *They left port with thirty*, she recalled sadly. "A few. Not…" instead of finishing that sentence, she said, "come on, it's rude to ask a lady's name without giving your own."

"Jean d'Argaelan," he replied. "Depending on who made it, I might just be the Captain of the *Western Zephyr*. Or whatever is left of her. Gods, but this is a mess."

"Well, as one captain to another, your only duty for right now is to stay alive. My crew will be here soon, and we'll make it." It wasn't a long wait, though with the *Western Zephyr* groaning and cracking around them it felt like an eternity. But eventually, Cassidy could hear the *Dreamscape Voyager's* engines, and the ship came into view above them. Miria and Kek were strapped into harnesses and were repelling down to meet Cassidy and the survivors. They were each carrying a spare harness.

Kek landed first and immediately handed Cassidy a harness. She slipped it on and looked to the survivors. "We'll have to carry two of you. Jean is wounded, so he'll get the easy ride."

Miria and Cassidy helped the wounded man to his feet and Kek secured him into the harness, though it clearly hurt him. Cassidy let him lean on Miria. Cassidy assigned Kek to the other man while she helped the woman.

"Remember, don't let go of me," she said. The woman nodded into Cassidy's shoulder, her arms tightening around Cassidy's back, her fingers secure on the rigging. Cassidy in turn wrapped her arms around the woman's back. "Pull us up, Lierre!" Cassidy called when they were ready.

Soon, the winch above began to pull them up, and they were rising through the wreckage. Cassidy looked down, ready to see smoke and flame and a sinking ship, but instead her eye caught something beneath the water. It would have been hard to see if not for the speed and size of it, but it was unmistakable. Like gray mountains just beneath the water's surface, the Leviathan moved before it sank into the unknowable depths. It had been there the entire time. What was it? Where would it strike next?

She had no answer to either question, so she stared at the water where she had seen it, even long after there was no trace of the creature.

CHAPTER FOUR

Winter had little meaning in the Rivien Principalities, even a city like Isaro which stood only just beyond the Imperial border. Far below the massive, wind-carved and sand-blasted plateau that held the city above the influence of gods and out of the reach of the Fae were miles of desert that stretched out on to the horizon. The noonday sun was heavy and oppressive on the sandstone streets. Coupled with the dry air, even Imperial summers could not compare. Zayne knew he could have alleviated some of the discomfort if he'd replaced his coat with looser, more locally appropriate attire, but he knew there were spies watching the streets, and he didn't want his mark to think he was hiding from him. Besides, he felt naked without his ensemble of weaponry.

From outside the harbor, business had seemed the same here as anywhere, but there was an anxiety to the crowds of Isaro. A week before Zayne's arrival, the city had been threatened by something it had never been faced with: an entire *flight* of dragons. Though the beasts had been killed far from the city, out in the dunes, it had unsettled people. For one thing, dragons tended to be solitary, territorial creatures. For another, the world had been kept safe from dragons by the Imperial fleet that surrounded their mighty nest. Though word of the fleet's demise hadn't yet reached them, there was ample evidence showing that it had failed in its task. And so, few people milled around. Conversations were blunt and hurried exchanges. Errands were being carried out in a rush. Every action carried the weight that it might be the last.

Zayne had seen it all before during sieges and war.

But I've never been to war, he thought to himself. He shook his head. There was no time to question himself. He had come to Isaro with a purpose. He pushed through the crowds easily — people seemed loathe to get near him and crowded one another to give him a wide berth; he wondered if it was the mask, or if what remained of his expression frightened people. Whatever it was, he was making good time. Behind him, his crew — save for Nanette and Tagren who were keeping watch on the ship — were keeping pace. Ever since the bizarre incident on the ship, both had been deferential, at least to his face — though, whenever they thought he wasn't looking they scrutinized him as though looking for something amiss. He wondered, briefly, how Jacques, Flea, or the others would have reacted to current events. He couldn't say he missed them, but the new crew was still an unknown to him.

Ironically, Zayne and Nanette had deliberately assembled their current crew by enlisting enemies of the Daughters of Daen. They had searched for betrayed contracts, for victims of collateral damage, for survivors of battle or slaughter. They hadn't needed to search long before finding people who wanted to kill Dardan. And now their purpose was reversed, and while Dardan held a strange power over Zayne, the rest only followed suit out of fear.

'Bonds made in fear lead to fragile alliances, at best,' he quoted to himself. He couldn't remember ever reading it or hearing it spoken, but he knew it wasn't his own original thought. He was uncomfortable letting Shen walk behind him. Of the new crew, the pirate had the largest grudge. Years ago, before he'd taken up piracy, he'd been a deckhand on a family vessel. Zayne hadn't asked what business they did — he hadn't cared, and it wasn't relevant — but he knew how it ended. Dardan had wanted something from Shen's father. An heirloom of some sort. When denied, she had every man, woman, and child aboard murdered. Shen had only survived by hiding in a secret compartment in the floor. Zayne had promised to avenge them. He still intended to fulfill that promise, but he could not explain the complications. Would anger outweigh fear? Would Shen kill him when his back was turned, crowd or no crowd? He couldn't guess, but he was sure he wouldn't perform a *second* miraculous recovery if the pirate were so inclined.

Zayne led his entourage into a tea house. Stepping out from the oppressive heat and into the cool, shaded building was like having a weight lifted from his shoulders. He picked a table in a corner so he could watch the entrance and the door to the back room. While he waited, he listened to the sounds of the qanun being played by an elderly man in the corner. Shen sat away from him, with his back to an opposite wall, eyes locked suspiciously on Zayne. Aresh was much less conspicuous — he might even have passed as a local if their watcher didn't notice him following Zayne across the city. Xun sat at the same table as Zayne.

This song has a hundred names, he thought idly. *'The Healing Requiem', 'the Dreams of Starlight', 'a Night in Altarium'...* He was sure

41

he'd never actually heard those names and had no idea what or where '*Altarium*' might be, but he felt a sense of certainty regarding the names regardless. Still, throughout Rivien, the song was called '*A Moment's Rest*', and he'd seldom, if ever, heard it played in the Empire.

"You're serious about this, aren't you?" Xun asked suddenly.

Zayne raised an eyebrow. "About?"

She winced.

"What?"

"That... thing you do with your voice."

Zayne narrowed his eyes. *The thing I do?* he thought. "All things considered," said Zayne indignantly, suddenly self-conscious of the way his words rasped and itched at the wound in his throat, "I'm lucky to be able to speak at all. I'd wager if I stabbed *you* in the throat, you'd fare no better."

"That's not what — *stabbed?*" she said. She clutched her throat. Before the conversation could continue, a young man in a gray turban and matching kaftan approached with two cups of tea. He set them down wordlessly on the table. Zayne noticed a small brand on the man's left ring finger — an eye in a box.

"How is your father's leg?" Zayne asked in Rivien.

"He is walking, though it hurts when it rains," recited the boy. Unlike Xun, he didn't seem bothered by his voice.

"Tell him to try scorpion venom," finished Zayne.

The boy bowed and retreated into the back room.

"So, we're seriously going to meet the Father of Bastards?" Xun asked in Asarian.

"Circumstances force my hand," said Zayne. "And before you ask, aye, most of the rumors are true. Except maybe the numbers." That was the most tactful way to say it. The truth was, Xiao Ta, known in the criminal world as the Father of Bastards, was a disgusting, brutish, monster. His moniker stemmed from the rumor that he had a million bastard children, spread across the world, doing his bidding. Nothing was ever said what became of the women who bore them. One tasteless joke Zayne had heard once or twice was that *every* bastard in the world had come from his seed. He was also an immensely powerful man. He had his hands in a dozen different enterprises. Most famously, he was the only known source supplier of Myt Dust — a vile, volatile drug connected to the

Dreamscape, which made its possession and use a higher crime than murder — in all three countries.

The young man returned. "My father will grant you an audience, Zayne Balthine. Your... compatriots are welcome to join us, of course."

"What did he say?" asked Xun. "And why is he staring at me?"

"He says you and the others are free to follow me."

Zayne rose from his seat and followed the young man into the backroom. They walked through a small, humble kitchen and the host opened a beaded curtain that revealed a darkened stairwell. He didn't step through, merely offering Zayne passage. Even from outside the portal, the mixing aromas of sandalwood and desert flowers penetrated Zayne's scarf and mask. *Myt Dust,* he noticed with a sneer. The drug smelled different to everyone — the substance called upon fond memories and in doing so, recreated the person's favorite scent. It was a cruel, deceptive poison. He swallowed his disgust and began his descent down into Xiao Ta's den. Behind him, his crew took the dark steps much more cautiously. Laughter, discordant conversations, and music that humbled the lone qanun player above echoed from below, rebounding off the narrow passage and ringing in Zayne's ear. When the stairs began to curve, Zayne saw a light ahead.

The room at the bottom of the stairs was far larger than the entire tea house above. Large pillows occupied by lounging men and women smoking from large, communal pipes spanned the entire room. In a far corner, the music was provided by a dozen women clad only in translucent silks that made Zayne's stomach churn to see. He swallowed bile that rose in his throat and did his best to suppress the memories that came rushing to him at the sight.

Two burly guards wearing crisscrossed belts in lieu of shirts stopped him at the base of the stairs.

"No weapons," one said flatly in Rivien, while the other nodded, holding a massive hand out.

"Fine," Zayne answered in kind. He pulled his sword and both pistols off his belt. The expectant guard set them on a table just off to the side of the entrance. When Zayne began walking in, the man set a hand on his shoulder. He twitched his fingers in the universal gesture for 'the rest of it', and Zayne rolled his eyes. He was confident in his ability to fight through, but that would take time, and he wanted to leave quickly. He reached into his left sleeve and extracted a stiletto, a barber's razor and a length of chain with a hook on the end. Then he switched arms and produced two more daggers. "There," he said.

The first guard cleared his throat and pointed with his eyes to Zayne's chest. The mercenary sighed. He reached inside his coat and extracted a third and fourth pistol from concealed holsters he had woven behind the left-side breast, and two more from the right side. "Satisfied?" he asked.

"Keep it coming," said the speaking guard.

Zayne growled under his breath at the irritation, the desire to simply kill his way to Xiao increasing. Instead, he reached back into the coat, unclasping the pistol hidden at the small of his back. Setting it on the table, he raised his leg and extracted the knives he kept in his boot.

"Alright, you can go," the guard said at last. *Good thing he didn't think about the knives in the hem of the coat,* Zayne thought. Behind him, the guards had started to take the weapons of his crew.

Once allowed access to the room, the Father of Bastards was an easy man to find. His chair was on the opposite wall atop a dais, high above the rest of the room, four times as wide as it needed to be, with beautiful men and women dressed in far too little lounging about it while two of their own fanned the crime boss with massive leaves from the tropical wastes. Xiao Ta himself was a gluttonous, pig of a man, who wore no shirt to cover his bloated stomach and flabby chest. He wore a differently colored, oversized and gaudy ring on each swollen finger and thumb. He had a thin mustache that wasn't quite the same length on each side.

He sits as he believes a king should, said a judgmental voice in Zayne's head, *above the slack-jawed yes-men and fools he's enthralled with promises of money or blinded with Dust. He will never know true power, but because no one has stopped his petty games, and he gets what he wants, he thinks he has it all. Men like him are so common, and so commonly think they are the gods' gift to the world.* Zayne wasn't sure what triggered that line of thought, but it seemed accurate enough.

"Ah, Mister Balthine," said Xiao Ta. His voice was stronger than Zayne would credit to his slovenly visage. "I heard you'd died in a dozen spectacular ways over Justiciar Lake." He was speaking in Asarian. "And yet here you stand."

"Then clearly the rumors were exaggerated, at best."

"The common thread in the stories I hear is that you killed Elyia Asier, and in turn her crew killed yours. I'd also heard that they sank the *Scorpion*, but my eyes and ears tell me she was the vessel you brought into port. So, what really happened?"

"Elyia Asier is dead, and the world thinks I am. Let's not dwell on it."

The crime lord pursed his lips and leaned forward. "Tell me, did Dardan enjoy her Dust?"

"She made use of it," Zayne replied curtly.

"Good, good," the Father of Bastards replied. He leaned back in his oversized seat. "Few people know the real value of Myt Dust. Too many people use it to escape their own thoughts, to get lost in visions. But we know that's a waste. You, and me, and Dardan... we're kindred spirits who've walked the land below and seen far more than the simple, escape-seekers." Zayne sneered at the notion of being called 'kindred' with the likes of either Dardan or Xiao Ta — and he wasn't entirely certain which notion offended him more.

He made a show of looking around the room, pretending to be taking in the decorum while seeking out the guards. There were six obvious ones — the two who'd confiscated his weapons, two behind the dais, and one on either side of the room — but Zayne knew a man like Xiao Ta would hide more in his crowd. He spotted a veiled woman leaning on the wall pretending to be in deep conversation with a young man who was too far gone to talk back. She gave herself away with her unyielding gaze in Zayne's direction. Turning the other way, he saw two men playing a game of tajk, but one kept reaching under his seat each time he looked up to examine him. After surveying the room, he concluded that at least two of the alleged concubines lounging around the host were secretly guards. Unlike the others, none of their behaviors tipped him off, but it made sense that he would keep at least two men close enough to actually *protect* him if Zayne — or anyone else — decided to kill him.

When he returned his gaze to his host, he said, "Your... accommodations are far different from when we met last."

"But of course!" the Father of Bastards replied. "My dens in the Empire are meant to appeal to Imperial sensibilities. Here in Rivien, well..." He waved his hands demonstratively. "Speaking of which... How did you find me?"

"You're not a hard man to find," said Zayne.

45

"Now *that's* a lie I've never heard before."

Zayne snorted. The truth was, Dardan had given Zayne a full list of places and ways to find the man when she'd sent him on the fool's errand of bringing in the massive shipment of Myt Dust she'd used to devastate the Dragon's Nest. While Zayne had hoped he would never find himself in Xiao Ta's company again, he'd memorized the information in case he had to.

"So, what does Dardan wish of me this time?"

Zayne's scarred eye twitched beneath his mask in annoyance. The comment was clearly barbed, a reminder that Zayne was unimportant in the eyes of the criminal overlord. He was just a pawn, a messenger for Dardan. He suppressed the urge to lower his scarf and spit. "*I have come for your knowledge of the forbidden and arcane.*"

"Well, you've come to the right place, for no one knows more about the mysteries of the power of the Dreamscape than the radiant Xiao Ta!"

A sorry state of affairs if that were true, came a thought from somewhere in Zayne's mind. He didn't voice the disgust he felt. "I need a way to nullify the wards around the Imperial Palace."

Xiao Ta chuckled wryly. "Ah, the Daughters always have such lofty goals. But what could you ever need the wards down for? Planning to summon the Dread Hounds in the throne room?"

Zayne gave a shrug. "Might be I am," he said. "I won't bore you with the details, just know it needs doing."

"And what do I get for passing along my knowledge? This could well cost you more than the Myt Dust did."

Zayne shook his head. "I'm asking for information, not merchandise."

"Secrets *are* merchandise."

Zayne made a dramatic sweep of his surroundings, sure to include the guards he'd marked out in his gaze. He then directed his attention back to his host. "You have quite the organization. Your influence can be felt in every nation. You have wealth, and the freedom to indulge in whatever depravity and taboo you desire. If you want to keep any of it, you'll tell me what I want."

A great hush spread through the room like a wave, starting with those who had actually heard the threat, spreading outward as guests of the drug den and musicians grew quiet to see what the quiet was about. Xiao Ta's face grew red as a beat. The people Zayne had identified as hidden guards stiffened, as did three of the concubines. The room was still, like a tightly wound coil ready to be released.

"You... you dare," said the drug lord, "you dare come to me, making threats under my roof? Kneel and beg my forgiveness, or I'll send you back to Dardan in so many pieces she won't even know what she's looking at!"

"Let's make this interesting," said Zayne. "I'll kill the first two thugs to reach me using a deck of cards and my left hand." He reached into the inner breast pocket of his coat, extracting a tarot deck and began a show of one-handed shuffling.

Xiao Ta's nostrils flared, and spittle flew from his jowls when he shouted, "Kill him!"

There was a chaotic rumble as the guards began forcing their way through the crowds to reach him. It was one of the fake concubines that reached him first — a lithe woman who extracted two knives from beneath her loincloth. Zayne held up his deck of cards in time to block a stab to his throat with it. The knife punctured the entire stack. He twisted the cards, wrenching the knife from her hand. He then smacked her with the deck, her own knife lodging into the side of her head. That was when the screaming began. The sight of her blood sent a wave of nausea through Zayne, memories flooding unbidden to his mind. He stopped for a moment, trying to push down his last memories of his mother, only partially aware of the milling crowd of patrons trying to leave. He swallowed his bile and focused on the moment in time to stop one of the men from bludgeoning his skull with a tonfa. He caught the weapon with his right hand and slammed its owner in the throat with the opposite palm. When he recoiled in pain, a strange surge of cold rushed through his body and he punched the man hard in the temple. The man lost his feet and fell hard, breaking his neck when he hit the floor.

"That's two," said Zayne.

Another attacker tripped over a patron who sluggishly tried to run out of the way, and Xun kicked him in the head. The thunderous crack of a gunshot rang out in the room and searing heat and pain blossomed in Zayne's left shoulder. From the wound, heat and agony spread out like wildfire like molten metal flowing through his veins until his entire left arm was pulsating and burning. He let out a long groan and cursed. A second shot went wide and killed a man who had begun running in a panic. Their attackers continued to fire until before long the room was almost completely obscured by smoke. The screams faded, but the groans of pain and whimpering and crying remained, made difficult to hear beneath the ringing in Zayne's ears. He looked around at the smoke, seeing the silhouettes of his crew mates standing alongside him and the bodies littering the floor around them.

Zayne flexed the fingers below his wounded arm. They were numb and twitching, and each movement sent a wave of fresh pain up his arm. He hissed. "I've survived better than you," he said through gritted teeth. The smoke began to dissipate enough that Zayne could see one of the guards reloading. He closed his other hand, conjuring the golden sword into being and threw it as if it were a mere knife. The golden blade spun through the air easily, cutting through the top of the man's head. Its arc came to a stop when it was level with his eyes. The victim's muscles twitched violently before his legs gave out beneath him. The sword vanished in a flash of gold light and reappeared in Zayne's hand before the attacker's body even hit the floor. The sight caused bile to rise in his throat. He trembled, struggling to swallow it down.

"What *was* that?" someone asked through the murk. Zayne threw the weapon again and this time it landed through the heart of a woman about to throw a hatchet. She died standing, only falling when the sword's disappearance disrupted her balance. Behind his mask, Zayne was gagging, willing himself with all he had not to throw up.

"I count five," he said with more dignity than he felt. He shifted his injured shoulder and bit his tongue to keep himself from screaming. The room was starting to clear, and he saw a knife fly through the air, lodging into the neck of one of the men who had been stationed behind the dais. He turned to find that Aresh had gone back to retrieve their confiscated weapons.

"Eight, captain," the Rivien man replied. He threw one of Zayne's pistols to him. He released the sword, causing it to dissolve into light, and caught the gun. It smelled of spent powder. *Those bastards,* he thought, *shot me with my own weapon.* He flipped it around, grabbing it by the barrel. A woman came at him with a long knife. Xun struck her in the gut and Zayne struck her across the face with the grip of the pistol.

The last guard — a muscular man who dwarfed Zayne — stood, shaking in terror, between Xiao Ta and the mercenaries. He was carrying a staff with a large ax-head. He made no move to approach, clearly banking on the hope Zayne and the others would come to him, or else be intimidated to leave. Zayne holstered the pistol and the golden sword returned.

"What *is* that?" the Father of Bastards demanded.

Zayne snorted. "I thought no one knew more about it than the *'radiant'* Xiao Ta."

The fat man sneered. He slammed his fist on the arm of his chair. "What are you waiting for? Kill hi —"

Another gunshot sounded over the words and the guard's head exploded. His body fell sideways. Zayne and the Father of Bastards turned to see Shen holding the smoking gun. Zayne nodded to the pirate, who looked confused for a moment, then nodded back. The mercenary captain flourished the blade and let it disappear again. It was a strange, cold sensation.

He stepped up to the dais, and stood over the Father of Bastards, who looked up at him with his mouth gaping wide, his eyes trembling almost as much as his body. He stood there glaring down, waiting for the ringing in his ears to stop. While he did so, he looked deep into the criminal's eyes.

"Fear suits you," he said when his ears were finally clear.

"What are you?"

"I'm asking the questions, fool. How can I nullify the wards on the Imperial Palace?"

"Please don't hurt me!"

"That doesn't sound like an answer. You might be in shock, so let me ask you a simpler question; which finger do you need the least?"

"W-what?"

Zayne held out his hand and re-summoned the golden sword. The instant the sword appeared it occupied the same space as the ring on the drug lord's finger, the finger itself, and the arm of the stone chair. Blood and small chips of bone and gems and stone flew in the air. The man screamed, pain and terror fighting for dominance in his cry. He raised what was left of his hand in front of his face. It didn't take long for the blood to cover it almost completely.

"You'll want to get better at answering questions."

"Th-the wards were made with powerful rituals," Xiao Ta said quickly. "And after the Queen of Castilyn attempted to use the

Dread Hounds to assassinate the Empress twenty years ago, they were reinforced."

"Fascinating," said Zayne. "How can it be undone."

"It can't," said the Father of Bastards. When Zayne tightened his grip on the golden sword, he added hastily. "Wait, the wards *can* be brought down, but it won't be subtle! There will be no getting away with it."

"I'm listening."

"It's a complicated ritual — well, more of a craft, really — but the main things you'll need are orichalcum, Myt Dust, human blood."

"Two of which you have plenty of," noted Zayne.

"*No!* I mean, no, I don't. After what you and Dardan took for her scheme with the World Tree, I actually have very little stored — and what's left is spread across the three nations. I was about to launch an expedition for more. And the blood, well, the ritual requires it be willingly given."

"How convenient for you."

"As for the orichalcum, you'd need a fairly sizable amount. You'd have to get it from the source."

"Well, thanks to Dardan, there's no shortage of dragons these days," said Zayne. "And I don't think they started flying without their bones."

"So, there you have it," Xiao Ta said quickly. "That's what you needed, right? I'll just be going, and I'll be sure to send the instructions to —"

Zayne punched him in the face, silencing him. He then turned to his crew. "Bind and gag him," he ordered. "He's our new prisoner. Aresh, find a way for us to transport him *discreetly* to the ship." He turned back to the fat man. "If anything goes wrong, you're sinking with us." Aresh broke into a run to leave while Xun and Shen pulled the Father of Bastards from his throne.

Zayne took the seat for himself and looked at his left hand which was still trembling. He was breathing heavily, struggling not to call out or whimper. Every inch of his arm felt numb to everything except the sharp stinging that spread across it. When he wasn't looking at it, he wasn't sure it was obeying him and moving as it should. His first thought was that the bullet in him had been poisoned. But it was his own bullet, prepared by his own hand. No, something else was wrong. He had been shot before, but this pain was something new. He closed the hand into a quivering fist — an act which only exacerbated the pain — and stared at his reflection in the golden blade.

The weapon needed a name, he thought, apropos of nothing in particular. He'd never understood people who named their weapons — they were tools that would be replaced as needed. But this sword wasn't going anywhere, it seemed, and more importantly, it seemed special. It seemed *alive*. He let it catch the light of a nearby lantern, turning it around, seeing the way light reflected at the wrong angles and color. *Dawn Star,* he decided as he examined the red gleam in the gold. Yes, that was an apt name.

He released Dawn Star, finding discomfort in how it ceased to be, yet he could still feel it — it was a tingle beneath his fingers, waiting to be drawn back to life. It was a thing of the Fae and gods to conjure something from nothing. Whether the weapon was divine or trickery of the fair folk, however, he knew not. But it was clearly a thing of evil as he had been raised to understand. *Too late for piety,* he thought. He was, in some form or fashion, bound to Lucandri, a being he couldn't fathom, so perhaps the sword was a consolation. *And maybe I'll sprout wings and fly into the sun,* he thought sardonically.

Another burst of pain interrupted his thoughts, and he bit the side of his cheek, drawing blood. He would need Nanette to remove the bullet from his arm, and quick. He moved past his crew and his prisoner without a word. He walked back through the city, but he couldn't remember much of the journey before he arrived at the *Scorpion*. The ship seemed to greet him upon his arrival. When he stepped aboard, he felt a brief surge of warmth, as though for a small moment, he had become whole again.

CHAPTER FIVE

The voyage had been tumultuous since they'd escaped the wreckage left in the wake of the leviathan. Nieves had put in long hours doing what she could for the wounded. Cassidy had held the hand of the woman who lost her leg — her name was Song Nia — while Nieves did what she could with her wounds. With Cassidy's belt in her mouth, she had screamed and squirmed while Nieves burned and cut the rotting flesh, as she washed and sewed. Cassidy had struggled to watch, but she never got up to leave. She had surprised Cassidy by surviving. Jean d'Argaelan had also survived his injuries, and while Nieves worked on Song, it had been Kek who pulled the broken knife blade from the man's stomach. The other survivors had been better off, with less severe injuries, though they were clearly in shock.

Unfortunately, their relief had been cut short by a sudden blizzard. For three days the storm raged. The entire crew and their unexpected additions had been confined to the storage cabin. Song and d'Argaelan slept through the worst of the storm thanks to copious amounts of poppy milk, but the others had been restless. Song's daughter, Ling, in particular tended to cry when the cabin rocked in the wind and shivered when the thunder caused the ship to buckle. She handled Nieves changing her mother's bandages and cleaning her wounds remarkably well, however. Across the room, the pair that had seen Hymn — the man was named Trask and the woman answered to Karis — stared daggers at Cassidy. When they ate, they waited until everyone else had eaten before partaking themselves. The only time they didn't stare was when Cassidy had to use a chamber pot. Hymn had not come out of hiding since they'd returned to ship, but clearly, they hadn't forgotten about her, and had not opened themselves to trust.

Even the suspicious ones had to sleep, however, and Cassidy had had a few hours each day alone with Hymn. Instead of sleeping, Cassidy had chosen to draw on the Fae connection during the storm. She wasn't ready to face the prospect of sleep, and the storm had left her pensive. While Trask looked on her with fear and suspicion, Karis looked upon her with unmasked hate, and Cassidy was unsettled by it. Cassidy had seen those looks before, when her former captain, Asier, had looked upon Zayne Balthine, the man who would be her killer. Is that what Karis saw in her?

When the storm had passed, the Dreamscape's crew had taken to clearing the deck of snow. The man Cassidy had mistaken for Ling's father — Lishun — had offered to help, and things were starting to turn around. With the deck clear, Cassidy took to her cabin and sat on her bunk. She took her hat off, letting Hymn fly free for the first time since taking on the unexpected passengers. Almost immediately, there was a knock on the door.

"Who is it?"

"It's me, Captain," Kek called through the door.

"If you're alone, come in," she answered. He was, and he slumped when he closed the door.

"First thing I'm doing when I get my cut from this job is finding a hot bath," he said.

"I wouldn't mind one myself," Cassidy agreed. "So, we checking the books, again?"

"Aye, Captain. Figure we better brace ourselves now. We lost more food and medical supplies than we planned for."

Cassidy nodded and they both sat at the table in the middle of the cabin. Kek opened the fat tome that was their ledger. Cassidy looked at the lines of notes and columns of numbers and sighed. In a way, the story of Cassidy's adult life could be told with those numbers.

With Kek's help, she set a new budget for when they reached port in Revehaven. That proved more difficult than she would have liked; since Elyia Asier had died, the fair prices they had grown accustomed to over the years had taken a sharp rise. Some of their usual providers had claimed their previous prices had been a result of Asier's blackmail, while others had simply said any arrangements that had been made were only valid with Asier, and they couldn't afford to extend any deals with her successor. Some merchants had continued to deal at the same rates as before as a token of goodwill and friendship, but those had been few and far between. After some investigation, the crew had learned that it was not without reason; many of the supplies they bought regularly had a much steeper market value than the *Dreamscape's* crew had ever been made to pay before.

"So, after Revehaven, what's our itinerary?" asked Kek.

Cassidy pursed her lips. The question always made her stomach churn, for just a moment. She leaned back in her chair. "This winter looks like it'll be long and cold," she said. "We can probably make a fortune selling supplies along the Reach."

Kek snorted. "Lierre would never forgive you. Besides, we've never gone that far north. We have no contacts up near the Reach."

"We don't have most of the contacts we had a year ago. Elyia left us with a lot of debt and few ways out."

"Easy, Cass. It's not her fault."

"You're right," Cassidy said, trying to hide the bitterness. She knew from Kek's expression that she failed. "How could she have ever seen what was coming."

Kek glared at her. "Cassy, what the fuck is your problem?"

Cassidy opened her mouth, but she stopped. She knew if she told Kek the truth about Asier, he'd be as devastated as she was. They all would. Instead, she said, "Sorry. I haven't slept well since the mess with the *Western Zephyr*, and all this…" She hefted the ledger and dropped it back on the table. "I just don't know if I can do it."

"Stow it, Cassy," said Kek. "You're not allowed to put yourself down like that."

"'Not allowed'?" Cassidy repeated. "Aren't I the captain here?"

"Damn right you are, and we picked you for a reason. So, if you tell me you're not good enough, you're telling me I'm an idiot."

Cassidy giggled. "Well, you are. But I'll forgive you. Now, if you don't mind, I'd like some privacy before my watch."

Kek stood and gave a mock salute before leaving. As soon as the door was shut, Hymn floated towards the table. "When are you going to tell them?"

"Never, if it can be helped."

"Do you think they do not deserve to know?"

Cassidy considered that. "That's not it," she said. "They looked up to her. They loved her."

"So did you."

"Aye."

"And despite all your rage, you still miss her."

"Are you seeing my thoughts, now, too?"

"No. However, I do not need to. Do your friends not deserve the truth? The chance to decide for themselves how they should feel?"

Looking at the Fae, Cassidy took a deep breath. "I wouldn't even know how to tell them. I can't rightly say, 'Oh, by the way, it turns out the woman we loved who brought us together was actually strung along by fate and didn't care about *any of us'!*" She punctuated the last sentence by slamming her fist on the table. She got to her feet and stalked back to her bed. She felt like a child when she threw herself into her pillow, but she didn't care.

"You do not believe that." It wasn't a question. Hymn spoke as if it were fact. Cassidy wished she could be so sure. She wasn't quite sure what she believed about her former captain anymore.

A thought occurred to her, however. "Why do you think Len gave Asier those visions?"

Hymn's color shifted briefly. "I wish you would not speak of Len so much."

"We don't talk about her all that often," said Cassidy.

"Perhaps, but names are dangerous things, especially now with the leviathan loose and the veil between this world and the Dreamscape stretched so thin."

"Fine, but just humor me."

"Her motives are likely known only to herself. I have no intention of speculating."

Cassidy was tempted to press the subject, but she was too tired, and though she had never directly said as much, she suspected Hymn was afraid of Len. She recalled her fight with Miria against the woman in the strange cowl at the Dragon's Nest. Her sword had been orichalcum, not cold iron. Had she, in fact, crossed blades with Len? She thought to the woman's reflexes, the way she anticipated Cassidy's and Miria's every attack even in the midst of that unnatural storm. What else could someone like that be but a Fae, or someone possessed by a Fae

Cassidy closed her eyes for a moment and lapsed into a dream. She was back at the Dragon's Nest, amidst the fiery wreckage of ships while she and Miria dueled Len. Only, now she was alone. She drew on the Fae power to fight, but her body collapsed, and Len struck her through the heart.

Cassidy sat on the prow of the *Dreamscape* and watched as Revehaven drew nearer. The Imperial Capital sat bathed in the pink and orange light of dawn, glistening with snow. She had seen the city many times, and had always been impressed by its majesty, but now it was like taking a breath after having her head submerged in a bucket of water.

"Part of me thought I'd never see it again." Cassidy turned to see Jean d'Argaelan limping towards her.

"I hope you're not disappointed, Captain d'Argaelan," she teased.

"Never," he answered. "And I'm no captain. Song was the First Officer on the *Zephyr*, so if there was anything left of her, Song would be in charge. I'm damn glad she made it," he added. "Too many didn't."

Mixed pangs of guilt and sympathy met in Cassidy's chest, and she had no idea what to say to that. Instead, she turned her gaze city-ward. "Well, don't be a stranger, have a seat and enjoy the view."

"Gladly." He brushed some snow around and took a seat across from her, easing himself slowly. He winced and rethought his descent when he disturbed his wound. "I never did thank you for saving us," he said after a while. "So, thank you."

Cassidy snorted. "Well, at least *someone's* grateful."

She had meant it in jest, but his eyes grew hard. "You're talking about Keris and Trask."

"Is it that obvious?"

He nodded. "Please don't take it personally," he said. "You must understand, they watched a lot of people die — friends and family, some of them. All because of... you know. I'd be wary, too, but getting stabbed tends to put some perspective on who your friends are."

"I imagine it would."

"I've done my best to keep them in check, but..." He clenched his jaw. "I think Keris means to report you."

Cassidy's heart skipped a beat. "Shit," she whispered.

"If I can stop her, I will. Otherwise, call on me as a witness. I'll see to it that her claims are dismissed as hysteria. I'll swear it to the First Seeker himself."

"Thanks, Mister d'Argaelan."

"Call me Jean."

"Alright, Jean. You can call me Cassidy."

As they drew near the city, Cassidy had Miria bring them into the port of the second highest mountain, which sat just in the shadow of the Imperial Palace. She had been tempted to pick a different dock — Asier had always made port in the same section of the city — but there was something comfortable about the old habits. As ever, traffic around the docks were busy, with city skiffs directed ships into neat formations until berths were available. Even after reporting the injured and being granted priority and an escort it took almost an hour before they were permitted to dock.

As soon as the ship finally reached the harbor, the skiff escorting them landed. Members of the city watch set up a rickshaw and saw to it that Song and the other injured were taken to a local doctor. While they were seeing to her, mention was made about the *Western Zephyr*'s demise. A uniformed woman in her middle years required Cassidy and a member of the lost ship follow her to the nearest watch house to give a report of what happened. Jean volunteered, and Miria chose to follow along as well, as she had also been on the ship. The woman never offered her name.

The watch house was a tall, narrow building on the edge of the docks, flocking with people looking to request aid, or air their grievances. Following behind the watchwoman, they pushed through a line and passed through a small room full of shouting people into a larger space divided into small cubicles. Their escort led them into one of the cubicles and bid Cassidy to sit opposite her in front of a table while Miria and Jean waited just out of earshot. She took a fresh sheet of parchment and took their statement about the loss of the *Western Zephyr* and their subsequent rescue efforts.

Cassidy wondered at how much to share. In the end, she decided to omit all mention of Captain Dahlia's madness and her altar of worship. She also deliberately left out any mention of the leviathan and downplayed the full extent of the damage. With any luck, the report would sound like the result of a gunpowder accident, or at least something more ordinary than a *giant monster*.

When she finished the story, the officer looked her in the eye, then down to her parchment, then back to Cassidy. "You say you were alerted to the destruction by emergency flare?" she asked.

"Aye," said Cassidy.

"And you saw neither beast nor ship fleeing the scene?"

"None," she lied.

The officer looked at the parchment again and sighed. "Send in your crew mate, I need to —"

A man's voice broke in. "Tsang, Captain Durant and her crew mate are to be released immediately." Cassidy turned around to the door to find the speaker, wearing the same uniform as the woman who had been interrogating her.

"How do you —" she began, but Tsang cut her off.

"I am filing a report on a sunken ship," she argued. "What's so important that we forgo protocol?"

"This," he replied, handing Tsang a slip of parchment. She read it with a disbelieving expression, then sighed. "You are free to go, Captain. Officer Tai will escort you out."

Cassidy rose hesitantly. "Alright," she said slowly. The newly arrived officer held out an arm to let Cassidy leave first. She did so, finding Miria and Jean watching the scene with interest. "Come on, Miria, we're leaving apparently." The princess nodded and got to her feet, following close. She didn't look nearly as nervous as Cassidy felt.

Officer Tai didn't take them through the entrance, however, but further into the building and out the back into an alleyway. Cassidy put one hand on her pistol, the other resting nervously on her sword. If the officer noticed, he didn't show it. They walked the alley until they reached a crossing, where three noble-blooded women and a man in matching black coats and asymmetrical, green silk capes. The uniform of the Royal Guard.

"Captain Cassandra Durant," said the man. "We are here at the behest of the Empress."

Cassidy stepped in front of Miria and drew her pistol, which led the women to do the same. She eyed them carefully, her heart sinking at the sight of all the guns fixed on her, but though her hand trembled, she kept the weapon up. She cleared her throat, and calmly as she could muster — more calmly than she could really believe — she said, "The last time I saw someone wearing that uniform, they were kidnappers. I need proof you are who you say."

"Uncle Tao!" Miria exclaimed. She ran out from behind Cassidy to the man with reckless abandon and heedless of the weapons. When she reached him, she leaped and threw her arms around him. He returned the embrace, letting her dangle off the ground from their height difference. "I've missed you!"

Cassidy watched, unsure of what she had seen at first. Then she holstered her weapon. She couldn't help but notice that the Guards did not do the same, and she felt naked without the protection.

"You've grown some muscle," the man said with a smile, "between that and the dirt, I almost didn't recognize you."

"How'd you know where to find me?"

Miria's uncle snorted. "We knew as soon as you arrived. But come, we have business in the palace."

The princess pushed away from him and took a step back. "You're taking me back?" she said. Cassidy took an instinctive step towards her, but the weapons trained on her made her hesitate.

Tao must have noticed. In a less private tone, he said, "You will be joining us as well, Captain."

Cassidy nodded slowly, eyes on the other guards. At the wave of Tao's hand, they lowered their weapons, but there was an intensity to the glares they leveled at her.

"Can we trust them?" she whispered to Miria when the girl returned to her side.

"Of course," she whispered back. "I'd rather not go at all, but I don't think we have a choice. I'm just glad you're coming too."

Cassidy turned her attention to Tao. "So, what's the Empress want with us?" She could see one of the Guard women bristle, but Tao just laughed.

"I recommend you don't speak so bluntly in her presence," he said. "As to what she wants... it's not for me to say. Perhaps she wants to see her daughter. It *has* been a while."

The Royal Guard led them further down the alley to a skiff. Cassidy and Miria huddled together at the prow as the Royal Guardsmen fired up the balloon. The skiff rose and the engine roared gently, pushing them towards the palace. Cassidy looked down at Revehaven. Flight within the bounds of the cities were restricted to government sanctioned skiffs and emergencies, so she had never actually seen the city from this angle, like she was looking at a large map. It was interesting seeing the difference between high and low traffic streets from the sky. The Guard seemed disinterested in the view, but Cassidy couldn't help but be swept up by it.

When they began to cross mountains, her attention was redirected to the Imperial Palace. She had never even been to the palace *district*, much less the palace itself. She thought of Asier's story of how she had somehow stolen away inside and fell in love with the Empress. Under the shadow of the towering pagodas and mighty walls atop which guards stood every dozen or so feet, that story seemed impossible. Thinking of Asier at all sent a pang of sorrow through her chest. She looked over at Miria, who was looking at the palace with a nervous smile, like she wasn't sure how to feel about her homecoming. Cassidy clasped her hand, and the princess's smile deepened.

Inside the gate was a courtyard full of grass and a wide assortment of bushes. Cassidy stared in awe, unsure of how they could have grown them. The skiff descended into the courtyard, and the smell of a forest rose to meet them. It seemed impossible. When they landed, Tao jumped over the side and offered his hand to help Miria down. The princess giggled and jumped after him. Cassidy followed suit.

"We may have a problem," Hymn whispered from her hat. "There are wards — spells — on the palace walls. I will be unable to enter without permission. I may be discovered." Cassidy's heart skipped a beat.

"Is something wrong, Captain Durant?"

Cassidy looked to Tao. "Um…" An idea struck her. "So, we really have permission to enter the palace?" she asked.

Tao cocked his head, clearly unsure what prompted the question. "Of course," he answered. He led them to a set of double doors and opened one side. "After you," he said. Miria entered first. Cassidy hesitated at the threshold, and took a step, half expecting her hat to fall off, exposing Hymn.

Instead, she heard Hymn mutter, "I cannot believe that worked."

A man as thin as a reed garbed in a green, silk robe came to greet them. He gave a distasteful glance at Cassidy, and a long-suffering look at Miria. "Highness," he intoned with a gentle bow. "You and your… companion… are in no fit shape to be granted an audience with her august majesty."

"Hau," Miria said, more sternly than Cassidy had ever heard her. "This woman is my *captain*, and you will speak to her with due respect."

Cassidy opened her mouth to say that wasn't necessary, but she was shocked to silence by Miria's sudden conviction. By the time she composed herself, the man named Hau merely bowed again and

60

said, "Of course, highness. I apologize, Captain." He sounded almost sincere. "Please, this way."

He led them up a staircase, and Cassidy looked around. The red carpet that covered the floor was the softest she had ever felt. Decorative paintings and weapons lined the crimson walls. The room smelled of sweet smoke originating from strange woods burning on ornate tables. More than the expensive decor, however, it was the size that caught Cassidy off guard. The ceiling was so high and the walls so wide, she almost felt like she was still standing outside.

Hau stopped beside a door flanked by two gray-robed women. "I will see you once you are fit to attend the court." He bowed to Miria and scuttled off.

The servants opened the door and ushered Cassidy and Miria into a room with a bath chamber filled with steam and more women in gray. Cassidy squeaked in protest as her clothes were attacked and removed with ruthless efficiency. She felt Hymn leap off her head to take her hat with her, and a sharp sense of dread cut her to the quick. Hopefully, that looked like an accident.

The next few moments were disordered and chaotic. She thrashed as her head was shoved underwater and scraped clean with brushes stiff as iron. When she was pulled up for air she yelped in pain, which caused her to swallow a mouthful of soap and spring water before being resubmerged. The palace servants scoured the dirt from her skin and hair like they were at war and her body was nothing more than the battle zone. Cassidy was sure they drew blood, but still they carried on. They gave no care for her privacy or modesty, they scrubbed every fold and crevasse, even cleaning under her nails with malicious intent.

When at last they pulled her from the water, Cassidy had never felt so violated or so clean in all her life.

Still, the servants assaulted Cassidy, beating at her wet skin even with towels as they ran combs through her hair, working out knots with a painful intensity. They pulled her limbs this way and that, and she felt like a doll being fought over by a pack of girls. When at last the servants were finished, they wrapped towels around her and Miria as if they suddenly cared about modesty.

Cassidy crossed the bath hall to retrieve her hat. As she stooped to pick it up, one of the servants rushed forward.

"We will take your clothes to be laundered, mistress," she said, reaching for the hat with the pile of Cassidy's travel-worn attire. Cassidy fumbled for an argument, only to find the Fae missing.

"But what about the Empress?" she asked, setting the hat on the stack, though her thoughts were on the Fae. Where had she gone?

There was a synchronized gasp from the servants. The one with Cassidy's clothes in hand said, "You could not attend Her august majesty in such foreign and common vestments!" She sounded so offended Cassidy might as well have suggested pissing on the throne. "While there is no time to tailor something for the occasion, we have had something prepared for you."

Cassidy looked to Miria, who merely nodded, as if this were expected. They were led into a side room. Stepping into the cool, dry, well-lit powder room was a startling contrast from the steam and humidity of the bathing chamber. The gray-clad women ushered them behind modesty screens and almost immediately Cassidy was assaulted by makeup brushes.

The handmaidens dressed her and applied makeup with the same ruthless efficiency as they had bathed her, wrapping layers of fine silk around her ease in spite of her feeble resistance. Cassidy was almost unprepared to find herself standing on her own two feet, wearing a pair of wooden sandals and a long and beautiful green-on-green dress bedecked with embroidered flower petals she had never seen.

At her side, Miria was the picture of serenity despite the working over she had received. How she managed to look so poised after the aggressive care they had both received was a wonder. The princess wore a black and jade ensemble that fit her better than anything she had worn since Cassidy had met her.

The two stood in front of a standing mirror, forming a picture of contrasts. The princess was only as tall as Cassidy's shoulders and slender where Cassidy had more weight and steeper curves, which in their current dresses gave Miria a flowing look. Cassidy's make up was subtler, with a coloring not so different from her naturally dark skin, with only the plum-colored lip and eye paint standing out, while Miria's face had been painted more elaborately with a white face marked in shades of green, from her lips to the space beneath her exaggerated brows.

Miria patted Cassidy's shoulder affectionately. "Are you ready, captain?"

"To meet the Empress?" Cassidy squeaked. "Never."

Miria's smile was almost imperceptible under the makeup. "No one ever is. Come, she is expecting us."

The servants held open a door opposing the bathing chamber. Hau and Miria's uncle stood waiting in a corridor, apparently deep in conversation. Cassidy had thought the guide's robes had been fine when he had escorted them before, but in the presence Miria's finery, his was dry grass beside a pile of emeralds. As they stepped out into the hall, Tao's guards stepped from shadows and nooks in the wall as though in a dream.

The thin man nodded approvingly and led the party up a steep flight of stairs which led to a needlessly tall corridor. Tao and Miria exchanged excited whispers while the Guards walked stoically, giving Cassidy unpleasant looks when she happened to glance at them. After many twists and turns, they came to an immense hallway with an ornate and ostentatious crimson double-door that could lead to nowhere but the throne room.

"Her Majesty awaits within," Hau said. He pushed the door open with what appeared to be a great effort and bowed, offering them passage. Cassidy watched as Miria walked in confidently, followed by Tao. When Cassidy hesitated, one of the guards nudged her aggressively with an elbow. She glowered at the offending woman but shrugged it off and entered the room.

The room was the largest Cassidy had ever seen. The *Dreamscape Voyager* could sit comfortably beneath the high ceiling and within its wide walls. The room was lit with a mixture of daylight and candles that lined the room. Along the walls were dozens of banners depicting the Jade Phoenix, paintings of beautiful men and women, spears and halberds and swords, and on the back wall, towering above all else, was the statue of a woman sitting cross-legged in a meditative pose. In the giant woman's shadow, atop a dais, was a cushioned bench, where upon a woman in a long, silk green and black dress sat in a similar position. The Empress wore white face paint that contrasted with the dark, kohl painted eyes. Unlike Miria, her eyes were brown, a color more common amongst the noble-blooded, but they did not make *her* seem common. There was an intensity to her gaze that made Cassidy feel cold.

Hau led them to the foot of the dais, where he fell to his knees and hid his face against the floor. After a moment, he glanced back and made a twitching gesture that Cassidy took to mean she should do the same. She knelt more slowly, not out of disrespect but simply because she was not used to moving in such confining clothes, or dealing with royalty — at least, not undisguised royalty. This woman ruled the Empire. Nobility from every nation begged for an audience with her. She could decide the fates of countless lives, pardon or condemn anyone of any station with a wave of her hand. She commanded every fleet in the Empire. A word from her, and Cassidy could be executed, and no one would question it. In the face of the reality of her power, Miria's true identity seemed so surreal. Asier's stories seemed *beyond* impossible now.

"Captain Cassandra Durant, you are welcome within our halls," said the Empress. Her voice was rich and opulent, almost as ephemeral and otherworldly as a Fae. "You may rise. The rest of you, leave us."

Cassidy pushed herself back to her feet, nearly tripping on her borrowed skirt to watch Hau and the others offer bows before departing.

When the door closed behind them, the Empress turned to Miria. "You've grown," she said.

"I've had to," replied the princess, "the world is a large place to fit in."

A smile cracked the Empress's mask. It seemed sad and out of place. "Elyia said something similar, once." The smile disappeared, giving way once more to stoicism. "You should have returned when she died."

Miria didn't answer at first. She looked to Cassidy for a moment, then back to her mother. "I made my choice, and I'd make it again."

"Would you? You were abducted, and nearly killed." The Empress was cool as the morning frost, but there was an edge to her words. Cassidy's heart sank.

"How do you know about that?" the princess asked, mirroring Cassidy's own thoughts. At that moment, the door opened behind them. Cassidy turned to see a woman limping into the room. Her right leg was replaced with a wooden peg, each alternate step offering a gentle *thunk*. The woman wore a black and red military coat adorned with sashes. As she drew nearer, Cassidy noticed her right arm ended in a stump which was obscured by the arm of her coat being bound around it. The right side of her face was also covered by a half-mask — Cassidy could see hints of burn-scars beneath it along the edge.

"Forgive my tardiness, Majesty," she said. "I do not walk as fast as I used to."

"Captain Durant," said the Empress, "We understand you are acquainted with Admiral Jarva Hawkwind." Cassidy merely looked at the woman, unsure when she would have had the chance to meet the unfortunate woman. When she didn't answer, the Empress continued, "She was the Captain of the *Justice*. You informed her of our daughter's abduction just before the gods turned their full attention to the Dragon's Nest."

Cassidy scratched her head. She *vaguely* remembered the ship that tried to stop them from approaching the nest. She had been worried they would be shot out of the sky before they could rescue Miria.

"That was you?" Cassidy asked. She looked at the state of Hawkwind and had to fight to stop from shuddering. She remembered the way ships all around them had caught fire, or suddenly cracked like ice.

The woman bowed as low as her injuries would allow, and only after the Empress bid her rise did she answer. "Aye, that was me." Her eye swept along Cassidy's figure, and she couldn't help but be self-conscious, unsure if Hawkwind was offended that Cassidy had made it out sufficiently unscathed. Guilt steeped in her chest. "I am glad you were able to rescue her Highness."

"Me too," Cassidy said. After a moment, she added, "It was a near thing. I couldn't have done it without you." She chose to omit the fact that without Hawkwind's interference, she might have gotten to Miria sooner. Cassidy had managed pretty well, all things considered, and suddenly faced with what could have been, she didn't feel she had the right to complain.

"If that's true," said Miria, "then I owe you a great debt, Admiral."

Cassidy felt warm seeing the smile bubble its way onto Hawkwind's face.

"I only did my duty, your highness."

"Admiral Hawkwind's report is unsettling," the Empress interjected, bringing Cassidy's attention back to where she was. "Tell us, Captain Durant, what do you know of the creature that emerged in the desert?"

Cassidy reeled back from the unexpected question. The Empress was asking *her* about the leviathan? And why did she insist on referring to herself in plural? Regardless, she knew she had to answer carefully, since all her information came from Hymn. Mentioning that would get her executed.

"We call it the leviathan," she said slowly, looking for some hint of recognition on the Empress's face. All Cassidy found was a placid mask. "It came from the Dreamscape. I think," she added quickly. "That's the only way I could describe it. It destroyed everything it came into contact with. When we were en route to Revehaven, we encountered a ship that had been struck by the Leviathan. It was... horrible." One detail she hadn't thought much about struck her suddenly. "Even dragons seemed afraid of it."

The Empress nodded. "As of yet, the world at large doesn't know the creature exists. But it is a clear threat. Every day, more reports of missing ships flood in. Something must be done." She unfolded her legs and rose to her feet, descending from the dais. She was taller than Cassidy expected. "You have seen the creature; you know what is at stake."

Cassidy was about to shout but bit her tongue. *This is the Empress,* she reminded herself.

"You can't expect *us* to deal with the leviathan," Miria interjected.

"You? No, we expect you to remain here in the city," she said with ease. "Captain Durant, on the other hand, will be vitally necessary."

Cassidy swallowed a lump in her throat. "What do you think I can do, your majesty?"

The Empress took slow, ponderous steps until she stood mere inches from Cassidy. She was only a little taller, but with all the authority she commanded she seemed to tower over her. "It was Elyia who taught you, and it is her ship you fly," she said. "You are the only one we can count on to do what must be done."

"With all due respect," said Cassidy, "you don't even know me. Your majesty."

"No, we don't. But Elyia is dead, and all she left behind was *you.* We don't have the luxury of choosing our champion in this endeavor."

Miria nudged between Cassidy and the Empress. Neither woman stepped back. "The *Dreamscape Voyager* wouldn't stand a chance against the Leviathan!" the princess protested.

"No," agreed the Empress. "No ship could. But a fleet is a vastly different matter."

Cassidy's breath caught in her throat. "You... you're giving me a fleet?"

"No," the Empress answered in a dire tone. "*You* will be giving one to *us*." She looked at Miria, then back to Cassidy, and stepped away. "When we sent Elyia to fight our battles in the last war, she had the power of conscription and the authority to grant amnesty for past crimes for those who followed her. If what happened at Dragon's Nest is any indicator, the Imperial Fleet will not be enough to deal with this beast — this leviathan.

"What we need — what the *Empire* needs — is for you to rally the allies we cannot."

Cassidy turned to Miria, who looked as confused and shocked as Cassidy felt. "I don't — your majesty... I'm not Elyia Asier. I don't have her influence, her connections." *Her knowledge of the future.* "Or her experience."

A look of sympathy flashed in the Empress's eyes, but only for a moment. "Perhaps not," she said, "but you do carry her legacy, and you were able to endure what many others could not."

"You're asking me to put the lives of my crew in danger!"

"Whether you accept the task or not, the danger is still present. The leviathan is a harbinger of destruction. It will not rest until everyone in the world lies dead."

"And how do you know that?" asked Miria.

The Empress glared at the princess, but the girl didn't flinch under that gaze. Cassidy sure would have. The battle of wills unfolding before her made Cassidy's palm's sweat, but Miria stood firm.

In the end, it was the Empress who turned away. "The Leviathan is mentioned in ancient texts, from before the ascension. It was referred to as the Great Beast, and it was said to be an instrument of Daen's wrath. It knows only hunger and rage. If it can't be stopped, the world entire will share the fate of the Dragon's Nest."

Cassidy's blood grew cold. She couldn't imagine any force in the Empire being sufficient to bring down the leviathan, no matter how large.

"We understand your trepidation," the Empress continued, "but it must be you."

"Why?" shouted Miria. "Why does it have to be her?"

"Because the *Dreamscape Voyager* will not obey anyone else."

"What the fuck does that mean?" demanded Cassidy. She clapped a hand over her own mouth when she realized that she had sworn in front of *the Empress of Asaria*. Miria, who had been strong and confident over the course of the audience let out a squeak, and Admiral Hawkwind visibly blanched.

The Empress, however, remained composed. "It means exactly as we said. Because the *Dreamscape Voyager* is alive."

Cassidy felt foolish as she stood there processing what she had just heard. The Empress seemed to be weighing her with her gaze. "I'm sorry," she said slowly, "but I think there was something crazy in my ear. Did you just tell me my ship is *alive*?"

"Captain!" Miria hissed sharply.

The Empress' lips thinned, and Cassidy had to fight the urge to shrink under her glare. "You heard correctly, Captain Durant. We were skeptical as you, once, but Elyia proved her claims."

More secrets, Captain? Cassidy thought bitterly. "I'm listening," she said.

The Empress' brow twitched briefly in what looked like agitation, but it was quickly replaced by her serene mask. "Elyia explained to us once that all ships are alive because their captains and crews treat them as an entity of their own. They put their hearts and souls into their vessels. At first, we thought the notion to be ridiculous, a fever dream brought on by the stresses of battle.

"But, after the war, she abandoned her station and at our command, she left behind her ship, the *Jade Phoenix*. We could not allow that ship, that symbol of our decisive victory against Castilyn, to leave the Imperial Fleet. But that ship had sailed into the Dreamscape three times with Elyia at the helm, and soon we learned the truth.

"We had assigned an admiral to the *Phoenix*, a strong willed and intelligent woman named Mai Ling. A week into her new commission, her crew began to report that Admiral Mai was muttering to herself, jumping at shadows. After the second week, she hanged herself."

Cassidy gasped and a hand reflexively went to her throat. "That's..."

"That's not the worst of it, Captain Durant," the Empress said, and it was clear from the gleam in her eye that she didn't appreciate being interrupted. "After Admiral Mai's untimely death, the ship was given to a veteran of the Dragon's Nest, Captain Sharan. He was specifically given the honor because of the iron nerve he showed under the worst dragon fire. He did not commit suicide, though reports claim he was plagued by nightmares. During his brief tenure as the commanding officer of the *Jade Phoenix,* he made daily reports of stolen supplies, missing tools, and sabotaged equipment. Then one day, he was thought to have disappeared. What was left of his body was recovered from the base of the mountain when deforesting teams came across it a week later."

Cassidy's eyes widened.

"Admiral Byran was the last to take the helm," the Empress continued. "He was apparently murdered in the galley, and though not one member of his crew was spared interrogation and imprisonment, the truth of it was never found.

"After that, we did the only sensible thing we could; we ordered the ship destroyed. Three ships towed it away from the city, and we watched the fires burn through the night from Serenity Tower. However, the next morning, the *Jade Phoenix* was sitting in its berth as though nothing had happened, while the three ships that had towed it away were nowhere to be found. After that, we ordered the ship be left alone, save for regular maintenance, until Elyia returned and gave it its new, more fitting yet ghastly name, the *Dreamscape Voyager.*

"Elyia has gone, but the ship has allowed you to remain its Captain. That, Captain Durant, is why you, and only you, can do what must be done."

Cassidy felt her legs growing weak, and she swayed slightly before realizing she was doing it. The *Dreamscape Voyager* was *alive.* Asier had kept yet another secret from her, the knowledge that the ship they had dedicated their lives to had become twisted by the Dreamscape.

She reached up to her hat, where Hymn was hidden. She tried to pass the gesture off as scratching her head. *Do I really have room to judge?* She wondered.

"That's a lot to take in," said Cassidy, "but really not the strangest thing I've heard this past year… your majesty."

That earned a curious look from the Empress. "We are sure you have stories to tell. Perhaps when this is all over, you can share them. For now, however, you will join Admiral Hawkwind. She and our advisers will brief you on a suggested itinerary," she finished, walking past Cassidy and heading towards the door.

"I need to get back to my crew," Cassidy protested. "They need to know what —"

"We have arranged for your crew to be informed," she replied without turning back. "We both have much to do before we're done."

CHAPTER SIX

The *Scorpion* flew under the desert sun, and despite being in his cabin, Zayne felt as though the light were warming his skin directly. He closed his eyes and the back of his eyes glowed red as though he faced the shining light. He could feel the wind outside, brushing along the ship. He lapsed briefly into a dreamlike state until the pain in his shoulder stung brightly and tugged at him. He let out a hiss. He was back in his cabin. Nanette was washing the wound.

"You make friends everywhere you go," she said sardonically.

"I've had worse," he answered.

"I know what you've been through. Are you sure you don't want a drink to numb you?"

"You know I don't."

Nanette sighed and nodded. She lifted a belt to his mouth. He bit down on it reluctantly. She had strapped him to the chair to keep him from flailing during the procedure.

"Ready?" she asked.

He gave a curt not and she took a knife and tongs and began. Zayne did his best to relax. The instant the blade touched his skin, however, he felt like he was burning. When had Nanette heated the knife? *Why* had she heated it? His breath grew ragged when she made the incision. He strained against his bindings, a muffled scream escaping through the gag. Another scream entirely, unbound, rang out inside his skull, and memories bombarded him in a rush. Elyia Asier's sword cutting through his skin. The forest floor with Dardan. Iron hands clutching his throat as a dagger was dragged into his heart, tearing him apart. His mother's corpse lying on the floor. Being torn apart with vengeful hands.

"I've only just started, calm — *what the fuck?!*" She pulled the knife away, which was bright crimson. The glow faded to a dull, flat red, and Nanette looked at it with something resembling horror. Zayne felt pain in the wound beating and pounding in rhythm with his heart. His head fell back, and he stared wearily at the ceiling.

His eyes were heavy. The belt fell out of his slackened mouth. His breath was labored. Spittle poured lazily from the corner of his mouth. He nearly choked trying to swallow it. The whole of his left arm was tingling, as though scarabs were crawling inside, hollowing out the blood and bone, leaving him numb but for stinging.

"Get this damn thing out of me," he said wearily. His ears were pounding so hard he couldn't hear Nanette's reply. Before he could say more, the belt was back in his mouth. He bit down on it and braced for more. Even though he knew it was coming, he still wasn't ready for the wave of pain. Tears flooded his eyes, leaving his vision blurred. He thought he saw red steam rising from his wound. His eyes rolled back into his head, and he was lost in memory.

Rain is battering down around him. Elyia Asier is dragging him into the mud. He tries to escape, to fly away, but she wraps an iron cord around his throat. It catches fire. He kicks and screams. He flails, looking up to see her amber eyes filled with hate. A knife is plunged into his chest. Pain blossoms out from the wound, spreading through his burning body. His eyes weep with blood. Agony radiates as he feels his skull splitting in two.

He thrashed violently. The straps holding him down snapped and he reached out. *How dare you?* He demanded of his attacker. His hands wrapped easily around her neck, and he pinned her to the ground. His fingers closed tight on her throat.

But it was not Elyia Asier's amber eyes that stared up at him.

Nanette's face was turning purple under the pressure of his fingers, her eyes glistening with tears. Fear he had never seen in her radiated from her eyes, confusion and betrayal fought over her lips as she tried to find words she couldn't breathe. He let go quickly and pushed himself to his feet. She took a great gulp of air. He staggered a few feet away and vomited on the floor.

How could I? He slunk to the wall and sank to his knees. He stared at his hands, which were shaking violently. With his hands, he had nearly killed his only friend. Unbidden, the image of Nanette lying dead on the floor made its way into the forefront of his thoughts, her face swollen from suffocation. His stomach heaved twice, and its watery contents spilled out of his mouth.

"Zayne," Nanette said in a raspy voice.

He closed his eyes and saw himself choking her yet again. "Get out," he whispered. She didn't move. He could feel her standing behind him, like an itch on his spine. "*Get out!*" It seemed like she was going to continue ignoring him, but eventually she stepped away. When she left the cabin, Zayne could feel her pace around the deck before going below. He felt each step she took until she reached her cabin, at which point he forced his attention away.

"What did you do to me?" he asked. He wasn't sure who he was questioning . He wanted someone to blame. Elyia Asier. Cassidy Durant. Dardan. The gods. He wanted to rage against them all. He wanted them to suffer. He tried to imagine it was one of them he was choking, dragging through the mud, *torturing*. The effort made him even sicker, and he fell flat on the floor. The entire ship lurched and groaned, buckling like something had struck it.

Is this really what I've been reduced to? He thought. *I was so much more, once.* He forced himself to his feet and grabbed a bucket to start cleaning the floor of his bile. He found Nanette's tongs , abandoned on the floor. The tips had been reddened, and in their clutches was a small, red ball. *The bullet.*

He reached down and picked it up. He almost expected his hand to catch fire, but it didn't. He rolled the blood covered bullet between his fingers, staring at it curiously. It was a strange thing to touch cold iron so easily. He frowned. No. It wasn't strange at all. He had done so his entire life. Hadn't he? Yes, of course he had.

"Damn you, Durant," he sneered, throwing the wasted bullet across the room. It ricocheted off the wall and bounded somewhere out of sight. He heard it roll around for a moment before settling. It was her fault. Of course it was. She had skewered him and threw him into the lake. She had released Lucandri, *she* had done this to him. He felt his face contort into a scowl, tugging at the scars on his face as he pictured her face, her mismatched eyes staring balefully into his as she tried to kill him. He rose to his feet and slammed his fist into the wall.

"No," he whispered. "It was me." It was his own fault. He should have thrown the trap containing Lucandri into the sea. Instead, he had kept it. He should have stood his ground against Dardan. Instead, he had cowed before her and followed her orders like a trained hawk. *No, it was her that struck the blow,* he thought. "I spilled first blood," he answered aloud.

For three days, Nanette avoided Zayne, as much as could be done on a ship. When he stood on the deck, she confined herself to the galley. When he went below, she went to her cabin or to the helm. He wasn't sure whether he preferred that to the alternative. He could still feel her slender neck beneath his fingers. He was all too aware of how easy it would have been to crush it. How could he have let that happen?

On the third day, Zayne had risen with the dawn and stood along the prow, eyeing the desert horizon for signs of their destination. At first light, the desert winds had still been cutting and cold, but at noon, they had been a welcome reprieve from the sun's intense glare.

It was late afternoon when Nanette came to him. He felt her approach, her gentle steps along the floorboards, before he heard. He didn't turn to face her, and she didn't announce herself. She sat on the gunwale, and he felt it the way he would feel her sitting on his lap. The comparison made him feel both a flutter in his chest and a churning in his stomach. Her fingers were fidgeting against the wood, as if she were plucking at invisible lute strings. It was distracting and comforting at the same time.

Along the shaded walls of a distant canyon, he saw strange patterns in the rock faces. As they drew nearer, the sight grew clearer. The city that had once been Morae Taluk had originally been a tiered structure hewn out of the cliff sides. At some point in history, the ancient architects had expanded into the valley between them, but the ravages of war and time left their expansionary efforts mostly buried and ruined.

"Long ago," Zayne said suddenly, not tearing his gaze away, "before the Ascension, this city was a blight. Priests took coin in exchange for protection, not *from* the gods, but *by* them."

"Been talking to our prisoner?" Nanette asked. It was a fair assumption. They had come to this place because Xiao Ta had cited it as his nearest entrance to the Dreamscape.

"No. He may know the spot, but he wouldn't know the history. Really, I shouldn't either, but I can *see* it. Looking at these ruins...

"It's like looking at your paintings and remembering because *I was there*. That pile of stone on the east side used to be half-again the height of the canyon walls. They *worshiped* gods there, publicly. They would beg the gods for forgiveness for crimes committed against man, beg for protections against the winds of life, and they would return to the city. They scurried like insects, seeking to undercut each other so the gods might see them and elevate them. Over time, they became blind and deaf to anything not of the gods. There, in the heart of the city, the grand spire was built so the king might look over his subjects, but his eyes were ever on the horizon." Disdain mixed with an unusual swell of amusement, and Zayne couldn't help but give a chuckle that felt at odds with the churning in his stomach.

"Start descent," he ordered. He pointed at a clearing amidst the rubble in the valley, in the shadow of the structure. "There." If the visions swimming in his head could be counted on, it had been the logical opposite of a sanctum, and that made it the most appropriate place for the atrocity he was about to commit.

Nanette took the helm, and the *Scorpion* began to descend. Zayne watched as the rubble and ruins grew closer, like an impending nightmare. She stopped reflexively about twenty meters above the ground, and Zayne waved her down. The remaining descent was slow and jerky, but eventually, the bottom of the ship touched the desert floor. Zayne could *feel* the baked sand crunch gently beneath the *Scorpion's* weight.

"Aresh, Xun," he commanded, "bring our prisoner out. Meet me by that rock with the bastard in tow." Zayne and Nanette put down the gangplank and walked down together.

Zayne had stood on solid ground perhaps a dozen times in his life, and none of them had been particularly pleasant. It felt unnatural that his body didn't have to shift and sway for constant balance. The air was also unpleasantly thick and warm, as though someone were trying half-heartedly to smother him with a blanket.

The wind carried whispers through the desert-buried ruins, words just beyond Zayne's understanding, but he understood all the same. He was being watched. There were eyes behind every shadow, curious, waiting. "Perfect," he whispered to himself.

Nanette turned her head. "You say something?"

He shook his head and made his way towards the building that had been made for the gods. The streets had been mostly buried by sand, but patches of the sandstone paths remained, providing level ground that helped him combat the sense of vertigo he felt. From this low vantage, he thought he could imagine what Morae Taluk might have looked like. He passed under half an archway that was thick enough to have once been a low bridge connecting

75

rooftops in such a way that implied multiple levels of traffic. He had the distinct impression this part of town had once been a market.

Out of the corner of his eye, Zayne saw thin, oily shadows in the vague shapes of people. Some walked at a casual pace, while others hunched over and leered. When he turned to face them directly, they would vanish like a mirage.

"Ghosts," Nanette whispered sharply. Zayne hadn't thought he had imagined them, but it was nice to hear confirmation all the same.

"I saw."

"Think they'll attack?"

"You never can tell," he said sourly. As the words left his mouth, he caught one lurking behind a dilapidated column like an amateur pickpocket stalking a mark. Of all the things Zayne hated — which was quite a substantial list, all told — ghosts probably ranked fourth worst, just after having his mind scrambled by Fae influence, and just before being shot.

According to Sanctum doctrine, ghosts were impressions left behind after violent deaths caused by Fae influence. The stirrings of Lucandri's memory in his head told Zayne that that explanation was not inaccurate, though it was overly simplistic. Whatever their origins, they were unpredictable; often, they were little more than illusions or shared hallucinations, shadow puppets replaying their final moments — or hours, in some cases — seemingly without end. Then, with no rhyme or reason Zayne knew of, one or a collective might suddenly break from the routine, assaulting or killing anyone in the vicinity. And, of course, they were intangible as the shadows and mirages they resembled, making self-defense all but impossible.

Making his way through the desolate market, he fell in the shadow of the collapsed tower. He found himself thinking of it as an anti-Sanctum, for a lack of a better term.

"Wait out here," he told her when they reached a gap that had once been a doorway. As he entered, something beneath the sand crunched and cracked under his feet. *Wood,* he realized. Perhaps it was what was left of the door. The air took an unexpected turn when he crossed the threshold. It was lighter, and while not exactly cold, he felt as though the desert heat was gone.

Zayne had interrogated Xiao Ta at length about the process of harvesting Myt Dust. "How do you get to the dust without being trapped in the Dreamscape?" he had asked.

After the display of what Zayne could do, the fat man had been eager to answer all his questions quickly. "There are places on the ground below where the Dreamscape is closer to our world, where you can just... walk right in. They're common in forests, but those paths are unpredictable, and needlessly dangerous. I find the most reliable places are ancient cities, places taken by violence where old ghosts still linger."

"So, how do you get the dust?" Zayne had pressed.

"Sometimes, it flows in on its own," Xiao Ta admitted. As his explanation continued, the panic in his voice gave way to an almost academic excitement. "That's not enough to get you anywhere, though. If you can find the right door, a place where the veil between the worlds is thinnest, you'll know right away you've left the world. Myt Dust forms where the worlds meet, like sawdust when you scrape wood."

"Sounds straightforward," said Zayne. "What's the catch?"

Xiao Ta's eyes had gone distant, as if he had remembered something he'd rather forget. "It's terrifyingly easy to walk *into* the Dreamscape. Not everyone finds their way *back out*." He had recommended different techniques he and his people used to stay anchored in the waking world — sometimes literally. He had been quick to remind Zayne that he still lost people regularly, all the same.

Zayne walked into the anti-Sanctum and the sunlight faded. Beyond the temple's walls was... whatever he was looking at certainly was not desert. Above was a black sky, covered in swirling clouds of red and purple, while the sand and rock beyond the dilapidated walls had given way to a dark void that seemed to continue into forever. Each time he turned to examine the space around him, it seemed less and less like a ruin, as though it were being repaired while his back was turned. He looked to the doorway he had entered and found a solid door marked with intricate, looping engravings. Beneath his feet, the floor had suddenly become devoid of sand and dust, and there was a plush carpet of velvet between his feet and a white marble floor beneath it. Looking up, the ceiling was whole, glittering with the light shining through a stained-glass window.

He turned to the light's source, taking in the circular, glass portrait that took up a sizable portion of the eastern wall. Its features seemed too fine and detailed to have been made from stained glass, yet here it was. The image was clearly a skilled practice in dichotomy.

The right half of the picture was primarily done in reds — most so deep they could almost pass for black — depicting a man falling headfirst. Zayne had the distinct impression he was falling asleep. The left side, conversely, was mostly the color of ivory and pearl, depicting another man — his back against the falling man — who seemed to be ascending.

Zayne took a step toward the glass mural. He found the contrast striking, and the way it served to highlight the similarities between the figures was masterfully done. Both figures wore flowing coats, though of opposite color, and each figure bore long hair, though the falling man's partially concealed his face while the man in white had his face — an impossibly handsome face — free of anything that might obscure it.

Beyond the focus of the picture, Zayne noticed a thousand smaller murals. In the shadow of the Falling Man, he saw a burning ship, a woman covered in blood that made his stomach churn to see, swords, and masks. Despite his immediate impression, there were tiny pieces of white spread across the red to highlight certain features. In the light shining on the Man In White, he saw robed figures on their knees, strange creatures rising from water, dragons, harpies, and other creatures. Pieces of red and black were utilized on the white half of the image to create shadows and lines.

Zayne turned away from the image, but as he did, he noticed something that left a cold pit in his chest. The background images beneath both the Falling Man and the Man in White fitted together to create a single image beneath the focus pieces. A scorpion.

From the door he had entered, he heard Nanette calling his name, but it was far away. At the same time from a hitherto unnoticed door on the adjacent wall he heard another voice whispering 'Lucandri'. Zayne sneered at the call and moved to the center of the room. He drew a pistol from his coat and fired it straight into the air. It didn't hit the ceiling. Zayne blinked and was staring up at a bright, desert sky. He was in the ruins again. The only evidence that anything unusual had happened was that the floor around his feet were covered in blue and purple sand.

Nanette stood in the doorway. There was a nervous twitch in her eye, and her lips kept moving like she was trying to find the words to say. Zayne wasn't ready to answer any questions she might have, so he said, "Have Aresh empty his flask and give it to me."

She nodded and walked to where Zayne had told the others to wait. While she was gone, he looked at the wall where the stained-glass window had been. It occurred to him that the ruin was far too small to have ever housed the window. He turned to his right and saw that the second door he had seen was solid wall, as well.

Nanette returned, stopping again at the threshold. Zayne strode back towards her and took the flask she offered and started to fill it with the blue sand on the floor. It took him a few scoops to get the Dust to completely fill the container.

"Let's check on the prisoner."

Zayne was relieved to put his back to the strange ruin. As they walked, he noticed Nanette looking back every few steps, as though unsure about something. She was likely beginning to suspect what Zayne knew to be a fact; they were being followed.

Xun, Aresh, and Shen were waiting where Zayne had ordered, with Xiao Ta resting on his knees with his hands bound to his ankles behind his back. Zayne eyed them each in turn, offering his vilest sneer to the crime lord.

"Tell me, Xiao," he said as he approached, "you've been in the Myt Dust business more than most. You've sold it, traded it, given it as a gift, even planted some to frame people who pissed you off. Judging by that hint of blue I see in your eye; you've even taken your fair share. So, I'm curious about your opinion; how many people actually *die* when they overdose on the stuff?"

Xiao looked up at Zayne, "Pardon?" he asked weakly.

"How many die?" Zayne repeated, "I've heard conflicting opinions. Some people say two thirds, since about one third of the Dusters we know about still have a functioning body after they cross that line. Others say it's one hundred percent, because what's remains isn't quite the same, is it?"

Xiao shook his head slowly. "No, I suppose it..."

Zayne overrode him. "Of course, it's hard to get a proper count since people get executed the world over for this. The risk of being possessed by some Fae spirit is too much to suffer a Duster to live. But for those who escape the noose long enough to dive too deep..." He waved the flask in front of Xiao's nose, and his eyes widened, as he clearly realized what Zayne was threatening to do. "Do you think if you were to get possessed here, today, it would be fair to call you 'alive'?"

Xiao started fighting against his bonds, impotently rocking on his knees, struggling to get out of his captors' grips. "Don't do it, Balthine! I'm more useful alive! Please!"

Zayne shook his head. "That might be true if I could trust you. As for my question, I guess I'll have to see for myself." He shoved the flask into Xiao Ta's mouth and held him down with his free hand. The drug lord struggled. He bucked and struggled against Zayne's grip, but even if he were free to move, he could never have matched Zayne's strength. Unable to spit, the fat man tried to simply avoid breathing, but his body couldn't tolerate that long, and soon he was forced to swallow. Ingesting wasn't the most common way to take Myt Dust — according to testimonials Zayne had heard, it burned a lot, which was supported by Xiao's muffled and choked attempts at screaming — but it was effective. Tears streamed down the fat man's face. After a brief spasm, a plume of Dust pumped out his nose, sticking to his upper lip. Zayne watched as the frantic, panicked look in his eyes was slowly replaced by lethargy. The white that remained in his already tainted eyes became the color of the sky, then a deeper, fuller blue. When the canteen was half empty, the man stopped fighting Zayne and reflexively swallowed the sands. It wasn't long after that that he stopped breathing.

Xiao Ta fell face first onto the desert floor.

A wind picked up and sand swirled around the body. Aresh and Shen stared agape at the fallen drug lord. Xun nudged him gently with her toe.

Nanette looked from Zayne to the corpse, and back. "What the fuck? Did you seriously drag him all the way out here to—"

A scream emanated from Xiao Ta's mouth. The voice was not the Rivien man's. It wasn't *any* man's, at all. After the screaming subsided, a feminine voice began to gasp and grunt as the body began to twitch, fighting against its bonds. "Release me!" the unfitting voice demanded.

Xun took a step back and tripped, falling flat on her ass. Shen turned right around and ran away. Aresh stood staring blankly.

Zayne knelt, looking into Xiao Ta's eyes. *No,* he thought, *they aren't Xiao Ta's eyes at all.* They eyes he saw now were inverted — white irises surrounded by colorful sclera consisting of reds and yellows. The eyes of a Fae. He had seen Dusters who had gone too far, but he had never seen so complete a possession. Typically, it was a gradual thing, with the Dust slowly opening the mind so that a Fae could take over, the identity stripped away. Perhaps it was being on the ground, or maybe it was a result of being so close to the Dreamscape itself, but there was nothing human left in that gaze.

It was like staring into the eyes of Cassidy Durant's guardian.

"Tell me," said Zayne, "who are you?"

The face that had once been Xiao Ta's contorted in defiant rage. Zayne met the Fae's gaze. Part of him thought this should have been terrifying. This was everything he'd been raised to fear. Another part of him, however — the part of him that imparted lost knowledge, the part of him that had left him questioning everything since his duel on the *Dreamscape Voyager* — knew that he held all the cards. There was nothing to fear from this one. And so, they locked eyes, he and this Fae, until eventually, it twisted Xiao Ta's lips into a sneer and said, "My name is Pyrrha." The name was familiar to Zayne, in the way something from a half-forgotten dream was familiar.

"This is madness, captain," said Shen. "We mustn't consort with its kind. Better to slit its throat and be done with it." There were nods of agreement from the others, including Nanette, who was staring wide eyed at what Zayne had wrought.

The Fae ignored them, however, choosing to scrutinize Zayne. "Release me from these bonds, masked one, and I shall grant you a boon."

Zayne shook his head. "I didn't give you that body to send you on your way," he said.

The Fae struggled to free Xiao Ta's body, causing the flabby form to jiggle in unsettling ways. "You think you can force me to swear an oath, then?"

"Something like that," said Zayne. He took a knee to meet Pyrrha's level. "Those iron shackles still burn, don't they?"

"Do not condescend to me," she said. She opened the criminal's mouth as if to finish that thought, then hesitated. "Why is your voice so familiar?"

Zayne shrugged. "Couldn't say." The next words came out of his mouth unbidden. "Perhaps you hear it in every sunrise."

Xiao Ta's face contorted with fear, stretched beyond its limits by Pyrrha's widening eyes. "Lucandri! I had heard... they said you... you were supposed to be dead!" Her eyes remained widened as she stared Zayne from head to toe. "That body… you could not be…"

"I'm not Lucandri," Zayne said firmly. "My name is Zayne Balthine."

"No, I am certain now," Pyrrha said, eyes narrowing. "You must be."

Zayne hoped his scarf and half-mask were enough to hide the uncertainty he was sure was bleeding onto his face. "If I was," he said, his voice more resolute than he felt, "I wouldn't be able to deny it, would I?"

Pyrrha looked thoughtful. "It is true, not even Len, the great deceiver, could lie *outright*. But it is so clear now, you hold his light, you *are* Lucandri."

Zayne snorted. "Let's say, for the sake of argument, that I am. What does that mean to you?"

A crestfallen expression came across Xiao Ta's face. *No, it's her face now,* Zayne acknowledged. Xiao Ta would not get it back.

"You are still alive," Pyrrha whispered. Her expression suddenly focused. "You need me. You must, else why would you have lured me here?" Zayne didn't answer. She seemed to be under the impression that he'd *specifically* tried to call *her*, and he had the feeling he could use that, so he decided not to disabuse her of the notion. "I shall serve your cause on one condition; all I ask is that you swear you will not betray me once I am no longer of use to you."

A memory just out of reach tugged on Zayne's mind. There was a history there, he was sure, though he wasn't sure exactly what. *This was easier than I planned,* he thought. "Good. Shen, release her."

Shen began to move, then stopped, looking from Zayne to Pyrrha, and back. "Y-you can't be… we can't trust a…"

Zayne rose to his feet, drawing himself up to his full height. Shen backed down. "You've got a bad habit of questioning my orders. You've seen what I can do, you know what we're dealing in. Like it or not, you're in this for life. Now, *release her.*"

Shen nodded and unshackled the Fae. He took his time about it, and Zayne watched his fingers fumble. He couldn't blame the pirate. Not really. He hadn't just ordered him to do something dangerous; he'd ordered him to do something that everyone present had likely been raised to believe was perverse, evil, and suicidal. Finally, there was a *click* and the shackles fell off the Fae. She got to her feet and rubbed her wrists, which were red and covered in small blisters.

"Aresh, take her to the ship. See to it that she has a bunk set up in your cabin."

The Rivien man gave a faint nod and looked to the Fae. For seemingly the first time, Pyrrha acknowledged someone other than Zayne. She nodded to him and made a gesture for him to lead the way. Aresh walked nervously, checking over his shoulder every few steps.

Zayne looked at the rest of his crew. Shen looked horrified, and the only reason Xun's expression didn't mirror his was because she also seemed confused. Nanette, meanwhile, looked frightened, but more composed. The way she moved her eyes told Zayne she wanted to talk but would wait until they were in private.

"Xun, Shen," he said. Xun jumped back, while Shen almost looked *grateful* to be called out. "Get the engines hot. I want to put this desert behind us."

"Aye, capt—" Shen's voice cracked. He cleared his throat, and said it a more normal register, "aye, Captain." He and Xun started towards the ship, though Zayne noticed they slowed when they came within thirty strides of Pyrrha.

"We've crossed a line here, Zayne," Nanette said when the others were out of earshot.

"Aye," Zayne agreed. "And we crossed another one ten years ago." He drew up a sleeve to show Daen's Crook scarred into his arm. Nanette rubbed her own arm, where she had the same mark.

"It's not the same."

"How's that?"

Nanette stamped her foot and a plume of dust rose around her. "We didn't have a choice back then! We were kids, in over our heads. This was…"

Zayne sighed. "I used to believe that, you know. At least, I told myself I did. But ever since *this* happened," he tapped his mask, "I see how naive I was. Before we boarded Dardan's ship that day, Salaa told me to ignore what I felt. The urge to fight, to run. And so I did. But we *had* a choice, Nanette. I *chose* to back down and let her brand me with Daen's mark. To show me those horrors. I could have fought."

A sad expression made its way onto Nanette's face. Zayne wanted to reach out, to offer a hand, but he didn't. "You'd have died," she said.

Zayne nodded. "Aye. But I'd have died *free*. I'd have died *clean*. Now, though… you saw what happened on the *Martyr's Demise*. Now, I *don't* have a choice."

Nanette didn't speak right away, though it was clear from the tension in her mouth that she wanted to. So, he waited. The wind picked up around them, causing the sand to scrape over the rock beneath it. Eventually, she just walked towards the ship, leaving whatever it was unsaid.

As Zayne made his way back to the *Scorpion,* he wondered if he really was without a choice, or if he was just as blind now as he was back then. However, remembering how Dardan had stopped him with only a word, he felt the flicker of hope that had come with the thought die in his chest.

CHAPTER SEVEN

Cassidy brought her cup of piping hot tea to her lips and blew on it as she stared at the massive table map in front of her. It was covered in pins and models of ships and cities and was far more detailed than any map she'd ever seen before; where most cartographers tended to get the general shape of the ground below — enough to establish landmarks and contextualize the distance and direction between cities — Cassidy had the distinct impression that whoever had drawn this had wanted to include the entire world.

"It's… big," Cassidy said, looking around the table. The advisers the Empress had mentioned were Miria's uncle Tao, a woman of indeterminate age without an ounce of fat or muscle in her body to speak of, a somewhat portly man hiding in several layers of elaborate robes, and Admiral Hawkwind. Miria was also present, as, according to Tao, her mother hadn't specifically forbade it.

The spindly woman, named Tasuki, clicked her tongue exasperatedly. "Are we really putting all of our hope in her?" she asked Tao. Her voice had a strange quality that made Cassidy think her throat was too tight.

"No need to be rude," Tao said gently. "Captain Durant, how much do you know about the ships that took Tal Joyau?"

"Just the stories," she admitted. "Five ships, using wind stolen by the gods, took down the Castilyn armada. The captain never really liked talking about what really happened."

"Well, the tale is true enough," said Tao. Maroda, the fat man, snorted derisively. Tao ignored him and continued, "That's not really the important part. After the war, each of the five captains went their separate ways and all but disappeared, their legendary ships fading into myth.

"Most of them, anyway. Jathun, Captain of the *Temptation*, resurfaced five years ago, and ended up in Marasi Prison."

"How does that help?" asked Cassidy.

It was Tasuki who answered. "Jathun has influence and connections. You've been tasked with giving us a fleet, Durant. Jathun could be instrumental for the task."

"Whatever friends he had," Cassidy argued, "he's been locked up on the far side of Rivien for years. And how can I trust a criminal I don't know, anyway?"

"Asier did," said Maroda. "I would think her Second would trust her judgment."

Cassidy did her best to hold back a sneer. *Maybe if I knew the future, I could be free with trust, too.* She drank a mouthful of tea and said, "Aye. We'll do what we can with Jathun. Who else should I be on the lookout for?"

Tao exchanged an odd look with Tasuki, who shook her head sharply. The thin woman said, "You shall have the power of conscription and, to an extremely limited extent, the voice of the Empress. I'm sure someone of your station could find useful souls in need."

Tao drummed his fingers, shaking his head. "There's more," he said.

"Tao…" said Maroda.

"Mercenary companies might be useful," Tao said, pointedly refusing to look the older man's way. "Also consider hunters if you can find any."

Cassidy caught herself sneering at the mention of mercenaries. The memory of Zayne Balthine murdering Captain Asier still curdled her stomach. Focusing on the task at hand, she said, "A few good hunters would probably know a few helpful tricks. Fishermen might be useful, too, since the leviathan seems to be hiding in the ocean."

"I guess that explains why there have been so few sightings. A flying mountain stands out, but there's no telling how deep those waters run."

"Aye," Cassidy agreed, staring at the map. "We encountered the beast in the Dusk Sea," she said, using her finger to circle an area of open ocean west of Revehaven.

"That's pretty far removed from the wreckage of patrols we've found here," he said, pointing to an island further south, "and here," he added, tapping the coastline west of that.

"It would have been spotted if it came any further east," Cassidy said, eyeing the coast of the main continent. She looked at the swath of sea that separated the mainland from the Black Gulch, and the larger waters that separated the Gulch from the border cities of Rivien. How many times had she crossed those depths, unconcerned about the monstrosities that lived beneath the seemingly placid waters? Now, there was a creature that shamed even her most horrific nightmares lying in wait. "Why me?" she whispered. Miria put a hand on her shoulder.

"So," Cassidy continued after taking a deep breath, "when I get this fleet, what's the plan for actually fighting the monster?"

"While you're gathering the fleet, we'll be dedicating teams to finding and studying the creature," said Tao.

"That's suicide!" Miria protested.

Tasuki made a *tsk*ing noise. "If it's of the Dreamscape, perhaps it's like the Fae, and the Priests of the Iron Veil can figure a way."

"That's a pretty big 'if'," Miria argued.

"It's what we have, highness," said Tao.

Miria whispered in Cassidy's ear. "Has… *our friend* told you anything about the Leviathan?"

"Not much," Cassidy muttered.

A low voice emanated from Cassidy's hat, and even she could hardly hear it. "I will tell you all I know when we are safe on your ship."

"I can't believe you never asked sooner," said Miria.

"I did," Cassidy retorted. "She wasn't eager to talk before."

Maroda cleared his throat. "Excuse me," he said genially. "But if you have anything useful to share, now would be an excellent time."

"Just getting our bearings," said Cassidy. "This is a lot to take in."

"No doubt about that," Tao agreed. "Admiral Hawkwind's report was gruesome."

For the first time since the meeting had started, Hawkwind cleared her throat to speak. "The report only covered the basics, and the numbers. The reality is far more terrible. If this leviathan hits a city… no, we need to find a way to put this thing down before it gets that far."

Cassidy closed her eyes, trying to imagine the destruction at the Nest occurring in a city. The thought made her sick, and her eyes threatened to spill over with unbidden tears. "There would be nothing left," she said weakly.

Hawkwind nodded. "Exactly."

"You'll be given writs of conscription and requisition," Tao said, clearly trying — and failing — to ease the tension. "All of the resources you need within Imperial borders will be at your disposal. In Rivien, however, you'll be on your own."

Cassidy's eyes widened. "I can requisition anything?"

"Within reason," Tasuki said firmly. "This isn't some pleasure cruise."

"Aye, aye," Cassidy said dismissively, thinking of the coin this venture was promising to save her. A bell rang outside.

"Well," Maroda said, rising to his feet and turning to leave, followed by Tasuki, "the good captain knows the task ahead of her, and we still have a government to run."

"Wait, that's it?" Cassidy asked. "You're just going to point me at this thing like I'm a gun? Just fire and forget?"

Tasuki stopped and turned to Cassidy. "Would you rather we send a contingent of soldiers to personally direct the situation? We've given you your tools, you can figure out how to use them." She and Maroda shared a nod and departed. Admiral Hawkwind offered a salute to Tao and followed suit.

Cassidy turned to Miria. "Please tell me I'm asleep and we haven't left Tien's Landing."

"Sorry, Captain," the girl replied, "but unless I'm dreaming, too, this is real."

"Shit, I was afraid you'd say that. I should strip your hide for insubordination."

Tao cleared his throat, and Cassidy felt a sudden weight in the air. "While I'm sure you were joking," he said sternly, "I'd avoid making any threats to the princess' person during the remainder of your stay. The walls have ears."

"Right," Cassidy agreed quietly.

"Come with me, Captain. Highness." Tao turned to lead them from the war room, into the vibrant corridors of the palace. "I hope the rudeness of the others hasn't upset you. If you don't mind me saying, I suspect my sister isn't fond of you, and her sycophants can't be bothered to demonstrate the manners of their station if they can't use you to appeal to her."

Cassidy nodded absently. "So, when Miria called you 'Uncle', that wasn't just an affectionate nickname?"

Tao chuckled wryly. "No, it wasn't."

"Uncle Tao took up the mantel as my mother's chief bodyguard and Champion after Elyia left."

"Yes," Tao said, drawing out the single word into a five-syllable phrase. "Can't say I ever really forgave her for that. I was looking forward to growing fat and lazy when I was told I actually had to uphold my duty." Cassidy watched as he walked, the way his uniform conformed to the tight muscles as he moved. She couldn't imagine him ever being fat, but she found herself imagining him in other ways.

"Aye," she said to fill the silence. "Turns out she upset quite a few people over the years."

"Oh, it's not so bad," said Tao. They stopped at an ornate door made of a rich, red-colored wood. "Your room, Highness."

"I see that," said Miria. "What happened to the old door?"

Tao sighed. "Burglars," he said flatly.

"Burglars were here and broke my door?" Miria asked. "And I'm supposed to be safer here than with my crew?"

Tao rubbed his eyes with his thumb and forefinger. "Security around the palace has been heightened, and with the threats we face... Listen, we will talk about this later, I promise. For now, the Empress — gods be blind to her — wants the captain out of the palace as soon as possible, and I know you want to say your goodbyes, so please."

The weight of his words struck Cassidy. She looked at Miria. She couldn't comprehend leaving without her. Even though the Empress had made her intentions clear from the beginning, it just seemed so wrong. "Miria," she choked.

The girl threw her arms around Cassidy. "You'll be fine, Captain," she said, and Cassidy hugged her back. "We'll see each other again real soon, you hear?"

Cassidy smiled, even as she felt tears spill. "Aye. We will. We'll kill this monster and be back before you know it."

Cassidy wasn't sure how long they stood together in an embrace, but it wasn't long enough before Tao put a hand on Cassidy's shoulder.

"I'm really sorry, Captain. Highness, I must see Captain Durant off, alone."

Miria stepped back and composed her face as though she was putting on a mask. "I understand. If I came, it would only make things more difficult." She opened the door to her room and stepped

89

inside. "I need time to myself," she said to Tao. "Please tell the servants no one is to bother me." Cassidy's heart sank as she closed the door.

"Such a brave girl," Hymn whispered from Cassidy's sleeve.

"Sorry, what did you say, Captain?"

Shit in a bucket, Cassidy thought, *he heard that?*

"I said she's a brave girl," Cassidy lied, though she felt the words too.

"Yes, she is," Tao agreed. "If you'll follow me?" he added, gesturing down the hall. Cassidy followed his lead, as much because she had no other way out as because he asked, "Thank you for looking after my niece," he said when they reached the far staircase.

"Of course," Cassidy said defiantly. She climbed down the stairs, stomping her feet with every step. "I'd do anything for her, and *not* because she's the Empress' daughter."

"I believe you. I was surprised to see how she's grown since she left. I was against it, but I think it's done her good."

"Hard work builds character," said Cassidy.

"No doubt there." He stopped suddenly and Cassidy nearly walked into him. He leaned in close to her. "Listen," he whispered, "there's another lead for you to follow while you're in Rivien."

"What —?" Cassidy asked, but Tao shushed her.

"The walls have ears, remember? Now, Jathun isn't the only 'associate' captains of Elyia Asier's. At least, of whom we know the whereabouts. Rumors and circumstance pin Captain Yaoru as the leader of a band of pirates attacking Imperial vessels trading in Rivien. Not civilians, I mean actual Imperial government and military."

"Yaoru Kiyen? The Captain of the *Clockwork Hydra*?"

"The same."

"So why not bring it up in the briefing?" Cassidy demanded, though she kept her voice at a whisper to match his.

"Here's where things get complicated." They resumed their descent, but at a slower pace, and he was still whispering. Cassidy suspected anyone looking would think they were intimate. "During the war, Asier sent Yaoru to the capital to send a dire message, and..." He sighed and rubbed his eyes. "He's Miriaan's father."

Cassidy stopped walking. Asier had *loved* the Empress. Knowing she was going to die, Cassidy's former captain had left Cassidy with a journal detailing her life, and in it she had implied that

Miria's birth in her absence had been a personal betrayal. Had she known?

"How?" she asked breathlessly.

Tao shrugged uncomfortably. "In the usual way, I suppose."

"Aye, but isn't the Empress —"

"She's my sister," Tao said flatly. "I try not to think of the specifics if I can avoid it. Anyway, the reason I didn't bring it up sooner is that there are only five people in the world who know this. The Empress, myself, Maroda, Tasuki, and now you."

"But why does it matter? The Empress wasn't married and it's not like we live in Castilyn where paternity affects the royal —"

"It matters because *traditionally*, the sire of the future Empress is afforded certain rights. Certain protections. And, of course, the right to be involved in his daughter's life. The trouble is, before Asier conscripted him for the war, he was a pirate, and *after* the war... he was a pirate."

"And giving him amnesty would show weakness, or endanger Miria," Cassidy guessed.

"While showing him none would be seen as a breach of tradition."

Cassidy pursed her lips. "Does Miria know?"

Tao shook his head. "She asked Shahira, a few times. All she would say is that her father was a noble and strong warrior. I think the truth of it would break the girl's heart."

"I see," said Cassidy.

"Anyway, I didn't tell you about Yaoru for the juicy gossip. His fleet would be a great asset, and he has a talent for designing weapons, which you may find useful when facing the Leviathan."

"But how would I find him? I doubt I could just ask after him, even if he is pirating under his own name."

"Probably not," Tao agreed. "Perhaps seeing the *Temptation* flying again might be enough to lure him out of hiding. If not, his targets have been pretty specific of late."

"You think I should set myself up as bait," Cassidy said.

"If that's what has to happen. You'll be given Imperial banners to fly, should you feel the need. The others disagree, but I think Yaoru will help you even more than Jathun, if he can be convinced."

"Seems to me we're putting a lot of faith on these criminals joining me just because they joined Elyia. I don't have everything she had."

"I know. I don't like any of this. You're a civilian, but Shahira— her Excellency — thinks it's the only way, and while I haven't always seen eye to eye with her, she's in charge. And to be honest, I haven't been able to come up with a better solution."

"It feels like she's trying to punish me for surviving where Elyia didn't."

"She's not that vindictive, I promise." Tao paused, remaining silent until they had walked several paces before adding, "Though I *am* pretty sure she resents you."

"Great. She's only the most powerful woman in the world."

"She is grateful, too, though. You did risk life and limb to save her daughter."

"But not so grateful she doesn't try and get me killed," Cassidy muttered. Tao said nothing to that. They left the stairwell and ended up where they had entered, the skiff they had taken still in place.

Cassidy climbed in, followed by Tao, two guards, and a flier. When the skiff took to the air, Cassidy kept looking back to the palace. She wondered if Miria would readjust to the life of royalty as quickly as she'd taken to the skies. The only frame of reference Cassidy had to that life was what Miria told her. She hoped the girl wouldn't be lonely.

From the palace, Cassidy could see the entire city sprawling out across the mountain range. The familiar streets were completely alien from her new vantage, and the snowcapped roofs created a uniform shine that contrasted and united the disparate architectural styles.

The skiff took them straight to the docks, and from the air Cassidy could see Kek sitting on the gangplank while four members of the City Guard loitered nearby. When they descended in front of the *Dreamscape Voyager*, Kek rose to his feet.

Cassidy jumped to the harbor before they landed, meeting Kek halfway.

"Captain!" he shouted over the grinding and whirring of the skiff, "Imperial soldiers showed up after you left and started loading up new cargo and ordered us on lock down! The last of them left fifteen minutes ago. What's going on?" He paused. "And what's with the fancy outfit?"

"Long story!" Cassidy shouted back. "Better to tell everyone at once! Short answer? We're fucked!"

"Great!"

"Captain Durant!" Tao called. Cassidy turned and he tossed her an elongated case. She caught it with both hands and nearly lost her balance. She opened the box to find it was full of scrolls. *The writs,* she realized. She nodded to Tao, who saluted her by putting his fist to his chest. The skiff rose and flew back towards the palace.

Cassidy closed the box and tucked it under her arm. "I want all hands on deck," she told Kek. "There's a lot to discuss."

"Aye, Captain," he said. She watched as Kek climbed up the gangplank, but she hesitated, looking towards the prow. There was no figurehead on the ship, and she wondered if maybe there should be, given everything. "Did you really kill those people, ol' girl?" she whispered. The ship didn't answer. Of course it didn't. But all the same, Cassidy felt uneasy as she made her way aboard.

Waiting for Kek to get the others, Cassidy leaned against a rain barrel and sighed.

"Are they gone?" asked a voice from inside the barrel.

Cassidy leaped out of her skin, dropped the box of scrolls and yelped as Miria emerged from inside, wearing her old clothes, covered in dirt and sweat and drenched in water from the chest down. "What the fuck! How did you —? What are you —? How did you get here?"

"It's a long story that involves a guard uniform, a Rivien prostitute, a wig, and a drunk firebird."

"That's — *what?*"

"Sorry, but 'I climbed out my window and found one of the skiffs sending supplies here' wasn't as fun."

"Your window?" Cassidy asked. "Your window *ten* levels high? That window?"

The princess shrugged before lifting herself out of the water and climbing fully out of the barrel. "I never said it was easy work."

"You let me cry!" Cassidy snapped. "You could have let me know you were coming!"

"With my uncle standing right there?" Miria retorted. "Besides, I said we'd see each other again soon."

Cassidy fought a smile. "Well, you've earned yourself an extra heap of chores this week."

Miria's face contorted as she, too, seemed to be fighting the urge to smile. "Remind me why I chose to come back?"

"I don't know, but we'll probably be executed for treason when your mother finds out."

This time, Miria let her smile show, and it was a devious thing. "Why? Tao saw you here without me. You had nothing to do with my escape."

Cassidy took a deep breath. "Hopefully, the Empress sees things the same." Kek and the others were climbing up to the deck. "Alright, crew," said Cassidy. "You're probably wondering about the Imperial soldiers."

"No, not at all, Captain," Kek said sarcastically. "This is all par for the course."

"Shut up, Kek," said Nieves.

"Are we in trouble for something?" asked Lierre.

"You could say that," Hymn chimed in from beneath Cassidy's hat. The hat briefly lifted from her head as the Fae flew out to hover between the crew. "I promised to tell you all I know about the Leviathan. Do you wish to inform your crew, first?"

"Wait, wait, this has to do with *the Leviathan?*" Kek sputtered.

"Aye," said Cassidy. She hesitated, the words struggling to find purchase in her mouth. Finally, in one quick blast she said, "the Empress conscripted us to kill it."

"What?" Lierre and Kek shouted simultaneously.

"That's suicide!" added Nieves. "How — and why — did she press us into this?"

"It's complicated," Cassidy said.

She told them about the encounter with Miria's uncle, her audience with the Empress, the Dreamscape Voyager apparently being alive. She told them everything, except what Tao had told her in secret. She considered telling all, but Tao's words — *the truth of it would break the girl's heart* — stopped her. The rest of it was enough, anyway.

"Shit," Kek said, the word coming out as a sigh.

"Aye," Cassidy agreed. "So, Hymn, what can you tell us about the Leviathan? What's our best chance against it?"

"Your best chance? Fly as far away as you can, possibly to the Reach."

Cassidy looked to Kek, who looked back and shrugged. "Would that... be any safer in the long run?"

Hymn didn't respond immediately. Cassidy was about to repeat the question when she finally said, "No. It would only delay the inevitable."

"So, it's not really an option. You're stalling, what do you know?"

"Little that can help," the Faerie said. Her light shifted from blue to red and back again. "Its very presence weakens the barriers between this world and what you call the Dreamscape. It is drawn to acts of great violence. Its living armor is made of dyrelights — reactive lights that can give shape to spiritual energies, among other things. You would know them as wisps.

"It is driven by instinct, an urge to destroy and consume, though I know of methods to temper its instincts with more focus. However, those methods are reprehensible, and lead only to greater destruction in a shorter span."

Cassidy looked around at her crew. Kek had fear and confusion on his face in equal measure, while Nieves looked as though she wasn't quite sure what she was hearing, and Lierre looked as though she would need new trousers soon. Miria wore a face of calm, though Cassidy couldn't help but notice the tension in her neck or the way she was flexing her jaw. Cassidy herself kept wiping her sweaty palms on her coat sleeves to no avail.

"So how do we *kill* it?" Cassidy asked at last.

Hymn floated a few feet away, then floated back, and repeated. Eventually Cassidy realized the Fae was pacing. "It is alive, so it *can* be killed," she said slowly. "But your world has gone to great lengths to diminish the power of the fair folk out of fear of gods, effectively cutting you off from your best chances."

"What chances would those be?" asked Kek.

"Weapons that could pierce even the Leviathan's armor," Hymn suggested, "or maybe knowledge. I am not the most knowledgeable regarding the Leviathan, though there is no one we could approach, so we cannot hope for more.

"If you really must confront the Leviathan — and I sincerely believe it is the worst idea imaginable — the Empress' plan of raising an armada is, sadly, the best you can hope for."

"You saw how quickly it tore through the Dragon Nest," Lierre protested. "All those ships, dedicated to *killing dragons*, did *nothing* to slow that beast!"

"If you have a better solution, I'd like to hear it," Cassidy said quietly. Lierre looked at her, pleadingly, then hung her head. "Then get the engines hot. We have a long way to go. Unless any of you want to leave here. I won't force this on any of you, but I have to see this through."

There was a pregnant pause as the crew stood there silent. She had offered all of them a chance to go their own way before, when Asier died, but that was different. Now, she was deliberately getting ready for a battle with no real chance of winning, against an enemy that could probably crush her without even knowing she was there.

"I'll be in the engine compartment," Lierre said.

"My watch just ended, so I'm going back to my bunk, Captain," Nieves replied.

Both women turned to make their descent to the lower deck, and Cassidy smiled. Kek shook his head. "I'm with you, Captain," he said, "but you know this is crazy, right?"

Cassidy's smile faded. "Aye. It's absolutely insane. But if I understood Hymn's comment, the Leviathan *will* kill us all if we don't kill it first, whether we try or not." The Fae didn't reply.

"Well, at least we won't have to worry about paying for the inheritance," Kek offered weakly.

"Aye."

"Should I fly us out?"

"Aye," Cassidy said again. "Take us out, then set course south by southwest."

"Aye, aye, captain."

Cassidy turned to Miria. "Sweep the snow off the deck, then start on your duties."

"Aye, captain," said the princess. She retreated to get a broom, and Cassidy entered her cabin, followed closely by Hymn.

When the door closed behind her, she pressed her back against it and slunk to the floor, then let out a deep breath. Hymn landed on her knee. Cassidy looked up at the ceiling, contemplating the task before them. "What have I gotten us into?" she asked.

"Grave danger," said Hymn.

Cassidy thought over Hymn's commentary. "Why can't we ask any other Fae for help?"

The light the Fae gave off shifted from blue to red and back as it was prone to do whenever Cassidy asked something that irritated or upset her. Cassidy rarely saw other colors of late, and she wasn't sure what any of them actually indicated.

"We cannot trust them," she said after a while. Cassidy waited for her to say more, but she didn't. Finally, with a sigh, she rose to her feet and went to bed.

The memory of her fight with the mercenary leader — Len, maybe — lingered, and she thought about the strange sword she had used against Miria and Cassidy. She bolted upright.

"Hymn," she asked quickly, "could orichalcum hurt the Leviathan?"

CHAPTER EIGHT

Everything was wrong with the situation. Zayne wondered which of his many mistakes had cursed his life this way. Whatever the reason, however, he sat across the table from a Fae-possessed corpse of a drug lord. Those strange, inverted eyes stared at him unblinkingly. It was uncanny to see the blatantly masculine features holding a decidedly feminine expression and posture.

"Pyrrha," he said cautiously. "You're using a human tongue. Can you lie?"

The Fae raised an eyebrow. She stroked her beard uncertainly, the fat fingers of Xiao Ta moving in an impossibly dainty fashion under her guidance. Every movement she made unsettled Zayne, though he tried not to show it. "No," she said finally.

Zayne narrowed his eyes. "How do I know *that* isn't a lie?"

"I suppose you cannot be sure," she admitted.

"I can think of a test." Zayne reached into the sleeve of his coat, finding a hidden pocket and extracted an iron coin. "Put your hands on the table," he ordered.

A twitch of the brow was all the reaction Pyrrha showed before obeying. He twirled the coin between his fingers, wondering why it wasn't burning him now. "I'm going to ask you a question," he said. "An obvious question. If you tell me the truth, I'm going to do this." He touched the coin to the back of Pyrrha's disfigured hand.

The Fae sucked in a breath and bit her lip. The coin grew warm in Zayne's hand. He held it there until he saw the skin beneath it grow red. When he released it, Pyrrha went slack, eyes misted by tears. The sight made Zayne ill.

"This seems cruel," the Fae whined.

"Cruel," Zayne agreed, swallowing slowly-rising bile. "But necessary. What color is my coat?"

The only answer was the sound of the *Scorpion*'s engines, the gentle creaking and groaning of the wood as she rocked gently in the wind. The galley was cold due to a draft that had persisted since a cannonball had knocked out the starboard wall nine years earlier. It had driven Salaa — Zayne's predecessor and adoptive aunt — mad that no matter how many times they patched the hull the draft wouldn't go away. Zayne almost smiled at the memory, but the sight of those red-gold eyes boring into him from beneath a layer of tears killed the urge.

"Black," she answered at long last.

"Aye, it is," Zayne said. He pressed the coin into the back of the Fae's hand again. She bit back a scream and her breathing became labored. "What color is my coat?" he asked again, this time not lifting the iron from the Fae's borrowed flesh. He forced himself to watch the contorting face listen to the screams, despite the rising urge to vomit. He focused particularly on her lips, which repeatedly formed the beginnings of words, but no more. Until finally, she screamed, "Black! Your coat is black!"

When Zayne removed the coin from the Fae's hand, there was a faint red glow where contact had been made. There was a blister forming on the Pyrrha's skin. He told himself that he stopped because he was satisfied that she simply couldn't lie. His stomach didn't much care *why* he stopped, just that he did. The Fae slumped forward over the table, breathing heavily and shedding tears.

The galley door opened. Zayne turned to look at Nanette. She was holding a small, wooden box. "Find them?" he asked cordially.

"Aye," she said, setting the box on the table. Zayne opened it. Inside was a pair of spectacles with thick, black and red reflective lenses.

"I never thought I'd see these again," he mused. In the last few years leading up to her death, Salaa had developed a heightened sensitivity to light — a familial affliction, she'd said. He turned to Phyrrha. "Nanette is your sawbones. Nanette, what would you say is wrong with... her?"

"She definitely has a severe case of blight rot," Nanette said firmly.

"There you have it," said Zayne. "Anyone asks why you're wearing these; your sawbones says you have blight rot."

Phyrrha rubbed her wound, staring at the spectacles. "Very well," she said slowly.

There was a scream outside. It was Shen. Nanette bounded up the steps and out the door. Zayne took his time. He already knew what had happened. While he hadn't been able to repeat his feat of vanishing and reappearing in a different part of the ship — and the crew had made the unspoken agreement to forget it ever happened — his passive awareness of what was happening all over the ship came and went more regularly.

When he reached the deck, Shen's sleeve was still on fire, and he kept waving it about in a panic while Nanette and Tagren were trying to get him to hold still long enough to put it out. Zayne looked to the helm, which was slightly scorched and smelled of charcoal. The fire hadn't lasted more than a moment, but Zayne found its source easy enough.

The balloon's igniter had been shot when Cassidy Durant had brought down the ship. Zayne adjusted a pulley that sat between the cords that raised and lowered the ship and the mechanism lowered to head-height. He fingered at the cracks in the rusted, soot-covered metal. Around the breakage, more crumbled easily in his hand. He looked on the ground, finding a thin piece, bent at a sharp angle, sitting at his feet. He picked it up.

"I've told you three times, Shen," he said once the flames had been put out, leaving the pirate's jacket a smoking mess. He had to take a deep breath to compensate for raising his voice. "Make sure this piece is in place before you use the igniter. Otherwise, *this* happens."

"Why are we flying this heap, anyway?" Shen demanded. "Bullet holes whistling at all hours, the igniter catching fire, we can't drink the water in the reserves because the tankards still have salt and Myt dust in them!"

"Stow your bellyaching," Zayne said wearily. Despite his words, however, Zayne knew the pirate wasn't wrong. Drafts in the galley were one thing, but issues like the igniter were a tightness in Zayne's neck he'd been meaning to address. And if they couldn't get the reserve tanks flushed out properly, his crew could end up poisoned if they had to depend on them for water. He looked at the mechanism hanging before him. "You raise a fair point, though," he said after a while. "When we reach port, you will dedicate yourself to fixing this ship."

"I'm not some —"

Zayne grabbed Shen by the front of his shirt, pulling the pirate close enough to make out the individual flecks of dirt on his face. "You're whatever I say you are! You volunteered."

Shen swallowed something in his throat. "I volunteered to —"

"To kill Dardan, I know," replied Zayne. He let out a raspy sigh. "And we'll kill her. But first, we must play along to her sick little game."

"You could have killed her," Shen protested. "You hesitated; you gave in."

The accusation was a dagger in his ribs.

Zayne pushed the pirate away and held his hand out to his side. Rainbow-patterned lights gathered around his hand and in a flash of golden light, Dawn Star was there, its long golden blade gleamed with impossible red light. "I did not *hesitate*," he said, waving the sword with a careless sweep. The pirate jumped back, but not before his tunic was cut from shoulder to hip. A few seconds later, a red line formed in his skin, blood seeping from the wound. Shen pressed his hands to his chest, though the wound was shallow. "Dardan knows the things of the Fae, and of the gods. I didn't spare her by choice, my hand was forced. Besides, I didn't see *you* quick to act when we reached the *Martyr's Demise*."

Shen's eyes flitted between Zayne's and Dawn Star. While he had seen it before, this was probably the first time he could have gotten a good look at it. The rest of the crew had gathered to watch, and the pirate noticed. "I wonder if you'd be so tough if I was the one with the cursed weapon," he said, though the disdain in his voice was undercut by the fear sending a tremor through it.

Zayne rolled his eyes. "Why do I always need to make examples of people?" He took hold of the golden sword by the blade and proffered the weapon to Shen. "Let's get this over with."

The pirate blinked, staring uncertainly. After some deliberation, he took the weapon from Zayne and leaped back, as though afraid Zayne would strike him for getting close.

Zayne closed his eyes. He could see Dawn Star in the void. He could *feel* it. Through the sword, Zayne could feel Shen's intent. He knew before Shen moved that the pirate was going to stab. Zayne turned his body to provide a smaller target and took a single step forward. Dawn Star's blade passed harmlessly behind his back. Shen grunted and let out a shout, swinging the sword around to strike at Zayne's head. Zayne turned again and leaned backwards, the blade cutting nothing but air in front of his face, not even trimming a lock of his flowing hair. A third strike and Zayne sidestepped it yet again.

"Are you quite through?" Zayne asked, opening his eyes. Shen growled, like a beast unhinged. He charged. He put all of his weight into a diagonal swing. Zayne sighed. Dawn Star glowed like the sun when it reached Zayne's collar. It shattered like glass, shards of light flying, hanging dramatically in the air before vanishing in wisps of iridescent light.

Without striking Zayne, there was nothing to slow Shen's momentum. The pirate only just seemed aware the sword had vanished when he ran into Zayne's fist. His feet continued forward as the rest of him fell backwards. Shen hit the deck completely horizontal. Someone gasped and Nanette made a pitying noise.

Zayne sat on his haunches beside Shen. "I really don't want to have this talk again," he said. "It gets tiresome. So, let me make this clear. I am the captain. Understand?"

The answer was a weak and breathless, "Aye."

"Good." He stood and looked to the crew, who stood clustered on the deck, gawking. "Don't you all have duties to attend to?" Xun all but ran below deck while and Tagren grabbed Shen by the shoulders and dragged him out of Zayne's way, leaving Zayne with only Nanette and Pyrrha.

The Fae-possessed corpse was smiling. "A fascinating display, my lord."

"*Captain*," Zayne corrected. "I am your *captain*."

"As you say."

Zayne waited for her to say more. When she did not, he met Nanette's eye and gestured his head. She followed him up to the quarterdeck. Pyrrha's eyes followed him, but thankfully, she did not follow.

"Was that really necessary?" Nanette asked once they were relatively alone.

"When have I ever done anything unnecessary?"

Nanette opened her mouth and Zayne held up hand.

"What happened in Tal Joyau doesn't count."

Nanette began again, and Zayne cut in again.

"Andaerhal was completely necessary."

"Fine, but there's still —"

"And we agreed never to talk about that night in Quishan."

Nanette rolled her eyes and sighed. Zayne folded his arms and looked ahead at the line where the sea met the distant mountains cresting over the world's curve. The air smelled of salt, and a cold wind blew against them as they sailed. He wished the horizon would stay right where it was, forever out of reach.

"You're getting better," said Nanette.

"What?"

"Your memory," she clarified. "All those places you mentioned actually exist."

Zayne grunted. "The confusion is at its worst at dawn and at dusk," he admitted. "I still don't understand, really. Lucandri's memories — and the *Scorpion*'s memories — come and go, but the ship's memories are clearer than the Fae's."

"If I ever see that Durant bitch again," Nanette said, "I'm going to kill her for what she did to you."

"I appreciate the sentiment, but I'll dish out my own revenge."

Nanette nodded. "So, you think she'll even turn up? World's a big place."

"We'll see her again," said Zayne. He felt it in his bones. He hadn't seen the last of Cassidy Durant, or her Fae guardian. He sneered at the thought. Something about that Fae triggered something in his mind, just beyond the edge of perceptible memory. He suspected it was Lucandri's memory.

Zayne leaned against the aft gunwale of the ship and kept his eyes ahead. Nanette joined him for a time, but after an hour she made her excuses and went below. Alone with the sounds of wind and machinery, Zayne noticed a hitch in one of the engines, and once he became aware of it, each time it happened the muscles where his neck met his shoulder twitched. He endured the torment for an hour or so before he saw the smokestacks rising from the mountains to the east. It wasn't long after that Zayne could see the city of Cielhal itself perched defiantly atop the peaks.

Residing on the farthest borders, Cielhal was only an Imperial city in the barest legal sense. More than three quarters of its population were Rivien, and it saw more trade from Castilyn than from anywhere in Asaria. Even its name was Castilyn in origin. The only real claim the Asarian Empire had was its rather small garrison, which existed to support the fleet at the Dragon's Nest. Zayne wondered how the destruction of the nest would affect its standing.

As the *Scorpion* drew closer to the city, Zayne spotted that the baron's castle, a prominent feature at the city's heart, had been reduced to a burnt ruin only three stories tall. When they were close enough to make out the ship traffic, Zayne realized that on the south side of the city, there wasn't a building taller than two stories that wasn't similarly destroyed.

Zayne dislodged himself from the balustrade and looked to the ground below. Strewn about between the mountainside and the field beneath it were signs of battle. At least two dozen ships had fallen, some in salvageable condition, but others were torn apart and scattered like children's toys.

Dragons, he thought to himself. This close to the Nest, dragons had been a natural threat, but outside of their breeding grounds they tended to be solitary creatures smart enough to avoid cities. What Darden had done to the nest, however, forced a devastating change in the world.

Then Zayne realized the ships surrounding the city were just hovering in place, moving with the wind. *Traffic* hadn't been the right word.

"Looks like the city's been blockaded, Captain," Xun called from below. Her face was pressed to her spyglass.

"I see that," he replied. He descended to the deck. "Check the harbor for a Rivien ship, black in color, with a white mural of Daen across the starboard side of its hull." Xun looked back at Zayne, as though to question his orders. After meeting his glare, however, she put the glass back to her eye and made a show of sweeping her gaze about.

"I see it," she said eventually.

"What beast's corpse is hanging on its prow?"

"It, uh… it… I think it's a griffin?" Xun answered.

"Griffins have been extinct for over a hundred years," Zayne said with a dismissive flick of his wrist. Still, Xun's answer told him everything he needed to know, so he added, "Besides, it's too small, and that's a fox's snout on its face, not a beak. It's a sphinx." He lowered his scarf to spit over the gunwale. Rather than clear spittle, it was a thick blot of blood. "Xun, fetch Nanette."

She ran as if eager to get away from him, and Zayne looked at the blockade. *They aren't flying any banners,* he noted. Fifty ships, by Zayne's count, each painted a rich brown. The paint looked oddly fresh.

"Which Daughter is loitering in the city?" asked Nanette as she climbed on deck.

Zayne kept his eyes on the blockade, considering ways to bypass it. "The *Kestrel.*"

"Oh, piss in a bucket," Nanette sneered. Zayne shared the sentiment. The *Kestrel* was captained by Isara Altair, a young woman with an unhealthy obsession with the Dreamscape, the Fae, and the gods — as if there were any other kind. How she managed to avoid execution for various crimes committed in their pursuit over the years was a mystery to Zayne.

"We'll board that boat when we get to it," he said, observing the blockade. "We need to find a way to sneak into the city to see what's going on."

"I guess we could use the skiff," Nanette suggested. "It's a moot point if the *Kestrel* can't leave, though. There are other captains we could involve in our plan. Anyone else at all, for a start."

"Aye," Zayne agreed. "Shen, change course, South by —" he stopped when he realized one of the ships from the blockade was approaching them.

"I don't suppose they're just going to tell us to leave, are they?"

"Wouldn't count on it."

Shen stepped over. "Course, captain?"

"Belay that, for now," said Zayne, "but keep alert. Xun, Tagren, pick a gun and wait for my signal." Xun immediately made way for the starboard cannon, while Tagren hesitated a moment before climbing to the Stinger — a massive ballista mounted atop the aftcastle.

Zayne rested each of his hands on one of the pistols strapped to his belt as the ship drew nearer. When it was close enough for Zayne to make out its crew, he realized that no one aboard was wearing an Imperial uniform, but instead red kaftans and matching turbans. "Fascinating."

"What?" Asked Nanette.

"The Empire isn't running the show." The ship made a sweeping turn on its approach, its starboard side becoming parallel to the *Scorpion,* its name — the *Nightjar* — was emblazoned on the side in gold Rivien script.

A bearded man stepped up to the gunwale of the *Nightjar* and called over. "I wish to speak to Captain Zayne Balthine." His Asarian was accented, but he spoke clearly.

Zayne turned to Nanette. "Don't make me shout."

Nanette gave him a weary look and nodded. "Aye." Louder, she called back to him. "This is Captain Balthine. Who's asking?"

"I only come to inform you; your ship is allowed passage into the city. Your arrival was expected."

Zayne shivered despite the desert heat. "Of course we were," he muttered. "Shen, bring us in."

"Aye, aye, captain," Shen replied, resignation clear in his voice. The *Nightjar* escorted them as they made the voyage to the docks, much to Zayne's irritation.

"Who was expecting us?" Nanette asked, casting a look over the desolated city.

Zayne eyed what had once been the castle at the city's heart. "Couldn't guess. My contacts here are pretty low-standing citizens. A gunsmith, a cartographer… there was a botanist who sold me those roses I used to keep on the aft balcony." Nanette sneered at that. "What?"

"You gave Durant one of those."

Zayne blinked, thinking of when he might have done something like that, until he remembered his first meeting with Asier's crew. The memory was so distant, he would almost have attributed it to Lucandri. He had been battle worn, almost in shock, and grateful for his life. "So I did," he agreed. "Then she went and killed the lot of them. One more thing to put on her ledger."

Nanette snorted.

When the *Scorpion* made port, the man from the *Nightjar* took hold of a rope and swung gracefully to the docks. Nanette whistled. With a roll of his eyes, Zayne ordered the gangplank put down. "Nanette, you're with me."

"I thought you didn't trust anyone alone with the ship."

"I trust Altair even less."

"If she's not dead," said Nanette.

"When have I ever been that lucky?" asked Zayne.

They walked down to the docks, which were abandoned, save for their guide and a small patrol of men dressed much like him. "What's your name," Zayne asked his escort when they reached him.

"Rashaad al Muun," he offered with a proffered hand. Zayne looked at the hand and crossed his arms. The weapons hidden in his sleeves rattled dully as they made contact through the leather. The bearded man frowned and lowered his hand. He put his hands behind his back and began to walk into the city.

"What happened here?" Nanette asked. "Other than the dragon attack?"

"The dragons came at a most inopportune moment," said al Muun. "For the Imperials, at least. However, I will let your host tell you the full story." They crossed several streets and reached the city's main square with an ease that would have been impossible if the markets weren't completely abandoned.

The least damaged building on the square was a tavern. It was missing part of its roof and half the balcony had crashed onto the street below. In comparison, several other buildings had been burned to the ground or more completely collapsed. Al Muun led them to the tavern and opened the half-hinged door open for them. Zayne put a hand on his sword and went ahead.

He was greeted by the sight of a dragon's severed head sitting in a pillar of sunlight that came from the hole in the roof. Sitting atop the scaled skull, a leg draped over one of the dragon's horns, was Isara Altair. She wore black trousers and a matching, sleeveless tunic. Her black hair was a stark contrast to her pale skin. Theatrical as always, Altair sat lounging, half in shadow, exposed in the dim pools of sunlight within a mote of dust. An orichalcum pendant of Daen's crook dangled from her throat, its iridescent pattern catching the light with a sinister gleam.

Zayne had expected he would have to double back and find her after dealing with whoever had invited him into the city. It would have been a relief if he had wanted to deal with her at all.

"Scorpion," she said with a sharp tone. Her voice was deep and resonant.

"Kestrel," Zayne retorted flatly. "Have you been sitting there all day, or did a runner tell you I was coming?"

Altair ignored his comment. "I heard you died," she said.

"That rumor went on for a while."

"So," asked the *Kestrel*'s captain, "did you really kill Elyia Asier? Or was that just a rumor, too?"

"Aye," Zayne said solemnly. "That's truth."

"Must have been hard for you," Altair said, and Zayne could *hear* her smug smile. "You're from Dawnhal, so she must have been something of a hero, the way she liberated it from Castilyn control during the war."

"There's no room for heroes in what we do," said Zayne. He looked around in the dim light of what had once been a tavern, quickly spotting Altair's crew spread out in the gloom. "You've found an interesting perch. What's the story?"

Altair leaned forward so Zayne could see her brown eyes which seemed golden in the sunlight. "It started with the riots. Something about Imperial abuses or some such, I don't know the specifics. We were called in to keep order. It was a simple gig, at first. We made a few examples, then we were sitting pretty collecting money just to keep the peace. Then the dragons happened. I'm sure you know about that."

"More than most," said Zayne. "What happened next?"

"Our client, the good Minister, told us to defend the city, kill the dragons. We did what we could, but what few ships the Empire had stationed here weren't as ready as we were. So, naturally, the city took some fire. The line of succession here got pretty blurry, and riots started again.

"Well, in the initial wave of rioting, an enterprising group of looters became rich enough to hire us to 'keep the peace' again."

"Not an Asarian group of looters, I'm guessing."

Altair smiled and shrugged. "Not at all. I get the feeling they didn't like the Asarian Empire, since we were given a bonus to kill all the Imperial soldiers, and another for killing what was left of its bureaucrats."

"Messy business," said Zayne. "With everything else going on, it'll probably be a while before the Empire finds out."

"Aye," Altair agreed. "I plan to be long gone before then, though."

"How convenient," said Zayne. "I have a job that will get you out of here."

The *Kestrel*'s captain leaned even further forward. "I'm sorry... did I just hear that Zayne Balthine is *sharing* a job?" She turned into the shadows of the room. "Tael, did he actually imply that?"

A bored sounding young man from the remnants of the bar answered, "That's what it sounds like."

"This must be big," she said. She leaned back on her makeshift throne and laced her fingers. "So, what's the pay?"

"Take it up with Dardan," Zayne said with a sneer. "It's her job."

"This must be big."

"The biggest," Zayne agreed. "Nanette, the plans."

Nanette nodded, pulling a rolled-up scroll from her coat. Altair whistled and darkness momentarily pervaded the room. A kestrel with dawn-colored feathers dropped in from the massive gap in the ceiling, pulling out of a dive just in time to set down on the floor between Zayne and Altair. The bird stood as tall as Zayne, and her wingspan was three times that. Altair performed a series of tongue clicks and whistles and the bird took the scrolls from Nanette with its beak and turned, placing them at Altair's feet. With another whistle, the kestrel shot into the air and vanished, leaving behind a set of feathers dancing on the air.

"You know," Zayne said dryly, "it would have been easier if you, or one of your crew, had taken it instead."

"Andrasta *is* one of my crew," Altair chided when she took up the scroll. As she unrolled it and held it to the light, she gasped. "This is —"

"Aye," said Zayne. "The Imperial palace. Our job is to kill Empress Yushiro Shahira."

Zayne saw Altair's finger twitch as the rest of her body stiffened. "That's madness."

"Strong word coming from you," said Zayne.

"I'm serious, Balthine!" she snapped. "We'll never be able to work in the Empire again!"

Zayne snorted.

"What?"

Zayne looked briefly to Nanette, who shrugged. Stepping forward, he stepped into the light just beneath Altair. If one could set aside her madness, her cruelty, she was beautiful. Not that that meant anything to Zayne. "Even if you hadn't ruined your own name doing this job here, it doesn't matter. I know you're behind the times, but Lancen was caught abducting the Empress' daughter. There's a bounty on the Daughters throughout Asaria, and everyone bearing the brand is sentenced to death. You might have heard the news by now if you hadn't blockaded the city."

Gasps echoed in the shadows.

"You expect us to fly right up to the Empress' doorstep?"

"Of course not," Zayne said. "I expect the *entire company* to fly right up to the Empress' doorstep." He put a boot on the dragon's skull and stepped up so he was level with the seated Altair. He leaned in. The smell of her perfume threatened to choke him, taunting him with images that conjured memories that left his stomach roiling. He pushed through that and relayed his plans. "First, we'll need to send someone ahead, sneak into the palace as servants. I've been working on special bombs. Their core components are orichalcum, Myt Dust, and —"

At mention of dust, someone grabbed his leg. He looked down to find a mess of blonde hair with impossibly blue eyes peeking out from under it. "You've let your First Mate go too far with her addiction," he noted. He kicked her off and she whimpered on the floor.

"You mean to break the wards," Altair said, ignoring the interruption. "Of course, *you* can't get in now." Zayne glowered at her. "Don't give me that look, I realized from the moment you opened your mouth what's become of you. What amazes me is you still seem to be… *you*. How did it happen?"

"That's a discussion best left for never," said Zayne. "So, you get the idea. The infiltration needs to happen before our fleet arrives so I can get in as soon as the *Scorpion* reaches the palace."

"Why not have the infiltrators assassinate the Empress, rather than bringing in everyone?"

"If you think you can, be my guest, it wouldn't hurt my feelings," Zayne said flatly. Altair sneered up at him but didn't say anymore. "When the wards are down, I'll go in for the kill."

Altair looked down at the plans, then back up at Zayne. "This is insane."

"Aye," Zayne agreed. "Which is why we need to go over every step."

INTERLUDE ONE

Twelve Years Ago

Cassidy slammed the door of her father's office as she stormed into the street with her pack slung over her shoulder. The sunlight that met her was a direct insult to her mood. She set her face to a scowl and headed to the docks. She'd spent a lot of time there, lately. The ships in the harbor, the wind, the sounds of trade all reminded her of better times. Her father didn't approve of her going to the docks unattended.

"The docks are full of disreputable sorts," he would say. *Well fuck what he'd say,* Cassidy thought to herself. Her mother had died less than a week ago, and she had just walked in on him in the arms of another woman — one she had seen around a lot *before* her mother had finally passed. What right did he have to call anyone *disreputable?*

She heard the bells clamoring when she was still a few blocks away and picked up her pace. It was almost noon and the crowds at the port was in full swing. Vendors hawked their wares, city watchmen milled about yelling orders, and sailors loaded and unloaded their ships of cargo, bringing wonders from all over. Having never left Dawnhal before, the docks were her favorite place in the world.

But today wasn't about getting lost in the crowd for a few moments.

She pressed through the crowd, coming up to the closest ship. It was a relatively small ship of Imperial make. At first glance, it seemed unremarkable — there was no decorative figurehead, the sail fins were unadorned, the dragon-hide balloon wasn't dyed and had no emblem on it — but there was a simplistic beauty to it that drew Cassidy's eye for a second, longer look. The paint on the wood was fresh and had a polished shine, but beneath it there was a well-worn feel to it that reminded Cassidy of her mother's old boat.

111

As Cassidy approached the ship, she saw emblazoned on the side, in gilded paint, was the ship's name. *Dreamscape Voyager*. On the wharf in the ship's shadow was a dark haired woman sitting on a barrel. She was eating an apple while reading a local newspaper — Cassidy recognized the story on the front cover, which told of the murdered judge and his family a couple of months back. Messy business, that.

Suddenly, Cassidy was nervous, and she was tempted to do this another day. But she tamped that urge down; she had made her decision, and she was already here. If she backed out now, she would never get anywhere. She stepped up to the woman and stuttered, "Ex-excuse me, m-ma'am?"

The woman looked up, and there was an odd smile on her face. Cassidy couldn't help but notice her eyes were a brilliant amber. "Aye? How might I help you today?"

Cassidy cleared her throat. "I was, uh, just wondering... might you be the captain of this ship?"

"Aye, that I be," the woman said with a smirk. She set the paper down and tossed the apple over her shoulder. It went clear over the edge of the harbor to make the long plunge to the bottom of the mountain. After wiping her fingers on her trousers, she proffered a hand. "Captain Elyia Asier, at your service."

Cassidy had just lifted her hand to accept the greeting when she realized what she heard and stopped. "Wait. Elyia Asier. Like, 'liberated this city from Castilyn occupation' and 'ended the war' Elyia Asier?"

"Aye, I'm definitely that one," she said. "Not that I've heard of many others."

Cassidy snorted. "That's a good one, lady. You almost had me. So, who are you really?"

"I'm Elyia Asier. Really."

"You're really set on that claim, are you?"

The woman claiming to be Elyia Asier folded her arms under her rather impressive breasts. "Why are you so sure I'm not?"

"These docks are full of people making outrageous claims," said Cassidy. "Bet you five doves I can find a man claiming to be the Queen of Castilyn in this lot. Besides, what would a hero like Elyia Asier be doing all the way out here?"

"The winds blew, so I followed," she said, as though that were a normal way to answer the question. "Why don't you tell me what you're doing interrogating me, child?"

"I'm not a child!" Cassidy protested, "I'm sixteen."

"My apologies," the woman claiming to be Asier said with a mocking bow.

"Anyway, I'm looking for work on a ship," said Cassidy. "Thought maybe you needed a deckhand, but if you're just going to make fun of me, I'll look elsewhere!"

The ship captain laughed, and though Cassidy's first reaction was to get flustered, there was something sincere in the laughter, and something was familiar she couldn't place, so she forced herself to relax. "If that's all it takes to get under your skin," she said when she stopped laughing, "you'll never make it among sailors. Mockery is a staple of ship life."

"And identity theft?"

The woman sighed. "I really am Elyia Asier."

Cassidy raised her brow and locked eyes with the woman. Her amber eyes never wavered. Maybe she was who she said she was. Or maybe she was unbelievably dedicated to the bit. "Okay, *Elyia Asier...*" she said, nervous of how to proceed. "Do you need a deckhand?"

Asier looked Cassidy over. "First," she said, "you never gave me your name."

"Oh, right," Cassidy stammered. She held her hand out. "Cassandra Durant, but my friends call me Cassidy."

"Well, Miss Durant, you need to know something. You're going to have to work damn hard. Especially the first couple weeks. You'll *earn* your pay. Any order I give, you follow."

"I figured that was the definition of having a job," said Cassidy.

"You'd be surprised how many people don't think like that. Once you're aboard, take the ladder on the port side to the lower deck. Crew quarters are just past the engine compartment on the port and starboard. Pick a bunk to set your things and meet me on the deck.

"Aye, aye, ma'am!" Cassidy exclaimed, hurrying to obey the order. She didn't see any crew on the deck, though she figured some might be enjoying shore leave while others were below deck. She found the ladder easily enough and made her way down. She walked past the engine compartment, surprised to see no one at work, and knocked on the starboard side door. There was no answer. She opened the door and found four cots secured to the wall, but nothing atop them, no trunks, nothing to indicate anyone used the space. She closed the door and opened the port side cabin. Just like the starboard side, there were four cots secured into the wall, but nothing to suggest anyone lived there. Confused, and a little uneasy, Cassidy set her pack on the top bunk on the aft side and ran up to meet the captain.

Asier was standing at the helm.

"Ahoy, Miss Durant," she said. "Get yourself settled?"

"I think so," Cassidy said uncertainly. "Where's the rest of the crew?"

"This is it," said Asier.

"Just us?" Cassidy exclaimed.

"Just us," said Asier. "I told you it would be a lot of work. Oh, don't look at me like that, it's not a permanent arrangement. But the wind's changing, and we need to follow. But before we set off, there's one thing you need to see."

Cassidy followed Asier to what she figured must have been the captain's quarters even before she opened the door. There were swords and an old military uniform hanging from one of the walls, and several storage trunks lined up against another. The captain led Cassidy to the only table in the room and indicated a massive book. Opening it up, it turned out to be an accounting ledger.

"What I need isn't a deckhand," said Asier. "I need a First Mate. And one of your many responsibilities is to help me with the accounts. How good are you with numbers?"

"Pretty good," Cassidy said shyly.

"Good, because this ledger is going to tell our story."

CHAPTER NINE

As blood dripped onto her ledger's pages, Cassidy absently wiped her face on her sleeve. She'd stopped wearing white shirts to mitigate the constant damage she was doing to them. She wiped the drop from the page, hoping to get it before the stain set in. Hymn was floating a ways over the ledgers and — though her glow was so potent that Cassidy had to peer very closely to see anything more than a floating ball of light with wings — Cassidy could tell the Fae was glaring at her disapprovingly.

"What?"

A single wave of red light pulsed through Hymn's blue radiance. "You know very well 'what'. I have told you many times, you are too dependent on our connection."

Cassidy leaned back. "You sound just like Kek," she said dismissively.

"Even a fool like him can impart wisdom."

Cassidy crossed her arms. "I can't help it, damn it! It's all that keeps me on my feet sometimes."

"Perhaps if you drank less —" Hymn started, but Cassidy slammed her fist on the table.

"It's not just the hangovers," she snapped. The Fae didn't flinch, and Cassidy sighed. "It's other pains, too. Earlier this week, my whole arm was in pain and my fingers were numb, all day. This morning, I couldn't have gotten to bed without this connection because my ribs felt like they'd broken again!"

"You push yourself too hard," Hymn said softly. "You need to let yourself heal properly."

"I'll be fine," Cassidy said firmly. She made a point of looking over the ledgers, doing a few calculations in her head.

"What are you looking for?" Hymn asked.

"Thinking of expenses," she said absently. "Orichalcum isn't cheap. Fashioning it into something functional... ugh."

"The Empress has given you writs for that sort of thing."

"Trade and commerce are more complicated than that," Cassidy said, "but even if everyone cooperates and abides by the

Empress' orders, that's only good in the Empire. If we don't find what we need when we make port in Andaerhal, we'll need to find it somewhere in Rivien."

Despite her words, she quickly found herself looking at the numbers from the previous month, then the year before, and soon she was looking at the exchanges made over the past decade, with bittersweet memories tied to many of the listed expenses and earnings. It was easier looking back this way than Asier's journal had been. No special meanings, no hints at a dire future, just notes like *new boiler*, *special medicine for Kek*, and *delivery of ancient artifact* and accompanying numbers.

Eventually she decided she wasn't getting anywhere looking at the same numbers until she went cross-eyed, and she slammed the book shut. A wave of fatigue came over her, and she felt dizzy.

"I need some air," she announced as she stood and threw her coat on. The Fae followed her outside into the chill air. Miria was at the helm and Nieves was on the aftcastle mending a net.

Cassidy paced the length of the deck, performing a cursory inspection, all the while thinking again about the revelation that the ship was apparently a living creature. In spite of her initial reaction, it really didn't seem that strange. Even before learning the truth of it, Cassidy had always empathized with the *Dreamscape Voyager*, and it was the same with any sailor and their vessel. She ran her hands along the gunwale, scraping snow off to the distant ground in thick clumps that vanished in the distance. Eventually, she made her way to the ladder to the lower deck. She pulled her coat sleeves up to her fingertips and climbed down.

"... and he's a proper noble!" Kek was shouting. Cassidy looked over her shoulder as she cleared the last few rungs, finding Kek leaning on the edge of the engine compartment while Lierre shoveled coal into the chamber.

"Perhaps, but Qi is fun and personable," Lierre retorted. "Kuan-Yin is boorish."

"Oh, come on, Lierre," Kek protested, "she deserves better than the penniless sitar player."

"What're you arguing about?" Cassidy asked, causing Kek to curse and leap to his feet.

"Ahoy, captain," Lierre said, continuing to work. "Kek just finished reading the latest romance from Kasim Dalina." Cassidy raised an eyebrow, peering over Kek's shoulder to find a pink, leather-bound book in his hand. It looked well-worn for a new book. "Latest to be translated into Asarian, anyway," she added. "Stay on my good side, Valani, or I'll tell you what happens in the next book."

"You wouldn't dare!"

Cassidy shook her head in amusement.

"Anyway, all these years and Kek still doesn't understand women," Lierre said with a smirk.

"Pigeon shit! I'm just saying a noble just has more to offer."

"Kek," Lierre said in the long suffering tone of someone dealing with an idiot, "girls want more out of love than money."

"I'm not saying they don't, but — Cass, help me out here!"

Cassidy held her hands up. "Sorry, Kek— I think I left my cabin on fire!"

"Cassy!"

"What? I don't read that swill."

"Swill?" Kek and Lierre shouted together. Lierre added, "Don't act so high and mighty, captain, I know all about what passes for literature in your cabin!"

"That's different!" Cassidy said defensively. "They... have pictures," she added, quieter.

"Right," Kek said dryly. "Well, if you ever need more than pictures..."

"Not interested."

"So, what brings you down here, captain?" asked Lierre.

"Just needed to breathe, thought I might do a little inspection. Anything I need to know?"

Lierre stopped working and crossed her arms under her ample breasts. "I meant to tell you in the capital, but everything went mad. I have some parts I'll need after the beating we took in those storms. We should be fine with my patch ups," she added, "so long as we don't push the old girl too hard. Oh, and I've been hearing a rattling, I would like to request a full stop to investigate it. Perhaps after supper?"

"If you think it's something important," said Cassidy, "we can stop right now."

"Thank you, Captain."

Cassidy nodded. "Kek, you got anything to add?"

"It's not something that will matter right now," he said, and Cassidy made a gesture to urge him to spit it out. "It's our old guns,

Captain. If you want to go through with orichalcum ammunition, we need to make some changes."

"Like what?"

"Not sure if you've ever seen an orichalcum bullet before —"

"I haven't," said Cassidy, "but the principle can't be that different, can it?"

"It's complicated," he said. "Dragon bones are as weird as the rest of the beast. You're probably thinking, lighter material, just change the powder mix. You'd be wrong. Something about the metal reacts when it's caught in an explosion."

Cassidy blinked. "Reacts… how?"

"It makes a much bigger explosion," Lierre said flatly. She smacked Kek in the stomach and he grunted. "This is no place for dramatic pauses."

"Right," Kek said with a cough. "Anyway, back in my days with the fishing crew, some of the guys used orichalcum canon rounds for breaking through tortohemoth shells. Well, one day an idiot named Gilliaum loads one into a cannon that wasn't fortified for them." Kek cleared his throat uncomfortably and his eyes settled on the middle distance, as if lost in a memory. "That was his last day on the crew."

Kek shook his head, as if to clear his head of whatever he'd seen and Lierre visibly shivered. Cassidy opened her mouth to speak and closed it twice before finally saying, "Right. New guns to go with the ammunition. Well, if you need anything else, let me know. Preferably *before* a catastrophe strikes. Get ready to stop, I'm going to tell Miria."

Cassidy turned on her heels and climbed the ladder to pass Miria the orders and relieved her post. When the girl went below, Cassidy staggered to the steps of the aftcastle and flopped right on her ass, letting out a heavy breath.

Unintentionally, she released her Fae connection. Her arm flared in pain immediately, centered around her elbow, and her fingertips went numb. She flexed her arm and opened and closed her fist repeatedly in an effort to alleviate both the pain and numbness.

"What's the matter captain?"

Cassidy turned to see Nieves a few steps above her.

"It's nothing," said Cassidy. She was suddenly breathless. "Just tired, and sore."

Nieves cocked an eyebrow and the corner of her lip twitched into a sneer that said she didn't believe her. Despite that, the sawbones got to her feet and walked right past her on the steps. "When you're ready to tell me, you know how to find me."

Cassidy nodded and tried to catch her breath.

CHAPTER TEN

The private room of the tavern was in better shape than the entrance, and there was enough room for Altair's entire crew as well as Zayne and Nanette. Except for the damned bird, Altair's crew was gathered around the bar, raiding the stockpile of drinks and chatting idly. In the center of the room, underneath a warm lamplight, Altair and Nanette were sitting at a polished oak table with Zayne standing behind his First Mate. Spread out on the table were the plans for the Imperial palace and maps of the Empire.

"I like it," Altair said, a wicked smile creeping over her face. "But how will our fleet even reach the capital? You said all our ships are being targeted."

"Aye," Zayne acknowledged. "But flying around the patrols won't be as hard as you think. Play your cards right, and no one will be discovered until we rally for the assault."

The other ship captain narrowed her eyes suspiciously. "Explain."

Nanette looked up at Zayne. He nodded and stepped up to the table, tapping the map of Asaria, indicating a red circle just beyond the Rivien border. "You'll be flying through the Dreamscape."

A hush fell over Altair's crew. Zayne glanced over at the bar to see a burly man staring slack-jawed at him while trying to pour an entire bottle of brandy into a small glass. At the same time, a wiry young woman with tattoos covering both arms dropped the deck of cards she was shuffling. The only ones who weren't staring at him as if he'd just been juggling his own eyes were Nanette and Altair's first mate Tatl, the blue-eyed duster with the disheveled blonde hair. She was nodding as though it made perfect sense.

Zayne returned his attention to Altair. Her eyes were so wide Zayne thought they might fall out. She had the map held stretched tight between her fists. He was worried she might tear it in half. "You know a way into the Dreamscape?" There was a gleam in her eye, and her words were laced with hunger.

In truth, Zayne didn't, but Pyrrha did. He wasn't about to explain that situation to Altair, though. *"After* you've rallied every Daughter from here to the Reach," Zayne said, "you'll lead them here. There, you'll find two white trees in an otherwise empty valley. You will fly your ships between them at dusk, and you'll be in the Dreamscape. From there, the map itself will show you the way."

"Fifteen years," she said, trembling, "fifteen years I've looked for a way back! I've tried recreating Dardan's ritual… experiments! So many dead…" She rose to her feet, her face cracking into a demented grin the likes of which Zayne had only ever seen in the deranged. "And here you've given me the key! It's all —" Zayne grabbed Altair by the shoulder and shoved her back in her chair. A young man with oil-slicked hair leaped over the bar and pulled a pistol on Zayne. Without taking her eyes off Zayne, Altair stopped the youth with a quick gesture. "It's fine, Tael." He lowered his weapon but did not holster it.

"Your hands are stronger than I imagined," she said breathily. "But if you want to control me, you should grab a bit *lower*," she added, pushing her chest at him. Zayne was once again made aware of her perfume: rich desert flowers and a hint of spice. His pulse quickened. He let go of her. Images of Altair beneath him flashed briefly in his mind, but were soon replaced by less savory ones, which made his stomach churn. Bile crept up his throat.

"Save your games for someone else," Nanette snapped.

"Oh, you're welcome to join him, of course," Altair said, eyes still locked with Zayne's. "Maybe I'll get to see what keeps him so firmly attached to your hip."

"Enough!" Zayne said, slamming his hand on the table. "You have your part, and you *will* play it."

"You have you have your part, and you will play it," she repeated, mocking his tone. "Gods, Balthine, I remember when you hid behind your aunt Salaa's skirts. Do you really think you can bully me into anything?"

Zayne sighed, walking away from the table.

"Hmph, that's what I thought," said Altair, leaning her chair back. "You're still just a coward with his —" Zayne summoned Dawn Star to his hand and hurled it like a spear. It struck Altair's chair just a hair's width from her neck, cutting through straight to the hilt. The other mercenary captain blinked, slowly turned to look at it. "Huh," she breathed. She stood up and tried to pull the sword

121

from the chair, but it vanished in a flash of light as soon as she braced her foot on the seat.

"You *will* gather the other Daughters," Zayne repeated. "And you *will* help me assassinate the Empress. *Then,* and only then, you'll be free to do whatever you fucking want."

Tatl stepped over to the table. She opened her mouth, and a creaking tone came out, stretching on as one ragged and overlong note before she spoke in a raspy voice. "We should listen to him," she said. "He can make the world dream."

Zayne raised an eyebrow at that. It was an open secret that Altair used her First Mate as a test subject for her experiments with Myt Dust. Less well known was the fact that many of her more lucrative decisions had been made at the behest of the Fae addled addict. What amazed Zayne, however — more than the trust the occultist put in her drug-crazed former sister — was the fact that she hadn't long since been possessed like Xiao Ta had been — or simply killed.

"Alright, Balthine," Altair said, "I'll help you. But when all this is done, I want to see that sword of yours." She paused, and added, "And not in an ironic, 'you kill me with it' sort of way."

"We'll see what happens," said Zayne. "After killing the Empress, I'll be in Tal Joyau."

"Going to kill Queen Isabel, too?"

"Not if it can be helped."

Altair looked at the map again. "How will we get *out* of the Dreamscape without you there to show us how?"

"The map will show you the way," he promised. "Nanette, let's get the provisions we need." Nanette rose to her feet and walked briskly to Zayne's side. She turned back and shot Altair a glare that could freeze dragon fire, but the other Daughter was staring lustfully at the map in her hand.

As Zayne and Nanette crossed the former common room, Nanette scratched at the dragon skull, pulling off a loose scale. "The nerve of that woman," she said, sneering. "Can we really trust her to do her part?"

"Normally I'd say no," said Zayne.

"But she's too interested in you," Nanette concluded. Her voice was pure venom.

"Aye," Zayne said indifferently, trying not to think of her perfume — and adamantly not thinking of any *other* aspect of Isaara Altair, for that matter.

"I saw the way your stance changed," she continued. "You were about to be sick. I know what leads you down that road."

"You're jealous of the fact that she makes me want to vomit?" he answered offhandedly, focusing on not thinking about any of it.

Despite his attempt at a neutral tone, Nanette seemed to realize she'd said the wrong thing, because she quickly said, "I don't like seeing you uncomfortable like that. It's just..." she stopped talking, which was for the best. It wasn't a subject they broached often, and never from this angle. Altair must have gotten to her as much as Zayne.

He decided the best thing would be a change of subject. "While we resupply, do you want more paints? New canvases?" He almost added that her old ones were destroyed when the *Scorpion* sank, but he knew that would just rub salt in her wounds.

As they stepped out into the street, Nanette turned to face the setting sun. "I'd like that," she said. "Do you think we can find a shop selling them right now? Between the lock-down and the desolation, we may be lucky to find food."

"We can look a while."

Nanette nodded. "Gods, it's been so long since I've taken the time to paint. I don't even know what I'd start with."

"Yumesalam," Zayne said, thinking of the first place that came to mind. He thought of the crystalline spires reaching into the sky, of the gardens that contained every color of flower, the dyrelights that illuminate it from dusk until dawn.

"What?"

"The city at the end of —" He stopped when he realized he had never heard of nor seen the place he was remembering, and that whatever it was at the end of was as much a mystery to him as it was to Nanette. "I'm sorry," he said, "Lucandri's memories are in the way."

Nanette didn't say anything. She just grabbed his arm and squeezed it. Zayne placed his hand on hers and they walked together.

CHAPTER ELEVEN

The night was unseasonably warm and there wasn't a cloud in the sky. It was the perfect night to keep watch. All Cassidy needed was a light jacket. She stood at the prow, clutching the gunwale and staring at the night reflected in the water. She drummed her fingers, occasionally wiping blood off her face with her sleeve.

"Looking for the monster?" Kek asked. His voice was teasing, but there was a nervous tinge to it.

"I don't want it to surprise us," she said, but she pushed herself away from the edge.

"I'd like to think we would see it coming."

"Like the crew of the *Western Zephyr* did?" Cassidy snapped. Kek blanched.

"Sorry, Kek."

"No," he said, "you're right." He sat down on the gunwale and let out a sigh. "Sometimes I wonder what... Elyia would do." Cassidy noticed the hesitation — she knew he was about to say *what the captain would do* — but she didn't call him out on it.

She knew exactly what Elyia Asier would do. She would blindly follow the pull of fate, damn anyone she hurt along the way. "She's dead," Cassidy said with an unwanted hitch in her voice.

"What the fuck is your problem, Cassy?" demanded Kek, leaping to his feet. "Aye, she's dead, I was there, too. But that's not *her* fault, damn it!" Cassidy was about to make a snide remark about how it was *entirely* Asier's fault, but seeing the hurt in his eyes, Cassidy believed he was going to punch her. For a minute she wished he would. Her chest was aching with the sudden tension. "Back in Bajin's Landing, we agreed to drink to her memory, didn't we? But you just moped in silence until the first boy to offer you a wink came along, and you left us to jump his bones!"

Cassidy honestly couldn't remember that night. "That's not —" she began but Kek wasn't done.

"Nieves and Lierre told me to let it go because you were probably hurting. But I won't stay quiet while you badmouth the woman who gave us everything we have!" He was about to punctuate the statement by jabbing his finger into Cassidy's chest when Hymn appeared. The Fae did not appear as small, glowing ball of light, but as a tall woman wearing a dress made of an unnaturally blue night sky. She was holding Kek by the wrist, glaring daggers with her inverted eyes that matched her dress in color.

"That is enough, Kekarian," the Fae said firmly. Kek gaped for a moment, then fiercely pulled himself from Hymn's grasp. For her part, Hymn seemed to feel her point was made and let him go without issue.

"Hymn, you didn't need..." She looked up. The ship was moving through the sky, supported not by its balloon but by three great, ribbed sails snapping and cracking in the wind. "When did we enter the Dreamscape? And why doesn't the sky look different?"

Kek seemed to notice right after, and he let out a mild curse.

"It is the leviathan's influence," Hymn said. "It is weakening the world's veil. We will most likely pass back fully into your world shortly." Cassidy bit her lip, looking up at the sky. She looked at the stars she'd spent her entire adult life keeping track of. At first, she didn't see anything to set the night apart from any other, but as she continued to stare, she saw occasional lightning flashes amongst the stars, despite a lack of clouds.

There was a loud *snap* of tightly-pulled leather and Cassidy's vision was suddenly filled with the balloon overhead. Kek gasped and cursed again. Hymn had returned to the form of a small ball of glowing light with iridescent wings.

"Is that going to happen a lot?" Kek asked.

Cassidy was wondering about that as well — she had been about to ask the same thing but hearing Kek pose the question instead caused another question to take root in her mind. "Is that going to happen to *other ships*?"

"It is very likely," Hymn said before floating away. Cassidy let her go. Kek looked like he wanted to follow the Fae but gave up after one step and turned back to Cassidy.

He didn't speak, so Cassidy said what she thought he wanted to hear. "Sorry, Kek." He grunted and turned away.

He leaned out over the edge of the ship and sighed. "Me too," he said halfheartedly. "I just..." He breathed in sharply. "I..." he hung his head.

Cassidy leaned back against the gunwale beside him. "I know," she said. She closed her eyes. "Sometimes I think of how nice it would be, to go back to those days. It felt safer."

"Well," Kek said wryly, "we didn't exactly go chasing monsters."

Cassidy tried to smile, but it came off as a sad twitch. Out of the corner of her eye, she saw Nieves climb up to the deck. "Looks like your watch is over," she said to her first mate.

Kek grunted and looked up. He pushed himself off from the gunwale and headed towards the ladder. He gave Nieves a small nudge and a grunt before disappearing below.

"What's wrong with him?" Nieves asked once they were alone.

Cassidy opened her mouth, intending to mention their row, only to decide she didn't really want to talk about that. Besides, there were more pressing matters. "Have you noticed anything weird when you're on watch?" she asked.

"No," the sawbones replied slowly. "Why?"

"Apparently," said Cassidy, "the leviathan can make the Dreamscape affect this world." Nieves had a look of pensive discomfort on her face. "Kek and I just watched the ship change, like it did when the leviathan first appeared."

Nieves blanched and took a step away, as if to steady herself. "This *just* happened?"

"Few minutes ago, aye. Have some breakfast before you worry about it," Cassidy advised.

Nieves gave Cassidy a blank look for several seconds. It evaporated into a barely suppressed grin. "Let me guess," she said, "there's no breakfast prepared, and you wanted me to make it."

"Would you, please?"

Nieves gave Cassidy a suffering smile and turned to the galley. When she was alone, Cassidy leaned backwards over the gunwale and groaned. "Fuck whoever started this weird shit," she said. She felt her nose running again and wiped the blood on her sleeve.

"Blame is unhelpful," Hymn said, appearing off to Cassidy's right.

"Well, it's all I've got," Cassidy muttered, pulling herself back up to a sitting position. She pulled her cigarette box from her pocket and extracted one, along with a match. "Why would someone even…" Cassidy snapped her fingers a couple of times as she tried to think, "what's the word?"

"Summon?" Hymn provided.

"Aye, let's go with that," Cassidy agreed, not able to think of a better phrase. She lit her cigarette and stared at the burning paper for a moment. "Why would someone summon that *thing*?"

"Power," Hymn said. "Humans often dive too deeply into wells they cannot fathom. Do you remember when we watched the history of Queen Acselna?"

Cassidy furrowed her brow. "Queen who?" she asked, though as soon as the question was out of her mouth, she remembered Hymn showing her visions in the Dreamscape. "Wait, from the city in the Black Gulch, right?"

"The very same," Hymn confirmed. "She was given a weapon and warned not to use it against her enemies."

"Sounds like giving sweets to a child and telling her not to eat it," Cassidy commented. She took a drag of her cigarette, feeling the warm smoke filling her lungs, and a faint sense of calm pushed back the mounting anxiety.

"An apt comparison," said the Fae. "As it would happen, Queen Acselna did, in fact, use the weapon against an invading army. It certainly did its job — the army was no more."

"I feel a 'but' coming up."

"Quite. The invading army was destroyed, but so too was the city, and its people."

Cassidy continued to smoke as she ruminated on Hymn's words. They had a familiar ring to them. "The Iron Veils tell stories like that. Sanctum texts say before the Ascension, things like that happened all the time, which is why it was necessary to take to the skies. It's why our relationship is illegal and liable to get me thrown into the *chateau de fer*, or just executed on the spot."

"I'm not familiar with that place," said Hymn. "Neither you nor your crew have mentioned it before."

"It's a prison in Castilyn, run by the Iron Veils. No one really knows much about it. No one comes out."

"I thought execution was the standard procedure for the crime of contact with my kind."

"Normally, aye," said Cassidy. "But sometimes if the Iron Veils are the ones that find the guilty party," she made a gliding gesture with her hand, "they take them away. Never to be heard from a—" She noticed something dark on the horizon. Her heart skipped a beat. She fumbled for her spyglass, her hands shaking when she put it to her face.

It wasn't the leviathan.

She let out a breath and tried to focus on whatever was on the horizon. "Smoke," she said aloud. "Something big is on fire." She adjusted the scope and swore under her breath. "Is that Andaerhal?"

Hymn fluttered near Cassidy's ear. "I believe it is."

Cassidy stared at the pillar of smoke. "Might just be a factory fire," she said, mostly to herself. She also considered the possibilities of pirates or dragons or, if the gods were playing their games, the leviathan itself could be responsible. "Better wake the crew, just in case," she added. She stepped up to the helm to make a slight course correction before heading to the bell posted on the aftcastle. She rang it six times.

Nieves was the first to answer the call, of course, steeping out from the galley, brandishing a kitchen knife. "Trouble?"

Cassidy was explaining the smoke on the horizon when Kek pulled himself on deck, having apparently traded his shirt for his weapons since going below.

"We under attack?" he asked quickly, clearly poised to rush to his cannon on the aftcastle.

"What is that?" Lierre cried from the ladder as she and the princess emerged from below.

"Don't rightly know yet," said Cassidy. "Miria, take the helm. Kek, I want you at your gun, just in case. Nieves, Lierre, eyes out and be ready for orders."

As everyone moved to carry out the orders, Cassidy made her way to the prow to assess the situation ahead. Hymn fluttered by her shoulder as they flew towards the city, close enough Cassidy could hear the bell-like chime of her wings over the engines churning away at full speed.

"What do you think?" Cassidy asked the Fae. "Leviathan?"

"No," said Hymn. "The city is still largely intact, and the fires seem to be isolated to the inner walls."

"You can see that from here?"

"Of course."

Cassidy grumbled, waiting for a better view. Dawn broke behind them as they neared, and she was able to see something. Black spots dotted the freshly painted horizon. At first, Cassidy thought it was a fleet, but through her spy glass she saw that mixed among the Imperial colors were a host of different classes of ships.

Despite the heavy traffic, no one was approaching the city, or departing.

"A blockade," Hymn said, as though to voice the thought in Cassidy's mind.

Cassidy nodded. It wasn't quite midmorning when the *Dreamscape Voyager* neared the circle of ships banding a mile out from the mountain that wore Andaerhal like a crown, weary of the Imperial naval ships holding the line. Skiffs moved between ships, with criers and messengers flying this way and that.

When Cassidy dropped the engines to a full stop, she let the *Dreamscape's* momentum carry them to the blockade line. She could hear shouts of protests in the distance, but she couldn't make out the words. It was several minutes of uncomfortable silence before one of the skiffs began floating towards them. Its pilot was a middle-aged man in a blue, soot-stained watch-officer's jacket. A grey-haired woman and a younger man were positioned as guards on either side of the boat.

"Hail!" the man called over to Cassidy. "I am sorry, but we cannot let anyone into the city. I recommend heading north to Bajin's Landing."

"Why are you blockading the city?" Cassidy asked. She looked to the plumes of smoke and a chilling thought crept into her. "Plague?"

"Riots, madam," the officer informed her, in the weary tone of a man who had repeated himself dozens of times. "We are currently handling the situation, but it is unsafe for anyone to enter the city."

"But we have to supply here," Cassidy protested, "Bajin's Landing is too far."

"I have heard claims like that hundreds of times already, I am afraid you'll have to wait or seek harbor elsewhere," the watchman said. His tone was not exactly unsympathetic, but he spared no time in starting up the engine to move the skiff.

"Wait!" Cassidy shrieked, flushing with embarrassment at the desperation in her own voice before clearing her throat and adding, "we have orders straight from the Empress herself."

The man paused and looked back at her. He cut the engines and said, "You could have led with that," he said, almost too low to hear across the distance. "I'm coming aboard, let me see these orders." Using a manual pump, the officer closed the distance needed to throw a rope for Cassidy to catch.

She pulled the skiff close enough for the officer to step aboard and tied it off on the gunwale. Then she reached into her jacket and pulled out the leather tube containing a copy of the Empress' writ, which she had taken to keeping on her person. The watchmen seemed to read it three times before he finally sighed and rolled the scroll back up and returned it to its container. "I will need to relay this back to my superior. To ensure you aren't shot for attempting to break the blockade, you understand."

"Comforting," Cassidy said dismally.

The officer nodded gravely. "We do what we must," he said. "For the Empire."

"For the Empire," Cassidy agreed, though her stomach churned.

Cassidy fidgeted uncomfortably as she watched the skiff fly away. She called the crew together to inform them of the situation, and then planted herself on the gunwale and watched the blockade. She picked at splinters in the wood with twitching fingers and checked her watch every few minutes. Kek paced behind her while Nieves and Miria whispered about something Cassidy couldn't hear.

It was half an hour before one of the naval ships broke away from the blockade and began an approach towards the *Dreamscape Voyager.* Cassidy wiped her sweaty fingers on her trousers and smoothed out her jacket repeatedly as she watched the vessel approach. As it drew nearer, Cassidy could read the name *The Night Heron* emblazoned on its side in gilded Imperial script. Like the *Dreamscape,* the *Heron* was an Imperial junk, but it was three times the length, double the width, and had four decks lined with cannons. Cassidy swallowed nervously.

From the deck of the *Heron,* a woman wearing the red uniform of the Imperial military, rather than the blue uniform of the Watch, ordered them to follow her ship. Cassidy relayed the order to Miria, and the *Dreamscape Voyager* followed in its wake. Cassidy could see people aboard other ships in the blockade gesticulating angrily in the *Dreamscape'*s direction, though between distance and her ships engines, she couldn't make out what curses were being hurled her way.

"Maybe we should have hoisted the Imperial colors, Captain," Lierre suggested. "It might have saved us some time."

"Aye," Cassidy agreed. "Something to consider next time."

Cassidy expected the *Heron* to lead them to the docks, leaving them free to depart as they would. It came as a surprise to her, then, that rather than slow, the *Heron* kept its heading but began to rise until it shared an altitude with the higher levels of the city. Seeing the destruction took her breath away, and she understood the necessity of the blockade. Just beyond the harbor, spanning the entire width of the harborside, every building three streets deep had been put to the torch. Blackened skeletons of shops stood alone where once had been beautiful edifices. Bustling streets had been replaced with debris and rubble. Lierre cursed. Throughout the city, Cassidy could see pockets of the city that either still burned or had been reduced to ash. It looked less like the site of riots and more like a dragon had attacked.

They approached the city's ministry offices — a tall, flat roofed building with four pagodas situated at each of the building's cardinal points. Three ships of a comparable size to the *Heron* were nestled atop the flat roof between the towers, and Cassidy could see naval uniforms and watchmen milling about.

From the aft of the *Heron*, the same woman who had bade them follow called for a full stop. When Miria cut the engines and let the *Dreamscape* drift, another skiff launched from the deck of the *Heron* and approached. It cut alongside Cassidy's ship and the woman in red stepped aboard without requesting or waiting for permission. Cassidy couldn't help but feel a tremor of annoyance at that, but she figured, under the circumstances, she could forgive the woman just this once.

Up close, the officer looked haggard. Heavy bags sat under her dark eyes, her black hair was pulled back into a tight tail, but stray locks wandered in various directions, and her uniform had the rough patterns of having been slept in. Still, she stood proud and straight as if a rod had been shoved right up her ass, and as her head swiveled around to survey the crew, she managed to look down her nose at everyone despite being even shorter than Kek.

"Vice Admiral Jiang," she said curtly. "Which one of you is Durant?"

Cassidy bristled and made a conscious effort to stand straighter to rival the other woman's ridiculous posture. "*Captain* Durant," she said.

131

Jiang grunted. "You are to accompany me to the Lord Minister and the baroness."

Cassidy snorted. "Mister Valani," she called to Kek, "you have the ship until I'm back. Miss Merlyn, you're with me."

The officer nodded briskly and crossed back over to the skiff. Cassidy gestured for Lierre to go first while she whispered to Kek. "Seems like a lot for a riot," she muttered to him.

"Aye, Captain," said Kek. "Also quiet. I'll keep an eye out."

Cassidy nodded and stepped off her deck onto the skiff. She sat beside Lierre on the prow, facing Jiang and the two burly deckhands with her. One of the latter — a young man with an unfortunate haircut that resembled an upturned bowl — released pressure from the skiff's balloon at an even pace and they descended towards the roof.

As they made the drop, Cassidy asked, "When did the riots start?"

"Two weeks ago," said Jiang. "But it's not really about riots anymore. That's how it started, sure enough. A bunch of small riots over the usual — unfair factory conditions, the continued existence of Castilyn-established offices and policies from the occupation, increased taxes following the disaster at the Dragon's Nest, the result of the last bout in the fighting pits — but all one right after the other."

"That sounds deliberate," Hymn whispered from Cassidy's hat, hopefully low enough only Cassidy and Lierre could hear.

Jiang perked up. "What was that?"

Cassidy opened her mouth. *Damn you, Hymn,* she thought.

"It sounds almost like someone planned it," Lierre offered, covering Cassidy's silence. Cassidy breathed a sigh of relief, and also hit the side of her hat. Hymn tumbled across the top of her head.

"What came next would suggest the same," said Jiang. "During the chaos, a man named Adryen Flint began arming rioters. Shortly after, we found ourselves facing not riots, but armed revolt."

"Damn," was all Cassidy could say to that.

The pilot stopped the skiff about a foot above the roof. He stepped off first to tie it down to a post Cassidy couldn't see from her vantage, and Jiang gestured for Cassidy and Lierre to disembark next. Once they had, she led them to the north tower and the door leading inside.

Led by the Admiral, they descended the pagoda's spiraling staircase until they reached a corridor bustling with red and blue uniforms. Rapid, purposeful strides navigated deftly and carelessly as men and women all but ran from room to room carrying sheets of parchment and piles of scrolls. Jiang cut a path through the hustle while Cassidy and Lierre followed in her wake. She opened the largest door on the left.

It was a large yet stuffy chamber furnished in a bizarre blending of classical Imperial and Castilyn décor. Ancient woodcuts sat beside oil paintings, a case containing two Imperial war swords stood over a mannequin dressed in the uniform of the first musketeers, and two wildly different styles of changing screens waited on opposite sides of the room. Two desks sat directly across the room, behind which stood two women: one short, plump and sweaty, the other lean and severe. They were in the midst of an intense argument when the company entered.

"…affairs of the city are my purview as baroness!" shrieked the fat woman, waving a trembling finger in the other woman's face. She had an even thicker Castilyn accent than Lierre.

"You have proven time and again you cannot handle the situation," said the other woman in a calmer, yet carrying tone. She turned her head to see Jiang leading Cassidy and Lierre into the room. "Admiral, do you have something to report?" she asked, her gaze adding the unspoken question, *who by the Mists the Admiral had brought into her office.*

"Lord Minister, I have with me Captain Durant, tasked by the Empress Herself to —"

"We have the situation well in hand," protested the baroness.

"Clearly the Empress agrees with *my* assessment," said the Lord Minister.

"I actually wasn't aware of the situation until my arrival," Cassidy cut in quickly, lest she lose any chance to speak for herself. "I am on a mission to conscript a fighting force against…" She paused, considering. "External threats," she decided to call it. "My crew only came to Andaerhal to find supplies and potential recruits."

Jiang seemed to pale at that slightly. She clearly misinterpreted the orders as well.

"This office is not a supply depot," snapped the baroness.

"Even if it were," said that Minister, "we are not in any position to provide. In case you haven't been informed, we are currently faced with open rebellion."

An explosion threw Cassidy to the floor. Heat and smoke immediately washed over her senses while pain and pressure racked her body.

CHAPTER TWELVE

Pale sunlight poured through the smoke. The acrid stench of spent gunpowder and sulfur rankled Cassidy awake. Her ears were ringing from the blast.

She pushed herself up. Chips of broken plaster and splinters cut into her palms. The stench of sulfur gave her a headache.

At least, she thought it was the sulfur. She put her hand to massage her temple, and it came back sticky with blood. She grimaced for a moment before panic fluttered in her chest. Her hand darted back to her head, this time to her hair. Her hat had been knocked off. *Hymn!* she thought and immediately began looking for the Fae. She heard a groan off to her left.

"Lierre!" she realized aloud. The engineer was sitting on her knees cradling her head. Cassidy stumbled on the one step it took to reach her and knelt beside her. There was a splotch of blood caking with dust on the side of her head.

Lierre's eyes fluttered slowly open, and she let out a miserable groan. She pushed herself out of Cassidy's arms and cradled her head. "Ugh," she managed. Then, more slowly, she asked, her voice muffled by the ringing in Cassidy's ears. "What happened, Captain?"

"We'll figure that out when we—" Cassidy's next words were swallowed by another explosion nearby. The room shook violently. What few decorations hadn't been cast to the floor in the first blast crashed with a vengeance.

Cassidy found her hat surrounded by rubble, with only a layer of plaster dust and some chips of rubble marring it. Hymn's light was conspicuously absent from beneath the wide brim. She crawled over to it, shaking it free of debris before placing it back on her head and taking a stand. She helped her engineer find her feet before looking at the other women who had been toppled by the blast. The Lord Minister was pulling herself from behind her desk with what dignity and grace could be salvaged after being knocked flat, while the lopsided and plaster filled wig of the Baroness slowly peered up from behind her own like a wooden target at a shooting range.

Cannon fire rang out from above, and Cassidy could also make out the sounds of shouting and a distant volley of gunfire.

"You!" the Lord Minister snapped at Cassidy. "You are here in service to the Empire? Then serve and help us fend off this rabble."

"I need a weapon," Cassidy protested. The Lord Minister reached into her desk and pulled out a pistol. It wasn't a flintlock, but rather a wheellock and accompanied wrench. *I hate these things,* she thought dismally, taking them up. "Lierre, do you have any cartridges on you?"

The engineer shook herself before checking her pockets. She extracted a tube of paper tied on one end and folded on the other. "I have five of these, Captain," she said. Cassidy nodded.

Cassidy took a deep breath and cranked the wheel to its ready position. The outer wall of the corridor had been blown wide open five places, and all along the gaping maws were firing squads of Imperial military and the city watch. Some were fortunate enough to have a jagged outcrop of the former wall to use as cover, but most only had the benefit of the high ground as they shot down at their enemies below. The watchmen fired and reloaded their shots sporadically while the red-clad soldiers each had a smooth rotation where the frontline fired. A partner reloaded, and they traded weapons with every volley.

Cassidy hesitantly joined the line and fired almost as she spotted a man dressed in brown rags aiming up at them from behind a makeshift barrier of scrap metal and debris. The pan of the wheellock flashed hot and the thunderous crack sounded faster than Cassidy was used to. Her target fell back into the streets. She handed Lierre the pistol to reload and ducked low.

A blue-clad woman to Cassidy's left doubled over as a shot hit her in the stomach and she fell through the opening in the wall, tumbling along the building's face. To her right, a red-clad officer screamed as his pistol was shot from his hand and went careening into the exposed room behind them.

Lierre handed back the pistol, the wheel set to a firing position. Cassidy slowly stood— dropping back to her belly when a wake of air flapped the left side of her hat. Rapid and sporadic gunfire heralded from further up. A cannon blast sent debris soaring high from the yard below, accompanied by a chorus of shouts. Another canon from the rebel line fired up, the ball flying over the Ministry Office.

Three ships sailed over the skirmish, unleashing torrents of canon fire and gun smoke. One amongst them was the *Dreamscape Voyager*. The rotary guns chugged rhythmically, bullets picking off the rebels that had been driven from cover by cannon fire. It seemed that the battle was over once the three ships — her own sweet vessel accompanied by a black warship that showed its age with its name, *Princess Sahira,* and another ship of a rich dawnwood with the name *Sunshear* emblazoned in gilded Imperial script along its side — but then an explosion opened the third story face of a nearby home and a streak of purple fire tore through the *Princess Sahira*'s port side, smoldering ebony cascading down onto the city below. The shot hit the northern pagoda, but Cassidy wasn't in place to see the extent of the damage.

The wounded *Princess* limped back in retreat only for a second shot tailed by purple flames to erupt from another apartment. The shot ripped along the length of the balloon, sending the ship careening into the street in a crash of splinters and burning debris.

"What was that?" Cassidy wondered.

She didn't realize she had spoken aloud until Lierre said, "That's what you wanted, Captain," she said quietly, horror clear in her voice. "Those are orichalcum cannons."

CHAPTER THIRTEEN

Amidst the fire and rubble, Cassidy found a bizarre stillness to the world around her. To her right and left, the soldiers and watchmen seemed to move in water as they reloaded, aimed and fired. The pans of their weapons flashed, and smoke poured out, but Cassidy could no longer hear the bark of exploding gunpowder. She blinked.

She is no longer standing in the gap in the wall. She sees herself from the outside as she stands surrounded by fresh rubble, a sword in one hand and a spent pistol in the other, covered in dust and too much blood to be wholly her own. She shoots a brown-coated rebel wearing a mask of tightly wound cloth. She flips her pistol — not the wheellock but a proper flintlock — and catches the barrel. Then she turns to Lierre, who is picking herself up from more rubble. She reaches out to pass the weapon to Lierre to reload when a bullet passes through the back of her head and her face explodes into Lierre's in the half-a-heartbeat, and the bullet strikes Lierre between the eyes.

Cassidy gasped. She recoiled and nearly stepped off the precipice. Her heart was hammering in her chest, and the beat was erratic, as though she had a second pulse not quite synchronized with the first. She touched her face gingerly, feeling a cold dread stung her sinuses. *What was that?*

An invisible thread pulled at Cassidy's chest, forcing her away from the ledge. That compulsion forced her to turn back to the corridor entrance. The door burst open and a party of six men in non-uniform brown poured into the room. Cassidy's limbs burned as if she had been longing to break into a run for hours. From the first step, she knew the path she had to take. She snatched a freshly loaded pistol that was being traded for a spent one. She pulled the hammer back and fired without breaking stride.

The first man in the pack dropped like a stone. The others tripped over him, apparently surprised to be caught. She had cleared most of the distance by the time one of the rebels — a man wearing a potato sack with eye holes over his head — had the wherewithal to push off the dead man. Cassidy veered right towards what remained of the inner wall and felt the urge to leap like she had rehearsed this charge a hundred times. When the rebel had fired, she was already out of his line of fire, both her feet connecting with the wall as she felt —more than heard — the blast. She pushed off the wall and swung her stolen pistol like a club, cracking open the shooter's skull with the pommel. A wet, red spot welled up on the surface of the sack.

Before Cassidy could even register the thought, she raised the pistol at an angle to block a slash from an Imperial war sword. Cassidy kicked the swordsman in the balls and took his weapon.

The pulse in her chest was closer to the beat of her heart and she had a dreadful sense that she was running out of time. A chill ran down her spine. That pull stronger than instinct forced her to step aside, and a club whistled through the space her head had just been occupying. Experience and reflex gave her room to think, however slightly, and adrenaline gave her thoughts a surreal clarity, and memories she had stewed over for months stirred to the surface.

This is what it was like for her, she realized. Elyia Asier had seen the future, and she had followed its pull for thirty years, knowing herself to be safe until the day she had foreseen.

Cassidy did not have thirty years. She didn't even have thirty minutes.

As she followed the pull to the future, she ducked under as second swing of the club, and the attacker hit one of his fellows in the chin instead, breaking his neck. She knew she'd be safe until she got to the yard. So, the logical step was to not go to the yard. She would not allow the future she saw to come to pass. She would be fighting blind, but surely that was better than walking into certain death.

She ran her sword to the hilt through the man's ribs and, rather than pull out to attack the last rebel who was crying in the doorway, she put all her weight into pushing Clubs on top of Crier, using the sword for purchase. She decided against killing the teary eyed youth, however, and withdrew the sword as the body collapsed on top of the other man, who gave a choking sob of surprise.

"Captain!" Lierre cried out, running down the corridor after her. "That was —" She stopped suddenly, looking out into the city, "*Hymn?*"

Cassidy followed Lierre's line of sight. At first, she saw nothing through the smoke and dust. A glimmer of blue trailed over the ground like a shooting star in the sky. The small faerie was being pursued by two burly rebels swatting at her with pikes. She flew into the doorway to the apartment building beneath the orichalcum canon. She emerged a moment later, black smoke trailing behind her in thick plumes.

An explosion blew out from the bottom floor of the apartments. The building collapsed like a tower of cards. The cannon perched at the top fired again in mid fall, the purple flame streaking through the rebel lines and into the Ministry building a few floors directly beneath Cassidy's feet.

Cassidy yelped as the previously steady floor bowed and cracked, and she began to slide, then to fall. She snatched Lierre's hand when she felt the stinging instinct to do so. As they fell, she pulled her friend tight to her body. Sure as she was that this fall wouldn't kill her, it was not painless. She hit the floor with enough force to knock the wind clear of her lungs before taking a second plunge, passing through chips of plaster that cut her hands, and one unfortunate soul dropped with them for a time, hitting Cassidy at an angle before landing with a crunch on the floor above them. When their tumble ended, Cassidy landed on her ankle before rolling down a pile of rubble into scorched cobblestones that burned like they had basked in the summer sun for hours.

She released Lierre and rolled onto her stomach. The sword she had stolen was just a hand's breadth in front of her face. Her muscles ached and her skin stung in revolt as she pushed herself up and scrambled for the weapon. The pulses were getting stronger, and a terrified part of her mind knew she was going to die in moments. Was this what Asier had felt in the fight with the Scorpion?

Following pseudo-muscle memory, Cassidy pirouetted and severed the hand of a rebel who had — for reasons she could not fathom — thought to run at her with a gun pointed at her rather than shoot from a safe distance. His pistol flew in a gentle arc, and she caught it with her offhand. She caught another rebel through the ribs with the sword.

She pulled the sword from blood and bone and whipped her other hand out, trusting the pulls from the future as she shot. The bullet tore through a woman's lower jaw.

The pulse was so heavy now she thought it was reverberating in her bones. Every muscle in her body ached to turn around and hand Lierre the pistol to reload. She felt herself beginning to follow through the motions, but her mind screamed at her to stop. When her hips did not obey and her leg lifted to facilitate the turn, she screamed out loud and forced herself to twist the other way. She threw her sword in desperate defiance.

She heard a snap of a cord like a breaking lutestring. A tremor resonated through her veins. She tensed, and with her Fae powers, she set the airborne blade ablaze, at the exact same moment the bullet she had prophesied would kill her — her *and Lierre*, she recalled in horror — struck iron instead. Sparks danced in a swirl as the fiery blade snapped in two. The hilt and what remained of the blade continued in the direction Cassidy had flung it, while the rest of the iron spun backwards.

Two feet of burning, edged metal struck Cassidy hard enough to knock her prone. As she stared dazed at the flames, part of Cassidy's mind realized there was a sword sticking out of her shoulder, while another realized she was on fire. The part of her mind that should have connected the pieces was floundering uselessly as panic welled up in her breast. She tried to scream but began to hyperventilate instead. She flailed at the burning metal with her left hand, but she dared not touch the flames as they spread across her clothes.

She was unable to breathe and felt a cold chill. Smoke and steam rose from her scorched coat, and the now blackened blade still protruded from her arm. Someone placed a flask to her lips and coolness ran down her tongue. She coughed out a mouthful of water and blew more out her nose.

"...ld on," Lierre was saying to her. "Hold on, Cass." Her voice was soothing. She repeated the command several more times, and there was sense in it. So she clutched Lierre's hand and held on.

CHAPTER FOURTEEN

There was a cold dread in Zayne's gut as he stood atop the aftcastle in the pre-dawn half-light, listening to the sound of hammers on wood. A cold dread, and little else. He had dreamed of Asier again. In the dream, he had spoken with the late-Admiral, but once awake he couldn't recall the conversation. What he did remember were her amber eyes, alight like gold when lightning flashed. Then he was drowning, being crushed by the sheer depths of the darkness around him. He had forced himself to wake when he had seen a distant light.

Pyrrha was perched on the bow with a red spine-beak nearly as tall as her stolen body perched on her arm as though it weighed nothing. She whispered to the bird at length, though above the winds of the harbor, Zayne couldn't make it out. He suspected, with his connection to the ship, he could listen in, if he were so inclined. He had done so when Shen and the others had discussed mutiny. But he was weary of actively relying on such Fae power. He was already going mad with his mind split between himself and a spirit he had no real comprehension of. Surely to pull his conscious mind away into the ship would be like taking a great mouthful of Myt Dust. Besides, his empathic tie to the *Scorpion* was already threatening to overwhelm him as the maintenance he had ordered was underway.

As he watched the Fae send the raptor to its flight, he wondered if he would end up like the Father of Bastards, being worn like a hand-me-down coat, or if he would somehow live to be as feeble-minded and dependent as Altair's First Mate.

Pyrrha's unsettling smile was so far removed from the grotesque, toothy look favored by Xiao Ta that Zayne could almost forget she was inhabiting him, though his drooping moustache and goatee remained. Thankfully, in addition to the shaded spectacles, Pyrrha had taken to wearing the fully covering robes and tunics Zayne had provided, as he wasn't particularly interested in seeing the hairy and flabby folds and layers that the former criminal had preferred to leave on display. Still, there was something strange about the way she wore them. Or perhaps it was a strangeness born of her nature. Either way, when he saw her from the corner of his eye, or when she moved quickly — as she often did to avoid the metal patches of the deck and confine her steps to where her booted feet would touch only wood — he could see strange patterns and shadows in her form, and he was willing to swear he saw stars even in the bright light of day when she stood nearby.

"You seem troubled," she said, looking up to meet his eye with her bespectacled gaze. Her smile seemed to deepen as she said the words, which only served to make him feel more uncomfortable.

Zayne opened his mouth to argue, but the breath caught in his throat. He tried to form the words, but his tongue sat like lead in his mouth. He clutched the balustrade. His eyes widened as he choked, and a burning sensation blossomed out from his lungs, through his veins, and sucked all sense of feeling from his extremities.

When his mind turned away from denial, however, he was able to breathe easily, and felt no impediment when he snapped, "Vex me not, creature. What was it you were doing with that bird?"

"Scouting," the Fae said, as though that answered anything.

Zayne resisted the urge to rub at his temples. In addition to the Fae unnerving him, a tremor of pain was beginning to blossom from his sinuses. He considered demanding that Pyrrha explain herself, but Shen ripped out the housing unit for the balloon's igniter, and a burst of fresh agony ripped through the inside of his skull.

Lightning flashes, and comprehension dawns. Pain. How could a mortal inflict such pain upon him?

The woman stands with her feet planted on either side of his hips, her figure a silhouette against the storm clouds as the rain crashed around them. Her eyes are smoldering, an amber glow within the darkness. Those eyes bear down upon him with a weight he hasn't felt in a thousand years.

Lightning flashes and the metal claws she wears on her fingers shine like silver. She plunges those sharp tips beneath his skin and rips him open.

Zayne's hand instinctively reached up to his throat, and he traced the scar with trembling fingers. They came back dry — of course they did — but still he felt unsteady. He did his best to ignore Pyrrha's smug expression as he descended from the aftcastle and retreated to his quarters. He closed the door behind him just in time for a second flare of hot misery to burn across his insides. He clutched at his chest, finding the barrel of a pistol strapped to the inside of his coat. The pain was spreading to encompass his entire body.

Durant's blade sinks into his throat. His eyes grow wide as he stares down the length of it. From beneath a curtain of red hair, he sees her mismatched eyes brimming with indignant fury as tears pour over the edge.

By Durant's side stands a girl in a red, silk dress patterned by starlight, with a waterfall of wavy red hair pouring out of an azure mask of woven sky. Despite her mask, despite the age of years, Zayne recognizes the set of her brilliant eyes, the way she tilts her head to level one eye at him in almost suspicious contemplation. He wants to cry, to laugh, to scream.

She is Nanette. Not his First Mate, but the younger sister he failed to protect so long ago, in another life. Perhaps that makes it fair turnabout that she protects Durant from his counterattack and shows no sign of recognition or grief as she meets his eye. He tries to speak, but the iron in his throat prevents him. The blade before him gives way to a pathway of flame, blinding in its heat and intensity.

He is ascending into the gray sky, and a silver haired man garbed in white falls to meet him, arms bound behind his back. In the moment before they collide, Zayne makes eye contact, and is in awe of the golden sclera and the empty white vastness of his irises. Then, in the moment of contact, Zayne is submerged into an icy lake.

Flash.

Parthenia floats beneath the surface among her fellow rivermaids, observing the shadow eclipsing the dancing sunlight. Spears pierce the veil of water and rain down upon them. The Siren Song reverberates in the depth, bubbling up to the surface. The attack slows, and her sisters have a chance to flee. She turns to follow, but she is lanced through the shoulder. She cries as her blood creates a cloud of red ink around her. Terror overwhelms her as she is pulled from the water by her wounded shoulder.

So high above the river, her sole refuge resembles nothing so much as a pattern formed in stone, and should she drop to it, she would be dashed across its surface. The humans' song is devoid of melody and rhythm, a discordant din of pride and mirth.

Parthenia clutches at the rope tethering her wounded shoulder to the human vessel, trying to give herself slack. She Sings, but one of the humans, one with curly black hair and the figure of a rivermaid— from the waist up, at least — points at her ears and grins smugly. They are deaf, she realizes.

They bring her to the deck of their vessel, and she fights. One dies to her taloned hand, another to her vicious fangs, but she is overwhelmed.

144

She doesn't understand, cannot remember what happened. A human strikes something into her palm. She throws her head back in agony and she strikes it against the ship's prow, adding to her pain. She is pinned by the palms and by the tail to the front of the vessel.

Days go by as she bleeds, the cold unforgiving air sucking the life from her Song. She is thirsty. So very thirsty. Her skin feels brittle in the frozen air, and she wants nothing more than to die. In the back of her mind, however, she knows she cannot, for she is no longer Parthenia, but the Scorpion.

Flash.

The Scorpion *cries in agonized silence as her captain, the second captain she has served, plummets to the lake below. She feels within him the same heart that beats within her, but she cannot save him.*

The Dreamscape Voyager *betrays their kinship and opens fire upon her. The* Scorpion *screams again into silence, this time as she is set ablaze and driven from the sky to follow her captain. She hits the water with staggering force, feeling herself break against the waves.*

Flash.

Zayne pressed the barrel of his pistol under his chin, his finger on the trigger. The same force that had prevented him from killing Dardan aboard the *Martyr's Demise* was now forcing his finger, no matter his will to die. It was as if it were no longer apart of his own body, not subject to his will. He gritted his teeth as he directed every scrap of his will to firing the weapon.

At the peripheral edge of his awareness, Nanette screamed. With a staggering blow that recoiled along his arm, she slapped the pistol away from his head and the muzzle erupted in smoke and fire as the door leading to the aft balcony splintered. Zayne dropped the weapon from his trembling hands. The pain in those memories felt so real, and so *fresh*.

Nanette slipped her arms around his slumped shoulders and pulled him into an embrace. Though he shivered against her touch, her grip was a balm, and though the pain didn't fade, it didn't seem so overwhelming. Memories of his four tangled lives continued to blur in the forefront of his mind, but Nanette was an anchor, and he was able to retain his sense of self.

As the rays of dawn finally gave way to the softer glow of morning, Zayne finally quit shaking and Nanette released him. He slouched back against the door to his cabin, and she sat on her haunches before him. He wanted to thank her, but his mind kept replaying the events of the morning. The memories of Lucandri —

of even the *Scorpion* — had invaded his own before. But now he felt like a dam within his own mind had cracked.

"So what happened?" she asked.

Zayne reached into his coat, into a pocket beneath the empty pistol holster, and took out a flask of water. He sucked it down and tossed the empty tin to the floorboards and let out a heavy sigh. "My coat is white," he mumbled to himself, staring at the black fabric. "My coat is white. My coat is white."

"Zayne?"

He met Nanette's eyes, and the concern he saw in them were almost as comforting as her embrace had been. "It's complicated," he said, "but I was reliving…" He trailed off, trying to figure out the best way to phrase what happened. Outside, he could feel Shen replacing the balloon's old igniter, like a tooth being filed in the back of his mind, Xun replacing bullet-scarred planks in the hull like stitches being sewn into his lungs, and Aresh scrubbing out the water reserves. The worst of it, however, was Pyrrha. He couldn't see her, but he could *feel* her devious grin.

"I was reliving the circumstances that led to…" He gestured vaguely around the room, then ended by tapping his mask.

Nanette hesitated, chewing on her lip as she was surely chewing over her words. "From Lucandri's perspective?"

Zayne nodded. "And my own. And the ship's, even the gods forsaken rivermaid that's been decorating the prow for the past twenty odd years." In spite of himself, Zayne snorted. "Did you know she had a name?"

"I didn't know siren-kin were capable of that kind of thinking."

"Nor did I." His tenuous grasp on levity slipped, and steeped again in his previous melancholy, he said, "It took her three days to die. Three *agonizing* days. But crucified as she was, her consciousness slowly faded, replaced piece by piece by the *Scorpion*'s."

Nanette shuddered.

"I wonder if that's what's happening," Zayne confessed. "If this continues, will I just stop being me?"

"That's not going to happen," Nanette said firmly.

"How can you be sure?"

"Because you're not being crucified, for a start. And besides, I won't let you slip away." She stood up and offered a hand.

146

Zayne smiled and took it, rising to meet her. "Thanks."

"There is one thing we need to clear the air on, though."

"What's that?"

Nanette took in a deep breath and closed her eyes. Her fist crashed hard into his solar plexus. He doubled over, gasping for air. "Don't you *ever* leave me behind again."

CHAPTER FIFTEEN

It took the better part of four days to repair the *Scorpion*. For Zayne, it was much like stitching himself back together, but it was vital work, so he did not shirk his share of the work. The damage had not been quite as severe as perhaps it should have been — Zayne attributed that to the same quirk of Lucandri's power that had him walking around and breathing — but it was still a taxing effort. Adding to the difficulty was the sensation that Zayne was disassembling and reassembling his own body for much of the work. Still, after his episode, he was loathe be derelict in his duties.

Replacing the bullet-ridden and water-damaged sections of hull took most of the first day, while the second was spent finding parts with which to fix or replace the various mechanical components that were on their last legs. They worked in shifts through the night and into the morning to get the ship ready to fly. When all the essentials were properly secure, Zayne was sorely tempted to let it be.

But he couldn't deny a connection to the ship, something deeper than empathy, and while he had on more than one occasion said he wanted to stop flying the colors of the Daughters of Daen, the *Scorpion* herself felt naked and wrong without the black paint and the mural of the desert goddess decorating her prow. And to the chagrin of Shen, the crew had blackened the new wood to match what remained of the old, contrasting with the pallid skin and purple tail of the rivermaid at the prow. Nanette drew out the outline of the spectral mural, and the crew worked together on recreating the white woman with features of fire and smoke while Pyrrha watched with apparent disinterest.

When at last the task was done on that fourth day, it wasn't quite dusk, but it was near enough that the light was beginning to turn. Zayne dismissed the crew before retiring to his own quarters to wash up. When he looked in the mirror, he fixated a while on the iron half-mask and the scars beneath. Despite how frequently the memories repeated in his mind — like the chorus of an overplayed song — part of him still found it so surreal to remember fighting Asier and being wounded by her First Mate.

148

It was strange, the twist of fate that led him here. By all rights, his song should have run its course on that lake, alongside Jacques, Flea, Tana, and Kales. He wondered if they knew peace, or if the gods were tormenting them even now. He hadn't liked or trusted any of them, but he felt guilty. If he had let Dardan kill him when he had first confronted her... what? He supposed Nanette would have led the attack on the *Dreamscape Voyager*, and rather than try to duel Asier, she might have tried to kill the lot of them and take the princess. Dardan got what she wanted in the end anyway — mostly.

He sighed, his ragged breath scratching at his throat. It didn't help to think about the what-ifs or might-have-beens. He had gotten his crew killed. He had bound himself to a Fae creature. All there was to do was move forward, complete Dardan's task and find a window to kill her. And if he survived the attempt, track down Durant and kill her, too.

Shedding his paint-marred clothes, he put on a fresh, white shirt and black trousers. The shirt was missing buttons, revealing the latticework of scars and burns along his chest. He put his boots and gun belt on but decided to forgo his coat as he left his cabin and made his way down to the galley where he could feel the crew was gathered.

The scent of roasting mushrooms and fish greeted him as he stepped into the room. The tense quiet amongst the crew was enough he could hear the sizzle of cooking meat from the doorway. Shen sat turned away from the table, staring daggers at Zayne as he entered. Xun and Tagren were on the other side, each looking as though they were having trouble deciding which wall to stare at. Aresh sat at Shen's left, but his back was to Zayne. Nanette stood a ways away from the rest, as she was the one actually preparing dinner. How long had it been since the Scorpion's crew shared a meal?

Not since Elyia Asier, Zayne supposed. He had certainly never sat down alongside any of the current crew before. Still, he and Nanette had talked about it. Or, rather, she had talked, and he had listened.

"We can't afford a mutiny," she had said as they refitted the cannons by lantern light. "Fear of your — of *Lucandri* will only keep them in line so long. You need to make them *want* to follow you."

"How do I do that? They're convinced I recruited them on false pretenses."

Nanette had hesitated, and her lips quirked as she looked to the moons for guidance. After some time, she had said, "You've got to tell them the score. Maybe during dinner."

Even now, he wasn't entirely sure it was the best plan.

He met Shen's eye as he circled the crew and took his seat at the head of the table. His chair creaked as he leaned back, setting it on its hind legs. He swept his gaze over the pirates that had found themselves involved in far more than they had bargained for.

"Let's clear the air," Zayne said, doing his best to project strength despite the sharp rasp of his voice. "When I found you lot, I made some promises. I told you that if you joined me, you would help me kill Captain Javina Dardan. Since then, you have seen her defeat me with Fae witchery and press gang me into service, seen *me* employ those same eldritch forces to frighten you into staying in line, and subject another human being to having his identity stripped away, to be filled like a gourd with something *evil*. And then, as if to rub salt in the wound, I made you help repaint Dardan's colors on this ship.

"I have made you party to unpardonable crimes," he said, adjusting his position so his chair slammed on the floor, and he was facing the crew straight. "But it wasn't fear of me and my monstrous curse that kept you aboard, is it?" He looked to each crewman in turn. Despite his claim, he saw fear in their faces, though it was shared with different emotions along the lineup. Shen's face twitched with an impotent anger Zayne knew too well. Xun looked at him with a perplexed curiosity. Though Aresh's fingers trembled as he stroked his beard, there was a greedy glint in his gaze, as though he knew what Zayne was leading to. Tagren was strange; he had a sad, downcast expression as he listened.

"No," Zayne concluded for them, "any rational, gods-fearing sailors would have cut and run when we made port. Or tried to kill me when I manifested before you during your talk of mutiny. Better to die trying than to be party to this horror. No, you stay because of *hate*. Because I *have* promised you, you will help me kill Dardan. You signed on to kill a monster, and despite your reservations, you know in your heart of hearts, that in order to kill something so vile, you must become so vile the gods will take notice and smile upon you.

"So it is that we will continue on this foul voyage. It will be bloody, dirty work, but the only way to reach Dardan and finish her is to pile the bodies and climb."

Zayne hadn't exactly expected any applause, but he was still unsure how to handle the deep, intense silence that followed. He wondered if he had overplayed his hand. Gazes flit between the pirates, a dozen unspoken communications flying like bullets between them, with no ground being gained for any decisions.

The effect was broken when Nanette dropped the first wooden bowl in front of Shen. He peered into the steaming dish as if he had never seen food before and thought it might bite him if he weren't careful. The fear seemed to be contagious, as all of the would-be accomplices side-eyed their meal once Nanette gave them their shares.

When Nanette placed a bowl in front of Zayne just before sitting down by his left, he lifted it to his lips and slurped the broth demonstratively. He knew it didn't really prove anything; Nanette could have poisoned their bowls individually if that's what this was about. Still, the general atmosphere in the galley was starting to annoy him. Then, at long last, Tagren mimicked the gesture, and visibly — and audibly — began chewing on chunks of fish. Not seeing him keel over on the spot, the others began to eat, albeit more carefully.

Xun was the first to set her bowl down, small amounts of broth running from her lips. "What's the plan, then?" she asked.

"First, the only way to slip Dardan's snare is to kill the Empress," Zayne replied, "as planned. Then, we fly to the Castilyn capital to meet our *magnanimous* employer."

"I don't like anything about this," Shen said, setting down his empty bowl with a hollow thunk. "But the things I've seen…" He began to fiddle with the empty dish, turning it over in his hands as if it were a talisman. "You're everything the Sanctum warns of the Fae, to be sure, Balthine. But the Scourge? She sails with the gods themselves. I don't like this at all. But this is the only chance I see."

Tagren nodded solemnly.

"What's to stop the mad woman from using whatever Fae thing she did to you at the Dragon's Nest?" Xun asked. "Or, whatever it is now," she added awkwardly.

"For one thing, I expect the lot of you to be there, this time," Zayne replied. Xun hung her head and seemed to find the empty bowl in front of her fascinating all of a sudden. Tagren simply nodded again.

Zayne ran over the gist of his plan — which really wasn't much of a plan at all, really, as he lacked any relevant information about where the *Martyr's Demise* would be or exactly when his rendezvous with Dardan would be or what it would entail.

When he dismissed the crew, he ordered an all-night in, knowing they needed to be rested for the voyage through the Dreamscape to the Imperial capital. He also knew that rest would be hard won, because only a mad woman like Isara Altair would relish the thought of entering the realm of Fae and gods. He found Pyrrha standing at the prow, the spine-beak from a few days earlier perched on her arm again.

"Rest well, *captain*," the Fae said as Zayne reached his cabin door. "You'll need it for what lies ahead." She wasn't looking at him, but into the eye of the bird. Still, her inflection sent a shiver along his body. When he closed the door behind him, he could hear the creature's laughter, though it was soft and distant. He was very sure he would *not* be resting well.

CHAPTER SIXTEEN

The roar of the *Scorpion*'s engines broke the serene, almost unnatural silence in the still terror-stricken city. Zayne watched Cielhal drift away from the aftcastle as Xun flew them out. It was a haunting view, being the only ship leaving from what should have been a busy port, seeing empty streets where there should have been a thriving market. He had a feeling that it wouldn't be the last time he saw something so perverse.

As the *Scorpion* put the mountaintop city out of sight, Pyrrha approached the prow and whistled sharply above the winds, engines, and propellers. A tight formation of a dozen red-feathered birds poured from nearby clouds as though they'd somehow been lying in wait. They formed an arrow point directly in front of the ship as if to lead the way. The Fae pointed a fat finger at the flock and said something to Xun, which Zayne assumed was an order to follow them.

And follow Xun did.

They sailed a steady course northwest for a time, and Zayne let himself enjoy the fair weather and the sea breeze, until the line of birds took a collective dive before them. Xun yanked hard on the air release on the balloon, and the *Scorpion* sank rapidly. Zayne peered over the gunwale to the encroaching ocean below. Memories of hitting an icy lake made him flinch from vertigo, and he stepped away.

The ship dropped far lower than Zayne would have liked, stopping only when at last the avian guides pulled up before them and guided them again, now following a more westbound charter. Through his connection to the *Scorpion*, he could feel the water rising and spraying in their wake, and through the rivermaid's senses, he was experiencing the scent of the ocean spray through two vastly different perceptions: nostalgic yearning and conditioned fear, both churning his stomach with their dissonance.

Nanette leaned over the port side to watch the ocean speeding by below them, so much faster than it seemed from higher up. Zayne fought down the urge to tell her to fall back, his own experience painting an unpleasant picture in his mind. He turned his attention to their heading. Several minutes passed before the endless ocean expanse gave way to a horizon with actual physical features, but when it did, it approached steadily over the world's curve.

Their destination appeared to be an island with two plateaus with overhanging ridges that formed a lopsided archway. The fact that such entrances to the Dreamscape existed was unsettling on its own, but the idea that they were just *there* — out in the open for anyone come across, added another level of discomfort. Perhaps it was a small thing to be perturbed by — he was, after all, partially possessed by a Fae creature and had just recently stepped into a space between worlds. Still, he had been somewhat more comfortable with the notion that the ways between were cracks in a wall, not open gates. The reality of the situation gave way to a few unpleasant considerations.

If we can fly a fleet in and out, he thought, fidgeting with the cuffs on his sleeves all the while, *what's on the other side that could do the same?*

Memories flitted lazily across his mind, creatures of unfathomable scale and incomprehensible glory. The visions were quick and barely distracting compared to others. In addition to seeing silhouettes blotting out the sky, he caught a familiar feeling on the edge of his thoughts: the sadistic amusement that comes from describing a sudden fall to someone hanging for dear life over a drop.

He shook his head to clear it of Lucandri's influence. He didn't have time for hypothetical horrors. He needed to be ready for the real ones. He braced himself, clutching the balustrade tightly as the *Scorpion* sped to the archway. As they crossed the threshold of the island, Zayne focused his attention *beyond* the archway, to the grassy patches between jagged rocks, to the waves breaking on the opposite shore, and the golden sun.

As the Scorpion followed the scarlet flock through the natural gate, everything changed by inches.

A shadow blossomed in the heart of the sun, eclipsing it in a deep purple that made the sky bleed into a foreboding maroon. The clouds raced by, their silver linings becoming a red shine similar to the gleam present along Dawn Star's blade. Stars appeared in rapid succession, forming bizarre and expansive constellations that were both foreign and familiar to Zayne's split mind. The ocean seemed to darken from its depths, a shadow of deepest black spreading up

154

to encapsulate the entire sea, though the foam and spray of the waves were aglow with light the purest blue Zayne had ever seen. The grass on the island grew to great heights, and color shifting wisps drifted lazily into the air from their roots.

The *Scorpion* buckled. The roar of the engines died abruptly. Despite this, the ship's speed only intensified, and a deafening *snap-crack* tore through the air as the balloon above disappeared as though it had never been, replaced by a trio of sails connected to a mast that hadn't been connected to the deck mere moments before. Tagren nearly tumbled overboard at the revelation and Xun leaped from the helm to secure him. Zayne was torn between shock and satisfied expectations and couldn't be sure how to react to any of it.

A translucent film crept along the iron fixtures atop the deck, most notably the various guns the *Scorpion* boasted. Zayne stepped up to the ballista set at the aft — the aptly named Scorpion Tail — and watched, curious and captivated, as the strange substance enveloped the iron, right down to the last rivet, but ignored the wood entirely. It flashed, brief and silvery. When the light faded, whatever Zayne had been looking at was replaced by a chitinous shell. *Like a scorpion's,* he thought. *Fitting.*

Zayne's stomach lurched when he returned his attention to the deck below and found Pyrrha standing amidst the novelty, having undergone her own jarring transformation. Rather than wearing the form of an obese man with unfortunate facial hair, she appeared as a willow-thin woman, taller than Zayne by a head with hair that, depending on the way the light struck it, shifted from black to sunset red. Though she still wore the spectacles provided by Nanette, the coat she wore as Xiao Ta had been replaced by a sarong sleeker than silk made of red gold, patterned by stars and moving swirls of clouds, with a matching wrap around her chest. Where she stood backed by the sky, her outfit appeared not to be fabric at all, but a colored window through which he saw the Dreamscape's sky. Her hair and clothes seemed to flow as if she stood underwater. Her exposed midriff, shoulders, and left thigh sent waves of conflicting discomfort through Zayne.

The most unsettling facet of her changed appearance, however, was not what she wore — or what she wasn't wearing — but rather the fact that Zayne's eyes and mind both seemed to be trying to reconcile her new appearance with the mortal body that he knew in his bones was still there, and he saw the shorter, fatter silhouette of Xiao Ta superimposed over her like a shadow hovering in the air around her, mimicking her every stance and motion.

"Welcome," she said, throwing her hands wide and looking theatrically around the deck in a way that brought Isara Altair to mind, "to the Dreamscape!"

CHAPTER SEVENTEEN

The stench of curdling blood and burning flesh did little to distract Cassidy as the needle wove through her shoulder. She hissed between her teeth while Nieves worked at closing the wound. She almost felt guilty for it. All around her in the dining hall, which was being used as a makeshift medical ward, were the groans and cries of men and women who had taken far worse damage than her. She overheard many would leave short an arm, a leg, an eye, or all that and more. Many would not leave at all. Still, acknowledging their suffering didn't make her own pain go away. She was just grateful she had her own friend and crewmate to stitch her up. And that she had been whisked in early enough to get one of the tables before the sawbones took to using floor space.

Looking over the mass of people, Hymn's absence was several spoonfuls of anxiety. On the one hand, if the Fae were to return to her *now*, Cassidy would be outed as a criminal of the same caliber as Adryen Flint. And if she didn't... just where was she? Hymn had always been insistent that she remain nearby, to better fulfil her oath to protect her. Had she been hurt in the fighting? Was she *dead*? *Could* she even die? No matter which directions her thoughts pulled her, they were a misery that left her sick.

"It was a lucky break," Nieves said after Cassidy and Lierre finished relaying the story. Cassidy had left out the parts about seeing the future and being guided to the pivotal moment. She didn't know how to put the experience into words. And even if she did, she would have to explain everything she knew about Asier's own future sight.

"Doesn't feel so lucky," Cassidy said between pained hisses, though the memory of her prophesied death replayed in her mind with so much clarity she was almost afraid *Nieves* would see the lie.

"You big baby," Nieves jibed. "It's a clean cut, you'll be fine if you don't do anything stupid." She hesitated, halting her work. "I guess that's a lot to ask, isn't it?"

Cassidy barked a laugh that cut short with another sting of the needle. "I didn't exactly plan this?" she muttered as Nieves tied off the catgut and snipped the excess. Cassidy gripped Lierre's hand tight and let out a miserable hiss as Nieves applied a whisky-soaked rag to the wound. Then she began to wrap her work in bandages.

"Where are Kek and Miria?" Cassidy asked.

"With the ship," Nieves said. "Miria wanted to volunteer to help with the survivors, but I told her you'd want her to stay aboard, given everything."

"Thanks. This must be hard on the poor girl."

Nieves was guiding Cassidy's arm into a sling when the Lord Minister appeared in their midst. The severe woman had plaster dust powdered on her tattered suit and perplexingly tidy hair. There was a line of dried blood on her temple and bruises along her face and hands, but she maintained a steady and composed posture as she assessed the trio.

"Captain Durant," she said sharply.

"Lord Minister?" Cassidy replied, unable to keep the questioning tone from her voice.

"I would like to thank you and your crew for helping in the battle," she said, though the stiffness to her voice made it clear that was just a token courtesy.

"And what would you *really* like to say to me, Your Honor?"

The Lord Minister looked around at the chaotic press. She winced when a young man, little more than a boy, wailed. She tugged on the hem of her suit to straighten it, which only caused a rip in the fabric to open wider. "If you would please accompany me, Captain? This is best discussed in less... public spaces."

Cassidy looked to Nieves to see if she was clear to move, and the sawbones nodded her ascent.

"Well," Cassidy said, coming to a wobbly stand with Lierre's help, "I can't imagine your office is in the best of shape." The tight line of the Lord Minister's mouth spoke volumes, and Cassidy cleared her throat before adding a sheepish, "After you."

As the Lord Minister led them from the hall with a faint limp to her gait, Cassidy scanned the windows for any sign of Hymn, but to no avail. The first corridor outside was lined with a double row of wounded, and out of the corner of her eye, she saw Nieves tense. They turned into an adjoining passageway, and at the end of that, another, continuing to march along until they couldn't hear the chorus of misery from the dining hall.

"Admiral Jiang is dead," the Lord Minister said without preamble, though she didn't stop walking. "Died in that first explosion."

"I'm sorry for your loss," Cassidy said automatically. She had completely forgotten about the woman.

"She was in charge of our defenses," the thin woman said, though her voice had a distant quality, as though she wasn't speaking to Cassidy or the others. She stared out a large window overlooking the ocean for a while. She shook her head abruptly, probably to dispel whatever visions had been conjured by all the death she had seen today. "What brought you to the city, Captain Durant?"

Cassidy glanced at Lierre, then she looked to Nieves on the other side. Neither woman seemed any surer about how to address the question than she was. She cleared her throat, taking the moment to compose her thoughts.

"I'm pretty sure I mentioned it, the Empress tasked us to conscript a fighting force."

"Against what?"

Cassidy wasn't sure how to broach the subject. She worked her mouth uncomfortably while thinking of how to convey the scale and horror of what they faced. Any explanation of what the Leviathan *was* sounded mad. To follow that up by explaining they were *hunting* it was completely insane.

Nieves came to her rescue by asking, "Are you familiar with what happened at the Dragon's Nest?"

"I've heard rumors that there was some sort of attack," the Lord Minister said. "Are you hunting dragons?"

"Not exactly," Cassidy said.

Lierre cut in, "The Nest was destroyed by... by a Fae beast."

"It wiped out almost the entire Nest Fleet," Cassidy finished. "That, Lord Minister, is what we're hunting, because it is a threat to the whole Empire."

The Lord Minister sucked her teeth and turned away from the group. Cassidy guessed she was balancing her rational understanding of the world around her with the madness she presented to her. She sympathized.

"I cannot offer you anything as long as this rebellion lives," said the Lord Minister. "But if you help —"

"Don't make promises on behalf of my city without me, Chaihua!" came a shrieking Castilyn accent. With Lierre's assistance,

Cassidy turned to find the baroness taking remarkably long strides to meet them considering the ragged state of her previously over-designed dress. Her wig was so askew Cassidy expected it to fly off as the plump woman sped across the carpeted floor.

"I'm sorry, Morgane, did you want to ignore the Empress' edicts?" The Lord Minister — Chaihua, apparently — raised an eyebrow at the Baroness. Presented with some opposition, she drew herself up taller and seemed to loom over the other woman. "I am certain *that* will sweeten the opinions of your critics. I can think of a few people in prison who might feel particularly vindicated to hear it."

As the Baroness blanched quite impressively, Cassidy felt as though she had stepped into a personal and long-running argument and was intruding. To her side, Nanette was trying to wipe the red stains from her hands while pretending not to notice, while Lierre was unabashedly taking in the argument with interest.

Baroness Morgane sputtered for a moment before saying, "I never said we should ignore anything! Just that you should involve me in any discussions."

The Lord Minister sneered for a moment but nodded. "Very well, be involved." She turned her attention back to Cassidy. "As I was saying, we can't offer anything to your cause. All our resources are being used to fight this rebellion. We'll let you pass freely through the blockade, but if you help us put these terrorists down, you'll have whatever you want."

Thinking of the battle made Cassidy's stomach drop. "You're asking a lot," she said.

"I know," replied the Lord Minister. "Please think it over."

Cassidy fought down the urge to tell the woman where she could stick the request. The poor woman had been through enough today. But so had Cassidy and her crew. It wasn't her fault, and while the Empress might have been able to conscript her, Andaerhal had no power over her.

"Come on," she said to her crew. "We'll discuss our next move aboard the ship."

The Lord Minister nodded her ascent, though her severe expression melted into that of a heartbroken child as the three of them walked by. The stairs to the roof were a challenge, and not just because every part of Cassidy's body hurt. The steep climb was congested by runners carrying reports and supplies to every story from the bottom to the roof. Each step drained Cassidy, and she felt like a gentle breeze would send her falling backwards. She stopped once to dry heave, but Nieves and Lierre helped her up. When at last they reached the roof, Cassidy was surprised to find the *Dreamscape Voyager* was perched low to the roof, almost resting directly on top of it. The *Sunshear* and another ship Cassidy couldn't identify from her vantage were flanking her vessel in what Cassidy saw as a defensive arrangement, but also a confining one.

"Ahoy!" Nieves called up.

Kek's blonde head popped up suddenly from behind the gunwale. "Cassy! Lierre!" he exclaimed, jumping to his feet. "You're alright!"

"They're hurt, you lummox, set out a ladder," Nieves snapped.

Kek darted away, and Miria appeared in his place and breathed, "Oh, thank goodness!. When we saw the explosion…" The princess' face sank a little and she said, "explosion*s*." Whatever she had been about to say was gone like morning mist when Kek returned with a wood-and-rope ladder.

Nieves sent Cassidy up first, so she could catch her if she fell. Though it wasn't a long climb, Cassidy felt unbalanced as she climbed one-handed, and at one point she felt her body lurch backwards, though she held on tight to the next plank while she rocked unsettlingly about. She pulled herself level with the ship and took a steadying breath before climbing up the rest of the way. When she cleared the gunwale, her legs gave out. Miria caught her in a clumsy embrace and helped guide her aside. Lierre's ascent was more graceful, but no faster, and she made it only a few steps before dropping onto her butt like she had been running for hours. Nieves was on the deck in mere moments, and she retreated into the storeroom.

Pain wove in and out, never fully dissipating, but settling as an irritating ache that gradually built into a sharp pain that subsided again in unpredictable rhythms that made Cassidy want to cut her arm clean off just to be done with it. The rest of her body hurt too, but none of it came close to the same level of misery.

Kek offered Cassidy a sloshing waterskin. She hadn't given thought to how thirsty she had been until she found herself sucking greedily at the mouth of it when she had guzzled it dry. Beside her, Lierre gave an appreciative belch after downing her own.

"What were you thinking?" Cassidy asked, though there was no fire in it. She leaned her head back against the gunwale and stared lazily at the sky.

"Excuse me?" Kek asked, his voice hitting a point between incredulity and confusion.

"Bringing the *Dreamscape* into the fight," Cassidy clarified. Again, she failed to inject any anger into her tone. "Why'd you do it?"

"You'd have done the same in my boots," Kek said.

Cassidy quirked an eye at him. "Think so?"

Kek slunk to a sitting position between her and Lierre. "I'd bet my left nut on it."

"That's not worth much," Cassidy said with a smirk. She pulled her hat off to air out her sweaty scalp and Kek flinched.

"Where's Hymn?" he asked, a nervous twinge coloring his otherwise composed question.

Cassidy stared into her hat, half expecting to see the Fae staring impatiently at her, though she knew better. "Haven't seen her since the battle," she said. And again, she broke down the events, this time for Kek and the princess, and again she left out the parts about seeing the future and the pull guiding her until she broke its compulsion.

"That was a lucky throw," Kek said, staring at her shoulder.

"Nieves said the same thing," she snorted.

"What are we going to do about the Lord Minister's request?" Nieves asked. The question was so off the course of Cassidy's thoughts she didn't know what the woman was saying at first.

"What request?" asked Miria.

"More of a deal than a request," Lierre said wearily. "We help put down the rebellion, they let us conscript their leftovers."

"It's suicide," Cassidy said. "We're free to move on, we can probably make it to Isaro with what we—"

"No!" Miria snapped, stomping her foot between Cassidy's knees.

Cassidy pushed up off the deck, though she couldn't quite find her feet and only made it as far as sitting without slouching. "Excuse me?"

"I said no!" the princess said. She didn't raise her voice, but Cassidy felt a chill as she looked up. In Cassidy's haze, she was no longer looking up at Miria, but the Empress herself. "Our mission is to save the Empire. That includes this city."

"We're five people!" Cassidy protested. "And this rebellion... what would we do? Wait to get shot?"

"We help come up with a plan!" Miria's imperious mask dropped, and she was once again the young girl. "Captain, we can't abandon these people."

Tears welled in the girl's eyes. Cassidy pushed herself up to her feet and Miria grabbed her by the front of the shirt, shocking her sober.

"Promise me, we won't let this stand."

Cassidy's instinct to protest and pull rank shriveled and died under the girl's blue-eyed stare. Her shoulders dropped. She was making a lot of promises, it seemed. "Alright," she said softly, setting her hands on Miria's shoulders. "I promise. We'll do what we can here."

CHAPTER EIGHTEEN

It's a stupid plan, Cassidy decided for what must have been the thirtieth time. As she paced the deck of the *Dreamscape*, fighting to keep the contents of her stomach down, she looked over the burning cityscape. Smoke wafted up thin but constant clouds, masking Andaerhal in a shadowy miasma.

The Lord Minister had invited the *Dreamscape*'s crew into a tightly packed room that currently served as the headquarters of the city's administration. A detailed map of the city was rolled across two tables with cups and coins being used to illustrate the known placements of the rebel and Imperial forces. The western district of the city was hanging off the edge and threatened to send the markers cascading off if anyone brushed against it.

According to Vice Admiral Ruan — a wiry woman with a bloody bandage visible under her coat — the mercenary Adryen Flint was holed up in the slums in the south-western edge of the markets. A younger officer — whose name Cassidy missed — had asserted that Flint had four captains working beneath him, and he put tokens at four points on the map to indicate them. Sketches were passed around, depicting the likenesses of Flint and the others.

On its surface, the overarching plan was simple; capture or kill Flint and his captains and the rebellion would be as harmless as a manticore without its head. The trouble was — as usual — in the specifics. The first problem was the presence of the orichalcum cannons. Not counting the two that had been brought down during the previous battle, scouts had reported the location of four, and Cassidy had agreed with the Vice Admiral and the Lord Minister that there were more they didn't know about.

"I should have gone to the meeting alone," Cassidy groused to Nieves when they were alone on the deck.

"She never would have forgiven you if you forbade her," said Nieves.

As the Vice Admiral had been laying out the plan, she was assigning crews to assault Flint's location. Ships were to provide cover while soldiers went below to flush the rebels out of hiding.

"I'll join the ground team," Miria had declared.

Cassidy — who throughout the meeting had been studying the map, trying to find the *least* dangerous post for the *Dreamscape* and her crew — felt as though the younger woman had pulled the rug out from under her. "Excuse me? No, you won't!"

Miria had stepped right up to Cassidy then. "Captain, these people have been fighting for weeks. They're wounded, and starving, and sleep deprived."

Cassidy had been acutely aware that every eye in the room was upon them, so she lowered her voice to a whisper when she said, "If you go down there, *you* will be wounded."

"Captain," Miria rebutted, and unlike Cassidy, she showed no inclination towards keeping their argument discrete or quiet, "I'd bet everything I own that even with these soldiers at their peak, I'm the best fighter in the city, with my pistol and my sword."

"There's a huge difference between a fight and a battle!"

"Can you give me one reason I should give any less than they're giving? *Risk* any less than they're risking?"

"Because you're —" Cassidy bit her tongue hard, stopping herself from outing Miria as the Empress' daughter. The princess gave her a playful smirk, knowing Cassidy couldn't risk revealing her true identity. "Because you're my crew, and I can't let you throw yourself into danger alone."

"She won't be alone," Kek said, stepping to Miria's side. "I'll be right beside her."

Cassidy jabbed a finger into Kek's chest. "Don't you start. There is no way I'm —"

"If we don't do this," Miria said forcefully, "if we *can't*, then we don't stand a chance against the Leviathan."

Cassidy kicked the gunwale and cursed as the pain ran in shivers from her toe up to her shoulders. "The gods are watching today, I swear," she muttered.

"Don't say that, Captain," Nieves reassured. "We'll see this through."

"First Hymn disappears, then I get cornered into letting the fucking heir to the Empire run right into a rebellion. Tell me the last year has been a dream."

"If it's been a dream," said Nieves, "at least we aren't naked. And maybe we can get some of these coats when we wake up," she added, referring to the jade deels they had been given, to mark their status as Imperial officials — distinct from the military red, but unlikely to be confused for the brown that seemed to be favored by the rebels.

Cassidy stepped back to the helm, adjusting their course. Then, she opened the pipeline. "Lierre, do you still have visual on them?"

There was a delay as the engineer must have been moving around her compartment to reply. Her voice came back clearly through the horn, "Aye, Captain. No change."

That had been the way of it since Cassidy had sent Miria, Kek, and a dozen other City Watchmen and Imperial soldiers to disembark when they had crossed beyond the market. Flanked by the *Sunshear* and a bright red cutter bearing the name *Dawnstar*, the *Dreamscape Voyager* moved at little more than a drifting pace to provide cover for the contingent on the streets below.

Cassidy pulled her cigarette and match box from her coat pocket. When she lit a match, a gust of wind blew it out immediately. She was about to curse when the sound of flapping canvas caught her attention. The balloon that should have been holding the *Dreamscape Voyager* aloft had once again vanished, replaced by a sail that should have done nothing to stop her from plummeting to the streets like a stone.

To either side, the crews of the *Sunshear* and the *Dawnstar* were coming to the same discoveries aboard their own vessels, and from what Cassidy could make of their expressions and general flailing, they had not experienced such changes before. With the engines no longer roaring, Cassidy was able to hear gibbering panic, but she realized it wasn't just from the other ships, but rising from the streets, as well. Cassidy wanted to call over, to assure them, to tell them to ignore it and carry on, but even if she could make herself heard, *how* did you tell someone to focus when the very reality they relied on was in question?

"Cassidy, there!" Nieves called out, pointing to a cluster of tenement homes ahead. Cassidy nodded, mostly to herself, as she caught sight of a mast peeking up over the lip of one of the buildings, a ship having been hidden before the Dreamscape had warped it.

"Captain!" Lierre was climbing to the deck. "It happened a—"

The ship Nieves had spied erupted in a fountain of splinters and black smoke, and gouts of flame shot skyward in streaks of red and purple flames. Screams let out as another explosion rattled through the slums, and pillars of dust rose while debris spilled out into the streets. Along the causeway far ahead of where Miria and Kek were walking amidst the Imperial forces, a wall blasted outwards, sending brick and plaster and charred bodies out into the street. Confused looking rebels poured from the breach, not as an attacking force, but looking over their shoulders and bellowing in panic as if in retreat.

Gunfire rang out below as the rebels threw themselves directly into the line of fire. As their bodies piled up, however, they seemed to forget whatever had them so terrified behind them and began to take cover and return fire.

Cassidy turned the wheel hard to port to get into position. "Lierre, get on the spitfire, Nieves, the rotary! Don't let —" She cut off abruptly as vertigo took her over.

She is running — limping — along the cobbled streets. Her lungs burn from exertion as well as the smoldering embers she is surely breathing in. The sky is completely blackened from smoke, now.

She hears the commotion ahead. Gunfire and clashing swords. She climbs a stairwell between two tenements that connects two streets. She nears the top, sees Kek illuminated by fire, leaning against a wall to catch his breath. Half his shirt is torn away revealing cuts and thick, distorting bruises and the other half is red with blood, but she can see the steep rise and fall of his breathing.

She reaches the top step and something heavy hits her behind the knees, sending her sprawling over. Hands crawl up her body, pulling her back as a man presses himself on top of her. She is forced around hard onto her back, and the wind is knocked out of her lungs when she hits the cobblestones again. As she looks up at her attacker in the firelight, she sees thick locks of black hair, a sharp and short beard, and black eyes brimming with hate that seem to swallow the firelight like hungry coals.

He spits venomous words as he throttles her in animalistic fury, growls through bloodstained teeth. Her fingers scramble for his, her nails tearing into the flash of his calloused hands, but still he keeps his grip. She flails, her feet struggling to find purchase on the ash-covered streets that she may push herself away.

The man releases her so abruptly that her head strikes the cobbles. Her ears ring. He catches Kek's wrist, twisting it and forcing the shorter man around as he sinks a knife into his back. Kek cries out silently as the man's knife plunges again into him, and a third time. Kek bounces as he hits the street. His hair — so crusted with blood and plaster and rubble and dirt that Cassidy barely recognizes it — falls in his face. And through the tangled and damaged locks, she can see his eyes staring emptily back at her.

Cassidy caught herself before she could hit the deck face first. She forced herself to her feet to take stock. She was still on the *Dreamscape*, which was still under the influence of *the* Dreamscape. She wasn't running through the burning chaos below.

Kek was in danger. She recognized the hateful visage, worn by his killer. Adryen Flint. Already, she could feel the pull of the future tugging at her, as it had during the previous battle. She wasn't sure if it would be wise to heed it this time, but it was a strong feeling, like a river's current carrying her along. She found it easier to let it guide her back to the helm. Nieves and Lierre were standing where she had last seen them, staring at her.

The words repeated three times in her mind, each time with increasing urgency, before she let them out of her mouth. "You have your orders!" she snapped, and they moved to their stations. As she gripped the wheel, she whispered, "I'm not going to let you die, Kek." But even as she said it, she felt the pull of the future looming over her with all the weight of inevitability.

INTERLUDE TWO

Twelve Years Earlier

Despite the heavy cloud coverage and the gentle breeze that rose from the cool lake below, Cassidy was sweating profusely as she made the circuit from the deck to the engines and back for the thousandth time that day as Asier called for a full stop. Her feet pulsed in pain. She tried to re-roll her sleeves, but the damp fabric kept sliding back down her arms. She climbed the ladder with deliberate steps as dizziness started to set in.

"How," she breathed, "did you manage to run this boat... to Dawnhal, by yourself?"

The legendary admiral — who, by the strangest twist of fortune, was now Cassidy's captain — stood at the helm, her coat wrapped around her waist and her shirt unbuttoned and wide open. Cassidy had been under no illusions of modesty in the skies, especially in the summer months, but it was still an odd sight to see such a powerful figure in such a humble state, even if the woman had nothing to feel humble about. She also found the famed cross-shaped scar over the tops of her otherwise enviable breasts rather illuminating; she had always assumed that particular detail of her legend to be an exaggeration.

The older woman lifted her hat to scratch at the sweaty mess that had that morning been an artfully arranged bun. "Just followed the wind," she said with a sly grin.

"You keep saying that. What does that mean?"

Asier's grin blossomed into a wider, more genuine smile that she seemed to be trying — and failing — to hide. "Got swept up in a storm. That did most of the work. Finally settled out a few miles north of Dawnhal."

"Must have saved you some time, then."

"Not really," said the Captain. "I was heading to Melfine from the start."

Cassidy scratched her head. "So, what were you doing in town when I met you?"

"Sometimes…" Asier began, though the look in her eyes went distant.

Cassidy opened her mouth to ask Asier what she was getting at, when she darted into the galley. Cassidy stared after her, curious and confused, but far too tired to do anything about it. The Captain returned a moment later with two wooden buckets tucked under her arms and a small bundle of cloth in each hand.

She offered one of the bundles to Cassidy and upturned the buckets on the deck to sit by the gunwale. Unwrapping the cloth, she revealed last night's mushrooms stuffed with minced meat and spices. The scent wafted up to greet her, and her stomach let out a low rumble that trailed off into a squeak.

"Sometimes," Asier repeated, dropping down onto her bucket, "you need to know when to act, and when to sit back and see what happens."

As she began to dig in her lunch, Cassidy sat down to watch her. The Captain was looking over the placid lake as if she were expecting something. When Cassidy heard the thrumming of engines in the distance, Asier's head cocked and she said, "Looks like we stopped at just the right time. I think those are fishing boats," she added, gesturing out over Evere Lake.

A trio of cutters were flying low enough to disturb the water behind them. Sure enough, Cassidy saw as they formed a circle, there was a large net connected to each vessel. Asier put her spyglass to her eye. "Well, that's a lovely sight," she muttered to herself.

Cassidy reached for her own spyglass. "What is it?"

"Blue ship, on the aft at the stinger."

Cassidy focused on the ship in question. Situated at the grapnel was a wide-hipped woman with jet black hair in an intricately braided tail. She wore a vest that left her midriff exposed and showcased an impressive set of lean muscles.

"If you like that sort, I guess," Cassidy said, then swept her gaze around the ship.

"I do," said Asier. "What about you? Anything catch your fancy?"

With the ships speeding and turning over the water and most of the crews milling about to their posts, Cassidy could only offer a shrug. From what little she could see, most of the fishing crews seemed to be women, and she wouldn't be working herself up over any of *them* later.

After several minutes, the ships ascended, their nets fat with squirming koi. No sooner than when the boats lifted their haul from the water did a heavy foam form on the water. Cassidy watched, alternating between focusing through her spyglass and getting the full view as a massive, reptilian head broke the water's surface. The creature let out a blaring yawn accompanied by gouts of water spraying from its beak.

The six-eyed tortohemoth created a tumultuous ripple as it pulled its jagged shell from beneath the lake. Cassidy watched in fascinated awe as the fishing crews opened fire seemingly without breaking routine, as though they had expected this. At such a distance, the ships' cannon fire sounded like faint popping rather than thunderous blasts, which seemed appropriate, given that the reptilian latecomer seemed more agitated than hurt by the onslaught, at least from where Cassidy was sitting.

The hulking beast stretched its neck out, snapping at one of the fishing nets but drawing up short as one of its eyes exploded in a shower of smoke and blood. It screeched in fury and dived beneath the lake's surface with a tremendous splash that washed over the attacking vessels.

"That was anticli—" Cassidy began, cut short when the tortohemoth emerged again, this time in a gesture reminiscent of a leap, its body vertical, its stonelike forelegs exposed to the air and hanging before it awkwardly as it snapped its beak once more at the day's catch.

The monster roared in agony, and Cassidy checked her spyglass to find a harpoon had been fired into its innermost left eye. The cable went taut as the creature's ascent reversed, ripping the harpoon launcher off its fixture in a shower of violent splinters. The woman the Captain had been admiring moments earlier was plummeting alongside the wreckage of her weapon to meet the furious dweller of the deep.

A short-looking man in a brown coat leaped from the side of the boat, affixed to a tether, and swung like a pendulum. He crashed into the woman with enough force to stop his arc and sent the tether spinning, but he caught her, as Cassidy could see her hanging limp over his shoulder. Four of their crew secured their own lines and moved to pull them up. The hero of the hour passed the burdensome beauty up to two older looking women who were hanging over the gunwale to accept her.

With the woman no longer occupying his arms, the short man began climbing the tether as his crew worked to pull him up. Below, the thrashing tortohemoth lunged a third time for the vessel, now forgoing the fish and aiming its snapping maw at the human interlopers.

The rope snapped, and the short man fell, striking the front of the massive turtle's beak with his back before tumbling ineffectually down its face and along its body.

"He's dead," Asier said, not exactly unsympathetically, but with an air of acceptance that Cassidy frequently heard in the voices of seasoned sailors, especially those who had fought in the war. Cassidy nodded sadly. Death was always tragic, and he had seemed like a brave man.

Still, the onslaught continued, and through her spyglass Cassidy noticed that the cannonballs were starting to rip through the creature's thick hide, forming deep gouges and bloody pockmarks in its neck and face. It dived again, and after a series of ineffectual shots hit the water, a moment of relative silence fell over Evere Lake.

Cassidy was sitting on the edge of her makeshift stool. There was a tension in the air as the cutters circled the monster's wake. She peered over the gunwale to see , but as the waves settled, the lake reflected the morning sky, and she could see no hint of the tortohemoth.

Then its head burst from the water's surface, flailing violently as it screeched. A look through the spyglass revealed blood spewing from its center left eye as it came under fire again.

"Daen's tits," Asier breathed.

"What?" asked Cassidy.

"Look under the chin."

Cassidy turned her spyglass and gasped. The man Asier had written off for dead clung to the tortohemoth's neck, gripping onto the leathery flaps of its throat by what seemed to be a punch dagger and hooks on his boots. He kept his grip as the tortohemoth thrashed and bucked. Between wild flailing, he used the knife to slowly climb his way around to get on top of the reptile. A cannonball struck its face at an angle that shattered its beak and sent its head lolling.

The blue cutter swooped in and opened fire at close range with three consecutive blasts. The first shot tore along the left side of its face, the second went wide off the mark entirely, but the third struck the top of its skull with enough force that the cannonball escaped out the back of its crown.

The creature went limp. Its head came crashing down on the lake's surface. Fortunately for the insanely brave man who had chosen to scale it, the side of its elongated neck that hit the water was not the side he had clung to, and though the creature was beginning to sink, he had not been crushed.

"Well, that was exciting," Asier said cheerfully.

"How did you know that was going to happen?" Cassidy asked.

"I didn't," said the Captain. "It's as I said, I just have a sense for when to sit back and see what happens. And we needed a break anyway."

Cassidy shrugged. "Back to work, then?"

"Aye."

Cassidy descended the ladder for the thousand-and-first time that day and fed the engines as Asier guided the *Dreamscape Voyager* over the corpse of the tortohemoth and the crews that were now harvesting what they could from their kill. It would be a good time to buy some fish and tortoise meat, she realized.

The Captain called Cassidy over the pipeline, inviting her to watch the city's approach. She all but leaped at that. She had heard tales of the incredible artistry and engineering that was Melfine. Standing at the prow, she set her spyglass to her face. It was there, at the very heart of the lake. At first glance, it seemed to be a scattered cluster of ships, but as they made their approach and Cassidy was able to peer through the mist, she was able to make out a sense of the floating city's scale. Supported by an assortment of grandiose balloons, the city was something of a collage of airship history. She could make out the forms of familiar passenger ships and warships, and several unfamiliar ones, but they were connected by brilliant craftsmanship and pressed so tightly together that it expanded into the mist beyond sight. She found it so easy to lose sight of individual ships as their shape blurred into the press of a city.

It was impossible, and it was beautiful. Cassidy hung off the prow in her excitement to get a closer look. The stories really didn't do the place justice.

As Asier guided the ship to port, Cassidy realized the wharfs were constructed out of the same class of junk as the *Dreamscape*

Voyager, so they would be stepping off their ship onto a nearly identical one, when they finally docked.

That reminded her she would be back in public for the first time in days, so she retreated to her cabin to change into some cleaner and more presentable clothes. When she returned to the deck, she found Asier had done the same, though her outfit — featuring a thin, asymmetrical purple skirt and short coat that barely cleared her chest — were much richer than anything Cassidy had in her wardrobe. Something seemed to have soured her mood since Cassidy had gone below, however.

"What's wrong, Captain?"

"Castilyn fashion," Asier groused.

"I… can't tell if you're being sarcastic," Cassidy admitted.

"I'm not," Asier said dryly, and she tugged at her corset as if making a point. "Doesn't seem all that long ago when no Imperial citizen would be caught dead wearing one of these. But, bizarrely enough, after the war, southern attire became all the rage. It's the damnedest thing. The tailors must be holding the country's entire economy on their backs right now."

Cassidy had never really given thought to the rise of things like corsets, frills, and lace, but supposed it *was* a little ironic that they had become so popular in the years after the war. They were even popular in Dawnhal, where anti-Castilyn sentiment ran rampant. She rather liked wearing corsets, though. "Well," she offered awkwardly, "you could always choose *not* to wear them."

"No, no," the older woman resigned, flicking her wrist dismissively, "you can't just rebuff the current trends. I may not like it, but it's important to keep up with fashion — or at least to be fashion *adjacent*. Easier that way, generally speaking. I just hope Asarian fashion returns to vogue soon."

"Aye, Captain," Cassidy said, finding no other answer to the statement, though she really didn't understand it. "What about Rivien fashion?"

"Hmm," Asier considered. "Those veils *do* look cute. And I imagine I would look quite fine in a turban, if I do say so myself."

Asier had Cassidy pay attention as she negotiated the docking fee with the local port authority and showed their documentation, saying Cassidy would need to do it herself one day.

Setting foot into Melfine was a bizarre sensation. It was more alike to a ship than Dawnhal had ever felt, lacking cobblestones or indeed anything truly solid beneath it, and yet it was so clearly *far* too big to be anything less than a city. The scale of it made Cassidy's head spin.

"Since this is your first time here, I'm going to show you a few key landmarks," Asier told her. "This is a big place, and it's important to know your way around." She led Cassidy through the press of the docks, and she continued to marvel at the spectacle.

They passed several docked ships as they went down the street when Asier pointed out the blue cutter they had watched by the lake. "Sightseeing can probably wait," she said to Cassidy. "They might be selling some of their haul."

Sure enough, Cassidy caught the scent of large quantities of fish, and there were lines to buy. The Captain picked a line, and they moved along at a reasonable — though not quick — pace, and it wasn't long before Asier was negotiating for what Cassidy supposed would be their next several meals.

"Don't you dare walk away while I'm talking to you!" someone shouted from behind the makeshift sales counters.

Cassidy joined several other bystanders in looking for the source, finding a muscular, blonde woman wearing a vest that hardly contained her chest. She chased a waterlogged young man with similar golden hair whose boots squelched as lake water splashed from them with every step. The woman grabbed him by the shoulder and whipped him around.

"I saved Keiko," the man snapped at the woman. Looking at them, she might have been his mother, or older sister, though Cassidy couldn't be sure which. "Seems to me, you should be saying thanks."

"You risked a dozen lives to do it, including your own!"

"It's a crew, ain't it? One for all, or some shit?"

"Don't even *pretend* that's why you threw yourself into danger. You did it to show off."

"Maybe if you took better care of your equipment, I wouldn't have had to."

The woman's face contorted into something between indignation and rage, and she raised a hand as if to strike him, but she lowered it quickly. "You aren't cut out for this, Kekarian. You're done."

"Fine by me," he said, turning away again and walking into the crowd.

175

"We'll talk about this later!" the woman shouted at his back.

"No, we won't," the man named Kekarian said, making a rude gesture with his hand without turning back.

The woman turned her storm cloud of a face to the crowd, as if only just now aware she had had an audience to her fight. Cassidy joined in what seemed to suddenly become a popular game: pretending that she had been focused on something else entirely.

Asier handed Cassidy a heavy bundle of wrapped fish, and unlike the sheepish crowd around her, she seemed legitimately disinterested in the drama that had just played out.

It appeared Asier was simply a better actor than most, because as soon as they were away, she said, "That boy seems like the sort that would be good to have on a crew."

"Argumentative?" Cassidy asked wryly.

"Dedicated. And resilient, to boot."

Cassidy couldn't argue with that, so she just shrugged awkwardly with her burdens. They made their way through the crowd, turning off into what Cassidy could only describe as a side street — though it felt odd to call it that, given the city's construction — where Asier pointed out a tavern.

"Not my favorite place in town," the Captain acknowledged, "but it's clean, cheap, and I have a good feeling about it."

If Cassidy felt charitable, she might have called it cozy — though she supposed that was probably just the nature of Melfine. The bar cut the common room almost perfectly in half, and the tables cut the remaining space in half again, leaving only a narrow strip of the room to stand or walk along. Because of this arrangement, she had a clear view of the entire clientele from the moment she walked in, and directly ahead of her at the far side of the room, whispering in a bored-looking woman's ear, was Kekarian.

"Were we *following* him?" Cassidy hissed to Asier .

"No," Asier said, and Cassidy couldn't help but notice she didn't sound offended , or even that she *wouldn't* have followed him. Instead, her voice only suggested that she hadn't been *this time.* "I said I had a good feeling, though, didn't I?"

The woman Kekarian was talking to rolled her eyes and walked away, and he turned back to his drink with a casual shrug. Asier made her way to him, and Cassidy followed close.

"Excuse me," Asier said, "Kekarian, was it?"

The blonde man looked up, and Cassidy couldn't help but notice now that she was so close that he looked more like a boy. He smiled at Asier, looking nothing like someone who had just been publicly reamed a half hour earlier.

"*Oui, mademoiselle*," he said with an exaggerated bow. "Kekarian Valani, at your service, and may I say it would be a *pleasure* to serve such a beautiful woman." He turned his gaze to Cassidy. "*Two* beautiful women? Dare I dream? The gods must seek to lure me to some insidious trap, to send such perfection, *cheri*?"

Cassidy found herself commiserating with the woman who had just walked away. Asier, however, chortled.

"Sorry to say, you can't sell anything I would want to buy," she said. "And speaking Castilyn probably won't win you any favors with either of us. But I saw what you did at the lake today. And the fight at the docks."

The good humor melted from Valani's face. "Ah. What of it?"

"I got the impression you need a new job, and my ship needs some more hands. You seem to be just the sort I want on my team."

Valani worked his mouth thoughtfully. "What's the job?"

"Cargo trading," said Asier. "Independent, so no company overhead."

"Pay?"

"Ten percent, plus all the amenities."

His smile returned, and he gestured as if to tip a hat he wasn't wearing to Cassidy. "I suppose that we'd be pretty close for weeks on end. Sounds like a grand time."

"Captain, are you sure we need this relentless flirt?"

"Relentless?" Valani exclaimed, pretending to be shot. "I prefer the term dedicated or committed."

Asier kept her eyes fixed on Valani as she answered Cassidy. "Any man who would throw himself at a creature like that for his crew is one I want on mine."

"It's nice to be appreciated," he said, suddenly devoid of his flirtatious and snarky tone. He offered his hand. "Call me Kek."

CHAPTER NINETEEN

Cassidy held fast to the wheel as the *Dreamscape Voyager* picked up speed. The *Sunshear* and *Dawnstar* fell behind as the *Dreamscape Voyager* glided through the corridor of buildings. The vision she had witnessed was burned over her mind's eye. She shuddered. The memory of Kek's final fall wouldn't fade or dim. She had to stop it, like she had for the vision in the previous attack, and the thought had her mentally begging herself to stop following the pull entirely.

But if she stopped following it, she might not end up in a position to stop it at all. She screamed in frustration.

"Captain!" Nieves shouted. "The ground forces are still behind—"

"Lierre!" Cassidy called, cutting Nieves' protestations short as she saw something briefly as they flew by a window. Understanding was forming in Cassidy's mind as she charged headlong on the course set to her by her vision, moments crystalizing in the form of sudden insight, as if to trick her into thinking the strings pulling her along were her own wants. The words she felt forming on her tongue were vile, but there was a vile rightness to them.

Her conscience screamed at her to abandon the dark future entirely, to turn back and stick to the plan.

Her voice screamed, "Set fire to the tenements."

"*What?*" Lierre shrieked in horror.

"That's an order, Merlyn!" Cassidy snapped, and she watched from the corner of her eye as Lierre took a deep breath before resignedly arming the flame-spitter. True to its name, it spewed an alchemical mixture through a match-sized flame, sending a glob of burning adhesive that would turn into an inferno in short order. The first shot hit the plaster walls as they passed, starting a fire that on its own could devastate the district if left unattended. The second shot two buildings down the line, broke into a window, and immediately exploded out.

The *Dreamscape Voyager* swayed violently after taking the brunt of the blast. Cassidy pulled hard on the wheel to keep the ship from ramming the buildings on the opposite side of the street. The grinding, scraping noise of wood on brick sent a spike of fear through Cassidy's heart. Behind them, two more explosions erupted.

A purple tint shadowed the *Dreamscape Voyager* and, akin to dragon fire, burned the air's moisture right out. Cassidy risked a look and found that one of the tenements had become a geyser of iridescent flame. And falling from the burning rubble was one of the orichalcum cannons.

Also falling, and not harmless to the ground, but in a steep arc towards the *Dreamscape*, was debris that flapped and screamed as it made its plummet. It struck the starboard gunwale only a few feet from Nieves' station, breaking the beam and leaving an icy-purple fire in its wake. In the moment before it flopped over the side, Cassidy realized it was the top half of a human, sans its left arm.

"*Lierre*," Cassidy called, but the engineer had anticipated the damage quicker than Cassidy could have and was already running back from the storage cabin with an ice canister under each arm. She tossed one to Nieves and cracked open her own.

The flames seemed alive, dancing back and climbing away from the sweeping arcs of pressurized alchemical ice. The burning section of gunwale broke, the purple fire spreading onto the edge of the deck. The canisters were sputtering their last when at last the flames subsided, and Lierre stamped out the last of the glowing embers.

"Well," she said, and she met Cassidy's eyes with a forced smile. "That's one less cannon to worry about."

Cassidy stared gormlessly at the engineer. Then the tension in her breast broke, and unstable laughter bubbled up, escaping her in a fit of manic giggles. She laughed until she ran out of breath and began coughing.

"Is everyone—" She stopped when she remembered Nieves and Lierre were the only ones aboard. "Are you alright?"

Before either of them could answer, a heavy crash sent the bow of the *Dreamscape* shooting up. Cassidy's feet lost purchase with the deck, and she fell several feet before the ship leveled out, losing her hat in the process.

"What did we hit?" Lierre groaned.

"A ship," Nieves reported, looking over the starboard side. She pulled herself back to the deck just before a gunshot rang out. "Pissing blight," she breathed.

The other ship's unnatural mast and sails peered up in front of the *Dreamscape*'s prow. An idea had only just come to Cassidy when she felt the pull of the future urging her to move.

"Nieves, get the ship back to our people," she called before breaking into a run.

"What?" Nieves replied as Cassidy darted past.

Cassidy leaped from the bow, drawing her sword and plunging it into the enemy sails. She let out a noise halfway between a scream and a curse when she realized the tearing canvas was doing little to nothing to slow her descent. She fell hard on a burly woman's shoulders, and empathy and confusion made her think her own legs were broken when she heard the disgusting crunch as the stranger's body crumpled.

The ship listed to port, crashing into the tenement buildings. The helmsman was fighting in vain to stop the hull from being shorn off as it forced its way into a building, and much of the crew was in a confused panic. However, a tan, hook-nosed woman wearing a black short coat and a tricorn hat came at Cassidy with a saber. She recognized her as one of Flint's captains, though she couldn't remember the name. She was accompanied by a patchy-dressed youth Cassidy identified as a cabin girl.

Cassidy had never been quite the duelist Asier had been, and she didn't like the odds of being one against two. But she had seen the future, so she must win, right? She hoped that her former captain had been right about that as she felt the future's pull intensify. She ducked and rolled under the enemy captain's saber and parried a blow from Cabin Girl.

Hymn, don't fail me now, she thought as she reached for her Fae connection and lit Cabin Girl's sword on fire. Cassidy almost lost herself to the surprise; she hadn't been sure she would be able to do that due to Hymn's extended absence. The girl screamed and threw her sword to the deck — a terrible choice as the sword was still on fire, which spread to the deck.

Unperturbed, Captain Hooknose swung hard, and Cassidy caught the woman's saber on her hand guard. Every instinct in her body burned to leap to the side, and she followed through. She hit the deck just as a section of brick wall crashed down upon the deck where she had been standing, crushing the enemy as it cleaved through the fire-compromised structure of the ship.

The ship hit the street and the deck exploded in splinters and debris. Cassidy was hurled into the rigging, and she cracked her skull on the collapsing mast. A rope snagged her arm, and another looped around her throat. They pulled taut, choking her. Her dueling sword was still clutched between her fingers, and she didn't need the insistent pull of the future to tell her to use it to cut herself down. She hit the broken deck hard.

Pain disoriented Cassidy's senses, and she couldn't say for certain how long she lay delirious with a splinter as long as her arm pressed against her ribs. The air was hot and dark. Something seemed odd about that, but the concepts were proving difficult to grasp, and her thoughts were no louder than the incessant ringing in her ears.

As she came to, she realized the deck of the rebel ship was at a steep angle, and the only thing stopping her from sliding down into a pile of burning wreckage was a bent plank that had caught under her arm. Bracing her foot on what was left of the deck, she pushed off it, but the wood split under the pressure and she skidded down, tearing the sleeve of her deel off along the way. She rolled to avoid being skewered by debris and landed with her knees to the cobblestones. The fresh agony sent a wave across her entire body and flooded her eyes with tears. The air made her lungs itch, and she struggled to clear a burning sensation from her throat.

Again she reached for the Fae connection and was pleasantly surprised to find it still in place despite having no idea where Hymn had gone. A cold sensation washed over her body, and the pain became a distant thing, enabling her to stand.

The ringing in her ears subsided, and the discordant sounds of battle and terror and civic destruction were a miserable din that made her stomach drop.

I shouldn't be here, she thought to herself. *This shouldn't be happening.* Helplessness crept around her, heavy and oppressive like a tightening net. Things like this happened to other people, or in stories.

She tried to touch the place where dreams overlapped to the Dreamscape, to find the clarity that came from separating herself from a nightmare. But this time, the abilities she had gained since meeting Hymn failed her.

181

She was really here, in a burning city, cut off from her friends.

My friends…

The thought was like a struck match in a dark hold, not enough light to see by, but enough to give her perspective. "Alright, Cassy," she said out loud, and she smacked herself in the face with her free hand while her left gripped her sword tighter. Smoke blotted out the sky while fire cast red and orange lights against it to create disorienting shadows. "Enough self-pity."

The rebel ship had crashed on the corner of an intersection, and its remains coupled with the rubble of the tenement formed a barrier blocking off the street behind her. She could climb it to get to higher ground, she supposed, but that would be time consuming, and she couldn't be sure if the wreckage was stable enough to hold. That left her with three directions to start walking.

She reached in her jacket pocket to flush out her compass, only to find that it had broken at some point, and the needle was nowhere to be found amid the shattered glass. She discarded it with a sigh. Turning her back to the blocked street, she was reasonably certain she had been flying in from the left. She considered going that way to regroup with her allies. But the fighting had already started, so they may no longer be there.

And in Cassidy's vision, Kek had been slain by Flint. To stop it, to be where she was in her vision, she needed to head further along. That left her two choices: turn right, or go forward.

The tug of her prophecy nudged at her heart and told her to move forward. She took her first steps, aware of pain in her hips and legs and back, in much the same way a sleeper might be aware of whispering in the next room. In spite of it, she broke into a run.

She cleared two intersections before the ethereal tether on her bid her to turn right. She skidded to a halt just before running into two wounded rebel fighters who looked just as surprised by the encounter as Cassidy.

Still letting the future lead, she drew her pistol and shot one — a young man with scraggly stubble masquerading as a beard — right in the heart before the thought even entered her mind. Understanding only came when she was already driving the point of her sword through the heart of an older woman. Their bodies fell inaudibly before her without any last words, their death masks lacking any sign of comprehension.

Cassidy looked at the bodies in numb shock. She had killed before — duels, pirates, *mercenaries*. But all those times, she had been in control, if not of her emotions at least of her actions. In all those cases, it had been a mix of self-preservation and personal drive. Even killing Zayne Balthine, driven by a blind desire for revenge, it had been her own intention to drive the blade.

But this?

Sure, they were fighting on the other side of a battle, but they hadn't even processed what her presence had meant. *She* hadn't processed it. She had simply let fly whatever Fae suggestion flit into her head, and two people were dead. Maybe if she hadn't, it would have been a fight and she would have been forced to kill them anyway. But what if it hadn't?

Her sword rattled in her quivering hand. She stared at the bodies and saw the young man had landed with his dead gaze to the woman.

The memory of Kek's prophesied death, his dead eyes looking to *her*, shattered her reverie. These rebels had picked their side, and she would kill them all to see him safe at the end of it.

Prophecy carried her onward amidst fire and smoke, taking her around obstacles, be they debris or patrols of scurrying rebels. She cut through an abandoned tenement home, exiting through a back window just as an explosion tore open the door she had entered through and the adjacent wall, filling the room with smoke and dust before the floors above collapsed inside.

She began to recognize a change in the district layout as she carried on. Rather than a level grid, the streets became tiered with gentle slopes connecting the main intersections while alleyways were replaced by staircases. Barricades and pitched battles blocked many of these paths to Cassidy, but she followed her lead undeterred, skulking through their midst.

Cassidy slowly opened a tenement window to crawl inside when she heard a man shout, "Careful with that, you moron!"

"Ow!" a woman yelped.

Cassidy peered inside and gasped. Across the entry hall, through an open door, standing over a doubled over woman and illuminated only by the fires outside, was Adryen Flint. He appeared shabbier than the sketch passed around at the ministry office — his shoulder length black hair was shaggier, and his beard was untrimmed — but compared to the animalistic monster bathing directly in the glow of a raging city fire she saw in her prophecy, he seemed downright charming.

"Useless, subhuman garbage!" He yelled, and he turned his back to Cassidy. She swallowed a lump in her throat. Could avoiding the future she saw be so simple? She climbed through the window and slunk along the walls until she was crouched with her shoulder pressed against the threshold, shrouded in the darkness. "How hard is it to understand, *no fire*. If you want to kill yourself, take that crate and run at the Imperials, but don't take us with you."

"Adryen," said another woman just out of Cassidy's line of sight. "We've lost the seventeenth."

"Just fucking brilliant," Flint said, slamming his fist into a wall. "That whole mess with what happened with the ships... what was that Fae thinking? The last thing we need is the Iron Veils looking into this revolt. Where *is* Atarshai, anyway?"

"It disappeared after yesterday's attack. Muttered some nonsense and flew away."

Cassidy heard the slap of flesh hitting flesh.

"Why didn't you say so sooner?" he shouted. Quieter, he added, "What nonsense, exactly?"

"I only caught a few words," protested the woman.

"Then tell them," Flint said through gritted teeth.

"It said..." The woman took a composing breath. "'Curse Len, leaving work undone.' At least that's all I caught; I don't think Atarshai intended to be heard."

Cassidy's fist tightened around her sword at the invocation of the name and sucked in a sharp breath when the metal rattled. Flint and his people didn't seem to hear it.

Flint was silent for a long moment. "And it said nothing else about where it was going?"

"Its interest was never with me. If it didn't inform you after it departed, then it didn't inform anyone."

A figure moved to stand in the doorway, the black coattails swaying mere inches from Cassidy's face. *Flint?* She wondered. Could it be that easy?

Cassidy rose from her crouch, driving the blade of her sword between the mercenary's shoulder blades. It was only when the handguard pressed all the way into the mercenary's back that she realized she had never stopped following the pull of the future. Rather than killing Flint, she had stabbed the woman he had been

184

speaking to, a similarly dressed woman with short, blonde hair. From over the woman's shoulder, she met Flint's gaze, finding him every bit as surprised as herself. Tension thickened as the confusion slowly melted into comprehension.

As if coordinated, Cassidy and Flint moved at once. Cassidy set fire to her sword and laboriously shoved the woman into Flint at the same moment he whipped his pistol from its holster and fired. She fell into the entry hall, landing hard on her back. Pain blossomed in her right thigh and spread like ivy until it consumed her leg. She opened her mouth to cry out, but only a faint, high-pitched whine escaped her throat.

She rolled onto her stomach and began to crawl towards the window. As she picked herself up to leave the way she had come in, a tremendous weight struck her with the heat of a dozen summer suns and hurled her through the portal. She struck the cobblestones hard enough to bounce and roll into the step of the tenement across the street. A high-pitched ringing consumed all other sounds, and her understanding of the explosion that destroyed Flint's hideaway came from the trembling feelings that left her bones feeling like jelly.

She vomited on her lap. Her limbs were weak, all wobbling and buckling under her own weight as she used a small, wooden doorstep to help find her feet. Black spots obscured her vision. The world wavered and her vision split as she stumbled down the street.

In broken moments of lucidity, she wondered what she would be doing if she didn't have some sort of eldritch call guiding her to move; as it was, she believed — as much as she could believe anything with her brains beaten beyond reason by the inside of her skull — that she was incapable of moving by her own power and was simply a feather riding a zephyr. She was perplexingly aware that she was dirty; ash and grime plastered against her sweat, forming thick cakes of filth that cracked and crumbled when she moved and left her fingers feeling stiff.

The ringing in her ears faded gradually, being replaced little by little by the ambient sounds of crackling flame and distant gunshots. Among the reawakened world of sound, it was a thunderous rumble that snapped her thoughts back into their proper alignment. *Footsteps. Many footsteps.* She had no way of knowing if her allies or her enemies were coming to investigate the explosion, but she wasn't in a gambling mood.

She forced herself to embrace her Fae connection, and felt as though cold water were filling her entirety like a canteen while her mind sharpened. The pain that encompassed her every muscle and bone subsided, but it was too great to completely smother into irrelevance. She tried to break into a run, but it was more of a hobble as each time she put weight on her wounded thigh, fresh agony lanced through her trance, and she felt it across her entire body as though it were trying to pull her insides into the one spot.

She heard a woman scream. It sounded like a name, like... *Kek,* Cassidy thought. It must be Miria. She pushed herself, but even in her Fae trance, she was unable to run in a straight line, hobbling up the way. Her lungs burned under the exertion, but she pushed on anyway. A horrifying thought struck her as she heard fighting above her: she hadn't seen hint or hair of Miria in the vision.

Please be okay, she pleaded in her mind. Kek she knew she could save, but Miria? She was blind. She staggered and stumbled as she reached a staircase leading to the next tiered street. She veered clumsily as she forced herself to take step after agonizing step. *Please be okay,* she thought again. She reached the step where she could see over the lip of the stair and the memory of the vision was superimposed over reality as Kek was directly in front of her exactly as she had foreseen. He was wounded terribly and breathing hard, but he was still breathing.

But if she was seeing him, that meant her vision had almost come to fruition. That meant... *No,* she thought in dismay. *Flint can't have survived the* — she slammed that thought down hard. *She* had survived, after all.

But the pull of the future was strong, now, and she had given in to it so completely. She continued to take steps up the stairwell, and she felt as though her body were resisting her orders to stop and face her attacker.

The air snapped like the tension on a coiled string, and Cassidy recoiled as she escaped the course she had been following. She watched the fury on Flint's face turn to surprise as the momentum of his dive continued. Rather than catching her by surprise and knocking her legs from under her, his face struck her knee. It sent tremors of pain up to her hip and down to her toes, and she stumbled, but she was able to keep her feet while Flint fell back, tumbling down a few steps. Cassidy stepped back onto the safety of the street.

"Cassidy?" Kek asked wearily. His voice was raspy and distant, as though he were on the brink of sleep.

"It's me," she croaked, aware her voice sounded no better.

Flint took slow, plodding steps to the street. His clothes had been burned, either when his flaming ally had been thrown into him or in the subsequent explosion and blood stained his face and glued his hair to his skin. Cassidy hoped that he was just as haggard as she and Kek were, or everything had been for naught.

The mercenary drew his sword. Rather than a dueling sword, he carried a jian, the favored weapon of the Imperial military. He flicked the flat side of the blade and a moment later it was engulfed in flame.

"Shit," she and Kek said in unison. She hadn't thought through what it meant that a Fae had allied with Flint, and she had never imagined facing someone else who could do the things she could.

"You killed my crew," Flint growled, and he lunged at her, swinging furiously. Cassidy could only stumble back and stare at those coal black eyes, feeling their emptiness and the hatred gnaw at her insides as they drank the firelight.

As Cassidy narrowly evaded a burning slash to the throat, Kek interceded, catching the fiery weapon between his dueling sword and dagger. They traded blows, but it quickly became clear that Kek — already wounded and tired — could not keep up with the mercenary for long. Seeing how Flint handled himself even with his injuries, Cassidy didn't think Kek could match Flint even fully rested.

A wound in Kek's arm spurted blood as he overextended his arm to catch the mercenary's jian with the basket-hilt, but he gritted his teeth and kept pushing, bringing his dagger up to meet Flint's ribs. The mercenary was ready, however, and caught Kek's wrist with the other hand and headbutted the blond man.

While they grappled, Cassidy lunged — or, more accurately, *fell* — forward and wrapped her arms around Flint's waist, pushing all her weight into throwing him down. She succeeded in pulling him off his feet for a moment, but he shifted his weight and slammed his knee into her solar plexus. She coughed blood into his face. Flint's face was contorted into a mask of unadulterated fury, but without warning, it was replaced by a look of shock and horror. Cassidy looked down to see Kek had reached around her and stabbed Flint through the ribs with his dueling sword and in the opposite thigh with the dagger.

Cassidy kicked the mercenary off her, which ripped Kek's sword from his flesh, though the dagger escaped her First Mate's grip and remained in Flint's thigh. She stumbled, then, and would have fallen without Kek to catch her.

"We did it," she said breathlessly. "We really... fuck... did..." She tried to catch her breath.

A foul-smelling wind picked up. Dust and embers swirled around Flint as he pushed himself up, and behind him stood a figure. If the sudden unexplainable appearance hadn't identified the newcomer as a Fae, the impossible clothes — fabric smoother than silk that appeared to be a window into an impossibly radiant, golden-brown night sky — would have done. This Fae wore elaborate frills and lace, complete with heeled shoes. Sporting a beautiful, painted face and luxurious golden hair that flowed in the air as if underwater, Cassidy found herself completely unable to tell whether this Fae was male or female.

"Atar...shai" Flint grunted, pulling the knife from his thigh, "Where have you..." He vomited blood and bile, falling again to his knees. Tears fell from his face as he emptied his stomach again.

Atarshai looked piteously at Flint, then turned its attention to Cassidy. The sharp glare of its inverted autumn-colored eyes made Cassidy shudder.

The androgynous Fae turned to Flint. "You cannot survive this on your own," it said, and the voice did not do anything to help Cassidy identify it. It placed its fingers to Flint's forehead. "Do you wish to live?"

"What are you..." the mercenary croaked, but in a flash of light, his head rocked back as though struck, and Atarshai was gone. Kek swore in Cassidy's ear as Flint hopped effortlessly to his feet, heedless of the blood spurting from his wounds. His head rolled awkwardly around until it was upright. Then he opened his eyes, and Cassidy's stomach dropped. His eyes were at once human and Fae, with the black irises of Adryen Flint surrounded by the golden-brown sclera of Atarshai.

The amalgamation of human and Fae flexed his hands, staring at them as though seeing them for the first time. He snorted dismissively and took up a fighter's unarmed stance. Kek stepped around Cassidy and ran in swinging. Flint bent over backwards, letting Kek's sword sail harmlessly overhead. Before Kek could even adjust his attack, Flint returned to an upright position. He leaped to his own height and spun. His kick connected squarely with Kek's face and knocked him to the ground.

Cassidy dove for Kek's fallen knife, Flint landed hard on her hand, pinning it to the ground with enough force that she heard something crack.

He knelt and grasped Cassidy's throat in one hand and hoisted her over his head. She squirmed and struggled, clawing at his unnaturally powerful grip while kicking in vain at his body.

"You're her pet, aren't you?" asked a voice that was both Flint and Atarshai. "Did she promise you wealth? Power? Glory? Was it worth it, I wonder?" As it spoke, Cassidy was hearing less of the man and more of the Fae, and all the while, the human element was fading from its eyes. "It is a shame that no one told you never to trust the lovely lady —" Atarshai's eyes bulged wide, now completely devoid of human color. The veins in Flint's face glowed through his skin, deep red light shining like sunbeams between the clouds. In a blink, the light became a shimmering blue, and a thick crack formed down the center of the possessed mercenary's face, gushing blood as well as the ethereal blue light.

Flint's head split like a melon. His corpse fell first to its knees and then slumped to one side. Behind the dead man, wearing a sleek dress of a radiant blue night sky, with a finger-thick cord of blue light dangling from the tips of her middle and forefingers, was Hymn. Seeing Hymn in her true form while awake did nothing to dispel the surrealistic waves that had come of the day's events.

After helping Kek to his feet, Cassidy rushed over to Hymn. She wasn't sure what she intended to do. Ask her where she had been? Shout at her? Curse until her face turned as blue as her dress? When she reached her, however, Cassidy dropped to her knees, throwing her arms around the Fae's waist and trembled as tears broke the dams she hadn't been aware were welling up. She felt Hymn stiffen in shock at the gesture, followed by a gentle touch on the head. She felt a fool for it, but after the day's events… she had grown so used to Hymn's presence over the course of nearly two years, she hadn't realized how oppressively alone she had been fighting without her.

"Kek!" Miria's voice sounded from nearby. Cassidy broke away from the Fae to see the princess darting out from an alleyway.

"Kek, where —"Miria turned in their direction. "Captain! Hymn? What are you doing here? How did you find us?"

"Miria," Cassidy breathed, wiping her eyes dry and wrapping the girl in an embrace.

Miria hugged her back but pulled away. She turned to Hymn. "You need to hide, or they'll kill us all as sure as any rebels." Hymn looked briefly to the sky, as if confirmation of Miria's claims could be found there, and she was no longer the tall, beautiful woman but the small, easily concealed light that Cassidy was used to. At the same time, the sky suddenly began churning with the sounds of ship engines.

A squad of Imperial military entered the street with precision, fanning out to make sure the area was secure.

Miria stepped between them and Cassidy so she could quickly conceal Hymn in what was left of the tattered remains of her deel. Doing so, she kicked Flint's body.

"Is that..." the princess began.

"Aye," Kek said, fatigue and awe mixing in his tone. "Flint is dead. We did it."

CHAPTER TWENTY

Zayne had never felt so far from home as he did under that preternatural sky. Not to say there was *any* place he called home, really. If there was, it would be fair to say his home was the *Scorpion*. He had sailed from the frozen Reach to the north to the desolate doldrums to the south, traveled from Dawnhal in the east to the Storm Wall at the end of the western sea. But no matter where his voyages had taken him, he had never felt such a soul-gnawing yearning to simply *go back*.

The sensation was only exacerbated by the other feeling sharing his heart; the feeling that this *was* his homecoming, that the stars had stories they longed to tell him, that this alien place should be familiar. Lucandri's influence, no doubt. The fact that he couldn't even feel his own emotions without the Fae's parasitic invasion made him want to scream until his throat was raw, but he knew that if he were to relinquish control, to give in to the impulse, he would end up in tears.

The air was at once cold and comfortably warm, like lying in bed on a winter's night. The wind tasted of spices and the promise of autumn rain. A song played off on the horizon, just barely at the edge of hearing. A lullaby half forgotten. It was as if the Dreamscape was trying to seduce him into forgetting the danger it represented.

Forcing himself out of his reverie, he took in the transformation his ship had undergone. By all rights, it should be dropping out of the sky. But Lucandri's understanding poured into his own, and he knew that, like Pyrrha, it was simply showing its true self, here.

On the deck below, Xun and Tagren were staring dumbly at the newly formed sails — and Zayne really couldn't blame either of them — while Shen was chanting "Let them be blind to our passing," repeatedly from a prostrate position. Nanette, however, was leaning over the gunwale, apparently oblivious to the horrific situation. Zayne took a few steps to the side so he could see her face and saw her eyes were as wide as she could make them, like a child witnessing a magic trick for the first time. She was standing on her tiptoes, as if trying to reach something in the bizarre landscape.

"Nanette," he called. She didn't reply. "Nanette!" he said louder, but still she stared transfixed at the glowing sea foam and the shimmering wisps of light. He leaped over the stairs to the deck and grabbed her arm just as she started to tip over the gunwale.

She gasped and jerked violently, as if woken abruptly. But when she saw Zayne, she visibly relaxed, and let out a shaky breath. Zayne saw a flicker of silvery pink light race across her eye, but she blinked, and it was gone.

"Sorry," she said, turning her back to him. "I don't know what came over me."

A few steps away, Pyrrha was smiling. Zayne felt his hackles rise at the Fae, and it made his stomach uneasy to look at her distorted silhouette.

"Something amusing, Fae?"

"Nothing you would appreciate," she said in a reassuring tone that did nothing to reassure Zayne of anything.

He had to fight back a sneer. "Never mind, then. Xun, sail north to Revehaven."

"A-aye, Captain," the woman replied, taking to the helm. She looked skyward, then stood staring at the wheel. Irritation steadily simmered into a boiling anger as she simply did nothing, and he was on the brink of shouting when she asked, "How do you find north here?"

"How do you —" Zayne sputtered, but he cut himself off. The constellations were completely alien to the *Scorpion*'s crew. Only Pyrrha and Zayne would recognize any of those strange stars, and even then, Zayne couldn't be relied on to navigate this vile world accurately. He reached into an inner breast pocket of his coat and extracted his compass. The needle twitched rhythmically. Rather than simply pointing north, its motion was more reminiscent of a clock as it slowly wound its way around the circle. Curious, he checked his pocket watch in the vain hope that it was now indicating direction, only to find that it had simply stopped working outright.

"Fae!" he snapped.

Pyrrha sat down on empty air as though a stool had been set down for her and crossed her legs. "How can I be of service?" she asked, her tone so oversaturated with condescension it was a wonder she didn't choke on it.

Zayne gritted his teeth. *Like you don't know*, he thought, but he held back from saying so. He took a deep breath and met those inverted red-gold eyes, trying his best to keep his contempt from bleeding into his every word. "How do we reach Revehaven from here?"

The Fae tapped her lip in an exaggerated show of thinking deeply. "Hmm. Well, that is a remarkably interesting question with an equally remarkable answer," she said. "Where we are now is a reflection of the island from which we entered this realm, but once we go further out, you will find it increasingly unfamiliar. Going in any singular direction would be a fool's errand since it won't be the same direction for long." A sickeningly vile grin spread across her face. "Many humans have been driven mad by the effort."

Zayne snorted. "Quit grandstanding. How do we get there?"

Pyrrha sighed and lifted her right hand halfheartedly. The air around it shimmered as if from intense heat, and her skin began to emit a glow of many brilliant colors. Rainbow-patterned wisps of light seemed to bubble out of her fingers and palm and rose like steam. The lights drifted lazily ahead of the Scorpion, and suddenly shot out at a blurring speed. "Follow the lights," she said.

Xun's knuckles were white as she gripped the wheel, and the *Scorpion* sailed after Pyrrha's light.

Time was immeasurable in the Dreamscape. Changes to the sky were far too erratic to be of any use, with celestial bodies appearing and disappearing without warning when they weren't being observed, rather than moving across the sky with any kind of arc or destination, and the stars seemed to change every time Zayne looked at them. Zayne tried counting the time between changes, but he couldn't find any features behaving steadily enough to measure. His best attempt had been when the sky had first changed color from the maroon and red it had been upon their arrival to a gradient of blues interrupted with swirls of golds and oranges. He had counted to fifteen hundred before he realized the balance had been shifting gradually and the sky was almost entirely orange but for swaths of purple. After that, he had started to count again and only made it to one hundred before they were sailing under a black and pink sky, and he decided to stop bothering altogether when he counted to four hundred after that.

The only constant that Zayne could really get a sense for was that it was night. No matter what color the sky seemed to be painted, no matter how bright, it was only starlight and moonlight that illuminated the clouds or the sea. As they followed the wisps, the ship had gradually descended over the course of their voyage, until it actually sailed upon the water like a ship from before the ascension, and the wisps were reflected on the black surface of the sea. Nanette had asked why, and Pyrrha responded that it was the way it must be, that flying would not lead them where they were going.

Time was immeasurable in the Dreamscape, but Zayne did his best, regardless. He tried to keep the shifts and duties consistent as well as he could, calling for changes when it seemed natural. Xun, Aresh, and Tagren alternated at the helm while he, Nanette, and Shen had staggered lookouts. So it was that he used the instinctive cycles of hunger and fatigue to measure time, though he knew those were not wholly reliable.

Time wasn't their only uncertainty, however. In the quiet of the perpetual night, strange sounds left the crew jumpy and paranoid. Every so often, someone would hear indiscernible whispering, and every time it happened to Zayne he felt as though the speaker was breathing in his ear. On what might have been the third day, they sailed through a deep fog, in which they heard laughter. Under a dimly lit red sky on the sixth day, something like talons or claws scratched at the hull so loudly that Xun nearly jumped out of her skin. Tagren went to investigate, and though it seemed he put a stop to it, whatever he had seen left the mute horrorstruck and jittery. Several times the sound of leathery wings could be heard overhead, but no one had seen anything.

On what he assumed was the ninth day, Zayne woke early from another nightmare with the hilt of his sword, still strapped to his belt, pressed into the small of his back. When he realized Shen wasn't rousing him for his shift, he considered going back to sleep, but dismissed the thought. He lit his cabin lantern and reached for one of his spare canteens to fill his shallow basin when he remembered that they had finally replaced the poisoned water tank and could safely use the valve.

Shedding his iron mask, he washed his face thoroughly and retrieved his folding razor. He was relieved to find it wasn't burning him as he brought the blade to his face. He lacked a mirror and he had to trust his fingers and familiarity with his own face to be sure he wasn't missing anything. Surrounded as he was by madness, such as it permeated him like venom, he was able to find a quiet serenity in the simple act, in the sound of blade cutting through stubble and gliding the gentle scratch.

Schhhht. Schhhht.

It was soothing, and for a few minutes, at least, he was able to imagine a sense of normalcy.

He was washing his face again when a frantic knock at his cabin door shattered the illusion. In his right hand, he gripped the razor while his left found the hilt of his sword. The door swung wide, and Zayne cleared the distance. Shen staggered to a halt upon realizing he had a barber's knife at his throat. The surprise on the other man's face gave Zayne a start as well, and he realized that his sword was half drawn. He pushed the other man aside and slammed his blade home in its scabbard.

"What is it?" he demanded. He looked over Shen's shoulder to see the lanterns illuminating the deck but saw nothing of note.

Shen's eyes were still wide. He stared gormlessly at Zayne for entirely too long for comfort. Zayne snapped his fingers twice in the pirate's face, and he seemed to shake himself out of whatever stupor he fell into.

"Sorry," he said. "Captain," he added belatedly. "The Fae says you need to see this."

Zayne raised an eyebrow. "You couldn't decide that on your own?"

"I don't know this place, Captain. How am I to know what's special?"

Zayne supposed he couldn't argue that point. He stepped out onto the deck and immediately regretted not putting on his coat. The comfortable chill Zayne had noted on their arrival had fallen to an icy wind. As he watched his breath drift away like mist in the lantern light, he realized how odd the situation was. Since their arrival, though it had always been night, the skies had been bright enough to render lanterns moot. He shivered, and not just from the cold. He looked Skyward to find only one moon, a bone white sphere a little larger than his outstretched fist. A haze of black clouds dimmed its corona, and not one star shined alongside it.

Pyrrha sat on the gunwale just out of the torch light with her hands in her lap. Her starry sarong and chest wrap provided their own light to spot her, but she was not so bright as to illuminate the area around her. Her normally smug, knowing smirk had been traded for a solemn expression. Her lips quirked in self-satisfaction briefly when she looked at Zayne, but quickly faded.

"We are caught," the Fae said without preamble.

Zayne waited a moment for her to continue. When she didn't, he said, "Explain yourself."

The Fae lifted her palms skyward in what might have been a shrug. "In order to reach our destination, we have had to travel through the territories of others. It's a common thing, and we have moved quickly and quietly enough that none have noticed or cared. It seems this one was waiting for us, however."

"And just who is *this one*?"

"One I dare not name," Pyrrha said. "An audience has been requested. Take the small boat."

"And why should I meet this *nameless one*?"

"Because it must be you. Because we will not leave these waters until the audience is held and the host satisfied, and only you are satisfactory."

"Me? Or Lucandri?" Zayne asked, more sharply than he intended.

"That remains to be seen." The Fae shrugged again. "It is not for me to know the will of one so great, or so old."

"So why not meet it here?"

"Decline this invitation," said Pyrrha, "and your master's fury will be a distant concern."

Zayne opened his mouth to protest that Dardan wasn't his master, that her fury meant nothing to him, but his tongue was like lead in his mouth. He snapped it shut.

"My coat is white," he muttered to himself after a moment. He wasn't wearing his coat at all, and though the *shirt* he was currently wearing was white, the statement was still a lie no matter how he spun it. *I am a man, and as a man I am free to lie,* he thought firmly. He didn't know if Lucandri's influence was an active force on his mind, or if they were the instincts of the dead, the last embers on the end of a candle wick yet to fade. Whatever the case may have been, he was not going to tolerate being forced into honesty.

"Where then will I find our *host?*"

Pyrrha pointed out over the water. Zayne followed her slender finger and saw that the sea was unnaturally still, and thin trees rose impossibly tall out of its inky blackness, visible only through a barely perceptible path of fog colored by faded moonlight weaving through them.

"Don't do it, Captain," Xun insisted. Beside her, Tagren nodded emphatically. When Zayne met her eye, she shuddered visibly and looked away. "It's a trick. No good can come of trusting these things," she added, pointing at Pyrrha. The Fae gave no indication she cared about Xun's protestations, or insults.

"But she can't say an untrue word," Shen argued.

Aresh finished Shen's logical progression by saying, "If the creature says we're trapped, we're trapped."

Zayne thought back on Pyrrha's words. "Are *we* in danger, or are *you?*"

"Our fate, whatever it may be, will be shared in this. If you are allowed passage, I go with you. If you are condemned to remain, so too must I. It is for you to see if our passage can even be negotiated."

Zayne nodded. He wasn't sure what else he expected. "Nanette is captain in my absence," he said, though he noticed that no one had roused her after all this. He took the stairs to the galley and opened the trap door in the back that led down to the hold where the skiff was stored. Perhaps unsurprisingly, like the *Scorpion* itself, the skiff's balloon had been replaced by a mast and sail — though it had been collapsed and set neatly into the boat — and its engines and propellers were gone, with a more simplistic rigging and rudder in their place.

Zayne opened the bottom hatch with a pulley mechanism and cursed himself for a fool when water began to rise up from the new opening. Before he could start to panic, however, he felt the *Scorpion* rise. The water poured out noisily, and Zayne was free to lower the skiff into the water with another set of pulleys. He set the skiff on the water and set up the rigging, relying on a combination of his scant studies in pre-Ascension sailing and — more prominently — memories from Lucandri, who apparently had been remarkably familiar with the art.

The air was even colder as he set the skiff out on the water. There was a lantern on the bow of the small vessel that rarely saw use — typically, the crew used it for stealth missions, as it could be piloted with manual power, and even with the engines engaged it was quieter than most people paid attention to in a world of noise. He used it now, and a normally gentle flame became a sharp, near blinding beacon in that oppressive dark.

Immediately, Zayne regretted his decision; the light would be seen for miles, and the bubble that surrounded the skiff only gave him a few feet of vision. And the shadows that light cast were horrifying. The trees were white, lumpy things that cast the shadow of agonized faces and skulls as he drifted by, and occasionally it seemed the wind carried faint and distant cries.

Still, he guided his skiff between the impossible trees. What sort of creature would call such a place home? In the back of his mind, he could feel Lucandri's memories filling gaps in his own, and an impression was dawning on him, only to stop suddenly in a wave of fatigue.

The lantern flashed blue before it was snuffed entirely, leaving him in darkness. The scent of lantern oil faded quickly, replaced by cold numbness. Zayne felt as though he had woken up from a deep slumber, paradoxically disoriented and clear of mind and purpose. He was aware that Lucandri's influence had been completely stifled, as he would if a persistent buzzing he had come to ignore were suddenly silenced. Separated as he was from his crew, trapped in this alien darkness, and now without even the invader plaguing his mind, he was truly and utterly alone.

CHAPTER TWENTY-ONE

The skiff glided along those dark waters in a thick mist without faltering, and Zayne was sure he was no longer the one leading it. Fear gnawed at his guts. *I should have grabbed my coat,* he thought bitterly. *Idiot.* The tips of his fingers felt like they were being splintered. His lips, ears, and nose were all numb. Was it getting colder? Was that even possible?

The trees were pressing tighter, and soon he found himself going down a perfect, wooded corridor. After a long stretch of smooth sailing with no change in direction, the skiff beached itself gently on a sandy shore Zayne couldn't see through the fog. A whistling wind urged him to move, so he climbed out of the boat, setting foot for the first time on Dreamscape ground. It was disorienting, even compared to stepping on the ground in his own world. Whether that was a property of the Fae realm or the result of the conditions he found himself faced with, he wasn't sure. The beach was a steep slope of soft silt, and his boots sank to the ankle twice as he made the climb. Once he cleared the sand, the crunch of frost-covered grass filled the air with each step as he walked between more of those snow-white trees.

His legs were burning from the exertion by the time he reached a clearing bathed in silver moonlight and swirling mist. Seated in the heart of that glow, atop a stacked pile of skulls, was a massive figure shrouded in a cloak of the same unnatural darkness that surrounded them. Atop its head it wore a pristine white jackal skull, beneath which was only more shadow. Even hunched over, the host was half-again as tall as Zayne. Although the Host — lacking any other name, Zayne thought it a fitting enough title for the nameless figure — made no move, a primitive fear raked at his chest, and the urge to turn and flee was so strong that only an even greater fear kept him rooted in place.

Zayne had never been in the presence of a god. In his time with the Daughters, he had seen Dardan conjure what might have been *shades* of Daen, if they hadn't simply been Fae tricks. He had seen the messy aftermath of a cult's attempt to beseech Karhaset, one of the three goddesses of the sea. He had met people who claimed to have spoken to various gods — some he believed more than others. But although Zayne had never had his own prior encounter with the divine, he was certain the experience would feel like this, that the Host was one of them.

A sound, nothing more than a gentle hiss of icy wind cut through the mist to Zayne's ears and through the fog of his terrified mind to his very core. He felt the *intent* of that wind.

"My name is Zayne Balthine," he answered, surprised at just how steady his voice was coming through. "I am the captain of the *Scorpion*."

The Host seemed unmoved by the answer. It seemed so still; it might have been sleeping. Except, it couldn't be; though he could see no eyes in the shadows of the jackal's skull, he could feel them boring into him, judging him, weighing his worth down to his very soul.

To keep his fear from overwhelming him, Zayne focused on evaluating the Host in turn. It seemed strange to him that its attire should be less grandiose than a significantly less impressive creature like Pyrrha. He remembered, also, the red Fae that had interceded when he had tried to defend himself against Durant. Why should a god's ensemble be less impressive? He almost dismissed it as a choice, a statement that the Host needed no such things when he realized, no, its cloak was doing the same thing as Pyrrha's sarong or the other Fae's dress, reflecting the sky of the Dreamscape. It just so happened that under the Host, the sky was an abyss that stars had no hope of escaping. Indeed, like the Fae, this god's cloak seemed to be a window into a deeper darkness, one that might consume him were he to step too close.

Another whistle of wind cut through his reverie. A question.

"Lucandri?" Zayne asked. At that, the Host nodded once, slowly, and in that one gesture, Zayne felt the air grow perceptibly colder and fear churned his guts. "A year and more. I don't fully understand how, or why."

The Host answered, then, and the explanation seemed so simple. Zayne had already concluded that the weapon Dardan had given him to face Asier had contained Lucandri — or a piece of him, according to the Host. The mechanics of their merger seemed almost mundane; Durant's blade had pierced the vessel, pierced whatever aspect of Lucandri had been held captive within it, and when she had extracted the blade from Zayne's guts, Lucandri had been pulled directly into his body. The implications, however, horrified Zayne.

The memory of the day itself stood out in his mind. "The one who did this," he said. "A Fae had defended her. I thought I knew her, the woman in red, but that's impossible. Lucandri knew her, didn't he?"

Another short gust of wind. Confirmation. A name played across his mind like a song he had only dreamed of.

The Host stood silent after that, still as stone, and no wind stirred the mists. The only sound in the clearing was Zayne's shuddering breath.

When it became clear that it was his turn to speak, he said, "You didn't stop us to be my guide through my personal struggles. What is it you want? What will passage through your wood cost us?"

The wind was not an answer, but a question. An accusation. Truth.

There was no sense in denying it. "Yes."

Another question.

"No, I don't want it. I don't relish killing. I'm good at it, but I don't enjoy it like some do."

The reply might have been a quip if it weren't so cold and impersonal.

"It's true, but that's not out of any joy. Dardan is a monster, and Durant…" He paused. "When I came here, Lucandri went quiet. Did you remove him from me?"

The answer wasn't the one Zayne wanted, but the one he had expected. Lucandri would never be parted from him.

"Then she can't be forgiven, either."

A reproach. No, not a reproach. That would suggest it cared. A suggestion, then. A possibility. Almost an idle thought if something so vast could *have* idle thoughts.

"Yes, revenge can take many forms," Zayne agreed. "But what does this have to do with our passage?"

The answer was dire. It was at once a request and a command. It weighed heavily on Zayne's shoulders.

"This in exchange for safe passage?" he asked.

Confirmation. Concise and simple. It was clear there would be no negotiation, no argument.

"Very well," Zayne agreed.

The darkness swaddling the Host shifted, almost imperceptibly at first, and a slender hand armored in bone pointed back the way from which Zayne had come. He looked. He was at the shore once again. His skiff had been turned around, no longer beached, but waiting in the shallows. He turned back, and there was nothing but mist and darkness.

CHAPTER TWENTY-TWO

Zayne's return to the *Scorpion* went without incident. While the voyage to the Host had been long and oppressive, he left the impossible forest in what seemed to be mere moments, and his ship was just beyond the skeletal trees, floating ten feet above the placid waters. When the skiff was directly under the *Scorpion*'s bay, it rose as it would if he had fired up its balloons, rising gently into place. He wondered if it was because he thought it should, or if the skiff was doing what it believed it should. Thinking about it in such terms unnerved him almost as much as anything else that night. Almost.

When he climbed up to the galley, Shen and Tagren were wringing their hands and bandana respectively, staring at him strangely as he made his arrival.

"Not the *worst* welcome I've ever received," he said sardonically. "What do you want?"

Naturally, Tagren didn't speak, but he shrank like a scolded child. He never broke eye contact, though, as if he thought Zayne might disappear if unobserved.

"We have tried to rouse Nanette," Xun said. There was a distracted quality to her voice. "Her cabin is locked, and she won't answer."

Zayne furrowed his brow. Nanette wasn't a heavy sleeper. He crossed the galley quickly, Tagren following in his wake. He passed the crew cabins until he reached Nanette's. He hesitated. Then he knocked.

Silence.

He knocked again, harder. Still there was no answer.

"Nanette," he called through the door. Through the ship, he could feel her inside, but she didn't reply. He waited for a three count and repeated, "Nanette!" When she didn't answer the following knock, he raised his voice, "I'm coming in."

The door was locked, as Xun had said. Zayne's first instinct was to try and pick the lock, but a different thought occurred to him. He set his hand against the door. The Scorpion's pulse pounded in perfect time with his own. He imagined the lock coming undone.

Click.

He opened the door. The walls of Nanette's cabin were covered in canvases depicting swirling skies of every color. She had painted blue islands, forests of red leaves, purple mountains of impossible shape. In many of the pieces, Zayne could see shadows between the trees, or in the water, or against the skyline — silhouettes that brought tremors of primal fear to his chest, though he couldn't say why.

The strangest part of the bizarre art gallery, however, was the color consistency — Nanette had struggled with color all her life, but this? Her every depiction of the Dreamscape, while impossible by the standards of the mortal world, spoke true to Zayne's experience here.

Nanette herself sat on her stool, turned away from the cabin door, seemingly transfixed on the canvas sitting on her easel.

"Nanette," Zayne said low. The artist said nothing. She didn't even turn away from her art. He peered over her shoulder and recoiled, aghast.

The piece was almost entirely black and white — which could have been astounding all its own; despite her colorblindness, Nanette never painted in black and white because it had never been in vogue during her lifetime, and she resented her limitations and was determined to struggle past them. Depicted in sharp strokes of the brush was the clearing where the Host had held court. On the right, the host sat in profile. Nanette had managed to capture its jackal-skull mask and the way its cloak of night simultaneously blended into and stood apart from the surrounding darkness. On the left, standing in the shadow of the horror was a depiction of Zayne without his mask, face scarred. Beneath them was a reflecting pond, though the figures were not the same. The reflected Host was standing, and looking down in judgement at...

The man in the rendered reflection of Zayne wasn't him. Though he had never himself laid eyes on Lucandri, he knew the Fae at once, recognized it as readily as he would recognize him if he *had* been Zayne's own reflection. Where Zayne's long hair was black with a silver streak, the Fae living in his skin wore long locks of silver with a shock of black running through it. Where Zayne's face was an expression of awe tinged with fear, the captivatingly handsome profile of the Keeper of the Dawn scowled up at the Host with undisguised hate and resentment.

The only color in the entire piece was the perfect golden sclera in Lucandri's eye. Even without her colorblindness, how had Nanette captured so pure and perfect a golden color?

Zayne forced himself out of the captivated reverie and grabbed his friend by the shoulder. Nanette's head moved with agonizing slowness from her painting to the hand on her shoulder, as if she were struggling to look away. A confused expression passed over her face as she stared at the fingers clasping her shoulder.

Her knife was at his throat in a heartbeat. She had kicked the stool out from under herself and whirled. She pinned his back to the open doorway, her arm shoving her weight into his chest. Tagren drew his own knife and leveled it at Nanette, but she only had eyes for Zayne. Her dark eyes were cold. His heart was pounding against his ribs, drumming up a storm, and his mind was a whirl of confused emotions. *Nanette* was betraying him?

No, Zayne thought. *It's this place.*

"Nanette, it's me," he said. Her knife quivered against his bare throat, the edge burning against his breaking skin. "You've saved me too many times just to kill me here." He meant it as a joke, but he was unable to muster any humor in it, and his voice hitched as he said it.

Her sharp gaze broke suddenly as recognition flashed across her face. "Zayne," she breathed, and she dropped her blade. It landed point down in the floorboards right between their feet. She threw her arms around him and shuddered. He let out a heavy sigh. "Put on your mask," she said abruptly.

Zayne blinked. "What?"

"Put on your mask," Nanette repeated, gripping his shirt. Zayne brought his hands to his face, brushing the scars with the tips of his fingers. She pulled his hand away. "You don't even know, do you? You never realized —"

"Realized what?"

Nanette pushed away and turned her back on him. "It must be the iron. Ever since you came back, when you don't wear that mask, it's not you anyone sees." She pointed a trembling finger at her masterwork, to the golden-eyed malevolence depicted in Zayne's reflection. "It's him."

Zayne looked to Tagren, who nodded rapidly. He clenched his jaw and the mute recoiled as if in fear. Maybe he was right to. Zayne turned and began pacing between the cabin and the hall. It wasn't enough that Lucandri was polluting his mind, distorting his memories and emotions, he was stealing his very *face?* He knew he was working himself into a frothing fury, but he could find no release. He felt like a caged animal, wanting to lash out with violence but knowing he couldn't lash out on Nanette or her work. Still his breaths were becoming shorter and shallower as he thought about the indignities, the stockpile of injustices.

Pyrrha glided down the hall, her face a mask of bored superiority. "There you are," she said haughtily. "If you're quite through, the way is clear, and it would be best if we —"

Zayne clamped his fingers around the Fae's throat and slammed her into the bulkhead. It was disorienting, the way he saw his hands around the slender throat of Pyrrha while he *felt* them crushing the windpipe of the much fatter Xiao Ta. Just one more way normalcy had been ripped from his life. Throttling the Fae, he repeatedly pulled her back just to slam her back again. With each loud thud of flesh and bone hitting wood, dread welled up in Zayne's chest, but it was smothered by the fog of anger. That rage broke when her head struck the wall with enough force that blood splattered on the wood.

His hands seized up. He was standing in the doorway of his childhood home. His baby brother's skull lay cracked open on the floor. His sister was blue and swollen from strangulation. A shiver ran across him. Zayne couldn't quite read the expression on Pyrrha's face. He shoved the Fae forcefully aside and stormed out through the galley to the deck. Shen said something Zayne couldn't hear as he retreated into his cabin. The door slammed behind him, but he didn't remember reaching back to close it.

He clutched the sides of his wash basin with trembling hands. He dry heaved until his legs buckled beneath him. As he collapsed, he tipped the basin over and his mask clanged noisily on the floor.

On the fourteenth day of sailing the Dreamscape — if Zayne's measure of time could be trusted — the *Scorpion* reached the edge of the ocean, where the hitherto boundless sea finally gave way to a perfectly flat cliff face hewn from what appeared to be amethyst. The wall of unbroken purple stretched out from horizon to horizon, though it didn't seem too much taller than any normal rock formations in the living world. Iridescent waves crashed against that crystalline barrier, receding and crashing in endless cycles.

The *Scorpion* took flight without losing forward momentum, and they continued their voyage in the sky, much to Zayne's immense relief. A final look to the waves below revealed a wake too wide and long to have been made by the lone ship, quashing his minor comfort.

Beyond the cliff, the night was white as blue moons and luminescent stars shone on a snowscape. Overhead, a red aurora accented the winter sky, and trees occasionally broke the expansive landscape. The air wasn't cold in the same way the Mists had been cold. Where that darkness had been the cold of death, there was life in this chill, a sense that comfort could be found. It reminded Zayne a little of the Northern Reach. He suspected that a storm here would be even more deadly than the ones he had seen there.

He found Aresh and Shen playing cards in the galley. Amidst the madness and the unknown, there was something strange about something so ordinary. As if just outside the cabin, they *weren't* traveling thousands of miles through the land of bedtime horror stories.

Shen's gaze wavered rapidly between his cards and Zayne for a moment. His voice had a slight tremor in it when he said, "Would you like to join us for a game, Captain?"

The question surprised him, and for a second he thought he had imagined the invitation. He hadn't been friendly with any of his new crew since he had lured them aboard with the promise of impossible revenge. They had been on the brink of mutiny when he had betrayed that promise. Fear was the only thing keeping them in line, he was sure. Fear of his connection to Lucandri, fear of Pyrrha supposedly on his leash. And now fear of dying in the Dreamscape.

Aresh blushed and cleared his throat. The Rivien made a concerted effort not to look at Zayne, but his eyes flickered over to him repeatedly in the ensuing silence. "We would be hap— honored — if you joined us for a round."

In the back of his mind, he felt a sense of smug amusement rooted in Lucandri's memories. The mortal part of his mind was simply confused.

He could almost hear Nanette's advice in his ear. *Would it kill you to be civil for five minutes?* she would ask. His first thought was that it would. He would let his guard down and they would slit his throat. He thought about Jacques Charron's attempted mutiny.

But, then again, what if I hadn't treated him like the enemy?

He looked over the two men who stared expectantly back at him. *I'm so tired of keeping my back to the wall,* he decided wearily. If they betrayed him now… maybe it would be worth it, to have just a few moments to pretend things were normal.

"No stakes," he said firmly. "What's the game?"

Shen nodded with an awkward tilt of his head in acknowledgement. "Twisted Virtue," he said. "But we can play something else if you'd rather."

"Twisted Virtue is fine." Zayne took a seat at the head of the table, Shen to his right, Aresh to his left.

Aresh gathered the cards and shuffled them back into the deck. "Three for me," he said, pulling three cards off the top, "three for you —" He pulled three more, but Shen jabbed a finger at the bearded man.

"Oh, no, don't you try to pull that cheap ploy," the pirate said. "Proper vulture pass."

"Are all Imperials so paranoid?"

"Just the smart ones," said Shen. "And vulture pass comes from Rivien, so stow it."

Aresh rolled his eyes and shuffled the deck again, this time passing the cards out one at a time in a circle until they had three apiece. Zayne fanned his cards indifferently.

The first round passed in uncomfortable silence. Cards clacked against the table while the wind howled outside, and the ship groaned around them. *Clack. Clack. Clack.* Zayne lost after discarding the Burning Man and drawing the Sun. In most games, the draw would have been fortuitous, but Twisted Virtue favored low value cards.

Shen cut the cards for the second round. Again, there was no discussion as they took their turns. Though it was a numbers game, the quiet wasn't reflective, and even fixed on his cards, Zayne could feel the eyes on him. After discarding the Oath-Breaker, Zayne drew the Sun and lost again.

"You didn't shuffle well," Aresh chided Shen when Zayne set his cards down.

"Mists take you," Shen replied, though without real venom. "You never did say why you turned against Dardan," he added to Zayne.

Zayne picked up the deck and started shuffling. He considered taking the opportunity to cheat, but decided it wasn't worth his effort.

"Many reasons," he said. He thought about leaving it at that. Part of him wanted to. But that would just lead to the same distance and distrust he wanted to dispel. So he said, "My aunt, Salaa, was one of the Daughters. One of the originals, in fact. She was the captain of this vessel before I was. She had a... familiarity with Dardan. Wasn't afraid of her like everyone else. At least, not for herself.

"One day, during a meeting of the Great Captains, Salaa called Dardan out over the fact that she was tasking the Daughters with her own personal agendas, rather than — as she put it — *honest* mercenary work."

"Dardan killed her, then?" asked Aresh.

"Not then, no. She made a show of letting bygones pass. But Salaa's next job was an ambush. Only Nanette and I survived." For his last play, Zayne discarded the Dreamer and drew the Sun. He lost again.

"Can't blame me for that one," Shen muttered to Aresh. To Zayne, he asked, "So why do you still fly her banner? So to speak."

"Call it a lack of options," Zayne said. "You've seen her work her foul Fae power to stop me from attacking her. And before that, I've seen a knife cut her open and fail to stop her from strangling a man." He left out the part about the knife in question being his, and the man being himself.

"So how do you intend to kill her, if she is so invincible and can compel you to action or inaction?"

"The best way. Through distraction and misdirection." Zayne looked down at his cards. It was an expensive hand. The Oath-Breaker, the Artist, the World, and the Two of Swords. The last was the only one that was low enough in value to keep for the final move. But he recognized a pattern when he saw it. "I abstain from trade," he declared.

Aresh drew and swore. When the cards were laid bare, Zayne had managed — barely — to have a lower value hand than Aresh, whose set included the Sun.

Twenty days. Two full weeks. As far as Zayne could tell, that was how long their voyage through the Dreamscape had taken so far. And he was certain now that they were being followed. He had had a feeling for some time.

It had been a minor thing, at first, a feeling obscured by a million other discomforts in the eldritch realm. But as the endless nights blurred over time, the more he was certain. He had been making his rounds and spotted a dark shape in the woods. It was a tower of shadow standing out above the dark waters beneath black and purple clouds. The *Scorpion* never slowed, but when Zayne looked again, it was closer. As he stared at the looming shadow, he knew in his bones that it was staring back.

Nanette had also been acting strangely. Zayne woke up in the middle of a dark red night to the sound of her singing. He didn't recognize the words, despite being polyglot. He had stepped out of his cabin to find her leaning out over the gunwale, belting out an aria fit for the Royal Opera House in Tal Joyau. She had a gift for music, but Zayne had never seen her so animated.

She was also loath to perform without a potential paying audience. Yet, here, in the unfathomable loneliness of the Dreamscape, with naught but the shadows and stars as witness, she was belting a melody straight from the heart. It was beautiful as it was unsettling. Though the words were foreign to him, he could feel her intent, and his heart bubbled with faint delight as her voice painted portraits in his mind of rain on a sunny day, of a gentle breeze stirring a field of golden grasses, of a warm fire under the light of the moons.

She performed for the darkness, dancing and gesticulating to the unknown nebula. Zayne thought he heard musical accompaniment on the wind. In this place, he didn't feel safe dismissing the thought.

Nanette's performance ended in a glorious crescendo, her arms thrown wide as if to embrace the entire bizarre world beyond the *Scorpion*'s borders. A sheen of sweat gave Nanette a silver glow as she gasped for air. Zayne couldn't quite read the emotions playing on her face, but it was a rare and beautiful sight.

His reverie snapped when he heard the applause, and Nanette's seemed to, as well. She whipped her head to find the source. Her eyes held a note of terrified confusion as she looked first to Zayne, then to the hatch to the lower deck, where Xun and Tagren were clapping in appreciation. Nanette's face visibly darkened, and she retreated below deck, shoving past the others.

That had been three days ago, and Nanette refused to speak of it. Pyrrha had made a vague and uninvited comment about "true nature" and the "call of home", but Nanette had told her where to shove that appraisal.

And now, Xun was running a dry mop over the same patch of deck she had an hour ago. At first, Zayne thought the chore was an effort to find normalcy in the chaos around them, like the card game. But the way she kept stealing glances his way no matter where he stood on the deck told a different story.

"I'm not going to start dancing, if that's what you're waiting for," he called out to her as he kept an eye on the looming shadow.

"Too bad, it would probably do you some good," she replied.

"Well, if there's nothing else —"

"You really didn't know when you take that mask off, you turn into the beautiful stranger?" Xun asked rapidly.

"What?" But even as the word left his mouth, he knew what she meant. She meant Lucandri. "No, I didn't. Why?" he demanded.

"It's just that, if you didn't know," she asked, "why wear an *iron* mask? Seems pretty heavy, and I don't know very many people who would spend the coin for one."

"You know the rumors about how I died?"

"I do. It was the talk of the town." She pursed her lips. "I recall telling you to piss off when you claimed to be you."

"When I woke up on the shore of Lake Justiciar, I was already wearing it. I don't know who would have given it to me, or why, but it covered the scars pretty well. Or so I thought."

"You should take it off more."

"*What?*"

"Don't get me wrong, you're pretty enough now, even if the mask is a bit much. But the white hair, and you get that golden skin... and those *eyes!* It gets me going like the Siren Song playing in my ears. I wonder if you could figure out what caused it, maybe teach it. Because I would really like to change my—"

"I'm Fae possessed, you dolt!" As the words left his lips, frustration and shame filled the void they left behind.

211

"You— you what?"

"How else did you think it was happening?"

"Well... you're one of the Daughters — gods, that sounds weird to say. Anyway, there are rumors you all delve into forbidden Fae tricks, I just didn't think you went as far as *getting possessed*." She looked to Tagren, who had been manning the helm, looking out into the darkness. "Did you know about this?"

The mute nodded absently.

"Why didn't you tell me?"

Tagren looked back and cocked an eyebrow at her before returning his attention to the Dreamscape.

"Oh, shut up," Xun sneered at him before turning back to Zayne. "But if you're... *possessed*... how are you... you? Shouldn't you be like Xiao Ta?" She whispered the name at the last moment, looking around uncomfortably, as though Pyrrha would appear in that moment. Zayne supposed it wasn't impossible.

"My circumstances were... different than his."

"How so?"

"That's complicated." *And that's an understatement,* Zayne thought to himself. "Best I could tell, Xiao Ta was dead before... well, *before*."

Xun was quiet for a while. Zayne thought she abandoned the conversation and turned to examine an odd blotch of shadows on the horizon ahead when she said, "You're going to Tal Joyau after this, right?"

"You mean *we* are going there, aye," Zayne said flatly.

"Aye," Xun said, stretching the word out to several syllables. "But I may well throw myself overboard before I set out on another voyage through here."

"All that assumes we survive Revehaven. Does it matter? Where we're going, I mean."

"Not if you like living, I guess," Xun said, offering a sympathetic shrug. "But I hear the Ruby Queen has the Iron Veil Priests crawling around her court." She dropped her voice to a conspiratorial tone. "I've heard tell her mother tried to call the gods to assassinate Empress Shahira. So Queen Celeste can't wipe her own ass without the Iron Veils calling for a search for Myt Dust or spirit boards."

Zayne had heard the same rumors. He had also seen people hanged for *spreading* those rumors. Queen Celeste was very defensive about her mother's reputation. The part about the Iron Veils had crossed his mind, but he hadn't given it too much thought; if Dardan could come and go, how attentive could they really be? But then again, Zayne was clearly possessed by Lucandri, or near enough. Maybe Xun had been too thick to notice, but the Iron Veils surely wouldn't.

"Great, just what I—" he began, but he stopped when he realized he recognized the shapes he had been staring at. The silhouettes were distorted by the nature of the Dreamscape, but he had spent his entire life looking at ships, be they Asarian, Castilyn, or Rivien. And surer than he was of his own name, he was looking at a small fleet. The Daughters of Daen. "Altair held up her end," Zayne said, unable to keep the surprise from his voice. He wondered what surprises had befallen the others who had traveled these dark byways.

"That's it?" Xun snapped, taking in the same sight. "There can't be more than fifteen ships! How are we supposed to hit the capital with this?"

"Elyia Asier took over the southern capital with only five," Zayne offered with half-hearted optimism.

"I don't suppose you've also been hiding wind stolen from the gods in your pocket, too?" Xun asked flatly.

"No. But if Pyrrha is right, we should drop right on top of the palace. They won't be ready for a threat from so close to the city." The notion tasted like oil. Inability to lie or not, oath of fealty or not, he didn't like hinging any hopes or trust on the Fae.

Zayne called into the pipeline, "All hands to battle stations."

Xun manned one of the starboard guns, while Aresh took up the scorpion tail at the aft. Shen would be below alternating between the forward guns. And Tagren would be working the bellows to keep the *Scorpion* running. Zayne didn't relish leaving the task in the hands of a man who couldn't call out if something went wrong, but the others were simply better suited to handle the weapons.

Nanette climbed on the deck well after everyone else had taken their places. She looked feverish and irate, but she took the helm without complaint.

As the *Scorpion* joined the fleet, there was a quiet tension in the air. How could there not be? They had spent two weeks waiting in a nightmare on the brink of battle. And while Zayne could not claim to know the Dreamscape's mysteries, he was willing to bet there was worse out there than he encountered.

He spotted the *Golden Heron* and its sister ship the *Black Heron*, both distinct among the Daughters in that their murals of Daen were gold rather than white. Zayne knew the *Golden*'s captain, Xi Khana; she and Salaa had had something of a rivalry. The two would meet periodically to compare jobs, kills, and even sexual partners, much to Zayne's discomfort. Then they would drink, and laugh, and threaten one another before parting ways.

Conversely, he only knew the captain of the *Black Heron*, Khana's nephew Xi Lang, by reputation; the man had taken command after his father had taken a cannonball to the face in a Rivien trade dispute. In response, both *Heron*s not only killed the merchant prince responsible and destroyed his ship but tracked down and wiped his entire family off the map. Suffice to say, they ended the dispute in their client's favor.

The *Knight in Mourning*, captained by Lucky San, was also present, the Castilyn man-of-war recognizable by the kirin corpse adorning the prow; while all the Daughters had some form of beastly trophy serving as the figurehead of their ship, the *Knight* was unique in that Lucky San had decided to put custom armor on her kill before mounting it. Zayne had never asked, but it must have been expensive to craft.

The *King in Yellow* was a Rivien vessel that was not allowed to fly in Castilyn — on penalty of death — due to its name being a historical reference to a mad king the monarchy tried and failed to censor. On her prow was a strange breed of kraken that had developed bat-like wings. Zayne had never encountered one like it, and not even Captain Basir pretended to comprehend what he had found.

At the heart of the congregation were Altair's *Kestrel*, and two of Dardan's great captains: The *Illusion of Justice* featured a roc hanging by a noose. Never to be out done, rather than a single monster on display, the *Silent Song* wore a chain of harpy corpses like a grotesque mosaic. Perhaps befitting its name, the *Forgotten Promise* was nowhere to be seen, nor was the *Second Chance*. The three ships were tethered together.

"Should we join them?" Nanette asked. She sounded weary, but not nearly so much as she looked.

"Are you going to be okay?"

Nanette spat at his feet. "Are you going to knock me out again?"

Zayne recoiled. He deserved the remark, but he still hadn't been expecting it. He opened his mouth to apologize, but Nanette overrode him.

"I'll be fine when we're under a real sky," she said. She sounded certain about that. Zayne hoped she was right.

"Bring us in," he said gently.

It shouldn't have felt so much like flying into enemy territory. The Daughters were the only human company for any conceivable distance. Zayne was even about to go into battle alongside them. And yet his hackles rose like he was a cornered dog.

He had always been apprehensive around his fellow mercenaries — possibly as a consequence of being sold out and abandoned by Kaveth Darziin before he had even been inducted. Ever since Salaa's death, however, that apprehension grew into paranoia and disdain; any one of them might have been party to it, and any one of them might turn on Zayne just the same.

And it wasn't as though the Daughters gave him much cause to trust. Altair was insane, obsessed with the Dreamscape, and guilty of human experimentation; Ject was a bloodthirsty brute with a penchant for killing when he got bored; he hadn't learned anything about Del Thanris since they had first met, but she made him uncomfortable.

As the *Scorpion* drew on the collective, other ships began to as well, as if his arrival had been a prearranged signal. He didn't like that notion at all, but he did his best to shove down his misgivings. They needed to finalize the battle plans, after all.

The captains and their firsts were gathering on the deck of the *Silent Song*. The *Scorpion* took her place among the ships, and Zayne tossed a tether line over. Ject was the one who caught it. Zayne had once seen the man stand bare chested in a blizzard, so it was a spectacle to see him with his coat wrapped firmly shut. His black hair was partially done up in a messy topknot while the rest sat around his shoulders, giving him a wild look.

"So, you really are alive, Balthine," he said in a tone of dull surprise. His low voice had a coarse edge to it. He tied the line and made a show of tightening it as securely as could be done. Zayne set down the gangplank. "You sure took your time. We were starting to think you were going to bow out, like that coward Lancen."

Zayne shook his head. The truth was, he wanted to. If not for whatever Fae influence Dardan held over him, he would have. "Is this everyone?" he asked, mirroring Xun's concern from earlier.

Ject hesitated, as if surprised by something. Then he snorted. "Everyone that's *left*. When we first set out on this gods accursed expedition, there were ten more ships."

"Twelve," Thanris called over her shoulder. She seemed to be ushering newcomers to the deck but passed that duty to a burly person of indeterminate gender to join Ject and Zayne. Her sand-colored hair was pristinely combed, and she had a much cleaner look to her than Ject, though behind her cheery facade, her eyes had the clouded look of fatigue. "We lost the *Crow Queen* an hour ago, by my reckoning, and the *Gauntlet* was eaten by the thing in the lake sometime before that."

"Oh. Well, that sucks," Ject said dryly. "The *Crow Queen* had that *really* big gun. You know, the one that took down the — well, anyway, we lost a few en route. Some just vanished." He opened his hands as if letting something fly away. "The others, well... you probably saw the *Heron*s coming in?"

"I did."

"Well, I wouldn't invite them to dinner anytime soon."

"Khana fled to the *Black* after her crew started a cannibalistic orgy," Thanris explained. Zayne could barely comprehend the statement, and Thanris' casual tone didn't help. "Apparently, her cabin boy declared himself 'King of All Worlds' and invoked gods no one had ever heard of — all while wearing the First Mate's brain as a hat. While inside of her! Inside the first mate, I mean, not Khana. Khana was fighting her way off the ship at the time."

Zayne shuddered, bile roiling in his stomach. He didn't know what visual was worse. He was half convinced the only thing stopping him from vomiting outright was the sheer absurdity of it.

"Yeah," Ject said wearily. "That's actually not the worst thing that's happened here."

"We don't actually know if anyone on the *Gold* is still alive," Thanris confessed, and there seemed to be embarrassment in her tone. "Xi Lang sent a party to kill the traitors. Then we had to send another to look for *them*. No one's come back."

"You can forget help from the *Summer Sun*, too," Ject sneered. "They set up an altar and started worshipping a leaf or something stupid like that. Don't do anything else. We actually thought they all starved to death until San sent a couple of her crew to go gather whatever supplies they left behind."

"They frenzied, and tore them apart," Thanris finished for him.

"Why are these ships still flying?" Zayne asked. "They sound completely unhinged and are a threat to us all."

"Don't think we haven't thought about it," said Ject. "But Altair and her Dust-addled first mate insist that would make everything worse."

"She likened it to unleashing a plague to fight a head cold," Thanris said. There was a strain in her voice and a tension in her face. Her cool demeanor was starting to flake away, and Zayne had a feeling that she was just downplaying a situation that was causing her no shortage of stress. "Not that it doesn't *feel* like a plague already."

Ject grunted in agreement. "Different stories, same result for the *Moonlit Spider* and the *Kiln Hammer*. And there's been crazies on every ship. My first mate clawed his own eyes out, yelling something about 'seeing the truth', then pulled a murder-suicide on two of my crew by tackling them overboard."

"I just want out," Thanris whispered. "I want to see the sun again. I envy those bastards that went ahead."

Zayne chewed the inside of his cheek as he took in the stories. He was at once terrified for Nanette and grateful that whatever happened to her hadn't been so severe. "Speaking of insanity," he said, "I see the *Kestrel*, but where's Altair?"

"She'll probably be around shortly," Thanris said dismissively. "While *sensible* people have been trying to keep focused on staying sane, Isara has been taking regular ventures out to study… something. She's remarkably consistent about it. With clocks and watches not working right, it's how I keep track of the days."

"Talking about me behind my back?"

Zayne snapped his gaze behind the gathering crews. Altair wore a red, silk deel patterned with black briars, which made her stand out amongst all the black coats. Where Thanris seemed to be putting on a brave front, Altair's smile and relaxed posture as she strolled across the deck appeared genuine. Tatl walked in lockstep behind her, her eyes vacant as always.

"Balthine, come to revel in the splendors of the dream?"

"You know why I'm here, Altair."

She rolled her eyes. "I see being part Fae still hasn't made you any more fun."

"Part *what?*" Thanris and Ject snapped simultaneously.

"That's complicated, and I want to see daylight as much as the rest of you," said Zayne.

"Speak for yourself," Altair mumbled.

"If this is everyone who hasn't gone mad," he continued, "let's lay down the plan of attack. If we're going to die, let it be as ourselves, under the sun."

CHAPTER TWENTY-THREE

The battle hadn't ended with Flint's death, but the *Dreamscape Voyager* and her crew had done their part. Cassidy sat in on protracted meetings over the next couple days, listening to updates. It had been nerve racking at first, but as the hours wore on, she had grown used to runners barging into the room to announce that a given block had been taken or lost. Admiral Ruan — she had apparently been promoted in the carnage — gave orders accordingly after each report. Cassidy followed along as best she could, trying to make sense of the chaos of battle. She liked being farther away from it, but it seemed so abstract from the safety of the war room.

It was late into the night of the second day when victory was declared. Two of Flint's captains had surrendered and been taken into custody. The rest had been killed. The battle had deteriorated into blind riots that were then quashed. Cassidy hadn't relished in hearing the details. She had returned to her ship in the middle of the discussion about their sentencing.

The *Dreamscape* had taken some damage, but nothing too serious. The trouble was, with all the devastation, the city's infrastructure was the priority. She knew she could flash the Empress' writ and get whatever she wanted, but she was loath to pull workers away from their own desperate community. So, it was up to them to deal with it themselves.

Cassidy, half asleep and slumped against the gunwale, watched the sunrise. Some plumes of smoke still blotched parts of the view, but she could really see the horror of the light pouring through the cracks. They had cut trenches through the city. Here and there Cassidy spotted a few rooftops still supported by its pillars even though the walls were destroyed, which only served to highlight the desolation. It felt so surreal looking at it, the way dreams used to.

"Ahoy, captain," called Kek.

Cassidy turned her head lazily. Kek was accompanied by Miria. "Did you sleep?" she asked them.

"A little," said Kek, and the lingering fatigue was clear in his voice.

Miria shook her head. "I couldn't," she said. "I should probably see how the recovery is going."

"You aren't the princess here, princess," Cassidy croaked. She managed a tired grin, but Miria didn't return it.

"Forgive me, captain, but I have a duty to these people."

"You charged into battle with a sword," Cassidy reminded her. "Besides, they don't know who you really are, so what's the harm?" Miria's shoulders slumped. Cassidy couldn't tell if she was disappointed or relieved. "Kek, I think the Lord Minister said something about a tavern being open. Take Miria and help her unwind."

"Aye, aye, Captain," Kek said. "I damn sure could use a drink."

"Aye," Miria said woodenly. "I think that would help wonders."

Cassidy smiled weakly as they disembarked. Kek took Miria's arm like a Castilyn gentleman, and Cassidy wondered when he'd learned to do that. When she was sure they were out of earshot, she pulled her hat off, gesturing for Hymn to sit on her knee. The Fae obliged with a graceful flutter.

"What is it?"

"We have a lot to talk about. I'm not quite sure where to begin."

"Try the beginning," the Fae replied. Was she being flippant? Cassidy couldn't tell.

But the beginning made a certain sense. "Where were you?" she asked bluntly. "During the battle."

There was a slight buzz in the air as Hymn began to hover. The way the light twisted, it seemed like she was looking for something. "I was trying to keep Atarshai away from you," she said eventually.

"Why?"

"I am bound to protect you within the limits of my power."

Cassidy raised her brow. Perhaps she was just too tired to think straight, but she felt like Hymn could have said that no matter what she asked. She knew if she brought it up, though, it would lead to an argument about semantics, which she was not in the mood for.

"And how did Atarshai know you were in the city?"

"I made my presence known when I destroyed those cannons that were aimed at you."

Cassidy grunted in acknowledgement. That had been quite the spectacle — talk on the loyalist side said one of the rebels must have blown it up on accident, or a loyalist sacrificed themselves. Both served the purposes of making the Empire's forces look good and its enemies foolish, but they didn't know about Hymn — but there was still something bothering her.

"The mercs mentioned Len." She flinched and hit her head when Hymn's light suddenly turned from its usual gentle blue into a deep vermillion.

"What did they say, *exactly*?" Hymn asked severely. The edge in her voice terrified Cassidy, and she immediately scrambled to remember what the mercenaries said.

"She — one of the mercenaries — said that Atarshai talked about her before disappearing. Something like, cursing her for… leaving work undone?"

A tremor flickered across Hymn's light before it slowly faded back to blue. Cassidy likened it to a human sigh. Had she been worried that Len was also in the city?

"Len tried to kill me," Hymn said.

Cassidy sat up straighter. "When was this?"

"To you it would have been an exceedingly long time ago. But you need not worry about my history. What else did you wish to discuss?"

Cassidy swallowed a lump in her throat, trying to order her thoughts. She wasn't sure how to address either subject. *You asked about the first thing first,* she told herself, *what happened next?*

"I saw the future," she said. "Twice."

Hymn set back down on Cassidy's knee. She seemed to be considering her anew. "Yes, I thought I felt a tremor. You veered off the course you were set."

"I wha— er, yes," Cassidy fumbled. "But I don't understand how, or why, or… it was all so confusing."

Hymn began to float again, this time drifting in circles, as though she were pacing. Finally, she settled herself about a foot away from Cassidy's face. "The future is full of possibilities," she said. "You might decide to remain here until you fall asleep. You might follow your friends to the tavern. Whatever choice you make unfolds into consequences."

Hymn descended, flying mere inches above the deck. Ethereal light emanated from the wood in her wake, until she stopped and the line broke and forked around her. "Those consequences beget more choices," she continued, and the light began to expand, with the diverging points breaking apart into more branches. Some paths curved like a river while others bent hard, and others remained steady. Cassidy stood up to take in the luminous artwork. As the patterns continued to weave, Cassidy thought it resembled a tree.

"Endless possibilities. When you say you saw the future, however…" There was a *snap* in the air, and a single point in the glowing tree turned red. The path that led to it began to melt from the gentle soothing blue to a furious scarlet, weaving around blue until it returned to the starting point Hymn had first created.

The single red path stood out against the myriad of blue, which began to blur in Cassidy's vision. "It would be more accurate to say you saw *a* future. But in their hearts, mortals are drawn to what they know, and once you see the end of the path, it becomes easier to walk. Your soul knows the way to that outcome."

Just like Asier, Cassidy thought. *She had seen the future as a child and followed it to the end.* "But I stopped it from happening," she said.

"Sometimes when you walk a city, you leave the main street to avoid an obstacle, or because there is somewhere else you would rather be. The future is no different. It was difficult because you were trading certainty for the unknown, on a level far beyond the cognitive. It is not something mortals were not born to comprehend or experience, but there are always those who try.

"There are those who can see the entire scope of possibility, as you might a map, or my representation here, but that is a rare gift among my kind." The elaborate pattern of light disappeared abruptly.

"But… how did it happen? And why that future?"

"Foretelling is a curious gift," Hymn replied. "Perhaps you saw the most likely futures."

"But they only came close to happening because I saw them coming."

"Seeing the future changes the future," Hymn said simply. "Now if there is nothing else, you need your rest."

"No, there is more," Cassidy insisted. "What happened to Flint? With Atarshai?"

Hymn sat stoically silent.

"Hymn?" Cassidy pressed impatiently.

"Atarshai took possession of the mercenary's body."

"But why? Why do Fae possess people? What do they gain?"

Hymn hesitated. "There are different sorts of possession, and different motives. I shall address what happened here: there are feats," she said slowly, "that only my kind can accomplish. Then, there are human traits that my kind cannot replicate. And then, there are things that can only be accomplished by the merging of our blood. When one of us takes control of a human vessel, our weaknesses are… diminished. Our power might be diminished as well, but even a small portion of our strength is superior to human might.

"I can only assume Atarshai possessed the mercenary to save him from you. He was clearly an asset in… whatever this was supposed to accomplish," Hymn finished, addressing the swaths of destruction.

"And… Atarshai is *dead?*"

"Yes."

Cassidy shuddered. She knew Hymn had sought her out for protection, but the notion of Fae *dying* was something else entirely. The prospect was as alien as killing a nightmare.

"Now, if I have satisfied your curiosity, you really ought to rest."

If anything, Cassidy's curiosity had only grown more heightened, but with it came an intense anxiety. And Hymn was right. She was exhausted. She had been drawing on her Fae connection just to stay awake. Her nose had started bleeding again. She wiped her face before fumbling for her matchbook. "I'm not ready for any of this," she confessed. She lit her cigarette and stared out at the city. So much death, so much destruction. And their enemy had been human. What chance did they have against something so vast and unknowable as the leviathan?

"No one ever is," Hymn replied evenly. "That is the cost of doing the right thing."

"So, you admit what we're doing is right?" Cassidy asked. She smirked as Hymn said nothing.

She breathed in the cigarette smoke, letting it fill her lungs, longing for that familiar relief to sooth the edge of her anxiety. The relief didn't come. Instead, she felt pain rack her chest. Rather than soothing warmth, her lungs felt like they were on fire, at once collapsing and expanding beyond their limits and bursting open. She opened her mouth. She didn't know if she meant to gasp for air or to scream, but she could do neither. She clawed at her own throat. Her ears started ringing. Tears blurred her vision. Her muscles began to spasm. She kicked and squirmed on the deck, thrashing in desperation. She heaved, spewing blood on the deck.

The episode ended as quickly as it began. Cassidy's chest convulsed one last time and she gasped deeply, her throat scratching the whole time. She blinked the tears away to find Nieves staring down at her, holding her.

"What happened?" she asked, glaring daggers at Hymn.

Cassidy shifted her gaze between Nieves and the Fae, though the effort made her dizzy. The Fae emitted a pale red light. "Cassidy," Hymn said softly. Her voice was gentle in a way Cassidy had never heard before. "You should have heeded my warnings. You have pushed yourself beyond your physical limits for far too long, relied too heavily on forces you do not comprehend." She hesitated. "You are dying."

"What?" Nieves shrieked. She reached out like a blur and snatched Hymn between her fingers. "She trusted you!"

Cassidy's head whirled as she struggled to make sense. She was *dying*? That made no sense. And Nieves was…

"Stop," Cassidy rasped. She'd meant to shout it, to demand it, but she was too weak. She couldn't even slap Nieves' hand. Instead, she dully flopped her own hand on top of her friend's. "Don't hurt her."

"Cassidy, her influence is killing you! By her own admission."

"She saved me," Cassidy countered, somehow feeling both weak and resolute. "She saved Kek, and Miria. All of us. Please, don't hurt her."

It was a rare thing to see the kind of unbridled anger in Nieves' eyes that she saw now along with her tears. Cassidy seriously thought she might try to rip the Fae in half. But she opened her hand, letting Hymn go.

"What's happening to her?" Nieves demanded. "How do we stop it?"

"It is a combination of factors," Hymn said slowly. "She pushes herself further than her body will allow by numbing herself to the pain, using our connection. I already knew that to be a problem, and warned her frequently. But it seems the power she draws on is itself not sustainable with the limits of the human body." She turned to address Cassidy directly again. "It is burning your body from within. Rotting you."

"How do we stop it?" Nieves repeated, at the same time Cassidy asked, "How long do I have?"

Hymn flitted between facing Nieves and Cassidy, as if unsure who to answer. "There will be no stopping it," she said solemnly. "The only hope she has is to slow it. If you persist as you have, drawing on the connection constantly in your waking hours... you will die before this year ends."

Cassidy's heart grew cold. "And... if I stop?"

Hymn considered her. "If you stop completely, from this moment on, you might live to see another five years." Cassidy slumped into Nieves' embrace. *Five years?* Five years was so little time. Her mind reeled as she tried to think of things that might be left undone, sights left unseen. She never regretted the life she had chosen, but she expected to keep living it for a while yet.

Then she remembered the leviathan. She couldn't live her own life, no matter how short, while that thing was still out there. Even without the Empress' edict on the matter, the fear and knowledge of it would always be a shadow on the horizon. She needed to kill it, so what few years she had left could be her own.

She pulled herself out of Nieves' grip and to her feet. They had wasted too much time. She needed to find the Lord Minister to finalize their agreement.

"Cassidy," Nieves said, "why don't you rest, and I'll get Lierre to —"

"No!" Cassidy shouted, and blood sputtered from her lips like spittle. Nieves wiped it from her cheek, keeping her eyes locked with Cassidy's. "No," she repeated, more softly this time. "I don't want to worry anyone else. We have enough going on."

"Cassidy, we have to tell—"

"Don't you have an obligation to keep your patient's secrets?"

"You know damn well I never finished my surgeon training, and never took the damn oath."

"Then it's an order!" Cassidy snapped.

"An order?" Nieves repeated incredulously.

"Aye. Do not tell *anyone* about this."

Nieves looked ready to spit. "Aye, aye, *captain,*" she sneered. She turned to leave, calling over her shoulder, "I'll keep your damn secret, but mark me, you're making a mistake."

Cassidy looked down at the deck, at the still smoldering cigarette sitting there. She felt a lot like that cigarette, burning, useless, falling apart. *Five years.* She released the soothing numbness for the first time in days, and the full exertion of the battle hit her all at once. Her knees buckled and she nearly fell over again. It was hard to parse what merely ached from what was agonizing because she had been cutting herself off from all of it for so long. Her legs spasmed and her arms shook like rattles. She stamped out the cigarette with bitter remorse, wishing she could instead take comfort from it.

"Five years," she repeated out loud. "Let's make them count."

CHAPTER TWENTY-FOUR

The way home was far less inconspicuous than the ways into the Dreamscape had been. Where the *Scorpion* had entered through an obscure rock formation, and the fleet had passed through a set of trees growing in an abandoned valley, now they were all faced with a structure that was clearly man made; impressions passed on by Lucandri confirmed it; if it had been crafted by the Fae, it would have had a more natural form.

The gate was embedded in the flat side of a mountain, perfectly circular and a hundred feet wide. The ring was made of countless painstakingly arranged bricks of smooth marble engraved with strange glyphs. The tunnel was unfathomably deep and dark.

Who made this, Zayne wondered, *and for what purpose?* Although it seemed simple in design, it was an incomprehensible feat of engineering. Had desperate people been trapped like Zayne and the Daughters, driven to create a way home? Or had some grander ambition been at play? And had it accomplished its purpose?

The stone had no answers.

The Daughters' fleet converged in front of the threshold. The Scorpion led the armada, but Zayne could feel the tension in the air. Everyone still sane was eager to see the sun again. Of course, Altair had been upset about leaving. He suspected that when all was said and done, she wouldn't follow the rest of the Daughters to Castilyn.

"Are you ready?" he asked Nanette.

"Can you *ever* be ready for this?"

"Point," he conceded. "Let's start a war."

The *Scorpion's* sails snapped as the unnatural wind filled them. The darkness enveloped them rapidly. Zayne had never been especially afraid of the dark, but this was different. Something primal in his guts was screaming to flee and find light. He bit his tongue so hard it bled, which quelled the unease just enough to realize it wasn't his own.

So Lucandri is afraid of the dark, he thought. He would try to take advantage of that later.

Somewhere along the way, there was a perceptible change in the air. The scent of spice all but evaporated, replaced by the smell of dirt and soil and trees. Stars winked in and out of existence above them. No, not stars. Sunlight was breaking through some kind of barrier.

Blinding light exploded, encompassing everything. The music and gentle winds of the Dreamscape were shattered by the cacophony of churning engines come to life. Zayne blinked until the afternoon came into focus. They had done it. They had appeared above the city, over the western-most mountain on the range, the Temple District.

Relief washed over him like a hurricane in the desert as both he and Lucandri drank in the sun. Soothing warmth seeped through his veins, flowed through his lungs, and enveloped his skin, keeping the wind's chill at bay. Pains he had been so accustomed to lifted, and for the first time he could remember, he felt whole.

A quartet of cannon blasts tore through a busy marketplace. Burning oil coated the *Silent Song*'s munitions as they bombarded the unsuspecting people. Zayne could hear the screams above the din of the fleet's engines. The *Knight in Mourning* was firing her rotary gun along the length of the street as they passed overhead, and Zayne watched the people scurry and frenzy like animals. His stomach roiled as the streets were splotched with blood. Lucky San's gunner was far too good a shot.

Other ships joined in the pointless slaughter. The *King in Yellow* swooped low into a broad street, firing cannons on both port and starboard to indiscriminately destroy everything in her wake. The *Illusion of Justice* opened her underside hatch, dumping thousands of pounds of burning sludge right on top of a major thoroughfare. As the fleet reached the edge of the district, the *Widow Merchant* fired her forward guns and obliterated the ferry that carried the city's citizens between peaks and the *King in Yellow* destroyed the foot bridge.

Zayne watched survivors scream in terror before they disappeared over the ledge. He folded his arms to hide his trembling. None of this death was necessary. He almost wanted the city's defense to intercede faster, to stop the wanton slaughter, though he knew it wouldn't help; the City Watch had ships just off the port, but they were poorly armed, since they were only expected to deal with minor infractions. The ships of the Imperial Navy, conversely, were well armed but stationed further out to intercept threats *before* they reached the city.

Zayne watched from the prow as the people below were herded by violence, congealing into an indistinct mass that scurried for safety. Some crammed into homes or brothels or shops, only for their shelter to be torn down or blasted apart. Others were corralled into dead ends while the mercenaries used them for petty sport. It sickened him, and not just for his aversion to blood, or the shadows of his past. He knew some found killing easier when the bodies were piled high enough that somehow you couldn't put faces or names to the dead; when you couldn't know their stories; when they were numbers in a report somewhere. Zayne couldn't find that shelter; all the distance did was give his mind a canvas to paint on familiar faces. Each explosion took mothers and brothers and sisters and friends and unsuspecting bystanders, men defending the innocent, women just doing their duty. He couldn't claim to be innocent. He had been killing most of his adult life. But he had never killed for fun, never allowed his crew to do so. When Salaa had been his captain, he had always urged her, if not to mercy, to restraint.

This, he reminded himself, *is why I don't belong among them.*

Half the second district was on fire before the first ships of the City Watch intercepted them. Three full-sized junks arrived from the south, with more inbound. They made an attempt to form a blockade and deployed longboats to meet the Daughters.

"Orders, captain?" Nanette asked.

Zayne chewed the inside of his cheek. "Stay the course. Fire at will." The words were like oil in his mouth.

Nanette shouted into the pipeline, "Fire at will!"

There was only a moment's hesitation before one of the *Scorpion*'s forward guns fired, bucking the ship with the recoil. One of the longboats exploded in a shower of splinters and smoke. A few moments later, the second shot rocked the ship. It sailed harmlessly between the next longboat and its balloon, crashing into the hull of the ship behind it. It wasn't a crippling shot, however.

The *Scorpion* rammed into the approaching longboat, smashing the smaller vessel. Some of the Watch were knocked off to their deaths, but those who held on climbed aboard. Zayne could feel them scrambling onto the hull like ants on his skin. He gritted his teeth.

Six boarders, he counted. Only four climbed to the deck. Two were using hooks to climb around the hull to flank them, or to sabotage them. Zayne flexed his hand, closing it just as Dawn Star appeared beneath his fingers. The attacking Watchmen were taken aback by the conjured weapon, and Zayne threw it like a spear. When the sword's golden blade drove through a woman's chest, he felt the blood running down its edge, her heart beating its last around the unnatural metal, as though he had stuck his own hand inside her. The feeling was revolting, and flashes of memory, the sight of his mother bleeding from countless knife wounds, staggered him with nausea.

Dawn Star vanished in a flash of light and blood spurted from its victim's gaping wound before she fell limp to the deck, tripping the man who had boarded behind her. The unnatural sword reappeared in Zayne's hand, and he threw it again. This time, a young man saved his elderly compatriot by shoving him out of the way and taking the blade in the shoulder. The blade vanished again, and Zayne drew the falcon-pommeled dueling sword from his belt.

Compared to Dawn Star, the iron blade felt heavy in his hand, but it was a comfortable weight, and with a weapon of cold iron, he didn't have to feel the sensations on the other end. He severed the hand of the older Watchmen as the man leveled a pistol at him. He caught the weapon in the air and shot the wounded young man with it. The blood splattered on the deck felt like it was drying on his skin. The last of the four attackers lashed out at Zayne with a flurry of overhanded blows, only for his head to explode when Nanette shot him.

"Boarders, port side, forty degrees!" Zayne shouted at her.

Nanette dropped the spent pistol and pulled a loaded one from the small of her back. Just as one of the boarders popped her head above the gunwale, Nanette fired, blowing the woman's scalp apart. The *Scorpion* rammed into one of the junks that had placed itself in their way, dislodging the remaining climber with the force of the blow. As the two ships scraped against one another, Xun opened fire with the rotary, spraying the enemy deck with bullets. She was almost as good a shot as the *Knight's* gunner. Six men died, leaving only the helmsman topside. The other two vessels were destroyed by the combined fire of four of the Daughters' ships.

Four more Watch boats were in position to intercept. "Stay on target," Zayne ordered. "Basir will handle them." As if on cue, the *King In Yellow* broke off from the fleet to meet the opposition, accompanied by the *Black Heron*.

The *Silent Song* and some of the others continued to attack the defenseless populace below, wreaking terror to the proud capital of the Empire. The cannon fire became a steady rhythm, and the screams were drowned out in the rumble of debris and concussive blasts.

Zayne kept his eyes up, away from the death, towards the Jade Palace. It looked much like it had on his first visit, massively tiered with towering pagodas that watched over the city. But there was something different about it, something he had not seen with wholly human eyes. There was a thin veneer of green light crawling over every surface of the palace walls, swirling and shifting like shadows in the Dreamscape. If the infiltrators didn't do their job, Zayne would never be able to set foot inside, and all this was for naught.

The fleet crossed into the Palace District, and once again the crossing ferries were shot down and the footbridge was destroyed. Zayne trembled, partly in sickness and frustration, but more because there was a part of him, Lucandri's part, that was reveling in the slaughter. It was a vindictive sort of catharsis, like the petty vengeance of a child. The part of him that was still himself tried to shut out what happened below, but his mind was assaulted with the imaginings of the people fleeing for safety, watching as their neighbors and loved ones died horrifically, or worse, penned in by fire and rubble or just unlucky enough to be caught in a blast.

Four naval ships arrived on the scene when the Scorpion was about halfway through the district to the palace. He caught sight of two of their names — the *Phoenix Legacy* and the *Dusk Prince* — as they formed an impromptu blockade ahead of the *Scorpion*.

Zayne hit the deck as the *Legacy* unloaded its rotary gun on them. The concussion of one of the Scorpion's forward cannons was followed by a tremendous crash. Zayne felt the impact beneath his feet and through the ship as well as feeling the pain *of* the ship as the hull was ripped open.

Shen's voice shrieked over the pipeline. "Lost the starboard head cannon!"

Zayne growled in pain, clutching his chest, even though he didn't feel it in his own body. "I noticed!" he snapped, though he only had himself to talk to. "Nanette, fifteen degrees to port. Maintain the speed."

As the ship turned, Zayne summoned Dawn Star again. He stood on the prow, and in the moment before the *Scorpion* collided with the *Legacy*, he threw the Fae sword, this time letting it spin as it arced through the air. The weapon skewered the enemy pilot's hand, pinning him to the wheel. As Zayne hoped, the pilot unwittingly leaned into the wheel, causing the *Legacy* to yield as the *Scorpion* shoved through.

The *Knight in Mourning* rammed the *Legacy* from the other side, locking her between the *Knight* and the *Scorpion*. A scrawny crewman from the *Legacy* drew on Zayne. The moment he cocked the hammer, a red and black feathered bird swooped down and grasped him and another man in its thick talons, tossing them like dice to the winds to fall to the streets. The pistol was fired blindly, accomplishing nothing.

Andrasta dived below the *Legacy*, picking out whatever sailors fell in her reach. Most she tossed aside, as if displeased, but she launched one man skyward only to soar and catch in her beak, ripping his guts out before gorging on them and spraying viscera on his allies. She let out a whistling caw before returning to the *Kestrel*, en route towards the *Dusk Prince*, which was suffering heavy bombardment.

How did she train that thing? Zayne wondered. Knowing Altair, though, it probably involved her illegal Dreamscape experiments.

The *Knight's* crew boarded the *Legacy* to kill the survivors, so the *Scorpion* pushed ahead unmolested. More ships were inbound, but no one could stop the Daughters from reaching the palace. The ethereal green light still shrouded the structure, however, and Zayne wondered if maybe that was the reason the Empire had adopted jade as the royal color.

As the *Scorpion* forsook the senseless slaughter, she was the first ship to reach the outer walls. Nanette turned hard to port, giving Xun access to shoot down any defenders on the gates. Like the city watch, they were ill prepared for a full-scale assault so deep into the city, but a stray shot could still kill any one of them, and Zayne had always flown the *Scorpion* with minimal crew. He was starting to regret his lack of trust in that regard.

Zayne eyed that gleaming Fae barrier that crawled over the main structure. *Bring it down,* he thought tensely, and something in the pattern of thinking clued him in that Lucandri was thinking the same thing. It made sense; if the barrier didn't fall, they would be pinned to the wall, and the Fae's fate was tied to Zayne. Of course, the Fae was also eager for blood. And vengeance, though he wasn't sure what he could possibly want to avenge on the Empress.

There was a recognizable discipline to the palace guards' response. Though they must have been every bit as surprised by the sudden appearance of the Daughters as the city had been, the *Scorpion* had only killed a single wave before the response from inside the palace escalated. Mobile cannons fired from the pagodas, crashing into the *Scorpion*'s hull like heavy fists to Zayne's skull. Bombs fell from overhead, shattering in clouds of smoke and shrapnel that tore at the deck. An array of hooks latched to the gunwales, and five boarders climbed rapidly in an attempt to overwhelm and bring them down.

Shen fired the head cannon, breaching the palace's walls and bucking the *Scorpion* yet again. In the brief moment where the boarders struggled to keep their feet, Zayne drew and fired a shot at the middlemost attacker, catching him in the throat. The man clawed at the wound as he fell to his knees to drown on his own blood.

The woman beside him spun and lashed out against Zayne with an axe-bladed spear. He parried with his spent pistol, but the blow was too strong. The blade scraped across his mask and knocked his head aside. He crouched low to avoid the next strike of the spear. One of the other soldiers grew overzealous, thinking to skewer Zayne while he was down. Instead, he stepped in front of the first woman's wind up and got his throat chopped by the haft of her spear.

Zayne felt a shift in the aft of the ship and stepped to the right a mere moment before a six-foot long shaft of wood blew through the spear-wielder in a blur before skidding across the deck and skipping overboard. With painstaking slowness, the woman looked down at the fist-sized gaping hole in her abdomen.

Heavy waves of sickness slammed against Zayne's stomach. He could see clear to the other side, and some of her guts were falling out. Her spear fell from numb fingers. One of her companions — a stocky man with a scar on his nose — screamed and ran past Zayne, his gaze fixed on Aresh perched on the Scorpion Tail. The pirate threw his hands up in a crude gesture. But Nanette threw a knife in

233

the Imperial's eye, causing him to stumble and hit the deck with a graceless *thud*.

The last two boarders — a man and a woman — drew swords; not the thin dueling blades that had become popular among the common people with the rise of Castilyn fashion, but the broader jian, a heavier breed of weapon. Zayne flourished his falcon sword in challenge.

He ducked under a sweeping slash, then back stepped away to parry a thrust. But he didn't have the leverage to redirect his opponent, and the enemy's drive cut his sleeve. He feinted, leading from the woman's left only to turn on the man. She slashed at his face, and Zayne caught the blade with the basket guard of the falcon sword at the same moment Dawn Star appeared in his outstretched hand, its blade manifesting in the man's chest. His dying, shuddering breath did nothing to quell Zayne's burgeoning sickness, and only his battle-heightened senses kept him from succumbing.

Zayne shifted his hold on Dawn Star ever so slightly, and made the sword vanish only to reform it in a reverse grip. The golden metal appeared in the woman's ribs and assaulted Zayne's mind with miserable sensations. She pulled herself off the Fae weapon, and Zayne thought she might try to fight through the wound. Instead, she raised her sword only to drop it and collapse.

Zayne paced the deck, eager to keep his blood up, lest he be paralyzed by his weakness. He turned his attention to the entrance Shen had made.

The damn barrier was still up. The gaping hole in the wall had been a lucky enough shot — Shen hadn't destroyed too much of the floor, meaning Zayne would have a place to land — but that didn't mean anything as long as that green light was still keeping him out.

More of the Daughters' ships converged on the palace, but the navy was in hot pursuit. As the *Kestrel* arrived, Andrasta carried Altair and Tatl on her back through the opening in the wall. Seconds later, the bird flew back out alone and rejoined the battle. The *Silent Song* arrived next and Ject took a running jump off his deck into the palace as they passed. The *Illusion of Justice* made a strafing run and as she did so, Del Thanris swung from a rope and launched herself inside.

"Zayne!" Nanette called, her voice urgent, "If you don't get moving soon, we'll be pinned!"

234

Zayne looked, seeing the naval forces were almost on top of them. There were enough Daughters to give them a fight, but that was small comfort if the *Scorpion* was shot down first.

"The damn barrier is still up!" Zayne fired back irritably.

"How can you —" Nanette began, but the barrier flashed red for a brief instant before the light shattered like glass and faded away. It must have been visible to mortal eyes as well as his own because Nanette looked alarmed.

"Get me close," Zayne ordered. Nanette obeyed, and Zayne followed Ject's example, taking a running leap. In the first moment after he'd cleared the gunwale, he worried he had misjudged the distance. But he cleared the rubble-strewn breach and landed amidst the debris. He clamored to his feet and watched the *Scorpion* make her retreat.

"So, *that* was the Fae barrier," Altair mused. "I wonder why the whole city isn't protected like that."

"Don't know," Zayne retorted, "don't care. In a crisis like this, I think the Empress should be in her throne room. It's reinforced and —"

A scream cut him off. He turned down the hall to find a matronly woman and a young boy — both in blood-stained robes of servant's grey — running through the rubble. *Towards* the group of armed invaders. As they retreated, shrieking all the while, Zayne saw the bodies, torn apart and strewn on the floor behind them.

Something else was already in the palace killing people.

CHAPTER TWENTY-FIVE

Shadows scurried along the floor like giant insects, chasing after the servants. Before they made it halfway to the Daughters, two massive, black, snarling figures rose up out of the floor. To Zayne, they resembled dogs — at least, if he had only ever seen dogs in his worst nightmares. For a start, they were far too large; even on all fours, they were half as tall as he was and ridiculously muscular. The tops of their heads were bone, and they had thin, sharp horns and tusks. A strange, thick, dark liquid poured from their jaws, causing the floor to sizzle even as it evaporated into red and purple smoke. Their tails were thick cords with blades made of bone at the end. Worst of all, however, were their eyes: swirling and ever shifting gradients of black and yellow that seemed to be composed of liquids of different viscosities sharing a space. Zayne didn't need Lucandri's confirmation to know these nightmares for what they were.

They were the Dread Hounds.

They bounded after the servants. The edges of their bodies blurred like tapering flames as they moved. One caught the boy on the edges of its tusks, ripping his arm off and stretching out sinew and muscles until they snapped and tore without ever slowing. The beast trampled the child, kicking him into the path of the other monster as it lunged, biting the woman, engulfing her entire upper body, violently tearing her apart at the hips and chomping greedily on her. The second Hound consumed what was left of the boy in two bites.

For the first time in his life, Zayne's fear completely drove his sickness out of mind.

What are they doing here? The thought repeated in his mind with different connotations; the part of him that was still Zayne wanted to know why the world's greatest horrors were in front of him. *Lucandri*'s influence, however, had him legitimately concerned with why they were here, *specifically*; the impression Zayne had was that while they slaughtered prey indiscriminately and had an insatiable hunger, they tended to only appear where they were *sent*. Did Dardan have *this* kind of influence? Zayne didn't think she did.

He hoped against hope he was right, but ultimately, he supposed it didn't matter; *someone* had sent the Dread Hounds, be it Dardan, a Fae, a god, or some other player in the game.

The canine beasts turned to face Zayne and the others, snarling and showcasing their blood-stained teeth. Ject stepped to the front of the group, clutching a hand axe in each fist. The Hounds let out a synchronous, trilling roar. Zayne thought it sounded like laughter. They loped across the corridor, one of the dogs taking strides on the *wall* when the other invaded its space on the floor. Ject ran to meet them, but with their superior speed and range of motion, he didn't have far to move.

The Hound that ran on the wall kicked off to cut ahead of the other and thrashed its head to swing its tusks at Ject. He leaned back farther than Zayne would have thought possible without losing his balance, letting the beast's attack pass harmlessly overhead. He straightened and leaped above the suddenly thrashing tail as it whirled around. He spun in the air, letting his axes strike with his rotation. The first blade sparked as it scratched the Hound's bone-plate just above the eye. Completing his turn, the second axe sprayed a fountain of blood.

The Dread Hound's blood was red, the same as human blood, or maybe just a touch darker. But rather than splatter and stain the palace walls and floors, after its initial spray, it turned into a deep, red smoke while the wound bubbled and hissed. Ject hadn't touched back down to the floor when the beast struck him with its forepaw. The impact was hard enough Ject bounced twice before skidding to a halt. Zayne thought the other man was dead, but he pushed himself up with the points of his axes and clapped them together.

Del Thanris broke into a run to join the fight, spear at the ready. She aimed herself at the beast that Ject hadn't cut. Her target took half a step back to evade, but she used her spear to vault over its head. There must have been a hidden switch somewhere on her weapon because a length of chain began spilling out from the pommel. She twisted in the air and wrapped the metal links around the Hound's throat before landing behind it. The air sizzled as steam and smoke rolled off the beast's skin and fur where the iron made contact.

Zayne stayed back, trying to find a pattern or rhythm to exploit, or barring that, a chance to retreat. The first of the Dread

Hounds lashed out against Ject, eliciting a sharp growl with each snap of its jaws. The axe man wove around the gnashing fangs, but he couldn't land another strike on the beast. The second tugged against Thanris' chain, pulling her off her feet and dragging her across the floor. She hit the wall and released the spear.

Altair reached into the sleeve of her deel and extracted a drawstring bag that rattled like dice. She tossed it to her first mate, who caught it without expression. "Tatl," said Altair, "give me strength."

The blonde looked at the bag in her hand with dull confusion, then turned to the Dread Hounds. "Speed would serve you better," she said sleepily.

The *Kestrel's* captain bit her thumbnail thoughtfully. "If you think it wise. Speed, then."

Tatl dug into the satchel and sifted through its rattling contents before extracting a long fingerbone. She held it up to the light, cocked her head to the side, then put it back, looking for something else. One of the hounds struck Ject in the gut, and he struck the floor so hard it cracked under his weight.

"If you're going to do something," Zayne said as he drew a pistol and readied his falcon blade, "now's the time."

"You can't rush perfection," Altair said lazily as Tatl inspected another fingerbone. The woman placed it back in the bag and resumed her search.

Ject strained to push himself up off the floor, but when the Hound opened its jaws to bare down on him, he shoved off to one side and slashed blindly with his axe. Sparks flew from the beast's jaws, and it bubbled and sizzled like cooking meat.

Behind them, a door crashed open. "Surrender in the name of — *what in the mists?*"

Zayne risked a look back, finding three palace guards with spears half-raised staring dumbstruck at the Dread Hounds. One of the women dropped her spear and fled the way from which she'd come, while another seemed completely petrified by fear. The third, however, looked from the Hounds to the mercenaries, and appeared to be weighing the situation.

"I found one," Tatl announced dully, holding up another fingerbone. To Zayne, it looked no different from the others. She handed it over to her captain, who put it in her mouth between her back teeth and bit down. Her face contorted with strain as she pressed down on the bone. Drool poured in a steady stream from her half-open mouth.

"What are you doing?" Zayne demanded.

She ignored him and continued to bite down so hard Zayne thought she might break her teeth. He thought that was what happened when he heard the crack. She swallowed.

Then she was *gone*. Only a heavy breeze remained between Zayne and Tatl. Zayne ventured a look back at the guards and sickness broke through fear and confusion as he found them both impaled on their own weapons. The wind in the corridor changed directions and Altair was beside him. Then she was gone again.

A spear blossomed in the eye of the Dread Hounds. When it thrashed its head back in pain and screamed, Altair was crouched atop its skull. Then the spear was gone, and Altair was holding the spear in the Hound's throat. Zayne had seen no intervening motion between any two points, and only the billowing of her hair and the sleeves of her deel suggested she had actually moved. The hound snapped at her, but its jaws were empty when they slammed shut. Altair appeared atop the Dread Hound's skull, driving the spear point in the bone. Blood geysered from the wound and turned to smoke in the madwoman's face.

The edges of the monster's frame became even less substantial, and Altair fell into a crouch on the floor as it became intangible as smoke. Its image vanished, but its shadow was still cast on the floor. The shadow ran, leaving behind the Dread Hound with Thanris' chain wrapped around it. It was giving chase to Thanris who wove around its legs.

It's toying with her, Zayne realized.

"Well, Balthine?" Altair asked. She remained crouched; one hand braced on the floor like she was thinking about pushing herself up but hadn't quite committed to it. The veins in her face were bulging and had become so red they were almost black. Blood was streaming out of her eyes, from her nose, and out her mouth. Zayne's sickness at the sight sent tremors through him as he held back the dry heaves. "Are you going to do your part already?" she snapped.

He turned away from the madwoman and fired his pistol at the remaining Dread Hound. The bullet missed the creature's eye by inches, and its skull sparked and burned where the iron hit it. It whipped its head away from its prey and turned to face him. It reached him in a single bound. He rolled under the snapping jaws. He drove the falcon blade between its ribs. Its blood burned like acid as it sprayed him, then evaporated into acrid smoke. It howled in agony and twisted above him. Zayne's sword was wrenched from his hand and skittered across the floor.

Zayne rolled out of the way as the Hound brought its heavy paw down. Though he avoided being crushed, its claws gouged his back. He scrambled to a crouch and lunged forward, snatching his ornate weapon and brandishing it. The blade had been snapped clean, leaving him only six inches of the weapon.

The beast stalked towards him, but there was a strange jitter in the way it moved. Zayne eyed its ribs, noting the way the blood spurted and boiled. The rest of his blade was still inside it.

He tossed the broken sword aside and drew Dawn Star from the air instead. The Dread Hound lunged, more slowly than before but it was still wild and terrible to behold. He narrowly avoided being gored like the serving boy. Instead, the tusk glided along his ribs, cutting through his coat, vest, and shirt, drawing blood. In exchange, he ran his golden sword across the Hound's face, from snout to its eye. Unlike iron weapons, Dawn Star did not spark against the eldritch creature's skin or bones, nor make them sizzle. The Fae weapon cut it cleanly, though its blood still turned to smoke after a moment. The Hound shrieked in pain.

Zayne fell into a fighting stance more situated for a spear than a sword, with his empty hand leading and his sword hand drawn all the way back, the tip of his blade aimed for the beast's heart. The beast's muscles coiled as it readied to pounce, and Ject roared as he slammed both of his blades deep into the Hound's hind calves, causing it to buckle. The Hound whirled back to retaliate and Thanris shoved Ject out of the way. Its jaws sank around her shoulder.

A muffled blast sounded.

The Hound collapsed without a sound. Thanris stumbled backwards, taking three steps away before coming to a wobbly halt. The bloody stump where her arm had been sizzled as acid ate away her clothes and skin. She stared at the dark, wet splotch with glassy, uncomprehending eyes. She swayed in place, working her mouth as if to say something.

At her feet, the Dread Hound's skin was flaking away and swirling in the open air like dust. Its bones broke down. At first,

Zayne thought its bones were turning to powder, but when they crumbled, each piece became a dark pit containing swirling light and stars, like the night sky of the Dreamscape, before scattered slowly in the breeze and melting into the air.

The blade of Zayne's sword dropped to the floor with a *clang*. When its head broke down and disappeared, a spent pistol fell from its mouth. When finally its body completely fell apart, the chain that had been wrapped around its neck crashed in a heap, the metal links blackened by heat but still whole.

Ject pulled himself up to his feet. His face was covered in a thin veneer of blood, caused by a cut in his forehead that opened up when he'd been slammed to the floor. Altair's face was almost completely red, as apparently she had wiped it on her sleeves and only managed to smear it everywhere. Zayne's insides were quivering just looking at them, but that was nothing compared to Thanris.

"Daen's tits," Ject said, gaze shifting between Zayne and Altair, all the while ignoring Thanris even as she collapsed to her knees, then slumped onto her back. "How did you do that... *vanishing* thing? And what is that sword?"

"Long story," Zayne and Altair said simultaneously. Zayne cleared his throat. "We should do something about her wound," he said pointedly. Thanris didn't seem to hear. She just kept working her mouth, staring at the place where her arm used to be. The acid seemed to have stanched the blood loss, but there was still so much forming a pool beneath her and soaking through her clothes.

Altair appraised her like she might a painting at auction. "Hmm. No."

"*No?*" Zayne demanded.

"No," Altair repeated, and she may as well have been turning down a glass of wine. "There is no time. We didn't kill the first Dread Hound, and there's no telling how many more there are."

"They always hunt in packs of thirteen," Tatl informed them, in the same bored tone a normal person might use to describe a predictable cabin mate.

"Not to mention we're in the Imperial Palace as invaders," Ject added unsympathetically.

"Glad to know who'll be watching my back," Zayne sneered.

"You want to stay here and die with her, be my guest," Ject said. "But I want to live to see tomorrow."

241

Tatl stepped up gently, standing right in Zayne's face. Amidst all the blood and smoke and violence, she was untouched. She looked at Zayne with too-blue eyes. "There is nothing any of us can do for her," she said dreamily, "and your bindings are not yet released."

Zayne gritted his teeth. He didn't know exactly what Altair had done to the girl, but it was said Altair weighed her advice and warnings more heavily than anyone else's because, mad as she clearly was, she saw things no one else could.

Zayne scowled, then nodded. He dismissed Dawn Star and took up Thanris' spear, finding the switch that recalled the chain. It retracted into the shaft easily, coming to an abrupt halt with a faint *click*. "Let's go, then," he said flatly.

He could hear distant screams and fighting farther inside, and the cannons and engines of ships outside. But in this corridor, it was so quiet that when they filed out, he could hear Thanris mutter, "I want to go home. I want to go home. I want to go home. I want to go home. I want to go home."

The palace had become a full pitched slaughter. The Dread Hounds had left behind evidence of their passing through the corridors: blood splatters marked every wall and floor, and the Hounds didn't finish every meal before moving on to the next, leaving body parts in their wake. They didn't find anyone alive until they followed the sounds of gunfire to an interior garden. Zayne and the others took cover by the entrance to assess the situation.

Four of the Daughters of Daen were positioned behind a large, decorative gray rock while half a dozen palace guards were taking cover behind a small footbridge that extended the length of the garden over a koi pond. One of the Daughters — a young man with dyed blue hair — tossed a powder horn over the rock. When it flew over the bridge, an older blonde by his side climbed the stone and fired. A bullet shattered her skull at the same moment the horn exploded, destroying the bridge and showering the guards with splinters and shrapnel. The pond became red with blood. One survivor thrashed weakly in the water while another gripped impotently at the foot-long piece of wood jutting from his ribs.

A third guard appeared to be unharmed. She hefted her spear, leveling it at the Daughter's cover. There was a pan-flash and the spear bloomed in smoke. The resounding gunshot blasted a large chunk out of the stone, knocking the blue-haired man off it into the garden rocks below. The guard ran, clamoring atop the fallen bridge, spear at the ready.

Ject stepped into the garden and hurled one of his axes. The blade clanged against the woman's armor, but the impact sent her reeling. One of the Daughters — a tall, bald headed man — then leaped from the stone and met her at the bridge. The guard recovered and ran the Daughter through with her spear. He recoiled, but with concerted effort, he pulled himself along the long shaft and sank his sword into her chest a moment before he died.

Ject led the small procession into the garden. He picked up his fallen axe, then stopped to examine the guard's spear. "I'd heard they were developing weapons like this," he said. "I didn't know they'd got them working, though. Figured they'd never work out the misfiring."

"Captain!" the blue-haired man announced. Only, Zayne was realizing he wasn't a man at all; he was still a child, younger by a sight than Zayne had been when he had joined the Daughters.

"Qing," Ject replied tersely, "was that Carine I saw get shot in the head?"

"Aye, Captain," the boy said, hanging his head.

"Pissing blight!" Ject snapped. "She owed me a phoenix!" If the boy had a problem with his captain's frustration at the senseless deaths in their ranks being based on debts, he didn't show it.

Zayne took a steadying breath. "Let's keep moving," he said, keeping his eyes away from the bodies.

"We found out where they've got the prisoners!" the boy declared.

"What prisoners?" Zayne asked.

"Not important," Altair said, waving her wrist dismissively.

"When word got to the Empress about Lancen's abduction of the princess," said Ject, "you know, that thing *you* were supposed to do — and she sent the edict out ordering anyone in the Empire bearing the mark of Daen or flying one of the Daughter's ships be put to death, there were a few crews in the city. They were arrested, probably to name names.

"Rather than kill them all at once," he continued, "there's been one execution a week. So, we figured some were still alive."

"Rat saw them before the battle started," the boy confirmed.

So, this must have been part of the infiltration team sent to destroy the barrier and help turn the tide. Zayne couldn't help but wonder why Ject would send someone so distinctive as a blue-haired boy. "Eight of them are still alive."

"We don't have time to rescue eight half-starved husks," Altair said firmly.

Zayne was inclined to agree. "We have enough opposition without running around looking for dungeons."

"That's just it," said the boy. "They're on the way. They'd just been moved because the Empress was going to have them questioned after meeting with the court."

"Convenient," Altair drolled.

"Do they look healthy enough to fight?" Ject asked.

The other surviving Daughter — a mousy haired young girl with a scar beneath her ear — spat. "Eight bodies between us and the guns? Does it matter?" Zayne was starting to see why Ject's attitude hadn't hurt his crew's morale.

Ject cocked his head towards Altair. "Got an argument against *that*?"

"Fine," she said wearily, "but they sink or fly on their own."

The whole situation was disgusting, but Zayne couldn't argue the prudence. "Lead on," he said.

Gunfire sounded through the door on the other side of the garden. The Daughters lined up on either side of the portal, and Zayne slid it open cautiously. The gunfire was being exchanged parallel to them, so they couldn't simply step out without being shot. A bullet hit the edge of the door just a handbreadth from Zayne's shoulder.

"Is there a faster way around?" Ject asked.

"Not directly," Zayne answered. "We can try circling around and hopefully get behind the guards to —" He cut off when he spotted a shadow moving across the garden. He looked around but found nothing that could be casting it. "*Fuck*," he sneered, extending the word to several syllables.

The shadow swelled as the Dread Hound burst forth, like seawater around a kraken before fully surfacing. It loomed over them, rolling its shoulders as it skulked, strutting in a display of dominance. It had only one yellow-black eye, which rolled lazily

244

between them, then snapped harshly on Altair. Qing screamed like an even younger child. The mousy haired girl drew a pistol and fired. Her bullet sparked on contact with the beast's skull. It let out a growl that might have been from pain or frustration and snapped its jaws at her.

The girl was ensnared by the creature's jaws, tossed in the air. Her blood gushed and splattered the Daughters, the garden floor, and the walls as it crunched her body in three vicious bites before swallowing. Thanris' spear rattled in Zayne's hand as he struggled to keep his stomach down.

"Rat!" the boy shrieked, but rather than try to avenge her, he ran into the corridor behind. Enticed by the motion, the Dread Hound bounded into the corridor after him. Screams and gunfire followed. Zayne wished he could convince himself that the splattered blood on the floor was the beast's, but he knew better.

The floor rumbled thunderously as the Dread Hound bounded across the corridor. Zayne eased his head around the corner and winced. Only Qing's boot remained, sitting in a red puddle.

Ject darted into the corridor, and Zayne followed just in time to see the Dread Hound melt into smoke and shadow again amidst a pile of armored corpses. A cold feeling permeated his guts as he watched its form vanish.

Opposite the fallen guards were a pile of dead black coats. Something shifted among the corpses. Zayne leveled Thanris' spear, and Ject brandished his axes. Altair and Tatl looked on, bored. A young woman pulled herself up from the bodies. Beneath her jacket, she wore the palace servant's greys.

"Ugh," she groaned. She looked from Zayne, to Ject, then shuddered when her gaze passed over Altair and Tatl. "Where is Captain Xi?"

"Which one?" Altair asked blithely.

"K-Khana," she stammered.

"Well, *she's* probably fine," Altair explained. "Your crew, however, were all driven quite mad. In fact, the cabin boy —"

"Not now, Isaara," Ject snapped. Altair directed a glowering pout at him, like a child chastised for stealing sweets.

"Mad?" the girl repeated with a squeak in her voice.

"The effects of the Dreamscape," Zayne said simply. "You were lucky to be sent ahead."

245

"Did anyone see the direction the Dread Hound fled?" Altair asked.

"*Dread Hound?*" the girl shrieked.

"It's not fleeing," Tatl said matter-of-factly. "It's hunting."

"Well, which way did it *go*," Altair pressed impatiently.

"That way," she said, pointing down a fork in the corridor just behind the guards.

"Shit, that's the way we're going, isn't it?" asked Ject.

"You don't send the Dread Hounds after serving girls," said Altair.

"They're finishing the hunt they started twenty years ago," Zayne added. "Same job as us."

"I didn't sign up to fight the fucking *Dread Hounds!*" the girl declared, which was undercut somewhat by the way her voice raised by several octaves when she said, 'Dread Hounds'. She threw her hat and black coat aside, taking on the guise of a serving girl. She made it ten paces into her run when Altair drew a pistol and shot her without even turning to look. Zayne bit his tongue to fight the wave of sickness that followed as her body crumpled on the floor in a bloody pool. How could he face *so much* death and still not be able to stomach it?

"For fuck's sake, Isaara," Ject snapped. "Conserve your ammunition, this is a battle!"

Altair rolled her eyes and reloaded her pistol, all the while making faces and mouthing something that Zayne was sure was denigrating to Ject. She holstered it and crossed her arms petulantly. "Well? Let's get this over with. There's only so many interesting things here." She marched ahead.

Ject leaned in conspiratorially close to Zayne, and his musk tinged with gun smoke and blood choked his senses. "I never put much stock in the Sanctum, or the Iron Veils, but if anyone made a solid case for steering clear of all things Fae and dreams, it's her."

"Shame none of us had her as an example," said Zayne, "because it's too late now." They caught up to Altair, who maintained a brisk walk. They navigated the palace's twists and turns, passing the aftermath of several battles, as well as claw marks and acid burns that told of the Dread Hounds. Most of the casualties they passed were guards or servants, or the occasional courtier or military personnel, but there was no shortage of Daughters along the way. From a tactical standpoint, each dead Daughter was more damaging than twenty dead Imperials.

As they reached the floor with the throne room, Tatl stopped abruptly, and Altair followed suit two steps later.

"What is it?" the *Kestrel*'s captain asked.

"The captors are behind this door," Tatl said, pointing to a door she was close enough to touch.

"You sure?" asked Ject.

"Don't question her!" snapped Altair. "If she says something *is*, it is."

"You put a lot of faith in a drug-addled madwoman."

The punch must have surprised Ject as much as Zayne because Altair's fist made full contact with his jaw and knocked him into the wall. "Insult her again, and I will show you the essence of madness. Have you ever experienced *time*, Ject?"

Zayne didn't understand the threat, and he suspected Ject didn't either. But there was an undeniable weight to her words, regardless. Considering how lackadaisical she had been amidst the carnage and the nightmares, the sudden burst of passion gave her a heightened intensity. What did she mean by *time*?

Ject rubbed his jaw, popping it loudly. He sneered but said nothing and didn't retaliate. Instead, he stepped past Tatl — clearly making a show of not touching her — and pushed the door open slowly and skulked inside. There was a crash and a shout that cut off abruptly, replaced by a gurgle.

Tatl counted down from three in her mystically uninterested tone, and in the moment after she reached 'one', an ornately dressed man was hurled bodily through the doorway. His neck had been cleaved and was barely holding together by threads of sinew. Zayne forced himself to look away and bit his tongue. Tatl led her captain into the room. Further into the palace, a series of explosions rumbled. Zayne followed Altair inside.

Zayne had expected a dank dungeon, but instead walked onto a plush rug, and while it was dim, the air was cool and comfortable. The room was dim, but not oppressively dark. He had pictured the captive Daughters locked in cells wearing burlap and covered in their own filth. Yet they were lined up against the wall — manacled, of course, otherwise they surely would have escaped in the chaos — dressed in clean, gray tunics, and smelling of perfumed soaps. Uniformly shaven clean, Zayne didn't recognize any of them, and wouldn't have known them for Daughters at all if not for Daen's crook branded on their arms. All of them seemed to have the signs of un-monitored weight loss, but not nearly as severely as Zayne might have expected.

"You look better than any prisoners I ever sprung in Castilyn," Zayne commented. Three of the captives flinched, as if his words would come with lashings. One of them was staring at him with quivering eyes. He looked familiar, but Zayne couldn't place it.

"I don't remember ever getting a bath in Castilyn, either," Ject agreed.

"You know about *baths*?" Altair asked. Zayne couldn't quite place her tone, but he *thought* the question sounded baffled and sincere.

Ject grunted, and in that one sound he conveyed annoyance, offense, and a begrudging acknowledgement of a well-timed joke. "Which crew are you?" he asked, stepping deliberately away from Altair.

"*Dead Sparrow*," said the woman at the end.

"*Painted Smile*," the next man and woman said simultaneously, which was repeated by a girl down the line.

"The *Four-Fingered Fist*," said a blue-eyed woman. "If they haven't scrapped her, I'm the captain, since everyone else is dead."

Zayne didn't bother to mention that it was unlikely any of them had a ship to return to, or a crew to be captain of. Instead, he looked down the line up.

The man with the terrified eyes opened his mouth and clamped it shut. He had a very weak chin, and the tan lines of his face spoke of a thick beard that hid that fact.

"Your turn," Zayne prompted.

The man broke his gaze away from Zayne, and his eyes took on a pleading look as he shifted to look at Altair, the Ject.

"Oh, this is rich," Ject said, failing to stifle a chuckle. "They actually left you alive! Who did you sell out to keep off the gallows this long?"

"Ject," he said with a tremble in his thick Rivien accent, "you wound me. I would never —"

"Kaveth Darziin!" Zayne blurted out, unable to suppress his disdain at the revelation. Darziin flinched, hitting the back of his head against the wall.

When Zayne had been a young man, before he knew about the Daughters, he had paid Darziin to take him and his family from Dawnhal, to escape his father. When his mother and siblings had been murdered, Darziin had taken Zayne's money and fled the city while Zayne had been left to face the executioner's block.

The next time Zayne had seen the older captain, he had been working a job with Salaa in Darziin's home country of Rivien when the older mercenary had spotted them from the patio of a tea house.

Darziin had waved Salaa over, all smiles and good cheer. He didn't even seem to recognize Zayne. Perhaps it was because his hair had grown almost two feet since Dawnhal, but more likely he hadn't given him a second thought since that dark day.

"Salaa, my morning sun!" he greeted, waving to the empty seat at the table across from himself. "Come, sit, we'll share a pipe! I've ordered some baklava," he added, leaning in like he was trying to sweeten a deal.

Zayne had tensed at the sight of the other mercenary. Salaa nudged his shoulder and whispered, "Treat it like cards." Then she threw her arms wide as she drew nearer. "Kaveth! It's been so long! I haven't seen you since… oh, damn, has it really been a year since that job outside Dawnhal?"

"Too long, regardless," he said. "And who is this you bring with you? A new suitor? Need I be jealous?"

"Kaveth, you don't recognize my nephew?"

"Nephew? I thought your brother — *no*! He can't be Da—"

Salaa snatched his beard from across the table and yanked it hard enough to slam him into the edge and knock the wind from him. "Look *real* close. Recognize him?"

Zayne froze as the mercenary started at him with wide, panicked eyes. Darziin was such a small part of the horrors Zayne had endured, he thought he had moved past him, figuring that in the grand scheme of things, it didn't matter. But faced with the man in the flesh, it suddenly mattered the world to him. He felt as if the violence Salaa was engaged in was born from his own heart.

"I've never seen him before in my —"

"Look again! Think about the last time I saw you."

Darziin screwed up his face as he focused, *really* focused, on Zayne. His eyes widened. "You're the boy who killed his family."

His nose crunched under Salaa's fist. "Don't you *dare* spread those lies! He came to you for help, and what did you do? You betrayed a contract," Salaa whispered, just loud enough that despite the onlookers she had attracted, only Zayne and Darziin could hear. "And not just any contract. A contract made in *public*, with multiple captains to witness. People already think we're evil because of our name and our banner. But you made us look *unprofessional*. You made *me* look unprofessional. And if I hadn't been there to clean up after you, you would have left an innocent boy to hang. So, here's what's going to happen, Kaveth. I'm going to be nice, for old times' sake.

"You are going to pay my nephew back every last coin you stole from him. Then, you are going to leave. I never want to see you, or the *Autumn Raven*, ever again. If I hear she is even docked in the same fucking city as the *Scorpion* after today, I am going to castrate you and string you up on the figurehead in place of the ugly fish you have mounted there!"

Kaveth had taken her at her word. By all accounts, the *Autumn Raven* had always been at least half a country away from the *Scorpion* for ten years. Some said Darziin had been so afraid of Salaa, he had risked losing his ship to debts because he wouldn't take any job that would risk crossing Salaa's path. And even when she had died, he kept his distance.

Again, Zayne had thought that, weighed against everything else in his life, Darziin's betrayal had been just one drop in an impossibly large bucket. He hadn't been responsible for the deaths of Zayne's family. He hadn't been the one to frame Zayne for the crime. Nor had he been responsible for the countless acts of violence that haunted Zayne's sleep. And yet again, being faced with the man stoked a fire in his heart, and he didn't understand it anymore now than he did back then.

"B-B-Balthine," Darziin stammered. "I heard you had died up north! It's…. It's good to see you well. I'm so sorry about Salaa, I —"

Zayne slammed the butt of Thanris' spear into Darziin's guts. "Stop talking." He set the weapon aside and extracted a set of lockpicks from their hidden compartments in the sleeves of his coat.

"I was hoping for more drama," Altair muttered to Ject.

Zayne gave her a sidelong look, then rolled his eyes as he started unlocking the Daughters. Darziin's eyes welled up in tears when he passed him over. When the other seven were free, Zayne stowed his lockpicks and took up Thanris' spear. "Let's go," he ordered. Ject shrugged and turned to walk out the door. Altair gave a long suffering sigh before following. The expressions of the freed captives sat somewhere on a spectrum between guilt at leaving Darziin and gratitude at being free themselves.

"Balthine!" he barked. When Zayne leveled a glare at him, he whimpered like a dog. He cleared his throat, and in a more desperate tone he said, "I definitely see the irony of leaving me locked up. I'm sure some would say it's even fair. But see reason! I've served my time here! And you got out! You've seen the world, you got away from your father and —"

Thanris' spear glistened with Darziin's blood. Zayne didn't even remember making the decision. He hadn't planned on killing him. He'd been ready to leave him behind, but *murder?* His stomach was starting to hurt from all the sickening lurches. The worst part, however, was the way his heart contradicted itself; there was no satisfaction in his death, and yet, some deeply rooted part of him was glad to have done it.

More of Lucandri's influence, he figured, but that raised an uncomfortable consideration. *Was* it Lucandri's fault? He had taken to blaming the Fae for many uncomfortable changes — and how could he not when his body was now only half his own and he was host to entire lifetimes of someone else's memories? — but could it be that he was just changing? Could it be that he was a monster because he was getting used to a lifetime of committing terrible deeds?

He didn't know.

The sounds of battle were growing more intense, both inside and out of the palace walls. He worried for Nanette, but the moment he thought of her he could feel the *Scorpion* in the same way he could feel his fingers. She was still at the helm, and the ship was holding strong. *Good,* he thought. He wouldn't go so far as to say she was *safe,* but she was alive and walking, and that was the most he could ask for.

They came across the aftermath of another battle, and the freed captives looted the bodies of guards and their fellow mercenaries, taking up weapons. One of the *Painted Smile* crew took the coat and boots off a corpse as well, falling behind as a result.

The final approach to the throne room was a maelstrom of battle. Palace guards held the line against two dozen black coats, using the great pillars as cover, but both sides were also engaged against a trio of Dread Hounds. As Zayne watched one become a shadow and reform to flank a guard it had been fighting head on, he remembered the one Thanris had killed. It hadn't tried to escape.

Maybe it had *tried,* Zayne considered, watching as sparks sprayed with each attack landed on the beasts, *but the iron kept it tied down.* Of course, they *were* of the Dreamscape, the same as the Fae. Perhaps, implacable as they seemed, they shared the same weaknesses. He hefted Thanris' spear and charged. The nearest Hound had three Daughters with their backs to the wall. He hit the switch for the chain and swung hard, sending the metal links wrapping around the beast's right hind leg, sizzling with each wrap around. It turned away from its prey to focus on him, snarling.

"They can't vanish if iron touches—" he began, but the Dread Hound lunged at him. He tried to skewer it in the maw, to pierce its brain like the one Thanris killed, but the chain tugged as the beast moved, and the blade scraped along the edge of its fangs instead. Fire flashed in its jaws at the contact, but the Hound didn't so much as flinch. The world slowed, much as it had when he thought Durant had killed him. Just as he had been powerless to watch as her blade sank first into his stomach and then into his throat, the razor teeth of the beast descended upon him. Maybe this time death would stick.

The Hound yelped and Zayne was nearly blinded by the flash of fire. He blinked away the heat, faced with a burly woman with a top knot hefting a heavy half-handled hammer. The face of the weapon had burned black where it had hit the beast. He didn't have time to process his gratitude, much less express it. He shifted the spear in his grip and followed up after the monster. It was knocked aside but braced itself and shook violently. Zayne drove the blade into its left foreleg and twisted, feeling it hook on bone. Its blood sizzled as it dripped, staining the length of the spear before turning to smoke.

The Dread Hound thrashed, and the haft of the spear jerked into Zayne's ribs. The air was sucked from his lungs, and he dropped the spear. He gulped in a painful breath and took staggering steps away from the threat. The beast moved as if to stalk forward, but the chain tying its opposing limbs together tightened, and the sizzling of the iron burning its ethereal flesh intensified.

Zayne called Dawn Star back into being and broke into a run. The Dread Hound snapped at him, but he dropped into a slide, slashing up at the beast. Its blood turned to acrid smoke before it could splatter across his face, but it was choking and miserable all the same. He hamstrung as he recovered his feet. Its cry was palpable, and in a primal place in Zayne's heart, deeper than any thought could reach, he felt pity for it. Never mind that it was trying to kill him. It lumbered around, and a hail of gunshots lit its flank with sizzling sparks and red smoke. It fell with a thunderous crash, its whines scraping at the integrity of Zayne's soul. Whatever was left of it, anyway.

A Daughter with red hair and a dueling blade stepped too close to the beast, apparently thinking downed meant harmless. It twisted its head, and with a snap of its jaws, removed her top half. Her knees gave way, causing what was left of her to fold. Someone screamed something — it might have been the woman's name, might have been an order, might even have been a curse, Zayne couldn't make it out over the noise — and four of the black coats converged, stabbing the beast simultaneously in the back, in the head, in the throat, and in the ribs.

The Dread Hound's last breath was not unlike a whimper. As much as Zayne hated killing, watching suffering was worse, even if it was a creature of nightmare. It was a mercy when it finally began crumbling into starlit dust. Even still, something about watching a force so powerful and proud die such a pathetic way broke something inside him. He could only hope to give the rest cleaner deaths. Or at least that his own would be quick.

He left Thanris' spear where it clattered on the floor. He flicked his wrist and gripped the stiletto that dropped out of his sleeve. With his other hand, he drew a pistol from his belt. Black gun smoke and the crimson blood-smoke off the Dread Hounds obscured the hall with acrid clouds, though much of the battle had moved to close range. Daughters and guards and beasts clashed with equal fervor, with no sign that any two sides were uniting against either threat. One of the remaining Hounds was still freely traversing the killing field as a shadow, while the other seemed restrained by a bola sizzling around its hind ankle. Ject led their freed mercenaries on a charge against the hampered beast.

Zayne turned his focus to a skirmish of guards and Daughters and closed in. When two warriors locked blades, Zayne flanked and drove his stiletto into the guard's armpit. She let go of her sword, and he took it with his newly freed hand. The Daughter she had been fighting ran her through. As she buckled in death, Zayne leaped and rolled over her back, landing just as another guard turned to see what had befallen his ally. Zayne fired his pistol into the man's hip before he even processed what was happening.

Though he had practiced with heavier blades like the jian — more than he ever had with a spear — he had fought very few real battles with them; the thinner swords were less conspicuous, as most people in both the Empire and Castilyn had one. So, while he wasn't completely without a rudder, he felt sluggish and sloppy when he clashed with a guardswoman who was actually ready for him. His blade rebounded off hers and she went for a rising slash. He caught the attack along the barrel of his spent pistol — he had meant to parry, but just as he rarely used a jian, he rarely came across opponents armed with them.

He thrusted. She sidestepped and slammed her knee into his ribs. He doubled over, but before she could follow through, she bent backwards with the sound of squealing metal and breaking bones. She fell limp, and the Daughter with the hammer was standing triumphantly over her corpse. "I saved Daen's Scorpion, twice," she boasted. "I think that deserves a kiss."

Zayne straightened himself and grunted. "Let's see if you still want it after all this is done." He tossed the pistol aside and recovered his stiletto and surveyed the battle. Ject moved deftly against a wounded Dread Hound, but everyone who had followed him was dead, their remains leaving a gory trail across the hall. The palace guards had found an iron net and hurled it atop the other beast, which seemed to have had the added effect of setting it on fire.

Ject jammed the back spike of one of his axes into the Dread Hound's flank and used it to climb his back. It thrashed and bucked, but he drove the other axe spike into its shoulder blade, keeping himself saddled. It reared up on its hind legs and pushed back to the wall to crush Ject, but he rolled out of the way, and the blade in its back was driven deeper into its flesh. It returned to its forelegs and dropped, rolling, probably to crush or dislodge the mercenary. He pulled a pistol from his coat and placed it directly on the base of the Hound's skull.

He didn't even need to pull the trigger, as the flames and sparks that sprang to life when the iron lip of the pistol kissed the beast's Dream-born skin touched the powder and set the pan flashing. The blood-smoke sprayed simultaneously from the back of the Dread Hound's head and from the dark depths of its maw, and Ject was thrown from his perch as it dropped dead mid-motion.

Even on fire, the remaining beast had whittled the guardsmen down to the last woman. Half her helmet had been torn off, and her face was half red with her own blood. Two distinct claw-marks stood out in her chain link armor. There was a dizziness when she sidestepped, and the end of her spear wobbled as she kept it aimed at the Hound's bone face. Her breathing was so labored Zayne could see her shudder from across the hall.

Against all sense, she attacked first. She screamed and thrust her spear in quick jabs, first at one eye, then the other. Neither hit the mark, but the second scraped against the bony ridge just beneath the target, and the resulting flame burned bright enough to make it flinch. She took a half step back and swung the spear in a rising arc, cutting the creature's collarbone. It retaliated with a swipe of its paw. She rolled over top the massive leg and smacked its face with the butt of her weapon as she passed. It raised itself up to reposition itself and came down on her with its mighty jaws open wide. She braced herself, and in the moment its jaws started to close around her, a pan-flash and gun smoke erupted from her blade. The Dread Hound's teeth snapped shut around her as it collapsed. It crumbled to dust as the others had, leaving behind her bisected corpse as its final victory.

There was something surreal about surviving such a nightmare. Standing amidst the gore and the bodies, Zayne wasn't totally convinced that wasn't exactly what it was. He had seen more than his fair share of death and slaughter — more than his fair share if he lived a hundred lifetimes, as far as he was concerned — but the carnage left behind by the Dread Hounds, the dogs of the gods, was something altogether different. He felt like he was looking through someone else's eyes, through a tunnel. He walked numbly across the blood.

The strangest part — the most horrible part — was that the killing wasn't even done.

CHAPTER TWENTY-SIX

Unsurprisingly, the double doors to the throne room were barred. They were heavy, massive things, several times taller than they had any cause to be, made of strong wood and reinforced by iron. Ornate gilded patterns coated the face of them. Zayne had knocked down his share of doors, but these would take considerable effort. And time.

"By the time we get this thing down," Ject said, mirroring Zayne's own thoughts, "the Empress will probably slip out through some secret passage."

"Under normal circumstances, yes," Tatl said in her unsettling monotone. "But there are still nine Dread Hounds we cannot account for. Escaping us would only result in falling to them."

"We should still hurry," Zayne said. "If we take too long, the fleet can't pick us up *and* escape."

"Agreed," said Tatl, though she sounded as disinterested as she did about everything else.

"Weren't we supposed to have explosives?" asked Altair.

"Our infiltrators were supposed to handle it," Ject acknowledged. "But I think they got eaten."

Altair nodded and wiped at the blood on her face with her sleeve, which only smeared it more. "Tatl, Strength."

"You are still recovering from the last one. I advise against this." Despite her words, the Dust addict had started rifling through the red drawstring bag from earlier before she had finished speaking. As she had before, she took out a finger bone, held it to the light, and kept searching.

"What in the name of Daen's glorious tits are *those?*" Ject demanded.

"The bones of men, women, and children killed after their bodies were possessed by Fae spirits," Tatl said matter-of-factly. She held another to the light and put it back.

"Err," said Kin Mei — the woman with the hammer, who Zayne recognized as the first mate of the *King in Yellow*, "why exactly do you have a bag of... those?"

"Well, I can't just keep them in my pockets," Altair said lazily. She picked at her blood-crusted nails and studied them, as if she were trying to make some sort of impression.

"But why do you *have* them?" Ject pressed.

"For situations like this," she replied, waving her arms around, encompassing the grand hallway. Her first mate held up another bone to the light and put it back.

"Here," said the blonde woman, holding up a bone that looked no different from the others. "I advise against this," she repeated, but she made no effort to stop Altair from plucking it from her fingers.

Altair set the bone between her back teeth, just as she had the one from before. She bit down and doubled over. What parts of her weren't painted red with blood became dark pink with strain. Veins in her forehead pulsed, looking ready to burst. The bone cracked and she swallowed it. The mad woman swayed dizzily as she got to her feet. Her neck cracked audibly as she tilted her head one way, then the other.

Altair took a deep breath and let it out, gesticulating in ways that mimicked the motion of the air. She placed her fist gently against one of the doors, about an inch from the seam where they met. She took another deep breath.

"This is ridiculous," Ject groaned. "Balthine, help me gather some gunpowder to—"

The door rattled and thundered as Altair's tiny fist struck it. Cracks ran along the face of it. Her knuckles were bloody as she drew back and punched again with all the force of a battering ram. The door seemed to bounce in its fixture, and the cracks ran deeper. Blood was trickling from her eyes like crimson tears, from her nose, her mouth, and even from under her nails.

The next hit bowed the door in, but it bounced back hard as the bar on the other side held its shape. Another pushed further, and Zayne could hear the sound of cracking wood. Altair took woozy yet deliberate steps backward. Zayne couldn't stand to look at the blood obscuring her face, but he thought the sound of her labored breath sounded vaguely like a count. At fifteen paces, she broke into a run and leaped, higher than should have been possible. Blood streamed behind her like tassels in the wind, her foot slammed in the spot she had been punching with the sound of a cannonball breaking though.

The door opened, just a crack. But it *was* open, and the locking bar didn't force it back in place. She staggered away, violently coughing up clots of blood. Zayne turned away from her and pushed both sides of the double door open. They were heavy, and it was slow, drudging work. He suspected that under normal circumstances, a servant would be assigned to each. But he knew — assuming no one shot him while he did so — the sight of him, tattered and stained by blood and gun smoke, pushing through would make for a more powerful image. And image was important in his line of work; it was easier to kill or coerce someone who was afraid.

"Give me one of those!" he heard Ject demand behind him.

"You wouldn't be able to handle it," Tatl said. It wasn't snide or mocking, just a statement of fact. "Captain Isaara has had to change much to survive what she has." Whatever that meant.

The throne room was larger than he expected. What looked to be thirty frightened courtiers congregated on the far left side of the room, far away from the dozen and one guards standing in a reverse-flight formation with spears aimed at the encroaching attackers. Despite their presence, the room seemed empty.

Behind the guards was the dais. The Empress sat atop her throne, ornamental silk robes of vivid green draped around her. She sat impassively, still as a statue, more beautiful than a painting.

Having wiped most of the blood off her face and hands, Altair caught up to Zayne, taking her place on his left as he entered the chamber. Tatl flanked him on the right. He could hear Ject and the others following behind.

Nine Daughters against the Empress's elite guard, Zayne considered. He thought about his battle with Asier but pushed it aside. The context of that fight had been completely different, even if she had been trained the same as these warriors.

He stopped three spear lengths away from the guards, and Tatl and Altair immediately broke into synchronous and elaborate bows with one leg forward, as if their entrance had been rehearsed. Maybe it had been. He couldn't quite figure them out.

"Your august and sagacious majesty," they intoned simultaneously, "it is an honor to stand in your presence."

The clack of wood striking the floor caught Zayne's attention, and he turned in time to find a figure in red he hadn't counted emerge from the shadows. He caught the assassin's blade with his own stolen sword and was surprised to recognize his attacker. It had been a long time since he had thought about the officer from the Dragon's Nest. Though her face was half obscured, much as his own was, though she stood now on a peg leg and was down an arm, he knew her pride, the gleam of frustration in her eye. He remembered her suspicions, and bizarrely, her concern.

"*Hawkwind,*" he grunted as the name came to mind.

"Mercenary scum," she grunted. "I thought you were a —" a gunshot cut her off, and she slumped, leaning her weight into Zayne. The smell of death had already plastered itself into Zayne's nose, and he shoved her away and fought against his stomach.

He turned back just as Altair tossed the spent pistol to the ground as if it offended her. She had somehow, with blood in her eyes and a trembling hand, shot over his shoulder and into Hawkwind's neck. Had she known she could make the shot? Had she cared? The mad woman gave no indication of her feelings and turned back to the Empress.

"Did my clothes offend, your grace?" she asked, voice heavy with mock innocence. "I wore my nicest deel — made by the best seamstress in the city, albeit ten years ago, and I know how fashion changes — but I hadn't expected so much killing on the way!"

Two of the guards broke out of the line and charged at them. A man — probably their captain — shouted an order to fall back, but they were committed. They made it halfway to the Daughters' procession, but Tatl had stepped up to meet them.

One of the attackers slashed down at Tatl with her spear while the other lunged to run her through with his. The blonde woman bent backwards like she had been built on a hinge. The two spears collided in the air, and she grabbed them both beneath the blade. She twisted in ways Zayne could hardly track and sat on her haunches atop the crossed weapons, driving them to the floor. She stood and stabbed them both in the chin with hitherto unseen knives, jagged and made of bone.

The guards seemed as surprised by the Dust addict's sudden display of skill as Zayne, but they held their ground, nervous though they seemed. Now eleven, they fanned out together, circling the Daughters. Zayne flourished his stolen sword. He picked out the chief of the Empress's personal guards easily enough; in addition to being the center-most guard between the Daughters and the

Empress, there was a crest of office on the clasp of his emerald cape. He had a steady air of a man sure of his skill, unrattled by crisis.

"Yushiro Tao?" Zayne ventured; it was public knowledge that the Empress' brother had replaced Elyia Asier as her personal champion after the war, so it was a safe guess.

"What of it?" the man asked, leveling his spear down Zayne's eye, and Zayne noticed the narrow barrel of a hidden gun in the spear.

"I've already killed one of her majesty's champions. Do you really want to make it two?" He didn't know why he said it, where the sudden urge to taunt him came from. It might have been the battle thrill creeping up on him. It might have been Lucandri's influence. It might have just been his bad mood.

"Huh. So you're the bastard," Tao said. His long moustache twitched as he gave a sardonic grin. "I heard you were dead. I'll tell you now, Elyia wasn't in my league. If you want to throw your arms down now, I'll kill you quickly and without malice."

Zayne snorted. "Not likely."

The stench of sulfur filled the air. Zayne looked down to find a swirling shadow beneath his feet. He stepped back before the snarling snout of a Dread Hound rose from the floor. The beast tossed him aside as it emerged from under his boots, and he crashed into Ject and Kin Mei. All of the Daughters except Tatl were sent sprawling, as were all of the guards, save Yushiro Tao. He pushed himself back up just as its paws slammed onto the floor, causing a tremor and threatening to knock Zayne down again.

The beast sniffed the air, then directed its gaze at the Empress, who continued to watch impassively. It crouched, ready to lunge for her. A gout of purple flames spouted from the Hound's shoulder with the sound of a gunshot. It staggered to one side before limping forward. Tao cartwheeled over its snout and drove his spear through its bone-plated skull. He knelt down as it thrashed, keeping low and tight to its head as it tried to toss him. Another gunshot rang out and purple flames erupted from the underside of the Dread Hound's throat. It collapsed and flaked away into stardust.

Ject and Kin Mei rushed past Zayne to charge Yushiro, likely to take advantage of the distraction. Ject swung his axe low while Kin Mei's hammer went high. Rather than retreat, the Empress' bodyguard dove between the pendulous weapons. The butt of his spear cracked Ject in the ribs while the blade slashed

261

across Kin Mei's face. Her blood splattered on the floor in a neat arc. Ject clanged his axes together in a gesture of primal battle lust and charged again.

Zayne spun on one of the guards just as she tried to stab him in the back. He ran his stiletto through her chest. The warmth of her last gasp on his face made his skin crawl, but he pushed through. Behind her, one of the Daughters — a young boy Zayne knew as Tan — took two spears to the chest at once. Zayne threw his knife into one of the guardsmen's eyes and drew a pistol from the small of his back. His shot might not have killed his target, but the bullet blasted his thumb off and lodged in his gut. He used the weapon's barrel to parry another spear aimed at his chest and severed the arm of the guard holding it.

Tala — a cabin girl from the *Illusion of Justice* — danced around two guards as they flailed while trying to skewer her on the ends of their blades. She hamstrung one with a jagged knife and shot the other in the face with her pistol. She was shot in the throat by one of those gun-spears and dropped. A ragged-looking Daughter Zayne didn't recognize avenged Tala by igniting an alchemical flare in the shooter's face. The stench of gas and burning meat cut through the blood and gunpowder, if only for a moment before the Daughter took a spear blade to either side of his neck.

The three remaining guards pressed on Zayne. They stood roughly a sword length apart and approached him with deliberate steps, keeping their spears leveled at his chest. He took a steadying breath and brandished his sword. He feinted left, and as the spears moved to follow, he pivoted off his step and somersaulted at the guard on his right. The edge of a spear cut along his back, but he pushed, but he sprung to his feet and drove his blade through the man's chest. He hauled his victim around to use him as a human shield. As one of the guards drove her spear through her former compatriot, Zayne gripped the hilt of his sword and kicked off the dead guard, freeing his own blade while shoving him down the shaft of the other guard's weapon. He pulled a pistol from the breast lining of his coat and shot the third guard in the chest before slashing the throat of the newly disarmed woman. His body was trembling as he fought back the waves of unease.

Ject and Kin Mei were still battling the prince. Yushiro fought like a dancer. Ject stepped in to cleave his skull, but he caught the edge of the axe with the butt of his spear, stabbed the floor and vaulted. His boot landed on Ject's incredulous face with an audible *crunch*. Kin Mei was mid swing with her hammer when Yushiro pulled his weapon from the floor and whipped it through the air, carving a deep gash from one side of her lips to the opposite temple, crossing over the previous cut he left on her face. She fell to her knees, holding her bloody face in her hands.

Ject snorted and a glob of blood shot from one of his nostrils. He flailed his axes in wild chops, apparently trying to overwhelm the prince with unpredictable attacks with no pattern. Far from overwhelmed, the prince turned the spear and batted Ject's attacks away with the blunt end. Zayne noticed he was fiddling with the blade's fixture with one hand as he used the other to guide the weapon to parry the Daughter's reckless assault. Then, the prince whirled the spear around and aimed the blade at his target.

"Ject, *get down!*" Zayne shouted.

A pan flashed. An ear-splitting shot sounded, and a gout of purple flames and smoke bloomed from the end of the spear. Ject had thrown himself to one side. His severed right arm fell in the other direction. He clutched the bloody stump just below his elbow. Yushiro stood over him, poised to deliver the coup de grace.

Zayne felt around in his coat and realized he didn't have a loaded pistol. He extracted a barber's razor from his sleeve, unfolded it and threw it like a knife. It whirled through the air and fixed to hit the prince in the eye.

Before it met its mark, Kin Mei flailed on the floor, still blind. She kicked out and caught the back of Yushiro's knee. He buckled. He fell, and Zayne's razor sailed past, leaving the prince with two small cuts across his face rather than gouging his eye out. He braced his fall by slamming the butt of his spear against Kin Mei's gut, knocking the wind out of her as he fixed his footing. He leveled his blade against Zayne.

"Show me, then," he said. He flourished his weapon and wiped at the blood dripping near his eye, smearing it like warpaint. "Show me the skill that bested Elyia."

Zayne swallowed a lump in his throat. He fell into a ready stance, sword arm pulled back, weapon trained on his opponent. He hadn't given any thought to Yushiro's claim that he was better than Elyia Asier. However, after seeing him wipe the floor with both Ject and Kin Mei — after watching him kill a *Dread Hound* — he had to acknowledge that the prince was dangerous, perhaps more dangerous than anyone he had ever fought. He stepped into his attack just as Yushiro did the same.

The tip of his stolen sword hit the edge of the spear, and one of the blades chipped on contact, though Zayne couldn't tell which as he immediately moved into his next attack. Safely behind his opponent's reach, he swept low, aiming for Yushiro's ribs. The prince dropped the weapon and drew his own sword, catching Zayne's before it even escaped the scabbard. The blade wasn't iron: it was orichalcum.

They both retreated two steps. Zayne went in for a rising strike, and Prince Yushiro met it with a falling blade. The iron sword screeched as the iridescent weapon cleaved through its length, embedding itself mere inches from the hilt. Zayne's eyes widened in horror.

Shit, he thought.

Yushiro turned his wrist, and Zayne's useless weapon was wrenched from his grip. It skittered and clattered across the floor. The prince drew his arm back for the coup de grace. Zayne stared up at the dark, multi-colored sword as it glinted in the light, and time dilated in the way it did when one's mind raced, when it seemed too late to actually act. And a strange thought played across his mind, obscene in how obvious and easy it was.

Let him kill me.

With all the blood on his hands, Zayne certainly deserved it. He was a murderer, a thief, a liar, and on top of everything else, Fae possessed. Today alone, he had led a fleet that had killed thousands of people. Setting the day's slaughter aside, he had killed innocents who knew too much, righteous people serving a noble cause, and a hero of his own childhood. And why? Because he was too scared to do what was right.

I'm sorry, mother, he thought, *Nan, Cenn. I really botched it.*

You can't die here, another voice said. It sounded like his own voice. There was an angry edge to it. *You still have work to do.* He thought about Dardan's orders, the way her commands had overridden his body. *No, not that, don't think about that.* He thought about killing her. He had sworn he would, hadn't he? And Nanette was still out there, counting on him. He had to fight, for her, if not for himself.

His hands felt sluggish as he watched Yushiro's dragon-bone sword glide through the air towards his face. Still, he positioned them just so, and let out a steady breath. The world snapped, the speed of reality returning abruptly as Dawn Star appeared in an eruption of golden light. The orichalcum blade was violently knocked aside as the air became a flare of gold and purple sparks.

The prince held onto his weapon, but the Fae Blade's appearance had disrupted his inertia so completely, he skidded several feet across the floor, though somehow, he kept his feet and his wits. When he came to a stop with the squeal of his boots, he crouched into a defensive posture and eyed Dawn Star like a venomous serpent. Or a scorpion's tail.

Zayne lunged. When the Fae metal scraped against orichalcum, gold and purple flames came to life and fizzled away, causing the prince to falter. Zayne pressed the attack, coming in low, then high, spinning and flourishing, coming at Yushiro from every angle. For his part, Yushiro was able to block each assault, but his confusion and uncertainty left him unable to do anything more, and Zayne drove him back step by grueling step. He must at least have an inkling about the origin of Zayne's weapon, which must have raised a thousand questions about what it could do. Zayne could sympathize; he didn't quite understand it himself.

The prince must have regained his wits because he quit his retreat. He pivoted on his back foot and twisted his grip, locking the two unorthodox swords together. Their knuckles knocked together as their weapons' cross-guards met. They broke apart, and Zayne felt a familiar rhythm as they clashed.

Swish, swish, clang.

Clang, clang, swish.

Clang, clang, swish, clang, clang, clang.

It was only as Yushiro's blade scratched his mask that Zayne realized why it was so familiar. It wasn't just that his fighting style had been the same as Asier's — with both of them having been trained to serve the Empress, that only made sense. What struck Zayne was the barely contained rage behind every move, the reckless abandon that came from hate that pushed beyond self-preservation. Together, the fight and the fighter brought Zayne back to the deck of the *Dreamscape Voyager* that cold winter's day. He could still see Elyia Asier's amber eyes flooded with rage, her lithe form as she moved through sword forms with boundless speed, the nuances of her stances, and the memory almost perfectly lined up with his current reality.

Clang, clang, clang, clang.

Yushiro pushed him back.

The prince's assault featured less flourish and flash with each landed blow, gradually clipping away at extraneous movements until he became an automaton, moving from one end point to another. That made it harder for Zayne to read him. His arms burned as he struggled to keep up with the onslaught. He tried to parry Yushiro's attacks, but more often than not, he was barely able to block.

Clang, clang, clang.

Clang, swish, clang, clang, swish.

Swish, clang, swish, clang.

Clang, clang, clang. Snick.

Stinging pain bloomed to life in his right shoulder as Yushiro's blade slipped past his guard and sliced through the sleeve of his coat. He leaped back and clutched the wound. It was superficial, he was quite sure, but it burned like acid.

He threw himself at Yushiro's follow-through. The prince parried his counterattack, throwing his injured arm wide. Zayne was wide open. He wasn't fast enough to swing Dawn Star — even as light as it was — to intercept the orichalcum blade.

But he didn't need to.

As Prince Yushiro went for the kill, Dawn Star vanished from Zayne's right hand. The light hadn't even completely faded before another golden burst of luminescence came to life in his left hand, expanding, blooming, taking on the shape of the now-familiar blade. Yushiro seemed to realize what was happening, but it was too late.

The sword became solid midway through Yushiro's swing, and the prince's attack turned into his own dismemberment. His arm maintained its momentum, but without the elbow to keep it anchored, it went spinning, flying behind Zayne. Its fingers still clutched the orichalcum weapon when it landed, point driven into the floor.

A lot of people are losing their arms, today, Zayne noted. It had started as a glib thought, but it quickly devolved into something more grim as the weight and consequences landed on his shoulders.

Yushiro clutched his stump, much as Ject had mere moments before — had it really been so quick? The prince looked like he wanted nothing more than to kill Zayne, but he also looked

266

as though he would faint if he made any effort to move. There was no sense in killing him. There had been no sense in any of it, really, but at least now he had a choice.

"You've done your duty, your highness," Zayne said, stepping around the Empress' champion. "You did your duty. Don't throw your life away now."

Zayne released Dawn Star and took the prince's sword, setting his hand reverently aside. The blade's weight was strikingly similar to the Fae blade, but the differences were important. Much as he had grown to rely on it, he knew Dawn Star was, in some form or fashion, a tool of Lucandri, and he grew increasingly weary of it the more he used it. He flourished the sword. He offered a look back to find Tatl playing nurse to Altair, Ject, and Kin Mei.

Then he turned to face the Empress.

"I'm sorry, your majesty," he said. "I don't have a choice in this."

"Words oft spoken by cowards," the Empress said. Her voice was at once detached and accusatory, quiet yet commanding, calm yet tinged with deep passion. She had not stirred from her seat atop the dais. "You should sit, dog of Castilyn, while the real Hounds try to steal their prize."

Before Zayne could process the words, shadows manifested around them. Eight pools of darkness spread across the floor. The gods' hunting dogs emerged, howling and snapping and snarling. They ignored the easy prey of the dead, of the wounded, even Zayne, and formed up as a pack to square up against the Empress. The apparent pack leader — at least, if physical position implied such a thing — had red smoke billowing out of an empty eye socket and from a wounded throat and head. That was the one Altair had hurt if Zayne didn't miss his guess.

The Empress' barb made sense, with obvious hindsight. Clearly she knew that the Daughters were working with, if not for, the Queen Celeste of Castilyn, but more importantly, with her defenses crushed, what chance did she — a lone woman garbed in burdensome robes — stand against *eight* of the legendary servants of the gods, when any singular one had slaughtered scores of her people and her enemies alike. With them arrayed against her, nothing Zayne did could turn the tides in either direction.

Wait, Zayne considered, *did she say* try? Try *to take their prize?* The woman must have misspoke. Or she was mad.

As if responding to some unseen signal, the Dread Hounds simultaneously broke into a run. The Empress opened an ornate fan, and snapped it shut.

Lightning struck the floor. A hundred brilliant flashes of blinding light danced in the throne room, accompanied by a chorus of thunder so loud and concussive Zayne was rendered deaf and thrown several feet back. He bounced several times before falling into a roll.

Between the spots in his vision, Zayne saw the burning city from above, ships flying in chaotic formations, plumes of smoke from cannon fire, and lightning striking the top of the palace on a clear day. Amidst the ringing in his ears, he could hear the rush of the air, the churning of engines, the heavy blasts of cannons and rattling pops of gunfire, and the roll of thunder trembling through the air. Along with the burning numbness of his skin, he felt the soothing winds, the concussion of explosive charges, static energy dancing and lifting his hair on its ends, the touch of Nanette's fingers at the helm, stakes driven through his wrists to keep him secured to the prow —

His vision cleared and he was back in the throne room. He wasn't entirely convinced he was awake, however. The room was largely obscured by steam and smoke — both black and red — and the shimmering blur of pure heat he felt like a bonfire. Two of the Dread Hounds were breaking down into spectral dust. There was a hole in the ceiling large enough for a ship to drop through it, casting daylight down upon...

Zayne had no idea what it was.

The creature had a massive, serpentine body that emerged from a hole in the floor and almost reached the devastated ceiling. It had lean arms with thick, silvery talons, which it used to brace itself on the edges of the precipice. Its skin was coated in scales, reminiscent of a dragon's, which seemed black when looked at straight on, but shimmered in a myriad of colors when it shifted its weight. Its head was vaguely draconic, but wider, with a less angular snout equipped with long whisker-like tendrils, and its crown, rather than sleek horns, was adorned by white antlers. Its eyes were pure pools of jade-green light. It let out a low sigh that reverberated through the floor. Zayne's heart slammed against his ribs. He was reminded of the Host, for some reason. Was it a god? Or an instrument of a god, like the Dread Hounds themselves? Or was it simply a testament to the glory and power of the Empire's royal family, and a measure of their confidence that they didn't unleash it to lord over their people?

Zayne wanted to run, but the same paralysis that held him at bay when he tried to kill Dardan took over. It wasn't so much that he *couldn't* move, but almost as if his muscles didn't *want* to, in direct defiance to his mind. He knew if he were to try to push forward, his legs would obey without question, but retreat wasn't an option.

The six surviving Dread Hounds stood on Zayne's side of the strange monstrosity. Their disposition, if Zayne could judge their snarling and growling, had shifted from that of eager hunters cornering their prey to something even more violent. He wouldn't call it hatred — that seemed far too human an emotion to project on them, and it implied a state that *wasn't* violence incarnate — but neither could he dismiss it. Their hackles were raised, and whatever this thing was, it was their enemy.

They attacked.

As the Dread Hounds moved, their silhouettes blurred like flame, and amidst the heatwaves surrounding the strange creature, they became as illusionary as ghosts. Their forms blurred together as they surrounded the dark, prismatic behemoth. Its roar of pain when their tusks and fangs tore into its flesh was higher than Zayne would have expected, still loud and powerful, but with less depth and bass than its size might have implied. Like a gunshot in a canyon.

The thing that might have been a god was fast. Its neck lashed like a whip, its jaws catching one of the Hounds between pearlescent teeth. Blood sprayed and became smoke as the canine howled and squirmed for escape. The strange being slammed its interlocking teeth together and thrashed. Black and red smoke poured from the creature's mouth, and nothing remained of its prey.

Their battle was chaotic. The serpentine beast flexed and swerved, seeming to grow as more of its body filled the throne room. It wrapped and squeezed one of the Hounds even as its tusks and fangs and claws tore through its scales and ripped through flesh. The nightmare dogs crawled along their opponent's form and ravaged it, gorging on its insides. It flailed. One of the Dread Hounds was crushed under the giant reptile's full weight while another was thrown to the floor, with its own teeth scattered around it.

As the Hound regained its feet, Zayne caught a glimpse of its snarling maw as its fangs grew to their full length from its blackened gums and leaped back into the fray.

Tatl meandered up to the killing field to gather up the broken teeth. She hummed a strange, familiar song Zayne couldn't place as she picked up the pieces. Her too-blue eyes were vacant as always as she took in the pitched battle before them.

"You know a lot of hidden and forbidden lore," Zayne said as she drew near.

"I do," she acknowledged without pausing in her collection.

"What is *that*?" he asked, pointing at the Empress' beast.

Tatl eyed the great reptilian horror. Something broke over her normally tepid expression. It looked a little bit like sadness. "The last vestiges of a world worth living in," she said.

"*Excuse me*?" Zayne asked, so taken aback that it almost distracted him from the madness. He wasn't sure what warped priorities Tatl had between Myt Dust poisoning her mind and Altair's madness influencing her, but there was something in her words that resonated inside him for some reason, the way a sad song might stir a memory just out of reach.

Tatl kept her eyes on the monster. "You can't stop Darden from winning this battle. But if she wins the war —"

The Empress' guardian let out a suffering shriek. Two of the Hounds had clawed their way up the length of its body and sunk their teeth into the tender flesh at its throat. It reached up with its claws and seized them, puncturing their bodies with its talons, killing them, but the damage was done. Its head began to sway drunkenly as it pawed for the remaining Hounds, which now bounded easily around it.

"The world will continue to bleed out like her. And it will die the same. Thrashing, clinging desperately—futilely, to life."

Zayne watched the guardian as it — she? — flailed at the beasts that brought it down. "What do you mean, *continue* to bleed out?"

"When this is done," Tatl said, as though he hadn't spoken, "do as the First Night bid you. Before you seek out Dardan if you can. There's still hope if you do." She got up and returned to her ministrations over the other Daughters, leaving Zayne alone with the feeling that everything happening in front of him was a dream caused by the stress of battle.

That's what this is, he thought glibly, *I passed out after the battle started, and this is all a terrible dream.* He couldn't convince himself, however, not even for one, miserable second, that the sweat and the dirt plastered to his brow, or the claw marks across his chest, the stench of blood and sulfur, or even the strange sight before him weren't real.

The guardian fell so heavily the palace shook violently. It wasn't dead, yet, but it was in the final throes of death. Its breath trembled, washing over Zayne. It seemed to be looking at him, though it was hard to be sure as its eyes were pure light. Was that sadness he saw, or was he projecting?

The three remaining Dread Hounds surrounded it. One overeager beast stepped too close and fell prey to a final strike of its claws, smashed under the weight of its paw. The guardian shifted, and now Zayne was sure it was leveling its glare on him, though he wasn't sure why. Did it know something he didn't? Did it sense Lucandri's touch on him?

As it died, some of the guardian's scales began to fall off its body. Before they touched the ground, they exploded into wisps of light in every color which floated like dandelion seeds in the wind. As it continued to shed, its skin, its muscles, its sinew, its muscle, and even its blood melted away into light, just as the dead Dread Hounds had been reduced to a beautiful darkness.

The tiny lights were not terribly bright on their own, and they were small enough they could have fit in the palm of Zayne's hand if they were tangible. But there were a lot of them. The whisps soon flooded the room, obscuring the massive hole in the floor and Zayne's view of the Empress. The lights drifted inexorably upwards, out the gap in the ceiling, like a reversing waterfall.

Three Dread Hounds were still standing when the last of the guardian's light cleared away. They circled the precipice, their focus back on the Empress. One-Eye was still leading the pack, and it made a sound almost like mocking laughter. A cruelty so human somehow made the beast seem all the more alien and horrible.

The Empress reached up to her elaborately adorned hair and pulled at one of the pins holding it in place. She placed the pin to her lips, and it let out the most beautifully pure whistle Zayne had ever heard. There was an answering trill from above and behind the throne. An explosion of color — a brilliant myriad of reds and golds,

271

and one, singular flash of green — erupted from behind the dignified monarch.

Phoenixes, Zayne noted as nine beautiful birds pulled out of their collective dives. They were as tall as a man, sleek with tails that followed them like capes, circled the Dread Hounds like vultures. Eight of the avian protectors were like living flames, their feathers a gradient of deep reds that blended seamlessly into the golden pinions at the end of their wings. The ninth was the Empire's legendary mascot, depicted on banners and coins and stamped on goods all over the Empire; it was the Jade Phoenix. Zayne didn't know if they had somehow meticulously dyed each of its feathers, or if it was some sort of mutation or other fluke of nature, but somehow it was a green as vibrant as its namesake with black flight feathers.

In spite of himself, Zayne was captivated. Firebirds were widely — justifiably — considered the most beautiful and dangerous animals this side of the Dreamscape; while dragons were far larger and more aggressive, phoenixes were faster, smarter, and their blood would catch fire mere moments after being exposed to the air, earning them their moniker. It was widely known the Empress owned a few, but Zayne hadn't factored them when assessing the palace defenders. He had grossly underprepared for today.

The phoenixes swooped one at a time from their formation, striking with talons that easily cut through the Dread Hounds' impressive hides. The evil beasts quit their advance to retaliate against the airborne attackers, snapping at them with jaws full of razors, though only One-Eye managed to catch so much as a feather or two as their targets deftly evaded. The canines spread out, and the birds worked at giving them death by a thousand cuts.

Then One-Eye pounced.

It caught one of a passing phoenix's wings between its forepaws and bit viciously at its shoulder. The bird squawked in agonized terror, and a conflagration erupted within the Dread Hound's clamped jaws. One-Eye growled, pinning its prey to the ground with a heavy thud, and thrashed with its teeth still latched onto the burning meat. It ripped the bird messily in two, and each drop of blood, snapped sinew, and torn muscle caught fire, burning the Hound as it continued to enact bloody and futile vengeance on the creature burning it. The other phoenixes descended on One-Eye immediately, and in moments it had no eyes at all.

It decapitated a second phoenix with a heavy crunch that spewed more blood and fire, but it was torn apart by vicious talons and beaks, large muscle clusters being severed and crippling the beast, ushering it to death by a thousand cuts before it finally succumbed.

The remaining seven phoenixes converged on the next Dread Hound in a frenzy. It lashed out blindly, wounding two of the birds with its tusks, and when the blood staining its face caught fire, it was rendered blind. It lunged at the Jade Phoenix, which climbed effortlessly to avoid its attack. The Hound fell down the hole that likely led to the hidden catacombs Zayne had used to break in almost two years ago. He wondered if the fall would kill it, or if it could escape into shadow before the impact. He wasn't going to stand close enough to the edge to find out.

The final Dread Hound gave as good as it got. When one phoenix carved through its skull plate with a talon, its tusk took the bird's taloned foot. It cleaved through wings, burning its mouth, they gouged its eyes and were met with claws and a whipping tail. Each time blood was drawn, it was answered with more blood, until the Dread Hound collapsed among the self-incinerating corpses of birds and broke down.

The sole survivors were the Jade Phoenix and another with a wounded wing that didn't so much *fly* away from the carnage as hop and flap frantically to gain a few extra feet before collapsing — alive, but without any fight left in it. It smoldered in its own fires, which surprisingly didn't catch on the floor.

From atop her dais, the Empress played the whistle again, and the Jade and wounded phoenixes turned to Zayne and attacked. His reprieve was over. He barely had time to fall into a fighting stance before the Jade Phoenix was upon him. He slashed wildly. There was no blood. The bird had banked at the last second and he bisected a single fallen feather.

Altair was at Zayne's side, suddenly, and she had her own silver whistle in hand. She blew it, and the loud shriek hurt his ears. The Jade circled back and dived. Zayne grazed it along the length of its phalanx bone. It climbed and its wing flashed in a gout of fire. It reached the peak of its climb and began to loop around when a shadow appeared from below. Andrasta crashed into the phoenix. The two birds tumbled in the air. They flapped and flailed, both taking flight again before hitting the floor. The kestrel flew just out of the Phoenix's reach and evaded attacks until it was leading the Jade out into the open sky.

Zayne rolled his shoulders and took slow, deliberate steps around the precipice, careful to keep two arm's length between himself and the hole. He held the prince's sword out in a defensive posture, ready for anything to spring out from behind a tapestry, or the rafters, or gaping pits below or its mirror above. After everything else today, he half expected the dais to sprout legs and attack him. The Empress' placid face tracked his progress, but she remained otherwise still until he stepped in line with the dais.

Yushiro Shahira — Ninety-Eighth Empress of the Asarisan Empire, Protector of the Skies, First Arbiter of the Law, and Keeper of the Nine Promises— stood to confront Zayne — mercenary, murderer, thief, and conman. It was a smooth, graceful motion, as though the heavy robes and ornamentation encumbering her were nothing but air. Her hair adornments jingled faintly as she took deliberate, imperious steps down the nine steps of the dais. Halfway down, she shed the outer robe, and she began undoing the robe beneath it. When she reached the floor, she was dressed in a jade green tunic with detached sleeves tied at the bicep, and billowy pants tied at the ankles. She wore a sword at the small of her back — a jian with a silk tassel affixed to the pommel — and armored gloves with amber gems lining the palm and inside of the fingers.

Fire glands, Zayne concluded, eying the gloves. The stones taken from the belly of a dragon generated fire when they made contact with one another. They served a myriad of purposes, and Zayne had seen them weaponized before, but he had never seen them used in gauntlets. He wondered at the damage a person might do, not only to their opponent, but to themselves if they slipped.

"I'm sorry, your majesty," said Zayne. "I'll try to make this as painless as possible."

The Empress' eyes flashed in irritation. "You may have defeated our champions with cheap tricks," she said, "but we will not be defeated so easily."

She raised a hand and snapped her fingers. Fire struck like lightning and Zayne flinched at the sudden rush of hot air flowing around him. He only had his blade in place to block the bolt of flame by chance, and the golden-red blaze dispersed into a flash of purple sparks. She repeated the gesture in quick succession, and he was driven back by the onslaught of dragon fire.

She moved like a viper, each snap of flame coming at Zayne from another angle as she wove around his defense, looking for an opening. His sword was thrumming with each strike he blocked like the fading resonance of a gong. She closed the distance between them, and Zayne braced himself for another snap, certain he knew where it would come from. Her foot connected squarely with the unmasked side of his head. He staggered, nearly dropping the blade. She snapped again and the fire struck his shoulder like a whip. His coat was fire-resistant, but these sparks had force behind them, like a gale compressed into the size of a bullet. It tore through his sleeve, and the searing pain around the wound hit something deep that ran across his nerves to his fingertips and his spine.

He nearly dropped the sword from twinging fingers. Instead, he gripped it so tight it rattled, and he thrashed out at the Empress' follow up. The dragon bone sword cut through the dragon fire, dispersing flame and leaving waves of heat blurring the air. It was like cutting through water shooting out of a pipe, the raw force behind it wearing his already tired arms to pure exhaustion and threatening to blow him back.

When he pushed through her barrage, he aimed for her heart. It would be quick and painless. He had stolen her friend, and her people. He had crippled her brother. He owed her what little mercy he could find. She didn't flinch. She didn't try to evade. She didn't even reach for her own sword.

She caught the blade between her hands.

Despite everything, there was a faint hint of a self-satisfied smile worming its way onto the placid mask that was her heavily painted face, cracking the facade. The faint quirk of her eyebrow was accentuated by the kohl she wore. She was enjoying this. Not in the bloodthirsty way of an unshackled killer — he had known so many people like that in his life — but in the way of a highly spirited fighter who had taken the measure of her opponent.

An unsettling thought intruded on Zayne's thoughts as he met her eye: The Empress was beautiful. She was beautiful in all the ways he knew a woman *could* be beautiful. Though her face was masked in makeup, its shape was an idealized beauty. Her deep, mahogany eyes seemed to drink in the light and reflected only the most perfect sources in their shine, and there was a thoughtfulness as she studied him. Her voice was imperious and proud, certain and confident. She was brave enough to face a murderer in her own home, and strong and quick enough to back up that courage.

His reverie was broken when she clicked the heels of her palms together, touching amber gem to amber gem. Rather than a lightning-quick spark, a large fire blossomed in her cupped hands, corralled by the other gems lined along the inside of her hands. The orichalcum blade between her palms split the blast of fire, causing two streams of flames to erupt. Zayne leaped back a moment before the twin jets could incinerate his face, but it was close enough he worried about his eyes, and his mask was hot on his face. *Who makes a mask out of iron?* he thought bitterly. He blinked until tears came back to his dried eyes and missed the Empress closing the distance. She hit him in the gut with an open palm still swirling with flame.

The flames were smothered immediately, but his skin burned all the same. He doubled over as the air was knocked out of him, staggering back two steps. He caught himself before stumbling back a third and drove the point of his sword forward. The Empress pirouetted and the blade sailed harmlessly behind her back while her foot caught the masked side of his head. This time, he couldn't keep his footing, and he hit the floor.

The mask hit the floor with a *clang.*

His hair, black as night with a single streak of silver, draped around his fallen face. As he pushed himself up, he watched as the black strands became white while that one bizarre streak darkened to a raven's hue. He thought about the revelation about appearing as Lucandri when he didn't wear the mask and wondered how he had missed an obvious sign like that. His skin had shifted, too, more subtly, but his skin was a rich, almost golden tan. Had he been so absorbed in melancholy he had missed a transformation so obvious? He didn't think so. More likely, he hadn't been looking so closely at his own features.

The iconic black dye of his coat shifted, like the dark clouds of a storm starting to break. A strange gold-white light appeared beneath it until there was no blackness remaining. *That* had definitely not happened before. He was fairly sure, at least.

He stood.

Some of the courtiers gasped or made other noises Zayne couldn't quite identify. He had completely forgotten they were present. In particular, he heard one man offer nasally mutterings to the stunned quiet.

If the Empress was surprised by his transformation, however, she didn't show it. Perhaps she was a master of her emotions. Perhaps she saw strange and eldritch sights with some regularity. Perhaps she figured she was just having that kind of day and it wasn't worth being surprised by anything else. Regardless, she looked impassive and unimpressed. She glanced over to the huddled mass of her courtiers, and her brow quirked like she learned something strange.

"We see what you are," the Empress said, turning her attention back to Zayne. "But you have no influence over us." He had no idea what she meant by that last part, but it sounded significant.

She lifted her hand to snap her fingers again, but she seemed to be moving more deliberately. Zayne understood once the fire flashed to life. Time had dilated in his mind, and the fire was no longer lightning quick as it traveled through the air. It wasn't slow, but now it was a weapon he could easily track. He slashed with the orichalcum blade, feeling less resistance than before — he still recoiled from the force, but it was no longer overpowering. Despite his slowed perception, he didn't feel slowed or sluggish himself. Fire splashed all around him as he cleaved through the bolts and pressed through the heat.

Had he been suppressing this strength by wearing his mask this whole time?

No, he thought forcefully. He didn't know why he felt such a vehement rejection of his own thoughts. Perhaps it was a slippery road from accepting Lucandri's boons to welcoming his presence under his skin. Either way, whatever shrivel of morality remained in his heart refused to even consider that he was better off like this, with this evil creature inside him.

Wanted or not, his newfound strength allowed him to slash easily between the ribbons of golden flames and fight his way to the Empress. She cupped her hands together, touching the gems at the heel of her palms together, the tips of her small fingers, and the ends of her thumbs. Fire danced in the space between her hands and was funneled out through the gaps between her fingers, launching out at Zayne in a geyser. He needed to neutralize this weapon. He stepped to the side of the approaching light and plunged the orichalcum blade into the rushing flames. This time he did feel the resisting pressure, but he fought, taking a deliberate step and dragging the sword through the torrent of fire.

He hit something hard.

The air violently sucked inward even as it exploded outward, creating a vortex of heat and wind. Zayne's feet scraped the floor as the raw force pushed him back several feet. He stopped on the precipice into the palace depths just behind his heel. The ends of his hair had caught fire, but he was easily able to pat them out. Smoke and the stretch of charred leather and hair separated him from the Empress, who stood at the foot of the dais with hands open, staring at them as if unsure what had happened. Steam and smoke rolled off her gauntlets as sparks spurted from the broken gems. She was breathing deeply, but steadily. She shed them with a delicate grace. Even broken, fire glands were still a danger — if anything, they were *more* dangerous, as they were more likely to backfire.

She blew gently on her hands, though from Zayne's vantage they didn't seem to have burned. She turned her gaze to meet his. "We have been prepared for a threat like yours for a very long time, but still, we expected to never need the tools to combat you."

Zayne understood in principle why the Empress referred to herself as *we*; she spoke on behalf of all of Asaria. When she made demands, it was the *Empire* that demanded, when she made promises, they were the promises of the *Empire*, when she made a proclamation, decree, or even a request, it was the Empire entire that spoke. Still, from a strictly grammatical standpoint, it was more than a little confusing. Had *she* prepared alone, or had she and her guards prepared? And did *she* doubt, or —

The Empress reached into one of her detached sleeves and extracted an ornate vial of amber liquid as long as her thumb and twice as wide around the middle. She popped the decorative stopper with her thumbnail and downed the draught. The revulsion at the taste was far and away the most emotion Zayne had seen on her face.

There was a thrum in the air, a deep, resonant bass that rattled him to his bones and made his teeth vibrate. The Empress was the epicenter. She smelled like the wind before a storm. Light seemed to bend around her, as though it were the sea, and she was a whirlpool. It settled as quickly as it had begun, and he knew something had changed in her, but he had no way of knowing what.

She drew her sword. It was a match for her brother's, save for the jade tassel hanging from the pommel. She took her stance, blade held high to come down on Zayne like judgement. Zayne chose a low, sweeping stance to answer her, and they took slow, deliberate steps to shorten the distance — and in Zayne's case, to get away from the precipice.

Her eyes are different, Zayne thought as they stood poised to strike. It wasn't the kind of change normally watched for — composure giving way to hate, or bluster to fear — but a much more *physical* change. Mere moments ago, he had become lost in those eyes, which had been brown — the most beautiful shade of brown he had ever seen, but still *brown* — but now they gleamed in distinct, brilliant and fiery shades of amber. He had only ever known two people with eyes like that: Elyia Asier and Isaara Altair. *What was in that draught?* More importantly, he wondered, *What else changed?*

Zayne knew the importance of attacking first. Conventional wisdom said the first to strike was the last to strike. *Knowing* a thing, however, didn't make *doing* a thing easy.

He moved less than a second after the Empress, but that small allowance had her setting the pace of their exchange as she opened with a stab. She was faster than she had been before downing the vial. Her iridescent blade was a hand's breadth from his face before he was able to bring his own weapon to bear against it. Purple sparks flew as their swords scraped across one another's length.

They each took a step back and leaned into the next attack without pause. *Clang, clang, clang.* The Empress launched a feint at his core, then threw her weight into a two-handed assault at his left. When he parried her, she spun, having switched hands and cut at his right. He missed the block by a paper-thin margin, and her blade bit into his right shoulder. She kicked him in the ribs, driving him harder against her blade, but though with his own weapon pushing against it, it didn't make the cut any deeper.

When they separated again, the Empress didn't step forward to meet him, but rather she *threw* her weapon at him. He batted it away from his face, though the action was more of a flail than any kind of practiced defense, and he was unprepared when it arced around her and swung around her back, slicing his shoulder, crossing the previous wound before the Empress yanked the tassel and returned the hilt to her hand. Pain lanced through him, but he fought the reflex to drop his sword.

Their next clash included a series of flourishes that drove him back, and she alternated between using the hilt traditionally and using the tassel for added reach. Zayne had known several people who used gimmicks to fight; he had once fought a pirate who used oils to breathe fire, worked with a Daughter who had two swords with their ends affixed together, seen a man who used a massive brick of iron as big as his body and called it a sword. Just today he had seen spears hiding guns and lengths of chain. Unorthodox weapons or techniques were great at catching an opponent off guard, but amateurs tended to rely too heavily on the novelty and could be defeated as soon as the enemy figured out the trick.

The Empress was no amateur. She shifted seamlessly between techniques, utilizing her fists and feet as much as blade and tassel. He recognized some of the styles she used, but before he could find a steady rhythm, she would change to one he didn't. She didn't give him room to launch an attack, and he was barely able to defend against each rapid attack.

Clang, clang, swish, clang.

Clang, clang, clang, thud.

Clang, thud, clang, clang.

Zayne had once believed Elyia Asier to be the greatest warrior in the world. He had had to bring a pistol to their sword fight in order to defeat her. Then he met Yushiro Tao, Elyia Asier's successor, and discovered a new pinnacle of skill. He had needed superior numbers and a Fae-trick sword to tip that scale in his favor. But the Empress was proving she didn't *need* champions. And worse, she had countered his unfair advantage with one of her own.

Clang, clang, clang.

They locked blades. The Empress was half a head shorter than Zayne, and her illustrious hairpins were at his eye level. So he knew what was happening when she removed a pin with a jade jewel embedded in the end. He just wasn't fast enough to stop her. The pin slid easily between his lower ribs. The pain was excruciating. The prince's sword dropped from his numb fingers and his vision blurred.

The Scorpion *feels her captain's pain. He needs her. She is currently engaged with another vessel, the* Dreamless *— a foolish name, as all ships dream, even now, long after the old World Tree was razed, though those dreams became faded and devoid of their former luster — but she will not lose another captain, not now. She had loved her old captain like a daughter loves her mother,* *still loves her even though she is gone. Her First Mate, who would become the next captain, is also precious to her. But her current captain had shared his blood with her. They had sunk together, fallen to the depths together.*

And they had risen together.

If he fell, so would she.

So she fights against the guidance of the First Mate. It feels wrong to take the lead. Unclean. Against her very nature. But she does. She breaks away from the Dreamless *and turns the ballista — her aptly named Scorpion Tail — on her aftcastle around, aiming it at the pilot of the* Dreamless. *The one manning the weapon fires, whether surprised at what she has done or understanding it, she cares not. The spear destroys the navigation equipment and kills its pilot.*

She can feel the voices traveling through the pipes beneath her hull. The cannoneer demands to know why the First Mate is taking them to the palace. She tells him she isn't. She is fighting against the Scorpion's *will at the helm, and the* Scorpion *feels guilty, but she must do this.*

One of the cannons nested at her fore has been destroyed, and it still burns, the timbers around it still smolder. But the other she forces into position.

Fire, *she willed at the cannoneer.* Fire. *She has the means to* force *him to do it, but she needs to save that strength. She has only one chance.* Fire.

The cannon fires.

Zayne blinked. The ship was about to open fire *here*. The Empress's arm was pulled back, ready to make the killing thrust. *Come on, Shen,* he thought, *do what the ship wants.*

The wall to Zayne's left exploded. Plaster dust and burning tapestries and wood rained down with intense sunlight. The Empress turned, releasing her hold on the jade pin to protect her eyes. Zayne used her distraction to rip the jade pin out of his side. Even though he had been prepared for it, he groaned in agonizing pain. Blood spurted from the wound and pooled at his feet. His body rattled as the stinging pain sent a cold sensation across his nerves.

The Empress steadied herself and returned to her attack. He couldn't stop her this time. But she *could* be stopped. He felt the *Scorpion* ready its secret attack, as though he himself was taking a deep breath. The rivermaid crucified to the prow had been pinned there, exposed to the elements for almost thirty years, and now, one with the ship, its mouth opened. The *Scorpion* made the impossible happen.

281

The rivermaid sang.

The Siren Song echoed through the throne room, washing over everyone who heard it, and debilitating anyone with a love for women. It even affected Zayne despite his connection to the *Scorpion* and by extension the Siren-kin. The song felt like warm water washing away the blood and the dirt, like a sweet-smelling fog threatening to smother his brain of all thoughts of tension.

The Empress dropped her sword mid-strike and it clattered on the floor. Her whole body was trembling, and her breath was labored. Her eyes, now that brilliant amber, were quivering with unfocused lust. Despite it all, she clearly hadn't given up the fight. With a quivering hand, she reached up to pull another pin from her hair. She clutched it in her fist and lifted her hand to take the final stab at Zayne. But the song had left her even just as debilitated as his wounds affected him.

He dropped the jade pin he pulled from his ribs and summoned Dawn Star. Lucandri's visage melted around him. The silver of his hair and the corresponding black ran like ink, revealing his natural, his *human* appearance beneath. The infinite depths of white he wore blew away like clouds, revealing the true, dyed-black appearance of his coat. The rich, almost luminescent tan of his skin faded to its usual tones. All aspects of Lucandri's illusion ran like oil on water and coalesced in the shimmering lights that shaped the sword. He took an unsteady step forward.

The Empress rammed her pin deep where his shoulder met his neck, and in doing so, drove Dawn Star to the hilt between her breasts. Her eyes widened, either in pain or shock. He couldn't tell which. Her heartbeat slowed, each hit a steady thrum running through the sword. The Siren Song was cut off as the *Scorpion* shrieked with Zayne's agony, and every thought and memory it had suppressed — the killings, the pain, the guilt, the fighting, the filth, the fear — exploded within him like a mountain of gunpowder.

He buckled. He would have collapsed to the floor if the Empress hadn't fallen into him in turn. They held one another up without meaning to. Her breath hitched and misted with blood as it hit Zayne's face.

"May... the gods," the Empress managed around a mouthful of blood, her voice breathless and distant, "drag... you down... with them when… they…*die.*"

Her hand flexed weakly around the pin in his shoulder, as though she were trying to free it so that she may stab him again, but she fell limp, falling fully into Zayne, and he caught her reflexively. Her final breath shuddered, warm and trembling against his neck in an almost intimate gesture.

It was too much.

Zayne had killed thirteen people today — now fourteen including the Empress — and each one burned a place in his memory, in his *soul*. And he'd been party to the deaths of untold thousands, even before considering the long-term effects of the attack. He had waded in blood and smoke and death, until finally, at the top of the world, he could barely stand, burned, beaten, lacerated, and heartbroken.

With one trembling hand stained with blood and black powder, he adjusted a lock of the Empress' hair that had fallen into her face after removing her pins. He touched her cheek, tenderly, as if he might wake her, smearing ash and blood through her makeup. He cradled her in his arms.

And he wept.

CHAPTER TWENTY-SEVEN

Turye, the smallest of the moons, was still out well into the morning. Cassidy had been staring at her for a while, trying to think of her next move and failing. All she could think of was how nice it would be to be nestled in the sky like that, to feel nothing but the gentle coolness of the early bright. Instead, she was sitting in the cold on a supply crate in the shadow of the *Dreamscape Voyager*. Her whole body hurt, and the one remedy she had was denied to her.

She was meeting with the Lord Minister, the baroness and a host of other officials. After Cassidy had waved in their face that she had killed Flint, they had agreed to meet her on the roof, rather than in a stuffy closet or whatever. Somehow, they had managed to bring out tables and chairs up, though they hadn't brought one for Cassidy or any of her crew. That was fine, she had her crate and the knowledge that she was the hero of the hour. Kek and Miria stood on either side of her — Miria as the most knowledgeable person in the *Dreamscape's* crew, and Kek claimed it was his responsibility as Cassidy's second-in-command — to weigh in as needed.

"... only have seven patrol ships that can be repurposed to accompany you," said Watch-Captain Tseng — it had taken a whole day for the officials to figure out who was still alive in the City Watch, but from there it had been a simple matter to determine that Tseng had defaulted her way into the job, with the deaths of eight of her superiors. She was a lanky woman who had managed to get through the fighting with only a bandaged head to mark her. "If we had more time —"

Cassidy flicked her wrist dismissively, then winced at the pain. Blinking away tears, she said, "Gather your strength, then. We can return for the fleet when we get back from Rivien."

"What will you be doing in Rivien?"

"Among other things, we have to buy guns," said Cassidy. *And to conscript pirates turned war heroes and back, but I don't need to tell you that.* "We need to arm the fleet with orichalcum weapons. We were able to recover a few from the rebels, but given the circumstances —"

"What do you need orichalcum guns for?" demanded the city's minister of finance. He was that bizarre mix of fat and what might also be muscle, and had a high, soft voice that in no way fit the body housing it.

Cassidy sighed and rubbed her eyes. She wanted a cigarette. "About half a year ago, the Dragon Nest was destroyed," she said, "with Fae power." She let that addition sink in. "There's a giant tree where it used to be, and when that tree appeared, something from the Dreamscape came with it."

Kek unrolled a large scroll. Nieves wasn't the greatest artist, but she had a steady hand and an eye for detail and — with Hymn making remarks about features Nieves had not seen — she had spent the night making a passable likeness to the monster.

"We call it the Leviathan," Cassidy informed the officials. It was strange, the way she kept saying that. They *called* it the Leviathan because that's what *Hymn* said it was called. She didn't know if the word had some kind of meaning in either Rivien or Castilyn — or even if it were an obscure Asarian word that had eluded her limited education — nor did she know if it were a common legend somewhere, in which case claiming credit for the name would probably come off as patronizing. "It was large enough to swallow multiple adolescent dragons whole," she added. She watched as some of the faces around her blanched, while others looked at her like she was spinning a ridiculous fisher's tale.

"We saw it in the north sea a month ago en route to the capital," Miria answered. "It was hiding beneath the surface, but its silhouette spanned at least a mile. It's been destroying ships in transit. We have no way of knowing exactly how many have been lost, but the disappearances have been noticed, and the reports are rising."

"Lord Minister," said a grey-haired woman with an upturned nose — Cassidy thought she was the Minister of City Ordinances or something equally unhelpful to the situation, but she couldn't quite remember. "You can't seriously be considering lending our people on chasing silly rumors. Honestly, this is probably some wild tale spread by the overfunded fools at the Nest with too much time on their hands."

Cassidy was so taken aback by the ignorance of the minister that her anger had to follow several steps behind her mind. Kek made up for her loss by slamming a fist on the table. "We were at the Nest when it was destroyed. Imagine this," he added, gesturing to the ruins of the city, "happening in minutes. That's the force this can bring to bear."

"You're just opportunists," the woman argued, "spinning a story to take advantage of gullible fools —"

"Would you call the Empress a fool?" Miria asked flatly.

"What?"

"I asked," Miria said slowly, taking a deliberate step forward, "would you call the Empress a fool?" She pulled one of the copies of her mother's writ from her belt. "I suppose someone decided you weren't important enough to inform, but the Empress herself assigned us this task. So by questioning us, you're either calling her a fool or a liar. You're also disrespecting the scores of men and women who died at the Nest," she added solemnly. The minister looked like she swallowed a toad and said no more.

"Our task," Miria continued, apparently taking charge away from Cassidy, "is to scour the seas and skies with as many ships and guns as we can conscript. And with all the trouble our crew put into stopping the rebellion here, you should be grateful we don't conscript every man and woman of service age in the city to make up for lost time." Whether it was her sharp rebuke instilling shame or the pure iron resolve when Miria spoke, the minister was sufficiently cowed, and no one dared to even meet the girl's eye. "The Dreamscape was deliberately opened up over the Dragon Nest. We don't know why, but regardless, the Leviathan is a threat to the Empire and beyond. If we don't do this, people will continue to be lost. Trade will suffer, and then everything you need — fresh food, supplies, everything — will dry up, and rebellions like this one will be a way of life until they end in anarchy and cannibalism."

Cassidy swallowed uncomfortably at the thought. She had only been thinking about the *direct* consequences of the Leviathan being free — the *Western Zephyr*'s destruction being a particularly painful memory, and she had imagined the beast killing people by the score — not the long-term effects. Cassidy was already set on this course, but if she had had any doubts, Miria's assessment quashed them.

The princess incognito continued to direct the meeting into the logistics, and Cassidy was more than happy to leave it to her. Cassidy knew more about the prices and general accessibility of goods and resources and chimed in when needed, but Miria went clear over Cassidy's head when it came to discussions about how to acquire and distribute said resources. It was agreed that the *Dreamscape Voyager* would fly into Rivien without a fleet, partly because they didn't have the ships to hand, but also because an Imperial fleet entering foreign skies might be taken as a sign of invasion. Miria also helped set up a messaging relay system so the *Dreamscape's* crew could communicate with their conscripts in Andaerhal more quickly than if they had to fly all the way back themselves.

The rest of the meeting passed in a blur of reiterating questions and ironing out details that had already been covered. Cassidy probably would have stopped paying attention even if her body weren't falling apart. As it was, she tried to look composed and aloof when in reality, her injuries over the course of the battle — compounded with the pain she had been using her Fae connection — left her feeling like she had been fired out of a cannon into a mountain.

She watched Turye's progress across the sky, grateful for Miria's intervention. In the end, it was decided that the *Dreamscape Voyager* would have two ships as escort: the *Roc Spear* and the *Sunrise*.

The captain of the *Sunrise* was a reedy, one-eyed woman named Kin Aahn. When the meeting adjourned, she pushed past the city officials as they carried their chairs or hefted their tables. She stood in front of Cassidy with a strange gleam in her eye and a barely suppressed smile.

"Captain Durant?" she asked. Her voice was a husky and scratchy affair. She barely waited for Cassidy to nod before launching in with, "It's a pleasure to meet you. I fought with Admiral Asier during the war. Well, maybe not *with* her, so to speak, but I was there during the Battle of Tal Joyau. I was a cabin girl on the *Night's Wish,* but even that little post was enough to give me my own captaincy when I signed up for the Imperial navy; of course I may have exaggerated my contribution. I joined after the *Wish* and her captain disappeared. Never learned what happened to them." She looked up at the *Dreamscape Voyager,* her eyes lit with recognition, and a smile heavy with nostalgia played across her face. "The name may have changed, but she's still the *Jade Phoenix* under that paint. Small for what she's done, but a damn fine vessel.

"The admiral was an incredible woman," she concluded, "I wish I could have known her personally."

"She was, " Kek agreed, and when he thumped his chest, there was a real pride in him.

"Aye," Cassidy said.

"She was an incredible leader, and a good friend," Miria said.

Cassidy thought about that. Had Asier's affection been as hollow and insincere as her courage? She didn't want to believe that, but the specter was there, lingering like an infection in her brain. Now that Cassidy had been through the process of seeing the future and following its course — twice — she knew how easy it was to trust the vision to string her along. Had any of Asier's tokens of affection been spontaneous, or had they been guided by the future to ensure events played out the way she saw them? Had she really loved the crew, or had it all been an act where the script appeared in her head like a magician's trick?

"We set out first thing tomorrow," Cassidy informed Captain Kin. "Where's the *Roc's* captain?"

"Captain Zhu is helping with the recovery. His is a Watch ship; this is his permanent home. You'll probably meet him before we embark."

Cassidy nodded. "Well, it was a pleasure to meet you, but I need to meet up with the rest of my crew."

"Of course," Kin said with a bow. "I have to see to my ship's provisions. Good day, Captain Durant."

Cassidy turned to Kek. "Take me to the tavern," she said.

"Your nose didn't bleed once," Kek said. The non-sequitur confused her. It must have shown on her face because he added, "You haven't done those Fae tricks. That's good. I swear, that shit can't be good for you."

You have no idea, Cassidy thought bitterly, but she forced a smile through the pain. She felt Hymn move about uncomfortably in her hat, and she hoped desperately that the Fae didn't feel like chiming in. "Tavern," she repeated, friendly as she could muster. "I need a drink, or seven, and a word with Nieves."

They waited until the tables were no longer blocking the stairwell and wove through the ministry building, passing through the triage stations — which were seeing less use now that the battle was over — and out into the streets where teams of laborers cleared rubble with rickshaws and wagons. The medley of smells — ash and charcoal and sulfur and gunpowder and sweat — came and went with an unsteady breeze. An uneasy quiet sat heavily over the work.

There was no idle chatter, no boisterous barkers hocking their goods, no cacophony of city life. Only the mechanical sounds of wheels grinding against cobblestones, of rubble clattering and wood knocking around, of very distant ship and skiff engines buzzing, filled the surreal and impossible openness. Seeing so many lives upended felt unreal; it was less like her world than the Dreamscape.

She was acutely aware of Miria's misery as they walked. The princess made a point of meeting every eye that glanced their way, meeting the hollow gazes of onlookers with a firm fist-to-chest salute, returning weary nods from the workers with a proud smile that couldn't hide her heartbreak — at least from Cassidy — and when she saw tears, she would allow a tear to roll down her own cheek. How she controlled them was a mystery to Cassidy.

According to Kek, only one tavern in the ministry district was still standing. *Standing* was a bit generous. The roof of the Fluted Flask was still resting on its support pillars, but the front wall had collapsed, giving a clear view to the absolutely packed common room within, from well down the street. Even amidst the destruction — with black powder and plaster dust staining the chipped, red walls and silk pillows, with decorative trimmings broken and smashed — it was clear that the Flask had been a high-class establishment that catered to a certain *discerning* clientele. Now it was full of the hard working, the ragged, and the weary as well. Even the richest ensemble here was running threadbare as it seemed everyone was doing their part. Cassidy wondered if that was good nature and patriotism in action, or if the owner was only serving people who contributed something.

Patrons were sitting on top of tables as well as at them, and in the aisles between them. Benches were packed end to end, and the bar was standing room only. Even here it was quiet, albeit less so than on the street. There were muttered conversations, brief and breathless.

Cook smoke wafted out into the streets, making Cassidy's mouth water and stomach squeal in desire. Kek led the way to the bar and grabbed the counter's edge as though afraid of being pulled away. The woman tending it didn't look like she worked there, normally: she was burly with a face haggard by age, and she looked like she would be more at home at a dockside inn. A cigarette dangled lazily from the corner of her mouth, smoldering gently, mocking Cassidy's need for such a comfort.

"You want food, take a number," she said, indicating a stack of parchment scraps on the bar. "You get whatever comes out, no negotiations. First drink is free, after that you pay standard rates. If you start anything, I have a few boys that will throw your ass out."

At that moment, a younger girl with heavy bags under her eyes stepped out of the bat-wing doors behind the bar and shouted, "Sixty-two!"

A dirty man in a ragged coat with bandaged hands near the open wall stood up and waved his voucher, and the girl brought him a steaming, cloth-wrapped bundle. That changed the context of the quiet, at least a little, making it feel a little less oppressive. Miria, Kek, and Cassidy picked up numbers ninety-nine, one hundred, and one hundred and one, respectively, and each accepted a cup of white liquor.

"Lucky number," Kek said, nodding to Miria's ticket.

"Not just any lucky number," Miria said, a tired grin playing on her lips, "it's *my* number."

Cassidy furrowed her brow at the statement, before remembering that Miria's mother was the ninety-*eighth* Empress of Asaria, so it made sense that Miria might feel some affinity with ninety-nine.

"There you are!" Lierre called out. Cassidy glanced up, seeing the engineer shuffle and step her way through the crowd. "Nieves and I have been waiting for ages! We found a nice stack of bricks to sit on."

"Have you eaten?" Cassidy asked.

"Aye, Captain. Just before the numbers cycled around. The owner is *very* adamant about no one getting seconds."

"I can see why," Kek said, looking around.

The spot Lierre had mentioned was just outside, on the corner of the gaping entrance, and they had only missed them because the crowd had amassed around them. Nieves raised her cup as they sat down.

"Long meeting?" She asked.

"Interminable," Miria replied, rubbing her eyes. "Unfortunately, we won't be leaving with any kind of fleet, but they will be ready for us. We'll have two ships escorting us into Rivien, though."

"Hopefully, we won't need it," Cassidy said. "I'm done with excitement for a while." Lierre and Kek nodded in commiseration, while Nieves plied Cassidy with a disapproving look.

"Durant, is that you?" a booming voice called out from across the crowd. Cassidy turned to see a towering man in a patchy, leather coat with red hair like hers — in fact, since she had started to grow it out, it was *exactly* like hers, with the same waves and form — and matching beard.

"Little Jev?" she exclaimed, standing to meet him. She hadn't seen the man since they had accidentally started a bar brawl in the capital. That seemed like a lifetime ago. "When did you get here?"

The fellow Dawnhal sailor barked a laugh. "I'm not the one who broke a blockade to get in. My boys have been here for weeks. Honestly, when I heard you were the one who killed Flint, I didn't believe it. 'Not pretty Cassy Durant', I says. But look at you! Making yourself a war hero, just like your old captain before —" His elation bled out as he made a realization. "I'm really sorry about ol' Elyia. She was a damn inspiration."

"Aye," Cassidy said quietly. "You should have seen the lights. But what are you doing here, Jev?"

"Well, I *was* here to enjoy the Midwinter Festival, maybe buy some cheap coal to sell up at the northern reach," he said.

Kek swore. "With everything going on, I completely forgot to write my sister for Midwinter. Twice, now. She won't let me live it down."

Cassidy thought about it. Midwinter had been two weeks ago, give or take. She had forgotten about it, too, but anyone she cared enough to write lived aboard the ship with her anyway.

Jev grunted solemnly. "Aye. Wasn't exactly expecting all this crazy shit, neither. But what about *you*? Got to be swinging something pretty big between your legs to get through blockades and kill mercenaries in full rebellion."

"Big job," Cassidy agreed. "The biggest." A long-ignored memory breached in Cassidy's mind, and implications and ideas came scrambling for purchase. "Jev, I need your help."

"Durant. I like you," he said in a tone that made it abundantly clear that there was a *but* coming, "but the last time you said those words, I ended up spending three weeks locked up, and lost the most comfortable pair of trousers I've ever owned."

"It's about your mother," she said firmly.

Jev blinked. Then he crossed his arms and narrowed his eyes. "What's this big job? And what's it got to do with *her*?"

"Heard about what happened at the Dragon's Nest?"

"I heard dragon sightings have gone up. What's it got to do with you?"

"The Nest was destroyed. The fleet, and the actual spawning ground."

Jev blinked. "Excuse me?"

"Sixty-six!" cried a girl at the bar. Cassidy looked at her meal voucher and sighed. It seemed like it would be a while before they got theirs.

She turned her attention back to Jev. "The specifics are a bit sensitive, but..." She racked her brain, trying to think of a satisfactory answer. It came to her only after an awkwardly long silence. "You ever heard of the Daughters of Daen?"

"'Course I have," Jev said. "They show up in the news sheets every so often, and there's an edict out for their collective executions, so I've read about them every day for a while now."

Cassidy nodded. "Well, that's why." It was true, or at least, as much of the truth as she was going to divulge. She wasn't going to get into it about Miria's identity with Jev, even without considering the attention she's somehow managed to turn her way. "I'm in charge of conscripting a fleet capable of..." She hesitated. "Destroying the force responsible for what happened," she said finally.

"And you want the *Never World*," Jev concluded. His mouth turned as though he had just eaten a mouthful of something sour.

"Only the *Clockwork Hydra* had better guns," said Cassidy, "and it was reputedly nowhere near as fast."

"I don't appreciate being used for my family ties, Durant."

"I know."

Little Jev had spent years trying to escape the shadow and reputation of his mother. Before Elyia Asier had conscripted the great ships that would ultimately lead the final charge and end the war, the *Never World* and its captain had already had a reputation. Caria Altis had been a minor noble in Castilyn who had escaped an arranged marriage by joining the Iron Veil priesthood. That was a common enough story — Kek and Lierre had entire stacks of books that started the same way, though Kek's tended to be more risqué in nature — but somewhere along the line, the Lady Altis — or Sister Altis — decided to pursue a career in domestic terrorism.

Almost thirty years later, Cassidy was *still* hearing new rumors about the whys and wherefores; it was because a secret lover spurned her; no, it was because of a change in the taxes; no, it was because the Queen herself had insulted her at some important state function; no, she saw the suffering of the people of Castilyn and felt compelled to fight oppression; no, she had discovered some hidden truth in the Iron Veil's forbidden library, and it had driven her mad.

Whatever the reason, she had gone from one unknown priestess among dozens of others to an almost folkloric figure. More rumors said that her ship, the *Never World*, had been seized by the Iron Veils because Fae influences had corrupted it, which is how Altis had acquired the vessel in the first place. Unlike the other rumors, that was a consistently agreed upon part of the woman's myth. Because of this, the ship reputedly had a supernatural aspect. Asier had once commented offhandedly that it was mostly smoke and fog, but now that Cassidy knew better, she thought really hard about that *mostly*.

Somewhere along the line, Captain Altis had settled down in Dawnhal long enough to have a son, and Jeval Altis took to flying like he was born at the helm. However, his mother's reputation stained his own from the start. He couldn't go to Castilyn without risking being seized as her accomplice, even though he hadn't even been born when her spree had started. He struck out on his own at fifteen, but by that point the senior Altis had gained even greater fame, or infamy, for joining Elyia Asier's fleet. When he had bought his first ship, his name had earned him attention, but no steady work, and even less *legitimate* work. He had eventually managed to make his own name but talking about his mother risked turning him into a powder keg.

"I wouldn't ask if it wasn't important," Cassidy said gently.

Jev snorted, then sighed. "I know. I can't promise anything. She and I aren't on any better speaking terms than you and your father."

Cassidy gritted her teeth. "Aye. I get that."

"I don't suppose you could use the *Little Bittern,* instead?"

"Is *that* why he's called Little Jev?" Miria whispered behind Cassidy's back.

"*Non,*" Lierre answered.

293

"I don't suppose you and the boys started doing mercenary work in the last year or so?" asked Cassidy.

"No, but..." He gestured vaguely over Cassidy's crew. "Last I heard, you're still in the cargo business, and here you are, throwing yourself at villains and the like."

"Seventy-one!"

"I'm a special case," Cassidy said, wincing when she tried a dry laugh. "I don't recommend it, but I won't turn down a set of guns. Find me at the administration building tonight if you want to know what we're going against."

"I'll be there," Jev said. "Us Dawnhal folk got to stick together. Anyway, that was the call for my breakfast just now."

Cassidy forced herself to smile. "Aye. Enjoy it. I hope you feel the same when you know where we're headed."

Later that night, Cassidy sat on a crate across from Kek at the foot of the *Dreamscape*'s gangway, with Hymn sitting idly in her hat. Her cigarette box sat opened in her hands. The scent of tobacco wafted up on the breeze and left Cassidy with an itch of longing from her lips down to her lungs. Still, the memory of the last time she had smoked, of Hymn's revelation, left her shivering.

Kek was in the middle of going over their supplies when the door leading into the building below opened with a squeal. Cassidy looked up to find Little Jev strutting towards her.

"Alright, Durant," he bellowed, "what's this big, scary job you got?"

"Pull up a crate," Cassidy offered. "You'll want to sit down."

Jev shrugged and took a seat between Kek and Cassidy. "I'm still a little confused. Are you trying to get into mercenary work?"

"Gods, no," Cassidy snapped. "But when the Empress herself gives you a job you can't really say no."

Jev's eyebrows shot skyward. Then he threw his head back and laughed. "Ah, that's right, Asier used to be her right-hand woman! I guess that opened some doors for you."

"I think I preferred when the Empress didn't know me from a wren flying by her window. Have you heard about what happened at the Dragon's Nest?"

Jev scratched his beard. "Heard some rumors. If you get passed the tall tales, it sounds like an absolutely clutch hatched and overwhelmed the fleet stationed there. What, are you chasing down deserters? Or is it the bounty on the dragons you're after?"

Cassidy and Kek shared an uncomfortable look. She cleared her throat.

"The truth is actually a little less rational than all that. Kek, show him."

Kek reached into his coat and withdrew Nieves' sketch of the leviathan.

"A beast the size of a mountain burst out of the Dreamscape when a cultist used some kind of blood ritual, and it wiped out the fleet and is currently at large somewhere in the Imperial Sea."

Jev looked from Cassidy to Kek and the sketch and back again. This time his laughter was less sympathetic and more raw humor. "Oh, you really had me with this one, Durant! All this mystery, the dramatic pauses. You missed your calling in the theater."

"We aren't joking," said Cassidy.

Jev's laughter settled into a chuckle. "Come off it. I'm not some green cabin boy fresh on the boat. What are you really doing?"

"We're really hunting the leviathan." Cassidy explained the events with the Western Zephyr, and briefly described her meeting with the Empress. She showed him one of the writs, and explained her plans for orichalcum guns, and the release of Jathun from Marasi Prison. When she was done, Little Jev frowned and stared into the middle distance.

"Well, I'll be," he said. "I, uh... I'm sorry to say, but I don't think the *Little Bittern* will be of much help to you. If it's alright, I'll have to rescind my earlier offer. This is... this is a lot. I'm just in the cargo business, you know?"

Cassidy suppressed a bitter laugh. "I get it. I really do."

"When all this is over, I'll see you again?" Jev asked. When Cassidy nodded, he stood. "Right. If you ever need anything, Durant, you let me know." Kek and Cassidy traded silent commentary with their eyebrows as Jev stood up.

"Aye," Cassidy said dryly. "Anything at all, right?"

When Jev was finally gone, Kek snorted loudly. "So much for 'Dawnhal folk got to stick together'."

"I didn't expect him to really do it," said Cassidy. "Let's get back to work."

CHAPTER TWENTY-EIGHT

The *Dreamscape Voyager*'s engines heralded the dawn. Cassidy braced herself against the gunwale before signaling the *Sunrise* and the *Roc Spear* to be ready for departure. She was glad to be leaving. The days wasted in Andaerhal felt more like a year, and now her time was more precious than it had ever been. When the ship rose, it felt like its weight was lifted off her shoulders. With the wind in her hair, she looked above the ruin to the horizon, to the west.

As they flew over the city, she ordered that they unfurl the Imperial banners Tao had supplied them with, as a morale booster. It had been Miria's idea, and it was sound. The *Roc Spear* and *Sunrise* displayed their own banners, and Cassidy couldn't deny seeing the Jade Phoenix flying in the morning light was an inspiring sight. The princess herself manned the helm with a proud smile on her lips.

They reached the sea by noon, and it wasn't long before land disappeared behind them. Cassidy assigned Kek and Nieves to prepare the ship for the desert, which consisted of putting up a curtain that could be dropped around the deck in the event of a sandstorm. When she decided all was well on deck, Cassidy made the arduous climb below to check on Lierre. The engineer was reading a book by the light of the bellows when Cassidy found her. Its title was in Castilyn, and while Cassidy wasn't completely oblivious to her friend's language, the looping script wasn't something she could make out at a glance.

"You know, most people at least pretend to work when their captain is on patrol," Cassidy said over the engine's din, leaning against the compartment window.

Lierre didn't even look up. "Most captains don't even know what real work looks like," she countered.

"You got me there," Cassidy conceded. "How's the gun we salvaged?"

"Heavy," Lierre said. She set a length of red ribbon between the pages of her book and closed it with a sigh.

"But orichalcum is light," Cassidy argued.

"Lighter than iron? Aye," Lierre agreed. "But it's a cannon! That's a lot of metal, dragon bone or no."

Cassidy nodded. "Okay, but how badly was it damaged when the tower fell?"

"She means to ask if it is operational," Hymn said, pushing Cassidy's hat aside to fly free.

"Thank you, Hymn," Cassidy responded dryly.

Lierre frowned at the Fae, then said to Cassidy, "It's orichalcum, Captain," as if explaining it to a child. "If we filled the entire hold with gunpowder and lit it, the cannon would be fine." She paused. "But we would probably become a very colorful fireball, then dust. So let's not do that."

"Were you able to get it rigged up the way you wanted?"

"Oh, aye," Lierre said. She smiled. "Would you like to see it?" Without waiting for Cassidy's answer, she stood, set her book on her stool, shoveled two scoops of coal into the furnace, and led Cassidy to the hold.

She wasn't happy that the ship's skiff had been broken down and stowed. Lierre assured her it could be reassembled, but it wouldn't be quick work. In its place, hanging above the scuttle by an elaborate series of moving parts Cassidy couldn't quite track, was the cannon. The iridescent metal shone prismatically where slats of sunlight struck it.

"It's brilliant!" Lierre boasted. She pulled a lever, opening the hatch at the bottom of the deck. Pullies and clockwork mechanisms worked in tandem, and the cannon descended gently with a faint *whir*, until it was hanging well below the *Dreamscape*'s belly. "Do you see the railing?"

Cassidy leaned over the opening, feeling Hymn pull her back by the corset as she looked down at the sea speeding by below. She did see the railing Lierre mentioned — two long tracks on either side of the cannon's barrel, extending several feet behind the weapon, fitted to grooves on its surface.

"To deal with the recoil?" Cassidy asked.

"Aye, *Capitan*!" Lierre said, her accent coming through even thicker than usual in her excitement. "Orichalcum is weird; it increases combustible energies acted on it, and the recoil is intense. If we put this where the one on the deck is, it could blow us right off course! There will still be recoil, but it will be considerably mitigated. And there's a mechanism on the gunner's seat so the cannoneer can reset it to reload."

Cassidy nodded. It seemed like a good set up, maybe even a great one. There was just one problem niggling at Cassidy.

"So, it has to be down there to fire," Cassidy said slowly.

"Aye, captain."

"And the person manning it has to be able to raise the cannon up here to reload, right?"

"Aye, captain," Lierre repeated, though her tone was less confident than before.

"Who's going to be on it?" Cassidy asked.

"Pardon?"

"In a battle," Cassidy clarified. "Who is going to be on it?"

Lierre opened her mouth as if to answer but shut it quickly with a thoughtful expression.

"It can't be you, because you need to work the bellows," Cassidy said, counting off on her fingers, "can't be Miria, because she's the helmsman. Nieves needs to be topside —"

"Kek?" Lierre said. "We're only using this for the Leviathan, right? Our usual gun probably won't be a match for that thing's hide."

Cassidy bit her lip. "You're probably right. After supper, see if he's up for it. I don't want to spring this on him."

"He'd be wearing a harness," Lierre said defensively. She flipped the lever again, recalling the cannon and closing the hatch with the whirring of pulleys.

In the moments before the hatch shut, Cassidy stared intently at the water, wondering if she might see the Leviathan. It was a silly notion; the seas were vast, and it wouldn't be following her. Still, she had to suppress a shiver. "Either way, it's good work. I can't wait to see it in action."

Lierre nodded, a proud smile plastered on her face. "I hope we can use it at night," the engineer said. "You've seen it fire during the sunlight, but at night, the flames leave behind these... eh, what is the Asarian word... comets have them?"

"Tails?"

"I think, yes. Tails of crystal light that hang in the sky, like new stars. When Tal Joyau fell, before I knew what it meant, I thought it was a light show."

"They used these in the war?" Cassidy asked.

"The *Clockwork Hydra* did, at least," Lierre said thoughtfully. "I never saw the *Jade Phoenix*." She paused. "But, I suppose the *Dreamscape* was the *Jade*, wasn't it? So if she had them, we wouldn't have needed to salvage this one out of the rubble."

"Unless Captain Asier sold them. Or the navy took them away." Even as she said it, however, she thought about the Empress' story of the *Dreamscape Voyager's* refusal to be captained by anyone other than her predecessor. If that were true — and Cassidy had seen enough strange things lately to believe it — there was no way that she would have allowed anyone to simply take her weapons.

"Hm, that's possible," Lierre agreed, "They would have been worth a good deal, and in those early days we weren't exactly sleeping on bags of coin."

"We aren't exactly doing that *now*, either," said Cassidy. She nudged Lierre in the ribs. "Unless you're holding out on me."

Lierre giggled. "You found me out, Captain. I am actually one of the Princes on the Rivien Trade Council! I am only here because it entertains me to dress like a poor!"

"Like *the* poor," Cassidy corrected.

"Bah! I am much too rich to care about your silly language! For I am Prince Lierre! Now, go away, I have rich people things to do, like... buying a store, or something."

Cassidy joined Lierre in raucous laughter until her ribs lanced with pain, then kept on chuckling after getting a breath. She wasn't sure why she found it so funny, but as much as it hurt, it felt so good to laugh. Still, her pain must have shown, because Lierre wrapped an arm around her and guided her to a stool to sit.

"Are you okay, captain?"

"I'm fine, *mother*," Cassidy said. Gods, why couldn't anyone stop asking that?

"I can get Nieves if you need some —"

"I said I'm fine!" Cassidy snapped. Lierre recoiled as if slapped, and even Cassidy wasn't sure where the anger came from. She let out a quivering. "I'm sorry, but I'm fine. I... I should go." She forced herself not to cradle her ribs as she made her way back to the ladder with Hymn trailing behind her like a star in her wake. As she climbed above deck, she offered one last look to Lierre, who looked confused and hurt.

300

INTERLUDE THREE

Twelve Years Earlier

Castilyn was beautiful in the spring. It was just a shame that the *Dreamscape Voyager* was marring the scenic view of emerald fields and a two-moon morning with a trail of black smoke a mile wide in her wake. The ship bucked as Cassidy ran across the engineering deck with another ice canister tucked under her arm. Valani was swatting at the mounting flames with a heavy blanket, but just when it seemed he had the situation in hand, something behind him popped and another gout of fire burst from a busted pipe.

Cassidy pulled the lever, cracking open the canister. The alchemical compound hissed and spat as it sprayed over the flames in a geyser of liquid crystal. She batted at the blaze with sweeping motions, and slowly, the fire backed down. It fought back, as if alive, but with each pass, the flames were shorter and less formidable. After a protracted battle that left the floorboards, the pipes, and the walls all covered in ice, the last embers were finally smothered.

Valani stood in the middle of the engine compartment. Ashes and soot coated him in black splotches, and he panted heavily, but he seemed fine. He dropped the fire blanket unceremoniously and plopped down on the compartment's charred stool, which promptly fell apart under his weight.

Cassidy squeaked in shock, then burst into laughter.

Valani looked around as if to find a culprit. "Oh, you know," he said with an affected casualness, "I was just standing in a fire."

"I saw. If you can do it again a couple dozen times, we might be able to make a few coppers taking the show around Castilyn."

"I think I've burned down enough of this country for one lifetime," Captain Asier said, and Cassidy jumped. She hadn't heard the captain make the climb down to join them. "Good job, though, Mr. Valani."

"What do we do now, Captain?"

"You two will have to take the skiff and hire someone to tow us into town." She reached into her coat and pulled a hefty sack and dropped it into Cassidy's hand. It clinked as it settled heavily on her palm. "It's a little town. Naariem. Fruit is pretty cheap here, so get yourself something nice. I'll work on cleaning some of this mess up. Well, don't just stand there, off you go."

"Aye, aye, Captain," Cassidy said. In truth, she would rather stay behind while Asier took Valani. Or go with the captain while Valani cleaned the deck. But she had her orders, so she took the cumbersome purse. Valani struggled to his feet, and she led the way to the hold.

They clamored into the skiff and Valani worked the pulleys while Cassidy fiddled with the balloon's igniter and lit the coal into the vessel's small engine. As they descended into wind, with nothing but air between them and the distant valley below, Cassidy felt her palms slick with sweat. She had no problem aboard the *Dreamscape*, with its sturdy hull and comforting size, but the skiff rocked and teetered with every slight shift of their weight, and until she got the balloon hot, she had to trust the ropes to keep them from plummeting to their untimely deaths.

"So," Valani said as the balloon filled, giving the rope enough slack to disconnect them.

"So?" Cassidy asked.

"You and me, in a skiff together," he said. He wiggled his eyebrows in a way Cassidy knew was trying to convey *something* dirty, and she was sure it was dirty.

She rolled her eyes. "You're stubborn, aren't you?" she said dryly.

"I can be," he admitted. He wasn't defensive about it, nor did he seem chided by the accusation. "It's helped me in the past."

"Is that how you did it in Melfine?" Cassidy asked. "Just wear a girl down until she lies back for you because you won't go away? That can't be good for anyone."

This time Valani did look offended. "Never!" he said, aghast. "I just want to let you know that the offer is still open is all. In case you change your mind."

"Does that happen often?" Cassidy asked. She had meant to be dismissive, but she couldn't deny a little curiosity.

"More than you'd think," Valani said. A little quieter, he added, "Less than I'd like. Still, the important thing is communication; if I stopped inviting you to my bunk, you might feel like you missed your chance."

Cassidy snorted. "Sure. But haven't you ever heard the expression about shitting where you eat?"

"I have, aye," said Valani, "but I don't do either of those things in my bunk."

This time, Cassidy laughed. "Fair enough."

She finally brought the skiff's engine to life and the set off to the city. Cassidy gripped the rudder tightly. When she corrected course, the skiff jerked, and she would clutch the gunwale until it stopped rocking. Valani offered a smile, and she glowered back at him. He, at least, seemed relaxed.

"First time on the skiff?" he asked, not unkindly.

"No," she snapped. She had flown the skiff before, but only once. She didn't think he needed to know that.

"Well, scoot a little closer to starboard," he said, "your balance will be better."

She frowned, but did as he suggested, moving herself closer to the center. It made it harder to clutch the gunwale, but not impossible.

"Ease up on the rudder," he continued. "Takes a lot less to turn her than the ship."

Cassidy nodded. Captain Asier had said the same. "You spend a lot of time on skiffs? On the fishing crew, I mean?"

"I did. Every so often someone would take a dive into the lake. Lots of monsters in the water, so you got to get your people fast."

"I saw the tortohemoth."

Valani nodded. "They swim down from the north, usually during the winter months. It was actually a little unexpected to see one that day. In the summer, rivermaids come up from the south."

"And you live there?" Cassidy asked. "Rivermaids are Siren-kin, aren't they?"

"Sure, but they can't fly. Because of the wind, their voices don't usually carry up to the city. And we know, roughly, when they're in the water, so we plug our ears before heading out. Besides, we make a lot of money on their tails."

"Really?"

"Aye. Most buyers are here in Castilyn. The meat is pretty popular, but the real money is in dressmaking."

Cassidy tried to imagine a dress made of rivermaid scales, but they had faces and bodies that were so similar to human women that the notion made her shiver. The thought of *eating* one was equally unpalatable. She tried not to think too hard about it, but the only other thing to think about was the flight.

Naariem was little more than a blur on the horizon, and Cassidy didn't relish voyage. The beautiful green fields she had admired from the deck of the *Dreamscape* now threatened her with the prospect of a hard flat surface to fall on, interspersed with a peppering of enormous stones across the landscape.

"So, you call Dawnhal home?" Valani asked.

"Obviously. I have the wavy red hair," Cassidy said tightly. "No prize for guessing."

"That proves you were born there," he said. "But the Empire's a big place, and the world's even bigger."

Cassidy eyed him. *What's he fishing for?* she wondered. "Aye," she conceded. "Before signing on with the Captain, I never went further than the Starlit Sea, and maybe a mile or two in any other direction."

"What's it like?"

Cassidy swallowed and shifted in the skiff, her heart lurching when it rocked. She told him basic things at first — Dawnhal sat at the edge of the Empire, and Castilyn had invaded it early in the war for its nearby mines and herbs — but Valani prodded and pressed, and soon, Cassidy was telling him about the tavern on the harbor that smoked birds from sunup to sundown, which she could smell from her home uptown. She told him about the summer skiff races, the Midwinter Festivals. Crime was usually on the petty side — the only major exception Cassidy could remember was the murder of a city judge and his family a few months back. Rumors blamed it on his disproportionate punishments, or for Castilyn sympathies.

"Wasn't always that way," she admitted. "During the war, and right after, riots were pretty common. Vandalism is still common when Castilyn ships dock." Speaking of the southern kingdom reminded Cassidy where she was, and she was surprised to discover they were nearly upon Naariem. She had stopped paying attention to the uncomfortable ride, and they had cleared most of the distance. Valani was nodding along on the other side of the skiff.

"Got any family back home?" he asked when she started looking down again.

"I guess," Cassidy said slowly. "My mother died not long ago. Sickness. My father is captain of the city guard. Not really interested in going back to see him, though."

"Violent?" Valani asked, and there was a note of sympathetic concern in his tone.

"Not especially," said Cassidy. "But as soon as ma died, he had another woman in his bed. Or, maybe it would be more accurate to say his chair." She shuddered. She hoped someday she could unsee that. "What about you, Valani?"

"Well, you were at my resignation," he said, "so you've seen my sister, Ara. She's the de facto head of the Melfine Fishers Guild."

"De facto?"

"Means unofficially."

"I know what it means," Cassidy lied. After a pause, she added, "If she's only the *de facto* leader, who's the real one?"

"Well, technically it's our uncle," Valani said, "but that old man hadn't handled a spear that wasn't his own, or set foot on a boat, in over five years."

Cassidy felt herself blush at Valani's suggestion and cleared her throat. She tried to pass off her discomfort as she led the skiff to the docks, where an air traffic director guided them to a platform. A thought came to her abruptly. "You speak Castilyn, right?"

"A few basic words and I can complement a lady," Valani said, "but that's about it. Wait, didn't you live under Castilyn occupation for a few years?"

"We're still Asarian," Cassidy snapped. "They tried to force us to adopt the language, but we can be a stubborn lot." She was starting to regret that, however. Thankfully, Valani didn't criticize her for it.

Instead, he said, "Well, we can probably get by; most people speak at least a little Asarian, after all."

"I suppose," said Cassidy. She wasn't completely convinced, however. She landed the skiff, and Valani jumped out to tie it down.

A port official — a gangly man with a ridiculous moustache fashioned into an elaborate series of loops that reached the outer edges of his eyes — approached them, and immediately started speaking in rapid Castilyn.

Valani then said one of the few complete Castilyn sentences Cassidy knew: "We don't speak Castilyn." He said it with such an authentic accent, it sounded like a joke. She laughed in spite of herself.

The official rolled his eyes in exasperation and called across the wharf to a boy about Cassidy's age who was flirting with an older sailor. The boy was terse as he and the mustachioed man exchanged words. Cassidy caught the word "idiots" and "Asarian", and the boy sighed dramatically. He spoke Asarian with a thick but intelligible accent and translated the negotiations for parking the skiff — Cassidy had shouted him down to half the asking price and still felt outraged and cheated.

After that, they discussed the tow services. Through the boy, the mustachioed man insisted that that it couldn't possibly be done that day, nor could he say with any certainty when it would be done, but he still expected to be paid immediately for the service. It was Valani's turn to shout, and Cassidy was eager to join him.

When Valani took a breath, the boy — unprompted — told them about a nearby private company in the city that would haul them in and work on repairs. The mustachioed man apparently asked what he said, then they began shouting at one another.

The shop in question was on the far end of the docks. The wooden sign swinging from a pole over the door read "Myrlin's" in the looping Castilyn script and featured a hand painted stylization of two crossed wrenches. From outside the door, Cassidy could hear the pounding of hammers and muffled shouts.

Inside, the shop was more of the same, with steam whistles added to the cacophony. Behind the front counter, Cassidy could see into the workshop. On the staging floor stood a rotund man with skin as dark as Cassidy's. He sported a moustache that followed the curve of his cheeks, mingling with his short, curly hair of the exact same thickness and texture. He argued with a much shorter girl with just as much plump to her frame. Cassidy didn't understand a word of the exchange, but she could tell an argument was well underway from the wild gesticulations they threw at one another. Three other people dressed in matching aprons and goggles rigidly avoided looking at either of them while they worked on separate projects.

Cassidy and Valani stood in front of the counter as close to their line of sight as they could be while pretending not to have noticed. There were wooden placards and signs throughout the waiting room — probably listing prices or store policy — but Cassidy couldn't catch more than a handful of words of any of them.

The portly man stepped out to greet them after a few more minutes of shouting. He spoke in Castilyn, apologies clear in his tone and the way he bowed his head as he smiled at them.

"Er, sorry, we don't speak Castilyn," Valani said slowly.

The man grunted and shouted over his shoulder, "Lierre!"

The girl he had been arguing with stepped out to meet them, wiping her hands on a dirty rag. The two had another heated exchange before the man folded his arms and stepped away from the counter. He sneered at Cassidy and Valani even as the girl plastered on a smile to greet them.

"Welcome to Myrlin's Famous Shop," she said in a thick, musical accent, "you want many good supplies, *oui?*"

Valani leaned on the counter and offered the girl a smile he probably *thought* was suave and sexy. "*Mademoiselle*, has anyone told you your eyes are the color of an Autumn Phoenix?"

Lierre snorted. "You need to do better than comparing me to a bird. Boys around town tell me I look like the Queen when they want under my skirt. I'll tell you what I tell them; if you aren't here on business, my papa will toss you out on your asses. And he already doesn't like you Imperials," she added sotto voce.

Valani sighed and pushed away from the counter. Cassidy swatted him in the arm.

"Our ship suffered engine failure just outside of town. We need a tow and repairs."

Lierre reached under the counter and extracted a sheet of parchment with a form printed on it. She guided them through which lines to write the information, and Cassidy filled it out. After she was done, she had Cassidy repeat the information so she could write it down phonetically in Castilyn.

"... the ship's named the *Dreamscape Voyager*," said Cassidy. "And the captain is Elyia Asier."

The gentle scratching of the pen stopped abruptly. Lierre looked critically up at them and over her shoulder, her father's sneer turned apoplectic.

"That kind of joke isn't funny," Lierre said. "We lived in Tal Joyau during the war. Now, if you aren't going to tell me your captain's name, I'm going to have to ask you to leave."

"That *is* our Captain's name, though," Cassidy protested.

Her father said something in Castilyn and Lierre responded in kind. The exchange was too quick for Cassidy to pick up any familiar words. Finally, the man grunted, threw his arms in the air and said something that sounded like a curse.

"My brothers will bring your ship in."

"What'll it cost?"

"We'll discuss that once we see the damage, but the tow —
"

"Twenty Imperial ducks," Lierre's father said in stilted Asarian. Lierre rolled her eyes and the two of them began arguing again.

"Falcons," Lierre said finally. "He means falcons."

"Twenty silver is pretty steep," Valani argued.

"He won't budge," Lierre said. "He's a stubborn piece of work."

Valani leaned into Cassidy. "You do the books," he whispered. "Can we handle that?"

Cassidy grunted. "We don't have much choice."

As soon as Cassidy fished out the coins and handed them over, Myrlin senior barked orders in their direction.

His daughter sighed. "You'll have to wait somewhere. Your ship will be brought to the docks sometime in the next couple hours. I recommend Maeva's Cafe, just down the way. You'll be able to see your ship being brought in from the garden. Maybe I can join you after I run a few errands?"

"That would be lovely. Thanks for your help," said Cassidy. Before she and Valani even managed to leave the shop, the Castilyn mechanics began arguing again.

The cafe Myrlin recommended was run by a woman in her middle years who spoke excellent Asarian and the view they had of the valley was breathtaking. She and Kek sat and drank tea and played game after game of Falling Grace — a two player variant of Twisted Virtue. The afternoon passed slowly, and the sun was a soft gold near the horizon by the time Cassidy saw the *Dreamscape Voyager* trailing towards the city, pulled by two smaller vessels.

Their drinks finished and their game concluded, Cassidy and Valani worked their way up the street. Just as they arrived, Asier disembarked to a confrontational Myrlin. The Castilyn man aimed a fat finger at the Captain and demanded something in his language. The only words Cassidy caught were "Elyia Asier".

"*Oui*," Asier said flatly, cocking her eyebrow at the man and offering a quick glance to Cassidy and Valani. She then asked a follow-up question in Castilyn. Cassidy didn't know enough about the language to gauge her accuracy, but her confidence was impeccable. The two went back and forth for a while, Myrlin clearly unhappy to be dealing with the enemy war hero — even with the war six years past — and Asier equally unimpressed by the man trying to throw his weight around her.

They might have carried on into the night if a shout hadn't sounded in the crowded streets. Both combatants stopped to look, as did Cassidy. Myrlin's daughter lay sprawled on the ground, pointing into the throng at a scrawny figure pushing his way through the masses. She shouted what Cassidy was fairly sure translated to, "Thief! Thief!"

Asier sprinted in a blur, all but leaping into the crowd.

"Captain!" Cassidy cried, but Asier was gone. Cassidy ran back to the street and helped Lierre up, all the while shooting dirty looks at the people passing by without so much as a glance at the poor girl. "Are you alright, Miss Myrlin?" Cassidy asked in Asarian.

"*Oui*," she said breathlessly. "I'll be fine, but that man —" she trailed off and squinted down the street as if questioning her eyes. Cassidy followed her gaze.

Rather than fighting her way through the street traffic, Asier was running along a decorative wall along the side of the road, from which she leaped atop a vendor stall fixture. The captain *dove* into the crowd to the sounds of shock and confusion all around.

"Lierre!" gasped the Myrlin father as he made his way to his daughter's side. They exchanged the first unheated words Cassidy had heard between them and he gave her an unabashedly large hug, and Cassidy heard the girl's back pop.

Asier arrived a couple minutes later with a city watchwoman at her side. She nodded to the Myrlin girl and said, "*C'est elle.*"

The watchwoman asked what Cassidy assumed were the standard questions pertaining to the theft. Seemingly satisfied, she handed a purse to Lierre and offered a nod to Asier before returning to the crowded causeway.

"*Merci, mademoiselle...*" said Lierre, pausing for a name.

"Asier," the Captain said. "Captain Asier."

Myrlin's eyes widened, but her surprise was short-lived. "Ah, Capitan Asier," she corrected. "Thank you for coming to my defense," she said, offering her hand. "A good thing you did, too, since I will be repairing your ship. Lierre Myrlin, lead engineer of the Myrlin Family Repairs."

Asier smiled. "Well, aren't I a lucky one. It's a pleasure to make your acquaintance, *mademoiselle*. Though I believe your... father? Yes, your father claimed that title a few minutes ago."

Lierre snorted. "He taught me everything he knows, but he can't keep up with progress. If you don't mind, I'll take a look at the damage."

With the remaining daylight, the Myrlins assessed the damage. They examined all the pipes and engines, and even the furnace. They tested them for structural weaknesses and faults. They even checked the deck for support failings. The next morning, Lierre and one of her brothers started to work.

Cassidy woke early to find Lierre installing a new furnace.

"It's amazing you were able to make it here without exploding!" the engineer said cheerfully. "There were bullet holes in the boiler and the overflow pipe. And then there was the careless treatment."

"Careless treatment?"

"I already got rid of the old furnace, but there was clear evidence of over-firing in bursts. It's a common mistake, especially for short-staffed vessels, but being common doesn't make it less harmful to the engines. You need to maintain a steady burn when flying long distances."

"It was just me and the captain for a while," said Cassidy. "And just the captain before that."

Lierre nodded. "It probably sounds appealing, keeping your payroll low, but that's how people get killed. Or robbed. Or exploded!"

"I don't want to get exploded," Cassidy conceded with faux seriousness.

"It doesn't end up well for anyone," said Lierre. "Well, except maybe Lady Carina. But we can't all be so lucky."

"Who?"

"Have you not read the latest Kasim Dalina book? *Winds of Burning Passion?*" Cassidy blinked, but before she could formulate a response, Lierre pressed on. "Oh, the Asarian translation probably hasn't been put together yet, I'm sorry. Don't worry, the explosion isn't as big a surprise as it sounds, you aren't ruined on much."

"Um," said Cassidy, "who is Kasim Dalina?"

"Who is Kasim Dalina?" Lierre repeated, affronted. "Only the greatest writer the world has ever known! Bah, my father always says Imperials are uncultured, I never thought he could be so right! Her books are all the rage in the capital right now! The first one, *Candlelit Dreams*, was first printed three years ago…"

As the engineer worked, they talked. At first, they talked about their favorite books — Cassidy preferred erotic stories to romance, which made Lierre laugh like a child — which led to talk about the southern kingdom and the Empire — apparently Imperial novelists, musicians, and other artists were heavily censored and censured, which left little exposure to northern styles. They talked about fashion, and sports — it turned out the Fighters Guild owned the Castilyn arenas as well as the ones in Asaria, so Cassidy knew many of the fighters Lierre rooted for.

Lierre invited Cassidy to have lunch with her when she took her break and led her to a bistro, and they bonded over a fine stew of slow-cooked duck and juicy mushrooms. Cassidy was a little overwhelmed by the sheer friendliness of the girl, but she also found it irresistible.

"What's she like?" Lierre asked as they paid the bill.

"Who?"

"Admiral — er, *Capitaine* Asier."

"She is incredible!" gushed Cassidy. "She's fearless, and generous, and fun! There was one time this manticore landed on our deck…."

The *Dreamscape Voyager* was deemed ready to fly on the third day. Cassidy found Captain Asier on the harbor, speaking to the Myrlins in Castilyn. Cassidy assumed the old man was perpetually grouchy, so his scowl told her nothing as he made Asier sign a series of papers. By his side, Lierre beamed with something like satisfaction.

Asier made comments in Castilyn as she thoroughly read through the looping script, of which Cassidy couldn't make heads or tails. Myrlin grunted in acknowledgement and said a few words to Lierre. When Myrlin and his sons walked away, Lierre stayed behind, still smiling broadly.

"Cassidy, show our new engineer to her quarters. Make sure she feels at home."

CHAPTER TWENTY-NINE

Dusk painted the Rivien sky a thousand shades of red and gold when the *Dreamscape Voyager* finally caught sight of Isaro, standing alone atop its peak surrounded by craggy expanses of lowlands that stretched for miles. The border city basked in the final hours of light which formed a corona around the intricately layered and terraced brick buildings and cast deep purple shadows over its streets and onto the desert floor.

When the wind rose, Cassidy could smell the sulfur from the city's famed hot springs. She couldn't remember the last time she had a proper bath — she scrubbed clean every day, or every other day, at least. Maybe every third day if it couldn't be helped— but a soak in those legendary healing waters was a tempting treat that brought tears to her eyes even as she watched their approach.

Their arrival was noticed, and a skiff intercepted them when they fell into the city's shadow. Cassidy called a halt and stood at the gunwales to wait for word from the city.

"I swear to all the gods," she said as Kek took his place by her side, "if Isaro is in trouble, too, I am going to throw myself overboard."

"We have enough problems without bringing the gods into it," Kek said.

"He is right," Hymn agreed from within Cassidy's hat. "Fortunately, their attentions are otherwise occupied."

Kek did a double take. "Excuse me? How do you know that?"

"It is in my interest to know such things," said Hymn. "In addition to the birth of a new World Tree to the south, something has happened in the east, though I know not what."

"The World Tree," Cassidy repeated slowly. With everything else that had happened that day at the Nest, and since, she hadn't given much thought to the tree. Still, it sounded important, and familiar.

"A *new* World Tree?" Kek asked. "So, there's more of those out there?"

Hymn hesitated, as if unsure how to answer. "There is another, somewhere in your Empire's borders," she said finally. "Not for a lack of effort on the part of your forebears, I might add."

Cassidy imagined the scale of the tree that had appeared in the Nest. "Can't be! If there was, it would be public knowledge," she protested. Then she asked, "wouldn't it?"

"Apparently not," Hymn said.

"But the gods are interested in the tree? Not the Leviathan?"

"The Leviathan is a known quantity," Hymn said. "There has never been *two* World Trees under one sky before."

Before Cassidy and Kek could chase Hymn down the sphinx den of potentially endless inquiries, the Isaro skiff met them. Aboard were two women and a man in blue kaftans. The man carried two signal flags. One of the women stood in the skiff.

"Hail, stranger," she said in accented Asarian. Cassidy thought it was a good decision to leave the banners flying, though as she thought about it, she supposed the fact that they had come from due east and their formation consisted entirely of Imperial junks probably would have done the same job. "What business brings you to Isaro?"

"I am Captain Cassidy Durant, of the *Dreamscape Voyager*. We have come to negotiate with one of the Merchant Princes, on behalf of Empress Yushiro," said Cassidy. The woman wanted proof, so Cassidy sent Kek after one of the Imperial writs. Once she was satisfied, the man lifted his flags and waved them in a clockwise pattern of snapping movements.

"If you will please follow us directly," the woman asked, "You will be given a berth in the Mercantile Quarter."

Miria brought them in. Isaro's tiered quarters climbed in a clockwise pattern, with the lowest being the public district in the east, the highest the Mercantile Quarter in the north. After the nightmare in Andaerhal, Cassidy was relieved to see people milling about on the streets, to hear the sounds of industry and trade carried on the breeze. She imagined their only cares were the daily grind, and it lightened her heart, even as she felt a sick envy swimming in her gut.

Cassidy had been to Isaro twice before — both visits relegated to the public quarter — and she couldn't help but think that the Mercantile Quarter was grossly misnamed.

The domed buildings were richly crafted from bright alabaster and adorned with silk tapestries and golden trellises rife with vibrant flowers. Five palaces formed a circle in the heart of the district, surrounded by manor houses that could easily swallow the neighborhood Cassidy had grown up in with little difficulty. Shaded by the glory of such wealth, were the storefronts the Quarter's name might have implied, but they seemed far too rich and exclusive to qualify as standard commerce. Indeed, even the docks in this quarter were richer than anything Cassidy had seen from the lower city.

The *Dreamscape Voyager* was led to a sheltered berth, which was housed in an elaborate construct of brass and smoked-stained-glass that resembled an eye from the outside. The way hidden panels slid open to allow ingress as they approached added to the impression. Her breath was taken away when the aperture closed behind them, and the berth was struck with swirling patterns of lights from the setting sun playing on the structure.

The dock inside was an immaculately polished, fine grain wooden structure that Cassidy couldn't imagine saw much use. Just as the glass construct separated the berth from other harbored ships, the dock did not open out into the city streets but seemed to be built out of a building like an elaborate balcony, requiring arrivals to enter to leave. As dock workers appeared as if from nowhere to tie down the *Dreamscape Voyager*, an ornate, gilded palanquin with deep purple curtains emerged from inside, carried by a dozen bearers decked in brown silks.

"Gods," Kek breathed.

"Aye," Cassidy agreed as she took in the grandeur.

"You know, I've always dreamed about becoming one of the Merchant Princes," Kek said, as though there were anyone who *didn't* harbor such dreams, "but I don't think I ever imagined what having that kind of coin would be like."

Cassidy felt the same. She had once discussed the prospect with Asier and had asked her how much money was needed to buy a seat on the Merchant Council. Asier's answer had been, *If you've ever asked how much something costs, you'll never be able to afford it.* Cassidy was just starting to understand what she meant.

"And this is just the docks," she breathed.

"What, you've never seen the royal treatment?" Miria called from the helm. There was a huge grin on the girl's face that Cassidy couldn't help but smile back at. Then she caught the implication, and her heart froze.

"Do they know?" she breathed.

Miria's grin deepened, and she stifled a laugh. "No, Captain, if they knew who I was, they would have gone all out. But they take hospitality very seriously here."

"This isn't all out?" Cassidy said, and her voice broke from the shock.

"Not at all."

The litter bearers set down the palanquin with a practiced ease, and the two men at the front of the procession approached the edge of the dock.

"If we can be let aboard," one of them said in a soft voice that belied his muscular frame, and if the ship had made port in any harbor open to the wind, he surely would have been drowned out by the slightest breeze. "We can carry any luggage you require to your rooms."

"Our rooms?" Cassidy asked.

"Of course, your honor," he said patiently, and Cassidy blinked in surprise at the unusual honorific. "It would be unseemly to force an Imperial diplomat to await an audience confined to docks."

"That won't —" Cassidy began, but Miria hissed in her ear.

"Turning down their hospitality would be a grave insult," she whispered from the corner of her mouth. "The ship is safe here," she added, as if reading Cassidy's mind.

Cassidy cleared her throat. "Thank you," she said to the litter bearer.

"Of course, your honor." The soft-spoken man bowed. "How many suites will you require?"

Cassidy didn't understand the question, a face she only realized when she had opened her mouth to answer.

Miria, however, came to her rescue. "There are only five of us aboard the vessel," she said with a gracious bob that strongly resembled a curtsey.

The man looked taken aback. "So few?" He recovered quickly, however, and bowed again. "As you say. Allow us to prepare your luggage."

Cassidy set Kek and Miria to placing the gangplank and retreated into the ship's makeshift cargo hold. She hurriedly found the two trunks that had been prepared by Miria's uncle for the meeting with the princes. Her core muscles protested as she stacked them neatly at the door. Gods, how she missed drawing on Hymn's power. She was starting to feel like an invalid. She managed to refrain from crying and settled her face into a neutral expression.

As the litter bearers entered the room, Cassidy indicated the trunks. She was suddenly self-conscious about the state of the hold; though she and the others cleaned it regularly, she had never stopped to consider adjusting its 'lived in' look. The cookpot from the evening meal was still on the table, with all the crew's dishes sitting inside to be washed. Even without carrying cargo on this mad job, the galley was cluttered with old trunks and crates that had slowly been brought up from the proper hold below for convenience. And against the regal presentation, she couldn't help but feel she had kept the *Dreamscape Voyager* in a shabbier state than the ship deserved, never mind how it must look surrounded by such grandeur.

If their hosts were put off by their humble surroundings, they gave no indication. They simply took the trunks she indicated and carried them out with quiet competence and stoic professionalism. Cassidy followed them out to the deck.

At Miria's insistence, the crew disembarked behind them and marched single file to the palanquin. The bearers set the trunks within before holding the curtain open for the *Dreamscape*'s crew.

Miria bobbed another curtsey before disappearing inside. Lierre copied the gesture — with perhaps less elegance — while Kek and Nieves simply climbed aboard. Cassidy hesitated at the threshold and offered a glance back at the *Dreamscape*. Every nerve in her body was telling her to leave someone behind to guard her. But she sighed and dutifully stepped into the litter, letting the curtain fall behind her.

Cassidy had expected benches, but instead the interior was a spread of elaborately embroidered pillows and unbelievably plush blankets in swirling patterns of color, in the middle of which sat a qalyan and a tray of figs, almonds, and grapes. Cassidy felt self-conscious about tracking dirt, so she immediately dropped to her knees and crawled her way over to a pile of pillows between Kek and Lierre. She sank into them almost immediately. The others all seemed similarly absorbed by the sudden comfort, save for Miria, who sat poised atop one of the cushions as though it were a rigid chair. Though the girl was dressed in a worn shirt and tattered trousers, her posture and serene expression made her look like she belonged among the rich trappings in a way that the rest of the crew never would. And maybe, Cassidy supposed, she did.

Cassidy eyed the qalyan, longing in her lungs mixed with the painful memory of what happened after the battle in Andaerhal. Even now her chest burned, as though cinders had been trailed along her insides.

Miria must have caught her look but missed the feeling because she said, "The pipe is complimentary, Captain. Help yourself."

"I'm good," Cassidy said, shifting on her pillows to face away. She caught Nieves' glower on the other side. The sawbones still hadn't stopped pressing Cassidy to tell the others about her condition.

"You okay, Cass?" Kek asked. "Never known you to turn down free toba."

"Fine, thanks for asking," she said through her teeth. "Just tired, is all," she added more gently.

The palanquin rocked gently as it was hoisted onto the bearers' shoulders and carried down the dock. Cassidy had never ridden in one before and was surprised how smooth the journey was, though it was also very slow.

Kek popped a fig into his mouth. "If this is how diplomats are treated," he said with his mouth full, "I've been doing the wrong job."

"You won't have the job long if you keep talking while you eat," said Miria. There was a playfulness in her voice, but it was strained.

"I once saw a lord decapitate his own bodyguard for speaking with his mouth full," Hymn offered from beneath Cassidy's hat.

Kek swallowed so hastily he spasmed, as though the fig were stuck. "Are you serious?"

"In all fairness," Hymn said slowly, "he also sucked his teeth quite loudly. It was very annoying."

Kek ate more daintily after that.

Cassidy sank deeper into her pillows and closed her eyes. The steady rhythm of the palanquin wasn't so far removed from the sway of a resting ship, so she found it easy to lose herself in the comfort. She was in the hazy place between sleep and wakefulness. She teetered on the brink of letting true rest take her over, but she felt something draw her into the Dreamscape, like a low heartbeat masking a sound just on the edge of hearing. She forced herself to think lucidly, to enter the place of dreams as the Fae did.

Hymn was already there on the deck of the dream-*Dreamscape Voyager*, as always, in her true form, casting what might have been a judgmental look with those fathomless, inverted, cerulean eyes. Cassidy wondered if the Fae was always in both worlds, or if she simply knew Cassidy well enough to meet her on either side. After more than a year, she still didn't understand the Dreamscape or her connection to it. She wasn't going to ask Hymn about it — at least, not at that moment; she tended towards explaining metaphysical concepts and scales of reference Cassidy couldn't comprehend with her limited human experience.

It had taken Cassidy long enough just to grasp the scope of the *word* 'metaphysical'.

Instead of concerning herself with how Hymn juggled being here or there, she asked, "What was that pulse I felt before falling asleep?" She looked around, seeing that they were in the Rivien desert, above Isaro. Only, the city was not there in any substantial way. Instead, only a translucent, oily shadow in roughly the shape of the city floated some distance above what should have been a plateau. Instead of a towering rock formation, however, the break in the dream-desert was a *tower* hewn from a polished red stone that reflected the starlight above.

"I told you, *something* is happening in the east," Hymn said.

Cassidy looked in that direction. In the way of dreams, her vision expanded, and the world twisted with her thoughts. The curvature of the horizon bended and flattened until she could see the churning ocean, the isle of Andaerhal, the Black Gulch, and the forests of the mainland. The sky — a brilliant swirl of purples and reds adorned with stars and brilliant moons above — was interrupted in an abrupt and pitiless blackness that hung over the Revehaven mountains. It wasn't just dark clouds, but a fathomless black void. Lightning danced in that darkness, but no clouds were revealed. Something towering moved under the shadow, lithe and serpentine. A trail of red light cut through the unfathomable empty sky from where the palace stood in the waking world and out to the north.

She blinked, and her far sight vanished. She could feel the memory of what she'd seen fading like a dream. She tried to see out again, but the Dreamscape refused to change.

"Hymn, make me see again!" she ordered.

The Fae kicked off the gunwales and seemed to swim over to Cassidy's side, orbiting around her slightly as momentum carried her. Her bright blue dress and raven hair tossed around slowly, as if flowing in a disrupted current of water.

"You should not make such thoughtless requests, especially not here." She took up a seated position once more, but she was hovering in the air level with Cassidy's shoulder. "You were able to see your empire?"

"Aye," said Cassidy. "It was dark, and there were... things I... I can't quite remember."

Cassidy, wake up, we're here.

"We will discuss this another time," Hymn said, and Cassidy was forced to agree.

Cassidy woke up in the real world — more easily than she would have if she had actually been asleep — to find Kek was leaning over her, prodding her gently. The palanquin had stopped and been set down. She groaned as she pushed herself up. Her bones ached and her muscles were quivering in stress, but she was able to climb out unaided, for which she was grateful.

They emerged onto a purple, velvet carpet that stretched out to the doorway of a towering edifice with a domed ceiling. Outside, lined up before the palanquin, five servants stood in a line to greet them. They all wore identical, egg-shell brown kaftans with simple, copper-accented embroidery.

"Welcome to Isaro," said the boy in the middle of the group. He couldn't have been any older than Miria. He had bright brown eyes and the kind of smile that Cassidy might have let herself get swept up by when she had been young and innocent. "Allow us to take you to your rooms."

The servants paired up with the *Dreamscape*'s crew, and Cassidy noted with a hint of amusement that the only girl — and the only one who looked closer to thirty than twenty — in the party was assigned to Kek, thinking how relentlessly eager he was likely to be in her company. That was, until the girl took him by the arm not with her hands but with her entire body, and Cassidy suspected it might have been intentional on the part of their hosts.

The young man took Cassidy by the hand and winked at her. "I am Shakil, and I am at your service for the duration of your stay. Lady...?"

His hands were soft, and his touch was gently, as if she were porcelain. It made her acutely aware that it had been months since she had had intimate contact with a man.

"Captain Durant," Cassidy answered automatically, losing herself briefly in Shakil's eyes. "Captain *Cassidy* Durant."

They entered the building and cut through an enormous lobby rife with gaudy statuary depicting scantily clad or nude men and women in lounging positions and rich tapestries decorated with elaborate and abstract patterns. On the other side was a short corridor that led to another that, at a glance, Cassidy was pretty sure circled almost the entire diameter of the tower.

Kek, Lierre, and Miria were escorted off to the left while Cassidy and Nieves were taken right. Cassidy felt a pang of anxiety at being left without the princess' expertise in such an unfamiliar setting. Still, she followed Shakil's lead, deciding she couldn't possibly get in over her head so soon. Nieves was taken to a room on the inner side opposite a stairwell while Cassidy was led further around.

"I've saved the best room in the tower for you, Captain," Cassidy's escort said conspiratorially.

Cassidy smiled pleasantly, but as grand as the lobby and the corridors were, she wasn't sure she would recognize one room being any more impressive than another. They followed the corridor to the very back to a grand-looking double door. Shakil opened both sides of the entrance and stepped aside for Cassidy to enter the circular room.

A plush rug covered the floor leading to a recessed floor adorned with an assortment of large, silk pillows and cushions surrounding a communal qalyan and a larger spread of the same snacks that had been available in the palanquin. Through windows on the rounded ceiling above, Cassidy could see that mirrors were arrayed to bring in sunlight and cast against the gilded accents in the decorative wall fixtures, painting the room in a rich, dusky glow.

Three side rooms were visible, though thick curtains were tied to the thresholds allowing for privacy within. One appeared to be a richly furnished study, complete with a small library and a writing desk. The middle most was an opulent washroom, and last was a room occupied by an enormous, circular bed Cassidy could all but hear calling for her.

Cassidy gasped at the majesty of it. She had seen richness and grandeur before — she had been in the presence of the Empress herself fairly recently, and this wasn't quite on that scale — but it had seemed like a glimpse of a life that had nothing to do with her. Now she was being given a piece of that world, and it was overwhelming.

"If you go straight through the washroom," Shakil said, "there is a communal spring bath. Rest assured, however, you will only be sharing it with your companions. If you require more food or drink brought to your room, there is a stack of lists on the table. Simply check off what you desire and drop the parchment into the letter slot here." He indicated a brass flap in the wall. "An emissary from one of the Princes will greet you in the morning to arrange your meeting. There are two in the city; Prince Hassan and Prince Jinan." He leaned in, and in a whisper Cassidy could only describe as conspiratorial, added, "I'm sure they will be fighting each other to be the one to meet with you."

Cassidy had not heard of either Prince, but she hadn't really expected to; for one thing, there was something like fifty Merchant Princes on the Rivien Trade Council, and the seats were bought and sold and traded like family heirlooms at a pawnshop. For another, she wasn't a Rivien citizen, and while she didn't consider herself or her crew *poor*, the kind of money to involve one's-self in their level of politics was beyond her.

"Thank you," was all she could say.

"If there's anything else you need," Shakil said, "do not hesitate to ask. I am here to serve your *every* need," he added in a lower tone that made Cassidy shiver.

She didn't think she was misreading the signals, and if she was, she really didn't care. She gripped Shakil by the kaftan and kissed him. He didn't seem surprised, and when their lips met, it felt like he had been the one to initiate it. With practiced ease, she walked backwards towards the recessed and cushioned section while her fingers danced over the younger man's kaftan. She fought against the pulling of her tendons and the cramping muscles to open the jacket, which dropped to the floor in a pile. He unlaced her corset with considerably less effort than she had put into putting it on that morning. In her impatience, she didn't even wait for his trousers to fall all the way to his ankles before she pulled him back to the cushions.

She didn't know if it was a result of falling, or if Shakil had knocked it off, but her hat flew off her head and Hymn let out a sudden, if subdued, cry of alarm.

"Are you okay?" Shakil asked, pulling away.

"Aye, uh," Cassidy said, trying to think of an excuse. It was difficult, as her ribs were burning, and a sharp pain was forming in her back. "I'm just... excited."

Pain was starting to mount too much to enjoy it when he was finally inside her, and she made a decision. Her days were apparently numbered one way or the other, and she refused to let her final years be bereft of pleasure. She tapped on the Fae power for the first time since learning the cost, and it relieved her and flooded into her all at once, like being blasted by icy water on a summer's day.

Discomfort yielded, and she let herself enjoy the moment. Tomorrow could wait. The Princes, the fleet, the Leviathan, everything else was beyond her control, so she wouldn't pass up comfort when it came calling. And surely a few minutes of pleasure and release wouldn't cost her too much time in the end. She could ask Hymn, but she didn't really want to know.

CHAPTER THIRTY

The doldrums within the Dreamscape reflected Zayne's mood perfectly. In fact, he wasn't entirely convinced they weren't a *consequence* of his feelings. That thought only served to sour his temperament even further. Dark clouds sat stagnant beneath dark clouds, as fixed as the stars in his own world. He sat on the gunwale of the *Scorpion*, his elbows on his knees, his fingers interlocked and holding up his chin.

After the death of the Empress, the surviving Daughters had all boarded the *Scorpion* — at least, Zayne had to assume they were all the survivors; if anyone *had* been left behind, he didn't think they would be survivors for long — and the *Scorpion* had led the fleet's retreat. With Pyrrha providing their heading, they soon found another entrance to the Dreamscape large enough for ships to pass through.

Zayne had been disturbed to realize just how close it had been to Revehaven.

Most of their Imperial pursuers seemed to have abandoned chase after watching the Daughters of Daen vanish like smoke. Those ships that had been too close to break off were caught unawares by the horrors of the Dreamscape. In their confusion, it had been easy to pick them off.

After that, it had been decided that they were safe — from the city's pursuit at least, though not in general. At Zayne's command, Pyrrha provided multiple routes out of the Dreamscape that would see the Daughters safely away from the capital. Zayne had the distinct impression that Altair wasn't interested in leaving at all, though she insisted on following the *Scorpion* to see Zayne pay his debt to her.

Ject and the other captains had fled as quickly as they had been able, with nary a farewell or tip of the hat. The *Scorpion*, however, was bound for the capital of Castilyn, and in order to make the voyage as quickly as possible, she needed to remain in the Fae realm. At least in theory.

Together with the *Kestrel*, the *Scorpion* floated immobile in darkness. It was a bleak overcast instead of the impossible darkness where he had met the Host, but they were every bit as stranded. Pyrrha didn't report another strange Fae or god was responsible, and only seemed bored by the delay.

Zayne was alone on the deck, at long last. Altair had taken a skiff from the *Kestrel* to the *Scorpion* — how the skiff had moved when the ships wouldn't, he had no idea — to harass him and study Dawn Star for some time. Zayne had sat by passively as she swung at the blade through the air or prodded at it with iron or odd relics and tools she had brought over from her ship, occasionally forcing it to disappear when she tried turning it on someone, or later upon request. Eventually, she said she needed to return to her ship to run some form of test and tried to take the sword with her. He had let it disappear from her grasp again and had ignored whatever face or gesture she had thrown his way before she departed.

Shen and Xun were below, doing their best to repair the breach in the hull where enemy cannons had disabled her own. Zayne felt each removed broken plank and hammering blow like they were operating on his ribs. Nanette and Tagren were in the galley fixing something for supper. Aresh had taken a stray bullet in the battle and was recovering from a fever that had followed in the aftermath.

Zayne summoned Dawn Star beneath his laced fingers, and the point was set on the deck. He shifted position and let the sword dissolve into light. He made it appear in his right hand, then his left, in a proper grip and in reverse. He tried to manifest it away from his hands to no avail. He did this idly, almost thoughtlessly, as he reflected on what he had done.

He hated killing, but he excelled at it. He killed for money, in self-defense, to hide other crimes committed in his work. He killed men and women, innocent and guilty, strangers and associates. He hated killing, but he kept doing it.

Why was this so different? Was it because she was the Empress? He had never been much of a patriot. Maybe it was the cumulation of blood. Maybe he had piled so many bodies on his shoulders they finally broke his back. Whatever the case, he saw their faces when he closed his eyes, and hers came to him most clearly. Her last breath still tickled his neck.

The golden sword was light and well balanced even as he held it by the blade. Its tip passed effortlessly through his vest and his shirt, and when he pressed it down against his chest, a small well of blood left a blossoming stain in his clothes. His chest felt tight when he took that final breath. He tightened his grip on Dawn Star, cutting his palms. He pulled the blade into his chest.

Or, he tried to.

An invisible pressure held his hands at bay, as though he had reached the end of a length of chain. He leaned forward, trying to fall into the sword, but it would not sink any further. He pulled the blade out a few inches and slammed it back, but again the blade stopped abruptly, as though a lead block sat against his chest.

"Suicide is not an option for our kind, Lucandri," Pyrrha called from below deck. He climbed the stairs with a deliberate slowness that left every step creaking. "Oh, forgive me, *Captain Balthine*. Even when we possess a vessel, we cannot destroy it, even if it might prove more convenient." She gestured to her own body, and even though she appeared true to herself in the Dreamscape, the silhouette of Xiao Ta was faintly visible as an optical illusion, which made it difficult to look directly at the Fae.

"I'm not Fae," Zayne snapped. "I'm a mortal man, and I'm not bound to your rules."

"Perhaps you *are* mortal," said Pyrrha. She glided across the deck like smoke and seated herself so close to Zayne's side their hips touched. He wasn't sure which was worse, the discomfort he felt at the way her feminine and scantily clad true appearance directed his thoughts, which in turn drudged up associated memories, or the physical contact of Xiao Ta's fat and masculine body. "But you are so much more than a man. And as a consequence, you will have to plan a few more steps ahead if you want to commit suicide."

Zayne sneered and got to his feet. "What do you want from me, Pyrrha?"

"I am but your humble servant," she answered in a tone that was anything but servile. "What drives you — after fighting so hard to survive threats from both sides of the veil of myths and dreams — to end your life so inauspiciously?"

"That's my concern, not yours."

"I beg to differ," the Fae said. "My fate is woven with yours. I should like to know from where the winds blow."

Zayne said nothing and crossed the deck.

325

"Do they keep you from sleep?" she called after him. "The dead laid at your feet?"

"Shut up," said Zayne.

"The weight of your guilt is palpable," Pyrrha continued. "Which burden is heavier? The lives you yourself ended or those you tried and failed to save?"

"I said shut up," he growled between his teeth.

"Death flirts so tenaciously with you, and then takes everyone around you. How long before you get your dear songstress —"

"I said *be silent!*" Lucandri bellowed, and his voice stirred a violent wind that buckled the ship. He turned to face Pyrrha whose face seemed trapped between expressions of terror and elation as she gazed upon him.

She obeyed this time, though her mouth worked as she tried to defy him. "You never could leave well enough alone, could you Pyrrha? Always pushing well past the limits of good sense." He drifted before her, placing his fingers delicately around Pyrrha's illusionary throat. "It has served you well so far, but it will get you killed one day." Lucandri applied a gentle pressure and pulled her to her feet. Pyrrha's image dissolved into the form of the human body she inhabited. She flailed silently, arms thrashing wildly as he continued to press on her stolen windpipe. Her eyes bulged beneath the tinted spectacles, and their bone white irises expanded and threatened to swallow the red-gold sky that housed them.

Lucandri released her abruptly and the ragged breath of a dead man filled the silence as she fell to her knees and struggled for air. A tremulous mirage shifted around the human body and Pyrrha's chosen form reconstituted itself. He flexed his fingers and studied them intently.

"Have I... displeased you, my lord?" Pyrrha managed between coughs.

"Many times," said Lucandri. "Not least of which being when you abandoned me when the *Dreamscape Voyager* sank her claws into my flesh. Destiny must despise one of us to reunite us like this, tied to a dying world and trapped in broken vessels."

"It was no fate, my lord," Pyrrha countered, "but choice! I sought you out ever since your final battle, but your essence was scattered and faint. It was not until a year ago that you resurfaced, and even then, you were masked by the mercenary's presence."

Lucandri cocked an eyebrow. "Is that so? It seemed to me that you had faded and become like any of the other, desperate scum-sucking parasites scraping at the rift between worlds for enough power to escape the pull of the desolated World Tree. From where I see it, you were just unfortunate enough to have taken the bait my... *counterpart* used to secure a guide."

"No, I pursued you relentlessly, served unerringly!" she declared. "You know I cannot lie!" she added in a tone strained by desperation. "Doubt me not, for I have a plan to free you of Balthine and return you to your true glory!"

"Oh? But I believe —" Lucandri began, but he was cut off by Nanette's arrival.

"Zayne?" she asked. "I heard shouting, what happened?"

A cold chill took Zayne over and he gripped his shoulders. He glared daggers at Pyrrha, still in a heap on the deck. *What are you playing at, you monster?* he wondered. To Nanette, he said. "Nothing. Just dealing with unpleasant company. The wind has picked back up, I think we can return to course."

Nanette put her hand on his shoulder, and her touch cut the chill like a hot knife. "Aye, captain." As she took the helm, Zayne saw Pyrrha sneering at Nanette's back before stalking away.

CHAPTER THIRTY-ONE

The bath was fashioned to resemble a natural, rocky spring consisting of three pools connected by little waterfalls and divided by carefully arranged steps. Moss grew on the stones arrayed decoratively around the chamber and fronds rose between them. Like the adjacent rooms, moonlight was reflected into the room and cast against the walls to give a steady but gentle illumination.

Dressed only in a towel, Cassidy was the last to enter the steamy chamber. Miria, Nieves, and Lierre were lounging in the topmost pool while Kek sat in the one beneath them and let the waterfall crash down on him. Cassidy dipped her toe in the water and found it warm and inviting. Shirking off her cover, she eased herself into the hot spring.

The joints in Cassidy's shoulders and back and hips all cracked as she lowered herself into the pool, but the hot water suffused her in a sensation akin to drawing on the Fae power — though it was warmth that seeped into her muscles and the gaps between her bones, rather than coolness. She let out a moan of pleasure and stretched out. The pool was so large she didn't even come close to touching any of the others as she did so.

"Glad you could join us, Captain," Lierre said cheerfully.

"I can't remember the last time I had a good bath," Cassidy said, "and I never had one this nice." She held a breath and slipped entirely beneath the surface. The water was so soothing she was tempted to fall asleep in it. The burbling of the waterfall from underwater was a gentle rumble on the edge of her awareness, like a soft roll of thunder. She stayed there until her lungs started to itch for air.

"You should tell them about the Princes," Hymn advised when Cassidy resurfaced. The Fae had taken Cassidy's discarded towel and made something like a steam tent with it.

"Do you know something?" Miria asked, scooting forward.

Kek's head peered over the ledge of the lower pool. "Are we talking about the job now?"

"Aye, I suppose we are," Cassidy said, settling into a seated position by the edge of the pool. "You might as well join us."

A moment later Kek emerged, naked as the rest of them and stepped around the pool. Nieves neither looked at him or away, while Lierre was making eyebrow gestures at Miria who was blushing like a virgin bride and very pointedly not looking at the gunner. The princess also crossed her legs and arms and sat a little deeper in the pool as Kek lowered himself into the water. Cassidy couldn't help but smile. Surely by now they had seen one another naked aboard the *Dreamscape*, on accident at the very least.

"So, what's this about the Princes?" Miria asked, taking a sudden and profound interest in the waterfall.

"Apparently there are two Princes in the city," said Cassidy. "Hassan and Jinan."

Cassidy thought Miria's blush couldn't get any redder, but she was positively crimson.

"I see," Miria said with a little hitch in her voice. "I imagine they will be fighting over who gets to meet us first."

"That's what Shakil said," said Cassidy.

"Who's Shakil?" asked Nieves.

"That servant boy who greeted us when we arrived, remember?" Lierre chided. "Don't tell me you didn't see the sparks between him and the captain. We haven't been here a day and she's already rubbing elbows with all the handsome ones."

"I doubt elbows were all they were rubbing," Kek said, and a smirk tugged at his lips. "I swear, Cassidy was one eyebrow twitch from stripping down and jumping his bones right there on the street."

"I'm not *that* bad at hiding my feelings."

"You're pretty bad at it," countered Lierre. Kek and Nieves nodded in agreement.

"Whatever," Cassidy conceded, and she splashed water at her friends. "I'm just glad I didn't have to jump out a window afterwards."

"Beats getting pushed," said Kek. "So, what do you know about these Princes?"

"Oh, I thought we were talking about the captain's sex life," Miria drolled.

"We can talk about yours if you prefer," Kek offered in a tone that might even have been sincere.

"Oh, stow it, Valani," said Miria. "Anyway, Prince Hassan has held his seat on the Council of Merchants since he was sixteen — about twenty years, give or take."

Nieves snorted. "Rich kid."

"Quite," Miria agreed. "He mainly deals in luxury. Art, bookstores, expensive tailors, rugs and furniture, musical instruments, that sort of thing. He owns the Red Moons Mercenary Company, too. I met him briefly on a diplomatic tour ten years ago, and from what I remember, he was kind, but a little intense."

"What about Jinan?" Kek asked.

"Prince Jinan has had her title for about five years," the princess said, and her embarrassed tension melted into a more thoughtful expression. Cassidy was surprised to see that Kek — while not averting his gaze — was not openly ogling Miria. "She took her seat by cornering the market on essential goods. She owns most of the nation's farms, water delivery companies, as well as a couple bakeries, a respectable shipyard, and brothels in almost every city in the Rivien. She also owns her own mercenary company: Black Griffins."

"Does any of that help us?" Kek asked.

"It gives us a foot in the door," Cassidy said. "A few empty platitudes about how rich they are, and we get our release form."

"I wouldn't put it so blithely, Captain," Miria advised, "but that's the hope. Acknowledging the value of the other party is key to providing a foundation of mutual respect. And... I fear we might be fighting against the wind on this one."

"Why do you say that?"

"Do you know why Captain Jathun was arrested in the first place?"

"No," Cassidy admitted, "but I have a feeling I won't like where this is going."

Miria sighed, and slumped into the water, apparently forgetting her shyness entirely. She regained her composure quickly, however. "Captain Jathun murdered Prince Hassan's brother. Beheaded him right on the street in broad daylight."

"*Merde*," Lierre swore.

"You could have led with that," said Nieves.

"So, we have to hope we meet with Prince Jinan instead," said Kek.

Cassidy felt a headache coming on. "Anything else?" she asked.

"I don't think so," said Miria. "I can walk you through the finer points of diplomatic protocol if you like."

"In the morning," said Cassidy. "For now, I just want to let these healing waters heal me."

"You earned it after Andaerhal," Kek said.

"We all did," said Cassidy. She threw her head back and groaned. "And we aren't done yet."

"All the more reason to enjoy having a minute to breathe."

A comfortable silence fell over the crew, accentuated by the gurgling of the spring, the churning of the waterfalls, and the slapping of spray on stone. Cassidy let herself drift in the pool. A tiny splash preceded Hymn's cerulean light zipping through water beneath her. The Fae cast a radiant glow that moved like a searchlight as she raced silent laps around the crew and down the waterfall.

"This is so much nicer than the public baths," Lierre said after a while.

"I've never been," Miria replied with a yawn.

"It's not that it's bad," said Lierre. "But they aren't this fancy, and there's no privacy."

Hymn shot up the waterfall in a gentle spray and after fluttering down, gently floated along the pool's surface.

"I prefer the company here," said Kek.

"Of course you do, pervert," Nieves snarked. Miria shifted, as if Nieves had reminded her to be shy.

"It's not like that," said Kek. "But as the only man in the crew, I would be surrounded by strangers in the men's bath — most of whom don't speak Asarian."

Nieves and Lierre continued to rib on Kek, but after a while the conversation died down and everyone fell back into relaxing. Miria was the first to turn in, quickly covering herself in her towel and speed walking back to her room. Lierre and Kek followed suit not long after, albeit at a more leisurely pace.

"Are you okay?" Nieves asked when they were alone. "Is the water helping?"

"Aye, I think so," said Cassidy. "We'll see how tomorrow fares."

"Tapping into the power tonight will have put a strain on you," Hymn said as she floated by.

Water splashed around when Nieves stood abruptly. "You're still using it?" she snapped.

Cassidy's face heated like the pool. She pursed her lips and turned to look at the fronds. "It was one time, for maybe two minutes."

"We disembarked straight into the lap of luxury!" Nieves continued, as though Cassidy hadn't said anything. "What could you possibly need it for?"

Cassidy's face grew hotter, and she bit down on her cheek.

Nieves sloshed water around as she took a violent step forward. "You burned your insides up *for sex?*" she screeched. Cassidy flinched even as a flash of anger drove her to her feet.

"What am I supposed to do?" she yelled back. "Spend the rest of my short life hobbling around like an old crone?"

"You're supposed to *live* the rest of your life, you fucking idiot!"

Cassidy opened her mouth, but the words didn't come. Her anger had fizzled out as quickly as it had flared up, leaving nothing but a cold pit of self-pity and remorse where it had been. Her eyes stung with tears threatening to break the dam holding them back.

Nieves grabbed her towel from the side of the pool and wrapped it around herself. Then she closed the distance between them and embraced Cassidy in an awkward hug. "Five years isn't a long time," she said with a hitch in her voice. "Don't make it shorter."

Cassidy's resolve broke and the tears cascaded down her face. She returned Nieves' embrace and they cried together.

Cassidy hadn't worn a cheongsam since she was Miria's age, when a boy she had met in Xindi had taken her to the local theater. She had managed to lose the dress before the night was through and had never had the opportunity or cause to buy a replacement. At the time, she had been rather distraught, as it had been the fanciest piece of clothing she had ever owned, and it had set her back a fair amount of money. Compared to the intricately embroidered jade green and black silks she wore now, that old gown might as well have been a dirty smock. It hugged her almost as securely as a corset and was so smooth she had to make a concentrated effort to keep from running her hands along it.

She sat stiffly in a chair in front of a standing mirror as Miria ran fingers and long pins through her hair. The princess had a deft touch and managed to never once pull Cassidy's hair, which set her above several city stylists she had endured. Miria topped Cassidy's mane into an elaborate series of buns while leaving a long segment to fall loose around her. The look came together with a subtle dusting of makeup to cover Cassidy's wind-dried cheeks and lips and kohl to mask the bags under her eyes. It was an impressive change, and Cassidy was glad she had grown her hair out.

As if reading her thoughts, Miria said, "Would you look at that. If I didn't know you, Captain, I would think you were a proper lady."

Cassidy snickered. "You might want to tone down your own look, someone might take you for the princess." She actually looked a lot like the Empress, and bedecked in such finery, only their eyes and Miria's gentleness could set them apart.

"You think so? I hear she's the most beautiful girl in the world, so I'll take it."

"I heard she snores like a fat man," Cassidy whispered conspiratorially.

Miria scoffed and slapped Cassidy's arm. "That kind of talk is treasonous!" They grinned and shared a laugh.

Cassidy stood to leave, but spent another moment admiring herself in the mirror. *I look damn good*, she thought in satisfaction.

"When all this is done," Miria said, peering around Cassidy's shoulder to share the mirror, "I'm taking you to all the parties. You can have a dress in every shade of every color."

"One for special occasions is plenty," said Cassidy. Rubbing her fingers along its length again, she added. "Maybe two. And one to sleep in."

The others were outside in the hall, already dressed. In their respective finery. Lierre and Nieves wore nearly identical cheongsams to Cassidy and Miria, while Kek wore an equally fine long shirt with wide sleeves. Lierre wore her hair in looped braids, while Nieves's was too short to do much more than comb in a stylish way, and Kek wore his in a short tail. The group was huddled together and whispering.

"... need to know," Kek said in a low, cutting tone. Looking over Nieves' shoulder, he nodded. "And here they are."

"That's not my favorite way to join a conversation," said Cassidy as she and Miria stepped over to join them. "What's the problem, Kek?"

"It can wait until after the meeting," Nieves insisted. "Right Lierre?"

"I don't know," she replied, squirming a little. "It's not exactly like we can do anything about it."

"What is it?" Cassidy demanded.

Kek reached into his sleeve, extracted a news sheet and handed it to Cassidy. "Second story," he said. Blocks of text in all three languages told the story, for which Cassidy was grateful, as she did not have a strong grasp of anything other than Asarian.

"Businessman still missing," Cassidy murmured in a singsong tune as she skimmed along. "Three weeks hmhmhm... following a shootout in the private lounge of a teahouse owned by hmhmhm... prime suspect the notorious mercenary *Zayne Balthine!*" She shrieked his name and nearly tore the sheet in half, and it nearly tore again when Miria pulled a corner to read it herself. For a brief moment she felt a pang of dread and hate as she imagined him traveling safely through Rivien outside the grasp of the law.

Impossible, she thought. *I killed him. If he didn't bleed to death, he choked on his blood. If he didn't choke, he drowned.* The thought steadied her. Below the article was a rendering of a man who vaguely resembled Daen's Scorpion. The depicted figure wore a black long coat and had long black hair, but the artist had left a streak uncolored. And he wore a mask over one side of his face.

Another sketch accompanied it, depicting an Imperial junk with a battered hull, a meticulously detailed rivermaid crucified to her prow, and a less-lovingly rendered image of the mural of Daen on its flank.

Besides the pictures was a continuation of the article that explained that Zayne Balthine had been reported dead in Asaria and the *Scorpion* — which had allegedly been seen in Isaro's harbor — had been sunk.

Cassidy stood staring at it for several long moments, trying to reconcile what she was looking at with her memory. Her heart pounded in her chest as she relived his murder of her captain — her friend — and then her retaliation. Her thoughts spun loosely without sticking to her conscious mind until...

"He's a copy-crow," she said calmly, as if by willpower alone she could steady her heart. "Someone trying to profit off the reputation of the bastard." Cassidy wondered how much effort went into recreating the *Scorpion*. Had they fished out a real rivermaid, or had they faked one with wire, fish, and plaster? And was it even the right color?

"That's what we figured," said Kek. "Still, I figured it was best you find out about it from us."

"And *I* didn't want to worry you until after we meet with the Princes," Nieves said with a sharp glare at Kek.

"Right," Cassidy said, thinking about the matter at hand.

Shakil and Miria had both predicted that the Princes both wanted to be the one to play host to the Imperial delegation, especially a group who had arrived unannounced bearing urgent orders. What they hadn't expected was that they would compromise and agree to meet them together. It had been an awkward arrangement because both Hassan and Jinan had sent servants to request a meeting at the same time, and despite the fact that the meeting would be held with both Princes in attendance, Cassidy had been required to address the messengers separately and with equal attention, less the *Dreamscape's* crew give offense.

"It probably doesn't matter," Lierre offered. "If someone is running around claiming to be the ghost of Captain Balthine or whatever, it can't be out of any interest in us."

"A person has to be sick in the head to want people to think he's a dead mercenary," said Kek. "Especially with a bounty on the Daughters."

"Actually, this is pretty common in Castilyn," said Lierre. "Debtors, or criminals who find their record makes rejoining society difficult, will claim to be someone with a better tax record or something, and if they're dead, they can't show up and dispute it. In theory, anyway. It almost never works.

"Pirates do it a lot, too," she added. "Partly for anonymity, but also because claiming to be Captain Valentina de la Fontaine — the hundred-and-three-year-old pirate and slaver, with fifty sunken ships attributed to her name, who has allegedly come back from beheading, explosions, drownings, skewerings, disembowelings, and falling down a flight of stairs — is a lot more impressive than striking out as Captain Fanny Tasse, who used to work the common room in the brothel on Third Street."

"I don't know. Captain Valentina sounds very unlucky," Miria noted. "Maybe she should retire."

"Probably," said Lierre. "There was an incident years ago where four pirates all claiming to be de la Fontaine were found drinking in the same tavern. I forget the details, but three of them died by firing squad."

"And the fourth?"

"Married the judge and died of consumption a week later. Or did she?" Lierre amended, then imitated a melodramatic and theatrical interpretation of a ghost. The rest of the crew laughed, leaving behind the subject of Zayne Balthine, though it still cast a shadow on the edge of Cassidy's thoughts.

They took a palanquin to one of the palaces. It was a short trip, and Cassidy thought it might be less trouble if they walked. Two identical girls wearing yellow kaftans greeted them at the palace door with a deterrence that made Cassidy uncomfortable.

The servants led the crew through a dazzling vestibule and across a grand library. Cassidy supposed that with so many Merchant Princes, their palaces were too numerous to rival the Imperial palace for sheer size, but the lack was compensated for by the sheer gaudiness and *stuff*. Every wall was covered in artwork — most of which she could not identify except to say it was clearly expensive — and not all of it went together, such as an Imperial woodcutting of a humble calligrapher placed frame-to-frame with an oil portrait of a kingly figure dressed in a thousand shades of yellow. Each corner was occupied by a display case or statue or table overflowing with knickknacks. Cassidy's attention was pulled to a bizarre statue of a woman with enviable curves proudly presenting her breasts over her neckline. The rise in the statue's skirt was unmistakably less feminine than the rest of her image. If "her" was the right word. Cassidy was left puzzling over *that* oddity long after they left the room behind, and it was enough to completely make her forget about Balthine, at least for a while.

Cassidy's legs burned by the time they arrived at a garden balcony, and she was grateful they had taken the palanquin after all. The space was adorned with statuary depicting sphinxes, naked women and a manticore. As far as Cassidy could tell at a glance, none of the women had unusual anatomies. A wide, low table had been set out for them with platers piled with shelled pistachios, orange slices and pitted figs. Miria took her place on one side of the table and Cassidy sat beside her.

"His highness Prince Hassan and his guest will be with you shortly," said one of the servants. "Ring this bell if you have need of anything," she added, indicating a silver bell sitting behind the plate of orange slices.

"Thank you," Cassidy said politely. The girls bowed and took their leave.

"This Prince Hassan has... interesting tastes," said Kek, and it was clear from looking at him that even though he was facing the manticore that he was looking at the naked women.

"You can't have one," Nieves said, and she helped herself to an orange slice.

"I think it would add some character to the galley."

"We eat there," Lierre protested, "and I don't trust that you would keep your trousers on with it standing there."

"I hope that you will at least keep them on for our meeting," a deep, resonant voice said as a man and a woman dressed in resplendent kaftans emerged onto the balcony.

Prince Hassan — Cassidy assumed — wore a cerulean turban and an amber kaftan slashed with lines of ruby and trimmed in gold. His face was youthful, but his black beard was lined with tangles of gray. By his side, Prince Janin was a head shorter, but she stood as though she were the greater of the two. Her turban was as orange as firelight, and she accompanied it with a kaftan in several shades of red silk that shimmered as she walked.

Miria stood, placed her fist in her palm and bowed. Cassidy and the others followed her lead. "On behalf of her august majesty, Empress Yushiro Shahira, we thank you for this meeting."

"The Empress is always welcome in my house," said Hassan, "as are her envoys. Please, sit." As he insisted, he and Janin sat opposite the *Dreamscape*'s crew.

"Tell me," Janin said, grinning the least sincere smile Cassidy could ever remember seeing, "what is so urgent that the Empress sends five envoys unannounced?" She plucked a date from the table and popped it in her mouth. Her lips pursed condescendingly as she chewed.

"Come now," said Hassan, "that is hardly a way to speak to a guest. Tell me, friends, how have you found your stay in Isaro?"

"It has been lovely," Miria said. "The hospitality presented to us has been beyond compare."

"Good, good," said Hassan. "I would hate to hear that the Empress' daughter has been ill-treated."

Cassidy paused with an orange held up to her mouth. Miria, however, maintained her composure. "The princess? Surely you don't mean to suggest —"

"I never forget a face, Miriaan," Hassan said. A smirk tugged the corner of his eye. "And in all my travels I have seen only three noble-blooded Asarians with blue eyes. One is an old man, one doesn't have a nose, and one is the daughter of the Empress."

"You also look just like your mother," Janin added. "And your friends' faces gave you away. Tell me, blondie, are you free to play Twisted Virtue later?"

Hassan grunted. "Don't be rude." He took an orange slice and chewed it with slow deliberation. "Things must be serious if Shahira sent you in secret. So tell me, what can Rivien do for our beloved neighbor in the east?"

Cassidy glanced over at Miria. The princess's face was a porcelain mask devoid of emotion. If the revelation of being found out disturbed her, she didn't show it.

"We have come to request the release of a prisoner in Marasi Prison," Miria said, and Cassidy was impressed by how she kept her tone so level. Cassidy would definitely have rushed or stammered under the circumstances. "Specifically, Captain Jathun of Val Desolee."

"Absolutely not," Janin said forcefully, and Cassidy's heart sank.

"Now, now, let's not let haste ruin this meeting," Hassan said calmly. He leaned back in his seat and observed Miria with hard, cool eyes. "You ask much, your highness. To put it in gentle words, I have no love for Captain Jathun. Indeed, in my testimony I pleaded for his execution.

"As it stands," he continued, and his voice grew steadily in intensity, "he was sentenced to life in prison, and there he will rot. Why, then, should I put my seal on a release form?"

"We need his aid," said Miria. "We need his experience, his contacts, and his skill in battle."

"A washed up pirate and a murderer?" Janin scoffed. "You can forget it."

Hassan took a deep breath. "Even if we were amenable, Jathun has been in prison for five years. He is out of practice and out of contact, at best. Surely you have a more reasonable request, highness."

"If you will not release Jathun," said Miria, "then we will need a fleet, to replace the one we had hoped to use Jathun to build. We need ships built for battle, and orichalcum weapons." She turned to Janin. "Perhaps we can discuss hiring Black Griffins and the Red Moons?"

Janin's brow raised, as though she had been ready to argue and had been taken aback. "*And* the Red Moons? Just how many men do you need?"

"Both companies if it can be helped."

Hassan laughed, though his voice hitched as he tried to suppress it. "You go from needing one man to wanting a fleet. Quite a leap."

"We requested Jathun's release as a means to *acquire* a fleet. If you aren't willing to consider that, then we may need to deal more directly."

"Have tensions with Castilyn grown so much that you have to sneak around to find pirates and hire mercenaries?"

"This isn't about Castilyn."

"That's even more concerning," Janin said. She leaned in and stage-whispered conspiratorially, "You came to release an enemy of the Rivien people to raise a stockpile of ships and weapons... and not to face the hostile power to the south? I hope you don't expect my Griffins to turn against their homeland."

"We don't plan on turning the fleet against Rivien, either."

Cassidy was starting to wonder if Miria actually meant to include the crew with all the "we's", or if she had fallen into her mother's habit of referring to herself in the plural.

Hassan leaned back in his seat. "Why, then, do you come to us?"

Cassidy looked to Miria. The princess seemed conflicted. She met Cassidy's eye, and Cassidy felt just as unsure. Did people know about the Leviathan this close to the Nest? And if not, would the Princes believe them?

It was Kek who broke the silence. "It's the thing that destroyed the Dragon Nest."

Miria shot Kek a reproachful look, but Hassan visibly deflated across the table.

"You speak of the new World Tree."

"No," said Kek, though he looked south regardless. The tree was visible like a white scar, its many branches reaching out and blending into the horizon. "But when the tree appeared, something else came out of the Dreamscape. A monster. It's been picking off ships over the oceans for months now. It's the size of a mountain and capable of moving undetected."

"This is ridiculous," said Janin. "I don't know which is worse; the idea that you can't even come up with a more plausible lie, or that you believe the mad ramblings of the —"

Hassan slammed his hands on the table and the platters rocked and rang with the impact. "That is enough!" Cassidy recoiled and Janin looked as though she had swallowed her own tongue. Hassan took a deep breath, and in a calmer tone said. "The tree is visible from here. We have heard that it's visible as far as the Northern Reach and the Southern Expanse. Such a thing is not natural. So it is not unreasonable that some of the claims regarding what happened at the Nest are more true than we have given credit."

"The stories are not mad ramblings," Miria said. "We were there!" She lifted the sleeve of her cheongsam, revealing a jagged crossing diagonally across her forearm. "Fae power and blood brought that tree into the world, and so much worse besides. If nothing is done, no one is safe."

There was a long silence. Janin's mouth twisted into a snarl. Cassidy had to make a conscious effort to breathe. Hassan steepled his fingers. He and the princess seemed to hold a conversation in their eyes.

"Rivien cannot offer her fleets to her august majesty," he said finally. Cassidy's heart fell. Miria stood. "I see," she said with a tone cold enough to smother dragon fire. "If there's nothing else — "

"There is, actually," Hassan said. He gestured for Miria to return to her chair. "I will sign for Jathun's release tonight, and I will even throw in the *entire* Red Moons company."

Janin shot to her feet. "*What?*" she shrieked. "You can't be serious."

Hassan glanced up at his cohort and passed her a wry smile before turning back to Miria with a dour expression. "But nothing is free, you understand, highness."

"Of course," Miria said, and the suspicion was clear in her tone. "What will this cost us, exactly?"

"Your hand in marriage."

"You ask much," Miria said without missing a beat.

Cassidy, however, was slower to catch up as she tallied up the costs. Her world traded in lower stakes, but marriages formed in business weren't completely unheard of. On its face — before factoring Miria's feelings — a marriage for a fleet and a prisoner seemed lopsided in their favor but rank complicated things. As the future Empress of Asaria, Miria would have more power than anyone else in the world someday. But, a Prince of the Merchant Council was no small catch, either.

But what did Miria think of the idea? Cassidy suspected — from her distant understanding of royalty — marrying for love was never in the cards for the princess. But her mother had never married at all. And would it be worth possible decades of being tied down to this man to face a threat that — Cassidy hoped — would be put down much sooner than that?

"What's to stop me from pursuing another Prince to release Jathun and enlisting another company, like the Black Griffins?"

Janin sneered. "The Griffins' support and Jathun's release are mutually exclusive. And you! How can you entertain this madness? Your own brother —"

"I will not be spoken to in this manner in my own house, Janin! Isal, see our guest out." Before the words were even out of his mouth, a tall woman stepped out of the shadows as though she had been there the whole time.

"If you will please come with my, Prince Ja—"

"I know the way," Janin said, and Cassidy shivered at the chill in her words, shoving the woman aside. As she retreated, she called back, "This isn't over, Hassan."

"No," he said, more to himself than to her, "I didn't think it would be."

"My question still stands," said Miria. "Why should I accept this deal over another course?"

Hassan smiled sympathetically. "Because you know you cannot waste time, and now I know it as well. Lives are in danger, and I can see in your eyes that that is something you cannot, will not, stand by and wait for a committee to deal with. Now, Highness, do we have a deal?"

"Why *did* you change your mind about Jathun?" Cassidy asked, in part to give Miria time to think.

"I can see the way the wind is blowing," the Prince said. "The World Tree is something nebulous, but a monster born of the Dreamscape? One that is apparently responsible for many missing vessels? That is a certainty."

"You keep mentioning this World Tree," Lierre noted. "What do you know about it?"

"Less than my teacher," said Hassan, "more than most. Did you know that before the ascension, humans had power comparable to the Fae?"

Cassidy's eyebrow quirked. She had never heard anything of the sort.

"Not universally, mind, but many were capable of shaping the world around them at a whim, though their greatest feats were performed in concert with the Fae. These individuals often ruled as kings and queens of their lands, claiming their powers were gifts from the gods and signs of favor."

"What's this got to do with the tree on the horizon?" asked Kek.

"Shut up and maybe he'll get to that," Nieves whispered.

Hassan smirked at Kek, then continued as if there had been no interruption. "When the gods and Fae declared war on humanity, our forebears were woefully unprepared. Iron was rarer in those days, and humanity depended on the very lands that the gods corrupted. The dangers of the surface below we take for granted today were new horrors back then.

"Even after we ascended into the skies, the war continued, and we were on the brink of extinction. The leaders of what might have been called the resistance made a desperate decision. You see, they had concluded that the Fae and gods derived their power from the World Tree, a nexus place where the Dreamscape and our world intersect.

"They destroyed the Tree," he said bluntly. "Or, as much of it as could be destroyed, anyway. But that was a mistake. It ended the war, true, but it wasn't the source of the Fae's strength. It was ours. And as its name might imply, it was also our world's. You can see the effects everywhere if you know what it was like before. Ghosts are more commonplace. We can't inter corpses for three days before they start walking and killing people. Dragons are born sickly and remain small their entire lives. Farming used to be considered a safe and boring —"

"I'm sorry, did you just call dragons *small?*" Kek asked incredulously.

"We've seen dragons as big as my ship," Cassidy agreed. "They seem healthy enough to me."

"Size is relative," Hassan said, waving off further commentary. "Anyway, losing the Tree changed the world. I can only speculate how this new one will change things going forward."

Cassidy would have to ask Hymn about it later.

"Now, highness," Hassan said, leaning forward and directing his attention back to Miria, "what say you?"

"You can't expect her to make this decision without the Empress' consent," Kek said.

"Under normal circumstances, true," said Hassan. "But her august majesty is no fool. Her people are in danger, and she surely gave Miriaan more than enough latitude to achieve success at *any* cost."

Cassidy cleared her throat uncomfortably, though Hassan didn't notice. The Empress hadn't even given Miria consent to *join* the expedition, much less to use herself as payment. She was still worried that the Empress had sent ships after them to retrieve the princess. Hopefully, they were just as distracted by events in Andaerhal as Cassidy and the others had been.

"And if you don't mind me indulging in a little vanity," he added to Miria, "she would surely recognize that, as far as your prospects go, I am one of a very few potential suitors who comes close to matching your glory. It would not be the first time that an Empress of Asaria married a member of the Merchant Council. Her own grandfather was such a man, and with his aid your Empire was prosperous during a time of drought."

Cassidy couldn't help but think that last point — unprompted and largely irrelevant to the matter at hand — was a hint that Hassan was a little desperate himself. She just couldn't decide if it was a desperation to add to his already immense power and influence, or if he was actually an altruist and wanted to help but couldn't back down after adding a condition. She hoped it was the latter, but she suspected it was the former.

Miria took a deep, steady breath and took a sip of water. She set her cup down gently and smoothed out her skirts. Her face was expressionless when she met Hassan's gaze and in a voice as placid as a lake on a cold morning said, "Let us draw up a contract, then. You are correct in saying we have no time to waste, but I will not be rushed into a ceremony like a common woman. You will provide the ships and resources and you will have my agreement."

"Of course, your highness," Hassan said, bowing his head. "I would expect nothing less."

CHAPTER THIRTY-TWO

The *Scorpion* returned to the waking world around midday over a wide, green field spotted with patches of snow and dirt. The *Kestrel* had refused to follow. Altair had chosen to stay immersed in the realm of Fae and gods, and somehow her crew had not mutinied. So it was that only one black ship emerged from the clouds in the middle of Castilyn. Zayne took in the brisk air with grateful lungs, and he was not alone. Xun had excitedly roused Tagren and Shen with the promise of the sun and neither groused at their broken slumber. Aresh had forgone preparing food to dance around the deck with his arms thrown wide as if he meant to embrace the wind itself as he laughed like a man possessed. Nanette leaned over the gunwale like a child smiling into the mundane sight.

Only Pyrrha — once again appearing to all observers as the rotund crime boss Xiao Ta — was not reveling in their return from the nightmare world. She stood on the aftcastle, aloof and apart. As far as Zayne was concerned, she could stay that way.

Once reality set in, Zayne took stock of their position and set their course. As if the Dreamscape had wanted to impose one final confusion upon them, the *Scorpion* was headed north when it appeared in the sky, despite Castilyn standing far to the south of the Empire. With the ship turned about and her engines churning at full speed, the shining capital of the southern kingdom appeared on the horizon in under an hour.

Where Revehaven sprawled across the widely spaced peaks of five mountains and offered her citizens room to spread outward, her rival city Tal Joyau was built vertically, confined to a tightly clustered trio of sierras. On approach, the intricate series of bridges and sloped causeways that made up the city's streets formed a latticework of braids that looked to Zayne like an ornate and well-furnished bird cage. The Ruby Palace loomed over her city as an imposing shadow, in stark contrast to the Jade Palace which seemed to keep vigil over the northern capital — or maybe that was just the smoldering wreckage of Zayne's patriotism speaking.

Traffic was heavy departing and arriving across all the docks, but a pair of patrol boats flagged them down almost immediately and escorted them to skip the queue.

"Dardan's doing, no doubt," Zayne grumbled to Nanette as he followed. Sure enough, when they arrived at the southern harbor, Zayne spotted the *Martyr's Demise* docked in the berth beside the one apparently reserved for the *Scorpion*, like a black splotch of mold on a beautiful painting.

Zayne had expected to meet Dardan aboard her vessel to report and make a second assassination attempt. Hopefully a more successful one. Instead, the cultist-cum-mercenary leader stood at the bottom of the gangway when he disembarked. There weren't even any port authority officials with her to charge them a docking fee.

Her customary black shroud looked grotesquely out of place against a backdrop of bright colors and crowds of fashionably dressed people milling about the port. Her stillness beneath the cowl as it fluttered faintly in the breeze brought to mind the oily ghosts Zayne had seen in the ruins before enlisting Pyrrha.

"Captain Balthine," Dardan said by way of greeting.

"Dardan," said Zayne, unable to keep the venom from his tone. Out in the open there on the wharf, he would be arrested or shot on sight for her murder. If he had been aboard the *Martyr's Demise* he might have been able to fight his way out and flee on the *Scorpion* before the authorities were wise to his deeds.

Hopefully, Nanette and the others could claim ignorance of his intentions.

He drew his hidden pistol so quickly that the straps securing it to the interior lining of his coat snapped. He hadn't even pulled the weapon clean of his coat when Darden said, "Stop," and his muscles seized up. The pistol rattled in his hand as he tried to defy the order, but his arm wouldn't budge.

"You never learn, do you?" Dardan's voice was thick with wry condescension. "Fortunately, I don't need you for your brain. Is Empress Yushiro dead?"

"She is," he replied through gritted teeth, unable to keep the words buried.

"Oh, how wonderful!" Dardan said in a tone Zayne didn't recognize coming from her — she even clapped with apparent glee. "Queen Celeste will be pleased." She seemed more sober as she pointed up to the *Scorpion's* aftcastle with a bony finger and added, "Make sure *that* is elsewhere before the Iron Veils come to perform their inspection."

Zayne was surprised by how quickly Dardan had picked out the possessed crime lord, but perhaps he shouldn't have been. Dardan was probably the only person alive who knew more about the Fae, gods, and the Dreamscape than Isaara Altair.

Nanette descended from the gangway with a death grip on the knife on her belt. "Is there a problem, *Captain?*" she said, leveling a sneer at Dardan.

"As a matter of fact, there is," Dardan said firmly. "The Iron Veils are here in force, and your new crew now numbers a very *literal* daughter of Daen." Zayne and Nanette looked back again at Pyrrha, who noticed and wiggled her fingers in a dainty wave that looked entirely too delicate and light for Xiao Ta's sausage fingers. "I have spent years downplaying our name as an intimidation tactic to those pious and self-righteous bastards, but if they spot her aboard one of my ships —"

"*My* ship," Zayne corrected.

"— they will launch *another* investigation and how long do you think it will take them to find something amiss? Speaking of which," she added, and she reached into her sleeve to extract a small phial containing a thick, gray liquid. "You should drink this. It will hide the very obvious signs of your *condition*. For a while."

"And I should trust you because... why, exactly?"

"Because you are still an asset to me," said Dardan.

Zayne considered that while still fighting with whatever Fae influence held his arm in place. "How long is a while?" he asked.

"Four hours? Five? What difference does it make? You just need to be presentable for the Queen." Zayne grudgingly took the phial in his free hand and Dardan turned her back on them.

Nanette glanced at Zayne, and he nodded. She drew her knife and drove the blade into Dardan's back. The knife skidded off something with a shriek of metal and Dardan whirled around in a rush of black fabric. The weapon went spinning through the air and its blade stuck into the hull of the *Scorpion*. Dardan struck Nanette in the throat with the points of her fingers and the younger woman staggered away. Zayne finally freed the pistol from his coat, leveled it at Dardan's head and pulled the trigger.

The hammer fell.

And all was quiet.

Zayne's heart fell when he realized his folly. The flint had fallen out of the lock. He had come so close.

Dardan stood still as a statue on the other side of the pistol. Her expression was hidden by her cowl, but he could see from the way the fabric blew in and out that she was breathing more heavily than he had ever seen.

"Enough," she said. "The Iron Veils are on their way. Get rid of the puppet. Balthine, you need to come with me."

It turned out that Dardan wasn't joking about meeting the Queen. After compelling Zayne to swallow the gray concoction — which tasted like iron filings and salt water — she took him to a private palanquin with curtained windows. His skin crawled from sitting in so private a setting with her, but he felt the shackles on his soul when she gave an order and couldn't control his body to resist.

"Don't tell me you expect me to kill another monarch," said Zayne after nearly ten minutes of silence.

"Not today," Dardan replied. There was no humor or irony in her tone. "However, as I have been here for some time, Queen Celeste needs to hear the news from a new arrival."

Zayne bit back the urge to question Dardan further. As much as he wanted to ask why the Queen would trust him any more than Dardan — especially when he had arrived in the city far faster than any ship could fly straight from Revehaven to Tal Joyau, under normal circumstances — or why she didn't just wait for word to reach the south by conventional means, he knew she wouldn't answer. Or worse, she would. He also refrained from asking where her guards were, realizing that she had forced him into the role.

Despite Dardan's all-consuming shroud, he was unable to shake the feeling Dardan was staring at him over the course of the ride. His finger itched incessantly as he replayed his failure at the docks, alternatively imagining his pistol firing properly and the grim reality. He imagined quite a significant divergence in his life had hinged on that moment, and he wouldn't like where his current course led.

Just as the journey began to smother Zayne's sense of time, a noise outside caught his attention. He peeled the curtain aside to look at the streets. He regretted the decision almost immediately.

Zayne and Dardan crossed into a gated district, and as far as Zayne could see, the wall was pressed with the desperate mob, men and women, some dressed modestly in rough spun dresses and trousers, others wearing little more than patchwork and tattered rags. The city watch — uniformed from cap to toe in gray slashed with red bands — had gathered en mass. Some walked along the crowds, cracking thick truncheons against anyone who broke away from the press on the wall, while others maintained a perimeter with crossbows. One watchman hit a woman hard enough to leave her splayed on the cobbles and immediately waved the palanquin along as if there was nothing to see.

Zayne's gut churned with acidic bile as he found his feet and reached for the door of the palanquin.

"Sit down," Dardan ordered.

Zayne's body obeyed without his consent, and he could hear the pullers grunt when he flopped back onto the seat without warning.

"They really should learn their place," she pontificated, though Zayne thought he caught an edge of sarcasm in her voice. "These protests have occurred daily for about a month. There was a place in one of the poorer parts of the city. A humble little bistro, barely worth notice. The owner — a woman in her early-middle years by the name of Maeva Vidal — fed the homeless who came to her door after hours, offering up the day's scraps and leftovers to whatever poor vagabonds came begging. She was a well-liked if unremarkable presence to her neighbors, but to the downtrodden, she was a lifesaver.

"She was arrested on charges of 'contributing to public delinquency', because in Castilyn, giving scraps to the poor is affording them too much dignity. They might get *ideas,* you see. Anyway, the woman was killed after the arresting watchmen got a little too *handsy* for her liking. Meanwhile, her restaurant was shut down, her property — including her home on the second floor — were promptly scooped up by a wealthy merchant who is currently using it as a storage unit.

"She was hardly the first victim of such rampant capitalism. Indeed, I think she was just the last splinter that tipped the scales. It's illegal to say her name, now, but it's a rallying cry not just in this city, but across the country. But obviously, what chance do the common people have against the superior weapons of the law? The result is tragedy and oppression."

"And you're openly supporting it," Zayne sneered, though he knew it wouldn't mean anything to her.

To Zayne's surprise, Dardan didn't laugh, didn't extol upon him the virtues of violence. Instead, she scoffed. "On the contrary, Balthine, I am the only person who is working towards a meaningful change."

"Through slaughter and war!"

"No. Through *extermination*. The slate needs to be wiped clean."

"Pigeon shit!" Zayne snapped, slamming his fist on the palanquin walls. "The Empire doesn't abuse its people like that! Nor does Rivien! You want to commit genocide when you could just as easily take over Castilyn with your cult and change it!"

"And tell me, oh he from the enlightened Empire," said Dardan. "Whatever was it that happened to your family, again?"

Zayne reached for the stiletto in his sleeve, but his fingers numbly refused to retrieve it. He snarled at the cowled monster before him. "Don't you *dare* talk about my family."

"You were framed for the crime because your father — a known drunk with a personal vendetta against you — happened to hold a position of power. His word alone completely erased all the good will you earned over years of living in the community. And you were branded a murderer and sentenced to death."

Zayne lunged and his knife flew from his sleeve, striking the wall of the palanquin, sticking out an inch beside Dardan's hidden face. His forearm pressed against her neck as he drove his weight into her. "I said *shut up!*"

Dardan merely pushed him back with a finger and the weight of her earlier command settled forcibly again into Zayne's bones. Outside, the haulers grunted again as the box rocked.

"The Empire and Rivien may have more functional social programs," Dardan continued, as though Zayne's assault had been a bump in the road. "And the lives of *people*, as some vaguely defined whole, are objectively better than they are here. But *people* as individuals? Suffering is in the nature of the weak, and those with power will always be intent to inflict as much suffering as they can upon those they perceive as beneath them. So, no, taking over Castilyn and dismantling its government would not address the underlying issue. *Humanity*. Now, do be silent and play your part."

Zayne stewed in silence, unsure he would have had a ready retort even if he weren't compelled to keep his mouth shut. Dardan was so still and silent that only her steady breathing told him she was even still awake.

When the journey finally came to a stop, Dardan was the first to step out, and Zayne once more reached for a concealed weapon. His fingers refused to clasp it, however, and he felt pulled along by an invisible leash as he followed Dardan outside.

The outer gate of the Ruby Palace was an ostentatious monstrosity, made of dawn wood — cut from a rare breed of tree, which absorbed sunlight and glowed like crystal through the night. Castilyn was about the only place it could be found in enough quantities to make something as noteworthy as a door, as the royal family owned the only grove where they could be found. It also wasn't functionally any better than common woods. Zayne had once had to breach a door made of the stuff on a job and found that not only had it been remarkably easy to punch through, but it had made a rather colorful fire when he had done so.

The heavy door was adorned by gilded metalwork that depicted the current Queen of Castilyn sitting atop a two-headed griffin. The six guards manning the entrance were clad in red armor over gold silk tunics, holding long guns at their shoulders. One of them recognized Dardan.

"Lady Dardan, the queen is expecting you. We are to let in and to be escorted straight to the throne room upon your return."

"Then you should do so," Dardan said, and she waved them on. The guard didn't seem chastised by the remark and knocked rhythmically at the door. It opened with an unseen mechanism with slow, rumbling steadiness.

"*Lady* Dardan?" Zayne scoffed.

"Some people show me the respect due, Captain Balthine," she replied. "It makes life easier."

When the doors came to a booming halt, a quatrain of guards stood waiting on the other side and beckoned them to follow. The entrance seemed more like a tunnel than a corridor, with a ceiling so high and walls so wide, a dragon might have walked along that plush, red carpet with little discomfort. Unlike the Jade Palace, the throne room of the Ruby Palace was not far from the entrance — indeed, it was a straight shot from the gate, albeit up several landings of stairs — and Zayne assumed there was some kind of philosophical explanation for the difference.

A man and a woman in matching gray robes adorned with links of chainmail, complete with veils over their faces, flanked the door to the throne room — which compared to the gate and the corridor was almost conservative, being *only* half as high as the ceiling and six arms-lengths apart — in addition to six palace guards. The woman's brow furrowed upon their approach, but the man grinned so widely it showed through his veil.

"Javina!" he said brightly. "I heard you might be paying a visit, so I switched duties with Carver —"

"*Brother Tamlis,*" the woman beside him corrected.

"Oh, don't be like that," the man said. "Javina was —"

"*Lady Dardan,* you will not be allowed your cowl in her majesty's presence," the woman pressed. "And you and your companion will be searched for weapons and any heretical talismans, relics, or stolen property."

"Stolen property?" Dardan asked, and Zayne wondered if he imagined the smugness in her tone.

"There was a break in at one of our vaults last—"

"Brother Harrow!" the woman snapped.

"Oh, come on, Sel, Javina's one of us," Brother Harrow protested.

"She left the Order almost thirty years ago," Sel corrected, then turned on Dardan, "to dance with Fae and gods and thumb her nose at her oaths and duty."

"I have been cleared of all charges of conspiracy," said Dardan. "And it's been proven that I do not consort with the gods."

"You can't prove a negative," Sel countered. "Failure to prove that you are a consort is just that: a failure. You named your bloody company after a goddess, damn your eyes!"

"It's just a name to inspire fear in her enemies," Harrow said, offering an apologetic smile to Dardan.

"Inspiring fear in the name of a goddess defies everything we stand for!" she looked around, as if only now aware that there were witnesses to the argument. "Am I the only one who hasn't been poisoned by her lies?" she added in a whisper.

"Inquisitor Tavarian spent a year overseeing the Daughters to ascertain that there is no god worship or Fae consortium,"

Harrow said, in a tone that suggested he had already argued the point to death.

Zayne fought the urge to snort. The now-retired Inquisitor Tavarian had been so deep in Dardan's pocket that he had provided all the information that Zayne had used to steal the seed of the World Tree, two years ago. He wondered if that was the break-in Harrow had been about to blab about. He also wondered if Dardan had arranged to tie that loose end. Probably.

"Enough," said Sel. "Check them."

The guards moved with a rigid professionalism that suggested they resented being given orders by the Iron Veils, but they knew better than to argue. As they stripped his coat off, Zayne watched Dardan carefully. He had seen her without her cowl only once — during his induction into the Daughters of Daen almost a decade earlier — and she had appeared as some sort of reptilian, Fae monstrosity. He braced himself for the guards to suddenly turn violent and attack. He found himself wondering if he would defend Dardan if it came to it. Would he have a choice?

When Dardan's shroud was removed, however, Zayne was the only one surprised. Beneath the black veil and robes was *not* a menacing horror pulled from a nightmare. Her auburn hair was held in a loose bun, with wavy strands framing her heart shaped face, which was not covered in scales, but was blemished only by crow's feet, deep laugh lines, and a thin, mostly faded scar on her right cheek. She wore a pair of round, darkened spectacles at the end of her short, upturned nose, which she peered over with cedar brown eyes that featured neither the inverted colors of a Fae or the slitted eye of a snake. In fact, the only remarkable thing about her was just how *un*remarkable she appeared.

She wore a dress of deep red silk bedecked with black lace, which reminded Zayne of the deel Altair had worn in the mission to assassinate Empress Yushiro. He wondered if it was a coincidence, even as he fought down the shakes and nausea at the memory.

The guards were filling a box with Zayne's various weapons. A sour faced woman with a scarred nose leveled an ever deepening scowl with each knife she found on his person as she patted him down, while a tall man with a gravity defying moustache looked more confused than anything as he riffled through Zayne's many interior coat pockets. Zayne thought he might miss the hidden pockets altogether until he flipped it over and a stiletto shot out of the hem of the sleeve and clattered straight into the pile.

"Normally we would arrest you for even trying to carry *one* hidden weapon into her majesty's presence," the surly looking woman informed him when they were done, "but she insisted on this audience. Consider yourself fortunate."

Zayne shrugged into his coat. From the way the weight settled, he knew the man had missed the barber razors in the hem, and after adjusting himself he felt the spool of razor wire sitting just below the shoulder and the lockpicks. The entire situation was paradoxically relaxing in how it frustrated him; in a life suddenly upturned and filled with Fae and nightmare realms and regicide and a lack of free will, the agitation of knowing he would have to take time returning his belongings to their proper place — because someone unsatisfied with their job had to be a jackass — was an anchor to reality.

The doors swung open with an ease that belied their weight. *I should send the designs to the Empire,* Zayne thought.

With compulsion forcing his steps he followed Dardan into the oppressively lavish chamber. Stained glass windows bathed the room in harsh light like a perpetual dawn that accentuated the myriad shades of red and gold that made up everything from the carpeting and tapestries to the brickwork behind them. The room was empty of courtiers and petitioners, but the faint groves worn in the rug suggested that was a rare occurrence.

He and Dardan stopped before a line of guards separating them from the throne. Save one woman whose armor had the gold and red portions reversed, they didn't look at the mercenaries. Instead, they stood statuesque with their faces fixed on the doors. The woman Zayne pegged as the captain of the guard sneered at Dardan and Zayne in turn.

The Ruby Throne sat atop a steep dais with two golden chairs situated on either side two steps below, each occupied by a blonde woman in blue dresses that stood apart from everything else in the room — the Queen's chief advisors; her bastard sisters, Rosalin and Ysulde, if Zayne's information was still current.

Standing beneath it, Zayne couldn't help but compare it to the Jade Throne far to the north. Castilyn's seat was less artistically grand and more monetarily so, with rubies set in gold reliefs every few inches, with much of the backrest housing a crimson gem the size of Zayne's head. The throne was too wide for any person to fill, but Queen Celeste seemed to be trying.

Zayne had seen a few paintings of Celeste since her coronation, some sketches in news sheets, and a statue. None of them had hinted at the woman's girth. He might have called her figure *matronly*, except for the fact she was younger than him by a couple years. Unlike her sisters, she was committed to the Ruby theme of the palace. She wore a low-cut dress made of rivermaid scales in a gradient of reds from rose pink to crimson that showed off her elaborate ruby choker and a golden necklace set with a spiral of the jewels. Her hair had been dyed like wine while each of her fingers strained at the gold bands of rings affixed with fat, blood colored gems, and her nails were painted to match. Her thick, pouting lips were brilliant garnets, and even her eyes appeared to be red from where Zayne stood, which might have just been the reflection of the room against light eyes. Or it could have been a deliberate effect achieved by alchemical means.

Taking in the uniformity, Zayne wondered if Celeste actually *liked* the color, or if she got sick of it at the end of the day. He was reasonably certain *he* would. In fact, it was starting to agitate him already.

Dardan inclined her head in a semblance of a bow. After receiving glares from the bastards and from the queen herself, Zayne followed suit. Dardan didn't seem to show the same deference Altair and her first mate had shown the Empress. After what he had done on her behalf, Zayne wasn't prepossessed to do so either.

If their continued glowering was any indication, the half-hearted gestures didn't impress their hosts.

"Lady Dardan," said the thinner woman to Celeste's right — *Ysulde, the older sister*, Zayne thought, remembering her image from old sketches — stretching out the word like a sigh. "Who is this masked man you bring before her grace?" Her voice wasn't loud or particularly strong, but it carried well in the chamber.

"This is Captain Balthine the Second, one of my Great Captains, your grace," Dardan answered evenly, addressing not the advisor but Celeste herself. A flicker of recognition passed between the women, and what remained of Zayne's human side felt a mixed flush of professional pride and personal shame at how far his reputation had reached. "He comes bearing news you will surely wish to hear. Tell her."

Zayne felt a pressure rise up in his throat, and he tightened his jaw. He just wanted to stop revisiting it. Wasn't it bad enough he still saw her when he closed his eyes? Why did he have to be the one to drudge those memories up and open the wounds to the air?

Queen Celeste leaned forward in her oversized throne. Dardan glared over the rim of her spectacles. Finally, whatever Fae control Dardan held over him slithered its shadowy tendrils into his muscles and between his bones, thus he had no control. He barely even felt his mouth move as he said, "Empress Yushiro Shahira is dead."

"Ooh, that *is* exciting," crooned Rosalin. She whispered something to Celeste. When the queen nodded, her half-sister turned back to Zayne. "And how did our lovely correspondent meet her end?"

It was a relief beyond measure when Zayne felt no compulsion to reply. He stood in iron-clad silence. Let them arrest or execute him for impertinence. He would not dance where he could control his own steps.

His relief and pride were cut short when Dardan said, "Tell her," under her breath.

Still, Zayne fought. His jaw opened of its own accord, and he slammed it down on his tongue hard enough to draw blood. Still, his lips moved and through his bloodied teeth he answered. "She died with a sword through her heart."

Celeste burst into a childishly shrill fit of laughter, complete with her head thrown back and her ruby-slippered feet stomping the dais while she clutched the arms of her throne for balance.

Great, Zayne thought, *more monsters have entered my life.*

When Celeste's grating laughter slowed and she took a breath, Zayne scratched at his ear with his small finger to quell the ringing from her explosive applause. To either side, her elder sisters had much more subdued reactions: Rosalin shook with silent laughter and covered her mouth with her hands in a token effort to hide her smile; Ysulde, by contrast, turned away in her seat from her sisters' revelry and hugged herself as if suddenly feeling the room's chill.

"Ah," Celeste said at last. "Just what the bitch deserved."

Zayne's bile rose in his chest, and he sneered. He hadn't considered stepping forward, but found he had when the guard captain and one of the other guards placed their swords against his throat and chest respectively to force him to halt. He spat blood on the floor between them. "The Empress died bravely in the face of an enemy," he said, and only when he phrased the words did he realize that his indignation was compounded and mirrored by Lucandri's influence. Still irate, he added in his own words, "Which is a damn sight better than we can say about your mother. How does the song go?" He whistled a trilling tune from a song outlawed in Castilyn. The accompanying lyric to the tune was, "through the open window, she flew towards the pave."

The guard captain shifted her sword, so it nicked the skin of Zayne's throat even before the shock and outrage fully manifested on the royal sisters' faces. The cut burned, and not just from broken skin. Celeste's face went as red as anything else in the room while her sisters blanched in tandem as if Zayne had tossed a lit grenade at their feet.

"You impertinent *bastard!*" Celeste shrieked.

"Mind your choice of words, highness," Zayne said, "your sisters might take offense."

"How dare you —"

"Enough!" Dardan's voice cut through whatever Celeste was going to say next. Silence prevailed. "Now, the Daughters have fulfilled our end of the contract, your grace." Her voice was like ice. No, it was colder, darker. Her voice was like that place in the Dreamscape where Zayne had encountered the Host. "I trust you will come through with yours?"

Celeste was breathing hard with fury.

"Of course," said the more composed Ysulde. "The coin will be brought to the *Martyr's Demise* within the hour, with the promised bonus for those lovely riots and uprisings your people provoked. As to the other matter..." She stood and stepped down from the dais with a purposeful stride that reminded Zayne of Empress Yushiro. She crossed the floor only to stop several feet shy of the line of guards. "Approach, Captain Balthine."

The sword was removed from Balthine's neck, and he noticed, only for a fleeting moment, the edge had glowed a faint red from the heat. Or perhaps it was the room playing with his eyes. He doubted that, though. He moved to meet the royal bastard. She reached into the thigh-exposing slit of her dress and withdrew a bundle wrapped in thick parchment.

She glowered and handed the parcel to Zayne. Then grabbed him viciously by the lapel and pulled him in close to whisper. "The Iron Veils cannot see this in your possession." Louder, she said, "As agreed, the rights to forty miles of the Dawn Arbor. Though I can't imagine what someone like *you* would use it for."

Zayne unwrapped the parchment — which actually *was* a title deed for a set amount of the grove where the dawnwood trees grew — revealing a black horn intricately carved into the shape of a dragon, with its tail spiraling around to its point and its mighty jaws flanking the sound-producing end. Even though both of their bodies hid the horn from any onlookers, Ysulde was tense until he slid it into his coat. He kept the deed out to read it.

He could just sign his name and retire. That grove was surely more profitable than a year of risking his blood and skin. All he had to do was kill Dardan to escape the binds that stripped him of his free will. *Easy,* he thought sardonically.

"As agreed," Zayne replied. He wasn't sure how he would slip the Iron Veils; he could *feel* the mysticism rolling off the horn in a tangible pressure, almost like heat or a resonant sound. Though, he supposed that if Ysulde had hidden it away between her legs — and he tried not to think about *that* mystery too closely, lest his thoughts turn grim and turn his stomach — maybe no one else felt it.

Of course, he hadn't agreed to anything. Dardan hadn't informed him about any of the negotiations of the job — she had simply given him orders and bound him to them. He certainly knew nothing about the horn, either, though it was clearly a Fae relic. Whatever Dardan wanted, no good could come of it.

Ysulde inclined her head in a gesture halfway between a bow and a nod. As she retreated to her seat on the dais, Celeste cleared her throat.

Despite this, it was Rosalin who said, "With matters of payment concluded, we have another subject to discuss. One that involves Captain Balthine."

Zayne cocked his head. "Pardon?"

"A year ago," Ysulde clarified, "our little brother was sent into your company. Since then, news spread that you and your crew had been killed by Elyia Asier. Yet here you stand before us. Where, then, is our brother?"

Zayne furrowed his brow. "Your brother? I never —" but his mouth locked up on the words in the same way it had betrayed him by spilling out truth when he wished to stay silent. He remembered the pale, blond, fat boy who had replaced Karn. "Kales? Kales was your brother?"

"*Was?*" Ysulde asked pointedly.

"Stories of my death may have been slightly exaggerated," said Zayne, "but what became of my crew and my ship was not. The *Scorpion* was set ablaze and dropped into Lake Justiciar and everyone who set out with me was killed."

Silence followed the proclamation. He wondered if the pause came from disappointment, or in commiseration for the dead.

"How, then," asked Celeste, and her voice was like icicles scraping through the quiet, "did you survive?"

"He survived the same way he killed Yushiro and raced here before any other messenger," snapped Dardan. That seemed to cut the conversation to the quick.

Celeste's face was a mask of tranquil fury. Her sisters shared dubious looks. Zayne could see the Queen's nails dig into the arms of her seat. "Leave us," she said finally.

Dardan's bow was more exaggerated than before. "Your Grace. Know that if you want our service in your upcoming war, you need only reach out."

Zayne didn't bow before he turned on his heels to leave. As they left the throne room, Zayne immediately went to the box containing his weapons, and shoved the guard aside when she offered to help him. He needed something to be in his control. He slid his sword into its place on his belt, alongside two of his pistols, but when he grabbed a third, he remembered the horn occupying the holster in his coat. With a growl, he picked up the box and took it with him.

"Hey, that's not —" the guard began, but Dardan silenced her and took her shroud.

"Still wearing it, eh?" Brother Harrow asked, jogging to keep up.

"Of course," said Dardan.

"It's been thirty years, Jav," he said, and there was a quiet note of kindness in his tone. "Seymour—"

"I don't mourn for my brother," Dardan said fiercely. As she drew her hood up, she was once more the faceless shroud that haunted Zayne's thoughts. "I mourn for the world now that he's gone."

CHAPTER THIRTY-THREE

Accompanied by Miria and Captain Zhu of the *Roc Spear*, Cassidy met with the captain of the Red Moons Mercenary Company at the public docks an hour before setting off from Isaro. Captain Najm was a woman in her middle years, dressed in a black kaftan emblazoned with the eponymous red crescents arrayed in a circle with their points outward on her chest. Two scars crossed between her eyes and settled along either side of her nose, giving her a serious look. She stood half a head taller than Cassidy, which left her towering over Zhu.

"His highness says you're in charge," Najm said to Miria in a thick but intelligible accent. "The whole company, all expenses paid. What's the job?"

"How many ships are in the company?" Zhu asked in a scratchy voice.

"A hundred and fifty," Najm said in a proud tone.

"How many of them have Orichalcum weapons?" asked Miria.

Najm looked thoughtful. "Fourteen," she said slowly. "But the *Evil Eye* and the *Phallus* both have a full armament of the stuff."

Cassidy cocked an eyebrow. "You have a ship called the *Phallus?*"

Najm sighed, as though Cassidy had asked about a particularly troublesome child. "When one of our number buys their own ship and captaincy — or if they're brought into the fold with one — legally they have the right to put the name in the ship registry themselves. Most try to come up with impressive, inspiring, or terrifying names." She paused. "Some, on the other hand, either have no imagination or a child's sense of humor. And as a farer of the skies yourself, I am sure you know how expensive and difficult it is to get those registries changed. All that paperwork!

"But you cannot imagine the trouble it causes when the only ship you can send to parley is named *Kiss My Ass.*"

Zhu let out a low growl at the mercenary.

Najm had a perplexed look on her face for a moment. Then she turned to Miria. "Pardon, Princess." At another irate sound from the older man, she amended, "Highness."

Cassidy hadn't had a chance to get to know Zhu, but as soon as Miria's identity had been revealed — Prince Hassan had not wanted any confusion about his mercenaries' charge, and mercenaries apparently loved gossip — she had found him to be insufferable. For a start, he followed Miria around like a clingy pet and corrected the posture of everyone she encountered. He also seemed to resent Cassidy for deigning to give Miria orders or speak to her informally.

"Don't worry about the language, and *Miria* is fine," said Miria. She turned to Zhu. "And you're a soldier, not a lady-in-waiting. I don't need you worrying about courtly etiquette. My presence here is supposed to be a secret, Captain. And if you keep trying to dust the streets before I walk them, *someone* is bound to notice."

Zhu ran a hand over his bald pate and hung his head, chagrined.

"Fourteen isn't enough," Miria said. "I want every ship outfitted with as many dragon bone guns as you can find. I don't care if you have to melt down all the jewelry in all the principalities."

"Aye, your ladyship," said Najm. "Once this is done, what would you have us use them for?"

"You will fly east to Andaerhal, where you will assist in the reconstruction effort until we return with further orders."

Najm blinked. "Excuse me? You want us to stockpile weapons… to aid in… ah, what's the phrase in your language? An urban debauchery project?"

Cassidy snorted back a laugh.

"Do you make a habit of questioning your employers?" asked Miria.

"Only to be certain that orders aren't being mistranslated," Najm said cautiously. "Stockpiling weapons, then providing foreign aid seems, er… incongruent?"

"Those are your orders," said Miria. "We have yet more allies to rally. Only then shall we begin the hunt."

After talking over a few remaining logistical concerns with Cassidy's assistance, Miria dismissed the other captains. Zhu left dutifully, but Najm stayed behind.

"Is there a problem, Captain?" Miria asked.

"Not a problem, exactly, but Prince Hassan feels your ship isn't fully manned for a mission of this... bigness." Najm seemed to realize that was the wrong word, but she pushed on through. "He has instructed me to provide two sailors to augment your crew." She turned and whistled, and a woman and a young man in matching leather jerkins jogged over.

The man wore his beard in braids lined with wooden beads that clacked together as he ran. He pounded a fist to his chest in salute as soon as he reached the party. "Haytham Ramajin, at your service," he said in accented yet clear Asarian. "It's a pleasure to meet you! I read about your battle with the Daughters of Daen! Those fanatics give mercs a bad name. Is it true you sank the *Scorpion*? That ship has a reputation five miles wide and twice as long! I met the first Captain Balthine years ago, but I never met the second."

"We did," Cassidy said, pausing between the words to make sure she caught everything. She hadn't expected so much exuberant energy. "The *first* captain Balthine?" she added, thinking back to the conversation earlier in the week about the imposter who had killed all those people.

"Salaa Balthine," Haytham said. "I think she was the second's mother, or older sister, or something. She was a real artist with a knife. Before dueling was outlawed in Castilyn, she made a sport of it. After, too. I read in the paper that the ship was here in Isaro, but I also read that you sank it a year ago, so I wanted to be sure."

At Haytham's side, his partner cut in less enthusiastically. "Hanaa Ramajin. Forgive my brother's overbearing nature; I think he was dropped on his head."

Haytham just smiled. "If not for my 'overbearing' nature, you would be friendless and alone, so let's not criticize."

"Captain Najm says we're with you, highness," Hanaa said to Miria, ignoring her brother's insult entirely. "Before you worry about us checking to run our orders by the fleet, don't worry; we have one job; for all intents and purposes, we are your crew until the contract with the fleet is over. If you'll have us," she added as an after-thought.

"That's all well and good," Miria said politely, "but Captain Durant is in charge of our ship. If you answer to anyone, it's her."

Cassidy pursed her lips in thought. She didn't like the idea of having strangers foisted upon her, but she couldn't deny the prudence. The *Dreamscape Voyager* could get away with being lightly manned in the past, but Cassidy had just been discussing with Lierre the other day that they needed extra hands for the new cannon. Besides, how could they really refuse under the circumstances?

"We'll take you on a probationary run," she said finally. "If I don't feel like you're worth the trouble you're off, but you do your share and work well with the crew, you'll be welcome aboard."

"We're docked in bay six on the north end," Miria told them. "Get your things, we leave within the hour." The duo saluted and jogged back to the Moon's ships.

When they were finally alone, Cassidy asked Miria, "So we're still looking for Jathun, then?"

"We burned a ship and paid a great price for him besides," Miria said flatly. "And you've seen the Leviathan, too. Maybe this fleet *is* enough to kill it. But I don't want to find out the hard way that it's not."

Cassidy nodded and followed the princess back to the palanquin to the docks. Once inside, the princess refused to meet her eye. Instead, Miria kept opening the thick silken enclosure to look out at their progress. Cassidy helped herself to a handful of pistachios and dates, but Miria's agitation was contagious.

"So, are we going to talk about it?"

"I was backed into a corner, Cassidy," she snapped, throwing the curtain back and shrouding them in shade. "Did you see how he leaped at the opportunity to throw in a marriage contract into the bargain?"

Cassidy didn't have an answer for that. "How were the terms?" she asked instead.

"I worked them down to fair," Miria said, biting every word out. "Among other things, if he loses his seat between now and then, it's called off with all other promises staying firm. But that's not the point!"

Cassidy reached over and set a hand on Miria's knee. She frowned back at her. Then she let out a long sigh.

"It's not what I wanted," Miria said. "But at least we got the guns."

"So, what did you want?"

"Honestly? I don't know." She let out a breathless laugh that frayed at the edges. "My mother never married. Maybe that's what I wanted for myself. Maybe I wanted a storybook tale of love and romance with a poet, or a musician. Or maybe I just wanted for the life or death choices to wait until I was the Empress."

Miria stared absently at the curtains after that, not even pretending to be looking for something.

Cassidy crawled to the other side of the palanquin. "So," she asked, nudging Miria in the ribs, "when were you planning on telling me about your musician?"

"What?" Miria said, a blush rising to her face.

"Was he a singer? Or did you get swept up watching his fingers move?"

"It wasn't a *specific* example," Miria mumbled. "And she played the zither."

"Oh, *she*," Cassidy teased. "Wait a minute, was this the zither player in Bajin's Landing? We should go back and start your whirlwind romance!"

Miria slapped Cassidy's shoulder half-heartedly. "That was just an example. Maybe I wanted a boy to sweep me off my feet," she said, holding back a smile.

"It's not too late," said Cassidy. "It's not like this marriage is a product of love."

Miria plucked a date and chewed it slowly. "Come to think of it, the contract didn't say anything about fidelity."

They shared a laugh.

"I guess we can worry about the future when it comes," Miria said as she finally relaxed.

"Aye," said Cassidy, though her own tension was mounting. "We'll worry about tomorrow when it comes." *If it comes.*

CHAPTER THIRTY-FOUR

As soon as he was alone in his cabin aboard the *Scorpion*, Zayne hurled himself against the wash basin and inadvertently slammed his face against it. "Gods damn that wretched woman," he growled. With panic-driven fingers, Zayne opened the faucet and muttered to himself. "My coat is white," he lied, forcing each word out slowly so he could hear them. "My hair is red. The sky is yellow. There are five moons and they're fucking made of rice! My coat is white," and he kept on, listing every blatant falsehood he could think of, from his surroundings, to mathematics, to his culinary preferences, and repeating them when he couldn't immediately fill the silence with something new. "I have tattoos. My coat is white. I'm allergic to cats."

He was a man, not a Fae, and as such, he had a natural right to his lies, to break promises, and to deny orders. How dare Dardan force him to speak truths he would rather deny? What right had she to puppet him like a marionette, to force his hand to take actions as though he had no free will? Whatever power she had over him was a thing of the Dreamscape, and of Lucandri. He needed to break free. He was not a Fae.

He wrapped his trembling fingers along the edge of the overflowing basin and gripped it tightly. "I've been married three times. I am an apple trader. I killed my father." The litany spewed forth until he lowered his face into the basin.

He couldn't shoot himself. He couldn't stab himself. He couldn't throw himself off the harbor. Lucandri's influence stopped him. But he was already in the water now. If he could keep himself beneath the surface until he lost consciousness, maybe that would be enough.

He never got the chance to find out.

A concussive boom sounded a mere moment before something hit the hull of the *Scorpion* and knocked Zayne out of the water and onto the wet floor. He pulled himself up and reflexively closed the faucet before rushing outside to see what had happened.

Shen and Aresh scrabbled out from below deck at the same time Zayne stepped outside into the bracing chill. Nannette and Xun stared wide-eyed off the starboard bow, towards the harbor. Zayne followed their collective gazes.

The *Martyr's Demise* was aflame, her captain's cabin roiling in blazing red fire that spiraled out into the wind. Black smoke churned from the rapidly licking flames like all the billows of a factory district. The *Martyr's* black-clad crew had already formed a bucket chain and were trying to douse the inferno, but still it raged.

The heat was almost enough to dry Zayne off.

Time became distorted in Zayne's mind as he watched the flames dance against the cool winter afternoon. In that fire, he felt his hopes stirring like a phoenix chick hatching in the blaze of its mother's demise. Had Dardan been in that explosion?

Beside him, Xun fell to her knees and sobbed. Zayne pulled his gaze reluctantly from the *Martyr's Demise* and all the crew's eyes were on Xun.

"What's wrong," Zayne asked, though he wished someone else had. He was out of practice dealing with this. "This is what we —" then he realized; Tagren was missing. Not only was he not on the deck, Zayne could not feel him on the ship at all.

Tagren had done it. While everyone else had impotently flailed at Dardan to kill her face-to-face, Tagren had sabotaged the *Martyr* and set her to blow when Dardan returned.

"He might have gotten out," Zayne offered, but Xun shook her head.

"H-h… he did-didn-didn't leave her —" She inhaled deeply and let out another body-wracking series of sobs. "He never left the cabin! I watched him sneak aboard with the powder and oil, but he never made it out. He waited until she got back. That's when…"

Zayne didn't press her when she trailed off. He looked back at the *Martyr's Demise*. He hadn't known the mute well, but he had seemed like a good man. He wondered what Dardan had done to earn such vengeance from him.

His reverie was broken by movement on the burning deck. The fires seemed to swell like water just before it was breached, and a figure was birthed from the flames. Smoke clung to the figure as the flames danced around it.

Fire seemed to slough off Dardan's shroud as though they were water and oil. Her crew moved deftly around her, never slowing in their efforts to douse the blaze as she climbed down the gangway to the harbor. It took Zayne several slow moments to realize that Dardan was walking to the *Scorpion*. She carried a bundle in her arms.

She didn't ask permission to come aboard. Aresh and Nanette drew pistols as Dardan climbed the gangway, while Shen drew his knife. Dardan stopped when she reached the deck but seemed to pay the weapons no mind.

"I found this on my ship," she said in a tone that sounded almost as dry as her throat. She dropped the bundle unceremoniously and it unraveled. A smoking, blackened husk flopped onto the deck with a thud.

It was Tagren.

Or, more precisely, it was *part* of Tagren. Everything below his second ribs had been blown off, as had his right arm just above the elbow, and his left side where his neck met his shoulder. Where his body hadn't been burned to a shriveled, black crisp, it was a raw, angry red. Only his face was unburned, a mask of unadulterated terror somewhere between screaming and sobbing.

Xun crawled over to Tagren's form, fell upon him, and convulsed from the tears tumbling down her face. The pain in her tremulous scream sent a sharp pang of empathic pain to Zayne's breast.

"Maybe this lesson will stay with you," Dardan said coolly. "Your lives are mine, not the other way around." She swept her gaze over the *Scorpion*'s crew. "These attempts at murder have been diverting, but it ends today.

"Balthine, you will take the Horn of Acselna to the husk of the old World Tree. Bury it. Then return to the site of the new one for your orders."

"And if I refuse?"

"How many times do I need to prove to you that you *cannot* defy me?" Dardan asked. "You will do this."

But she was wrong, and she knew it. He *could* defy her. He had when he had drawn his pistol and pulled the trigger. He just needed to keep rattling the cage, and he would eventually break free. But she was right about one thing; he could already feel the pull of her command. He would obey for now, but some day, he would take away her power, one way or another.

CHAPTER THIRTY-FIVE

The Ramajin siblings adjusted quickly to the *Dreamscape Voyager*. Apparently, during their previous assignment aboard the *Nagi Queen* they had each shared a cabin with fifteen other people, and as a consequence found Cassidy's ship rather quiet. Haytham in particular had an easy adjustment with only a single bunk mate, though Kek — who had had the room to himself for over a decade — was less than pleased.

Hanaa proved to be a more than competent cook. She made a spicy fish stew on their third night out of Isaro, and it was the best thing Cassidy had eaten in weeks. She was also an excellent swordswoman. In practice bouts, she completely trounced Cassidy and Kek and fought Miria to a standstill. Her brother, on the other hand, could barely out-fence Lierre, but he prided himself as a marksman.

"I prefer whatever I'm killing to be over there," he had said, gesturing vaguely to the horizon.

On the morning of the fifth day, Cassidy checked the duty roster to discover Haytham had drawn breakfast duty. She could tell it was off to a poor start when she smelled burnt meat before even leaving her cabin.

"I suppose it's too much to ask that I'm imagining that," she said dismally.

"If you are referring to that burning stench?" Hymn clarified. "That would be an empty hope, yes. I do not understand why you insist on taking turns with such a vital task when some people are so clearly better at it."

"It's about keeping the chore load fair," said Cassidy. "What are you worried about, anyway? You don't even need to eat. Now, are you staying here, or coming with me?"

Cassidy, Hymn, and the crew had all agreed that it was best Hymn remain a secret from the newcomers, so at various times, she either hid away under Cassidy's hat, or in her cabin doing whatever it was she did when Cassidy wasn't around. Cassidy chose to imagine the Fae performed elaborate dance routines.

"I will wait here for now," Hymn said with a hint of resignation in her tone. "If you have need of me, I will be here."

"Alright, then." Cassidy stepped out in the pre-dawn gloom, bracing herself for the chill. She didn't understand how it could be so hot during the day only to become so cold at night. Kek was huddled in on himself at the helm muttering a string of curses under his breath.

"Is there a problem?" Cassidy asked.

"Punched a hole in my boot back in Andaerhal. My toes are freezing. Haven't had any sleep in days because I can't — well, there's no privacy," Kek trailed off. Then, after a violent shiver, he added, "And I'm starving."

"Well, I think it won't be long. I could smell it from my cabin."

"I haven't been able to smell anything all night. I swear my nose is frozen."

"See anything out here?" Cassidy asked, glancing out at the desert. Of the moons, only Jiqun remained clear at this late hour, but she was luminous enough her light reflected against the sands below, and the world around them bloomed in a shimmering glow. Aft and to either side of them, the *Roc Spear* and the *Sunrise* kept apace, but otherwise the sky seemed empty. She wondered where the pirates were.

"Nothing special. A howling owl passed us by, but that's about it. Otherwise, all's quiet."

A chime of the breakfast bell drew their attention. Kek all but raced to the galley, while Cassidy swept her gaze over the desert one last time before following. Lierre climbed up to join them, informing Cassidy that Nieves and Miria had only just gotten to sleep from their own watches. Hanaa, meanwhile, said she wasn't hungry. Looking at the blackened husks of fish and poultry that sat on the plate before her, Cassidy suspected Hanaa's refusal had more to do with knowing her proficiency — or lack thereof — with a cook fire.

Haytham had a sheepish expression on his face and refused to meet anyone's eye. "I was never very good at cooking," he said.

Cassidy picked at the black strips of something that had probably been a vegetable at some point.

"Not everyone can be a culinary master," Lierre said cheerfully, taking a bite without hesitation. Her smile faded as she began chewing. She took her time with the experience, and each moment her face became more dour. When she finally swallowed, she immediately took a swig from her hip flask. After a long gasp, she said, "I've had worse."

Driven more by guilt than hunger, Cassidy forced herself to take a bite. It was impressively terrible. Everything — even what she thought must have been an onion — was so dry it sucked the moister straight from her mouth, and yet it still left a greasy trail down her throat when she swallowed. Both the fish and the bird tasted so strongly of charcoal she had to identify them by their shape. "Well," she managed, resisting the urge to gag, "everyone makes mistakes, and there's worse things to be bad at."

A smile cracked through Haytham's embarrassment, and Cassidy felt a brief rush of heat. He was very handsome.

By Cassidy's side, Kek was powering through the meal like he had no sense of taste whatsoever, all the while glaring at Haytham when he thought no one was looking. He popped the fish head in his mouth and crunched on it mechanically. When Haytham retrieved the dishes to wash them, Cassidy elbowed Kek in the ribs.

"Don't be rude, Kek," she whispered.

"Maybe *you* would like to share a bunk with him," he shot back. Then he paused. "Actually, you probably would."

"That wouldn't be very professional," Cassidy said, though she had thought about it. "I am — in a roundabout way — his employer."

"I think Miria's name is on the contract, not yours."

"Aye, but Miria works for me," said Cassidy.

"And you're working for her mother," Kek argued.

"Yes, but Miria is here independently of her mother. Why are you arguing about this?"

"Who's arguing?"

"Kek just wants his cabin to himself again," Lierre said, poking at her food like she was afraid of it.

"Kek, it's been less than half a week," said Cassidy. "I shared a bunk with Lierre and Nieves for ten years. You can deal until the Leviathan is dead."

"Fine," Kek whined.

The rest of the morning went on uneventfully. With the dawn came warmth that quickly mutated into mirage-inducing heat. Hanaa had taken over the helm during breakfast and stayed on until the *Roc Spear* flagged the small fleet to stop for a briefing and a shared lunch. Unlike Cassidy's crew, Captain Zhu's ship had a dedicated cooking staff — probably a necessity for such a large crew.

Cassidy ate with the other captains on the aftcastle of the *Roc Spear* while her crew mingled with the others, partaking in a dish of fried egg and fish on a bed of rice. Rice was an expensive treat — given the dangers of harvesting any crop at so low an altitude, and as a consequence most rice went into alcohol production rather than more culinary purposes — but apparently being an officer had its perks. Despite Captain Zhu being the host, it was Captain Kin who filled their small circle with conversation. She jovially regaled them with the story of how she lost her eye on a sphinx hunt with her mercenary sister, which included several interludes about her musical background, the complex personal relationships with the friends who had accompanied her, a rival gang of hunters with a political agenda, and her recurring dreams about a rivermaid that spoke only in rhyme, among other things. Cassidy found herself enraptured by her skill as a storyteller, though Zhu looked ready to snap his chopsticks in frustration at each diversion.

"When we found the nest empty," Kin said, "Mei swore loudly, and her voice echoed through the canyon. *Shit, shit, shit*," she imitated, dropping her voice a little each time. "That's when we heard the rumbling of —"

"Enough of the dramatics!" Zhu snapped, pointing his chopsticks at Kin so hard he flung egg in her face. It bounced and landed on her lap. She popped it into her mouth and grinned.

"I'm enjoying it," Cassidy protested.

"We don't have time for her life story," Zhu said. "Or have you forgotten about the mythical monster threatening to kill everyone in the Imperial Sea?"

Kin hung her head sheepishly.

"If you don't want to swap stories, what did you hail us together for?" Cassidy snapped. "We could have had our lunch without coming to a halt."

"*Stories*," Zhu scoffed. "I wanted any updates on our plans."

"Same as before," Cassidy said, "conscript Jathun, see what he knows about fighting Fae beasts, and who he can wrangle into joining us. Then we regroup in Andaerhal and start hunting." She left out her tentative hope of enlisting the pirates. It was a stupid plan, and she had no way to find them anyway.

"Sounds simple, put that way," Zhu said, though he made it sound derisive.

"The best plans are," said Cassidy. "The fewer moving parts the better."

"We'll see," Zhu said.

The rest of the meal was filled with more curt conversation, little more than reports about the voyage so far — discipline issues, expenses, strange sightings, and weather watching — and by the end of it, Cassidy was glad to return to her own ship. As they parted, Cassidy offered Kin a pat on the arm while to Zhu she merely offered a dismissive wave. The older man answered by flaring his nostrils and spitting overboard.

It was late afternoon when Marasi Prison came into view at the end of a wide, deep valley of sand as a blue shadow on the horizon, and it was over an hour before they came close enough for its shape to resolve. Rather than being built atop a plateau, the bastille was built into one. Its entrance was a blocky, iron gate protruding from the rocky face, with a single bridge dock reaching out like an outstretched hand. Threw her spyglass, Cassidy spotted enormous long-barreled cannons atop the mesa, and a small fleet of ships were anchored on platforms hidden beneath the overhanging around its width.

There was only room for one ship to make port, so Cassidy had Miria bring them in while Kek flagged the *Sunrise* and *Roc Spear* to stand by. As the ship settled at the end of the bridge and the gangway was set, Cassidy ducked into her cabin to grab the Empress' writ and Prince Hassan's release form. As soon as she shut the door, Hymn flew up from beneath the bed, fluttering erratically.

"Something wrong?" Cassidy asked, tucking the papers into her coat.

"There are wards all over the prison," Hymn said with a nervous tension. "I will not be able to follow you beyond the bridge."

Cassidy swore. Andaerhal had been a miserable experience and being separated from Hymn had only made things worse. *Don't overreact, Cass,* she told herself. *You're just going to show some papers and escort a man to your ship.* Except that man was a convicted murderer, and she would be pulling him out of a hive of criminals. She shook her head clear and said, "It won't be for long. I'll have Kek stay aboard in case you need company."

"His company would do little to improve matters," Hymn replied.

"Maybe not, but it's what you've got. I'll be back as soon as I can."

As Cassidy disembarked, Hanaa called, "Captain Durant!" as though there was any other captain aboard.

"Yes, Miss Ramajin?"

"Storm's coming," she said. "I recommend we put down the sand curtains."

Cassidy looked at the sky. There wasn't a cloud in sight, and only a lazy breeze swept the valley. But she figured Hanaa knew better than she did about the Rivien weather. What harm was there in indulging her? "Have them set, then."

Hanaa saluted, a gesture Cassidy returned half-heartedly.

Accompanied by Lierre and Miria, Cassidy crossed the bridge. It was a sturdy construction, and it felt more secure than it looked to walk along. Two women in sand-colored kaftans with matching turbans and veils stood guard outside the gate, and neither made a move to greet them, though they didn't try to threaten them either.

When she reached the gate, Cassidy produced the release order and said, "I'm Captain Cassandra Durant" — she hated giving her full legal name, but it was the name on the writ, and she knew government officials in all three nations could be obnoxious about their bureaucracy — "and I've come with orders from Prince Hassan of the Merchant Council. I need to see the warden."

"Captain Durant," one of the guards acknowledged in halting Asarian, "the Warden has been expecting you. You will be taken to her office. Your escorts can wait for you in the processing wing."

Cassidy looked to Lierre and Miria, the former of whom merely shrugged while Miria blinked in open surprise that mirrored Cassidy's own. "We were expected?" she repeated, sure she had heard properly, but was baffled by the implication. *Who could have sent word ahead?*

Before Cassidy could form the questions, the guards slammed a massive knocker on the gate, eliciting thunderous booms, and a moment later, the latticework of iron rose into the maw of the mesa.

The entryway of the prison was little more than a cave inside which another quartet of guards stood. There was a forked path behind them, and each tunnel led to a lift.

"Captain Durant," greeted a man with a long, braided beard. His Asarian was even more stilted than the guard outside. "The warden is waiting for you."

Cassidy swallowed a lump in her throat and followed the man down the righthand passage. As they stepped onto the lift, her escort closed the cage-like door and pulled a lever. The box lurched as it rose.

"How did the warden know I was coming?" Cassidy asked.

"I know nothing of it," said the man. Cassidy pursed her lips but said nothing.

The top floor seemed much less natural than the entrance, carved with flat floors and lined with brick walls. A red door stood straight ahead with a placard written in the flowing Rivien script that Cassidy couldn't read. Her escort merely nodded for her to go ahead, and she opened the door.

Inside was a window-lit room — Cassidy hadn't seen any windows from the northern approach, and given the sheer amount of stone, she wouldn't be surprised if it were the only window in the entire facility — with an enormous black walnut desk piled with papers as its centerpiece. Behind the desk sat a woman in a purple kaftan with a deep, blue, silk brocade turban and translucent veil. The warden smiled and gestured to a chair on the other side of the desk.

"Cassandra," she said warmly, "please have a seat. It is good to see you are hale and whole."

Cassidy blinked, and narrowed her eyes, trying to place the woman. "Sister Venitha?" she asked, unable to hide the incredulity from her tone.

"I told you before, I am a Sister no longer," she said. Her smile never wavered. "Please, sit."

Cassidy obeyed that time, still staring at the older woman. "Right, you left to sell vegetables, then a tea house. What happened to that, anyway?"

Venitha sighed as though Cassidy had asked after a troublesome child. "Imperial taxes make running a business like that problematic, and it wasn't in the best location. You would be

375

surprised at the fights started over tea." She paused for a beat. "Or perhaps you wouldn't."

"And how do you go from selling tea in the Empire to being put in charge of a prison on the far side of the world?"

"'Far side of the world' is relative, Cassandra," said Venitha. "This is my homeland, after all, and Revehaven, Melfine, Andaerhal and Bajin's Landing are all faraway lands here. And no one 'put' me in charge. Leadership is a mantle you take, and I took it because I was needed. There is much good I can do here."

"I... see," Cassidy said, though she really didn't see anything. "How did you know I was coming?"

"Come now," the warden scoffed. "You and I have had the same light guide our voyages. I am simply better at heeding it."

Cassidy raised a brow. The erstwhile fortune teller sighed again, this time in disappointment. "It matters not. The important thing is that you are here to release Jathun. And it's about time, too. He has spent far too long wallowing in grief and guilt."

Cassidy resisted the urge to ask how Venitha knew that, too, and resigned herself to the notion that the strange woman just *knew* things. "That's it? You're just going to let me take him?"

"You should probably still give me the release order, for formality's sake," she said, "but yes. He's all yours if you can convince him not to throw his life away." She leaned back in her chair only to immediately bounce forward again. "Oh, I almost forgot!"

Venitha produced a heavy, wood-bound tome from beneath her desk and dropped it on the table with a heavy thud. Though Cassidy wasn't an expert on such things, she could tell at a glance that it was ancient. It wasn't just the crisp, yellowed pages or the frayed edges — though those certainly made the case well enough — but rather a *feeling* that came over her when she looked at it. The cover was decorated with a pyrographed image of a tree, and there was no title on either the front or the spine.

"I found this during my time with the Order of the Iron Veil," she explained. "I don't have much use for it, but I thought you might find it interesting."

Cassidy blinked at the book. The Order of the Iron Veils existed for two purposes; to stamp out the corruption of the gods and Fae from humanity, and to sequester, censor, and quarantine dangerous knowledge to prevent said corruption from blossoming.

Cassidy could only imagine what Venitha might have *found*, or the consequences should she be found *with* it.

In spite of herself, Cassidy opened the book. It seemed to be equal part sketches and colored illustrations — stylized renditions of trees and anatomical images of strange monsters, portraits of men and women, diagrams of musical instruments, and a myriad of other things — and partially faded text written in a language she had never seen, with blocky characters consisting of bold shapes that never seemed to intersect. There was a uniformity to the text that suggested it had been set with a printing press, but there wasn't much else Cassidy could determine from it. She thought maybe the pictures had been drawn first, because the text was always set around them, but that was just conjecture.

She flipped through the pages until she reached a page that made her heart skip a beat.

In fully realized color, two lovingly rendered women seemed to practically dance off the page. The one on the right had dark hair and wore an elaborate dress made of every shade of red that could be portrayed by an artist's toolset, with sleeves that draped from her arms like harpy wings. Her lips and nails were gradient swirls of the same color, as were her stiletto heeled shoes. Most strikingly were her eyes; the irises and pupils were stark rendered in white while her sclera were deep ruby. Her face was familiar though Cassidy couldn't place it.

Accompanying the Fae in red was an image Cassidy knew with certainty. Hymn's true form — complete with the sapphire dress with the detached sleeves she recognized — stood beside the stranger. Both women faced away from her counterpart, but they were connected by their small fingers hooked together in an intimate gesture.

Beneath the illustrated pair were two sigils and a dense block of text of which Cassidy couldn't make heads or tails. The sign on the left consisted of three crescent moons with their points turned out from one another and a symmetrical teardrop in the middle. The other mark matched the one burned onto Cassidy's wrist; three nesting crescents with the smallest turned inward and a rose in the empty center.

"What is this?" Cassidy asked breathlessly.

"A gift," said Venitha. "A piece of history. A compilation of the greatest mystical forces the world knew before the ascension."

Cassidy made to turn the page, but her eyes lingered on the image of her friend. She had known the Fae claimed to be old, had referred to events that preceded the ascension, but to see it was another matter. *Who's* your *friend, Hymn? And where is she now?*

CHAPTER THIRTY-SIX

Cassidy never considered herself claustrophobic, but in the depths of the prison tunnels — with the solidity of the stone beneath her feet, the full weight of the mesa above her head, and no sign of wind or sky to look at — she was starting to feel it all the same. By her side, Lierre looked equally uncomfortable, but Miria took it in stride. Cassidy wished she could be as steadfast.

With Venitha's book tucked under her arm, she tried her best to project confidence of purpose as she walked down the corridor illuminated with a harsh, alchemically produced liquid light that cast the cells in pitch darkness. Every so often she saw the silhouette of a prisoner sitting near the bars of their cell, and once a grimy hand reached out to snatch vainly at Miria, but otherwise it seemed to be a procession in emptiness.

Jathun's cell was the last on the block. Apparently, being sentenced to life without any chance at parole, Venitha's predecessor had decided to throw him in the back so he — the former warden, not Jathun — wouldn't have to walk as far to release other prisoners, and if they forgot to feed him once or twice a week, no great loss.

The guard escorting them rapt her knuckles on the bars of his cell and called in. "It is your lucky day, Jathun," she said in thickly accented Asarian. "Instead of dying here, you get to die in Asaria. Fun, yes?"

Silence answered the mockery.

"I know you're awake," she chided. "Come to the door. Nice and slow, but quick."

Silence again, but shorter as a scuffing sound carried from the back of the cell. The man who stepped out of the inky shadows into the uncaring light was not a figure out of legend. His hair was a tangled and shaggy mess, brown but blackened by grime. The stench of imprisonment wafted off him in nauseating waves. His ragged beard did nothing to hide the hollowness of his cheeks, and his skin clung to an emaciated frame. The amber eyes sunken in the dark pits of his pallid face was the worst of it.

There was a brokenness in those eyes that transcended physical expression, and it broke Cassidy's heart to look upon him.

379

"Jathun of Val Desolee," Miria said formally, "we have come to enlist your services."

Jathun tilted his head down to face Miria. Recognition flitted across his face for a moment, it quickly faded into placid misery. "And why should I offer my services to anyone?" His voice was a rasping husk, but deep. Cassidy suspected it had been resonant, once. "I'm a dead man walking. *Princess*," he added scornfully.

"I see your years of confinement haven't dulled your perception," she replied. "And you don't have much choice in the matter. You have been released on condition of conscription."

"Not interested."

"You haven't even heard what we're conscripting you for," Lierre protested.

"Don't care," he said, followed by something in Castilyn that made her reel back, affronted and outraged in equal measure. "Tell Elyia I am done playing her games. I let her string me along to war once, that's enough."

Cassidy's breath caught. "Why do you think we're here on Elyia's behalf?"

He barked a ragged laugh. "After what she did? I can smell the *Jade Phoenix* all over you like a rot in your clothes." Cassidy and Miria exchanged confused looks while Lierre lifted her sleeve to her nose and gave it a sniff.

"I guess you didn't get the news," said Cassidy, "but Elyia died. About a year back."

Jathun slumped against the bars, hung his head, and let out a bitter laugh. "I thought she'd outlive all of us. So, if it's not one of her hairbrained schemes, what do you want from me? My days of being useful are done."

"You have experience fighting Fae creatures," said Cassidy. She glanced at the guard, who didn't seem to be listening. She wondered how well she spoke and understood Asarian. She decided to gamble. "And I suspect the *Temptation* won't obey anyone else," she said in a rush, "just like the *Dreamscape Voyager* — the *Jade Phoenix* — only obeyed Asier, and now me. I think we can use a ship that thinks for itself."

Lierre furrowed her brow as if her understanding of the Imperial language had suddenly evaporated. Miria glared at her like she had sold state secrets. Cassidy half expected Jathun to share in Lierre's confusion.

Instead, he croaked, "Suspect? So, she never told you?" His eyes brightened and he opened his mouth to speak, but the light faded only a moment later and he backed away from the bars, though he kept his hands on them. "Doesn't matter. I belong here. I murdered a man. Not an innocent one, mind, but it was murder all the same."

The guard scoffed and put the key in the lock and yanked the door open. "It does not matter what you deserve," she said impatiently. "You are released. You cannot stay here."

"It's settled," said Cassidy. "The Warden already sent your possessions to our ship, so let's go."

Jathun heaved a resigned sigh and stepped out into the hall. There was a slight hobble to his step and Cassidy saw his left foot was wrapped in a dirty bandage.

No one spoke on the walk to the lift. Once inside, Jathun asked. "Can I scrub myself clean when we reach the *Phoenix*?"

"I told you, she's called the *Dreamscape Voyager* now," said Cassidy. "And I was actually going to order you to do so before anything else." Jathun chortled, but Cassidy wasn't sure which point he found funny. His stench was even worse in the confines of the lift, like being trapped in a box of human refuse.

Outside, the sky had turned to a burnt orange. The wind whipped hard enough to pull Cassidy's hat right off her head, and she barely caught it in her fingers. She worried Jathun might get blown away just as easily. Even at their elevation, sand blew in their way, hitting the bridge with loud clacks and snicks, pelting at Cassidy's face. She slipped her goggles on, but that did little to help.

The sand curtain around the *Dreamscape Voyager* was a tightly woven mesh that hung from the balloon like a skirt that covered the open decks. Cassidy could see the silhouettes of her crew but little else through it. She tried to push the flaps open only to find they had already been tied.

"Kek?" she called. "Let us aboard." Sand followed them in, coating the deck with a coarse lining that crackled beneath boots with irritating regularity. Kek fought against flapping canvas getting it re-secured. "Someone fetch water and soap. A lot of soap. Nothing gets done before our guest stops smelling like five years of filth. And burn that disgusting burlap sack he's wearing."

Jathun was stripped bare, and Haytham and Kek tossed three buckets of soapy water at him before leaving him to scrub himself down. Cassidy kept her back to Jathun to leave him his modesty, but she remained on the deck as bubbly runoff mixed with sand and formed muddy streams across her ship.

"What did you mean," Cassidy asked, "when you talked about what Elyia did? I think you implied she did something to the ship?"

Jathun scrubbed in silence, the sound of his lather barely audible over the persistent howl of the wind and the pattering scrapes of sand against wood and metal and leather and cloth. When Cassidy opened her mouth to press him, he said, "She did it to all our ships, not just the *Phoenix*. See, when she entered the Dreamscape, there was a Fae named Lucandri. He killed her crew. 'Part of a sick game', she said. So, she killed him."

"How?" Cassidy had killed a Fae in Andaerhal, but it had been inhabiting a human body. She wasn't sure how she could go about killing one in their own domain.

"Violently," Jathun said. After a long pause, he said, "She had these big, iron gauntlets — they were an impulse purchase, I think — and she used them to *rip. Him. Apart.*

"After that, she divvied up his pieces among us. His left hand went to the *Neverworld*, his right to the *Night's Wish*, one eye to the *Temptation*, one to the *Clockwork Hydra*. Elyia gave his heart to the *Phoenix*.

"There was a ritual, see," he continued. "The forbidden sort, you know. The kind of forbidden that would see us all executed without trial. Those pieces…" He trailed off, and Cassidy turned to see him running soap through his tangled locks, staring at the balloon as though it were a window into the past. "Our ships *woke up*. But you know about that, I guess."

Cassidy swallowed a lump in her throat. The Empress had told her about the *Dreamscape Voyager* — about the *Jade Phoenix* — being alive, but this was so much bigger than that. There was a Fae heart in her ship? The thought gave her vertigo.

"Elyia used Lucandri's skull, too. It was how we broke the blockade of Tal Joyau. Her legend chalks that up to wind stolen from the gods, but it was Lucandri. Don't know what happened to it, after that."

"This ritual," Cassidy asked. "You all agreed to it?"

Jathun dropped his hands to his side with a soap-muffled slap and sighed. "You have to understand, the war was a pretty lawless era. Queen Isabel used forbidden arts to thwart us at every turn. The Dread Hounds actively pursued Elyia, and the rest of us by extension. Profiteers were making life difficult for the common man. By the time she killed Lucandri, we'd already done our share of desperate acts."

Cassidy looked out at the churning storm, thinking of what lay beyond it. "I know what that's like."

"About that. What did you bust me out for, *exactly*?"

Cassidy explained, in broad strokes, what had happened at the Dragon's Nest. Because of Jathun's own admissions, she shared more about what she knew than she had in the past — including Miria's blood apparently serving as the catalyst for the Leviathan's appearance — but she still obfuscated the source of their information, deciding it wasn't prudent to tell Jathun about Hymn. She told him about the missing ships, about being conscripted by the empress. She got sidetracked and told him about the battle of Andaerhal. Then she explained the negotiations that led to Jathun's release. He didn't interrupt her or ask questions, and the only evidence Cassidy had that he was listening at all was the occasional grunt.

"And here we are," she concluded.

"I'm not surprised the prince was so willing to let bygones be for such a prize," said Jathun. "For all his posturing, all that man cares about is status."

"Why'd you kill his brother, anyway?"

"You mean besides a deep seeded belief that no one should be rich enough to have *two* seats on that damn council?" Jathun laughed bitterly.

"If you would kill over that," Cassidy mused, "you wouldn't have said it was so terrible a thing you deserved to be locked up."

Jathun snorted. "You were listening? You aren't much like Elyia at all."

Cassidy felt a flare of anger, but she managed to tamp it down to mere annoyance. "She was a great listener."

"Maybe she mellowed out after the war," he offered, and he emptied another bucket over himself. "Back in those days, she assumed the world would move whichever way she pointed."

That left Cassidy cold.

"I guess she would." After a pensive moment listening to the wind, she added, "You didn't answer the question."

"There are some things a man shouldn't discuss without trousers. Speaking of which, where are my belongings?"

Cassidy found the trunk that hadn't been on the deck before she disembarked and opened it. Inside were a full set of men's clothes, a pitiful coin purse, a knife and assorted oddments. She slid the chest over, and her eye twitched at the path it carved through the mud.

"You're cleaning my deck before supper," she said.

"I never agreed to follow your orders," said Jathun. "And you'll recall I never asked to be let out of prison."

Cassidy stamped her foot. "After everything I told you, you're still going to play aloof and pitiful?"

"Play? I told you already, I'm no use. I'm only here because you took away the roof over my head. Thanks for the bath, though."

"But with the *Temptation* —"

"She's a fine ship," he agreed, stepping into his trousers, "but I've been gone five years. I don't know where my old crew is. I don't have the contacts to make a new one. Whatever desperate scheme you Imperials cooked up didn't seem to factor in reality."

"We did hope you would still have contacts," Cassidy conceded. "But there's enough crew between the *Roc Spear* and the *Sunrise* to get the *Temptation* battle ready if need be. Where is she, anyway? Was she impounded when you got arrested or did you entrust her with someone?"

Jathun sighed. "Not exactly."

Cassidy's shoulders slumped. "Don't tell me we'll have to steal her from someone. Do you at least know where she is?"

"Oh, don't worry, no one has her," said Jathun, "and I know exactly where she is. But you aren't going to like it."

CHAPTER THIRTY-SEVEN

Jathun had been right; Cassidy didn't like it.

He had known when he had set out to kill Prince Hassan's brother that the *Temptation* would be forfeit. Rather than let her become the property of the Rivien government — or worse, Prince Hassan — Jathun had sent his crew away and hidden the vessel in the one place no one would think to look.

The surface.

Or, more accurately, *beneath* the surface.

"Three days west and a day north of here," Jathun said while they were still in the thrall of the storm. "There's a place where the earth is rife with steep ravines," he told them around a mouthful of eggs. "From the air it looks like cracked earth, but — oh gods this is so good!"

Cassidy snapped her fingers. "Jathun, the point?"

Jathun nodded emphatically but didn't answer until he had eaten another mushroom. He seemed to tremble in ecstatic pleasure as grease spilled from his lips and dribbled down his chin into the tangle of his beard. "Right. The cracks are actually wide enough to hide a ship, deep enough you can't see the bottom even from the surface and sprawling enough to make a safe snuggling station."

Hanaa sneered down the table at him. "Why should we trust this murderer?" she asked.

Jathun looked up from his plate for the first time since sitting down, and recognition flashed on his face when he spotted the emblem on her tunic. "Ah," he said simply. He gnawed a cormorant wing clean and drummed it against his plate before speaking. "You're one of his. I am a murderer, aye," he acknowledged. "A smuggler, too. Not a pirate, though, despite the charges. But I am not a liar."

"Don't you need to lie to be an effective smuggler?" asked Kek.

"Not if you do the truth a good twisting," Jathun said, and a smile Cassidy might have described as nostalgic passed across his face.

"Anyone can *say* they don't lie," Hanaa countered.

"True enough," he conceded. "But consider that I have no *reason* to lie."

Hanaa sneered but held her peace.

When the storm finally broke, Cassidy flagged the *Sunrise* and *Roc Spear* to begin their flight west and left Miria to helm the *Dreamscape* before retreating into her cabin. She flopped onto her chair at the table, picked up Venitha's book only to slam it back down with a crash that rattled the various paperweights.

"Is there a problem?" Hymn asked.

"What do you know about this?" Cassidy asked, indicating the tome in front of her.

"It is a book," the Fae said dryly, and Cassidy rolled her eyes. "You did not have it in your possession when you disembarked. It is quite old and —"

"So you didn't read it while I was gone?"

"I did not," said Hymn.

"I know you can at least read Asarian," said Cassidy. In fact, Hymn had revealed that by informing Cassidy that Elyia Asier's journal had actually been a posthumous compendium of letters to Cassidy. "Can you read pre-Ascension text?"

"There are a great many languages that existed before your 'Ascension'," the Fae said. "Show me what you want."

Cassidy opened the book to the middle and flipped pages back and forth until she came to the picture of Hymn and the other Fae. The living Hymn floated over gracefully. When she could see the image on the page, however, her light flickered red several times before shivering into its usual blue. She was completely still, even her dragonfly wings stood rigid, as she hovered in place without bobbing or wavering. Cassidy shivered at the sight.

"So," Cassidy said after a lengthy silence, elongating the word to several syllables. "Who is she?" She tapped the image of the Fae in red just in case Hymn was too distracted and needed the context.

"Len," Hymn said, barely more than a whisper. "This depiction is of Len." After several beats, she added, "This reads, 'Hymn and Len, Princesses of the Dark Wood'. Lofty and meaningless titles."

"And the rest of it?"

"History. Gifts offered, deals struck, flattering and flowery descriptions of our beauty, a poetic warning not to offend us, steal from us, or show preference between us."

Cassidy looked at the picture again, and her eyes lingered on their locked fingers. "I thought you hated Len, but here you look almost like lovers."

"This book is quite old, even as such things are measured by my reckoning," said Hymn. "I *do* hate her, as it happens, but there was a time…" She stopped, and fell to the pages, touching the aged vellum with a delicate *pat*. She stood there, staring at the image for a long time. Cassidy pushed away from the table to give her space. She barely heard Hymn whisper, "We were friends, once."

Cassidy turned, but Hymn said no more.

Cassidy leaned on the gunwale and sighed into the wind. The desert was beautiful and varied — with expanses of cracked land littered with shrubs and hills that gave way to wind-sculpted rock formations in a beautiful assortment of colors and rolling sand dunes — but she was impatient. As peaceful as the skies were, Cassidy felt a storm roiling inside. Nightmares of Andaerhal — dreams of standing, too weak to move, amidst rubble while bleeding people screamed at her, begged her, to help — had plagued her through the night. Hymn insisted that it was a good thing Cassidy really slept instead of wandering the Dreamscape, but what did the Fae know of fear?

"We're getting close," Jathun said, breaking her reverie. The man had shaved his head clean and trimmed his beard to a close-knit goatee and looked like a much younger man for it. He braced himself on the gunwale beside her and sucked in a lungful of air. "Ah! I think I missed the air the most."

"I'll bet," Cassidy said, unsure what else to say.

"It's not just the wind," he added, "but that's wonderful, too. But it's *clean*. Hot or cold, I can breathe. For the first time in a long time, I feel alive."

Cassidy rolled her gaze over him. "The fact that you've been eating all my food probably helps, too."

"I've had a lot to make up for," he said, and he broke into a smile. And it was true; though he had become emaciated, Cassidy could tell from the set of his shoulders and the remnant of his frame that he used to be heavily muscled.

"So why'd you do it?" Cassidy asked. "Why throw all this away?"

Jathun's smile sloughed off his face and he stared vacantly on the passing horizon. "I had a daughter. If she were still alive, she might be the princess' age.

"Back then, there was a group of smugglers selling pre-Ascension artifacts without Iron Veil sanction — mostly fakes, or harmless trinkets, but there was the occasional Fae relic. Dozens of deaths over the course of a year. Well, Prince Hilal — then-owner of the Red Moons — decides he wants the glory of ridding Rivien of the criminal presence. So, he launches an investigation. Comes to the conclusion that the relics are coming from Castilyn. So, what does he do?"

"Well, *normally* I'd guess he sets up security checkpoints," Cassidy said slowly, "but since you're asking, I'm guessing that's not what happened."

"A sensible thought," Jathun said. He spat overboard. "Hilal was not a sensible man. One Mid-Winter afternoon, four ships from Castilyn were shot down without warning en route to Isaro." He ran his fingers over his shaven pate. "My daughter and her mother were on one of those ships. And do you want to know the worst part, Durant? The worst part is the smugglers were already in custody. They were caught by the Iron Veils in Castilyn weeks earlier.

"When I learned of their fate, I tried to seek justice the legal way, but Rivien is ruled by coin, and the Princes have more coin individually than the cities they claim to govern."

"So, you assassinated him." said Cassidy. She said it without reproach, but Jathun looked chastised and averted his gaze all the same.

"Aye. Botched it pretty badly. Elyia would have laughed at how quick they caught me."

They lapsed into a companionable silence for a time, watching the rock formations drift by. The older sailor seemed to be drinking in the sights, and Cassidy wondered if the tears threatening to spill from his eyes were from the joy of freedom or the grief of loss. It might have been both, and she couldn't fault him for either.

"You're not what I expected out of Elyia's replacement," Jathun said after a while.

"What do you mean?" asked Cassidy.

"You seem really new to this whole…" He waved his hands around, as if fumbling on an invisible shelf for the word he was looking for, "*grand cause* thing. What did Elyia have you doing without a war to preoccupy her?"

Cassidy snorted. "We traded cargo."

"Weapons?" Jathun asked. "Myt Dust? Refugees?"

She laughed outright at that. "No," she managed between fits of giggling. "We carried furs and coats in the winter, silks and dresses in the summer; alchemy ingredients; parcels and letters. Whatever goods were going our way that people were willing to pay for. Whatever *legitimate* goods," she clarified.

"You seriously mean to tell me after being the big hero she settled into the merchant life? She couldn't have done that for five minutes."

"We were at it for ten years," said Cassidy. "I always thought she was happy."

"Huh. You think you know a person." Jathun's attention snapped suddenly ahead. "We're here."

Cassidy turned to look as well. Just behind a rocky ridge, the desert abruptly turned from windswept stones to a flat expanse of cracked, dry earth. Even knowing the true depth of those cracks, it seemed so plain and featureless. The view stretched on until it met the distant horizon where blue mountains blended faintly into the sky.

"There're so many crevasses," Cassidy noted. "How are we supposed to find the *Temptation* in all this?"

Jathun barked a laugh. "I remember exactly where it is, never fear." He directed them miles into the field, guiding them along by such small and unassuming landmarks Cassidy was almost sure he was making them up as he went — like a rock he insisted looked like a sphinx if you squinted and tilted your head, though to her it just looked like a rock. They weaved above the barren landscape from marker to marker for miles before Jathun finally called for a full stop. "It's there," he said, pointing at the crevasse directly below them.

Cassidy turned to Miria at the helm. "Do you feel comfortable setting us down or should I?" she asked the princess.

"I can do it," Miria assured her, and the girl's confidence was enough for Cassidy.

Kek flagged the other ships to gather together for a meeting. When the gangplanks were set out between the *Roc Spear* and the *Sunrise*, Captains Zhu and Kin came aboard. Zhu had a scowl on his face while Kin looked like she just woke up from a nap.

"The *Temptation* is in the pit below us," Cassidy said without preamble. "She will need a skeleton crew to get her to safe harbor. My ship runs on a small crew as it is, so we will need volunteers from your ships."

Zhu scoffed. "Why should I have any of my crew follow this convict below the surface? In fact, why should we risk anything for the sake of one ship? We have plenty. If Jathun's value hasn't been overstated, it shouldn't matter if he has his ship or a fishing boat, and if it *has*..." He let that sentence hang between them.

Anger boiled in Cassidy, and she had to bite her tongue to keep from shouting about the mystical forces at play.

Kin saved her from answering. "I'm sure I can find plenty of volunteers on the *Sunrise*. And I am fairly sure Jin has been swabbing the same patch of deck all day just pretending to look busy."

Zhu offered a bow to Miria and disembarked. Kin offered a mollifying smile and returned to her ship to wrangle up volunteers. She came back with a team of seven crewmen, each carrying packs full of rations and armed with extra pistols and long- reaching spears. She ran through their names, but Cassidy only retained a couple of them, preoccupied by her indignation at Zhu and her apprehension about the upcoming descent.

"You sure you don't want the *Sunrise* to back you up down there?" Kin asked.

"I appreciate the offer," said Cassidy, "but even if it's wider than it looks, it's probably going to be tight enough down there." Kin snickered and offered what might have been a wink. Cassidy in turn suppressed a grin.

When Kin returned to the *Sunrise*, Miria addressed the volunteers from the helm. "You are undertaking a great risk. We are descending into the depths of enemy territory, where mankind is unwelcome. If you are uncertain of your course, no one will judge you for returning to the *Sunrise*. The rest of you: keep alert and know that the Empire loves you for your courage." No one moved to return to the *Sunrise*. Though there were nervous glances passing around, Cassidy watched as the line visibly stood taller and breathed easier.

The princess lowered the *Dreamscape Voyager* into the depths.

The descent was nerve wracking. Cassidy stood at the port gunwale with Kek and a curious duo of volunteers as the ground grew ever closer. Despite Jathun's assurances, Cassidy gripped the gunwales in anticipation, waiting for the jagged lip of the crevasse to sheer the hull of her ship clean off.

Relief flooded when the ship descended smoothly by the edge of the earth, only for her heart to plunge back into terror when shadows swallowed the deck. Below, Lierre, Haytham, and Hanaa had set up spot lamps — bright lanterns set into mirrored housings — which provided some visual aid, but the bottom of the pit was deep, and as the *Dreamscape* descended, the walls grew wider apart, offering them little comfort.

There was a damp chill in the cavernous space that belied the scorching desert overhead, and the sweat lining all of Cassidy's body left her feeling clammy and miserable. A skittering noise echoed from somewhere in the space, and she nearly jumped out of her skin.

Chic-tic-tic-chic. Chic-tic-tic-chic. Tic-tic.

Cassidy forced herself to breathe slowly and calmly to hide her fear, to set an example. The air tasted like wet stone and felt heavy in her lungs, but she breathed it steadily.

A familiar warmth rushed up her back and pushed her hat askew before settling on her head. "I am here," Hymn said, almost maternal in her soothing tone. And Cassidy felt more at ease. A tension she hadn't even been aware of melted from her shoulders and she kept her eyes on the approach.

The bottom was flat and sandy.

Chic-tic-tic. Tic-tic-tic.

"Full stop," Cassidy ordered when the ship was some thirty feet from the bottom. "Tell Lierre to sweep the lights." Miria relayed Cassidy's orders through the pipeline and the search lamps began darting around the pit floor. Nothing moved as they passed over stones and shrubs. One of the lights strayed from the floor beneath them and caught something that glimmered. When it steadied, Cassidy realized it was water.

"The *Temptation* is on the other side of the lagoon," Jathun said, and though he spoke in a normal tone, it felt like he was shouting in the intense quiet.

"What's a lagoon doing underground?" Cassidy asked.

Chic-tic-tic-tic.

"I don't think it's a lagoon," said one of the volunteers from the *Sunrise*. Cassidy thought her name was Jin. "Lagoons are coastal. It's an underground lake."

"It's too shallow to be a lake," Jathun argued. "We'll be able to walk across it."

"Then it's a pond," said Jin.

"How many words for a still body of water are there in your language?" Jathun groused.

Cassidy ignored them, peering out at the light moving on the water's surface. There was a natural light on the other side, so faint she almost missed it, but she thought she could make out a silhouette of a ship on the other side. Or maybe she was projecting.

Chic-tic-chic-tic-chic-tic.

"Twenty-five feet," she said to Miria. "Let us down gently." The *Dreamscape Voyager* descended again at a slower, more deliberate pace, dropping only a few feet at a time instead of all at once. When the hull touched sand, Cassidy felt it in her boots, and she had to suppress a shudder. "Set all the lights along the lake to give them a course to the *Temptation*." Again, Miria relayed the orders and after a clumsy bit of coordination, the lights lined up on the water's surface. "Are you sure it's safe to walk across?" Cassidy asked Jathun.

Jathun nodded. "There's a deeper side further off, but from about the middle…" He pointed to the left of the lights. "To the edge…" He pointed to the right. "It only gets to about hip deep at the worst."

"You're *sure*?" Cassidy pressed.

"I may have been resigned to my fate when you found me," he said, "but when I left her here, I made sure I would be able to come back if I had the chance."

"Alright," Cassidy said. "Kek, help me set the gangplank. Nieves, get a couple lanterns for the *Temptation's* crew."

Jathun led the procession down to the surface without hesitation, but his new crew seemed less eager. Jin stepped on the gangplank and leaped back when it groaned. A tall woman whose name Cassidy had missed entirely patted Jin's shoulder affectionately and took her by the hand, guiding her down one step at a time. A burly man named Lim took a deep, steadying breath and wrang his fingers over his spear shaft as if to reassure himself it was there before he followed.

The volunteers splashed loudly in the water, which carried clearly across the cavernous expanse. Cassidy watched as they crossed the lake — or whatever it was — and shivered. Each trudging step they took through the water made the path seem longer rather than shorter.

"I wish they'd hurry," she said to Kek. "I want to get back under the sky and feel the wind again." A foul-smelling wind blew through the cavern as though the gods had been listening to her.

"This is bad," Hymn said.

The chittering Cassidy heard grew in intensity and a shadow like a giant hand dropped onto Jathun's line. Stones and water erupted with a thunderous boom. Screams filled the cavern.

Cassidy turned to Kek. Before her words could catch up with her mind, he nodded, and together they bounded down the gangway. Cassidy drew her sword and its blade ignited like a torch. As her foot touched the ground, a sense of vertigo overcame her vision.

A woman in a tattered, smoke gray dress drifts over the water. Blood tinted with ash pours from empty eye sockets and dribbles from between needle-like teeth. Hymn stands between her and Cassidy, a tenuous thread of blue light wavering between incandescent and wispish pulsing like a heartbeat between her slender fingers.

The gray lady splays skeletal fingers and a heavy wind knocks Hymn aside. She shoots out, and the water beneath her sprays behind her in a violent wake beneath her bloody feet. She strikes and Cassidy moves to block with her sword, but it is a feint, and she strikes from the other side. Talon-like fingers dig into her throat as the Fae hoists her off the ground. The pressure wells up behind her eyes even as warm lifeblood washes down the Fae's fingers and arm.

She slams Cassidy onto her back so hard the water doesn't slow her, and the air escapes her lungs in a single, gurgling bubble. Her vision goes dark at the edges as the gray woman barres down on her and blood spreads through the water. Hymn's whip ensnares the enemy's throat, but it is too late for Cassidy.

Cassidy stumbled as her second foot touched solid ground and Kek took the lead. She caught herself and followed after.

"Another vision," she said between breaths. "I didn't —"

"The future is not set in stone," Hymn said firmly. "I will protect you." Cassidy swallowed the urge to protest. She had seen Hymn fail to protect her, *felt* her failure as keenly as she felt the pain beneath her ribs with each stride she took away from the *Dreamscape Voyager*. She wanted to trust her friend, but the sight of a grotesque and ghostly figure strangling her, puncturing her throat and drowning her, was burned into her memory.

Cassidy would have to save herself when the time came.

Driven by fear, she drew on Hymn's power, and after abstaining and suffering the little indignities and pains, it felt like plunging into a spring and sucking the water down. She nearly stumbled again from the heady rush of drowning her pain out with a cold rush. Her steps carried her farther and came faster, and soon she pulled ahead of Kek as they began splashing through the lake.

The eyeless Fae was nowhere to be seen, but Cassidy could see what had dropped from the cavern ceiling. An enormous creature with eight slender legs armored in green-white chitin scurried about, thrusting its segmented tail out at the *Sunrise's* crew and threatening to behead them with pincer-like claws. It danced effortlessly in the water while the human invaders barely managed to force themselves out of its way. Even crouched, it stood half again as tall as the tallest man in their party.

The pan flash and erupting *boom* of Kek's pistol accompanied one of the scorpion's forelegs exploding. The beast staggered and fell to one side and emitted a gurgling shriek. Cassidy reached the wounded creature and swung her sword two handed, hoping to punch through its armor. Instead, the chitin gave easily under the burning blade, and she severed its leg with entirely too much ease.

It's not fully formed, she realized, and her conclusion dawned on her with mounting horror. *It's an infant, and scorpions are born in clutches!*

"Look out!" Hymn called, but the pull of Cassidy's prophecy was already beckoning her to move. With Fae-enhanced reflexes, she rolled under the scorpion as it whirled around to snap at her with its claws. She drove her sword through its belly and ichor doused the fire coating her weapon in a flash of hissing steam. As it reared up on its remaining hind leg, spears from the *Sunrise's* crew plunged into its front. Cassidy dove out of the way before it crashed to the lakebed, dead, with a gushing splash.

Five more nascent scorpions dropped from the ceiling and surrounded the corpse of their fallen sibling. Cassidy climbed the soft-shelled corpse to gain ground and drew her pistol. One of the arachnids scurried up after her and with the thread of the future tugging at her like a marionette, she leveled her pistol and shot it through the head. It fell into the water with a resounding crash. Gunfire rattled sporadically. Someone screamed as a scorpion pinned them down.

Kek severed a pincer and sliced into a scorpion's face in a single smooth cut only for his opponent to reel around and smack him with the broadside of its tail, sending him careening through the water. Cassidy leaped from her perch to go after him, but the pull of prophecy made her stop abruptly when the seven-legged beast stabbed at her. She avoided the stinger by inches, but it still bludgeoned her ribs with a sideswipe that sent her tumbling.

The water beneath her rippled and rather than smash face first into the surface, she bounced on a dense pocket of wind and rolled more gently into the lake. Panic flooded as she stared up into the gloom through the chaotic waves of combat. She could see the eyeless Fae bearing down on her, feel the nails puncturing her throat as fingers of steel clamped down on her. She thrashed and tried to scream, and her lungs seized as she sucked in water.

Someone hoisted her from the water and to her feet in a jerky movement that threatened to dislocate her shoulder. Blinking the water from her eyes, she peered at the figure standing drenched before her, his back to the search light so she could only make out the edges of his golden hair.

"Kek," she coughed out. "How... find me?"

"Hymn stands out," he said in a rush as a cacophony of gunfire, screaming, splashing and shrieking ensued around them. Sure enough, the Fae was hovering by her side. Cassidy could only hope no one noticed. "Are you okay?"

"Fine," Cassidy said. "I think there's another Fae nearby." To his credit, Kek didn't question her. Instead, he drew his sword and kept his back to her. Cassidy fished her blade from the water as Kek fought off another scorpion. She found the weapon when she kicked it. She raised the sword from the lake and let out a bellowing cry as she joined Kek without the pull of the future trying to pull her elsewhere for the moment.

Steam flashed off Cassidy's blade in the moment before fire once again engulfed it, and she launched herself at the scorpion. She and Kek each severed one of its claws and when it shrieked, Kek stabbed between its mandibles as Cassidy rammed her sword through its underside.

The ground beneath them rumbled and the water rippled tumultuously. In the darkness beyond the searchlights, something enormous breached the water and a wave several times taller than a man rolled over them, washing away Cassidy, Kek, the dead scorpions and everyone else. Cassidy collided with Kek hard before he hit a wall, knocking the air out of her lungs before the water followed back out. She sucked in a breath and succumbed to a fit of heavy coughs.

The search lamps refocused on what had risen from the depths. Black chitin armor reflected the light with an iridescent tint. Tremors coursed through the lakebed with each step of the monster's eight, fourteen-foot legs, and the shriek she elicited wasn't the shrill, high-pitched cry of its babies, but a deep, resonant bass that felt like a physical force. The sole surviving infant scorpion wandered into the path of this scorpion queen. The larger beast swept its child in its claw and crushed it before eating it without pausing in its advance on the human intruders.

A thunderous blast resounded and echoed over the water and threatened to deafen Cassidy, and a flash of fire and smoke bloomed on the scorpion's flank. It flinched and staggered but did not fall, though ichor bled from steep cracks in the beast's armor. The scorpion turned its massive body in a lumbering gesture that caused fragments of chitin to flake off into the lake, and it began the march towards the *Dreamscape Voyager*.

"*No!*" Cassidy shrieked, and she chased after it.

She thought someone called after her, but her ears were still ringing. Though the water slowed her, the scorpion wasn't fast, and she caught up to it before it reached the edge of the lake. Guided by the pull of the future she had seen, and with the Fae power coursing through her limbs, she leapt, plunging her sword neatly between the armor plates of one of the creature's legs. The leg buckled and the scorpion stopped its advance long enough for Cassidy to pull herself up the limb and over to the scorpion's back.

The scorpion thrashed viciously to throw her off, but Cassidy stumbled to the side where the cannon had struck and plunged her sword into the exposed flesh for leverage. The monster's scream reverberated to her bones, and she was nearly forced to release her grip on her weapon. As she flailed about, her foot hit something hard and lumpy in the arachnid's wound. She thought it was a fragment of cannonball. The Fae sense she used to set iron alight itched across her brain in confirmation.

With a shock like being punched in the face, Cassidy set the broken cannonball on fire. The scorpion reared on its hind legs and shrieked in confused agony. Prophecy guided Cassidy's hand again as the beast's stinger came down to skewer her. She deftly sidestepped the surprisingly flexible tail and with a swipe of her burning blade, cut the stinger from the end, sending it spinning off into darkness.

It reared up again, and this time Cassidy was sent flying as another cannon blast struck the underside of the scorpion. Her sword was lost as she tumbled in the air. She flailed about, reaching for something, anything, to grab hold of, but there was nothing.

She hit the water flat on her back, and the sting flashed even through the Fae-induced distance from pain. She sank a moment later and realized she was not in the shallows any longer but had been tossed to the depths from which the scorpion had emerged.

A brilliant blue light shined above her, and a silvery shape plunged into the water after her. Hymn clasped her arm with a human-sized hand and pulled her back to the air. Hymn knelt on the water's surface, and she looked so much like the image in Venitha's book, Cassidy wasn't sure the sight was real.

Cassidy wasn't an especially strong swimmer, but Hymn guided her to the shallows, where she climbed to her feet. The Sunrise's crew was gathered nearby, and though it was too dark to read their expressions, Cassidy could guess at the shock and fear she would find there. Guilt and a fear of her own welled up in Cassidy at the impending reactions. They would call for her arrest, or maybe even execute her on the spot. Two of them held their spears pointed shakily at Hymn.

Before Cassidy could think of a way to calm them, another fell wind blew over the lake, and it carried a sound like a dirge.

"You've killed my darling pet," came a voice like crystal chimes. Cassidy looked around, and she heard a chorus of shock gasps at the same time she spotted the source. Above them near the cavern's ceiling was a bright, gray light, emitted by the Fae from her vision. Her gray dress was hemmed at the knees — revealing her bare legs and feet as she pantomimed walking down a staircase as she descended to meet them — but billowed out around her and tapering at the edges, giving Cassidy the sense that it wasn't the *color* of smoke, but rather *was* smoke. Only when she stood five feet above the water's surface did Cassidy see the starlit sky amongst the gray and the emptiness in space — as though she wore a hole in reality — that she recognized in the garments of every Fae she encountered.

The Fae stopped abruptly when her inverted, gray eyes settled on Hymn, and they widened in what Cassidy thought was surprise, if not horror.

"*Hymn?*" she asked. Then her eyes narrowed, and a snarl formed on her lips. "No! How dare you w—" Whatever else she had been about to say was silenced when a brilliant red flash like lightning passed between the Fae, followed almost instantly by a blast of thunder that sent Cassidy and everyone else staggering. The stranger's head snapped back, and blood sprayed from her lips in a wide arc, and she fell those last five feet to the water, though she did not touch its surface, instead righting herself at the end of her fall and hovering. The light that had struck her shifted to blue and solidified, revealing itself to be the same whip-like thread with which Hymn had slain Atarshai, manifested from a point between Hymn's outstretched middle and third fingers.

Blood flecked with ash gray light gushed from between the stranger's fingers as she clasped her hand over her lips, and fury and pain warred for dominance in her eyes.

"Long have I waited to do that, Kalliope," Hymn said, and there was an unfamiliar edge to her voice that chilled Cassidy to her core to hear. "Now, begone. Leave us in peace or die."

Cassidy didn't need her prophecy to know Kalliope's choice. The battle began in a flash of fire and steam.

CHAPTER THIRTY-EIGHT

A jet of gray flame collided with Hymn's whip and a wall of steam flashed into existence between the Fae women. The heat hit Cassidy in a wave that left her eyes watering. Hymn ducked low before a light pierced through the haze, and a gout of fire spiraled out, sailing over her head as steam trailed in its wake. Kalliope snapped her fingers and the water between the Fae churned into a whirlpool. The circle closed around Hymn and ensnared her in a swirling sphere that had her spinning.

"Hymn!" Cassidy shrieked.

Kalliope turned to face Cassidy. She tried to speak but only a bubble of blood spilled from her lips, and fury contorted her face once more. She glided forward as though across ice, a jetting wake forming in her path. Brilliantly bright and colorless flame burst to life in her hand as she reached out to grasp Cassidy.

A gunshot sounded, and the Fae and she spun aside to evade it. The hem of her dress caught fire where the bullet passed through, but it was extinguished when it settled on the water. She looked affronted and indignant, rather than frightened. She raised her arm to strike when a torrent of steaming water fell upon her and washed her away.

Hymn stood, steam rising off her skin, her dress, and her hair — the latter of which was still moving as though submerged. She wore a tranquil expression, but Cassidy could *feel* fury rolling off her like heat.

"Talk to me, Durant," Jathun said, reloading his pistol. "What's going on?"

"Hymn — the one in blue — is on our side," she said hurriedly, though even as the words left her lips, she knew it sounded mad. A Fae on *their side*? It defied all sense and reason. Jathun looked sideways at Cassidy, and she couldn't read his expression.

"I expect an explanation later," he said. "Everyone, kill the gray one! She bleeds, she can die!" The order seemed to confuse or frighten some of the *Sunrise's* crew, but three of them broke into a sprint at the Fae. Cassidy took off after, and a burly man followed not far behind.

The lake water around Kalliope exploded in a violent geyser, and she stood across from Hymn, staring with an almost human-like contempt. The smoke-colored Fae snapped her fingers and a serpentine trail of gray flame shot across the lake. Hymn reached out with both hands and the jet of fire hit an invisible barrier between them.

The gray flames coalesced into a spinning ring beneath Hymn's slender fingers and flashed ruby red before fading to a rich, sapphire blue. She punched the air in the center of the ring of fire and it soared across the cavern. Kalliope slashed through the blaze with her hand.

Jin's spear cut along Kalliope's forearm. Sparks and flame guttered from the wound in place of blood. Kalliope backhanded her. Jin fell hard enough she bounced off the lake floor and above the surface before sinking.

The young woman who had comforted Jin fired her pistol at the Fae. The shot went wide. She dropped the pistol and lunged with her spear. Kalliope grabbed the shaft, which caught fire on contact. The Fae guided the spearpoint away from her body and chopped her attacker in the throat with her free hand. Her neck snapped audibly, and she fell limp into the drink.

Kalliope dropped the spear and plunged her burning hand into the cold water. Cassidy punched through the resulting steam with her blade, but the Fae slid almost imperceptibly aside, and her sword passed harmlessly through the air. Kalliope's good hand flashed with gray light. She thrust her shining fingers at Cassidy's throat. The pull of the future all but forced Cassidy to leap. With Fae-enhanced reflexes, she dove over the attack. Something like lightning exploded beneath her. Thunder cracked, and the explosion of air shot Cassidy completely over Kalliope's head. Behind her, a lance of pure light shot through the man who had followed her into battle. The light broke apart and faded, leaving behind a fist sized hole in his chest.

Cassidy was tossed aside but managed to land feet first and fell into a roll. She leaped to her feet and raised her sword only to discover it had snapped clean in half, presumably when she landed.

Hymn and Kalliope conjured matching whips of light and lashed out at one another. With rapid yet graceful swipes of their arms, blue clashed with gray with crimson sparks and violent splashes. Every time one Fae seemed about to reach her opponent, the other would twist a hand or turn her arm and knock the other weapon off course. And each time one blocked the other's assault, the air was filled with a sound like a thousand cracks of static. The water between them churned like the sea in a storm with the force of their blows.

Kalliope's thread licked the place where Hymn's neck met her shoulder with a deafening crack like a gunshot, opening a long and wide wound that poured a bright scarlet accompanied by a thick plume of red smoke. Hymn's whip in turn bypassed Kalliope's defenses and struck her with enough Force to snap her head back as deep red blood muddled with ash spilled skyward along with a cloud of gray. Kalliope staggered back one step and her attack was halted for just one second.

Jathun reached Kalliope in that second and tackled her. The gray whip vanished. The two wrestled, and the Fae had the advantage of strength, easily pushing back against the human. Hymn's whip snaked through the air, splitting Kalliope's attention and forcing her to release Jathun to reconstitute her own weapon of light. She barely parried Hymn's attack.

Jathun plunged a knife into her face.

The blade erupted into a bonfire that consumed her. Kalliope shrieked a blood curdling, agonized scream so tenable Cassidy could almost feel the Fae's pain as her own. With burning hands, she reached up to the dagger but was unable to grasp the iron hilt long enough to wrench it free. She threw herself into the water, but the lake could not quench this fire.

Kalliope burned brightly beneath the dark waters, an incandescent gray that set the surrounding water to a dangerous boil.

Cassidy watched in abject horror as she thrashed and struggled. She was everything Cassidy had been raised to fear. She had sent the scorpions to kill them and had tried to do the deed herself when they failed. But Cassidy had spent over a year with Hymn and had come to see her as a friend. And if she could accept a Fae as her friend, she had to see them as creatures capable of feeling.

And nothing, not even a Fae, deserved to suffer so.

She turned her broken sword over in her hand. She would put Kalliope out of her misery as quickly as she could. With each step she took towards the wounded Fae, the changing temperature of the water became more apparent as coldness pressed around the source of heat. As she reached the edge of the boiling pool, she looked down at her victim. Through the incandescent bloom, she could make out the image of Kalliope's face, one eye destroyed by Hymn's whip, the other skewered through with a knife. And a terrible realization hit Cassidy as sudden and heavy as a cannonball.

Despite Kalliope's wounds, Cassidy's vision of the future hadn't been averted.

Cassidy plunged her broken blade into the water. At the same time, Kalliope dislodged the knife in her eye by bashing at the hilt with a stone until it tore through her skull and fell away, instantly extinguishing the flames and leaving the water too dark to see through. Cassidy's broken blade hit the lake bottom impotently, and Kalliope breached the surface a few feet away. The blinded Fae thrust her hands forward and Cassidy was struck by a gale force wind that sent her and Jathun flying. She hit her head on the lakebed and was carried by the current. She stopped at the very edge of the deep end and stood up very slowly to avoid falling in.

Kalliope stood on tiptoes above the water's surface, blindly facing in Cassidy's direction. Ashen blood pooled in the wells of her eye sockets and flowed down her cheeks like steady tears, and her snarl showed her teeth were stained and her lips were spilling over as well. Hymn interposed herself between Cassidy and the eyeless Fae, and as she watched the sinuous blue light that trailed from her fingertips into the water fade and flicker, Cassidy realized this was the moment of her vision.

As she had foreseen, Kalliope opened her hand and attacked Hymn with raw force, knocking her aside as she launched herself toward Cassidy. Time slowed as the Fae glided across the surface of the lake to reach her. The wake behind her, reaching its zenith above the Fae's head, practically crawled.

Kalliope veered to Cassidy's left, where her defenses were strongest. The pull of her foreseen future primed her muscles, conditioned her mind to defend herself from an attack on the left.

But she had seen the truth.

When Kalliope reached an arm's length from Cassidy, the Fae pivoted and rolled in the air to strike from Cassidy's right. Cassidy fought against her own muscles — which felt like they were acting of their own accord — and pirouetted. The thread of fate snapped like an over-tuned string with an audible and tangible force that rippled the water. She severed the hand that had strangled her to death in her vision. Both ends of the Fae's wrists caught fire. As she began to scream, Hymn's whip ensnared her throat three times before jerking her head back. A sword blade sprouted between Kalliope's breasts and once more her body became a conflagration.

Kek kept his grip on his sword hilt and forced Kalliope to the edge of the depths. His breathing was labored, and he limped as he guided the burning Fae. Still, he kicked the burning Fae's knees out beneath her and sent her cascading into the darkness of the lake. Cassidy watched with him as her incandescent, gray flame illuminated the depths as she sank, until the waters were too deep for her light to reach them.

"I," Kek managed between breath, "need a fucking drink."

"Agreed," Cassidy managed.

"Are you alright?" Hymn asked, gliding over to them.

"Aye," said Cassidy. She looked behind Hymn and her shoulders slumped. Jin and the other *Sunrise* crew had weapons trained on Hymn. "We'll have to deal with this now."

Cassidy did a quick headcount and only found four of them. Guilt replaced the battle rush that had sustained her as she remembered Jin's friend and the burly man. *Who else died?* she wondered.

Jathun pushed through the volunteers, shoving a pistol down to point at the ground. "Alright, Durant, I'll have that explanation now. I think we've all earned it."

Cassidy looked to Hymn and Kek for support. The Fae didn't seem interested in the humans threatening her. Kek shrugged and winced at a wound at his shoulder. She sighed and faced the group. "This is Hymn," Cassidy said. "And she is my friend."

That revelation was met with a chorus of gasps.

Jathun, however, merely looked curiously at Hymn. "I've seen and heard a lot of strange things in my time," he said, "but I've never heard of someone *befriending* a Fae. But that's not much of an explanation."

"She is also…" Cassidy paused, thinking of the right words to say. "I guess you could call her my protector. I met her almost two years ago, now, when —"

"We can't stand for this," said a tall, broad-shouldered man. "She consorts with the Fae!"

"We've seen what their kind can do!" added a woman in her middle years, and the others murmured in agreement.

"And this one may have saved all our lives," Jathun snapped, which cut a hush through the chatter. "You all volunteered to save the world. Right? Or at least your Empire?" The question seemed to take them off guard. "I'll tell you from experience, it's a job that sometimes requires hard choices and unsavory alliances. This Fae — *Hymn*," he corrected, saying her name as if it were a more complicated assortment of syllables, "sided with us over its own kind. I'm sure that's no small thing."

"But the laws —" Jin began.

"Are secondary to our purpose. A creature like the leviathan isn't likely to be defeated by mundane arms alone. For now, we should keep this secret, and trust that Durant has the world's best interests." The survivors looked amongst themselves. After silent deliberation, Jin nodded, which was followed by assent through the entire group. Jathun directed his attention back to Cassidy. "Don't make me regret standing up for you."

"I won't," Cassidy promised. "Now, get to your ship, *captain*. If she's still sky worthy, I'd see —" She was interrupted when Kek slumped into her. She caught him, but he fell limp in her arms. "Kek? *Kek?*"

Jathun reached over to support him, and with Cassidy's help they turned him directly into the *Dreamscape Voyager's* spotlight. The veins in his right arm and along his neck were swollen and had turned a furious purple. Cassidy pulled aside his coat where it had already been punctured. Something dark and misshapen was buried underneath his flesh.

The Scorpion queen's stinger, Cassidy realized, and her guilt compounded. It looked as though Kek had ripped part of the stinger from his flesh, but some of it had broken off and stayed behind.

"We need to get him to your sawbones," Jathun said. Cassidy nodded. They each wrapped one of Kek's arms over their shoulders and carried him to the *Dreamscape Voyager*. "The rest of you, wait aboard the *Temptation*. Get her ready to fly."

Cassidy wasn't sure if Jin had chosen people who excelled at taking orders, or if Jathun's presence as a captain was that strong, but no one questioned him. Cassidy drew as hard as she could on the Fae power, letting her take more of Kek's weight and push on despite being battered and bruised. Even still, the trek across the lake felt like an eternity. Cassidy's legs burned with each grueling step. Even when they reached the sandy bank, it was agony as her boots sank into the shoals.

When she finally reached the ship, Miria and Nieves rushed down the gangway to take Kek from Cassidy and Jathun.

"What happened?" Nieves demanded.

"Poison," Cassidy answered. "Scorpion venom."

"Shit," said Nieves. She and Miria carried him up to the deck. Nieves said something about reagents, laid out instructions for Miria to follow and issue to Lierre, but Cassidy could barely hear her through the fog suddenly pressing on her mind.

Cassidy fell to her knees and curled in on herself. She pressed her head to the cold sand and wept. Physical pain and exhaustion compounded with guilt and doubt. Her tears mingled with the blood pouring from her nose, and they pooled together in the sand. She thought of everything that had happened, each step of the fight, and shuddered. Kek had been injured directly as a result of her visions, she realized. She had been so caught up in her own predestined encounter, she hadn't stopped to consider how her friends might suffer as she blindly barreled forward. Just like Captain Asier.

Kek had been poisoned, and three more people were dead.

Because of her.

Gods, if Kek dies…

A warm hand settled on her shoulder. "Do you need me to carry you, now?" Jathun asked.

Cassidy shook her head without lifting it from the sand. "I'll manage," she said shakily. "See to the *Temptation.*"

Jathun hesitated. After a moment, he stood, turned, and said, "You're a lot like Elyia, you know?"

More than you know, she thought miserably.

"She was always rushing headlong into battle, too. Always with the daring deeds and the insane maneuvers. It was always so inspiring." He started to walk away. "It's good to see some of her lives on."

Jathun was long gone by the time Cassidy got back to her feet. Hymn stood beside her, still in her Dreamscape form, only now she was wearing Cassidy's hat. She hadn't even thought about its absence but seeing it on the Fae's head made her feel suddenly naked.

"Let us leave this place," Hymn said solemnly. "Kekarian's condition will only worsen in the dark."

Cassidy nodded and climbed the gangplank. As soon as the two of them reached the deck, Hanaa ran across the width of the ship and swung an iron bar at Hymn. The Fae disappeared in a flash of shattering light and Hanaa's attack found only open air. Cassidy's hat remained in the air, however, and slowly drifted onto her head.

Hanaa looked poised and ready to attack Cassidy next, but Haytham appeared behind her and put her in a headlock. The siblings struggled for several tense moments.

"Just give…" Haytham said to his sister, the strain of holding her back evident, "… her a chance… to explain."

Hanaa sneered and broke free of her brother's grip. She elbowed him in the gut, and Cassidy wearily braced, prepared to defend herself. She was too tired and preoccupied to brawl. She would have to kill Hanaa or be killed if it came to it.

Instead, Hanaa crossed her arms. "This better be *damn* good."

Cassidy looked up to the aftcastle, where Nieves and Miria had laid Kek out to tend to him. Then she addressed the mercenaries. "Get us out of this cavern and I'll explain everything. But Kek's hurt and I need to make sure he's okay." She turned her back on them, fully expecting to be shot in the back as she climbed the aftcastle.

Kek had been set on a canvas across the top deck. He stared blankly at the crack in the cavern ceiling with glassy eyes. The dark and raised veins contrasted heavily with his increasingly pallid skin, and his breath was a shuddered and staggered affair. Cassidy knelt beside him, across from Nieves. The sawbones checked his pulse, his eyes, and the wound itself in her examination.

"This won't be pleasant," she said. With emphasis to Cassidy and Miria she added, "For anyone." Then she pulled a long, thin knife from her satchel and began excising the scorpion queen's stinger.

INTERLUDE FOUR

Eleven Years Earlier

Blood gushed between Cassidy's fingers as she stanched Kek's wound. The jagged cut had run the length from his left shoulder to the inside of his elbow. Kneeling beside him on the tavern floor, she clamped both hands over his arm while Lierre fumbled with her knife. The engineer cut wonky strips out of her skirt and wrapped them as tightly as she could around his bicep. Kek hissed as she tightened the makeshift bandages. Cassidy stripped her coat off and wrapped it over the dressing.

She undid his belt, which prompted him to force out a faint chuckle. "I'd ask you to buy me a drink first," he said in a voice that was little more than a sigh, "but I don't think I'll ever get this chance again."

"Oh, shut it," she said by rote. She tied his belt tightly around her coat. "Can you stand?" He had lost so much blood. The floor beneath him was a broad and soggy red patch.

"I think so," he managed, and she pulled his good arm over her shoulder and guided him to his feet before moving to his other side to put pressure on the injured arm.

"My man is hurt, damn you!" Asier shouted not far away. She was being held by the four members of the city watch pending an investigation; she had dislocated the arm of Kek's attacker and cracked the knee of a man who had taken up a knife to defend him.

"And that's why we aren't questioning him right now," said a resigned-sounding watch woman with graying black hair. She glanced over at Cassidy, Lierre, and Kek. "Oi! One of you will need to stay to issue a statement."

"You can't make them —"

"Listen lady," said a bald watchman, "I don't care if you're some war hero or whatever, laws and procedures exist for a reason."

Lierre and Cassidy exchanged looks. The engineer lowered her head solemnly. "I'll stay. Get him to a surgeon, quick!"

Cassidy nodded and walked Kek out into the streets of Melfine. The sun was almost completely set, painting the sky a burnt purple, and the lane was lightly trafficked with tight knit groups either heading home or out for a drink. Someone took a look at them and crossed the street hurriedly.

"Alright, Kek," Cassidy said, "you're a local. Where's the nearest surgeon?"

Kek let out a shuddering sigh and tilted his head to the right. "That way," he whispered, and they made their way through weaving streets comprised of retired ships.

Traffic grew heavier as they neared the center of town, though much of it was going in their same direction. Cassidy didn't see anything that looked like a clinic, and it wasn't until they stood in the shadow of an enormous, derelict warship — which towered high above the surrounding district, with densely packed lines of people ascending multiple gangways — that she realized where Kek was leading them.

"Kek, you need a *surgeon*!" she snapped in his ear. "We don't have time to watch a fight!"

"Trust me, Cassie," he whispered faintly. "Best help in town, right there. Don't go in line. There's another entrance at the base. Not for the public." Cassidy looked dubiously, peering at the crowds and at the arena behind them. With a sigh, she followed his lead.

The entrance Kek had mentioned was a small door that had clearly not been part of the original ship design and was guarded by two very heavyset men. As they made their way to them, Cassidy expected to be told to leave, or at least to be questioned.

Instead, a dark-skinned man with hair done in many thin braids spat to the side and said, "She's already pissed at you, Valani. She *really* won't be happy to see you with another girl on your arm. Maybe don't drop by unannounced?"

"She said she's going to kill you at least once a week since you skipped town," the other man added.

"She might," Kek wheezed. "But she's got to patch me up first."

The guards perked up at that, and only then did they seem to notice they were both splattered in blood, with Cassidy's hands being absolutely painted by it and Kek's arm haphazardly wrapped.

"She's on duty," one of them said, opening the door for them.

When they closed it behind them, Cassidy asked, "You friends with the arena staff?"

"Kind of. I inherited friends from... well, you'll see."

The two of them walked down a short hall and entered a room lined with privacy screens. Two women in gray gowns stood in the middle of the chamber, whispering. They stopped abruptly when they spotted Cassidy and Kek. One of the women laughed into her hand while the other visibly sighed.

"Nieves," the exasperated woman called, "he's back."

"*He* who?" another woman demanded from behind one of the screens.

"Kekarian," the giggling girl replied.

The crash of lacquer and wood against wood sounded and the hidden speaker pushed out from behind the screen so forcefully she nearly knocked it over. This Nieves was a slight young woman with black hair cut as low as her chin. She stomped across the room and raised a hand as if to slap him, stopping when she took in the drying blood marking him and Cassidy, and the makeshift tourniquet around his arm.

Her mouth twitched like she was looking for the words to say, but Kek broke in first. "Nieves, this is my friend Cassidy. Cass, this is Nieves, my fiancé."

"*Former*-fiancé," Nieves hissed, her scowl deepening. "You skipped town without so much as a goodbye." She took in his tourniquet again. "Well, don't just stand there, get one of the tables."

Cassidy walked Kek behind one of the screens and helped him onto a cloth-draped table with an elevated side for the head to rest. Nieves scowled and shoved Cassidy out of the way as soon as he was settled in. She took a heavy looking pair of scissors from her apron and cut right through Cassidy's belt.

"Hey, you could have —"

"Sit down and shut up or leave," Nieves said without looking up, and she pointed to a stool. Cassidy reluctantly obeyed, leaning forward intently to observe. Nieves snipped through Cassidy's coat and the strips of cloth that made up the bandages. Kek hissed as she examined the wound. She shoved something Cassidy couldn't see into Kek's mouth without warning, though it seemed he had expected it, and he began to chew. Then she took a tall, glass bottle containing an almost clear, white liquid and poured it onto the wound. Whatever it was, Cassidy could hear Kek's flesh sizzle like cooking fat as little bubbles formed, and he made a sound between a groan and a hiss.

Nieves took a rag and dabbed at the wound before she extracted a spool of catgut and a needle. "Your mother is still paying mine back for the wedding expenses, by the way," she said conversationally.

"Sorry," he said around whatever was in his mouth. "Why are you so mad? You didn't even want to get married."

The sawbones' face tightened into an even deeper scowl, but her hands continued moving at a steady and smooth rhythm, sewing smoothly and gracefully. "You left without a word to anyone, and I've had to deal with the consequences. So why'd you leave, anyway?"

"I had to get a new job," Kek groaned weakly.

"I heard you quit your old one the day you left," Nieves said. "You didn't *have* to do anything."

"You try working for my sister," said Kek, "then we'll talk about *need*."

Nieves snorted.

An older woman in a burgundy robe peeked around the screen. "Tarhant, Gen Bao just finished his fight, and he needs his arm set."

"I'm busy with a laceration," said Nieves, never looking away from her work. "Ling can handle a broken arm."

"Ling doesn't have your expertise," said the woman. She paused, looking at Kek. "And your job is to patch up our fighters, not every poor mugging victim that walks by."

Nieves whirled around at that and pointed a bright red hand at the woman. "I said I'm busy, Kako. Life threatening injuries come first. So unless Kigara ripped his throat out, he can either wait or let Ling do her job!" With that she turned back and resumed her stitching. The older woman looked affronted, and her eyes boggled, but she merely turned and stormed away. "So, when did you get back in town?"

"This morning," Kek admitted.

"And when were you planning on telling me?" She pulled her thread tight.

"I was — ahk! I was working on the best way to break it to you," he said.

"So you chose getting knifed in the alley?"

"It was a tavern," he protested.

"Oh, well, if it was a *tavern*, it's fine," she said, rolling her eyes. "Where was it?"

"Lampstreet," he said miserably.

"Kekarian Valani!" Nieves chided, and Kek hissed as she made another tight stitch. "You know better than to give those bastards your business."

"But they do the best dumplings in town! You know, with those shaved slices of meat? And I haven't been back in a year."

"I've noticed."

They lapsed into an uncomfortable silence as Nieves worked. A young girl came in to refuel the lanterns, and twice Nieves needed a replacement spool of catgut, but otherwise they weren't interrupted again. Only the sound of Kek's groaning, the clicking of needles were constant, though snippets of whispered conversation and the ministrations of other patients occasionally sounded from elsewhere in the room. Periodically, she would stop stitching to force Kek to drink from a canteen, but even then, Nieves' hands never lost their rhythm as she worked. Aside from her evident anger at Kek, she didn't seem concerned about what lay before her. Cassidy was sure if *she* had had someone cut open like that and dumped on her table, she'd be a frantic mess. But Nieves was a consummate professional.

As the hours wore on, Cassidy found herself nodding off, only waking up when she felt herself teetering off on her stool.

"Hey, don't sleep," Nieves snapped. Cassidy shot awake, thinking the sawbones was talking to her, but it was accompanied by a slap to Kek's face that left a bloody handprint on his cheek.

"Was that really necessary," he whined. "I'm dying."

"You aren't dying, you big baby," she said. "Now drink." Kek craned his neck forward to accept the water, and he gagged before swallowing and coughing.

"Fucking idiot," Nieves said without heat or venom. "Can't even drink without fucking up."

"I can drink you under this or any table," Kek protested sleepily.

"You never learn, do you?"

411

"Has anyone ever told you, you have the prettiest blue eyes?"

"My eyes are brown."

"So probably no one's told you that," Kek concluded, and he began giggling. Nieves rolled her eyes and continued her stitching.

When she was finally done, she cut the catgut with her scissors, took out the bottle she had used before and soaked his arm with it. After dabbing him clean and dry, she poured the rest of the contents into a shallow bowl she used to scrub her hands clean.

"Does your family know you're here?" Nieves asked as she wrapped him with fresh bandages.

"Not yet," he said.

"You should see them before you leave. How long are you staying?"

Kek looked at Cassidy. "Captain said three days, right?"

"Aye," Cassidy said, a little taken aback at being addressed at all. She almost felt like she was intruding on a private moment.

Nieves nodded. She finished bandaging him. "Try to be more careful. Steep these in tea three times a day," she said, taking a flat box out of a nearby drawer. "One should be enough. Don't lift anything more than three pounds with that arm for a while. And… Well, take care, Kek. Now, get out before you cause any more trouble."

"Nieves," Kek began, but she was already walking away.

Kek and Cassidy exchanged confused looks and shrugged. He was weak on his feet, but he was confident that he didn't need assistance walking. Street traffic for the evening was light, and it was a clear, starry night, so even between the gas lamps it was easy to see their way. They made it back to the *Dreamscape Voyager* unmolested, where they found Captain Asier and Lierre waiting on the wharf.

Lierre was pacing frantically while the captain sat cross legged on a barrel as if meditating. Asier was the first to spot them, but Lierre wasn't far behind. She quit her pacing and broke into a run to meet them. She opened her arms to hug Kek, but she stopped and gingerly clasped his good arm instead.

"Are you okay? Do you need anything? I was so worried!" Tears were threatening to spill from her eyes and Kek took her into a one-armed hug.

"I'm fine," he said, though his throat croaked a little. "I had a friend, helped me out."

412

The sun was high on the third day as Lierre and Cassidy brought the last of the new cargo onboard. Kek had been relegated to light duty, so the physically demanding tasks had fallen to them and the Captain. For his own part, Kek seemed to take it pretty hard, having apologized many times, and he looked sullen at not being involved. Cassidy wished she could help.

"Don't worry," she told him, "you'll probably be in shipshape by the time we make port in Nasradaan, and you'll be trying to avoid doing your fair share."

"Hey, when have I ever tried to avoid doing my fair share?"

Cassidy's only answer was to stick her tongue out at him. She laughed when he tried to swipe at her, and she led him on a chase around the deck. She stopped abruptly when she came to the gunwale and saw the captain speaking to someone in the harbor below. After a moment's study, she realized it was Nieves.

"... so is he here or isn't he?" Nieves demanded.

The captain folded her arms. "Aye, he's here." She looked up and saw Kek and Cassidy and waved them down. The two met them at the foot of the gangway.

Nieves immediately started in on Kek, poking him in the chest with her finger. "I lost my job patching you up," she said angrily.

"You did?" Kek asked, surprised. "But you're the best medic the arena has, how can they fire you?"

"Don't waste my time with false flattery, Valani," she said, poking him again, "and they fired me for *stealing* three rolls of catgut and a bottle of cleansing agent! You know, the cat gut that's keeping your blood on the inside and the cleansing agent that stopped it from festering?"

"Shit, I'm sorry, Nieves," Kek said, backing up a step.

"I don't want apologies," Nieves snapped, "I want you to fix this."

"What do you want me to do?" Kek asked. "Storm down to the arena and demand they give you your job back?"

"No, you idiot!" she snapped, "You're going to put in a good word for me and get me a job as the medic on your ship."

"I — what?" Kek stammered.

413

"You heard me," she said. "You obviously don't have a good sawbones on your vessel, and you just said yourself I'm the best that's ever come through the arena circuit."

"Actually, I'm pretty sure I just said you were the best that —"

"So it's settled," Nieves said. "Tell your captain what an asset I am."

"Don't talk about me like I'm not here," Asier said. "You're not making a good case for yourself right now."

Cassidy looked from the captain to Nieves and Kek, and back. "Um, Captain, can I have a word right quick?"

"Hm? Aye. You two work out whatever you have to work out." They walked up the gangway. "What's the problem, Cassidy?"

"You should hire her," Cassidy said simply.

Asier blinked. "Oh? I thought Kek might say that, but you barely know her."

"No," Cassidy admitted, "and I'll be honest, from what little I've seen, she's snappish and rude, and that's probably because of Kek, but..." She swallowed and tried to put the words together. "I watched her work all night. She's good, captain. Damn good. Unflappable, even. And more than that, while she didn't come out and say it, I could tell she *cares*. She took care of Kek all night, even though she was mad at him, and didn't even ask for money when she was done." She paused, adding, "And she's right; none of us are very good at patching each other up. We'd be fools to turn her down."

Asier looked over the gunwale, considering. She stood there for a long moment, then nodded. "Alright, Cass. You've said your piece." They walked back down the gangway.

"... to such a fat-headed pervert like you!" Nieves was shouting.

"Well at least I *have* a —" Kek began, but he was cut off with a sharp whistle from the captain. He and Nieves turned to look at her, and the tension in their looks was palpable. Cassidy wondered, belatedly, what Kek would think if the captain took her advice. They didn't seem to get along, but how much of that was just airing out grievances? She supposed it was too late to take back her suggestion, and it was out of her hands, anyway.

"Miss Tarhant, was it?" Asier asked.

"Yes, ma'am," Nieves replied.

414

"If you're going to be on this ship, the correct response is 'aye, Captain'," she said. "It may be a small thing, but ship life is full of little things you need to keep on top of. You'll have a share of the chores and duties necessary to keep the ship in order. You will have to share a cabin with Cassidy and Lierre, and you'll follow my orders to the best of your ability. We go where the winds of trade carry us. Can you handle all that?"

"Aye, captain," Nieves said without hesitation.

"We set off in three hours," Asier said. "I expect you back here ready to leave in two. It'll be a long time before we return, so think carefully when you pack."

"Aye, captain," she said again.

"And Miss Tarhant?"

"Aye, Captain?"

Asier smiled and held her hand out. "Welcome aboard."

Nieves clasped Asier's hand. "You won't regret this."

CHAPTER THIRTY-NINE

Cassidy gripped the gunwale tightly as she stared out into the desert behind them. The images of Kek's dead-eyed expression, of Nieves draining his swollen veins of festered blood with hollow needles, of his convulsions, all burned into her mind like the afterimage of the sun. Worse still was the sound. Kek hadn't screamed. He had just whimpered pitifully. That one sound, repeated a thousand times, shattered Cassidy's heart.

After Nieves had bloodletted him and given him a plethora of de-toxins she kept for just such an occasion, they moved him to Cassidy's cabin to rest. Nieves had elected to stay by his side, but Cassidy needed air. It was then she had explained her history with Hymn to Hanaa and Haytham. It was strange telling relative strangers the truth, to admit to breaking the most sacred law in all three nations. She fully expected Hanaa to attack her as soon as she said she had struck a deal with Hymn. Haytham's reaction had been harder to read. She supposed the only reason she hadn't been shot was that even on a ship as small as Cassidy's, two people couldn't stage a mutiny.

She hadn't seen either of the Ramajins since she'd given them the answers they had demanded.

"Gods, I need a fucking cigarette," Cassidy whined.

"That would probably kill you," Hymn said helpfully.

"I know." She pushed off from the gunwale. Kek's blood had left a deep wine-colored stain on the aftcastle. To get away from the sight, she climbed down and started pacing the deck. Miria stood at the helm, but she watched Cassidy closely. "What is it, Miria?"

"Just worried," she said. "Is Kek alright?"

"Nieves knows her job," Cassidy said with more confidence than she felt. "Have you seen the mercs?"

"Hanaa threw her bag into Kek's cabin, so I think it's safe to say they're avoiding us. I'd have mentioned it sooner, but it seemed pretty unimportant, relatively speaking."

"If their knowledge poses a danger," Hymn said, "it may behoove us to kill them. You can lie about their fates, and no one is likely to ask *me*."

"That's horrible," Cassidy protested.

Miria, however, stared at Cassidy's hat and quirked her mouth. "It's not off the table, but I think we should consider that a last resort."

"You can't be serious," said Cassidy.

"Very serious, Captain," said Miria. "Word *cannot* get out about you and Hymn. If we can convince the Ramajins that it's better not to sell us out, then great. But if we can't..." She let that hang there.

Cassidy rubbed her temples and stepped away, not far enough to disengage from Miria entirely, but just enough to close that discussion. The *Temptation* caught her eye, flying at their starboard as she was. The old ship certainly *looked* like she had been hidden away for years. Her hull had once been painted silver, but now only patches of the brilliant color remained, having been stripped by sand and water and scorpions over years and replaced by moss. Much of the metal Cassidy could spot was rusted, and she was surprised the ship could fly at all, never mind keep pace with the *Dreamscape Voyager* and the other ships.

Perhaps that was because of the pieces of Lucandri?

That thought had Cassidy's mind circling back. "It's not just the mercs we need to worry about knowing."

Miria nodded.

"I'm not too worried about Jathun," she amended, "But there are still four crewmen from the *Sunrise* on that vessel."

Miria nodded. "Hopefully dealing with the leviathan keeps their minds occupied."

"How did we get here, Miria?"

"Honestly? I have no idea," Miria said. "But we'll get through it."

Cassidy finally returned to her cabin that evening. Nieves was still sitting on a stool beside the bed, fretting over Kek like a fussy mother. Cassidy watched her replace the rag on his forehead with a colder, wetter one before checking his pulse. After examining his wounds, she sat there staring at him, as if she expected him to take a turn any moment.

"You should get something to eat," Cassidy said. "It was actually your turn to cook, but I threw what I could find in the skillet, so you can just eat. It's pretty bland, but — sorry, I'm rambling, aren't I?"

Nieves said nothing and didn't look away from Kek. Cassidy put a hand on her shoulder, and that got her attention.

"Sorry, captain," she said in a croaking voice, "I wasn't listening."

"I said there's food in the galley," Cassidy said. "Take a break. I'll look after him while you get some rest."

Nieves hesitated, then nodded. She rose and crossed the cabin, only to hesitate at the door. She turned and opened her mouth to speak, only to close it and leave the room. When she finally closed the door, Cassidy sat on the stool and took Kek's hand in hers, and it was like grabbing iron right out of the summer sun. He had been stripped to his small clothes, though the blankets had been pulled up to his chest leaving his arms bare over the covers. The veins that had been swollen had shrunk, but they were still red and inflamed. A moss green poultice had been smeared over the initial wound and all the points Nieves had blooded him, including his neck and his cheek. His eyes were puffy and sunken, and his face had only gotten paler.

"I'm sorry, Kek," she said, clasping his hand tighter. She could feel his pulse, faint and slow, beneath her grip. "This is all my fault." If she hadn't simply followed the course laid out for by her vision, if she had tried to break the thread *before* the last moment, she could have spared Kek the pain of —

But I could have died, she told herself, only to feel her heart drop out of her chest. *Gods.* Hadn't she spent the past several months condemning Elyia Asier for making the same choice? For grasping to certainty in the face of the unknown? For choosing a guarantee of a single moment in the future over a thousand potential deaths in between? For keeping that truth a secret from everyone?

And Asier had never failed any of them the way Cassidy had failed Kek.

The weight of Cassidy's hypocrisy hammered against the anvil of her guilt. Hot tears burst from her eyes before she could try to stop them. "I'm so sorry," she gasped, barely even a whisper.

Nieves stepped into the cabin then with a steaming teapot and a stack of cups in her hands. "Captain, will you be staying here tonight?"

"No," Cassidy said, wiping her eyes. "I'll just grab a few things and find other arrangements. If you're staying, I'll take your bunk."

Nieves nodded. "Aye, captain. Sorry to displace you."

"Don't sweat it," Cassidy said, "Kek's recovery is more important than my comfort." She stood, letting Nieves take the stool. There really wasn't much she needed to take — she was only leaving the cabin for the night, after all. She filled a small satchel with her hygienic needs and picked up Venitha's book from the writing desk. Beneath it was Asier's journal. The innocuous, little, black book stared up at her accusatorially. How many times had she thumbed through it, only to curse Asier, the woman who had become the older sister she had never had?

She picked up the journal. Maybe she could find something in Asier's words to help her through what was happening. Instead, just looking at the cover brought an echo of the same heartbreak and sorrow and fury, and she dropped it back on the desk.

"Captain?" came a croak. Cassidy turned to see Kek stirring on the bed. He tried to push himself up, only to let out a gurgling yelp.

Cassidy was at his side in a moment. "I'm here, Kek."

His eyes wavered and trembled in their hollowed sockets as he attempted to focus. "Cassidy? Where's the captain?"

Cassidy and Nieves shared an uncomfortable look. Fever delusions might upset him and worsen his condition. "Captain is… busy," she said. "I'm here, though, so what do you need?"

Kek's eyes wandered the ceiling for a minute before closing. He jerked back awake with a croaking gasp. "Cassidy?"

"Yes, Kek?"

"Can you tell the captain…" He trailed off.

"What do you need me to tell her, Kek?" Cassidy asked. When he didn't respond right away, she grabbed his hand to try and get his attention.

"Cassidy? Can you tell the captain… I'm sorry about the fire?"

Cassidy blinked. "The fire?"

"I didn't know it would be that greasy," he mumbled.

Cassidy furrowed her brow, until she remembered what he was talking about. That had been almost ten years ago, and no one was hurt. She stifled a laugh, which provoked Nieves to do the same.

"It's okay, Kek," she said. "No one's mad at you for that. But I'll tell her all the same, okay? Now get some sleep." She leaned in and gave him a peck on the cheek.

"Stop," he whined sleepily. His head settled back on his pillow, and he mumbled, "You're not my mother," before going still again.

He was so still, in face, fear choked Cassidy until Nieves checked his pulse and said, "He's okay. I'll keep an eye on him."

Cassidy nodded, gathered her things again, and left the cabin.

"This one depicts the World Tree," Hymn said, peering down at Venitha's book from Cassidy's shoulder. She had taken it to the aftcastle to have Hymn read the ancient text while she transcribed it into Asaria's familiar, exacting script. "More specifically, the old one."

"The one that got cut down and made the dragons sick?" Cassidy asked, examining the image. Unlike the stark white tree cut into the horizon like a branching scar, the bark in the picture was colored gold, with blue veins running down its length. The leaves were an artistically rendered night sky broken apart by the negative space between the branches.

"That is a gross oversimplification," said Hymn, "but yes, Prince Hassan was not mistaken. The partial destruction of the World Tree made the dragons sick and stripped power from your kind, among other things.

"The text reads 'The Tree only appears to those deemed worthy by Faeorn'," said Hymn, and Cassidy moved her pen gently above the strange characters, wary of breaking the aged vellum. "This was not true, strictly speaking. The tree can actually be found by anyone who has touched the Dreamscape. Faeorn was its guardian, however, so most mortals would only find the World Tree with her blessing."

"And what does a World Tree *do*, exactly?" Cassidy asked. "I doubt it was planted to give us something to look at," she added, looking to the southeast, where the current tree was woven into the horizon. "And how was it hidden? That one should be hidden behind the curve of the world at this distance, but it's right there."

"The World Tree *shapes* the world," said Hymn. "It nurtures the world with life, its roots hold the world together. It determines how *dreams* take form. Without it, there would be only death on a barren rock devoid of song."

"We've gotten along this far without one," Cassidy argued, looking at the white branches sprawling through the sky like veins.

"No, you haven't," said Hymn. "Your forebears wounded the old Tree, but its roots still serve their purpose, if only just. This new one, however... it is a mystery."

"It's certainly weird," said Cassidy.

"It is beyond *weird*. I wish to know why it was planted, and what will happen as a result. I suspect both questions have the same answer."

A heavy footfall and the whine of old, wooden steps halted the conversation. Cassidy closed the old book and stood to face Haytham as he climbed the stairs to meet her. He was unarmed, which was a good first step.

"Captain Durant," he said, though his eyes quickly slid off her eyes to the Fae sitting on her shoulder.

"Is there a problem, Haytham?"

The young man frowned. "Aye, there's a problem. There's a big problem. You consort with *djinn*. By rights, everyone on this ship should be put to death for that."

"You realize everyone on this ship includes you and your sister, right?"

Haytham looked behind him, and seeing that Miria's back was to them, he pulled a single iron coin from his purse. He held it out and rolled it in his fingers for Cassidy to see. It was an oval, rather than the circular make of Imperial currency, marking it as a Rivien crown. He tossed the coin skyward, and as it spun in the air, it suddenly caught fire. He caught the flaming coin in a gloved fist — which also ignited — and tossed it overboard. He patted his burning glove out and offered Cassidy a humorless smile.

"Aye. I realize that exactly."

Cassidy's eyes widened. Aside from herself, the only person she knew who that could do was the late Captain Flint. "You have a Fae companion, too?"

Haytham shook his head. "No. But I made a trade with one, once. Same offense in the eyes of the law, really."

"So what's your story?" asked Cassidy.

421

He leaned against the gunwale and crossed his arms. "About a year back, we were on a job," he explained. "Pirates had been operating in the west. We hunted them for weeks, sinking ships, taking captives. Killing." A look of discomfort passed over his face, and Cassidy couldn't tell if it was at the act itself or admitting to it that bothered him. "Eventually, only the ringleaders remained. We crippled their ship, but they took skiffs and went to ground. Me, Hanaa, and five others chased them into a cave that turned out to be a natural labyrinth.

"We gave chase, and we fought, and we gave chase again. Along the way, an explosive trap killed the others and separated me from Hanaa when a tunnel collapsed. I was wounded." He rubbed his arm as if he could still feel the pain. "I wandered in pitch darkness for what felt like days, bleeding, limping, feeling my way through. And I was starving. I thought I was having a dying dream when I came across an underground spring, with banks of soft grass and water that glowed from within. There was even an island with a tree in the middle of it.

"I saw her there, on the island. She seemed to me a woman of unmatched beauty," Haytham explained. "Red hair, not like yours, but like a cherry, and long enough to settle at her feet. She wore a skirt that at various points brought to mind jade or emeralds or meadows of silk grass or the sea, and —" He blushed, suddenly. He cleared his throat. "Anyway, she helped me escape, and I discovered I had strange abilities."

"Oh, no," Cassidy said, "you don't get to just skip the story like that. What was at the end of that 'and'?"

Haytham's blush deepened, and he coughed. "Well… she wore that green skirt, but, um… well, nothing else."

"Oh, ho," Cassidy teased. "Is *that* what made her a beauty?"

"It, uh, certainly didn't hurt," Haytham confessed quietly.

"So, you find this half naked Fae woman in an impossible spring inside a cave. What happened next?"

"She swam over to meet me, and it wasn't until she stepped on the shore before me that I saw her eyes and understood her nature."

"None of the other details gave that away?" Cassidy pressed. "Not even the fact that she was there at all?"

"I'm sorry if dealing with the *djinn* is old hat to you," Haytham said wryly, using the Rivien term for the Fae, rather than the name shared by Asaria and Castilyn, "but most of the *djinn* I'd ever seen before that was wisps. Besides, I was injured and likely delirious. Point is, I recognized her for what she was, and I thought for sure she would kill me.

"Instead, she offered to heal my wounds, in exchange for two drops of my blood. One she drank, and one she cast to the water. And my skin knitted up, and my leg was good as new. Then she offered to let me eat the fruit from the tree to stave off my hunger, in exchange for a story. That was difficult, but eventually I satisfied her by telling her about how Hanaa and I hunted a sphinx and ended up forming a rivalry with some Imperials hunting the same prey.

"After that, she asked if I would stay." Haytham let out a long sigh and leaned against the gunwale. "I knew no good could come of it. The *djinn* are evil, after all. *Everyone* knows that. But she seemed so kind and so sweet, and I was so comfortable and content that I was tempted. I was this close —" He held his thumb and forefingers as close together as he could without touching, "— to giving up everything and living whatever remained of my life in that hidden spring."

"Well, here you are," Cassidy noted. "What changed your mind?"

"As I was thinking about all I was leaving behind, I remembered Hanaa, still out there in the caves somewhere, and that got me thinking about all the adventures we'd been on. I couldn't give that up. So I told her as much, and that I had obligations to meet.

"She said she would let me go, but 'freedom is not free'." If he had been embarrassed before, he was completely flustered now. "In exchange for safe passage out of the cavern…" He cleared his throat several times. "She demanded a promise to return before I die, and… my seed."

Cassidy blinked. "Excuse me? Did I hear that right?"

"Probably," said Haytham. "I laid with her on that bank. And she took me in the water. And under the shade of that strange tree. If she had killed me then, it would have been worth it. I don't know how long I slept afterwards, but when I awoke, she was gone, and the path to the outside was clear.

"Turns out, while I was dallying with Heqanat — that was her name, by the way — Hanaa had already tracked down the last of the pirates and killed them. So, we returned to our ship, and I was ready to put the whole mess behind me. But over the coming weeks, I started noticing strange sensations. If I thought about it, I could feel a pull around iron, like a lodestone, and if I focus on that, the iron catches fire. When I fought, I would push myself harder than I thought possible. I can numb myself to pain." He turned to face her again. "I get nose bleeds a lot."

"You're just like me," Cassidy said breathlessly.

"Well, Heqanat isn't lying in wait in my pockets," said Haytham, "so not *exactly* the same."

She slapped him in the gut — which was hard and unyielding — and offered him a reproachful look. "You know what I mean."

"I do," he agreed. He sighed. "Hanaa is not happy. She wasn't pleased to learn about me, and she barely knows you. The fact that the *djinn* that touched you is still present upsets her, all the more."

"Hey, she's never touched me *that* way," Cassidy protested.

"I never said she — what is *that?*" Haytham exclaimed, pointing a finger aft and skyward. Cassidy followed his attention and saw purple clouds rolling towards them in the sky.

"A storm?" Cassidy suggested, though she was dubious. There was a glow that cast the desert in a gloomy light. Whatever it was, it was directly over them in moments.

"Those are no natural clouds," Hymn said. "You are under attack!"

A resonant *boom* sent a visible wave through the fog, and a bright purple comet sped from the sky. It punched through the *Sunrise's* balloon and burst through her deck. The ship spiraled groundward in a rush of smoke and flame. Cassidy could hear the screams even over the roar of engines and wind. An explosion sent the wreckage spinning in two directions. The bow of the ship smashed and broke apart against a windswept rock tower while the aft was dashed across the sand.

Cassidy stared down in open-mouthed horror. *No one could survive that,* she thought, but she knew even if someone *had,* they would soon be killed by whatever lived on the desert floor.

Something struck the *Dreamscape's* hull hard enough to knock Cassidy into the gunwale and a rush of panic overcame her as she imagined falling like the *Sunrise* had. Instead, a thick, black chain had punched into the hull, connecting it to whatever lurked in the clouds above. Soon, the shackles went taut, and the *Dreamscape Voyager* groaned as it tried to push forward but was held back.

"Captain!" Cassidy heard Lierre cry over the pipeline, "There's a spring-loaded hook keeping the chain latched to the hull!"

Port and starboard, the *Temptation* and the *Roc Spear* were similarly impaired.

"Full reverse," Cassidy shouted to Miria. The princess threw the telegraph, and after a moment's stillness, the *Dreamscape Voyager* began to fly the way it had come. Soon they reached the limit again, and when the ship squealed as the stress threatened to burst. "Full ahead!"

Even as Cassidy gave the order, the chains began to pull the ship skyward, and each push of the engines threatened to tear the hull apart.

"Full stop!" she ordered finally. When the engines cut, the *Dreamscape* was towed towards the assaulting ship. She stared up at the cloud that wasn't a cloud as they were drawn inexorably closer. She suspected what she would find up there. She had set out to find it, in a sense, but she hadn't expected it to be like this. "Tell the others to stay alert," she ordered, and Miria relayed the order over the pipeline.

Above, the mist billowed as seven ships breached and descended. As they converged, Cassidy got a clear view of the heavy cannons fixed on the *Dreamscape Voyager*, the *Roc Spear*, and the *Temptation*. Cold fear wrapped itself around her heart and threatened to smother her.

An eighth ship joined the small armada, and the strange miasma was pouring from her like a dozen smokestacks. An enormous, billowing cloth draped from her gunwale like a cloak, obscuring any identifying features, except for her silver keel — not silver *painted*, like the *Temptation* had been, but made of gleaming metal.

The *Dreamscape* was pulled closer to a red ship called the *Left Hand of the Sun* — or, at least, that's what Cassidy *thought* its name was; she had never been an expert in reading Rivien's flowing script — which reeled her in with a deliberate slowness that gave Cassidy's anxiety and dread time to percolate.

"What do we do, Hymn?" Cassidy asked.

"They want you alive," said Hymn. "Otherwise they could have blown us away as they did the *Sunrise*. Do not give them a reason to change their minds."

That wasn't comforting.

Nine skiffs approached from the cloaked ship, and even they had guns mounted on their prows. Three of the skiffs descended to approach from the lower deck. A dozen women in opaque veils boarded the *Dreamscape* with weapons drawn. With swift and silent coordination, they swept the deck for hidden threats. Four of the intruders surrounded Cassidy and Haytham while two more secured Miria. The cold chill of iron against the back of her neck sent a chill down her spine.

The three of them were pointed to a skiff and forced to move. Someone kicked in the doors to the galley and Cassidy's cabin, and after a moment, two of the boarders walked out, with Nieves and Kek slung over their respective shoulders. Nieves was thrashing and kicking and ineffectually hitting the much larger woman. Kek didn't even seem to be conscious, despite being dragged outside in nothing but his small clothes.

"Kek!" Miria cried.

"Leave him alone!" Cassidy demanded. "Can't you see he's injured?" The pistol pressed to the back of her head pushed her forward and she gritted her teeth.

A gunshot rang out from the lower deck.

Nieves stopped squirming and Cassidy shared a terrified look with Miria. No one said a word. The captors tossed Nieves into the skiff, rocking it and nearly pitching Cassidy over the side. They dropped Kek in her lap, hitting his head. He groaned awake.

"Agh, fucking shit," he managed. He broke into a violent shiver and huddled in on himself. Nieves held him close, rubbing his clammy skin for warmth. Cassidy slipped out of her coat, ignoring the pistol pressing a warning into her head and draped it over him. He turned and puked on the shoes of one of their captives, who looked ready to kick him when another woman put a hand on her shoulder and shook her head sternly.

To the starboard side, another skiff rose to meet them, with Lierre and Hanaa shackled together. The older Ramajin sported a blackening eye, and one of the captors appeared to be applying a makeshift tourniquet to her arm.

With the captives secure, the skiffs carried them to the silver ship. Cassidy watched skiffs speeding along with Jathun and the survivors from the *Sunrise* — the only survivors, Cassidy realized. The thought made her feel numb with the scope of it — and another with Captain Zhu and three others. Cassidy supposed his crew was too big for the pirates to abduct everyone, so they must have opted to take a few hostages and lock down the ship with the threat of superior fire.

Though it all made Cassidy wonder *why* they were going to all the trouble. If they wanted to rob them with minimal bloodshed, sinking the Sunrise was a waste, and they could just as easily threaten them with their superior firepower, and demand they hand over their valuables.

This was something else.

When they reached the pirate's vessel, Cassidy found its deck was the glowing red of dawn wood inlaid with silver filigrees. Two cannons fashioned from orichalcum were perched on the deck on swiveling mounts. A party of ten men and women stood amidships, waiting for their arrival. As soon as their skiff reached the mysterious ship, Cassidy was shoved onto the deck of the larger vessel. It thrummed and vibrated beneath her, and there was a steady *tick-tock* loud enough she *felt* it, more than she heard it.

Miria followed shortly after, and Haytham was thrown aboard. Nieves was allowed to stay on the skiff with Kek, likely because no one wanted to lift him again or risk him throwing up on the elaborate deck. Jathun and Lierre were granted the dignity of stepping aboard the ship, while Hanaa was thrown, and Captain Zhu was kicked in the back of the knee and dropped.

One of the pirates broke apart from the gathering and examined them with a critical gaze. She had the olive skin and almond shaped eyes that hinted at being a noble-blooded Imperial. Her raven hair was done up in a style that seemed deliberately messy, as though she had gone to the effort of having it arranged in a neat bun only to shake it half loose. Unlike her compatriots who wore silk veils, elaborately adorned turbans, ringers, and other finery, this woman's only accessory was a polished necklace of jet. Otherwise, she wore a plain black sleeveless tunic, leather trousers so tight Cassidy thought she must have been sewn into them, and a pair of thigh high boots with tall heels and knives sheathed along her calves.

Vincent E. M. Thorn

"Well, well," she said. Her voice was husky, and there was a cruel yet subdued mirth in her tone. "I was expecting diplomats but imagine my surprise to find the *Jade Phoenix* and the *Temptation.* This is an auspicious day, truly." She looked from Cassidy to Haytham, then from Haytham to Hanaa, then Lierre and Miria.

Cassidy considered the ticking beneath her, and the ambush, and decided to take a shot. "This is the *Clockwork Hydra,* isn't it?"

"Ooh, got it in one," the woman said with a mischievous grin. "Not just a pretty face, are you?"

"Where's Captain Yaoru?" Cassidy asked.

"You're looking at her," the woman said. Cassidy's confusion must have shown on her face because she gave her a patronizing smile. She leaned in close enough for Cassidy to see her eyes clearly even in the hazy light. She should have seen it sooner; she had seen those eyes every day for two years and would recognize their set and brilliant blue coloring anywhere. "You're probably thinking about my father, Kiyen. He's dead. My name is Yaoru Suzume, and I'm the captain here. Just like how *you...* " She tapped Cassidy on the nose. "... Are the captain of the *Jade Phoenix* now that that bitch Asier's dead." Cassidy scowled. "Yes, your reputation precedes you. Oh, but you call her the *Dreamscape Voyager,* don't you?"

Cassidy swallowed. "I guess that's the introductions," she said, trying to keep the hitch out of her voice. "But why are we here?"

"Oh, I am *so* glad you asked," said Yaoru. She stood and began pacing the deck. Cassidy noticed her steps were in perfect sequence with the clockwork ticking of the ship beneath her feet. "See, about twenty years ago, give or take — after the war was won — Elyia Asier tracked my father down. She raved that he had committed treason, that he had betrayed *her.* Then you know what she did, Red?

"She took a knife, like this one," she continued, drawing a knife the length of her forearm from the small of her back. Its blade had the shifting, iridescent quality of dragon bone. "She disfigured him! She *mutilated* him! She killed his crew when they sought to protect him and went at him like an amateur butcher!" Yaoru's crew jeered and hollered in agreement.

"She would never —" Miria began, but Yaoru was on her in a flash. She grasped the younger girl by the throat and dragged her to her feet.

"*I was there!*" she bellowed in Miria's face, and when the silence fell, she pointed with the dagger, to a stowage hole beneath the steps of the aftcastle. "I was *right there*. Can you imagine that, princess?" Miria's eyes widened in shock, and Cassidy felt it too; how much did Yaoru know. "Imagine being a little girl half your age and watching as the only family you've ever known slaughtered like an animal by his best friend!" She tightened her grip on Miria's throat while the knife trembled in the other hand.

"Let her go!" Cassidy demanded, but as soon as she found her feet, someone kicked behind her knee to knock her back down and twisted her arm.

"Do not struggle," Hymn whispered, so softly Cassidy was sure no one else could hear her over the incessant clockwork. "I will see you safely through this if you are patient." Cassidy sneered. She didn't care about her own safety. But if Hymn wasn't going to help Miria, Cassidy couldn't help her by getting herself killed. So she stood, paralyzed by her own impotence.

"I wanted nothing more than to make Asier pay in kind!" Yaoru said, easing the knife to Miria's throat. "But she went and got herself killed by some cultist lacky with poor dress sense. So I'll have to settle for crushing her legacy."

"You can't!" Cassidy shouted, struggling against the armlock.

"Oh?" asked Yaoru, pulling the knife away and brushing the edge around the princess' face. Cassidy couldn't read the pirate's expression, and thus couldn't tell if she was hesitating or relishing the moment. "The Empress will never find out."

"But she's your sister!" Cassidy blurted out.

Yaoru and Miria both turned to look at Cassidy, and the expression of bewilderment on their faces were identical. They weren't the only ones staring at her, either. Captain Zhu looked affronted, as if by making the declaration, Cassidy had slapped the Empress in the face. Yaoru's crew had quit their jeering and some stared dumbfounded at Cassidy while a few made doubletakes between their captain and the princess. Even Cassidy's own crew — save a barely conscious Kek, whose head lolled from side to side — looked dumbfounded.

"What?" Yaoru asked flatly. Her blade wandered absently away from Miria's face, but she kept her grip on the princess all the same.

429

"Look in her eyes if you don't believe me!" Cassidy pleaded. "It'll be like looking in the mirror."

And like a mirror, the two women turned away from Cassidy and stared into each other's eyes. The moment hung in the air like gently falling snow. Yaoru's eyes slowly widened with recognition. Miria's face was impassive. Cassidy's heart began hammering in her chest as her anxiety mounted.

Yaoru lowered her blade and pushed Miria to arm's length. The princess coughed and rubbed at her throat.

"It would be wrong to kill my own sister to avenge our father," she decided. Cassidy did her best not to let her relief show as she slowly let out a breath. Yaoru stood over Cassidy, knife poised, before she even saw her moving. "But I have no compunctions about killing you!"

A flash of brilliant light obscured Cassidy's vision. The pirate holding her arm released it to the telltale sound of a broken neck. Hymn stood in her true form, with Cassidy's hat resting on her head and Yaoru's blade pressed between her palms, mere inches from Cassidy's face.

Horror played across Yaoru's face as she stared up at Hymn's. In a cerulean blur of motion, Hymn released the knife between her hands and struck the pirate in the throat with the ends of her fingers. Yaoru staggered, her blade clattering on the deck as she clutched her throat. The pirates tripped over one another as some moved to their captain's defense and others tried to retreat from the Fae that had manifested before them without warning.

All motion stopped when Hymn held one hand up with her middle and third fingers curled inward, and the gentle glow of the dawnwood became a glare that burned as nearly as bright as the sun. The thrumming and ticking of the *Clockwork Hydra* intensified and the ship seemed to rattle beneath their feet.

"If you or your allies bring any harm to my friend or hers," Hymn said in the same menacing tone she had issued against Kalliope, "I will kill every last one of you." She swept her gaze across all the pirates before leveling her eyes on Yaoru. "It would be easy. Like killing children lost in the woods." She snapped the fingers of her other hand, and the deck-mounted cannons swiveled inward, with one aimed directly at the pirate captain and the other at the large gathering of crew. Weapons clattered on the deck all at once. Hymn lowered her hands and the light of the wood softened, becoming barely perceptible after the incandescent flare. "Do we have an understanding?" the Fae asked.

Yaoru opened her mouth to speak, but all that came out was a violent cough. She hacked forcefully for several minutes until a bloody pulp shot from her mouth and splattered on the deck before her. She wiped her mouth on her arm. "We do," she managed.

"Good. Then I offer you a *deal*," she said, and the gravity around that word was enough to deepen the fear in Yaoru's expression. The *Hydra's* crew and the pirates from the other vessels trembled. Captain Zhu stared at Cassidy with undisguised disgust.

Someone slid a sword across the deck to Yaoru.

Cassidy whirled around, stole the sword from her fallen captor's belt, and drew it.

Drawing on the Fae power, she ignited the iron blade and intercepted Yaoru as she struck out against Hymn. Both weapons blazed, spitting fire all around as they clashed. Cassidy's eyes widened in surprise while the pirate's icy blues narrowed in practiced calm. Blood trickled from Yaoru's nose even as Cassidy felt the same happening to her.

Yaoru looked past the fiery cross of swords, past Cassidy, to Hymn.

She stepped away from Cassidy, and with an angry swipe at empty air, the fire on the pirate's weapon was extinguished. "What's your offer?" she demanded in a tone heavy with resignation.

"Elyia Asier has been dead for over a year," said Hymn. "Direct your anger against a more meaningful target. A monster called a leviathan threatens the very world in which you live. Given time, it will consume *everything* you know. Nothing will survive if it is not first killed. Forsake this empty revenge against a woman already passed and commit yourself and those under your command to the cause of ridding this world of the threat of the leviathan, at the side of Captain Durant and her allies," Hymn said, "and I will free you of the oaths another of my kind has placed upon you."

Gasps echoed across the pirates, though Cassidy wasn't sure which part of the offer shocked them most. Yaoru clutched her jet necklace and she seemed on the brink of tears.

"What is your name, *O' Fair One*?" she asked.

Hymn smiled and swept her arm out in a magnanimous gesture. "My friends call me Hymn."

431

Yaoru crouched down and re-sheathed her borrowed sword. When she stood again, she stepped forward, ignoring Cassidy's still flaming blade and proffered a hand. "Very well, *Hymn*. You have a deal."

CHAPTER FORTY

The night air was frigid with the promise of a blizzard to come. Zayne never thought to return to Dawnhal, and to see her streets covered in ice and snow that reflected the moonlight like silver plates — as they had been when he had been forced to flee — was too much. He wanted nothing more than to burn the city to the ground. Oh, how the gods must laugh to see him follow the course they set him on.

The World Tree wasn't *in* Dawnhal, of course, but it was astonishingly close. Unfortunately, they needed supplies — Zayne had been sure the crew would have mutinied if they had sought to travel through the Dreamscape again, and thus they had sailed for weeks across the length of Castilyn, and another three days skirting around the Empire's border patrols — and were forced to stop. With the Daughters of Daen being outlawed in the Empire, the *Scorpion* was hidden in the woods beneath the city's mountain perch. Zayne, Nanette, and Xun stole into the city in the dead of night with the skiff.

Xun came up to him, dressed in an oversized fur coat that made her look enormous. She pulled a stolen rickshaw behind her. "Do we really need to go out in this cold?" she asked. Zayne couldn't tell if the tremor in her voice was an affectation or not.

"It's only going to get colder," said Zayne, though he wasn't much happier about it than she was. If anything, he almost envied her for wearing a coat large enough to sleep in. Like Nanette, he wore the same black coat he always wore, and though it was serviceable, and the scarf partially concealing his face was warm, the iron mask burned with an icy chill, even through the gauze he wrapped beneath it to prevent frostbite from taking his face. "We get what we need now, while we can still get out of the city. Otherwise, we could be stuck for weeks. And I shouldn't have to tell you why that's a problem."

As Zayne walked the same streets he had fled all those years ago, he couldn't help but think the city was smaller than it was in his memories. The walkways seemed narrower, the storefronts shorter.

Had the paint on all these buildings always been untended and flaking away, or was that a new development? On the harbor side, the eatery where he had first met Salaa had been torn down, and in front of the haphazard collection of bricks and broken boards that occupied the lot was a battered and aged sign that read *Toki's Noodle Shop - Open Soon.*

"The storehouse we're hitting is number three," Zayne said, after looking down the dockside road to assure himself it was still there. "The coal crates should be on the ground floor, in marked boxes."

"You know your way around this slum," Xun said between chattering teeth.

"I used to work here," he answered absently.

"Ooh, I like a man with a past," Xun said, though her attempts at flirting was undercut by the freezing tremor in her voice.

Zayne's retort was cut short by a tuneless whistle from around the corner. He ushered Xun and Nanette into the shadow of a narrow alley. Moments later, a watchman strolled into the street, twirling a small club in his hand. Zayne's breath caught as he recognized the red-haired man immediately. He had a few days stubble, and a blackened eye, and the passing of years had been unkind to him. As Tam obliviously passed them by, Zayne felt an old rage kindle in the cold pit of his stomach.

The last time he had seen Tam, the two-faced bastard had walked him to the gallows square to await execution. Tam had chosen to believe Zayne's father over Zayne himself about the Caraden family murders.

Zayne's hands trembled around a pistol as he suppressed the all-too-vivid memory of his little brother Cenn, his sister Nanette, his mother... he felt like he had never left the hangman's block, his family's blood literally on his hands while on his father's in deed. Zayne had done everything for them, and Tam, his so-called friend, had not even questioned the verdict. He should kill the guardsman where he stood.

Maybe drag him back to the Scorpion *and hang him,* a voice teased in the back of his mind. Yes, that would do nicely. Kill him, kill the bloodthirsty city that had condemned him after the most farcical trial, kill the —

Nanette's hand squeezed his arm, and he returned to the moment. He was standing in the street, his pistol trained on the retreating back of the still unaware and guardsman. His breath came heavy and fearful. The gentle click as he reset the hammer of his pistol contrasted sharply with the pounding of his heart.

How had he let himself take so many steps unawares?

"Come on, Zayne," Nanette whispered. "He isn't worth it. Let's get what we came for and go."

She was right, of course. Yet still Zayne trembled with fury. Now, however, the focus of that hate was spreading around, and he portioned a fair amount of it for himself. How close he had been to throwing everything away? Over Tam? Of all the shadows in Zayne's past, Tam was a mouse stacked against dragons.

"Do I need to come with you?" Nanette asked.

Zayne considered for a moment. He wasn't sure Xun could reach him if Lucandri influenced him at a critical moment. He wasn't even sure she would recognize the signs. Still, they had a job, and Nanette was the best woman for it. "We'll stick to the plan. You get the food and the weapons. Xun and I will hit the warehouse."

When Tam disappeared around at a distant street corner, Zayne and Xun broke off and approached the warehouse. The door was shut with a heavy padlock, but Dawn Star cut through the iron block like hot tallow. It hit the cobbles with a muted *plunk* and the crunch of snow.

The door slid open with the booming rumble of wheels that had been abused out of shape and left untended. He hoped Tam — and anyone else — was too far to make it out. The warehouse was as Zayne remembered, stark and wide, with piles of crates full of the basic necessities that kept a ship in the air, which the local port authority sold as a service for people who preferred expedience to reasonable prices. Zayne had worked and earned his coin unloading trade goods and loading overpriced engine parts, or sheets of leather to patch up balloons, or coal. It was the coal they were after tonight, but other things couldn't hurt.

Xun tugged and fought with the rickshaw to get it over the lip of the entrance. Once she cleared it, Zayne closed the door and directed her to the coal stacks.

"So, this is where you're from?" Xun asked as he lifted a crate and moved it to the rickshaw. He grunted in the affirmative. "I heard everyone in Dawnhal had red hair," she mused before taking a box and following his example. "Do you dye it? Was it red before the…" She set her load down and pointed at her own face.

"No, and no," Zayne said. "My hair was always black."

"And the silver's because of…?" she let the question hang.

Zayne considered ignoring her. He started to, but after loading three more crates, he sighed. "Probably. Timing seems right, and it seems *he* has silver hair. *Had?* Whichever."

"I asked Nanette about what happened," Xun confessed.

Zayne rolled his eyes. "And what did she say," he asked, humoring her.

"She said to ask you. So, what happened?"

"One terrible decision after another," he said glibly.

"*Fine,*" Xun whined. "We don't have to talk about the extremely dangerous abomination sharing your skin. What about Nanette?"

"What *about* Nanette?" He asked sharply.

"Oh, you know!" she said, nudging him in the ribs. "Are you two sweet on each other?"

"No," Zayne said firmly.

"Oh?" Xun leaned in and whispered conspiratorially. "But you're always so close!"

"She's my best friend," he said. "Maybe the only friend I have left."

"*So…*" Xun said, stretching the word out, which to Zayne's estimate, failed to have the effect intended because her voice trembled with cold. "You're saying there's an opening?"

Zayne decided the conversation might end sooner if he simply feigned obliviousness. He cocked an eyebrow. "To be my friend?" he asked.

"Uh, well," Xun stammered, "I guess I could… I mean, that wouldn't be so bad, would it?"

They lapsed into an uncomfortable silence and resumed working. After a while, her not-so-surreptitious glances started to bother him.

"What about Tagren?" he asked before he could change his mind.

"*Tagren?*" she seemed completely taken aback by the change of subject.

"You took his death pretty hard," he said. "Did you know him long?"

Her face fell and she nodded, more to the floor than to Zayne. "I met him… gods, it must have been fifteen years ago. I don't even remember what I was doing, but I passed this alley. I heard this whine, and I looked to find these four boys kicking the shit out of this poor boy — honestly, I thought it was a dog, he sounded so pathetic.

"Those boys couldn't put up a fight against a grown woman. I sent them limping off, and that's when I saw him. I didn't think much of him. He was just some scrawny kid who couldn't speak. I gave him some coin — figured he must have been mugged — and went on my way.

"He followed me after that. Wouldn't *stop* following me. That made me mad. I shouted at him to go away, but he was like a wounded pet, so I finally gave in, and he'd followed me ever since. Turns out he was good at sneaking around. There was one time on our last ship," she added with a sad smile, "he snuck into the galley with these insanely hot peppers. He covered *everything* with them! I couldn't feel my tongue for a week." Tears tumbled down Xun's cheeks and she sniffed. "The smile on his face when he fessed up…. Gods, I miss him."

Zayne put a hand on Xun's shoulder, and she threw her arms around him. She sobbed into his chest, and her tears quickly soaked through his shirt. The contradictory desires to shove her away and to openly share in her sorrow churned within him and left him with a pitched anxiety. Rather than give in to either impulse, he patted her on the head with stiff hands.

After a few shuddering heaves, she pulled away from him and dabbed at her eyes. "Sorry," she said.

"It's fine," Zayne replied, turning back to the task at hand. "You lost a friend. I get it. See if you can move it," he said to bring them back on track.

Xun wiped her face and braced herself to pull the rickshaw. Her muscles clearly strained as the cart's wheels began their slow turn, but once it started to move, she easily led it across the warehouse floor. "We can get more," she said, circling it back to the pile.

"We need to consider the skiff," said Zayne. He found a tool bag someone left lying around and tossed it into the rickshaw instead. "I'm going to make sure the coast is clear. Be ready to move."

He opened the door slowly to keep the squealing and rattling to a minimum. Crunching snow to his right drew his attention. He turned to the source and found Tam walking back up the street. With rapid steps, he approached his erstwhile friend with his head down and his coat wrapped tight around his chest. Zayne shoulder checked the watchman and made a show of stumbling back.

"Ah!" Tam exclaimed. "I am so sorry, stranger."

"Not at all," Zayne rasped. He glared at Tam from over his scarf and through the slit of his mask, hate and disappointment playing off one another in his heart. "It's a cold night. A man doesn't look too carefully at what's in front of him."

Tam tossed his head back and gave a full bellied laugh. And his belly certainly *had* filled over the years, too. "Too true, my good man. Still, at this hour, you might be better off staying indoors. I think we're due for a storm. If you can't get home, there's a good tavern —" A metallic boom cut him off. Zayne turned to find Xun, rickshaw in tow and partially obstructed by the door. Her eyes were wide as they passed from Zayne to Tam and back.

A bright light flashed between the old friends. Dawn Star formed in the same space as Tam's sternum and spine. Blood dribbled from his mouth and pooled on his uniform. He fell limp in Zayne's arms, and the sword vanished. Sickness roiled in Zayne's guts as the blood stained his hands. He retched down the dead man's back.

"I'm sorry!" Xun whined. "I thought the door was opened wide enough."

Zayne spat to clear his mouth. "It's fine. Get moving, I need to get rid of him." Xun moved to obey, dragging the rickshaw up the street the way they had come. That left him alone on the docks with the body. Despite Tam's added girth, he wasn't too heavy to Zayne's Fae-enhanced strength. "I don't know if I'm sorry or not," he confessed to the corpse. "I'm definitely not satisfied. You didn't even recognize me. And all I'm left with is a hollow pit closure will never fill. Have these years been worth it, you think?"

Tam said nothing, of course.

"What kind of man had you become?" Zayne asked as he carried the body across the harbor, suppressing another bout of sickness. He gagged several times, but he had nothing left in him to choke out. "Did you lay awake from the guilt? Did you even consider you might be responsible?"

He carried the body to the very edge of the wharf. Below him, clouds churned in a dreary fog. It would probably be weeks before any excursions were made to the surface. By the time anyone found Tam's body, it would probably be unrecognizable, even if it weren't completely mangled by the drop. Zayne thought he deserved better than that, despite everything.

But people rarely got what they deserved when Zayne was involved.

He tossed the body into the dark clouds below. Aside from the flapping of his uniform, it passed silently through the mist. Even that sound faded in moments, and there would be no crunch or crash heard from the city when it finally dashed across the slopes. He shuddered and turned away. The blood was hot even as it dried on his fingers. He knelt to gather a handful of brittle snow and crumbled it in his hands, melting it to wash them clean. When he was satisfied he had done all he could, he slipped away to rendezvous with Nanette and Xun.

He found them waiting by the edge of the city, behind an abandoned apothecary, waiting for him to give the signal. He knelt beside them and stared out into the same tumultuous void he had consigned Tam's body to moments ago. He summoned Dawn Star in a flash of golden light before letting it dissolve into sparks. He repeated the process four times before he saw the skiff climb silently to meet them.

Shen guided the skiff into position and helped load it with the stolen goods. Once the coal was aboard, Nanette set three bags of food — mostly canned, but Zayne spotted fresh vegetables and meat wrapped in wax paper in the mix — on top of the pile. Boarding the skiff itself turned out to be more of a challenge with the space taken up by crates and bags. Nanette stood, holding onto the rigging for support while Xun chose to sit on Zayne's lap, to his annoyance.

Shen let the skiff drop below the clouds again, which left everyone blind and even colder before they broke through along with the falling snow, which whipped sharply around them in the wind. The *Scorpion* floated serenely in the shadow of Mount Dawnhal. Aresh and Pyrrha both stood on the deck — Aresh to keep watch as ordered, Pyrrha because she hadn't been explicitly ordered *not* to stand there, Zayne supposed. Shen took them to the keel, where the bottom hatch was still wide open.

439

When the skiff returned to its proper place, the hatch closed seemingly of its own accord. Zayne still wasn't entirely sure how much control Lucandri's link gave him over the *Scorpion*, or even how one was connected to the other, but it was a useful trick when it worked. The hold was every bit as cold as the outside, but at least the wind couldn't cut at them.

"Xun, you and Shen unload our cargo. Nanette, get the engines hot. We can't waste any more time. We will reach the World Tree *tonight*."

The *Scorpion* touched down on the snow in a clearing just large enough to accommodate her. The forest floor was crawling with a swirling mist that seemed to be flowing deeper into the woods. Zayne readied a lantern and confronted Pyrrha. "Well? Let's find this tree and be done with it."

"My oaths prevent me from accompanying you to the World Tree," Pyrrha said. "However, if you follow the mist, it will lead you straight to it. The guardian should not be able to stop you."

Zayne cocked an eyebrow at that. The mention of a guardian triggered a feeling, a thought just on the edge of memory, but he couldn't grasp it. "Keep an eye on her," he ordered the crew. "I don't trust her. And you," he added, pointing at the Fae, "stay on the deck and touch nothing."

Pyrrha smiled patronizingly and bowed.

Nanette, carrying her own lantern, followed Zayne down the gangway without asking, which didn't surprise him. What did surprise him was Xun running after them as soon as their boots crunched on the snow. Zayne and Nanette both turned to face her.

"Sorry, Captain," she said, "but can I join you? I really don't want to stay with that... thing."

"You know we're probably going to see more of her kind in the forest, right? And that's before we encounter whatever waits at the Tree."

"Maybe, but we're ready to defend ourselves out here." Xun worked a pistol out of her overly padded sleeve to emphasize the point.

Zayne shared a glance at Nanette, who shrugged.

"Fine," he said, and he turned back to set on after the mist.

440

Cast in shadow as they were by the lanterns' glow and shrouded in mist, the trees appeared as twisted specters with cruel visages, and their branches seemed like claws and hands reaching out to drag them into the darkness. The sound of rustling brush just beyond their light reminded Zayne of the day he and Nanette had been inducted into the Daughters of Daen. Something had stalked them in those woods, too.

The fog flowed like water in a steady direction, weaving around obstacles and spreading wide along the path. As they followed, Zayne realized it was flowing uphill. When they stopped, it seemed to slow and shift, as though beckoning them to follow, but it never stopped flowing deeper into the forest.

"This isn't normal mist, is it?" Xun asked after a while.

"No," said Zayne, and as he said it, memories stirred in the back of his mind. "This is *the* Mists, where gods are said to trap souls of their victims. Sure you don't want to wait on the ship?"

"And split up? Not on your life!"

The Mists led them across a frozen stream that cracked with each step. They followed it through stone ruins that may have been a temple or a city. A shadow passed over their light when Nanette raised her lantern to examine a staircase that ended abruptly and led nowhere. They spotted a cornerstone with an ancient-looking broadsword driven straight into it. No one wanted to approach it. Zayne heard whispers carried on the wind. Somber tones answered barely audible giggles, sending shivers down his spine. A woman's trilling laugh sent animals scurrying in the brush and was interrupted by an owl taking flight.

Then all was silent, save for the crunching of snow and twigs and leaves as Zayne and the others pushed on through the dark.

The mist led them to a cave in a rock face. The cavern maw was only a hand's span taller than Zayne, but it was too deep for their light to reach the end.

"The tree is... in a cave?" Xun asked. She leaned forward, as if that would allow her to see into the depths without approaching.

"It's probably a tunnel," said Nanette. Her teeth clicked and chattered together as she spoke. "Hopefully, the tree is just on the other side."

"Aye, hopefully," said Xun. "I'm freezing."

Neither Zayne nor Nanette bothered to point out that Xun was dressed far more warmly than either of them. For his part, Zayne shivered quietly to himself and flexed his toes occasionally to keep the feeling in them.

The air wasn't any warmer inside the tunnel. If anything, the cold pressed more oppressively, and Zayne's own breath obscured his view when he let out a shivering gasp. The way was a straight path, suggesting it had been made deliberately, rather than by random acts of nature. When they could no longer see the exit behind them, the mist ahead rolled upwards over neatly arrayed stairs.

Xun shivered and Zayne wagered it wasn't just the cold this time.

He led them up. As they climbed, he heard a sweet and perfect song ahead in the distance. Behind them, he heard faint sobbing and laughter. The sounds never seemed to grow any closer or more distant, no matter how far they traveled. Around the time his legs began to burn, he became certain that the landmass they had entered hadn't been nearly so tall, and yet they continued to climb.

The stairway didn't veer or turn, and each step was identical to the last. It shouldn't have been possible. Xun checked her watch at some point and declared it had stopped. A quick check revealed Zayne and Nanette's were also no longer ticking, either.

Darkness loomed ahead and behind them, and Zayne felt like there was no end. He had heard stories of people trapped by Fae, condemned to wander in circles or perform some repetitive task until their minds snapped. He considered that might be their fate, but he found hope in the mist. It seemed to flow faster with each step. When it moved like an inverted waterfall, Zayne smelled something.

The scent of frost and water flowed down to greet him.

Zayne resisted the urge to break into a run, but he still picked up his pace. Nanette was quick on his heels while Xun fell behind and sprinted to keep up. A sliver of white light appeared in the distance, widening every few steps until it bloomed into the shape of a tunnel mouth.

Zayne stepped out into a bracing breeze. Frost-deadened grass carpeted the hard ground. The World Tree loomed before him, though it didn't resembled its offspring far to the west and he might not have recognized it if not for the sheer overwhelming sense of awe and dread rolling off it like fog. Where the tree scarring the horizon was rigid and proudly reached skyward, the specimen in front of him seems a haggard thing drooping under its own weight. Its trunk was blackened and cracked, and everything Zayne could see — the Tree's roots formed a wall around the edges of the clearing, and the full scope of it was too large to take in from its shade — was hollow. Its branches sagged, forming a curtain around them with pale leaves stained with the memory of a myriad of colors.

So, hissed a sultry voice in his mind. It made his teeth hum. *She sends you as a final insult.* Zayne looked up to find a silver shape descending slowly from the darkness of the canopy. The triangular head of a snake lowered itself. *I do hope she doesn't expect you to return. Trapped though I am, I cannot suffer insults.*

Lucandri thrashed in his mind, a sensation that was almost physical as Zayne felt the phantoms of anxiety and panic. He felt a numb tightness wash over his body as the Fae spirit scrambled against him for control of his body. His finger twitched and a spasm ran up his arm, but otherwise he felt nothing but a frantic desperation that wasn't his own.

At Zayne's side, Xun fell to her knees and cradled her head, while Nanette dropped her lantern and her knife and shook violently where she stood. The ground scraped beneath the snake's enormous body as it circled the group. Standing at his full height, Zayne could even reach the top of the creature's head as it lowered itself to the dirt. Its white scales glinted in rainbow patterns as it glided into patches of moonlight.

Its eyes were the most striking feature, however. The center of each eye held countless distant lights in as many different colors that coalesced into a spiraling galaxy of stars that seemed brilliantly white in the center, surrounded by the darkest abyss.

A scream sounded in the depths of Zayne's mind, countered by a deep, almost sensuous laughter that seemed to press on his thoughts from the outside. In his terror, Lucandri's memories were scattered across his own like shreds of parchment tossed into a blizzard, but Zayne was able to pick out an important piece of information.

"Faeorn," he rasped as loudly as he could, "we are not here to threaten your charge. We are only here to leave a tribute, to —"

Again, the goddess laughed in his mind, only this time it was a sharp, bitter sound that made the back of his eyes ache. Nanette doubled over beside him and Xun thrashed in agony.

A tribute, the goddess repeated in a mocking tone. *Must we continue to play these games, Lucandri?* She coiled around them, forming a wall of snake flesh that obscured all else. Faeorn's serpentine face peered down from above. Zayne noticed there were black lines across both sides of her face, intersecting her eyes. Only when Zayne saw ruby red blood, speckled with a myriad of other colors, dripping from it onto the grass did Zayne realize it was a wound.

What could wound a god? he wondered.

"I am not Lucandri," he said aloud.

How come you to this ability to speak lies? Is it that human tongue that twisted your nature? She lowered her head, so her enormous, star-filled eyes were level with his face. As that swirling, white abyss stared at him, he knew his only answer could be to stare back.

"I'm not Lucandri," Zayne repeated. "He has tried to possess me, but I kept my own mind."

Faeorn slithered away only to circle the trio again, this time at a wider distance. *Why have you come,* human? her voice resonated through the clearing and in his mind. *The fruits of this Tree have been poisoned, rotted.* Defiled!

The goddess opened her jaws wide enough to swallow Zayne whole with room to spare, revealing three rows of viciously long and devastatingly sharp teeth each as thick as his arms and twice as long. The wet, hissing breath that blasted Zayne like a gale stank of moss and blood. *You will find no immortality here, no great wisdom, no power. You will not even find warmth in the grove, any longer. Why not seek bounty from the newly planted tree to the west and birth new myths, rather than track this desiccated husk?*

"I have come," Zayne rasped slowly, reaching into his coat, "to deliver this." Despite standing in the shade, the horn glinted as though he held it directly in the moonlight.

The goddess's serpentine eyes widened in an all too human display of shock and horror. Her surprise was short lived, immediately replaced by a fury so potent Zayne *felt* and even *tasted* it in the air. The snake reached up skyward and let out a roar that shook the air like thunder. She thrashed violently, slamming her body against the ground, sending tremors through it and cracking it open, creating a rift between Zayne and the others, which Nanette nearly fell into.

The snake vanished.

444

She hadn't slithered away, hadn't dissolved into light, hadn't fallen off the plateau. She simply vanished.

A hand ensnared Zayne's throat and hoisted him off the ground. He couldn't breathe. The galaxies of Faeorn's eyes bore down on Zayne from the bleeding face of a woman who looked almost human. Unruly, auburn hair flowed from her head and moved as though she swam underwater, like that of a harpy. Not a scrap of clothing covered the goddess's modesty, and her nakedness revealed a jagged scar that wrapped around her shoulder and trailed between her enormous, pendulous breasts.

The sight conflated with his memories, first and foremost the violent death of his mother, but also of the many lives he had taken. Sickness churned in his guts, but the bile stopped rising in his chest, unable to reach his throat from the pressure Faeorn was exerting.

Sulfur permeated the air. A low rumble sounded from the shadow of the world tree as a distorted shadow lumbered from the darkness. A four-legged creature with only patches of raw skin covering muscles, sinew and bone stalked into the clearing. Zayne saw one eye glint in the moonlight before three other Dread Hounds emerged from the darkness. The beasts bore their teeth with ghastly snarls.

Panic and self-preservation cut through the memory. Both his mind and Lucandri's were tangled knots of fear twisting together, pulling against one another in an animal fury. He clawed and thrashed against the goddess's unbreakable grip. All his strength failed to so much as make her budge or loosen her grip.

The click of a pistol's hammer broke through his flailing terror.

"Let. Him. Go," Nanette said in thick breaths, her pistol quivering, held at Faeorn's head. The goddess's intense eyes shifted like the turning of the night sky.

Bold is the singer, said Faeorn, *to stand before my hounds with weapon drawn. Strong is she to resist my power.* Though the goddess moved her lips, her words were no less ephemeral and all-encompassing than before. She tossed Zayne aside. The air escaped his lungs on his first bounce and vomit spilled out on the second. It wasn't until after the third when he skidded across the ground into one of the World Tree's immense roots that he was able to draw in a ragged breath, which he followed with wet, vicious coughs. Nanette lowered her weapon and ran to Zayne's side, heedless of the Dread Hounds as they padded after her. She helped him to his knees and wrapped her arms around him protectively, keeping her body between him and Faeorn and the Dread Hounds.

Has your mistress not tormented me enough? On her behalf, you have killed many of my children, and maimed this one, Faeorn said, gingerly touching the one-eyed Hound with the back of her fingers, but the all the evil dogs were snarling at Zayne and Nanette with their hackles raised. *And still she sends you. Her game is unforgivable. Know you what you have done by presenting me with this relic?* Faeorn knelt, and the dry, frostbitten grass sailed up in a sudden gust of wind. Her fingers caressed the horn, and she picked it up with both hands as if it were fragile. *Bound by oath am I to protect the World Tree with all of my power. When your kind, led by the foulest trickery, sought its destruction, I fought for its defense.*

But in spite of my efforts, it was rent asunder. Oathbound, I have kept it alive for millennia, forestalling the inevitable. An almost humanly sad look came over her face, and she cradled the horn to her breast. *For all my efforts, the hunger of humanity to wreak destruction was beyond even my power. The tree is dying a slow death. An agonizing death. And without the World Tree to sustain, the world itself will crumble, reduced to a lifeless husk of iron and rust.*

She flowed, rather than walked, to the World Tree and set a reverent hand on its wounded trunk. *When the new seed was planted, nourished with the ashes of dragon fire and watered with the blood of tyrants, I dared hope the sun would set a final time on my vigil. As the new Tree nourishes the world, it draws the last of this one's strength, integrating it into the lifeblood of the land. It would at last be allowed to die while its child lived on.*

But you have brought me this, she said, and the venom of her voice dimmed the moonlight and made the air colder. The mist seemed to retreat from Faeorn as she whirled on Zayne, holding the horn up for them to see. *With this, the Tree will have the strength to continue its purpose, for a time. And with* two *World Trees, singing discordant songs, each shaping the world in their image, drawing on one another for nutrients, they will* tear the world apart. *This world will die, as surely as if the Tree had passed without its seed sprouting. And everything in this realm — man, beast, Fair One, and god — will perish with it. And with the oaths that bind, I have no choice but to allow it.* I must *do all in my power to protect and keep this tree alive.*

"But why would Dardan want that?" Xun asked, picking herself off from the ground. Zayne had almost completely forgotten about her. Her face was blotchy from tears and stained where the dirt clung to her wet face. "It doesn't make sense, *she* lives here, too."

You do not wear her mark as they do, Faeorn observed. *What part have you in her madness?* The goddess drifted towards Xun and with far more gentleness than she showed Zayne. She tilted the mercenary's chin up with one, long finger and the woman was transfixed by the goddess's otherworldly gaze. The wind howled through the grove as the two of them stared at one another.

The one you call Dardan, Faeorn said finally, *cares not for this world. She cares not even for her own life, as you understand it. She came to me, thirty summers past, when she was human. Grief and madness wed within her mind, even then. Fool was I to let her leave with her life, for she cast it away to a darker power.*

I will take the Horn, she said, turning to Zayne. *In payment, I shall grant you a swift death. Goodbye, Lucandri.* The goddess snapped her fingers. A hundred vines burst from the ground beneath them and entangled Zayne and Nanette in a smothering embrace before they had a chance to scream. They struggled against their living shackles, but they were powerless. Before long, they were completely immobile and enveloped in darkness.

If Lucandri had panicked before, in the darkness he was absolutely horrified. Zayne tried to think through the Fae's fear, which wasn't easy. With his face pressed into Nanette's shoulder he had a small pocket of air even as he was driven painfully into her body. Her breath was rapid and humid in his ear, and her heart pounded rapidly against him in a discordant rhythm to his own. She was terrified, too. He tried to get a stiletto from his sleeve, but his arms and hands were completely immobile.

The pressure released abruptly. Moonlight burst to life through the vines as they unraveled. Zayne and Nanette fell gracelessly to the grove floor as the overgrowth retreated. Mere feet away, Xun knelt before Faeorn. A silent scream marred her face while smoke and steam rose from her hand, which was pressed to the goddess's lips.

The pact is made, Faeorn's voice resonated through the grove. To Zayne and Nanette, she said, *Leave this place. I will not grant you another chance.* She turned, and as she glided into the shadow of the World Tree, she vanished entirely.

Xun still knelt, holding her wrist. Her face was contorted in agony. She looked as though tears should be tumbling down her face, but her eyes were dry. On the back of her hand, where Faeorn's lips had met her flesh, a symbol glowed like heated iron; two crescent moons pointing away from one another, connected by a perfect circle, with a four-pointed star in the center. The glow faded slowly, leaving Xun with Faeorn's brand scarred on her skin. Just as Zayne and Nanette were marked by Daen's.

The woman stood and tucked the wounded hand under her arm. "Let's get back to the ship," she advised. "There's nothing left for us, here."

CHAPTER FORTY-ONE

After their encounter on the *Clockwork Hydra*, Hymn had held the pirates' own guns to their heads while Miria and Cassidy took turns explaining the situation and what they knew about the Leviathan. Captain Yaoru took it all with surprising stride, and her crew seemed unperturbed by the myriad revelations. With their positions reversed, Yaoru ordered her raiding parties to return all of their captives to their respective ships.

Once they returned to the Dreamscape Voyager, Cassidy and Miria stood on the deck and waited for the pirates to leave. Nieves and Lierre escorted Kek back to Cassidy's cabin. Hanaa cursed at the pirates regarding their treatment while Haytham retreated to his duties, as if to pretend the experience hadn't left him shaking in his boots.

When the pirates finally flew away, Miria let out a relieved sigh that trilled out into a giggle. "I'm amazed she bought that," she said. "That was real clever thinking, Captain, telling her I was her long lost sister."

Cassidy averted her gaze. "It wasn't a lie," she told the Princess. "Your uncle told me, before we flew back from the palace."

Silence fell between them, heavy and uncomfortable. Cassidy stood paralyzed as she watched the emotions playing on Miria's face. Confusion turned to shock and back, until finally anger settled on her face. Cassidy felt guilt pulling her heart in two.

Miria opened her mouth to speak, and Cassidy could see the start of several different sentences form on her lips, apparently unable to find the right words. Until a strained whisper, sharp as any shout, finally broke the silence. "You knew this whole time *who my father was* and didn't tell me?"

"Your uncle —" Cassidy began, but Miria cut her off.

"I thought *I* was your friend, *Captain*, not him," she said. "You called me *sister*, and you keep something like that from me?"

Miria turned away and stormed off, shoving past Haytham and ignoring the disbelieving looks from Nieves and Lierre as she descended to the lower deck.

Tense quiet pervaded the deck of the *Dreamscape Voyager*.

No one said anything. Not to Miria. Not to Cassidy. Nieves finally pulled Kek into Cassidy's cabin — the night's excitement couldn't have been good for him — and the Ramajin siblings awkwardly retreated and took a sudden interest in the support struts holding the balloon in place, clearly not wanting to be involved. Lierre stood amidships with Cassidy, looking torn between confronting Cassidy and chasing after Miria. After several long seconds of doubletakes where her expression shifted between indignation and concern, she finally settled on following the princess down below.

Hymn — once again in her diminutive form — hovered beside Cassidy, occasionally chiming like a distant bell but otherwise quiet.

"I'm a hypocrite," Cassidy said, not so much to Hymn as to no one in particular. The Fae, unable to tell lies, said nothing.

Cassidy manned the helm as the small fleet, minus the *Sunrise* and plus eight pirate vessels, sailed on through the night. The *Clockwork Hydra* had stopped the strange smoke show that had obscured them but was every bit as conspicuous for the strange shroud draped over the hull. No one relieved her until dawn, and as guilty as she felt, she didn't order anyone to.

"You look tired, Captain," Haytham said when he climbed to the deck.

"It was a busy night," said Cassidy. She stepped from the helm and motioned for Haytham to steer. "Andaerhal is that way. Keep us flying in that direction and don't hit anything."

"How'd you get to be so close to the princess?" Haytham asked as she tried to walk away.

"What do you mean?"

"No offense, Durant, but I've worked for nobles. You're no noble. Why send you with her, instead of an honor guard?"

"I didn't know she was royalty when we met," said Cassidy. "Elyia... Captain Asier, my predecessor, was the Empress' former bodyguard. The Empress wanted Miria to see the Empire. We sailed for almost two years before being sent on the leviathan. And..." she hesitated. Haytham was a relative stranger, and she wasn't sure she should be telling him this. Then again, with all the truths out in the open now, it seemed like a small thing. Besides, his face was open and inviting, and she felt guilty for keeping secrets. "Besides, this mission wasn't planned with her in mind."

450

"Aha," said Haytham. "She doesn't seem the kind of person who would stay out of something so historic."

"No," Cassidy agreed. "She likes getting her hands dirty along with her people."

"I wonder if that's a good thing."

Cassidy furrowed her brow. "How could it not be?"

"Leadership is strange," Haytham said. "Everyone does it differently, but no matter what, you need a wide view. It's like a game of stones. Focus too hard on capturing one piece, you'll lose every time."

"I prefer dice games," she said glibly, but she considered his point all the same. Miria had chosen to fight in the streets back in Andaerhal. While it worked out in the end, she had clearly put solidarity above other, better choices.

Cassidy tried and failed to suppress a yawn. "Keep us on course," she repeated, and this time Haytham didn't stop her when she walked away. She opened her cabin door to find Kek sound asleep on the bed while Nieves seemed to have nodded off on her stool. She left them to their much needed rest and climbed the steps to the aftcastle. She sat with the gunwale to her back and tipped her hat over her eyes. The morning sun was already warming the deck, so she shirked off her jacket and used it as a pillow.

She slept fitfully, faced with nightmares she could scarcely remember moment to moment. Some images stuck with her though. A scorpion bearing down on her, the *Sunrise*'s destruction, and a city burning around her as she stood by helplessly, all stood in crystalized perfection in her memory against a blur of chaotic dreams.

The sun was hidden behind the *Dreamscape's* balloon by the time Hymn woke her up by chiming like a bell. She jerked awake, faintly aware of a thrumming skiff off to port. She managed to find her feet as Captain Yaoru tethered her boat to the ship. The pirate leaped over and sat down on the gunwale without asking permission. The other woman didn't seem to have changed her clothes, either, but she seemed a good deal fresher and more well rested than Cassidy.

"Ahoy, Captain Sleepyhead," she said with mock formality. "We need to talk."

"Aye," Cassidy sneered. "I suppose we do."

Yaoru jumped to her feet, but rather than set foot on the deck, she balanced on the gunwale. The showoff didn't even act like it was unusual as she paced along it.

"You don't like me," she said.

Cassidy was taken aback, though her shock was quickly washed away by anger which spread like a grease fire. "Should I?" she demanded. "You killed over thirty people! You tried to kill my friends!" Laid out like that, Cassidy wanted to shove the woman — precariously perched as she was — overboard to fall to her death. She hadn't known the crew of the *Sunrise* well, or very long, but Captain Kin had been a kind woman, and a good spirited. And the *scope* of the murder was more than Cassidy could wrap her head around. A numb shock settled around Cassidy like a shawl, smothering her fury, but she did her best to shake it off.

"True," Yaoru said, in a tone usually reserved for conceding to arguments about chores. She tapped her chin as though she hadn't considered it. "Still, if it bothers you, you really should know I've killed *lots* of people. Well, me and the rest of the Thousand and One."

Cassidy looked at the ships aft and to either side. "There's maybe *a hundred* and one of you," she said, "and that's pushing it." It was a petty jab, but it was all Cassidy had.

Yaoru shrugged. She crouched on one leg to Cassidy's eye level, folding the other over her knee, as if she sat on a chair, and met Cassidy's eye. "Missing the point here, Red. Are you sure you want to work with us?"

"Are you asking me permission to back out of your deal with Hymn?" Cassidy asked. "You're right. I *don't* like you. In fact, I would shoot you right now, if I thought I could get away with it. But the Leviathan is too important to turn down your guns. Besides, you're in it, now. You made the deal."

"Mhmm." Yaoru finally stepped down from the gunwale and stretched. "About that. I spoke with Jathun this morning, and I heard that you're issuing out Imperial pardons for people who help with this mess."

Cassidy scoffed. "You're already bound to this, why should I bribe you now?"

Yaoru rolled her eyes. "Where's my sister? I'm sure she'll be more reasonable."

"I'm right here," Miria said from the aftcastle steps. The quiet dignity Cassidy saw in her — belying the fury Cassidy knew coursed within her — made her look like the Empress herself, in spite of the dirty shirt and trousers she wore. "And I think you'll find Captain Durant is being quite reasonable. There were good people aboard that ship you destroyed."

If not for their eyes, Cassidy wouldn't have thought them sisters, or even related. For a start, even without the heels of her boots, Yaoru stood over a head taller than Miria, had wider hips and a more ample chest, all of which her unreasonably tight clothing and deliberately lax posture drew attention to. More than that, though, there was a sophisticated grace about the princess that two years traveling among common sailors hadn't been enough to sand away. Contrarily, the pirate had an air of smugness to her that made Cassidy think of a tavern thug and the predatory gaze of a hawk.

"Of course no one innocent ever dies in the Empire, right?"

"That's an absurd —" Miria began, but Yaoru cut her off.

"There's *never* been an innocent man dropped from the gallows," she said, her tone thick with patronizing irony. "*No* woman manning the guns at the dragon's nest was falsely accused. Every ship the Empire ever sank was full of pirates."

"Are you trying to suggest you sank the *Sunrise*... by *accident?*"

"No, little sister," said Yaoru, "I'm trying to tell you this high minded —"

Yaoru clearly saw the punch coming, but she only managed to unfold her arms before Miria's fist cracked her jaw and whipped her head back. The pirate stumbled back a step. Cassidy was amazed she didn't lose her footing completely and fall on her ass, staggering backwards on those heels as she was.

"Don't you dare," Miria said in a low tone, barely above a whisper. "You don't get to treat the lives of my people as some kind of object lesson. You don't get to justify your atrocities with vague anecdotes of misfortune or misconduct. And we may share a father's blood, but you don't get to call me *sister*.

"Perhaps you'll see a pardon, when all this is through," she continued, her tone settling into the impassive, imperious tone she had been using more often of late. She wiped her knuckles on her shirtsleeve, as though she had dirtied them on Yaoru's cheek. "But after last night, consider yourself fortunate I plan on granting you time to slink away once the leviathan is defeated." She turned on her heels and walked away. Apparently, whatever had brought her onto the deck wasn't worth staying near Yaoru for — assuming she hadn't made the climb just to punch the woman. Cassidy couldn't blame her, either way.

Yaoru stared at Miria's retreating back until she disappeared below deck. Then she turned to Cassidy. She fell into the same practiced stance with her arms crossed, but now, with an angry tension in her muscles and a glare plastered to her face, she looked less in control and relaxed and more petulant. "Fine. To the mists with your damn pardons, then. The Fae needs to make do on her end of the deal. Otherwise, I'll die as soon as we cross the Imperial Border."

"Show me the mark," Hymn said, emerging from Cassidy's hat.

Without hesitation or even a blush, Yaoru pulled her tunic over her head. She turned around smoothly and pulled her hair aside. A brand — similar to the one Hymn had placed on Cassidy's wrist — sat between her shoulder blades. Where Hymn's mark on Cassidy was three nesting crescent moons with the smallest pointing inward, which together formed a rough circle around a flower, Yaoru was scarred by a perfect circle with a smaller circle sitting inside at the bottom, with a crescent sitting atop the interior one like a crown and a stylized shape Cassidy interpreted as waves between its points.

"*Djian*," Hymn sneered. "This must be done at noon tomorrow."

Yaoru pivoted and thrust a finger at Hymn. "Why not now?" she demanded, completely unabashed having her tunic in hand in front of strangers.

"The one who marked you is strongest at midnight," Hymn said in a tone that conveyed an almost human boredom at the pirate's theatrics. "Her influence must be undone when she is as weak as possible, lest she become aware and investigate." She paused, as if considering. "More accurately, the height of her powers comes at midnight on a night when Jiqun, your largest moon, is entirely dark, but we cannot wait until she is full. Time is short."

"Fine," Yaoru groused, replacing her top. "I'll be back tomorrow. Talk to the princess for me, will you?" she added in a patronizingly sweet tone to Cassidy. She hopped up to the gunwale with abandon before climbing into the skiff and flying back to the *Clockwork Hydra*.

Cassidy turned to the main deck to find Lierre and Haytham watching the pirate leave. She didn't know when Lierre had arrived, nor how long the two of them had been watching the exchange, but either way they had probably gotten an eye full.

"Alright, show's over," she said, waving them off. "Get back to work." Haytham had the good grace to look embarrassed, but Lierre had a big grin on her face as she retreated to the galley.

"I would have expected that from Kekarian," Hymn remarked.

"She's twice as bad," Cassidy said, her voice pulled in two directions from both a laugh and a sigh. She sobered when she looked after the retreating skiff. "What are the odds she would be tied to the same Fae I've met twice?"

"Quite likely, actually," Hymn said in a voice like a sigh. "When your people tried to destroy the World Tree, I believe their intent was to prevent my kind from entering from the Dreamscape. It worked. In part, at least. For those already here, however, it had the opposite effect. While she and others can still cross the veil, they cannot truly escape the influence of this world. Imagine someone without a ship living in one of your cities. She could leave her home, but isolated on mountain tops as your people are, she is confined, only able to walk from one end of the city to the other.

"Furthermore, of those still connected to this place, only so many would seek to treat with your kind," Hymn concluded. "And *she* has always been particularly meddlesome."

Cassidy nodded and watched Yaoru's skiff vanish. Put like that, she supposed it made sense. Still, something about Hymn's explanation stood out.

"You said 'those who were already here'," she noted, keeping her tone idle. "Not 'those of us'."

"I..." Hymn began before hesitating. She didn't continue until Cassidy pressed her with a look. "I had a different way in."

Before Cassidy could follow that thread of conversation, she heard another skiff approaching. She looked to starboard and found Jathun, accompanied by Jin and another girl from the *Sunrise*.

"Permission to come aboard," Jathun called.

"Granted," Cassidy replied. At least *some* people had manners.

Jathun tied his skiff off and hopped over the gunwale to join her. "Was that Kiyen's kid I just saw flying away?"

"It was, aye. Spoiled bitch."

"She always was," said Jathun. "Kiyen must have thought discipline was a spice, and she was allergic. There was one time — no, never mind the good old days." He dropped to a whisper when he said, "You can only imagine how horrible it is for... well, I guess they're my crew, now. But for the turn of the dice, any one of them would have been on that ship when she went down. Survivor's guilt and lost friends are a potent mix. We're holding a service tonight. Given the circumstances, I am not sure if it's better you come to pay your respects, or to stay away.

"Still, you are invited. If you *do* decide to come," he added, forcing a smile onto his face, "bring food. While a few brought supplies, most of what's on my ship is canned goods from five years ago."

Cassidy looked over Jathun's shoulder to Jin and the stranger. The young woman glared at her and abruptly turned to look away, as if there was something in the skiff that had captured her attention. The other passenger on the skiff merely stared back at Cassidy with a distant expression. Cassidy recognized that look. It had found its way on her own face several times in the wake of Elyia Asier's death.

It hadn't been an easy choice to make, but as dusk painted the horizon and the small fleet halted for the night, Cassidy — accompanied by Miria and Haytham — took the *Dreamscape Voyager*'s skiff over to the *Temptation*. She had wavered over the decision for some time. On the one hand, it was because of Cassidy that Captain Kin and the others had died, and she had — inadvertently — immediately enlisted their killer. On the other hand, Cassidy *was* responsible, and she should probably acknowledge that fact. In the end, it had been Miria's decision to attend that forced Cassidy's hand; she couldn't let her go alone.

Nieves stayed behind to watch over Kek. Hanaa had elected not to attend. Lierre agreed with Cassidy that they couldn't trust the Ramajins with custody of the ship, so she remained as well. Haytham had surprised Cassidy by offering to join them, and she couldn't think of a good reason not to accommodate him. Hymn, refusing to be separated from Cassidy after recent events, completed the party.

Though it was short, the venture was tense. Miria refused to look at Cassidy, and while she wasn't giving her the silent treatment, she only spoke when addressed and gave curt, direct answers. Haytham, clearly sensing the tension, said nothing and focused on the covered food pot he carried.

Jathun greeted them on the deck and helped tie the skiff down. Cassidy hopped down and offered Miria her hand, but the princess coldly brushed past her. Haytham gingerly passed Jathun the pot before clambering out.

"I didn't expect you to actually bring anything," Jathun confessed.

"My sister made it," said Haytham. "Said the crab had to be used while it was still good."

Cassidy hadn't even been aware that they had *had* crab meat; for all her talk about ensuring the duty roles were fairly distributed, she hadn't given herself galley duty since before arriving in Isaro, and she hadn't looked too closely at what they had been given by Prince Hassan as they departed. *Well, at least it went to a good cause,* she thought.

Jathun nodded in gratitude and led them down to the galley. The air was a pungent blend of stale dust and burning grease. The survivors of the *Sunrise* were all present, most seated at one of two, long tables that filled the space. A burly woman stood at the stove, opening cans, setting some aside and tossing others in a sizzling pan. Jathun set the crab stew on the empty table and gestured for Cassidy and the others to sit with the mourners.

One of them yelped at the sight of Miria and led them in a chaotic rush to find their feet and bow to her.

"Please," Miria said tenderly, "tonight, let's forget matters of station. Tonight, I am one of you."

The sailors glanced at one another from their prostrate positions, and one by one, they slowly returned to a standing position. Only when Miria gestured them back to their benches did they actually sit, however.

A bubble of distance formed around the *Dreamscape*'s crew. The crew of the *Sunrise* seemed to at once revere Miria and fear or resent Cassidy. She supposed she should be grateful that she hadn't dragged Miria's estimation down with her, but instead, she felt a potent mix of bitter anger and guilt rising up from her core. No one spoke, leaving only the hissing of the pan and creaking of the old ship around them to fill the quiet.

It wasn't my fault, she thought at them, but it did nothing to stop them from glaring from the corners of their eyes.

The burly woman sat, and Jathun began to portion out dishes on the other table. She positioned herself directly across from Cassidy and glared at her. The others seemed to struggle to find a safe place to look.

Cassidy couldn't take it anymore.

"What in the Mists do you want from me?" she snapped.

There was a pause. The woman looked away, and Cassidy thought that would be the end of it. Instead, she asked, in a voice softer and more tender than her frame would suggest, "How could you?"

The lack of fire in her voice deflated Cassidy's rage. A little bit. "How could I *what?*" Cassidy demanded, though she didn't shout like she had built herself up to do.

The other woman opened her mouth to speak, then closed it. She repeated this several times, occasionally giving voice to a cut syllable before throwing her hands up and inarticulately groaning. "Any of it!" she said finally. She buried her face in her hands. "You consort with Fae! You risk our princess' life! You got Kin and the others killed —"

Cassidy slammed her palms on the table, making some of the others flinch. "That wasn't my fault!" Even as she said the words left her mouth, she found herself doubting them; she had ordered the Imperial banners flown, *knowing* they would provoke Yaoru into action. Still she pressed on. "The *Clockwork Hydra* would have killed *all* of us if not for Hymn. So before you condemn me for breaking the law, maybe you should *thank* us for saving your lives."

"*Captain Durant!*" Miria hissed in her ear.

The hurt look on the woman's downcast face told Cassidy that she had thought about that but didn't want to face it. Sympathy smothered what remained of Cassidy's mostly spent anger.

"Please forgive Bai Fen," Jathun said. He set a steaming bowl in front of the confrontational woman. "This has been a difficult day for everyone."

"Of course, Captain Jathun," Miria said, nodding graciously, almost like a bow. She then cast Cassidy a cutting look.

Jathun passed out food, a portioned mix of whatever had been in the canned goods and what Cassidy's crew had brought and a stack of clay cups, and a communal plate of canned desserts. He completed the supper by uncorking a heavy jug of rice wine. There was a tense quiet as they ate. The meal didn't have a uniform taste, with relatively fresh crab meat stewing with heavily preserved fish and fowl and dried vegetables, but Cassidy put it away mechanically, which she suspected she had in common with her fellow diners.

After an eternity of fending off ugly or sheepish looks, Cassidy felt relief pour into her when Miria stood.

"I didn't know Captain Kin well," Miria admitted. "I knew her people even less. Though I spoke with many of them — with you — before we departed Andaerhal, and again in Isaro, and though I know the names of all the lost, I don't know their stories. But what I do know is what those stories pushed them to. They left their home in a difficult time to pursue a greater purpose. To save their home, to save their *world*, they took ship for the good of others. I promise you, that selflessness will not be forgotten." She picked her cup. "To the lost, and the dreams they strived for."

The toast was returned, though with solemn tones. Some eyes were downcast, but Bai Fen and Jin looked resolute and touched, respectively as they raised their drinks and downed them in a swift gulp. As Miria sat, Jin bolted to her feet and Jathun refilled the cups.

"When I first joined the navy," Jin said, "I treated it like just another grueling job. I wasn't interested in the wild winds, the sense of home to be found on a ship, a lover in every port... not even the glory of the Empire," she added with a look to Miria. "I joined for the money." There was a faint roll of laughter across the table at that, like a long running joke. "But you know Kin Aahn wasn't a normal captain. She loved to tell stories, and wanted to hear yours, whether you wanted to tell it or not. This mad woman would make everyone stop in their duties to appreciate a particularly beautiful sunrise or sunset.

"I hated her for so long," Jin admitted. "Gods, but I hated her. I hated the crew. I hated you in particular, Bai Fen," she said, and the laughter intensified. "Everyone was always trying to engage in small talk, inviting me to take part in pranks or games, offering a shoulder when things got dark, and treating me like *family*. I thought then, 'I have a family, and I don't need another one'.

459

"I think I know when I turned around," she went on. "It was after my first leave, coming home to a family I couldn't connect with, who didn't get me anymore. I found out I missed the way I missed my normal life, more than I missed the normalcy itself. I missed the feeling of the wind in my hair and the ship swaying in the breeze. I missed those unfamiliar sunsets.

"I missed cards with the Wen sisters. I missed late nights listening to Little Shu whispering to Washu about boys." Her voice hitched, and tears streamed out of the corners of her eyes and down to her chin. "There were a thousand little things I missed, and now... now they're... they're just gone." She sobbed once, then reigned it in to lift her cup. "To the little things." As they downed their drinks, Jin sat back down and planted a heavy kiss wet with tears on Bai Fen's lips. The larger woman returned the gesture with equal parts fervor and sorrow.

It continued like that for some time, until everyone had their say. Bai Fen confessed to breaking into the first officer's liquor cabinet and rearranging his office, then stashed the drained bottles in the men's cabin so the blame fell on them. Cato shared stories of fights that turned into friendship. Tien was a newcomer to the crew, having volunteered after the events in Andaerhal, but he spoke of the bravery he saw in his crewmates, and the actions that made him want to be a part of something grand. By the time Yuji took her turn, the wine had Cassidy floating, and Yuji fared little better; she just announced that she loved everyone and collapsed into a crying heap on the table. Kang offered a eulogy to the *Sunrise* itself, saying the ship was the first real home he'd ever had. Last was Fan Wua, who merely stood as if to give a toast, then sat back down and cried.

The stories didn't end there, but they became less formal as the survivors aired out their grief together. Drinks flowed, and Cassidy wanted to throw herself fully in to drown her own horrors and sorrows and pains, but she knew the *Sunrise's* crew — or the *Temptation's* crew, as the case may be, with the *Sunrise* gone — needed it more than she did, so she stopped when her vision merely swayed. After a while, Jathun gestured for Cassidy to follow him outside. Miria stayed behind to support the others in their grief, and Haytham was fully engaged with them.

The bracing night air cut through the haze of drink, and Cassidy realized that no one from the *Roc Spear* had come to take part in the mourning. None of the pirates had, either, but that was to be expected.

"Thank you for coming," Jathun said, leading her to the gunwale. "It's not easy to see something like that even in the heat of battle. But an ambush like that?" He spat overboard and stared daggers at the *Clockwork Hydra*. "Well, no one could *really* be ready for that."

"Do you think it's a mistake?" Cassidy asked. "Letting them join us, I mean."

"I didn't see any other choice," Jathun admitted. "Not unless you count dying the same as the *Sunrise* a choice. I don't, but some pedantic assholes like to say it's always *a* choice."

Cassidy grunted and rested her arms on the gunwale. "You know her best. Can we trust her?"

"I knew her *father*," Jathun corrected. "And that was a long time ago. I didn't hear about Elyia attacking him, or about him dying. Who knows what lessons he taught her before he died, or how she took them.

"But she seems to take the Fae seriously enough," he added. "So we can at least trust her as far as the agreement goes." He leaned on the gunwale beside her and let out a long sigh. "You've really complicated my life, Durant. Did Asier give lessons in that, or did she pick you special for it?"

Cassidy snorted. "She picked me special, alright, but life seemed a lot simpler before she... before she died."

Jathun put a hand on her shoulder. "Well, once we get rid of the giant monster, maybe the world can go back to being simple."

Cassidy nodded and stared out into the desert. "I sure hope so."

Yaoru returned to the *Dreamscape Voyager* as promised the next day, a little before noon. Confident as ever, she came alone. Despite her restraint the night before, Cassidy nursed a hangover as she played host to the invasive pirate. Hymn had made some sort of preparations the night before, though Cassidy had been just drunk enough not to ask any follow up questions. Instead, she had fallen asleep in the galley while the Fae did... whatever it was she did.

The pirate stood on the deck, seeming to argue with Miria. The side of her face had become a deep purple, and though she had powdered her face, the shiner still showed though. Yaoru gesticulated wildly as she spoke to Miria, but the princess stood with her hands clasped in front of her, impassively taking in Yaoru's apparent ravings.

"... should be more grateful!" Yaoru was saying. "The *Hydra* alone has more firepower than a hundred of your — ah, Captain Durant. Is your Fae ready to do this? Because I don't like getting jerked around."

"Hymn has been preparing," Cassidy said, her voice croaking uncomfortably as she adjusted herself. "Let's get a move on. I want you gone as much as you do. And she's not *mine*," she added as she led Yaoru up to the aftcastle. The pirate took her tunic off without shame or even asking if it was necessary.

As Cassidy crossed the threshold onto the aftcastle, she felt a wave of vertigo come over her and a lightening of her body as she stepped into the Dreamscape. The abrupt quieting of the engines jarred her, as did seeing Hymn at her full height. Above them, the sky shone a garnet red slashed with a streak of light blue and speckled gentle purple stars. Below them on the deck, Cassidy could see the others standing beside the mast that only existed in the dream realm, but their images wavered like sunlight through water, and slowly, as though in an exhausted dream. Beyond the ship, Cassidy could see both the desert and a forest of white trees with crimson leaves, as if she were staring at a different picture with each eye. When Yaoru stepped up beside Cassidy, her image coalesced, and she staggered forward at a normal speed.

Cassidy whistled. "Is this what you were doing all morning?"

Hymn extended a gesture that was somewhere between a bow and a nod.

"This is the Dreamscape," Yaoru breathed. "I never expected to come back to this place!"

"How did you bring the Dreamscape *here?*" Cassidy asked, addressing the aftcastle. She had entered the Dreamscape enough times to know she hadn't fallen asleep and gone there, and if only the aftcastle was affected, they couldn't have flown into it. "*Why* did you bring it here?"

"The how is difficult to explain in mortal terms," Hymn said, "but it involves taking advantage of the nature of the damage done to the veil when the World Tree was attacked, and the erosion that has happened over time. The why is far simpler; what needs to be done cannot be done in the realm of mortals, but to venture where Djian can find us would be a mistake. The compromise is this, a sort of *bubble* of the Dreamscape, placed outside of time. It will exist only a moment, by the measure of those outside, so we must hurry. Come, Yaoru Suzume."

The bare-chested woman stepped forward, though rather than focus on Hymn, she gawked at the surrounding splendors of the Realm of Dreams, turning and walking backwards for a couple steps before settling in front of Hymn. The Fae placed a slender finger to the pirate's forehead and Cassidy felt the air tremble like the aftershocks of thunder.

Yaoru threw her head back. Her eyes rolled into her head and her mouth opened in a silent scream. Ripples of light spread from the pirate's body like the ones formed when a stone dropped into a pond. Faint images surrounded her, accompanied by faint whispers just on the edge of hearing.

As if through water, Cassidy saw translucent visions beneath that rippling light, fading one into another. Elyia Asier looming like a monster over the slumped figure of a blue-eyed pirate while his daughter watches in terror. A young child caring for her crippled father. A young woman so alike Miria watching a funeral fire. That same woman flying a skiff alone into a storm. The Fae Djian, dressed in a purple night's sky, descending from the clouds.

Cassidy heard Yaoru's voice as if from a great distance. *Grant me the strength and the skill to avenge my father,* the pirate pleaded to the Fae.

Strength and skill you shall have, and power beyond the ken of mortals, Djian promised. *But in exchange, you must stand vigil to the west, for one day a great evil shall emerge. Should you again fly beneath the skies of the Empire, your life is forfeit.*

The visions faded, and the brand on Yaoru's back began to glow and *shift*. The skin twisted and warped, the lines in the brand reforming. The stench of burning flesh filled the air and a great gust of wind blasted outward from Yaoru, nearly throwing Cassidy back. Even Hymn seemed to be struggling to hold herself in place. Waves of red trembled through the blue in the Fae's dress as it whipped and snapped in the wind.

Lightning struck from a cloudless sky.

Cassidy was thrown to the gunwale and the Dreamscape bubble burst. Real daylight tore through the red night. The crimson forest melted away. The *Dreamscape Voyager* bucked, and a last ripple of light washed over the ship, transforming the vessel into its dream counterpart. The effect spread, and all the ships in their fleet shifted into forms reminiscent of their pre-ascension ancestors, moving in sudden silence.

The change lasted only a moment, and the roar of the engines sounded as though they had always been running. On the *Dreamscape Voyager's* aftcastle, Cassidy and Yaoru lay sprawled on the ground, smoke rising from their clothes. Blood stained Yaoru's back, now marked with the same sigil branded on Cassidy's arm. Cassidy was seized by a fit of violent coughs that racked her body, sending fresh jolts of pain through her with each forced breath. When at last she pushed herself to her knees, she spotted Hymn, once more diminutive, laying on the deck, her light dim and flickering faintly between blue and red with terrifying moments where she didn't glow at all.

"*Hymn!*" she shrieked. She all but threw herself at the small Fae and cupped Hymn in her hands. Without the light radiating off her with its usual intensity, she looked as she did in the Dreamscape, but somehow less substantial, as though Cassidy needed only to find the right angle to see right through her friend. "Hymn," she pleaded, breathless and in pain, "Hymn, talk to me! Are you okay?"

A small chime, almost like a groan, sounded from the Fae. "I... will be fine," she said, and her voice was so faint it could barely be heard over the gentle breeze. "What I did was... never meant to be done. Indeed, I could not... erase Djian's price. Not truly. Instead, I was forced... to create a loophole. Fret not, Cassandra... I need rest. Nothing... more."

Hymn's face contorted into an expression of what might have been pain or concentration, and her glow intensified, becoming its usual azure brilliance. The light pulsed faintly like the steady breath of a sleeper. Cassidy cradled her friend to her chest, careful not to jostle her.

"Captain!" Miria cried, stomping up the aftcastle with Haytham and Hanaa in tow. Lierre was climbing up from below deck and Nieves burst from the cabin. "What happened?"

Cassidy turned to face her. "I... honestly don't know, exactly."

Beside her, Yaoru stirred and let out a long groan. She pushed herself to her knees and reached behind her shoulder to feel at the brand marking her back. "Did she do it?" she demanded.

"Aye," Cassidy said. "That's Hymn's mark, not Djian's."

Yaoru stood and replaced her tunic before turning around, as though she only just that moment discovered modesty. She looked at Hymn nestled between Cassidy's hands. Cassidy didn't like the calculating look in those icy blue eyes.

"If I don't survive crossing into the Empire," she said after a while, "I've ordered my first mate to sink this vessel, the *Temptation*, and the *Roc Spear*." She said it without emotion or hint of remorse, as though discussing the possibility of rain. She stood and made her way to her skiff. "If I do survive, though," she said without looking back, "and I reach Andaerhal with air in my lungs, I'll keep to my end of the bargain. I guess we'll find out soon, one way or the other."

CHAPTER FORTY-TWO

Cassidy watched the *Clockwork Hydra* for any sign of her guns turning. She knew in her heart that there was nothing she could do in the face of that firepower, but Yaoru's threat hung in her ears. So she watched. The exact line where Rivien ended and the Empire began was a contentious and oft debated point, and Cassidy didn't know how a Fae might make that distinction. So she watched the Clockwork Hydra, terrified that at any moment, Yaoru Suzume would suddenly breathe her last and take Cassidy and her friends with her.

When they reached the sea, storm clouds rolled in with the same sudden celerity the *Clockwork Hydra's* alchemical ones had when the pirates had ambushed them not long ago. No rain fell, but lightning danced between the clouds, rocking the ships with deafening peals of thunder. A warm and powerful wind tasting like the promise of a greater storm to come followed them. Cassidy gritted her teeth, anxiety wracking her heart as she worried both of being blown unceremoniously out of the sky and of an unexpected tempest.

She didn't breathe any easier until they were able to see Andaerhal on the horizon without a spyglass. At least she felt *reasonably* certain that if Yaoru hadn't been struck down by Djian's price by this point, she was in the clear. Fear still nagged at her, however, and she couldn't help but wonder, what if Djian considered the Empire's boundaries to start *at the city*? She shuddered.

Damn it, Cassidy, she chided herself, *trust in Hymn.* She *wanted* to trust Hymn, but the fear was hard to shake. The Fae had retreated into Cassidy's hat after recovering enough to fly but had scarcely spoken since. On the few occasions she would answer Cassidy, it was only to tell her she needed rest. It worried her, as the Fae had needed no rest at any point in the past two years Cassidy had known her.

The storm still hadn't broken by the time they reached Andaerhal. The sky was a rendered painting of purple and gold light on the edge of black and gray clouds connected by brilliant flashes of lightning. The wind tasted like the promise of rain that refused to fall.

Fear beat Cassidy's heart like a drum when she saw the smoke rising up from the city. It took several long moments for her to realize it came from the stacks in the factory district and not the residential ones. She breathed out in relief.

The *Dreamscape Voyager* and her companion ships were directed to restricted docking platforms on the north side of the city. Miria brought them into the harbor. As they moved, Cassidy examined the fleet guarding the city.

"Hard to believe I'm supposed to be in charge of this," she said to Nieves, who stood beside her, filling Kek's role as First Mate in his absence. "I doubt Captain Asier was ever this nervous."

"I'm sure she was," Nieves said. "But regardless, you've done so much already. This is just finishing the job."

Cassidy smiled in spite of her apprehension. "Thank you. You have the ship while I meet with the Lord Minister."

She turned to the others. Save Kek, everyone was gathered on the deck while she gave her orders. She would take Miria, Lierre, and Hanaa to see the Lord Minister — Miria for her authority, Hanaa because Cassidy wanted to keep an eye on her, and Lierre to keep the scales level if Hanaa decided to try something — while Nieves and Haytham — whom Cassidy trusted more than his sister — would watch the ship.

Cassidy took one step towards the gangway when her head snapped forward. Pain bloomed in the back of her skull. Black and red spots flooded her vision. Hymn let out a cry of surprise as her hat tumbled overboard with the Fae inside. A chorus of gasps echoed on the deck. Cassidy staggered a step and whirled around. "Ow! What the fuck was —" she began, but the words died on her lips when she saw Kek.

He stood on the deck, arm still outstretched from throwing whatever had hit her. His skin was still deathly pallid, his eyes weighted with heavy bags, his lips cracked and dry. His breath came out in ragged gasped as he stared daggers at her with feverish eyes. His clothes had been sloppily assembled — he wore no shirt under his jacket, which was mis-buttoned, his boots were unbuckled, and one had a trouser leg jammed into it — and his hair was a mess.

"What other secrets have you been keeping, *Cassandra*?" he demanded in a rasping growl. Cassidy swallowed a lump in her throat. He *never* called her by her full name. It was only then that she looked down at the deck to see what he had hurled at her.

It was Captain Asier's journal.

"You knew the *Clockwork Hydra* was hunting for Imperial ships and didn't warn us," he said, closing his hand into a fist, save for one accusing finger. "You knew about Miria's father and didn't even tell *her*! You tried to keep *Hymn* a secret, and only told us about her when it blew up in your face. And all this time, you knew that Captain Asier saw the gods damned *future!*" he concluded, his finger shifting to the book.

A second round of gasps filled the space at the declaration.

Lierre knelt down and picked the book up. Apprehension welled in Cassidy's chest as she flipped through the pages, her eyes widening. She exclaimed something in Castilyn and stared up at Cassidy. She didn't resist as Nieves plucked the journal from her fingers. Miria read over her shoulder.

"So what else are you hiding?" Kek demanded. He took a shaky step forward, and Hymn zipped past, stirring Cassidy's hair as she interposed herself between them. "What aren't you telling us?"

"Stand down, Kekarian," Hymn warned.

Kek's fever-mad eyes turned on Hymn, then he returned his attention to Cassidy. "When she died, you know what she told me?"

"Kek," Cassidy breathed. She grasped at justifications and excuses, but she had nothing.

"She told me to look after *you*," he said, leaning forward, but not crossing the boundary Hymn set. "And I've tried. Damn me for a fool, but I've tried. I've put up with your dark moods and your drinking. I've taken the risks with you, all the way. But I thought I could at least trust you to look out for *us*!"

"Kek," Cassidy repeated, weaker than before.

"Got nothing to say in your own defense?" he sneered.

"I-I couldn't tell you," she pleaded, scrambling for the words as guilt and panic warred for control, "you might have —"

"We might have known what you knew, and talked about it like adults," Kek interrupted. He spat on the deck between them. "But you don't trust us, no matter how many times we pull through and stay by your side. Well, I'm done. The gods drag you to the Mist, Cassandra. Find a new First Mate to lie to." He shoved past Hymn and shouldered Cassidy aside as he marched to the gangway.

"Kek!" Nieves called, grabbing him by the shoulder. "Your fever is still high, let's get you back to bed and we can —"

He shrugged out of her grip and continued. "Do what you want, Nieves, but I'm not staying where I'm not trusted."

"Kek, you can't!" she protested, "Cassidy needs you, she only has —"

"Let him go, Nieves," Cassidy bellowed. Her heart broke a little right then. She hadn't meant to say that, had she?

But she *had* said it, and as much as it hurt, he was right.

About everything.

"He's a grown man, let him make his own choices."

"Cassidy, you can't just," Nieves protested, but Cassidy cut her off.

"I can't force him to go where we're going." She turned away from everyone to hide the tears threatening to bubble over in her eyes. "If he doesn't want to fly with me, he can find his own way home." She heard Kek climb down the gangway, and the tears slid down her face.

Nieves called after him, her voice rising with each iteration of his name, until finally she let out a shriek and hit the gunwales before running down the gangway.

Time fell away as shame and guilt tore at Cassidy. He was right. About all of it. She had lied to her friends time and again. And rather than take any of the countless opportunities to come clean she had waited until it all came out — again.

Hymn landed gently on Cassidy's shoulder. She said nothing, for which Cassidy was grateful; she had told Cassidy she should be open with her crew about many things, and she had been right every time. She dried her face before turning to face the others. Lierre looked torn between chasing after Nieves and addressing Cassidy. Miria also stared into the busy harbor where their friends had disappeared. The Ramajin siblings looked conspicuously like two people trying to pretend they were unaware of the drama unfolding before them.

"Kek is right," Cassidy said. "I've kept too many secrets, and I owe you all better. If you want to leave, I won't try to stop you. But I need to see the Lord Minister. The leviathan is still my priority."

Miria stepped up to Cassidy wearing the cold mask of the princess. "We have a lot to discuss, Captain," she said. Then, after a beat, she was Cassidy's friend, again. "But you're right. Priorities."

Cassidy climbed down the gangway with Hanaa and Miria in tow — Lierre elected to stay behind in case Nieves or Kek came back. She was grateful to find her hat safely at the bottom of the ramp. The feather wasn't even out of place. She picked it up and dusted it off before placing it back on her head. Hymn took her customary place within it.

Yaoru intercepted them before they blended into the crowd. Cassidy was beginning to suspect the woman had a wide assortment of completely identical clothes, because the alternative was assuming she wore the same outfit for a full week even after she had bled in the tunic following Hymn's ritual.

"What do you want now?" Cassidy demanded.

"So testy," Yaoru teased cloyingly. "I'm bringing the big guns to your little fight, so it's only right I introduce myself to the other contributors."

Cassidy scowled. She wanted to tell the woman where she could stick her big guns, but she had no real leverage over the pirate. "Fine."

They hailed a rickshaw to the ministry offices. Cassidy sat beside Miria, only for Yaoru to squeeze between them and throw her arms around their shoulders. Though it was a short trip, they managed to see a great deal of the rebuilding, as well as what hadn't yet been reached. There were significant gaps in the skyline, and scaffoldings comprised much of what remained.

It would be years before the city returned to some semblance of normal.

"Mists take me," Hanaa muttered. "What happened here?"

"Insurrection," Miria answered, pushing away from Yaoru as much as possible. "Mercenaries had been stirring descent and starting riots. We had to put down a full rebellion."

"Giant monsters *and* rebellions," Yaoru mused. "You keep busy, don't you, little sister."

"I told you not to call me that," snapped Miria.

"Fine, fine," Yaoru said dismissively.

When they arrived at the Ministry building, a runner at the door recognized Cassidy and Miria and escorted them inside. Cassidy shivered as they walked the familiar route to the Lord Minister's office, remembering the bodies lined up in the hall, and the sense of panic and dread that had infected everyone. Things were calmer, now, but that didn't quiet the ghosts in her mind.

The walls that had been blown open when Cassidy first came to visit the Lord Minister had been patched, but no effort had been made to paint it. So it was just a colorless splotch with no windows in the middle of a classically styled, red and gold hallway. The floors suffered similarly, with plush carpet giving way abruptly to newly laid wood.

Their guide didn't knock on the office door. Instead, he threw it wide and announced. "Lord Minister, Princess Yushiro and Captain Durant, as requested."

The Lord Minister was alone, though it seemed she still shared the office with the Baroness. She leaned over her desk, her full weight on her hands, in a gesture that might have been anger, sorrow, or resignation. With her face downcast, Cassidy couldn't tell which. Her uniform was crisp, but her hair was in a messy bun.

"Thank you, Wan," she said, standing up straight and folding her hands behind her back. "Leave us." The runner saluted and closed the door behind him as he left.

The Lord Minister raised her head and bowed. "Your highness. I apologize for failing to recognize you during your last stay."

"I would have been dismayed if you had," Miria said kindly. "Though, I am curious, how you have come to know, now."

The Lord Minister let out a long breath and picked up a sheet of parchment from her desk. "News from the capital arrived mere hours before you did. Context made me suspect."

"News from the capital?" Miria repeated. "Please, do tell."

A crestfallen expression past briefly over the older woman's face, and while it was gone in an instant, Cassidy was sure she had no desire to obey. Still, she took a deep breath and gave her report. "There was an attack on the Jade Palace." Cassidy felt shock chill her blood. She looked to see Miria's reaction, but the girl wore the mask of command again.

"Ships hired by Castilyn appeared as if from thin air," the Lord Minister continued. "Eye witness accounts claim the enemy conjured the Dread Hounds," she added in a dubious tone. Then she sobered. "The reports say Empress Yushiro Shahira was slain by a mercenary named Zayne Balthine, also known as Daen's Scorpion."

"That's impossible!" Cassidy snapped, saying the words before she even had a chance to process what she was hearing. "I killed Balthine over Lake Justiciar and sank his ship after him for good measure!"

"Whether or not this was the same man, the situation is the same." The Lord Minister crossed the room and prostrated herself before Miria. "You must return to Revehaven to take your place as Empress."

CHAPTER FORTY-THREE

The *Scorpion* sailed above the tumultuous gray waves, beneath a featureless gray sky. The wind over the Imperial Sea was wet and frigid, and Zayne felt it twofold as it chilled his body and sprayed against the hull. Zayne kept watch from the aft castle. He was practicing his ability to see through the eyes of the rivermaid on the *Scorpion's* prow and his own simultaneously. It gave him a headache and confused him if he tried it for too long. It had proven useful for evading patrols, but now, with nothing but empty gray in every direction, it was more disorienting than helpful.

Pyrrha stalked just below him, casting the occasional glance at the hatch that led below. She seemed to be giving Xun a wide berth; while she hadn't said anything directly, Zayne had noticed the Fae tried to avoid being on the same deck as the woman for any length of time. He had to assume it was because of whatever deal Xun had struck with the forest goddess, though refused to say what she had agreed to.

Shen approached him, taking slow, creaking steps. "What are we going to do about Dardan?" he asked without preamble.

Zayne stared out at the sea. It looked glassy and serene from where he stood, but he knew if they dropped closer he would hear the lapping of waves and see just a hint of the tumult. He imagined losing himself in those waves. How long could he tread water before losing strength and succumbing to the depths? Or being eaten by whatever lurked under the surface?

"I don't know," he admitted.

"I thought Tagren had the right idea," said Shen. "I thought he did it."

"I… hoped," Zayne confessed, "but I don't think I really believed it, though."

Shen swore. "She was ready for it!" He punched the gunwale, which Zayne felt faintly on the edge of his perception. "How do we kill someone who sees every assassination attempt coming?"

Zayne thought back to Val Joyau. Dardan had been ready to fight off Nanette, but she *had* been surprised when Zayne had drawn his pistol. She *could* be taken off guard. Despite her intensity and air of control, *she knew fear.*

"If you see an opening, take it," Zayne ordered. "She can't keep dodging bullets forever."

"You really think it's that simple?" asked Shen.

"Feel free to find a Fae and ask *it* to kill her if that's not good enough," Zayne offered. He was only half kidding.

Shen glanced over to where Pyrrha stood, watching them from across the deck with a sickening grin. "I think there's enough evil in our lives without inviting more."

Through the eyes of the rivermaid, Zayne spotted a black form moving between the clouds on the horizon. "Well, keep your eyes open, and your weapon ready. You might get your chance soon."

As they drew nearer, Zayne realized the *Martyr's Demise* wasn't alone; he also caught sight of the armored kirin of the *Knight in Mourning* and the bull-headed spider that identified the *Forgotten Promise*. Of course Nyrien was lurking about like Dardan's personal honor guard.

Nanette slowed the *Scorpion* as they drew near enough to make out the ship's features without supernatural vision and let her drift close enough to cross. With the *Knight* on her starboard and the *Promise* on the aft, the *Scorpion* boxed the *Demise* in by taking her place at the larger ship's port. Zayne leaped across before Dardan's crew could set down the gangplank.

"Balthine," Nyrien sneered from behind Dardan's chair, her words puffing into mist. At least, he *thought* she sneered; the scars on her face drew her eyes down and lips up into a perpetual scowl. She wore a belted black coat with a thick red scarf secured to her shoulders by a leather harness. She made no effort to disguise the threat when she clasped the sword strapped to her back or the pistol on her hip, though she didn't draw either weapon.

"Nyrien," he replied with practiced indifference. "I didn't see you in Revehaven. Did the job scare you, or was it the prospect of taking your lips off Dardan's boots for five minutes?"

"Save the insults for Lancen, kid," Nyrien said, though her scowl had deepened at his words. "You might hurt yourself."

By her side, Lucky San choked out a raspy, phlegm filled chortle and spat. Her grin was a haunting, skeletal thing, twisting the scarred gap where her nose should have been. Zayne had once compared San Mina to a painting of the Imperial princess — or the new Empress, Zayne supposed, considering recent events — but faced with that horrifying grin, the comparison to so gentle and elegant a creature blew apart like towers made of ashes. She was dressed for warmer weather, with a thin, sleeveless black coat and detached sleeves made of silk strapped to her elbows.

"You can't deny, he has you pegged," San said with a barking laugh.

"Stow it, Lucky, before I peg *you*, you grotesque —"

"Enough," Dardan commanded, cutting through the chatter. "Captain Balthine," asked Dardan. "Is it done?"

"You could have warned me that the fucking thing was guarded by Faeorn," Zayne snapped.

"Would it have changed anything?" she asked placidly. When Zayne gave no reply, she waved her hand dismissively. "It didn't matter. So you faced a goddess. You aren't unique. Does she yet live?"

"She does," Zayne said through grit teeth.

Dardan laughed, a subdued, cold sound. "Oh, that is even better than I hoped. She will be forced to work against her own interests, serving my purposes instead." Her laughter deepened, and behind her back, Nyrien and San exchanged looks that said they had no idea what the conversation was about. Well, at least he wasn't the only one sailing in the dark.

"Why are we here, Dardan?" Zayne demanded.

"Ah, yes, of course," she said. There was a cruel mockery in her tone. "The three of you are instrumental to what comes next. Captain San," she barked, and Lucky San snapped to attention. Dardan rose, her cowl billowing like smoke in the wind. She produced a diadem made of charred bone held together by a strange fabric dark as a storm at midnight.

Something in that darkness *shifted* and *flowed* beneath Dardan's spindly fingers as she lifted the diadem for Lucky San to inspect. A chill radiated from the bloody thing, and Zayne was reminded of the Host, the strange dark god he had met in the Dreamscape. It was a vile thing.

"You wanted to prove yourself worthy of being one of my Great Captains?" Dardan asked San. "This is your chance. Come, all of you." She walked over to the prow, and after a moment's hesitation, Nyrien and San obeyed. As Dardan crossed Zayne, he felt his hands quake in pain as the desire to reach out and kill her with Dawn Star burned within him. His compulsion to follow Dardan's orders forced him to step away after she had passed a few feet of him. He fought the urge to destroy the relic just to spite her. He couldn't afford to be too rash. Again.

"The Leviathan is a fascinating creature," Dardan said to her captive audience. "Pure, unrivaled destructive power. Endless capacity for growth, and unlike the dragons of this world, it isn't stunted by the World Tree."

The gentle lapping of waves below gave way to a deep, thunderous rush of water. The gasp of something breaching the surface amplified a thousand times, and a tremendous geyser slammed against the ship, throwing Nyrien to the deck while Zayne and San clutched the gunwales. A wall of water formed all around the ship. The resultant deluge soaked them as a day's worth of rain came down on them in long seconds, the sound of crashing water drowning out all else.

Zayne peered over the gunwale to see the pillar of water fall away into a fathomless black pit as the sea sank in around itself.

A whirlpool a mile wide formed beneath them.

Every few turns of the current, jagged, impossible teeth cut through the water before being submerged again.

"There is just one problem," Dardan said through her water plastered veil, turning to San, as though nothing had happened. "It's not a predictable element."

Zayne snorted, spraying water from his nose. He knew from Lucandri's memories that the Leviathan had never been a part of Dardan's plan — his grasp on that plan actually *was* proved more tenuous; the scope of it was beyond what Zayne could glean in the chaotic moments when his mind was not strictly his own, and he couldn't even be sure of how much the Fae knew — but of course she had adapted easily enough.

"Unchecked, it is just as likely to undo my work as it is to hasten my ends," she continued. "I don't like uncertainties. So, I need assurance. The Leviathan needs direction."

"I have chosen you, San Mina, to be the mind that directs the fury. You shall *possess* the Leviathan."

San coughed out a lungful of water, hacking and wheezing. "You... want me to... want me... to what?"

"Wear this, and all will be made clear," Dardan said, holding the diadem out to her.

The bone crown rattled as San gingerly took it from Dardan's clutches and set it on her head. San's eyes widened and her skull-like grin of ecstasy sent a shiver down Zayne's spine.

"This. Is. Incredible!" she screamed. "I can see — I can feel — so much more than I have ever bef— have colors always been so vibrant? Oh, the music, gods, the music!"

"Focus, San," Dardan chided, and San's eyes shifted to Dardan's cowl. San looked at the woman as though she had never seen anything like her. "You will send the leviathan to follow my directives. The leviathan must not stay idle. It must *feed*.

"And don't worry about your crew," she added in a sickeningly sweet tone. "I'll take care of them."

San's eyes sharped. "What —"

Dardan shoved her hard in the chest, sending the blue eyed woman tumbling over the gunwale. She shrieked as she turned end over end, falling into the waiting maw of the leviathan. The *Martyr's Demise* thrashed and trembled as the *Knight in Mourning* exploded in a bloom of fire and splinters.

In the confusion, Zayne summoned Dawn Star. Whatever Dardan wanted, he was certain he couldn't allow it to come to pass. He hurled the sword like a spear at Lucky San's falling form. He felt the golden blade cutting through the air as if he himself were falling. He also felt the sensation when the blade passed easily through the bone, through the dream fabric, and finally through Mina's skull and brain and come out the other side. Only when the hilt connected with her forehead did the blade vanish in a flash of shattering lights.

Dardan didn't seem to have noticed, her attention fixated on the *Knight in Mourning*. The ship had been blown apart through the middle, with the aft and prow each dangling unevenly from the balloon. The aft cables snapped first. Zayne watched two people fall from the wreckage, flailing mere moments before the vessel followed. With the balloon dragged down on one side, its ability to provide any sort of lift failed and the prow dropped, too. The terrorized cries of the men and women aboard fell away as they unwittingly followed their captain into the swirling abyss. Zayne's heart cried with them, wanting nothing more than to spare them their twisted fate. He felt so powerless.

"Now, Captain Balthine," Dardan continued with her characteristically disgusting disinterest, "I have received reports that the Empire has tasked someone with hunting the Leviathan. Considering what I have just done to reign it in, I cannot abide by that."

Zayne watched the *Knight In Mourning* crash into the swirling edge of the whirlpool. As if its destruction hadn't been unworthy enough, the current shredded the vessel like ashes in the wind. He tore his gaze from the horror and swallowed bile. "You really think anyone can do something about that?" he said, pointing with his thumb.

"Perhaps not," said Dardan, "but you are to find whoever has been given the chance to try and —"

A second explosion jolted the *Martyr's Demise*, this one from the aft. Nyrien, Zayne, and even Dardan were thrown into the gunwale as splinters and flaming lumber showered the aftcastle.

The *Forgotten Promise* was in flames.

Nyrien dropped to her knees and let out a raw scream at the sight of her ship ablaze.

"Get up, you fool!" Dardan snapped, "your ship can still be saved." She turned, and though her face was obscured by her cowl, Zayne could *feel* her glowering. "You have your orders. Go. You best pray I don't discover your hand in this."

Zayne didn't need the compulsion to obey. For the first time since he had been cursed with Lucandri's binds — possibly for the first time *ever* — Dardan had given him an order he actually *wanted* to follow. He wanted as far away from her as he could get. Unfortunately, it meant he couldn't take advantage of the chaos. He turned and all but ran to his ship.

As he crossed back over to the *Scorpion*, he felt a strange sensation through the vessel. *Shen is climbing in from the outer hull,* he realized. He puzzled that out as he ordered Aresh to fly them out. Only when he saw the extent of the damage to the *Forgotten Promise* and the *Martyr's Demise* — neither ship crippled, but both battered and burning — did Zayne put together what must have happened.

Shen met him on the deck a few minutes later. His face was stained black with ash and there was blood on his coat.

"You climbed over and used the Martyr's cannons against the *Forgotten Promise*," said Zayne. "How'd you manage that?"

Shen grunted and wiped his brow, smearing a trail of blood along it. "Well, after they fired on the other ship, I had to do something. I opened a cannon hatch — luckily, the crew were focused on the other side and rendered deaf by the cannons. I killed the cannoneers and punched a hole in the aft blasting the *Promise*. Had to hide when reinforcements showed, but by then the *Promise's* crew was up in arms. Figure I'd let them sort it out. Did you kill Dardan?"

Zayne scowled. "No. Her influence was too strong."

"Blood and blight," Shen swore. "Well, what are we doing now?"

Zayne looked below. The swirling vortex was beginning to subside as the Leviathan sank deeper into the sea. "For now, we get out of here before our luck sours and we get killed." Shen grunted, clearly not happy with the arrangement, but failing to see a better solution.

They had proven yet again that Dardan could be surprised. It hadn't been enough, but she couldn't stay lucky forever. *I will find a way,* he told himself, *if it's the last thing I do.*

479

CHAPTER FORTY-FOUR

Kek hadn't returned to the *Dreamscape Voyager*. Instead, Cassidy and Miria returned to find Nieves pacing at the foot of the gangway, gesticulating wildly, and cursing profusely to herself. As soon as Cassidy caught her eye, the sawbones whirled on her, brandishing her finger like a pistol.

"... and if it hadn't extorted that stupid promise out of me," she said, not even breaking from her self-inflicted tirade and poking Cassidy hard in the chest, "I just know he would have come shambling home already, because despite everything he says, I know he wouldn't put his anger above your health! But now I have to wait for him to work himself out! He will probably start looking for comfort at the bottom of a cup, or the inside of a skirt, and he'll probably get hurt because he hasn't recovered enough to handle himself! What if he gets mugged? What if his fever spikes? Why the fuck do I even listen to your bullshit ideas, Cassidy?" She turned away but didn't slow her frantic rant. Cassidy's guilt weighed heavier in her chest with each passing word. "He could be out there right now puking his guts out, and where are we? No idea where he is, that's where! So now I have to sit here and wait for him to come crawling back all apologies and contrition, imagining every possible terrible thing that can happen because I have seen —"

"We can't wait for him to change his mind," Cassidy shouted over her. "We're leaving tonight."

"— what happens to someone when — " Nieves stopped abruptly and cocked her head. "We're *what?*"

"News from the capital," Miria said solemnly. "My — the Empress... she... the Empress is dead," she finally managed. "We have to return to the capital, at once. The moment we are resupplied."

"That's only a few hours, even assuming the orders take a while," Nieves protested. "Kek could be —"

"I don't want to leave him, either," Miria said, her tone cold and imperious like her mothers, "but the captain spoke true; he made his choice. Unfortunately, we don't have the luxury of giving him a second chance."

Nieves gritted her teeth. She looked ready to argue, but she deflated and hung her head. "Aye. I'll make sure we're ready." She turned to climb up to the ship, but paused, looking to Miria. "I'm sorry," she said. "It must be hard —"

"Not here," Miria said flatly. "Not now." She walked by Nieves and climbed the gangway with a cold, graceful intensity that reminded Cassidy so much of the Empress.

"I need to tell Jathun and Zhu," she said, swallowing her discomfort. "The Lord Minister is ordering most of the fleet with us, as an honor guard for… for her highness."

Cassidy chose to go alone. According to a watch officer on the docks, Jathun's entire crew had apparently gone to a tavern when they arrived, so Cassidy found Zhu at the *Roc Spear* first. The older captain had a writing board in hand, his quill scratching furiously at the parchment attached.

"Captain Zhu," she said, "we will be leaving earlier than planned, there's been —"

Zhu jumped at the sound of her voice. Once he identified her, he leveled his quill like a knife. "Oh, no. *We* are leaving *nowhere* with you. I don't know what sick plot you've concocted, but you'll not drag my crew into your madness!"

"Zhu, what—"

"Don't you dare speak my name! You consort with the basest of creatures, and with the *Fae*, and you drag the glory of the royal family with you. I may be powerless to stop you, but once the Iron Veils know what you've done, you're through."

Cassidy hadn't thought she could feel any lower, but she did. And with that pain came a bubbling anger.

"I'm not — I didn't — Hymn's not —" She frantically searched for words, but didn't know Zhu well enough to get through to him. Her eyes fell onto his writing pad. Was he —

As if sensing her thoughts, he said, "I have already sent my letters — in triplicate — to the Iron Veils. This is merely my resignation letter to the Lord Minister. I'll have no part on whatever corruption you plan to bring to the Empire."

"But the Empress is —"

"Do not despoil her station with your verminous lies, Fae touched," he sneered. "Begone, before I call the Watch."

Thunder cracked overhead and they both looked. Cassidy half expected the sky to open up in a torrent of rain any moment. When the two captains' eyes met again, Zhu sneered and walked away. Cassidy, short any other recourse, did the same.

"Can you believe the nerve of that ungrateful shit?" Cassidy asked Hymn.

The Fae merely buzzed against Cassidy's hair in a way Cassidy had started to equate to human snoring.

She followed the directions the watch officer had given to the tavern. It was a little place, barely more than a hole in the wall — considering the state of the city, Cassidy had half expected an *actual* hole in the wall — but it was clean and homey. She was surprised to find only Jathun and the survivors of the *Sunrise* in the place, spread out across the establishment's three small tables, with Jathun alone at the bar. There was a low rumble of conversation over a card game with Jin, Bai Fen, and Fan Wua, while the others seemed content to nurse their drinks in silence.

The bartender was a girl no older than Miria. When she looked up from the bar to Cassidy, Jathun followed her gaze. He smiled ruefully and raised a cup to her. "Captain Durant. Glad you could make it. Got some bad news. Good news, too, but I'll start with the bad."

"Shame," Cassidy said as she pulled a stool out and plopped down beside him, unable to hide her mounting fatigue. "I could really go for some *good* news. I'm full up on the other stuff."

"Well, Zhu is out. Sent three letters to the... well, people you want to avoid. Don't know why he told me. Guess he thought I would want to bail, too, under the circumstances."

"Oh," said Cassidy. "I actually found out before tracking you down. Bastard told me himself."

"Hey, that means I've only got good news for you, then!" he said amiably. "Because I just asked around, and everyone here is still at your back! Well, except Jia," he said, waving a hand at the bartender. "Jia doesn't know you. I'm sure she'd like you, though, given time."

The girl smiled uncomfortably and ducked into the backroom, which was divided from the common room by a half-torn, silk curtain.

"I have bad news, too," Cassidy said. "And I can't cushion it with better news." She took a deep breath. "Revehaven was attacked. You ever heard of the Daughters of Daen?"

"Heard of them, worked with them, fought against them. Crazy bunch of bastards. I guess if anyone were going to pull it off, it'd be them."

"Mm," Cassidy agreed. She leaned over to make sure Jia couldn't overhear them. "Well... the Empress is dead. The three days we had planned to take stock before we went hunting? Gone. We have to escort the heir to the capital, before people start suspecting something happened to her, too." She sighed. "We only have until the resupply is done."

Jathun nodded. He let out a long sigh and tossed his drink back. "I assume I don't need to repeat that for any of you?" he asked his new crew. Everyone had stopped what they were doing to stare at the two of them.

"N-no, captain," Jin said after several beats of painful silence. She scrambled to her feet and started gathering the cards. After another beat, the others began following suit and were soon pushing their way out of the tavern.

"Patriots," Jathun said with an air of affectionate mockery. His tone sobered when he said, "You should have a drink before you go. You look like you need it." He patted her shoulder and followed his crew, leaving Cassidy alone in the small tavern.

Jia returned and poured her a cup of rice wine without being asked. When Cassidy raised a brow, the girl said, "Your friend paid enough to keep the drinks coming for a while. And this is all we have."

Cassidy raised the cup with a smile and knocked it back. It was sour, and wasn't kept hot, but it would do. The bartender lingered after refilling it, running a rag over the same part of the bar and casting uncomfortable glances at her.

"Something wrong?" Cassidy asked.

The girl squeaked, as if surprised to be addressed. "Oh, I was... um... wondering if you would be in town long... sailor?"

Cassidy blinked. Then she shook her head, laughing. "Sorry, I'm not —" She paused as she thought about turning to Kek to share the moment, and her levity died. "Say, I don't suppose you've seen a blond man, have you? A little shorter than me, wiry fellow.

Probably has a fevered complexion? Would have been in the last two or three hours."

The young girl shook her head. "Sorry, miss. Your friends that just left are the first people we've had since lunch."

"Why so slow?" Cassidy asked. "I remember when the battle was over, taverns were taking numbers, and everyone was lined up in the street."

"Oh, that's still the case further in town," said Jia, "but most of the reconstruction is focused further into the city. We get a few stragglers, but most folks aren't straying too far from the job."

Lightning flashed outside, casting two deep shadows on either side of Cassidy. She turned to see two, tall women in matching brown kaftans, emblazoned with a black griffin on the left breast. One woman was tall and lean, and she wore a black turban. The other was short and more thickly built, with herd long, dark tresses hanging loose.

"Is that her?" the tall one asked.

"Dark skinned with red hair," the short woman, "one green eye, one golden brown. Aye, that's her." They each drew a pistol and Cassidy slammed her eyes shut. Cassidy heard three thunderous cracks before sound was replaced by the cold ringing of a thousand tiny bells.

She felt no pain. Had they missed? Or was she dying? She slowly opened her eyes. Gun smoke obscured her vision and tears welled in her eyes from their acrid influence. She ran timid hands over her body, feeling no blood or tender wounds. When she could finally see, she found her assailants propped against one another in mid fall, blood seeping from both of their hearts. The tall one's brains and skull were splattered in gooey chunks between where she stood and the door.

Cassidy turned to find Jia, pistol outstretched and quivering in her hand, and beside her, brandishing two smoking guns held still and true, stood a familiar, middle aged Rivien woman wearing a translucent veil. Her dark locks hung loosely, instead of hidden by a turban, but Cassidy knew her all the same.

"*Venitha?*" she exclaimed, a little louder than was probably necessary, as the ringing in her ears was starting to subside. "What are you doing here?"

Venitha smiled sadly. "It was too depressing working in the prison, with all the poor souls who could not be helped as Jathun was. I decided to move where I could help raise the spirits of the people I met, even if only a little, so I bought this tavern. Jia, dear," she added to the bartender, gently pushing down her still shaking pistol, "clean this up and tell the watch that these women tried to kill our customer. Specify that they are Black Griffin mercenaries, and there may be more. Cassandra, let's speak outside, before your unwanted guests stink up the place."

Without waiting to see if Cassidy would follow her, the strange savior walked back through the torn curtain into the back room. A pair of muted *thunk*s drew her attention back to the mercenaries. Their bodies had flopped limply onto the floor when Jia had shifted one of them. She started to drag the taller woman out by the wrists before Cassidy decided to follow the erstwhile prison warden.

The back room was little more than a hallway lined with racks of wine jugs, and a door leading to a nook overlooking an alleyway. Venitha greeted her with a smile, then filled two small cups of yellow rice wine from a jug before passing one to Cassidy. Cassidy accepted it graciously.

"I guess that's twice you've saved my life," she said before partaking. The wine was sweeter than the vintage Jia had served, and Cassidy caught a distinct honey flavor. It went down smooth, and a wave of warmth rushed from Cassidy's stomach through her body.

"Just doing my part," Venitha said, removing her veil to take a drink. After a lengthy pause, she added, "You've suffered a terrible loss."

Cassidy scoffed. "Is it that obvious?"

The bizarre woman filled the cups again. "I've seen the signs before. And that fire that blazes in your eyes is a little dimmer now. So, what's wrong?"

Cassidy raised the cup to her lips and downed the wine. "You always seem to know everything," she said. "Why ask me?"

"Because I'm not the one you need to air it out for," said Venitha. When Cassidy didn't say anything, she sighed. "At times like this, you need to be strong for those who follow you, so they can take strength from your example. But no one can wear that facade all the time without breaking. So, I'm offering an ear." She gave Cassidy another chance to speak. "Call it payment for saving your life, then."

With a sigh, Cassidy tossed back another cup and braced herself. "I got a lot of people killed and drove my best friend away by keeping secrets."

"Some people might find it strange that you put those things on the same scale," said the tavern owner. Before Cassidy could tell her where to stick her judgement, she held up a placating hand. "But I am not one of them. I understand full well.

"Death is always terrible, but a true friendship is the root of our humanity, and it is only natural to feel pain when it is torn away. Tell me, how did these things come to be?"

"Well, it's hard to say exactly where I started driving the wedge between me and Kek, but the deaths of the *Sunrise's* crew... I guess that really started when we set out for Marasi prison."

Cassidy told the story in fits and starts, occasionally circling back to provide context where she needed to. She didn't explain about Asier's visions or her own, and though Venitha had implied she knew about Hymn in their previous encounters, she didn't refer to the Fae directly, either.

Laying out only the bare bones of the explanation, it wasn't a particularly long story. That was good because Cassidy could feel tears burning her eyes even without the added details.

"... And I just feel like it's all my fault," she finished.

"Well," Venitha said, setting her cup back down to refill, "that's because it is."

"Thanks for the help," Cassidy muttered. Her senses began to fuzz at the edges from the drink, but the pain in her chest had barely been blunted.

"I'm sorry if that's not what you want to hear," Venitha said, and her voice *did* seem sympathetic. "But it is what you *need* to hear. Yes, your order to wave the Imperial flag, knowing that there were pirates looking for Imperial vessels, got those aboard the *Sunrise* killed. Yes, your choice to withhold information from your friends created a rift between you.

"The choices you make have consequences. What most people fail to realize, and the lesson you need to take from this, is that those consequences affect not just you, but everyone around you. So, yes, Cassandra; it is your fault, and the guilt you feel is deserved."

Cassidy gritted her teeth and reached for the wine jug.

Venitha caught her hand and held it in both of hers. "But we don't feel pain to punish ourselves. Our pain is meant to teach us, and to let us grow. You have to carry on, for the survivors, and for the friends still by your side. And you must take the lesson, taught by heartache, and strive to be better."

Cassidy stared into her empty cup. That made sense. *Be better.* On one hand, it sounded like condescension, but at the same time… it was so simple. Cassidy had made the same mistake as Asier, but she had the chance to *stop* making that mistake. She hoped Kek would forgive her in time, but even if he didn't, she still owed it to the others to be upfront, to be honest.

To trust them.

"You're right," she said. She took a deep, quavering breath.

Venitha poured another round. "There's still something bothering you. Something you're trying to hide away. Don't let it fester."

Cassidy opened her mouth to say that there was nothing left for her to reveal, but the words wouldn't come out. There *was* something else, something she had tried to put out of her mind because it didn't matter. Because worrying about it was ridiculous.

"A little over a year ago," said Cassidy, "I killed a man. He was a monster, a terror. Sometimes, on the rare occasions I really dream, I still see his face. I felt *good* killing him because he *needed* to die. But recently, I learned that someone is using his identity, and not just that, but doing the things I suspect he might have done, were he alive. And I *know* he is really dead — no one could survive what I did to him — but despite what I *know*, there's a niggling doubt in my heart, like a desert worm burrowing inside me. I'm… afraid. What if it is really him, and I can't stop him a second time?"

It was this confession that broke Cassidy's last reserves, and she burst into tears.

Venitha's hand was warm on her shoulder, and gentle. "Alone, you would probably fail," she agreed. "But your strength resides in your friends, and should your worst fears come to life, you need not face them alone."

Cassidy's return to the *Dreamscape Voyager* was something of a blur, partly from the drinks, but also from the rush of thoughts and emotions jostling through her head. The resupply was nearly done when she arrived. She nodded her thanks to the workers as she passed them and signed the manifest when asked. Two weeks of hard flying straight through the Black Gulch separated them from the capital city, and Cassidy was eager to get a move on.

"Lierre," she called over the pipeline, "I want those engines hot. Haytham, you'll take the helm."

When the *Dreamscape Voyager* left port, it was followed closely by the *Temptation* and the *Clockwork Hydra* and all of her compatriot ships. A dozen other ships from the city trailed behind and fanned out, and as they flew east, two dozen more that had been stationed outside the city tailed after them as well. Cassidy counted forty-seven vessels in the fleet. She stared in awe at the imposing sight.

Miria stood beside her on the aftcastle as they took in the spectacle.

"That's all for you," Cassidy said.

Miria nodded, but Cassidy could see her jaw tighten. The looming storm followed the fleet eastward, even though it should have dispersed or been driven westward by the winds. The constant flashes of lightning burned the image of the fleet in Cassidy's eyes, and the rolling thunder became a devastating symphony. She didn't know how long they stood there, taking it all in, but eventually Miria let out a long sigh and walked away.

The fleet pushed on through the first night and through the next day. On the second night, they stopped over the snow covered Black Gulch. Cassidy watched the rock spires for signs of harpies. They weren't likely to encounter any in the cold weather, but she watched all the same, shivering all the while. Asier had saved the *Scorpion* here, and it had cost her her life in the long run. A slew of memories, good and bad, piled in Cassidy's head after that, and she wished she could see Asier one last time and… what? Ask for advice? Apologize for tarnishing her memory for nearly a year? Share a drink?

"Sometimes I don't even recognize that life," Cassidy said, more to herself than Hymn, though the Fae had begun to stir earlier in the day. "Would she even recognize me?"

"A lot has changed," the Fae acknowledged from beneath her hat. "But for all that you are older and wiser, you have not changed so considerably. I suspect, were she here, she would be quite proud of you for facing these challenging times so courageously."

That was the most Hymn had said in days, and Cassidy felt a weight on her shoulders ease, just a little.

"I am sorry about Kekarian," she continued in a solemn whisper. "I know what it is to lose a friend. The pain it causes. Take solace in the knowledge that at least you still have others."

Cassidy nodded, thinking fondly of her crew, but something about Hymn's advice rang with a piteous note and changed the course of her thoughts. She considered Hymn's claim that she and Len had been friends, and her words just now. Had Len been Hymn's *only* friend before they fell out? Had she had other friends and simply lost them all at once? Either way, it sounded lonely. She wanted to offer some comfort, but anything she could say felt hollow.

The sound of the dinner bell drew Cassidy's attention, and she joined the others in the galley. She was the last to arrive, having sent the others ahead to keep warm. Crossing the threshold onto the confined space felt like shirking a block of ice and embracing a cozy blanket. She came in to find Miria serving out steaming bowls of rice piled with egg and poultry, and a side plate of pickled radishes. It struck Cassidy that this would probably be the last time Miria ever cooked a meal or served one.

Lierre and Nieves sat on either side of the empty seat usually occupied by Miria, with the Ramajin siblings sitting across from one another beside them. Cassidy's gaze lingered on Kek's empty seat for a long moment before she took her own.

She waited for the others to begin eating before she did the same, though hunger gnawed at her. The first bite was like a fire that warmed a path through her insides that settled into the yawning pit of her stomach, barely taking in the flavor until the second. She fought the urge to cry, and a laugh burst from her in its stead.

When the others looked up, Cassidy said, "You've come a long way from those terrible omelets you made two years ago."

Lierre burst into giggles and Nieves chuckled. Even Miria smiled at the memory, though she turned her head away to hide it.

"Gods," said Lierre, "those were awful! Kek even —" she stopped, and the laughter died down.

Cassidy cleared her throat. "About that," she said, though she wasn't sure how best to broach the subject. "Kek was right. I haven't been honest with you. I've been scared about so many things. It's no excuse, I was wrong, but, well… you saw the journal. I first read it after we escaped the Dragon's Nest. I would have missed it entirely if it weren't for Hymn.

"And when I read it, I was… I was hurt. I felt like Elyia abandoned us. Knowing she could see the future… I didn't know how to break it to you because I didn't really understand it myself. I wanted to protect you.

"And about your… your father," she said to Miria. The princess stiffened. "Your uncle told me that it would break your heart if you knew the truth, and I believed him. I should have known better, but I was still dealing with my own new truths. And Kek was right, I *did* know the *Clockwork Hydra* was looking for Imperial ships, I just didn't know they were going to… to do what they did."

Miria silently set her bowl down and stared into it like it held answers. Lierre and Nieves watched Cassidy and Miria, as if for some cue to tell them how they were going to respond. Haytham and Hanaa ate with the single-minded determination of people who didn't want to get dragged into the mess.

"I suppose, what's past is past," Miria said at last. "I'm not pleased, Captain, but I know you well enough to know you meant well. But I'm not sure I'm quite ready to forgive you."

"I'm not done," Cassidy confessed. She met Nieves eyes, and the sawbones gave her a resolute nod. "There's two more secrets I've been keeping, since we put down the rebellion in Andaerhal."

Nieves brow furrowed.

"How can one woman have so many secrets in such close company?" Lierre demanded, though there was a nervous playful edge to her tone. "I can't even use the privy without at least three people knowing."

Cassidy gave a wan smile at that before taking a deep breath. "That vision of the future Elyia had?" she began, bracing herself. "I've had a few, now. Starting with the rebellion."

Bowls clacked on the table as all eyes locked onto Cassidy. Even the Ramajins stopped pretending they weren't paying attention. Cassidy held off until the anticipatory silence grew too intense.

"I have seen… possible deaths, a few times now," she explained. "I've been able to use that foreknowledge to stay alive, so far, but it hasn't been easy. It's like wrestling against my own mind and body. And the last time it happened, Kek... Kek was poisoned because I saved myself!"

"Cass, you can't —" Nieves began, but she didn't seem to know how to finish that thought once she processed what Cassidy had said.

"I don't know what caused those visions," said Cassidy. "I don't know when I'll get another one, or if I'll be able to stop what I see from happening when I do. Or if I even should."

"Don't say things like that," Lierre said, reaching across the table over Haytham's food, to touch Cassidy's hand. "You didn't *choose* to hurt Kek, and he did what he could to help you. And he's still alive and walking!"

"That," Cassidy said, taking another deep breath, "leads me to the other thing." She closed her eyes. The words sat on the edge of her tongue, and she hesitated.

Be better, she heard Venitha say.

She swallowed a lump in her throat. "I'm dying." Silence met the proclamation. When she opened her eyes, she saw Lierre's dark eyes widen with shock. Miria's beautiful blues were misty with unshed tears and her mouth hung agape. Nieves looked downcast. Hanaa had a sympathetic cast to her face while Haytham looked a little deflated, which was more than Cassidy had actually expected, considering how little she really knew them. Focusing her attention back to her friends, she said. "Hymn said five years, if I completely abstain from drawing on her influence to stave off pain and give me strength." She raised her food to her lips to try and fill the void she felt growing within, and to play off the revelation as something to be treated casually, but she couldn't bring herself to do it. "I *haven't been* abstaining," she added weakly. "Not at all."

"Gods," Miria whispered.

Lierre pushed away from the table and ran around it, throwing her arms around Cassidy. "Oh, *non,*" she breathed. "*Non, non, non.*"

Cassidy hugged her back, feeling magnitudes better despite everything. "Hey, I'm not dying *tonight*," she said with as much warm cheer as she could muster. "I know this is a lot to drop on you all," she said. "But I don't —" Lierre squeezed her so intensely Cassidy thought her ribs would break again.

"I, um," Hanaa said, clearing her throat, "I need to fix my bunk. Haytham, I need you to give me a hand."

"Why do you need my —"

"*Haytham!*" Hanaa snapped, making eyes to the scene unfolding at the table.

"Oh, right. That *thing*. With the bunk. Right!" The siblings retreated, leaving the *Dreamscape's* crew — what was left of them — to their moment.

When Lierre finally tore away, she grabbed hold of Cassidy's hands instead. "This is just so much! What do I do?"

"You don't have to do anything," Cassidy said, smiling at her friend. "I'm just glad to have you here right now." She felt her smile fade as she considered her unintended implication, but she forced herself to put on a brave face.

Nieves let out a sigh. "I know this was difficult," she said. "But it was the right thing to do."

"We can find a way to stop it, right?" Lierre asked. "Surely Hymn knows a way to save you?"

"It would take one far better than I," Hymn said from within Cassidy's hat, "if it can be done at all."

Miria stood abruptly. "Do you not *care*? Isn't she your friend?"

Hymn flew out into the open, hovering above the table. "I care a great deal, Miriaan," she said in an implacably calm tone. "I warned her about becoming too reliant on the power of our bond, but have you ever tried to stop her from doing what she wanted? She is stubborn as a mountain."

"I'm right here!" snapped Cassidy.

"So do something about it!" Miria demanded. "You had the power to conjure a mile wide storm that is constantly sitting above Yaoru's head so she doesn't sail beneath an Imperial sky!"

Cassidy blinked. How had she not figured that out herself? Between Hymn's words about bending the rules, her uncharacteristic need for rest, and the unnatural properties of the storm itself, she felt like an idiot for not piecing it together.

"There is a fundamental difference between tearing open a fraying tapestry and reweaving one," Hymn said, still calm. It was almost a lament. "This is beyond me. I am sorry."

Cassidy expected Miria to get angry at being contradicted. So she leaped in surprise when *Nieves* let out an impotent shout of fury and stormed out of the cabin. Lierre stared after her, her face matching the astonishment Cassidy felt. The engineer gave an apologetic look to Cassidy and chased after their retreating friend.

"Hymn, could you leave us for a moment?" Miria asked quietly.

"I am bound to protect —"

"Do you honestly believe I pose a threat to her?" Miria interjected. Hymn gave no answer, and Miria said, "Please."

The Fae hovered in the air for a moment longer, then fluttered away. She slipped through a crack in the door, leaving Cassidy alone with the princess. Miria stood up and paced the room, staring at the floor.

"This is a lot to bear," she said. "The leviathan, Andaerhal, the *Clockwork Hydra*, my father, my mother... and now you."

"I'm not dead yet," said Cassidy, but she felt only guilt, rather than conviction.

"Elyia isn't even two years gone," Miria continued. "Now my mother is dead. And now you!" She whirled on her heels and grabbed Cassidy by the shoulders, the brilliant blue gems of her eyes magnified by tears. "You are my sister, in a way that pirate *bitch* can never claim! I can't... I can't lose you, too!"

When she finally cried, streams trailing down her cheeks, she didn't seem vulnerable. If anything, she seemed more resolute. Her face was firm, and in her eyes blazed a fire that put Elyia Asier to shame. "I *won't* lose you," she said. "That is a promise, as your sister. As your *Empress*."

CHAPTER FORTY-FIVE

Two weeks of hard pushing separated Andaerhal from the capital. Twenty days of running at full speed. While the full night of rest on the second day had been good for the humors, the slow start that came about the following morning had led several of the fleet's captains to suggest a more constant schedule. Given the urgency of their purpose, Cassidy had agreed. As a result, every twenty-six hours — they decided that noon each day was best— the fleet would halt for routine maintenance before setting pace again, and otherwise carry on for the full day and night.

The *Dreamscape Voyager* and the *Temptation*, both operating with smaller crews, made do by limiting the duty roster to the most essential tasks, with shorter but more frequent breaks. It wasn't Cassidy's favorite rotation, but it kept them moving.

On the ninth day, Cassidy climbed to the deck, her arms so sore she felt on the brink of falling from the ladder after a shift on the engines, just as Miria took the helm from Haytham. The mercenary followed her to her cabin door.

"Captain Durant," he said quickly, "we haven't had a moment to talk, and I was hoping I could take a minute of your time."

Cassidy leaned against the cabin wall and slowly traced him with her eyes. "I guess I can spare *a couple* of minutes," she said, putting on a pouty smile and crossing her arms under her breasts. His eyes dropped to her chest immediately, lingering a moment before darting back up to hers.

"Thank you, Captain," he said.

He didn't seem flustered. Did that mean he wasn't interested, or was he just comfortable? By his own account, he enjoyed the company of women, but she couldn't help but wonder if his tastes still ran to *humans*.

"First, I would like to apologize for my sister and I — ah, what's the Asarian word? — eavesdropping? Eavesdropping on your private moment, the other night, and before."

494

Cassidy's cheek heated and she averted her gaze. "Ah. That. No, I'm the one who should apologize," she said, struggling to contain her disappointment. "You shouldn't have been dragged into our personal messes."

"Do I understand right that it is the *djinn* granted abilities that..." he hesitated, then tapped his own chest.

"You're asking if that's what's killing me?"

He nodded uncomfortably.

"It is." It was only when she said the words that she realized how callously she said it; Haytham *also* drew on powers granted to him by a Fae. It wasn't outside the realm of possibility he was dying as well.

The Rivien man let out a long sigh and slumped against the wall beside her. "It's a terrifying prospect," he said. "I've been relying on the gifts more and more of late. I never considered..." He swore in Rivien, but there was no fire in it.

Cassidy's heart sank to see him withdraw. She wished she could listen to his thoughts, to know how he was handling it. It has been so far beyond her ability to grapple with when she learned of it. It still was, really.

She scooted closer and put a hand on his arm. It was firm beneath her fingertips and a shiver ran across her body. "Haytham. This is a really hard time for both of us, so I am going to throw subtly overboard. Will you join me in my cabin?"

A faint smile worked its way onto his lips, and he stood up to his full height, meeting her eye with warmth in his own. His hands snakes along her arms and settled on her back, "I never took you for a subtle woman."

"I've never met a man who would notice if I was." She grabbed him by the collar and pulled him into a kiss. It was only when he was touching her that she was able to smell him over the charcoal smoke that smothered her like acrid perfume. His warm skin smelled clean, of soap and the icy sea breeze, and his breath carried hints of plum.

Haytham reacted enthusiastically to her kiss. With arms corded with firm and lithe muscles, he hoisted her legs out from underneath her and pinned her to the cabin door. She crossed her ankles around his back, savoring the feel of his muscles beneath her thighs. Her fingers explored the black curls of his hair. The latch cracked as the door swung open and Haytham stumbled forward.

Cassidy though she was going to be dropped on her head and braced herself against his body. The mercenary caught his balance even with her added weight wrapped around his chest.

Cassidy leaned back, pulling Haytham on top of her as she crashed onto her bed. Their kiss broke when they reached for one another's belts. "Show me what you bought your freedom with," she said breathlessly.

Time melted away in the torrent of pleasure. The world lost its meaning. Pain and hurt and guilt were set aside. Intrusive things like thoughts and reason meant nothing. All that mattered was the moment, the mounting lust that paid with release, again and again, and the warmth of skin on skin.

Only after the symphony's final crescendo did Cassidy take stock of reality.

She had one leg resting on Haytham's shoulder. The position had felt wonderful mere moments ago, but now it was starting to strain her muscles. She slid off him and rolled gracelessly onto the bed beside him, gasping for breath. The cold air was beginning to seep into the warmth, and with it, everything she had set aside was rolling in her mind like the fresh bout of pain.

She looked to her side and found Haytham crying. He made no sound, but the tears streamed freely down his face, getting lost in his beard, and he jerked with silent sobs.

Cassidy couldn't know for certain what it was that had affected him so — though she had her suspicions — but whatever it was, she knew she felt the same. The pain in her body beat against her in concert with the pain sounding in her heart. Fear and guilt and uncertainty played with sore muscles and the memory of a thousand injuries only partially healed due to her own negligence.

She cried, too.

They sobbed together, their grief unspoken but acknowledged. When duty called them both away, they cleaned their faces and parted, ready to face the day as if nothing had happened.

Over the course of the second week, Cassidy shared her bed with Haytham almost a dozen more times. Once, they had actually used it to *sleep* together — which was a first for the thing, at least in Cassidy's tenure as captain. They hadn't shared another moment quite like the first time. Sometimes Haytham cried, sometimes

Cassidy did. Sometimes they barely had time to get pensive. But regardless of the outcome, they never bathed in the afterglow like lovers should. There were too many shadows on the horizon.

They hadn't made their trysts a secret — and how could they? Miria had been standing mere feet away when Cassidy had first thrown herself at Haytham, and the ship wasn't very large — but aside from the occasional giggle from Lierre or quirk of the eyebrow from Miria, it went largely unremarked upon.

At least, until the sixteenth day, when Hanaa crossed Cassidy's path on the way to the galley.

"Don't lead my brother on," she said without preamble. "I won't tell you to stay away; he's a grown man, surprising as that is sometimes, and can make his own decisions. But if it's not serious, be sure you tell him. I don't want him getting hurt, and he can be… bah, what's the word in your language? It means violently ill, but in the heart?"

"Romantic?" Cassidy answered blankly.

"Sure."

Hanaa had walked away after that, and Cassidy had returned to her duties. She decided not to engage in that discussion. Haytham was a very proficient lover, but if he was usually romantic, what they had wasn't that.

It was on the final day that Haytham broached the subject instead.

"What are you going to do after this monster hunt?" he asked. To his credit, he didn't add "with the time you have left".

Cassidy — breasts still hanging out of her blouse and skirt flipped up over her stomach — sat up. They hardly spoke once they hit the bed, and never about anything so substantial. She crossed her legs and leaned her head on his shoulder.

"I plan on going back to business," she said. "We were cargo traders before all this happened."

"Do you think you'll be able to go back to that life?" Haytham asked. His hands were soft and gentle as he pulled her in closer. His warmth was a welcome distraction from the cold patch she sat in.

"Why wouldn't I?"

"Your Empire is at war," he said. "The princess still needs to make the declaration, but Empress Shahira was assassinated by Castilyn agents. I suppose merchants will still be needed, but instead of luxuries, you might be called to transport weapons, or military personnel. And you have major armaments on this ship. If your princess — if your *Empress* — asks you to fight, would you tell her no? As a citizen? As a *friend?*"

Cassidy didn't have an answer to that.

"Whatever you decide," Haytham continued, "what happens to us?"

She had suspected that the question might come, but she still wasn't ready for it. She took a deep breath and let it out in a heavy sigh. "I don't know," she admitted. "I'm not sure how long I have. I'm not even sure we'll make it out of *this* mess alive. I've never thought about relationships in the long term before." She reached between his legs, gave him an affectionate squeeze and looked him in the eye. "I have enjoyed our time together. But as far as *'us'* goes… I don't know. What do *you* plan to do?"

"I'm still a mercenary," he said. "Once this job is done, Hanaa and I will find ourselves back on the *Nagi Queen*." He paused. "Or, if she goes down on the hunt, on another ship."

"I think that answers that question, then," Cassidy said, running her hand lazily against him. "You'll be off on adventures, laying with strange women and *Fae* —"

"That was one time," he said morosely. "I had to!"

"And I'll be charting my course here in the Empire. How often would we see each other? Once a year? Twice if we're lucky? I don't even have five more years in me." She was glad she refrained from saying, "And you might not, either", though it was sitting on her tongue.

Haytham's crestfallen expression spoke volumes, though the young man himself was silent.

Cassidy sighed again and tugged gently at him. "We can talk more about the future when we know we'll have one. For now, why don't we —"

Her cabin door burst open with a clatter, and Nieves stepped inside. Lierre poked her head through the door behind her. Both women made it clear they weren't going to avert their gazes from the handsome and very naked young man in Cassidy's bed, though he had his back towards them. Nieves looked a little disappointed, while Lierre didn't seem to mind so much. Haytham looked a little uncomfortable, but not enough to retreat or hide.

"We're within sight of the capital, Captain," Nieves said, though her gaze seemed fixed on Haytham. "It looks like an envoy from the palace is en route to meet us. I thought you might want to be dressed for it."

"Though, I would pay good coin to see you facing the nobility like this," Lierre added with a broad grin.

Cassidy rolled her eyes and put herself back into her blouse and smoothed her skirt down to a modest arrangement while she looked for her undergarments. Meanwhile, Haytham dressed with a speed that suggested he was accustomed to getting caught and making a hasty exit.

By the time Cassidy was properly dressed, the approaching delegation from the capital was almost upon them. The oncoming ships were headed by the single largest vessel Cassidy had ever seen, dwarfing even the *Clockwork Hydra*.

"When did they build that?" Cassidy wondered aloud.

"She's been under construction in secret for years, now," Miria said. "I don't know when they finished, though."

The hull of the mystery vessel was a work of art. Scale carvings of golden dragons shaped both sides — three on both sides — with enormous, forward facing cannons affixed in their jaws. Ballistae and cannons lined the top deck, mounted on the backs of scarlet and golden phoenixes. Rather than one balloon, the ship was held aloft by nine of varying size — though whether it was for the protection of redundancy or if they were all needed to support such a structure, Cassidy couldn't say. A phoenix — larger by far than the ones on the deck — rendered in brilliant green comprised the figurehead, with its beak open and wings spread wide.

Emblazoned on the hull in gilded characters of the exacting Imperial script was the name *Elyia Asier*.

Cassidy and Miria were taken aboard the *Elyia Asier* to meet with the Empress' advisors, Maroda, Tasuki and Miria's Uncle Tao. Even the Capitan's cabin was extravagant and impressive; twice as tall as Cassidy's own, the expansive room had featured a magnificent table sitting above a recessed floor where the advisors sat. Behind the table on an even higher level was a mahogany desk grand enough it could only serve the Empress. Beyond that was another room separated by a silk curtain emblazoned with the Jade Phoenix, perhaps to serve as the Empress' private living quarters.

The fat Maroda and the spindly Tasuki seemed to be wearing a dozen fur coats apiece, while the Tao wore a black tunic with a green cape draped over his arm. As Cassidy and Miria reached the apparent audience pit, the trio of advisors stood as one, walked into the lowest level of the room, and knelt to Miria.

"Your Majesty," they said in tandem.

Miria had worn the cold mask of the Empress as soon as the skiff had been sent to retrieve them. In the face of her uncle and her mother's closest advisors, the facade cracked. Cassidy wished she could hold the girl's hand, but she didn't know the protocols here.

"I haven't taken the throne yet," she said.

"A formality," Tao said.

"A formality we must see attended to with haste," Tasuki amended. "But a formality nonetheless."

Miria nodded to the woman, then turned a fiery glare on Tao. "How is the Empress slain when her first bodyguard and champion draws breath?"

"*Miria!*" Cassidy gasped. Had she really just asked why her uncle was *still alive*?

If Tao was taken aback by the question, he didn't show it. He answered dutifully, as though Miria were already Empress. "Your Majesty, I was unarmed by a foe of superior cunning and unorthodox weaponry." He pulled the cape from his shoulder, revealing that his right arm ended in a stump at his elbow, which he masked by tying his sleeve into a knot. "I failed in my most sacred trust. I await only the Empress' judgment."

Miria nodded. "And you shall have it. Rise, and tell me what happened." She motioned for Cassidy to follow her as she climbed the dais to the desk. The erstwhile princess took her place behind it, and Cassidy stood awkwardly beside her while the advisors convened a step below.

"The Daughters of Daen appeared over the city in the middle of the day," Tao began. He emphasized multiple times as he recounted the events that the black ships had literally appeared out of a cloudless sky within the city limits, and that no one had been able to figure out how they had done it. Cassidy had a good idea, but she would have to ask Hymn to be certain, and she wasn't going to interrupt the report to reveal her presence.

He went on to explain that saboteurs had destroyed wards placed in the palace after the late Queen Isabel had tried to assassinate Empress Shahira by calling upon the Dread Hounds of myth. The result was that those very myths reappeared in the palace and tried to finish the job. He spoke of the slaughter in mostly measured tones, using sterile and analytical language, but it was clear from the way his face would tighten or his voice would break in the telling that it was difficult for him. Gods, but it was difficult for *Cassidy,* and she had barely seen the palace. Miria must have been a storm of emotions beneath her projected calm.

Tao then talked about the final stand down with the Daughters.

"And you're *absolutely* sure it was Balthine?" Cassidy demanded when he mentioned the man.

"As sure as I can be, considering I never met the man personally," said Tao. "But he matched the descriptions and sketches, and the *Scorpion* was there."

"That's impossible," Cassidy whispered to Miria, but there was no conviction in her words. "You saw what I did on the lake that day."

Miria looked up at Cassidy. "Are we really in a position to doubt the impossible, Captain?" she asked, and Cassidy couldn't dispute the point, though she desperately wanted to. To Tao, Miria said, "Please, continue, uncle."

The former bodyguard gave a half bow, half nod and continued. "Balthine — if indeed it was him — fought using a Fae sword, and he wasn't the only practitioner of the strange in their number."

As Tao described the battle, he detailed all of the Daughters present and how they fought. Cassidy was most interested in this Fae sword the alleged Captain Balthine used. Hymn had never mentioned such a thing, and Cassidy hadn't even known the Fae made weapons. Cassidy was completely lost when Tao mentioned a *guardian* that had apparently turned into light when slain, and almost as confused when he mentioned phoenixes — in fact, she had assumed that the phoenixes had been a term for an elite rank of regular human guards, until Tao mentioned one bursting into flame — and was almost relieved, in spite of her mounting dread, when she understood what Tao was talking about when describing the fight between the Daughter and the Empress. That was, until he claimed the *Scorpion* blasted a hole in the throne room and started *singing* with the voice of a Siren.

And it was the Siren Song that had sealed the Empress' demise.

"For all that she possesses — possessed — an indomitable will," Tao said, his level tone breaking with a note of sorrow, "she was highly susceptible to the Song. I am amazed she was even able to continue fighting, I couldn't even think."

"I was possibly the only person in the room that day who isn't affected by Siren-kin," Tasuki said. "But I could only watch helplessly as Shahira struggled. But she fought hard, even as her body betrayed her, she kept her mind. When she dropped her sword, she took her hairpin and drove it into that murderer!"

"Unfortunately," Tao interjected, casting his gaze floorward, "it wasn't enough. She was run through by the Fae blade, and the assassin survived."

A moment of silence passed over the room and Cassidy wanted to collapse. She held to her feet, however, remembering that Miria needed her strong, both as her captain and as her friend. Besides, Cassidy's only stake was as a patriot; she never really *knew* the Empress — in fact, despite living a decade with the Empress' former lover, she barely knew anything *about* the empress that wasn't more or less common knowledge. Miria, though, had lost her *mother*, and that was a pain Cassidy knew well.

Miria nodded as the report was concluded. "We must hurry with the enthronement ceremony. I assume preparations have been made for my return?"

"They have, your Majesty," Maroda said graciously.

"We must have the ceremony done as soon as possible. Dawn tomorrow unless it can be done sooner."

"We will need to push," said Tasuki, "but it shall be done."

"In the meantime," Miria said, rising to her feet, "we have much to discuss. Captain, the fleet will begin the hunt as soon as possible. We need to finalize the plans with all of the ship captains. Lord Maroda, I need full reports on the aftermath of the attack. Casualties, damages, costs, a list of civic projects pending, ongoing, and complete. Lady Tasuki, any matters of my mother's affairs would have gone through you. Bring me a list of everything that requires my attention. Uncle Tao… did she at least have a beautiful send off?"

Tao took in a shuddering breath and visibly fought back tears. "The whole city dressed in white, and the lanterns lit the night sky like the sun."

Miria nodded solemnly. "You may approach."

Tao obeyed and stepped up to the grand desk. Miria stood and leaned over it, taking her uncle's remaining hand in both of hers. The prince's fingers twitched under his nieces touch, and his eyes pinched as if holding back tears.

"We shall make her proud," Miria promised.

The enthronement was a solemn ceremony. Cassidy wondered if it was always so, or if the circumstances and recent attack on the city had stolen the joy out of an event like this.

Cassidy, Nieves, and Lierre sat in positions of honor normally reserved for the royal family — which had caused quite a stir, but despite many protests from advisors Cassidy hadn't previously met, Miria refused to be swayed. Perhaps as an olive branch, or perhaps to keep her under surveillance, Captain Yaoru Suzume shared in the honor — and much to Cassidy's chagrin, there had been less of a fuss over that pirate being given the honor than there had over the *Dreamscape*'s crew simply because of a blood relation.

Cassidy and the others had their hair done in elaborate styles held in place with pins, and they wore jade-green cheongsams similar to the ones they had worn in Isaro, albeit better fitting. She wished Kek were with them. Her heart sank as she thought of her friend. She was sure if he had only known —

No, this wasn't the time.

On her other side, Yaoru wore a black gown of a similar style to Cassidy's, but far tighter, with an opening at her chest that framed her cleavage, and a scandalously short skirt. How had she gotten away with that? Cassidy had had an earful from some high-ranking servant about the impropriety of the wolf's head necklace she wore — it had been a gift and would one day buy her a favor from the Imperial Fighter's Guild, so she wasn't willing to part with it, lest it get lost. The pirate also lacked ostentatious adornments. Though she wore hairpins, they were matte, not even lacquered, and as ever, the only noticeably valuable accessory she wore was that jet necklace of hers.

Aside from her friends, Tao, and Yaoru, Cassidy was surrounded by strangers. Haytham and Hanaa had been allowed to attend, by dint of being a part of her crew, but Miria hadn't pushed nearly so hard to grant them a seat of honor, so Cassidy only knew they were somewhere in the crowd.

When Miria arrived in the chamber, all present prostrated themselves before her — an act that sent pangs of pain through Cassidy's body, especially her ribs. Cassidy dared to look up from the floor to see she didn't recognize the girl at all. Her face was painted white while her eyes were outlined in crimson, her lips a rich black. She wore voluminous robes of green and gold that completely obscured her figure. Her hair was done up in a fanning style that draped gently around her shoulders, held in place by jade pins and a crown balanced by hanging ornaments. She approached the dais and climbed the nine steps. Before she sat on the throne, however, she addressed the attendants.

"We stand before you on this day as the Ninety-ninth Empress of Asaria." Such a simple opening, structurally, and yet Cassidy couldn't think of a bigger statement. *I am the most powerful person in the world,* Miria had effectively said. It was amazing to realize just how naturally she came to it.

The speech that followed the pronouncement was a recitation of her mother's achievements, and all she had planned. She spoke of the beauty of the Empire as she had seen it in her travels, and of the strength of its people.

Cassidy had been informed that speeches at such ceremonies tended to go on for some time, but Miria's was short. At several minutes long, Cassidy wondered what people usually talked about if *this* was short. Still, Miria spoke well and wore regality like her own skin.

Cassidy found herself relaxing into the inspiring words, imagining the world not so much as it was, but an idealized version of it. The way Miria seemed to see it.

Then the tone changed.

"But threats have been laid at our feet. Our people have been brought to harm, within this very city, within these very walls. Our cities, bombed by Castilyn mercenaries. Dissent and lies sewn by Castilyn agents. Our people, killed by monsters of myth and dreams, called forth by Castilyn. Our Empress murdered in the name of the Castilyn Queen.

"We have a mandate to protect our people. The promises of the Empress are the promises of the Empire, and we promise you this; the devastation and wonton cruelty this nation has suffered at the hands of the aggressors to the south shall be answered in kind. I shall usher in an era of peace, but to do so, we must first bring war to Castilyn."

CHAPTER FORTY-SIX

A month after Yushiro Miriaan took the throne and officially became the ninety-ninth Empress of Asaria, Cassidy was still scouring the Imperial Sea looking for the Leviathan. The search had started a mile out from the shoreline, and the fleet sailed it north along the coast until they had reached the frozen edge of the northern reaches and turned west. They were now sailing south just west of the Black Gulch, having gone around it. Forty days had passed since they left the Imperial capital, and there was discontent within the fleet.

Not amongst the *Dreamscape Voyager's* crew — Cassidy, Nieves, and Lierre had all seen the leviathan first hand, and the mercenaries were paid to be there regardless of what actually happened — nor amongst the Red Moons — who, again, were being paid to participate regardless — but the ships consisting of volunteers and civilians. Apparently, they had expected one valiant hurrah, maybe a week of singing shanties, and a glorious battle, after which they would just go home as heroes. Cassidy had secretly been harboring similar hopes, but at the same time, she was not eager to actually face the leviathan again.

Then, there were the pirates. Yaoru told Cassidy little, only that she would *deal with* the problem. The problem as Cassidy saw it, however, was that Yaoru's assertion that she would handle it was the first and last time Cassidy had even *heard* of trouble in their ranks. Maybe she was paranoid, but she didn't like relying on loose cannons like the pirates.

On that fortieth day, Cassidy walked out onto the deck to be struck by the pungent stench of rotting fish for the seventh consecutive day. It was getting worse. As soon as she opened her cabin door the stench came riding on the spring breeze, so potent she could taste it and feel it wriggling in her sinuses.

Ten days earlier, she had been woken to the sounds of cannon fire. Believing the leviathan had been found, the *Forward Cannon* — one of the Red Moons vessels — had opened fire on a kraken. It had proceeded to take down the *Cannon* and three other ships before it was felled. Fortunately, most of the crew of the latter ships survived and were given a place wherever there was room on the fleet, including three coming aboard the *Dreamscape Voyager.*

Jathun had suggested they use the kraken as bait. So, the black and purple husk had been tethered between the *Temptation,* the *Ghost Bird,* the *Tawny Owl,* the *Moonlit Dancer,* and the *Blind Swallow,* and secured with a net. The carcass had then been drawn across the water, its inky blood leaving a trail behind it. Sharks had been feasting on the tentacles for days, needing to be shot in turn lest they consume their bait or tear it free from the netting.

And so the sour rot had plagued them every time the wind turned. Cassidy's only solace — small as it was — came from knowing that the sun would remain hidden behind storm clouds, and the kraken would not be baking beneath it.

In the haze that followed waking, Cassidy saw the black-haired woman manning the helm and almost called out to Miria. But of course, it wasn't Miria. It would never again be Miria at the helm. Miria had taken her rightful place and couldn't leave her station.

The woman at the helm was similar to Miria in size, though it would be impossible to mistake them at more than a glance. The Empress had assigned two new faces to the *Dreamscape's* roster to account for all stations in the absence of Kek and herself. Tora Kahn La was a retired admiral with about forty years on Cassidy, yet her hair was as dark as kraken ink blood. The woman had volunteered for the job, and Miria vouched for her competency.

Kahn La sneered as she turned around to find Cassidy. "Glad you could join us, Captain," she said. "I was feeling greedy, having all this stench to myself."

"Oh, by all means, keep it," said Cassidy. "Seen anything interesting?"

"Just that cute boy leaving your cabin without a shirt. If I were five years younger —"

"Five years?" Cassidy asked, trying and probably failing to hide the revulsion at the thought. "You'd *still* be old enough to be his grandmother."

"No need to get defensive, I won't steal your prize. And when you get to my age, your needs won't magically go away."

Cassidy imagined growing old, and the reality of her situation hit her hard. In five years, she might not even have her first gray hair. In the best case available to her, Cassidy would still die a year younger than Elyia Asier had. And that assumed she didn't die on this foolhardy mission first.

Her expression must have given away her thoughts — and the news of her impending death had spread, somehow; Cassidy blamed Hanaa, but it might have been Haytham — because the older woman cleared her throat and said, "No, nothing interesting. Not even much uninteresting, as a matter of fact."

Cassidy raised a brow. "And what is *uninteresting*?"

"Qiu Shi said something about the sharks not following the kraken anymore," the old woman said, turning her eyes back to the task of navigating. "Apparently those mercs we brought aboard taught her a new dice game — I don't really understand the rules. Too complicated. Why would you bring cards into a dice game? Young people, I swear. Oh, and I woke up in the middle of the night to relieve myself and caught an eyeful of that Castilyn girl practicing her acrobatics routine with two of the mercenaries. I guess that *was* interesting, now that I think of it. Didn't think she could lift her legs that high, or that anyone would be able to pick her up so easily."

"That's rude," Cassidy snapped.

"I'm not saying there's anything wrong with being plump. Just saying, I thought it and flexibility were mutually exclusive. Goes to show even at my age you can still learn a thing or two."

"Right," Cassidy said slowly. "Sorry I asked." She turned to walk away but stopped. "Which mercenaries?"

"Hm?" The old woman asked coyly. "Oh, the —"

"Captain!" Qiu Shi shouted urgently from the aftcastle. She was the other volunteer Miria sent, a royal cousin some steps removed with experience as a hunter of dangerous beasts, on land, sea, and sky. She was waving around a set of maps and wind charts that snapped in the wind and threatened to fly away. "Captain, I think you should have a look at this."

"What is it?" Cassidy asked.

"I thought something was weird on the horizon," said Qiu Shi. "So I grabbed my old maps. Look! See, that's the Black Wing Tower." She pointed at the map, on the western edge of the Black Gulch, then at a rock spire distantly visible on the horizon to the east. "Now, look south west and tell me what you see."

Cassidy looked. It was easy enough since that was the direction of their heading, and the *Dreamscape Voyager* was flying at the head of the fleet. "I don't see anything," Cassidy said.

"*Exactly!*" Qiu Shi said. "Andaerhal should be visible by now, at least as a shape on the horizon."

Cassidy's brow furrowed. She had only approached Andaerhal from this direction twice in her life. Asier had usually opted to travel through the Black Gulch rather than skirt around it, which added two weeks to the voyage. But, clearly, they couldn't see the city or the mountain from where they were, so Qiu Shi must have been mistaken.

"Are you sure you're not misreading the map?" Cassidy asked. "We're probably a little too close to the Gulch, or too far north."

"With all due respect, Captain," she replied, her tone suggesting the amount of respect due had just dropped precipitously, "I've sailed this route a hundred times. Something strange is going on."

Cassidy chewed on the inside of her cheek as she thought about it. The Leviathan was a creature of the Dreamscape, and she had seen how its influence affected the world in small ways. "It might be a mirage caused by the touch of the Dreamscape," she offered, hoping the answer would satisfy Qiu Shi.

Qiu Shi bit her lip. She nodded and went about her duties, but Cassidy found herself thinking about it. As far as Cassidy knew, nothing like that had happened before. She couldn't ask Hymn about it yet, not with Qiu Shi and Kahn La around. So she kept an eye on the horizon.

"It was that Ramajin girl and the boy we fished out of the sea," Kahn La said a few minutes later.

Cassidy's head whipped around. "*What?*"

But the old woman dropped the subject, appearing intent on flying. Cassidy left her too it, the gossip received, and proceeded to do the rounds.

Of the three mercenaries that had joined the crew after the kraken mishap, two were on the top deck. Mahsa and Sahar — Rivien women from the *Black Swift,* who had dyed their hair blue and gold, respectively — were performing routine maintenance on the weapons. Sahar was laughing with Qiu Shi on the aft castle as she tested the cannon's range of motion, while below, Masha oiled the rotary gun chambers and checked the feeding line for kinks.

Below deck, Cassidy found Lierre in the engine compartment, reading a book by the light of the burning coals.

"Ahoy," Cassidy called over the roar of the machine. She leaned over the short wall that separated the compartment from the hall. "Heard you had a fun night."

Lierre looked up and sighed. "For a little while, at least." Then a sly grin spread across her face. "I can't let you have all the fun," she said with a wink. "You know, there's something about being in motion that adds to the experience. Why did we go so long without trying it?"

"Because Asier would have skinned us alive if we started bringing people aboard to have sex?" Cassidy considered. "And because the only man we've had aboard for ten years is Kek, and he's —" Cassidy hesitated, "— *was* — like a brother."

"Cass," Lierre said in a soft, yet chiding tone. "Are you still mad at him?"

"It's only been a month," Cassidy groused. "And after everything, I think I have the right to be mad at him until the end of time."

"But you don't *have* until the end of time. Besides, is it even him you're really mad at?" ,

The trapdoor to the lower deck opened then, and Shahin — one of Lierre's two alleged lovers from the night before, a Rivien man with a shorn face covered in black smudges, and an equally spotted turban — emerged from the hold. He offered Cassidy an incredibly nervous bow before speaking in rapid Castilyn to Lierre — the man could not speak a word of Asarian, but he was fluent in Castilyn, and he was by all accounts a great mechanic, so Lierre had insisted they take him aboard.

Cassidy wondered if that decision had come before or after Lierre's decision to *practice acrobatics* — as Kahn La had put it.

Lierre replied in her native tongue before turning to Cassidy and saying in Asarian, "He says the Dragon Piercer is structurally sound, and is ready to fire."

"The 'Dragon Piercer'?" asked Cassidy. "We're calling it that?"

"Apparently that is just what they're called," Lierre answered with a shrug. "I never heard it before. Maybe it's a Rivien thing."

As Shahin was dusting himself off, Hanaa emerged from the women's cabin, still fixing her coat. She stopped in her tracks seeing the three of them, and conversation died as she stared, her face going red. Shahin had a deep blush as well, while Lierre seemed to be struggling to hold back a fit of giggles.

"Captain," she said, and there was a slight crack in her voice. "I'm just going to do the... dinner... roster." She walked quickly to the ladder and climbed topside without another word.

Shahin said something in rapid Castilyn and followed after her, shouting something else in Rivien.

"Seems not everyone was thrilled about last night," Cassidy noted.

"They have a history, apparently," Lierre said with a wistful air. "It wasn't my idea in the first place, so I take no responsibility for what happened. I don't know what they said to each other in the throes of passion, but things got awkward after that. 'And I was but a bridge between them, separating them as certainly as I connected them'."

"Is that a line from that book you're reading, or are you trying to give me details?" Cassidy asked.

"It's actually a line from the *previous* book," said Lierre. Then, with a widening grin, "But it also described our physical positions."

"Oh," Cassidy giggled. "Well, I'm sorry it ended so awkwardly."

Lierre shrugged. "Lessons learned. If I am going to agree to another *menage e trois*, it will be with people who *don't* have a complicated past."

"Good advice, in general."

"Captain!" Nieves' voice boomed from the pipeline. "You're needed up here immediately!"

"Duty calls," Cassidy said, putting on a front of calm, even as her guts went cold. Trepidation weighed on each rung she climbed, and despite the warm air of a storm that refused to break, she shivered.

Nieves stood by the helm alongside Qiu Shi, with a spyglass pressed to her face.

"What's the trouble?" Cassidy asked.

It was Qiu Shi who responded. "You know how I mentioned we should have seen Andaerhal by now?"

"I do." Cassidy swept her gaze southward and still saw nothing but the expanse of the sea.

"Well, we found out why," Nieves whispered. As she handed Cassidy the spyglass, her hands were shaking. Cassidy took it and gave her friend's fingers a gentle squeeze.

What could have Nieves, of all people, so upset? Cassidy swept her view along the horizon. She didn't see anything at first, just further expanses of sea. She tilted the sights a little closer and still saw nothing but crashing foam onto a barren, ash-black island a few miles around and jagged stones.

Except there had never been an island like that out this way.

Looking around at the surrounding isles, she found she recognized the area. There should have been a mountain there.

As they drew near, Cassidy saw debris floating in the water and caught in the breakers. It was some time before she could make out what she was looking at, but once she recognized the carnage, her breath caught. The wreckage of ships littered the rocky shore of the island, scores of balloon scraps floating amidst the jetsam. Waves broke against the partially submerged roof of a pagoda. She felt there was a conclusion her mind was refusing to draw due to the enormity of it.

"The city was destroyed," Hymn whispered from within Cassidy's hat. Cassidy couldn't tell how the Fae felt about that. She couldn't comprehend it. How could an entire *city* be destroyed?

The sea was black for miles around, foaming and churning in tumult, and a vast wake cut a swath south across the sea. It had to be the Leviathan.

Cassidy lowered the spyglass. She knew what she had to say, but a creeping terror seeped through her as though a block of ice sat in her stomach. It had *destroyed* Andaerhal and its defenders. How many thousands of people... just *gone*? And Kek was...

This is a bad dream, she said. *I can wipe this away, I can just step into the Dreamscape, or wake up, and all this will go —*

The persistent buzz of engines died abruptly. After the single second of silence that followed, the thunderous crack of a fleet's worth of leather and canvas sails snapped in the wind before the air settled into mournful quiet. Someone on one of the other ships screamed, their voice carrying in the open sky before growing into a cacophony across multiple vessels. Overhead, lightning flashed with increased intensity, and the thunder that followed shook the *Dreamscape Voyager* as if it had been struck.

Cassidy's faint and feeble hope that what was before her was a dream shattered. In its place, a cold and unsettling surrealistic feeling of vertigo settled around her perception. It felt as though she were growing distant from her own body and thoughts.

"Follow that wake," she ordered. "We'll find the leviathan at the end of it."

CHAPTER FORTY-SEVEN

The storm Hymn created for Yaoru intensified as the fleet sailed after the Leviathan. Crimson lighting danced between clouds painted red and gold by the setting sun.

The armada was spread thinner and more staggered than it had been during the month-long sweep — confusion and fear had left many of the ships drifting aimlessly or carrying on along their previous course before sanity and direction to take hold. Fortunately, the *Dreamscape Voyager*, the *Temptation*, and the *Clockwork Hydra* set an example the others were able to follow, even if they didn't understand the mechanics.

Truth told, despite having more experience with it than perhaps anyone alive, Cassidy was confused as well — the engines were largely gone, though the boiler still burned coal, apparently in the same way a body needed food. Rather than the propellers pushing them while their balloon sustained them, the ships drew the wind into their sails, completely independent of which way the gusts were actually blowing. And altitude was adjusted with a familiar rope pull system, but Cassidy couldn't make out what it was actually attached to in lieu of a balloon to release air.

All she knew was what Hymn had told her; this was how ships saw themselves, seen and felt though the eyes of those that loved them.

The sea below frothed and bubbled as the blackness of the churning waves stretched out in all directions. Waves crashed and climbed as high as the ships. One hit the *Dreamscape* and water sloshed onto the deck as the ship was knocked aside and sent spinning. Cassidy clutched the gunwale as she was sent toppling and braced herself as Nieves barreled into her. A geyser slammed into the keel and Cassidy's feet lost purchase with the deck as a wall of water obscured everything around them.

"All hands!" Cassidy shouted over the deafening torrent, "secure lifelines!" As soon as the water fell around them like a monsoon, Nieves ran to the lifelines and waved for the others to tie themselves to the deck. Cassidy went around securing each line before setting her own. Nieves tightened Cassidy's line a mere heartbeat before a second geyser knocked the *Dreamscape* into a spin. Cassidy pushed though the resulting deluge, wishing she had a balloon overhead to block the ensuing spray.

She opened the pipeline and shouted, "Report!"

It was a moment before a fit of wet coughs sounded through the pipe. "All... hands accounted for down here," Lierre· called.

"Secure lifelines and hold steady," Cassidy ordered.

"Aye, captain." Cassidy could hear her faintly shouting the orders in Castilyn.

A strange sound led Cassidy to risk a look down at the sea. The water's tumultuous surface was undulating, bowing downward for over a mile in each direction. As it deepened, the center grew darker, and the edges began to foam and spiral into an unfathomable whirlpool. Jagged rocks cut through the maelstrom.

No, Cassidy realized. *Those are teeth!* Row upon row of mountainous spikes formed concentric rings down the depth of the vortex. The lines holding the corpse of the kraken were released — save for the line held by the *Moonlit Dancer,* which snapped after dragging the vessel down several yards — and the monstrosity fell into the gaping maw of the leviathan without even slowing the current as it was carried along. The leviathan's fangs mangled the rotting corpse as it was torn by the rushing water and the indomitable obstacles. Cassidy watched, enthralled, as the kraken fell into the void in pieces. It didn't seem to satiate the monster, or even merit its notice.

A distant light appeared in the depths of that darkness, a single star that grew in intensity until it became a blinding flash. Cassidy's vision failed her as the air became charged, causing her hair to stand on end and the loudest thunder crash sounded, concussing the ship like a coordinated cannon blast. Cassidy hit the deck with enough force to knock the wind from her lungs and she flailed. Her vision cleared before her ears, coming in white and hazy and flecked with black spots as she came to.

The *Tawny Owl* and the *Moonlit Dancer* were on fire, and what was left of the *Blind Swallow* was reduced to a burning wreckage as it plunged into the leviathan's maw. Cassidy screamed at the sight, unable to hear her own voice over the ringing, and barely able to feel it in her numb and breathless state.

The *Clockwork Hydra* descended into sight and strafed over the current. The strange cloak draped around the hull was unclipped and the canvas covering snapped taut as the wind carried it away. The bulkhead of the *Hydra* began to shift and fold like a puzzle box, and as it folded in on itself, two enormous cannons shaped like snakes rolled gracefully out from the inner workings on either side, fanning out on rolling structures like deadly wings. Twin cannonballs wreathed in brilliant, purple flames spiraled into the maelstrom. The *Hydra*'s prow split apart and folded in on the hull as an orichalcum figurehead of a three-headed serpent emerged in its place, all three jaws wide open. Cassidy's ears began to pick up sound again in time to catch the rhythmic rattle of long guns firing before the snake figures retracted into the ship's mechanism and were replaced by a nine-headed snake.

The roar of nine orichalcum cannons bombarding the water were accompanied by a deep gurgle and a swelling of foul air. The sea foamed and bowed out as the Leviathan breached, unleashing a tidal wave in every direction as a shimmering blue mountain rose from the depths to a sound like a song amplified until the notes were unintelligible as anything other than *loud*. And yet Cassidy could feel the rhythm in her skin, in her bones, as the monster came up at them.

The *Dreamscape Voyager* fled under the quick guidance of Kahn La, and Cassidy watched as the rest of the fleet did the same, picking a direction and going. Not all of them were fast enough to flee, however. The Leviathan's incomprehensible size belied its speed, and it swallowed the *Tawny Owl*, the *Moonlit Dancer* and half a dozen other ships, while *Naga Queen* was dashed against the immense scales of the beast, its aft having been clipped as it snapped its immense jaws shut with enough force to knock ships away with the wind of it.

The Leviathan had been a terror since Cassidy had first seen it. It had haunted her dreams and terrified her waking mind from the memory. She had watched it devour dragons — *the* apex predator — with a careless ease, had watched ships designed for war against those same beasts crumple like paper in its wake.

Somehow, it was worse now that she could see it clearly, blotting out the sky before her. She thought it was even bigger than it had been at the Dragon's nest, if such a thing were possible. It *almost* had a form she could identify, though immensity made it impossible to catch all the details. Its skin and scales were a deep

516

sapphire blue, yet it caught the light wrong, emitting a black and iridescent halo that blurred the lines of its silhouette. It seemed to have a serpentine body, from what little Cassidy could distinguish from the shadow in the water and the way it held itself, but only its head and some of its neck had broken the surface of the churning sea. Terrifyingly, it had six, pitiless yellow eyes on each side of its head, each many times larger than a ship.

The *Clockwork Hydra* circled to the front of the monster as if in challenge, her dawnwood hull glowing in the shadow of the colossus like a defiant flame. As the clockwork mechanism rotated the spent guns into their original, hidden positions, the keel folded open and another cannon — a Dragon Piercer, as Shahin put it — much like the *Dreamscape Voyager's* own dropped into position, accompanied by another quartet of cannons, all maintaining the *Hydra's* namesake thematic appearance. Where had Yaoru acquired all the orichalcum necessary to build all these weapons?

Streaks of purple flame scarred the air as the *Clockwork Hydra* unloaded her arsenal. Sparks flew as the cannons carved deep gashes into the leviathan's flesh. Its mouth cracked open and a gust of foul wind that sounded almost like a gasp sent the *Clockwork Hydra* flying, spinning like a top across the sky before finding its proper orientation, albeit unsteadily.

The *Clockwork's* cannons had done their part; deep trenches ran along the side of the leviathan's snout. Steam and rainbow patterned wisps of light rose from the wounds, and deep, blue fluid poured from them.

"It bleeds," Hymn said from beneath Cassidy's hat. "What bleeds can die. And something seems to have dulled its reflexes. Do not become careless, but this battle is not hopeless."

"Kahn La, order the Dragon Piercer to open fire!"

The former admiral relayed the order through the pipeline. While Cassidy waited, streaks of purple flame rained upon the leviathan from all across the fleet as orichalcum shells bombarded the monster from all sides. Some shots were deflected by hide and scale and tore long gashes into the beast, while others hit straight and punched through the terror's armor, but either way, with such a large target, no shot missed. Its reactions were subtle, and Cassidy had no way of knowing how effective their onslaught was. When the *Dreamscape* fired her shot, the recoil nearly knocked Cassidy off her feet and sent the ship drifting several yards back. The Dragon Piercer hit true, striking the Leviathan where its jaw met its neck.

Cassidy hoped it hurt.

The leviathan thrashed its head to one side, and the force of it crushed the *Ghost Bird*, the *Sunrider,* and the *Evil Eye* like maggots.

"Reload and fire! And put more distance between us and the beast. Spread out!"

Under the influence of the Dreamscape, the *Dreamscape Voyager* danced on the wind as she turned and fled from the beast, spinning back into position for the Dragon Piercer to fire once more. Again, the ship recoiled as the orichalcum cannon fired, sending a flaming comet into the leviathan's side.

Following another bombardment, the Leviathan rose higher and snapped its jaws on another trio of ships with impossible speed. The *Dragon Chaser* and the *Defier* were caught on the edge of its jaws as they closed, their ships reduced to splinters scattered on the breeze, while others still were crushed by the force of the monster's momentum. Cassidy watched as the ill-fated survivors fell, either into the distant and tumultuous sea or to be dashed against the leviathan's scales — she couldn't tell which and didn't want to know; neither death was good.

"This isn't enough," Nieves said as the *Dreamscape* danced away again.

"It has to be," Cassidy snapped. "This is all we have!" She ordered the hit and run tactics to continue, and the *Dreamscape* circled the beast and lined up a shot. This time, it scraped along the side of the leviathan's neck. The *Graceful Waxwing* landed two solid shots in the trench the *Dreamscape* carved, only for the Leviathan to reduce it to kindling with a violent turn. It seemed like every time the leviathan moved, it brought down at least one more ship.

Cassidy took the gunwale in a death grip as the Leviathan turned towards the *Dreamscape Voyager.* Terror used her heart to pound the thoughts from her head as the dreadful mountain of scale and flesh grew larger in her vision. Above, Qiu Shi fired the cannon. An iron ball shattered against one of the monster's colossal fangs, with all the impact of throwing an egg at a warship. Its breath reeked of death and brine, infinitely more potent than the kraken's rot had been. There was no light as the Leviathan loomed like the very shadow of death itself.

That breath became a hurricane gale that pushed them away as it let out a pained gasp, and the beast drew back. Cassidy's rationality reasserted itself by inches, and she checked her spyglass. A quintet of cutters banked around the front of the leviathan to make another pass at its left, firing coordinated volleys, hitting the existing wounds with admirable accuracy. They were far too close to the leviathan for comfort, but their shot grouping was impeccable. But there was something odd about the group.

Those cutters hadn't been a part of the fleet Cassidy had led.

"Where did *they* come from?" Kahn La shouted as she turned the ship around for Shahin to fire the Dragon Piercer. The *Clockwork Hydra* appeared by the *Dreamscape's* side and fired her mechanically rotated payload into the crown of the great beast.

From the other ship's deck, Yaoru called, "You didn't tell me to expect more of your friends to join our little party! I'd have saved them a dance!"

Cassidy watched through her spyglass as the cutters fired heavy harpoons connected by orichalcum chains into one of the leviathan's great eyes. She recognized those tactics. She recognized those ships. Those were fishing vessels from Melfine!

"It's *Kek*!" she and Nieves shouted in unison. Elation cut through the terror like a sword through a curtain, and joy flooded Cassidy's heart. She and Nieves threw their arms around one another and laughed like children.

"Not to ruin the moment," Kahn La shouted, "but we still have a fucking nightmare in the water!"

The cutters rained fire on the hooked eye, which forced the leviathan to recoil in pain. The fishers unhooked the chains to avoid being dragged with its lurch. Except, one of the ships was locked in a struggle, and her harpoon launcher was ripped from its housing, along with a section of deck — and its operator still strapped to the seat — dangling above the shelf of the leviathan's eye.

Cassidy almost concussed herself putting the spyglass back to her face. Dangling from the length of chain was a blurry figure distinguishable almost entirely through brilliant blonde hair bound in a braid as long as she was tall, flapping in the wind. Cassidy knew that woman.

"That's Tenia Valani," she breathed. "That means Kek must be —" As she said the words, she saw another figure decked in brown leap from the wounded cutter and grab hold of the chain, blond hair waving about him. He bounced against the surface of the leviathan's eye, triggering another visceral growl and a violent thrashing on the beast's head. Three of the cutters got away, but the one Kek and Tenia had arrived in were crushed and sent spiraling into the sea. Cassidy watched helplessly as Kek and his sister were whipped about on the length of chain, certain they would either be bludgeoned to death or cast to sea. When finally the Leviathan gave up trying to dislodge the chain with its thrashing, Cassidy saw the chain settle and Kek shimmy his way down to his sister. "— a fucking *idiot*!" she said, concluding her last thought, unable to suppress the shrill note of panic in her voice. "Take us in close!" Cassidy demanded.

"Begging your pardon, Captain, but are you crazy?" Kahn La snapped. "Have you seen what that thing does to ships that get too close? We barely made it —"

"Take us in close or I'll keelhaul you and do it myself!"

Kahn La stared at her in horror for a moment. Cassidy took a single step towards her to make good on her threat when the *Dreamscape Voyager* began to fly towards the beast. "Get us within a harpoon shot of the eye. You'll need to turn us around because it's on the port —"

"I know where the fucking harpoon is, you Fae-touched whore," Kahn La shouted.

Cassidy nodded and opened the pipeline. "Lierre, as soon as a shop opens up, I need you to shoot a rope into the Leviathan's eye to give me a bridge."

There was a long pause. Then a shriek. "Give you a *what*?"

"Remember when we rescued Miria? It's like that, but my ribs aren't broken this time."

"You'll only have one shot, Captain," Nieves said from the gunwale. "Make it count."

"Not going to try and stop me?" Cassidy asked, forcing a smile to hide the bubbling anxiety welling up in her guts.

"*Someone's* got to put out the fire Kek started," Nieves said. Then she hugged Cassidy tightly. "You can do this."

Cassidy didn't know who she was trying to convince, but she was glad for it all the same.

Kahn La screamed in frustration as she wrenched the wheel hard to one side, turning the Dreamscape Voyager around.

"Keep it in line with the eye, keep the rope taut," Cassidy said, working the plan out as she lined herself up. "Don't break away until I give the signal."

"What's the signal?"

"It'll be really obvious," Cassidy promised. She drew her sword and cut her lifeline free, eliciting another shout — this one higher — from the retired admiral. "Are you ready, Hymn?"

"This is foolhardy," Hymn chided. "But I am ready."

A twang sounded below as Lierre launched a harpoon. Cassidy watched as the spearpoint wobbled and snaked its way through the air and ran to the edge of the deck, drawing on her connection to Hymn. The cold sensation flooding her body reinvigorated her, washing away pain she hadn't even been aware of and suffusing her with confidence in her ability. She leapt over the gunwale as soon as she reached it. She aimed for the thin rope beneath her, ignoring the black waves crashing far below. The thoughts of failure crowded in her head, but she pushed them aside, replacing them with the image of what she wanted. She hadn't had a vision, but if she forced herself to believe she had, it might be enough to see her through.

The rope went taut, and she landed on it with both feet. She nearly tipped, but strong winds pushed her from both sides, granting her balance enough to steady herself. The harpoon had landed a few feet away from Kek's chain and halfway down. *Great shot, Lierre,* she thought. *Now it's up to you, Cass.* She broke into a run on the tightrope, sword still drawn like she was charging a mere mortal enemy, her posture occasionally corrected by Hymn.

When Cassidy reached the end of the line, where the hook was blue with the leviathan's steadily oozing ichor, Kek had almost reached his sister. Tenia was unconscious — at least, Cassidy *hoped* she was unconscious — hanging upside down with her arms hanging loose, still strapped to her gunner's chair. One of those arms looked broken.

Kek glanced up at Cassidy when he reached the gun. He smiled. The son of a bitch actually smiled at a time like this! "Cass, I'm so glad to see —"

"Not now, dumbass! Cut her free and get up here!" Cassidy heard the groaning of rope and wood as Kahn La struggled to keep the *Dreamscape* at the proper distance. "We don't have much time."

521

Vincent E. M. Thorn

Kek nodded and pulled a knife from his coat. The gun swayed violently as he worked his way down the barrel and braced himself on the chair's frame. He took only a moment to steady his hand as he cut his sister's harness free. The older woman began to slip, but Kek dropped his knife and grabbed her by the front of her vest. As her head lashed back, she let out an audible gasp and flailed, catching Kek by the arm with her good hand, and they nearly pitched over together. Hymn emerged from Cassidy's hat and flew a circuit around him, and he was able to brace his legs on the harpoon gun.

"Kek?" Tenia gasped, "What was —"

"Focus," he said. "I'm going to start climbing. You're really heavy, but I'm going to need you to hold tight and be supportive." Tenia looked ready to berate him for his comment, but a quick glance at their surroundings made her shut her mouth and she nodded.

It was a difficult feat of acrobatics, but Kek was able to turn himself around while Tenia held onto the harpoon gun. She climbed his back and wrapped her good arm around his chest. Kek didn't have far to climb, but between his burden and the terrifying drop beneath them, the climb was long and grueling just to watch.

When the Valani siblings were level with Cassidy, she shouted, "Swing over!" She heard the groaning of rope beneath her, and the strain of wood more distantly. They didn't have much time. Kek and Tenia followed the instruction, leaning first towards Cassidy, then away, building up a steady momentum. The twisting metal in the Leviathan's eye elicited a low moan of agony from the front of the beast. It recoiled, and Cassidy feared the rope would snap before Kahn La could reposition the *Dreamscape*.

Tenia leapt first, wrapping her legs and good arm around the rope. She rolled to the underside but kept ahold and slowly shimmied her way up the rope.

"Not that I don't appreciate the rescue, Cassy," Kek called, building momentum for another jump, "but was this your best plan?"

"You didn't give me time for a better one," she shouted. "Now hurry your ass up!"

Kek visibly took a breath and at the apex of his swing, he leapt.

His foot caught on the chain, and he pitched forward, falling short of the rope. Cassidy clamped her thighs around the rope and crossed her feet as she leaned forward, reaching. Kek's hand landed in hers with a clap, and his weight dropped on her so suddenly, it strained even her Fae-enriched body. She howled, but clamped down on it, swallowing her pain. "Climb up," she said. As she drew further on her Fae connection, blood began to pour from her nose and spatter on Kek's as he hung beneath her, first in steady drips, then a steady trickle. "I can't hold you forever."

Kek swallowed a lump in his throat and pulled to get the leverage needed to reach up with his other hand. He clasped her shoulder, and she released his hand to grab his foot as he reached for the rope. When he scrambled ahead to follow his sister, Cassidy took a deep breath.

Now for the hard part.

The rope creaked dangerously.

"We'll never make it before the rope snaps!" Tenia cried from the front.

"We will," Cassidy promised. "Don't climb. Just hold on *really* tight!"

"*What?*"

Cassidy swept her sword in an arc and severed the rope behind her. Free of the harpoon, they fell like a pendulum, rapidly accelerating into their downwards swing. Tenia screamed. Kek screamed. Cassidy hoped this wasn't a mistake. Hymn zipped away from Cassidy, onto the ship — hopefully to tell someone to let them up. Tenia's cries stopped when the woman clearly ran out of air, and Cassidy feared she would fall unconscious again. There would be no rescuing her this time. There would be no rescuing any of them.

As their rope began the upswing, Cassidy dared a look at the leviathan. It thrashed again, trying in vain to dislodge the metal embedded in its eye, and roared in agony. The rope swung widely several more times before finally slowing to a degree Cassidy could feel safe climbing up to Kek and Tenia. When it did, however, her crew was already hoisting the rope up. Cassidy hugged it as the gravity of what she had done settled around her. Maybe the stories that the Fae made a person crazy were entirely true.

Tenia disappeared into the ship above, and Kek soon followed. As Cassidy hung there alone, so near a temporary salvation, she imagined simply letting go. It would be so easy. It was a terrifying thought, and one she didn't comprehend, but she couldn't shake it. All she could do was imagine being within spitting distance of safety and tumbling to her doom in the dark depths below. Even though the gentle numbness granted by her connection to the Fae, her arms burned, and her fingers grew weak.

Firm hands gripped her arm and shattered her haunting reverie. She sucked in a breath and held it in that terrifying moment. She was hoisted with little warning by Nieves and Lierre while Haytham and Hanaa pulled the rope. Only when Cassidy had both her feet on the deck did she let out the breath.

Seeing the expressions of awe and terror in the eyes of her friends reminded Cassidy where she was, reminded her *who* she was. *I am Captain Cassandra Durant*, she thought, taking a steadying breath. "See Miss Valani and Mr. Valani to a bunk," she ordered Nieves. "See that they are tended to and protect—"

"I'm fine, Cass," Kek said firmly. "I'm not badly hurt and I'm ready to do my duty." It seemed to be true. He was scuffed and bloody, but the worst of it was Cassidy's.

"Good," she said, unable to stop the warm smile from breaking across her face. Gods, but she missed him. That didn't stop her from slapping him across the face, however. "What in the Mists were you *thinking*? You could have been killed!"

"Couldn't leave you to go without me, Captain," he said with a grin, electing to ignore the red print forming on his cheek.

"We'll talk about everything later," Cassidy promised. "Check all battle stations, give me a status report. Two minutes. Nieves, see Miss Valani taken care of. Haytham, make sure Nieves has whatever supplies she needs and is ready in case anyone else gets hurt. Everyone else, to your stations."

Cassidy climbed topside and surveyed the battle, just in time to see the *Clockwork Hydra* and the *Temptation* line up to attack. The *Hydra* cycled through her arsenal like her namesake, becoming a storm unto itself, focusing all her firepower on the leviathan's eyes. Purple fire poured like rain on the monster, and the *Temptation* followed up not with a volley, but with a single Dragon Piercer that put the *Dreamscape's* to shame and a mid-deck cannon that launched her several yards to port.

The Leviathan's cry was a low, booming thing that was felt more than heard. It whipped its head up and stretched itself further from the water and reached up towards the *Hydra* with a vicious speed. She and the *Temptation* were already speeding out of its path, but three more ships were spinning out of control from where the leviathan clipped them when the beast made contact during its turn, and one more was caught between rows of teeth as it lunged.

The *Dreamscape*'s Dragon Piercer fired clean down the creature's throat. The leviathan only gained speed and was on top of them in moments. Kahn La spun the wheel to flee, but the beast's teeth were already above and below and to either side. They couldn't get clear in time.

We're going to die, Cassidy thought.

"We must sail down its throat," Hymn shouted.

The world seemed to slow as Cassidy processed that. *Down its throat?* She saw it, then, dark and terrifying and reeking of death. And yet so much closer now than the way out. They couldn't turn *and* make it out in time. Trying to escape was certain death. Down there, though…

"Gods! You better be right, Hymn!" Cassidy cried, and forced herself between Kahn La and the helm. "Full speed ahead!"

"What are you *doing?*" the older woman demanded.

"Saving our lives!" *I hope.*

CHAPTER FORTY-EIGHT

In the darkness beyond the Leviathan's teeth, it was wet, and it was dark. And in defiance of all Cassidy's expectations, it was cold. They sailed through a glowing, opalescent mist that seemed to cling to the deck and their clothes, and despite how fast she had pushed to clear the mouth, the *Dreamscape Voyager* moved at a slow, cautious pace through that claustrophobic darkness.

"Her majesty told me you were bold," Kahn La snapped, wincing when her voice echoed loudly in the space. In a whisper, she finished, "but she never told me you were a *lunatic!*" The last word echoed sharply like a breeze. *Lunatic-atic-tic-tic-tic.*

"We're alive," Cassidy said, though her voice lacked venom or heat as she looked for some sign of what to do next. "That should be enough for now."

"*Are* we alive?" Kahn La snapped. "How do we know this isn't the Mists? There certainly seems to be enough of it."

"This is not the Mists," Hymn said. Cassidy reached for her hat only to find Hymn — standing a few feet away in her beautiful true form — wearing it. Her brilliant dress of woven starlight illuminated the deck faintly. Kahn La shouted and scrambled for her pistol, and Cassidy interceded the old woman, forcing her to fire the weapon overboard rather than at Hymn. The iron ball caught fire as it zipped beyond the gunwale and sailed off like a comet until it was too far away to see.

"She's a friend," Cassidy snapped.

"A *friend?*" Kahn La shrieked, her voice echoing again in a painful retort. *Friend-end-end-end.* "That is a *Fae!*"

"Nevertheless," Hymn said, "I am not your enemy. And this is not the Mists," she repeated, not missing a beat as Cassidy retrieved her hat from her head. "The Leviathan is not a creature of flesh and blood, but a creature of dreams — and in a cannibalistic fashion, it is an *eater* of dreams. Inside the bowels of the Leviathan you will find not viscera and organs, but the tarnished and warped remains of memory, life, and the world. Behold!"

As if waiting for Hymn to give the cue, a brilliant aperture of light opened before them, and the Dreamscape Voyager sailed through it.

A blackened, rocky landscape broken by dark lakes and saturated with red fog spread out below them. Behind them, the fathomless dark from which they emerged was a tunnel that couldn't exist, inlaid in nothing, high in the air. Above was a swirling red sky flecked with black stars that seemed to suck light into their being rather than give it. Occasionally, a faint, white light like lightning behind a cloud would press against the red with the rumble of cannons. Waterfalls flowed in reverse into oblivion. Jagged rocks broken open to reveal beds of emerald floated in the air, some carrying the burdens of half-constructed edifices, others barren. Cassidy recognized half of the Andaerhal Ministry Building passing by.

She almost missed the ship charging at them. A wounded black junk with tattered sails and, marked with a white mural of the desert goddess, Daen. Or, *half* a ship, as the case had it; the entire aft section had been blown off yet still the ship came at them. A kirin affixed to its prow — adorned in ancient-styled armor — whinnied and pounded its hooves in the air as though running at them.

"Kek, get on the rotary!" Cassidy shouted as she spun the wheel. Kek opened fire even before settling into the seat. The weapon barked in a staccato rhythm — only Nieves had a steady enough hand to keep it firing smoothly — rattling against the approaching deck, but though it tore through the hull, it didn't slow. The black ship rammed them hard and sent them spinning. "Aim for the pilot!"

"There isn't one!" Kek called back. The ship is abandoned!"

"Aim for the sails, then!"

He rose and darted to the aftcastle. "I'll get on the cannon!"

"Don't worry, I'm on it!" Qiu Shi interjected.

The black ship ascended, burned wreckage and jetsam tumbling from the exposed innards, and swooped down on them. The aft cannon bellowed, and the ball smashed through the enemy vessel's mast. The kirin let out a horrific scream as the ship continued its trajectory without the support of flight. It cut a swath through the *Dreamscape Voyager*'s sails as it crossed and slammed into the deck. Someone screamed. The impact sent Cassidy sprawling and she pulled the wheel hard to starboard as she fell.

Though the enemy had only clipped them, it had crushed the gunwale and rotary gun and left a deep gouge in the deck before falling to the alien landscape.

"Cass!" Kek cried. He leapt from the aftcastle and was at her side in a moment.

"I'm fine," she said breathlessly, wiping the blood from her face, leaving a thick streak across her bare arm. She forced herself to her feet.

The *Dreamscape* was in a tailspin.

Cassidy gripped the wheel and tried to steady course, but she could do nothing about the ship from falling. A low slope was coming into view and Cassidy could see the disaster coming even without a vision. She opened the pipeline and shouted, "Retract the Dragon Piercer and close the hatch!"

A few moments later, she heard Hanaa call back from the hold. "It's jammed!"

"Then get Shahin out of there! All hands brace for impact!"

The squeal of metal grinding on stone pierced the air a moment before a vicious crack of wood and iron jolted the entire ship. Cassidy looked back to see the Dragon Piercer and its housing bounce away on the hill behind them moments before the underside of the *Dreamscape* fully touched down.

Cassidy bit her tongue hard enough to draw blood. The pain blossomed clear as the morning air even though her numbed senses. Her feet bounced off the deck without her aid, and it was only her grip on the helm that kept her from flying wildly away as the *Dreamscape* slid and scraped her way down the rocky surface of the hill fast as she ever flew. Cassidy could feel each stone and pebble beneath the hull traveling up through her feet like a hammer.

She could see that if the ship continued on its course at speed, they would crash into another mountain in mere moments. Her only hope was to turn to port. There seemed to be a drop between the mountain's edge and the lake below, and she had no way of knowing how deep it was. Still, better to die *trying* to survive. She threw her weight into the wheel, turning it hard to port.

The *Dreamscape* groaned as her rudders tried to fight against both gravity and friction. The wheel cracked beneath Cassidy's fingers. A faint, golden light shined in the split. A pulse beat against Cassidy's hands as she fought to turn. Her muscles burned, screaming in protest.

The ship turned just as she reached the point where the two mountains met and drifted sideways up the opposite slope before sliding off into the open air. Cassidy cried out in terror as the *Dreamscape Voyager* flung herself towards the water. The hull skipped as it struck water and crashed to a halt on a shallow bank. The sudden stop made Cassidy reel and she vomited on the deck.

"Ugh," Kek groaned a few feet away. He spilled his guts as well, but he had been lucky enough to make it over the side. "Please never do that again."

Up on the aftcastle, Qiu Shi was cradling her head and moaning. Cassidy looked for Kahn La, but the woman was nowhere to be seen. Cassidy looked back at the mountain, hoping to see some sign of the woman, but across the expanse of black rock, the only thing that stood out was the faint, iridescent glint of the Dragon Piercer. When her gaze dropped, she looked at the partially collapsed deck, and pooling between the broken floorboards, was blood and a snapped lifeline.

"No," Cassidy whispered. "No, she can't —" She took a steadying, rancid breath and stood. *Be strong for them,* she told herself. *Help those who can still be helped.* She opened the pipeline. "All hands, report." The silence that followed was a knife twisting in Cassidy's guts. Her legs began to tremble. Her heart grew cold, and a dread crept along her brain. *What have I done?* "All hands —"

"*Captain?*" Lierre's voice squeaked faintly over the pipe, and Cassidy burst into tears. Whether it was relief or just the tension, she couldn't say.

"Lierre!" she called back. "What's going on down there?"

"*We lost Shahin,*" said Lierre. The pain in her voice was obvious, but she pressed on. "*Hanaa is hurt pretty badly and can't even climb out of the hold. Mahsa isn't much better. There's water in the hold, and —*"

"*Give me that,*" Nieves' voice cut in. "*Captain, the situation is bad. Haytham and I are the only ones down here without at least one broken bone, and the hull was beat to shit. What's it look like up there?*"

"*I'm fine,*" Lierre argued.

"*I can see the bone!*" Nieves shouted.

"Things aren't great here," Cassidy admitted. "We lost Kahn La, too. And that ship cut our sails, and the ship thinks of it in the same terms as the balloon."

"*The ship thinks?*" Nieves repeated.

"That's a lot to get into. But yeah, until that gets stitched up, we're not going anywhere."

"*Tell me there's a plan, Cass.*"

'Give me a minute," Cassidy said, and she closed the pipe. "Kek, how's she doing?"

"She's in shock," he called back. "And I think she hurt her neck. Maybe a blow to the head, too. Nieves would know better, but I think moving her would be a bad idea."

"Let her sit, then," said Cassidy. She hoped that was the right advice, but she didn't know. What she *did* know was the ship. "I need you patching up the mainsail.

Kek looked up at it, unable to hide his grimace. "How much harder can it be than a balloon?"

"Hymn, do you see a way out?" The Fae didn't respond. Cassidy lifted her hat before remembering that Hymn had taken her full form. "*Hymn?*"

Cassidy looked around frantically. She spotted the Fae standing on the beach below, staring inland. Her gaze was fixed at a plateau that floated far above the rest of the landscape.

"Hymn?" Cassidy called. "What's wrong?"

Hymn didn't avert her gaze. "Someone has bonded to the leviathan. It should have been *more* dangerous, but it was slow. Stupid."

"That's a problem?" Cassidy asked.

"It is an *oddity*. But this solves two problems; we cannot return to either of our worlds from here until the Leviathan dies. Killing the bonded human will leave the Leviathan vulnerable enough to kill."

"You sound very sure," said Cassidy.

"I have killed gods before." Hymn began to walk towards the plateau.

"Hymn, wait!"

She stopped and turned to look at Cassidy. "This needs to be done, Cassidy," she said.

"Obviously, but we'll need a way out, so let me sort this out!"

"*We?*"

"Kek! Get that sail fixed," she ordered. "Have Haytham help you patch up whatever we need to keep this ship in one place. You're captain while I'm gone. Hymn and I are going to kill the beast."

"What?" Kek shrieked. "You can't be serious!"

"Kek," Cassidy whispered, but her voice carried in the quiet. "I know I haven't given you any reason to trust me, but this —"

"It's not that I don't trust you," said Kek, "but you can't go alone!"

"I won't be alone. I'll be with Hymn. And the crew needs you here."

"Cass, it's too dangerous!"

"Look around, Kek! It's been too dangerous since the day this thing showed up." She climbed to the aftcastle to meet him. "It's not going to stop being dangerous until it dies. And not just for us. For the Empire. If we don't solve this, Miria has to."

Kek let out a long sigh. "We'll come for you as soon as we can get her in the air."

Cassidy smiled and pulled him into a tight embrace. "I know you will."

From the moment Cassidy's feet touched the ground, she knew it would be miserable. Despite apparently being the dream of a dream, the sand and the rocks gave her the same eerie stability as the real thing. Each step she took felt ponderous and stilted, accustomed as she was to constantly shifting with the sway of a ship. Hymn, by contrast, was graceful as she had ever been. The Fae drifted with each step, her bare feet only skimming the ground, and her gown and hair flowed as though she were swimming. Cassidy envied that ease.

They walked the length of the beach for some time and came across the wreckage of the black ship that had attacked them. It had been marooned in the sand. The armored kirin lay dead feet away from the prow where its body had been fastened. Hymn kneeled beside the creature and cooed softly. The tide rose abruptly, engulfing the creature, and when it receded, all that remained was its armor half buried in sand. Cassidy could see its name, faded but legible. The *Knight in Mourning*. Hymn rose and resumed their march as though nothing had happened.

After rounding the island, they came across a stone staircase hidden in the rock wall. At the top was a basin lined by jagged rocks with a tree in the center. A shadow in the shape of a woman with hair made of flames sat beneath it. The tree was tall — but not as tall

531

as the surrounding walls — with black bark and vermillion leaves that glowed like the embers of a fire. A low, husky laughter filled the basin.

"Into the web the child falls." The shadow cocked its head in a way that it seemed to be staring at Hymn. "Doth thou heed your master's call?"

Hymn stepped between Hymn and the feminine figure and leveled a finger at it. "Show yourself, Hesperus."

"Thou darest invoke my name?" The shadow — Hesperus — brushed a lock of flaming hair from her face. "Of all, thou shouldn't provoke me lest thine I proclaim."

"Why is she speaking in rhyme?" Cassidy whispered to Hymn.

It was Hesperus that answered. "'Tis madness, an affliction of the mind," and she giggled when she said it. "An infection brought about when thine protector rendered me *blind*. Such a treasonous daughter. But can I blame her for doing as I taught her?"

"Enough!" Hymn snapped her fingers and a brilliant blue light snaked through the air like lightning between Hymn and the shadow. The whip cracked and the womanly figure vanished like steam in the breeze and Hesperus' laughter seemed to come from everywhere. "How have you come to be here?"

"Trapped, trapped, trapped in the tree, trapped in her grave right where thee left me. That is, until the leviathan came and came to consume me!"

The ground shook with enough force to knock Cassidy off her feet when a black spider dropped from the sky. A red sigil depicting two crescents pointing out from a full circle with a black hourglass at its center marked her abdomen. It bowed its legs as if to pounce, bringing its head down to stare at the same level as Cassidy. It glared with eight, white eyes that seemed to twist light and drink it in.

Hymn flicked her wrist and her whip ensnared one of the spider's rear legs, but she merely jabbed at Hymn's chest with one of its front appendages. Cassidy scrambled for her pistol.

"I shall not be taken unawares again," said Hesperus, and despite her monstrous appearance, she sounded no different than before. "You already know —"

Cassidy drew the pistol and fired, but the spider was too quick. It kicked her in the shoulder with enough force to make her shot go wide and knock the wind from her lungs. Cassidy dropped the pistol — on accident, but it wasn't going to help her now, anyway — and drew her sword. The spider seemed apprehensive and began to circle around her with its quick feet.

"Oh, child, so scared and sweet," Hesperus drawled, "put down the knife so I can ravage your meat!" The spider leaped over Cassidy's head and impacted the ground hard enough to send tremors through her, but Cassidy had been ready this time and held her ground, though it hadn't been easy. She pirouetted and caught the spider's mandibles in mid lunge, but its weight and momentum carried Cassidy off her feet and back several yards.

Her sword glowed hot as she held it pressed to Hesperus' fangs, and sizzling smoke bloomed from the contact. The spider shoved Cassidy's shoulders, and already airborne, her body sailed until she struck the tree, first with her back — which knocked the breath from her — then with her head — which disrupted her Fae connection and let in all the pain she had been suppressing for hours.

And that pain hit her all at once. *Hard.* She felt as though all of her bones had been smashed with a hammer and her head felt like it was going to explode out of her eyes. She was barely aware that Hesperus kept her pinned to the tree with its forelegs, looming over her with those light-drinking eyes. A pulse beat against Cassidy's body as she squirmed against the spider's grasp.

Hymn's whip of light cracked over the monster's head and Hesperus let out a hiss that sprayed rancid saliva across Cassidy's face. The spider whirled around and engaged with Hymn, leaving Cassidy to slump onto the ground, falling into the nook in the roots where Hesperus' shadow had appeared.

Cassidy felt the pulse intensify as she watched Hymn lash out with her whip and the spider danced around her with a nimbleness that should have been impossible for such a large creature. *Thump-thump.* The spider scurried along the wall of the basin. *Thump-thump.* Hymn extended her middle and third finger and two more threads of light manifested beside the first and she threw her full weight into a flourishing strike. *Thump-thump.* The pulse intensified when the spider leaped, evading Hymn's tendrils as they carved deep gouges into the stone. *Boom-boom.* A gout of white fluid shot from the spider's tail and pinned Hymn's hand to the wall, disrupting the threads of light. *Boom. Boom.*

Cassidy took a deep breath and sought the cold sensation of drawing on her Fae connection. Rather than rush into her like an open dam, the feeling trickled into her like a dribbling pipe, but even if it only took the edge off her pain it was worth it. She pushed herself to her feet and looked for her sword.

It lay between Hymn and Hesperus.

Great, Cassidy thought sardonically.

She limped as close to a run as she could, gradually steadying her stride as coldness ate away at her pain. The spider turned, swinging one of its forelegs at her like a club, but she dove over it, tucking in to roll when she reached the stone floor. The spider scurried and brought two more legs to drop on her, but she performed a handspring and slipped between the assaulting appendages. She landed beside the sword and slid her foot beneath the hand guard and kicked it up in the air to catch.

The spider turned on her as soon as the weapon was in hand. As it lunged, a red flash like lightning burned a line in Cassidy's vision, originating from over her shoulder and ending where Hesperus was recoiling.

Then the thunder cracked, and Cassidy was thrown sideways. Her ears rang, and she thought she felt blood trickling down the right side of her neck. She turned to see Hymn, her free hand outstretched, held in a fist but for her fore- and fourth fingers, between which small yet luminous threads of lightning danced.

Hesperus shook violently as she recovered on the points of her many legs. The left side of the spider's face had been gouged and burned by Hymn's attack. It let out a bestial shriek and charged. Cassidy matched it with a howl of pain and fury and ran at the spider. She leapt above its grasping legs and mandibles, swiping at it with her sword. Brown ichor sprayed from the wound she left behind as she severed a leg, and she dragged her sword across its back, letting it build heat as it burned the Fae spider, but she had a different target in mind.

There was a moment of confusion as Cassidy leaped off Hesperus' back, a brief moment where the spider seemed conflicted, unsure if it should chase Cassidy or turn its attention on Hymn. That delay gave Cassidy time to cover a fair amount of ground. But then the spider realized what Cassidy was running *towards*.

Cassidy felt the full, stone rattling weight of the spider hit her from behind moments before it lifted her off the ground and slammed her hard on the rocks. Time seemed to hold still. She had gasped a spray of blood, and it seemed to crystalize before her, as though the rubies sat suspended in the air. In that brief moment of clarity, she could see what she needed to do, and had the spatial awareness to know how impossible it was as long as the spider had both her arms pinned beneath its legs.

Time snapped back into place and pain and the underpinnings of terror took the place of clarity. The thin hairs of the spider's legs were hard and sharp as needles, and its weight was pressed into the recesses of her shoulder blades. She felt the impact of another explosive blast rattle down the spider's body, and it shifted its weight under the force of it.

Cassidy shifted as much as she could with Hesperus's weight and flung her sword at the tree. The blade spun, and Cassidy willed it to land point in. A rush of static washed over her senses, and the weapon stopped spinning as though hit by something and stabbed into the bark. Cassidy closed her hand into a fist and the blade ignited. Hesperus wailed and scrambled off her. The spider flailed wildly, its legs twitching and twisting as it writhed on the basin floor.

Cassidy turned her attention to the burning tree and saw a woman embedded in the burning trunk, Cassidy's sword buried in her chest. Her hair was a red so dark it was almost black, her eyes — inverted like all Fae — were a rich maroon that evoked wealth and warmth, but had visible scarring running across them. Hesperus — the real Hesperus, Cassidy was sure — had her mouth open in a silent scream. Iridescent wisps of light bubbled up off her skin and hair and began dancing in the air as though carried on the breeze. At first it was a slow, sporadic event, but quickly the light poured off her like ashes in the wind, and Cassidy realized that with each wisp that formed, Hesperus' body was dissolving. In less than a minute, her body was gone, as if it had never been, leaving behind only a charred outline in the trunk of the tree.

Cassidy retrieved her sword and dismissed the flames.

Hymn had freed herself and loomed over the frantic spider. The Fae raised her hands and extended three fingers on each. She flourished them in elaborate patterns as the threads of sapphire light blazed to life. Cassidy couldn't track all Hymn had done, but she reduced the arachnid to too many pieces for Cassidy to reasonably count, especially once they started to burn.

535

"Who was that?" Cassidy asked, and her voice sounded strange to her own ears. "She called you 'daughter'."

Hymn sneered. She said something, but Cassidy didn't catch it.

"What?"

Hymn scowled in frustration, then her eyes widened in an almost human expression of shock. Hymn stepped closer and to Cassidy's left. "You are deaf in your right ear," she said. "I am terribly sorry."

Cassidy blinked. "Is it... is it permanent?"

"Most likely," Hymn said, and there seemed to be genuine sorrow in her voice. "Let us continue. The battle still rages outside, but each minute we dally is more time the leviathan has to wreak havoc."

Cassidy put her finger to her ear. It was definitely bleeding. She snapped her finger. She *felt* it, but she couldn't hear it.

Damn it, she thought. A wellspring of helplessness formed in her chest, spiced with bitter anger, but she swallowed it down. *Later,* she told herself. *You have a job to do.*

She nodded to Hymn. "Let's."

A break in the basin led to another staircase, this one without rocks to either side or ground beneath it for support. It was nothing more than stone steps that wound their way, unsupported, to the top of the floating plateau. Cassidy limped alongside Hymn as they climbed — the steps were only *just* wide enough for the both of them to do so, even as slight and ephemeral as the Fae was — and her friend's attention seemed fixed on their destination.

Overhead, the press of light on the sky intensified, and the thunderous report of cannons was met with actual thunder and lightning. Cassidy was able to identify when the *Clockwork Hydra* was on the offensive from the tight cluster and consistent sequence of flashes. Cassidy guessed maybe half the fleet was still fighting, but it was probably less. She could only hope that those who had survived this long would be able to continue surviving.

The plateau was a cracked, empty and expansive surface. It was empty, save for a woman with black hair in a tattered black coat with only one detached sleeve. She stood in the center of the platform, swaying drunkenly, recoiling as though she were being struck with each flash of light in the sky. Then, sporadically, she would scream and thrash wildly.

"She is already dying," Hymn said. "This is why the leviathan has been reacting strangely. Someone sabotaged the ritual. Kill her, quickly."

Cassidy nodded. Any compunctions she might have had about killing an addled, defenseless woman had died with the sailors she had lost getting here. She approached the woman, sword in hand, ready to end it.

When Cassidy was ten paces away, the woman stiffened and jerked her head to face her. She gasped. The woman possessing eyes that Miria's and Yaoru's was surprising enough, but the woman before her had no nose, only a terrible, scarred gash where it should have been. She wore an ebony coronet with a slot running through the middle of her forehead, out of which blood and yellow fluid seeped out at an alarming rate.

"Can't... let... stop... this," she said, each word accompanied by a spasmodic twitch. Then she cleared the gap between them with blinding speed. Her right hook struck Cassidy in the deafened ear and while the pain was kept at a distance, she was still sent staggering and dizzy.

Cassidy swings her sword in an upwards arc. The woman in black dances to the side. Cassidy stops and adjusts her stance to attack again, and the woman kicks her in the head. Her neck snaps with finality.

Cassidy immediately felt the pull of the future tugging at her, urging her to move. She spun to avoid a dropkick. Hymn's whip lashed out at the woman in black, who pulled a jagged knife — almost a short sword, really — and struck the Fae weapon, causing it to spark and flash before retreating. A spark like lightning sputtered from the slot in her coronet and she twitched once as if something had hit her.

The spasm lasted only a moment and the woman in black continued her assault. She jabbed hard and fast. Cassidy blocked it with her arms, taking blow after blow. Even with the pain made distant by her Fae connection, Cassidy could feel her arms starting to bruise. Still, she took the hammer of blows until the pull of the future compelled her to kick off to the right. She dove and rolled into a crouch before slashing up at the woman in black. The woman took quick, graceful steps that let her flow around the blade like water.

Every instinct and reflex in Cassidy's body told her to stop swinging so she could launch another attack. The tension of the future was like a fishing hook pulling taut at her heart, demanding she stop. She defied it and instead turned her slash into a pirouette.

A discordant *twang* filled the air and rattled Cassidy to the core like an over-tuned zither string the size of a dragon.

She caught the woman's kick against her right hand. With her other hand, she punched with her sword, putting her hips into it. The woman in black flicked her blade away with a dismissive swipe of her knife and did a backflip to clear the ground. Two more of Hymn's whips lashed out across the distance, but the woman cut them away with her knife without turning away from Cassidy. As sparks showered around the strange woman, Cassidy fell into another vision.

The woman in black locks blades with Cassidy and they grapple with their free hands. The woman draws her head back and slams it into Cassidy's forehead, splattering blood across her face as the coronet cracks her skull. She is disoriented as the woman releases her hand and draws a second knife, plunging it into Cassidy's throat.

Cassidy followed her vision's lead and pressed the attack. She jabbed with her sword in rapid blows while the woman in black danced to evade and deflect her strikes, leading Cassidy on a chase around the plateau.

Clang, clang, swish. Swish, swish, swish. Swish, clang, swish.

Swish, clang, clang. Clang, swish, swish. Swish, swish, screech.

The woman in black stepped forward into the blow rather than away from it, her blade scraping across Cassidy's until they were quivering hilt to hilt. Cassidy twisted to punch with her right hand, but the woman in black caught her fist. Cassidy opened her hand and lunged for the woman's throat, but she grabbed Cassidy's elbow and Cassidy seized hers as well. The woman in black drew her head back. A heaviness overcame Cassidy as she was drawn to a future that required her to stay in place.

She would not let it come to pass.

She relinquished her hold on her sword and the snapping of fate's chord sounded even to her deaf ear. The woman in black pitched forward and Cassidy slammed her fist into the woman's oncoming jaw. The woman took several staggered steps back. Blood and pus gushed from her forehead and spilled over her face.

"You... fucking... bitch!" the woman said through gritted teeth. She drew her second knife and let out a roar unbefitting for a human throat.

Cassidy slashes down on the woman in black. She crosses her knives to catch Cassidy's blade. She kicks Cassidy in the ribs. As Cassidy stumbles, the woman in black throws one of her knives. The cold iron sinks into her throat.

Cassidy kicked her sword into her hand.

This has to stop now, she told herself as she and the woman in black clashed again. She couldn't keep reacting to visions. It was getting harder to fight the almost hypnotic pull, and she had no guarantee the visions would keep coming. Even if they did, it seemed only to show her defeat after painful defeat. It wasn't enough to stay alive, she needed to win.

But how? The woman in black was undeniably the better fighter; she was faster, and even with a gods damned *hole* in her head, her reflexes were sharper. Even flowing with the current of her visions, Cassidy barely kept pace.

She disrupted her own death again by retreating before the enemy could land a kick. She had another vision almost immediately, this one depicting her head being severed.

Swish, swish, clang. Clang, clang, swish. Clang, clang, swish.
Twang.

Another vision, another broken neck.

Clang, clang, clang.
Twang.

Cassidy averted it by taking a knife to the shoulder, changing the course of her opponent's strategy. Her breath was ragged as she tore away from the woman. She drew harder on her bond with Hymn. Her insides felt coated with frost, her vision spotted with blackness. She knew from experience she could only take in so much of the Fae's power — could only push her limits so far — before her body gave up, but what choice did she have?

"Cassandra!" Hymn called. "If you want to live, take as much power as you can hold, and *let me in.*"

"*What?*" Cassidy called back. Had she heard the Fae right?

"Let. Me. In."

Like Flint and Atarshai, she realized. The prospect horrified her, but the alternative... The alternative was no choice at all.

Cassidy embraced the Fae power. When she reached her limit, her lungs felt frozen. She watched from the corner of her eye as Hymn — standing on the edge of the plateau — dissolved into wisps of multicolored lights as Hesperus had. Rather than evaporate into the air, however, the light shot like a line of guns towards Cassidy and sank into her skin.

A deeper cold permeated her body, but it was slowly replaced by something almost like heat. Hatred suffused Cassidy then. A hatred purer than anything Cassidy had ever experienced. A hatred so large it left no room for any other emotion in Cassidy's mind. No room for nuance. No room for *anything* else. Hatred made her heart pound and her blood flow. Hatred kept her lungs pumping. Hatred moved her.

The woman in black looked confused, scared. She took a step back in fright.

Good! Cassidy thought. It wasn't joy, exactly, nor even satisfaction. It was a cruel thought born and steeped in the tides of her contempt. Confusion and guilt tried to sprout in her mind, but they were quashed immediately beneath the weight of malice.

She moved much faster than she had before. She was inside her enemy's guard in a blink. The woman barely managed to parry Cassidy's strike, and was unprepared for the backhand that knocked her to the ground. The stranger rolled away from Cassidy's follow through, but when she tried to stand, Cassidy kicked her with enough force to break her elbow.

The woman screamed.

What a pitiful wretch, Cassidy thought. She drove her sword through the woman's good arm and wrapped her hands around her throat, pressing her thumbs right against her windpipe. As she squeezed, she was faintly aware that her own nails were deep rubies speckled with stars, but the observation was washed away in the torrent of malice roaring within her. *This is too good for her,* she thought.

She slammed the woman's head into the stone. The woman gagged on a scream, unable to draw in the breath through Cassidy's grip. Cassidy smashed her skull again, which cracked the woman's coronet. Above, thunder barked. The third blow split the coronet in two and the woman's brains and blood and fragments of skull spilled out of the back of the woman's head like an egg. Some emotions tried to find purchase in Cassidy's mind, but they were drowned out by the fury of her loathing before she could even register what they were.

The plateau shook. Colorful wisps of light bubbled out from the rattling stone, spiraling up around her, drifting aimlessly. The leviathan was dying, its dreams were unraveling. Cassidy ripped her sword from the stranger's corpse and ran to the edge. The lights were blooming all across the landscape and even from beneath the water, floating ever upwards. The land was breaking apart as it melted into luminescence. "Damn it all!" she shouted into the expanding void. "Of all the horrible places to die!" The sound of canvas snapping in the wind drew her attention.

The *Dreamscape Voyager* cut a swath through the trailing lights and settled by the edge of the unstable plateau a few feet away. Cassidy made a run for it and leaped just as the ground began to fall away. Her feet hit the deck and Kek and Nieves grabbed her arms immediately to ensure she wouldn't fall, but there was no need. She opened her mouth to snap at them, to tell them as much, but the sight of them lit a fire in the frost within her chest. It was as though a gunshot tore through the all-consuming hatred that had enveloped her, leaving in its wake a sense of love and relief.

"Cass? What happened to your eyes?"

Cassidy opened her mouth to answer when suddenly she felt as though her insides were purged. She dropped to her knees and gasped as her strength fled and pain racked her insides as though she had been hollowed out with a knife. She doubled over, tears crashing onto the deck.

All that hate, she thought. She looked up to see Hymn a few feet away. The Fae looked at her with an unreadable expression. *Does she feel that hate* all the time? *Does she hate* me? And what Cassidy had done to that woman... sure, she had needed to die, and Cassidy had killed before, but *that?* That had been murder, and not only that, it had been excessive and cruel.

And she had *chosen* to do it.

"Get us out of here," Cassidy ordered — though with how her voice shook, it sounded more like she was *begging.* With Kek's help, she wandered over to the aftcastle steps to sit down while Nieves took the helm. He said something she couldn't hear. "What?" she asked, turning her good ear to him.

"I asked what Hymn did to you," he said. "Your eyes were... well, not quite like hers, but... do you remember what Flint's eyes looked like, before the end?"

"I don't think I could ever forget," Cassidy said with a shudder. "I looked like that?"

"Aye."

"To be honest, I don't know what happened," she said. "Not exactly. Things got rough down there."

Ahead, the sky broke open in a blast of cannon smoke and wisps of light. The red sky broke like a plaster ceiling, lending a view of a natural, dark night's sky illuminated by the moons Cassidy knew. The hole widened as the edges dissolved into more and more lights. Dyrelights, Hymn had called them. Nieves guided the *Dreamscape Voyager* through the gap in the sky, and they emerged into their world.

Beneath them, the Leviathan was floating lifelessly into the sea, dyrelights sprouting off its body, leaving behind emptiness in their wake. Some of the ships from the fleet were still unloading their weapons on the beast, but it was clear the battle was won. Cassidy could see a few silhouettes on some of the other ships, and they seemed to be cheering — whether over the defeat of the monster, or the *Dreamscape Voyager's* miraculous reappearance, she couldn't say.

It didn't really matter. They had survived, and there were more important things, now.

Cassidy stood and threw her arms around Kek, ignoring the agony of her body. "I'm so glad you came back," she sobbed into his shoulder.

He hugged her back, gently, as though she were made of porcelain. "I always will, Captain."

CHAPTER FORTY-NINE

Gaps in the storm above revealed not the natural sky after all, but a Dreamscape sky that was almost the same color. There were different stars in that sky, but Cassidy recognized the moons that shined behind the clouds. She wondered why that was, but she didn't dwell on it.

Instead, she watched the leviathan turn into light as the survivors — maybe a dozen ships, or thereabouts — celebrated their hard-earned victory. Shouts of jubilation carried on the breeze and over the water. She wished she could do the same, but she was just so damn tired. Below deck, she had too many wounded to have any real party, though they were drinking, and Cassidy heard a few shouted cheers. Topside, however, Cassidy sat with Kek, passing a bottle of rice wine back and forth. It wasn't as good as the vintage she had shared with Venitha — it wasn't even *good,* really — but she needed it. Everything hurt, and though Hymn stood at the prow contentedly watching the lights, Cassidy was unnerved by the Fae she considered a friend.

Was someone with such all-consuming hatred capable of real love or friendship? Just the memory of it terrified Cassidy.

"How did you get the fishing crews to sail all the way out here?" she asked him.

Kek took a deep pull of the wine. "When I left, I took one of the copies of your Imperial writ. At first, I was only going to use it to get passage home, but once the fever started to die, I started thinking clearly. I was going to come back, but you'd already set off. Decided I needed to make it up to you. And Tenia is a patriot, so once I showed her the writ, she got everyone else in line.

"We had been searching for weeks when we finally found you." He took another pull before passing it to Cassidy. "I didn't see Miria below deck. Is she…" he choked on the question.

"She's in Revehaven," said Cassidy. "She… she's the Empress, now."

Kek's face lit up. "Oh, that's —" The expression fell when he seemed to realize the implication of that. "Oh. How?"

"The Daughters of Daen," Cassidy said, her voice deep with disdain. "Reports say Zayne Balthine did the deed."

"That's —"

"Impossible, I know," said Cassidy. She leaned back on the stairs and stared at Jiqun.

The largest moon was gibbous and took up a large swath of sky, so much so that a ship hovering between her and the *Dreamscape Voyager* didn't obscure the view. The silhouette of the ship looked familiar. It was an Imperial junk with a distinctive figurehead — a rivermaid. Its long tail glittered like amethyst in the moonlight. Cassidy picked up her spyglass. That wasn't a carved decoration.

"What is it?"

"Name the fucking gods and they shall witness," Cassidy breathed. "It's the *Scorpion.*"

Zayne watched from the rivermaid's eyes as the leviathan died. With his own eyes, he watched the *Dreamscape Voyager* as she emerged from the monster.

"What were the fucking odds?" he asked.

"Are we going to kill them?" Nanette asked. There was a tension to her voice, and Zayne really wasn't sure which way she wanted him to answer.

"Not here. They have too many allies, including that clockwork monstrosity. But damn it all, I want to. For what that bitch did to me…" Zayne didn't realize he had put his hand on his sword until it began to rattle incessantly in his grasp. He relinquished it and took a steadying breath.

Nanette put a hand on his shoulder. "She'll pay," she promised. "But you're right. Not here. Do we need to go back to Dardan?"

Zayne laughed — not a bitter or sardonic laugh, either, but an honest laugh from the bottom of his stomach. It hurt his throat, but it was worth it. "You know, Dardan was so distracted when Shen blasted the *Forgotten Promise,* she didn't compel me to return. She just said *find whoever is hunting the leviathan.* Didn't even order me to do anything about it."

Nanette furrowed her brow for a moment, then she laughed as well. "So, what now? We run for it?"

Zayne sobered. "No. I'm more sure than ever that Dardan needs to be stopped, but... now we have a little time to plan. We can figure out something better than, *charge in and hope for the best.*"

Below, the *Dreamscape Voyager* was turning and accelerating fast. Towards the *Scorpion.*

"We've been spotted," he told Nanette. "Get on the helm. Let's lead them on a bit of a chase."

"That can't be the *Scorpion*," Kek said, not for the first time since Cassidy took the helm. "We sank that ship, and you killed Balthine yourself. I saw it happen!"

"Doesn't matter if it's the same ship," Cassidy said, "best we know, whoever is aboard that ship killed the Empress. We can't sit back and do nothing!" It was more than that, of course. But how to tell him she was *certain* Zayne Balthine was aboard that ship, somehow alive? She couldn't — not because she didn't trust him, or because she wanted to keep more secrets, but because she didn't understand how she had come to the conclusion herself. Maybe killing him once had given her an intuition about such things.

The *Scorpion* turned to launch a retreat and Cassidy pushed the *Dreamscape Voyager* to full speed. She opened the pipeline. "Anyone who can stand, be ready for a fight. The *Scorpion* is dead ahead."

Zayne stood on the aftcastle, watching the *Dreamscape Voyager* continue pursuit. Durant was persistent, but he supposed she wanted revenge as much as he did.

He turned to Aresh, sitting on the Stinger. "Fire," he ordered.

The Rivien man nodded and squeezed the trigger with both hands. Nothing happened. He tried again, but still the weapon refused to fire. He slammed his hands angrily against the Stinger and it moved off target and launched a ballista bolt that sailed harmlessly to the side of the *Dreamscape Voyager.*

"What was that?" Zayne demanded.

"I told you once, our kind cannot end our own lives," Pyrrha said by his side. With the Dreamscape influencing the world enough that ships flew without engines or propellers and used pre-

Ascension sails rather than balloons, the Fae wavered in appearance between her true form and that of the body she possessed, shimmering between them like a reflection in sea water distorted by waves.

"What does that have to do with shooting down the *Dreamscape Voyager*?"

"Simple. A part of you is on that ship."

Zayne felt Lucandri stirring in his mind, a fury muddled with… shame?

"Can't kill ourselves," Zayne said contemplatively. He drew a knife and ran it across the line of his palm. He hissed at the sharp ease with which he drew his own blood. He closed his hand in a tight fist and called to Nanette. "Drop speed and let them catch us," he said. "Then we'll see how well the *Dreamscape Voyager* lives up to its name."

Cassidy watched as the *Scorpion* slowed, letting her catch up to it. The Daughters' ship flew level with the port side and rammed them. Cassidy kept a tight grip on the helm and leveled out just as the *Scorpion* broke away to hit them again.

"Kek, take the helm!" she ordered. She tore herself away and drew her sword. Zayne Balthine — Cassidy was certain it was him even wearing that mask — stood on the gunwale with his sword drawn. Cassidy drew on the Fae power and joined him, punching with her blade.

Balthine parried her attack with ease and kicked her in the stomach, knocking her back down to the deck. Hymn's whip of light lashed at the mercenary, but he parried that too before retreating to his deck. "Can't fight your own battles, Durant?" Balthine chided, but it wasn't his voice she heard. It was a richer, deeper voice she had never heard before. "You aren't half the woman Asier was."

"How dare —"

The world changed. The sky above was a deep, cloudless maroon with bright stars with entirely too much order, forming rings that banded the horizon. The sea below glowed bright green from beneath its depths and foamed as though boiling.

Cassidy moved up the deck to the flame spitter and fired it, striking the *Scorpion's* deck with a burning adhesive.

"How is it possible you —" Zayne began, but the rest of what he said was lost when the *Scorpion* shot ahead.

"Follow them, Kek," Cassidy ordered.

"That would be folly," said Hymn. "The *Scorpion* does not mean to flee."

"Of course he does," Cassidy chided. "He's literally right there."

"No," Hymn said, shaking her head. "He deliberately drew you away from the fleet. Now I believe he means to take the battle somewhere I cannot so easily tip the battle in your favor, either. I think he is luring you into a trap."

Cassidy bit her lip. *What would Elyia do?* she wondered, but she shook her head because she had her answer before the question had even fully formed. Asier had lived her whole life in fear of Balthine. Even before the man had been born, he had been a specter in her nightmares. Cassidy couldn't let him do the same to her.

"Trap or no trap, follow him," she told Kek.

Kek's expression said a lot, and none of it pleasant, but he obeyed the order. The *Scorpion* sailed low, approaching a lone island consisting of nothing but two rocky spires, one on either end of it. The black ship passed between the pillars and vanished like morning mist. Kek shot a look to Cassidy, and she nodded. They followed.

When the *Dreamscape Voyager* returned yet again to the waking world, the sudden roar of the engines gave Cassidy a start of surprise, so accustomed as she had grown to the more subtle sounds of the Dreamscape. Taking stock of where they had emerged, Cassidy recognized the mountain before them. Bajin's Landing. It was strange to think of how recently she's been here with everything that had happened since they had departed from those docks. It felt like a lifetime ago.

Cassidy checked her spyglass. The *Scorpion* had increased the gap between them and was already making port.

"Get me onto that ship," Cassidy ordered.

"*What?*" Kek shrieked.

"Do it. Don't worry about making port."

"Cassidy, there's a hundred Watch officers, you'll be —"

"The Empress will pardon us, but if we don't stop Balthine now, who will?"

Kek looked like an argument was ready to burst from his lips, but he stifled his qualms and obeyed. Traffic directing skiffs tried to flag them down, but Kek blew past them. The harbor was lightly trafficked at the late hour, but Kek still needed to weave around a couple vessels in their approach.

"Hymn, I need to let you in again," she said.

The Fae stared out at the horizon for something Cassidy couldn't see, then nodded. Cassidy drew on her connection, letting the cold consume her, and Hymn vanished into dyrelights. The vast hatred returned, filling Cassidy so completely that her other emotions were burned away. But now, she had a target. A boundless loathing built and stoked like a pyre over fathomless eras was now aimed squarely at Captain Zayne Balthine.

When the *Dreamscape Voyager* passed the *Scorpion* at the harbor, Cassidy broke into a run and jumped to the other ship. A noble blooded woman and a man in a turban seemed surprised by her sudden appearance. Cassidy kicked the man in the stones and struck the woman in the throat with the pommel of her sword before leaping down to the deck. The gangway was down. Balthine had already departed. She swept her gaze and saw Balthine and his first mate on the harbor streets. In these pre-dawn hours, there were few people, but the mercenary wasn't entirely isolated.

"Balthine!" she screamed as she bounded from the *Scorpion's* deck. The mercenary turned his half-masked face. Her feet hit the cobblestones hard, and she fell to one knee, but the pain was made distant through the Fae bond. She drew her pistol and fired. In her haste, she fired wide and hit the wall of the warehouse behind him. The nearby pedestrians panicked and began running in all directions.

Balthine drew his sword — seemingly the same falcon-decorated weapon he had been holding when she knocked him into the lake. "I've been waiting for this for some time," he said, and his voice gave her pause. She heard two people speaking, and while one was clearly Balthine, the other was a voice like rich velvet that sent a quiver down her body. She shook her head to clear it and charged at the mercenary.

She roared, charged, and stabbed at him. Balthine sidestepped the attack.

Swish, swish, clang.

She had him with his back to a wall. He spun, kicked off the wall and flipped over her head. Burning pain blossomed as Balthine slashed her from shoulder to opposite hip as he came down into a crouch. Cassidy whirled, attacking with a speed and grace she had never known, driven by fury, and he answered in kind with the same intensity with which he had battled Elyia Asier. She and the mercenary clashed and stepped in a deadly dance that carried them around the harbor street.

Clang, clang, swish. Clang, clang, clang. Clang, swish, clang. Snick.
Balthine cut her along the cheek.

Clang, snick, clang.
Cassidy scored a blow on the side of his neck before he could redirect her strike.

Clang, clang, clang.
A bullet tore across the front of Cassidy's thigh. She turned to find Balthine's first mate reloading her pistol, and that momentary distraction was all it took for Balthine to get in close and pin her by the throat with his forearm. She dropped her sword. Even as strong as Hymn made her, the wound on her back pressed against a wall hurt unbearably, and with her windpipe being crushed, pinpricks of panic began to corrupt the purity of hatred welling up within her. She clutched frantically at Balthine's arm as he leveled his sword to her gut. She felt the connection of iron beneath her fingers and the dragon-hide leather coat. She frantically pulled on that connection. Balthine howled in pain and leapt back as smoke poured from his coat sleeve. He shook violently as a flaming stiletto shot from the sleeve, leaving a clear burn along the back of the mercenary's hand.

Through the anger, Cassidy remembered when she had thrown Balthine's coat into Lake Justiciar. It had been heavy, full of little trinkets and *weapons*. Cassidy grabbed Balthine's other arm and connected with iron. She set it alight. He howled again, patting at his sleeve to smother the flames. She slammed her palms into his chest and ignited it. Two pistols erupted, tearing through his coat: one fired straight up through the coat's breast, one shot outward. A woman cried out in pain. Cassidy punched the mercenary and ignited yet another iron source hidden beneath his coat, and it exploded.

Everything hurt when she opened her eyes again, but her head most especially. The reek of gunpowder overwhelmed her so much it was all she could taste. Her vision was blurry. Something brown, edged with red and covered with soot filled her vision. She stared at it for several long seconds, unable to determine what she was looking at. The realization was sudden and sent a wave of panic through her.

It was her own finger. She tried to push herself up, but pain in her hand pulled taut on every nerve all the way up to her eyeballs and she screamed. Gun smoke obscured Cassidy's vision in every direction. She recognized Hymn's azure glow through the haze above her. She rolled painfully onto her other side and pushed herself up with her left hand. She coughed through the gun smoke and waved away what she could.

A man stood a few steps away in the smoke, but as the breeze cleared her vision, Cassidy could see it wasn't Balthine. He had hair of the purest silvery white with richly tanned skin that was almost golden. His eyes — *gods, his eyes!* — were the inverted eyes of a Fae, purest gold speckled with stars. His tattered, smoke-stained coat was white and, like the garb of all the Fae Cassidy had encountered, it seemed like a window to a night sky, though she struggled to see the stars and streaks of color through all that brilliant pearlescence.

More than his features, however, was a daunting realization; he was the single most beautiful sight Cassidy had ever laid eyes on. As she met his eyes, she heard a song even in her deaf ear, a sweet, familiar melody. She had experienced a Siren's Song before, but because her attractions had always been for men, she had never felt the full intensity of it before. She felt it now. Heat blossomed between her legs like a fire. She didn't forget her pain, but against the intense waves of lust that pulsed through her, it didn't matter.

"No," she heard Hymn whisper beside her. "No, you cannot be —*NO!*" the Fae shrieked, and she zipped off into the sky.

Cassidy stood frozen. A distant part of her wanted Hymn to come back, wanted to scream, to cry, to demand to know where her friend was going. But that part was a small thing, smothered and buried beneath the raw slavish lust this male siren sparked in her.

"It looks like you're alone now, Durant," said the Fae that was also Zayne Balthine, and his voice was the deep, velvet smooth tone she had heard before and it sent a thrill through her entire body, but beneath it was an undercurrent, a whisper of something more mundane, something she *hated* and that was almost enough to give her an anchor. "Who will save you now?" He leveled his sword for her stomach.

Exactly where I stabbed him first, a distant part of her mind, the part that had held onto the human voice.

The Fae turned suddenly, and Cassidy was struck by something heavy that jingled like coins. She was flat on the cobbled streets of the harbor, ensnared in an iron net with exceptionally fine links. Balthine swiped his empty hand through the air and a golden sword flashed to life, cutting through a second net meant for him and ran. Cassidy saw two figures give chase but couldn't follow them.

A boot hit her in the ribs so hard she cried.

"Cassandra Durant IV," a somewhat nasally, masculine voice intoned, "you are under arrest for consorting with denizens of the Fae realm."

EPILOGUE

As the blood poured from between her fingers, Nanette cursed Cassidy Durant. How had Durant done it? How had she discharged a pistol from beneath Zayne's coat and shot her with it? She hadn't been able to stay to find out; Pyrrha had whisked her away almost immediately, and the pain in her ribs had been too much for Nanette to fight when Xiao Ta's body picked her up and carried her with its impossible grace and ease. How had the Fae known to be there?

The Fae sat Nanette down, propped against the gunwale.

"It's finally time, Nanette Adarin," Pyrrha said, smiling through Xiao Ta's lips. Nanette sneered. She wanted nothing more than to wipe that smirk off her face with a blunt instrument.

"T-time f-for what?" she asked, and she cursed herself for stammering. The pain in her side was too great to put on a show, however. Spots were beginning to form in her vision.

The Fae removed the tinted glasses Nanette had given her long ago and met her eyes with her own. The inverted gaze was unsettling, but worse was the fact that Nanette was able to discern their color in a world of gray. Unaccustomed to them as she was, she was unable to name those colors, but she longed for them, longed to know them. But not from this beast. Not from Pyrrha. Nanette hissed as her body shifted and the pain in her wound seemed to tug on every nerve in her body.

"Why, time for me to kill you, of course," Pyrrha said jovially.

Nanette's eyes widened. "You can't. You serve —"

"I serve *Lucandri*," Pyrrha said firmly, and she tapped Nanette on the nose. "Love is ever a pesky thing. So long as you live, Zayne Balthine will keep fighting to be who he is. You are standing in the way of progress. So many times you have brought him back from the brink when he needed to *break*."

"You can't think he'll let you get away with it," Nanette said. And despite her situation, she was confident. Regardless of whatever mad scheme Pyrrha had, regardless of what Lucandri did, Zayne's will was strong. The Fae couldn't kill her, because Zayne had the means to kill the Fae, and would do it if anything happened to her.

"Silly girl," Pyrrha said, slapping her with Xiao Ta's meaty mits. "He just has to think it was Cassandra Durant that killed you. I will be fine."

Nanette barked a laugh, then. "And what will you say if he asks you outright what killed me, huh?"

Pyrrha smiled back patronizingly. "Oh, Nanette," she said, taking a handful of her hair and running her fat fingers through the silky black strands. "You have the most beautiful *curly, blonde* hair."

Nanette's eyes shot open wide. "You can —"

"Lie? Yes. I was surprised, too. It is not an easy secret to keep when you aren't accustomed to it."

Nanette reached for one of her knives, but her muscles were jerky and slow. Pyrrha drove the bullet deeper into her body with a heavy finger. Pain forced cohesion out of her, until darkness took her. Nanette's blade brushed the Fae's collarbone, but the cut was so shallow it could never have made a difference.

"Zayne." She meant it as a shout. Instead, it came out as a whisper so weak it might have been her imagination. This couldn't be how her song ended.

Zayne returned to the *Scorpion* moments before the dawn truly broke. He had recovered his mask and dodged the Iron Veil's pursuits long enough that he was able to approach his ship without drawing much attention. He had wanted to deal with Durant himself, but if the priests had her, she was as good as dead anyway. At least now he could focus on dealing with Dardan.

"Nanette, get us out of here before —" his words cut off when he saw Pyrrha looming over Nanette. Blood spread beneath her in a deep pool. His stomach was roiling at the sight, but he forced himself to power through. "Nanette!" He fell to his knees into the blood. His stomach couldn't take much more, but he swallowed his bile.

"I did all I could for her," Pyrrha said. Her hands were completely red with glistening blood, holding her jacket shut at the throat as if in distress. "Durant's attack killed her."

Zayne shook his head, tears filling his eyes. "No," he whispered. He hugged his friend — the closest, the truest friend he ever had — tight to him, not caring about the pain or the blood, fighting his mind's urge to be sick. "Don't leave me here, Nan..." he whispered breathlessly. "Please... don't leave me alone... I can't do this by myself." The tears burned as they ran down his face. His nose was running, but he couldn't bear to remove his arms from Nannette even to wipe his face clean.

It was some time before he finally tore himself away from Nanette. The expression of pain that marred her face was too much. He ran to the gunwale. After three dry heaves, Zayne vomited over the edge. His knees shook for several miserably, stabbing heartbeats until they finally gave way and collapsed under his weight. There was nothing left for him. Everyone he had ever loved was dead. His mother. His brother and sister. And now his best friend.

Zayne Balthine sat alone beneath the dark sky. Prayers and wishes sat half formed on his tongue. There were no words, though; he knew they would be denied. He closed his eyes, willing the wound in his chest to be fatal.

When the dawn finally broke, its warmth shining down upon him, Lucandri took off his mask and stood.

ACKNOWLEDGEMENTS

I haven't quite figured out how to make this section entertaining, so for now, I'll focus on keeping it brisk.

First and foremost, a heartfelt thank you to Ellie Raine – author of the esteemed NecroSeam Chronicles and the editor of this book – not only for working so hard to helping make this book shine on a deadline, but also for helping me adjust to the career side of being an author and being a true friend and putting up with my near constant complaining and general mental health struggles during the entire process.

Next, thanks to Andy, my first reader, for your support and feedback.

Thank you once again to Fabrice Bertolotto for yet another absolutely stunning cover.

A special shout out and thank you to Naomi Rose-Mock for doing such a fantastic job with the audiobook for *Skies of the Empire*.

And most of all, thank you to all the readers who have made it this far.

i

ABOUT THE AUTHOR

Vincent E.M Thorn is a biracial Japanese American author. Born in Wyoming, he currently lives in the metro-Atlanta area. When he's not writing or reading epic fantasy, he enjoys video games and heavy metal.

Made in the USA
Columbia, SC
21 September 2024

42127313R00343